THE HOLLAND FAMILY SAGA

THE HOLLAND FAMILY SAGA

PART ELEVEN

WHAT THE GAME GAVE BACK

ISBN# 978-0-692-90000-0

This is strictly a work of fiction. Any references to actual events, real people, living or dead, or actual localities, is to enhance the realism of the story. Events within the novel that coincide with actual events is purely coincidental.

It's always a special moment for me when a book is released. It's like a rollercoaster ride. When I first started, there were a few, now there are many, and it's steadily growing. There are way too many names to mention, but if we've ever had a convo, I'm talking directly to you when I say thank you for giving me an opportunity. You chose to spend your hard-earned money on me and read my stories with appreciation. You all keep me on my toes, threatening me with a lynch mob (LOL), tick-tock and 'where my book'. LOL! But I love it all because it let's me know I'm doing something right over here. I hope you find this installment of the saga just as enjoyable as the rest, and I look forward to your feedback.

Sincerely,

Clever Black

CHAPTER ONE

THE FIRST PLAY

May, 29th 2009

"Who is Tanya Weinberger, Agent Vanguard?" thirty-seven-year-old Arata Moto asked in a low, inquisitive tone as he sat inside a black Lincoln Town Car limousine. The car sat parked on a busy Seattle, Washington pier tucked in between a long warehouse and that of Arata and his brother's hulking cargo container ship, The Red Dragon. Forklifts were everywhere and there were container trucks slowly creeping over the docks. Two dozen or so Asian men in denim jeans, boots and bright green safety vests and helmets, moved about atop The Red Dragon's deck untying lines. Six other Asian men with weapons concealed inside their custom-fit silk suits stood at the foot of the ship's gangway keeping an eye on the black on black limousine that their bosses had just climbed into just a few yards away.

Arata, the eldest of the Moto brothers was a 5'8" man of Japanese descent who had a clean-shaven face with short, black hair that was cut into a triangle at the top. The well-dressed muscular Asian with youthful appeal had eyes so slender, you could barely make out their greyish color. Minutes ago, Arata had been informed by Lisa Vanguard that his sister, Tammy Moto, had been murdered in her New Jersey home. He'd heard of Lisa Vanguard, but he didn't know her all that well. She claimed to be a federal agent who was a partner to, and a friend of his sister, but he didn't trust her just yet. He sat in silence staring blankly out the tinted window as he let sink in all that he'd just been told.

Thirty-five-year-old Raiden Moto sat to the left of his brother. He was pained over the loss of Tammy and it showed. He sat with his legs crossed t-style looking down in his lap with wet, watery dark brown eyes full of anger. He kept gritting his teeth inside his

7

square-lined jaw while running his hands through his pony-tailed hair in stunned disbelief.

"Tanya Weinberger is the woman who killed your sister," Lisa fabricated. The manipulative red-haired federal agent knew who it was exactly that had killed Tammy and more concerning the Moto family, but she was holding back certain truths for now in order to gain the upper hand.

Brenda had told Lisa that she didn't know who took out the contract on Tammy just before Lisa sprung her from a jail in Philadelphia, but the astute agent had figured it out all on her own, which was her reason for having lied to the Moto brothers. Brenda said a crew of Asians inside the Holland family had killed Tammy, and for Lisa that meant that only two people could've been behind the job if they didn't do the deed themselves: Phillip Tran and Grover Kobayashi.

Faye Bender was the one inside the German organization who'd ordered the hit on Tammy was what Lisa was also told by Brenda. The rogue agent wanted Faye dead as well, had been wanting to off the woman, but for a different reason other than her having ordered the hit on Tammy. Lisa wanted Faye dead because she'd killed her father back in Bentree, West Virginia in 1976. She'd paid her back once by killing her family back in Patterson, Iowa a few years later, but it seems as if the battle was starting to heat up again.

For a long while, Lisa had been letting sleeping dogs lie between her and Faye. Her having won the last battle was reason enough for her to disengage; but when Tammy went down and she learned that Faye Bender was partially responsible, Lisa knew the battle was on once again. Faye was coming for her, so she had to launch a preemptive strike. Her way of doing so was to hit Faye by taking down one of the leaders inside her crew in Tanya Weinberger. Lisa had every intent on letting the Moto brothers know who'd pulled the trigger on Tammy and then some, but before she did so, she and the two other women with her wanted the Moto brothers to do their bidding.

"I want to kill this Tanya Weinberger myself," Raiden declared as he looked over at the three women sitting before him.

"You can kill her if you want. She lives over in Cincinnati, Ohio." Brenda Marshall, a forty-six-year-old dark-skinned, voluptuous woman with sexy, full lips and deep, dark eyes, stated as she patted her large afro and placed her hands atop her crossed legs. "She was a friend of mine, but it doesn't matter to me because I want the bitch dead too."

"And just what is your deal in all of this matter, black woman?" Arata looked over and asked Brenda.

"Wud yuh mean wen yuh say 'black woman'?" forty-two-year-old Bridgette Fischer interjected as she looked up and removed strands of coarse blonde braids from before her vanilla white face. "Mi fren Brenda is part of duh crew and deserve yuh 'speck!" the conceited green-eyed Jamaican snapped as she removed a pair of dark sunshades from her slender, pale face.

Arata and Raiden looked at one another somewhat mystified before turning to Lisa. "What is she saying?" Arata asked as he eyed Bridgette suspiciously.

"She wants you to respect our friend Brenda," Lisa responded. "Save your pomposity for the streets, gentlemen. Brenda is working alongside me and Bridgette and is an important ally to all of our Causes."

"Excuse my arrogance early on, but the question still stands," Arata stated in a calm voice as Raiden nodded in agreement. "What's her deal wanting to kill her own friend?"

"My deal is that my old crew left me and my friend Vivian behind inside a Philadelphia prison. Nobody sent word, a lawyer, nothing. They left me and my friend out in the cold about to get stuck with thirty years. Even more important, they cut a deal with the same muthafuckas that killed your sister Tammy by using my son's death as a bargaining chip. I'm going my own way, but before I do, I wanna send my old crew a thank you message."

"Where's your friend Vivian?" Arata asked as his shifty his eyes scanned the motley crew of women sitting across from him.

"She's still in jail back in Philadelphia." Brenda answered while eyeing the Japanese men.

"How did you get out, Miss Marshall?" Raiden asked.

"Come now with yah decision, Asian man, yuh askin' mi fren Brendah too many personal questions now," Bridgette interjected, nearly singing in her bombastic voice.

"Agent Vanguard seems to know plenty about me and Raiden,"

Arata countered. "If am I going to sit and discuss business with you three I have every right to ask whatever it is that I want about you women."

"I helped her get out," Lisa confessed. "Brenda feels as if her organization has betrayed her. I offered her a place working alongside me and she's accepted my offer. We're setting up our own heroin distribution ring and we feel will can be of use to you guys."

"I know nothing about any heroin, Agent Vanguard," Arata disavowed as he eyed Lisa while rubbing his chin.

"Let's not bullshit one another here," Lisa objected while shaking her head and sliding to edge of the seat. She pulled a cellphone from her business suit jacket and played a message. *"Tammy, Arata here. You went to sleep on me? Our ship, the Red Dragon, will dock in Seattle on May twenty-ninth at three in the afternoon. Me and Raiden will be on board and look forward to seeing you when we arrive. Talk to you soon."*

"That's how I knew you were coming," Lisa said as she slid back into the seat and crossed her legs. A large forklift passed by, blowing a horn and pausing the conversation briefly. When it faded off into the distance, Lisa resumed. "Raiden? You and Tammy were in talks before she was killed. You and Arata didn't know of her death until you touched down here, so you're not here for that. I'm not sure what it is you two are here to oversee exactly, but I'm willing to bet it has something to do with drugs," she smiled.

"And if it were?" Raiden asked.

"If that is what it is, gentlemen? Me, Bridgette and Brenda are here to pick up where Tammy left off."

"We don't need your help for anything," Arata calmly protested. "Raiden and I are here on legitimate business. We own a fashion industry back in Japan and we're overseeing the delivery of high end leather purses from Burberry, Michael Kors and Coach. It's a five-million-dollar container so you should understand our concern."

"You really are going to make me lay it all out for you, aren't you?" Lisa chuckled in a condescending manner. "And do either of you give a true fuck about Tammy?"

"You don't ask us how we feel about Tammy!" Raiden retorted

as he lunged out at Lisa from his seated position.

"Now, now," Lisa calmly stated as she, Brenda and Bridgette all drew down with nickel-plated .9mm Berettas with infrared beams. "Do we really want to take it there, guys?" she asked, seething as her nostrils flared.

Raiden paused and slowly eased back into his seat. "You would kill us. Here? On a busy port?" he asked as a red dot landed on his forehead.

"Wid all dis noise 'round no one wud eva hear tha' gunshots," Bridgette disclosed. "Wi leave yuh stankin' right here on tha' dock wit out givin' it ah' second dought doncha know?" the blood-thirsty Jamaican purred while waving her .9mm back and forth between the Moto brothers.

"You'll never make it out alive," Raiden warned unnerved as the infrared beam danced off his rugged facial features. "We have men watching us. If you step out of this car before we do, they will kill you all."

"Is that so?" Lisa asked without cracking a smile as she held up a small letter. "See all those men on the forklifts streaming by? They're all federal agents. I have a subpoena to search your ship based on that phone message you just listened to. Now, we do well to make us a deal here today. I'll tell my people you two men had all the proper documentation for your freighter, call off the search and we meet again later, or, I can play it by the book and strip that cargo ship down to the hull. I'm more than sure I'll find more than just a bunch of name brand purses."

"What sort of a deal are you looking for exactly?" Arata inquired as he eyed Lisa cautiously.

Lisa smiled over at the Moto brothers audaciously as she placed either of her hands on the wrists of her comrades, gently lowering their guns as she sat in between the two. "Good. You know a good deal when you see one," she complimented. "The deal is a sixteen-million-dollar deal."

Arata and Raiden looked over to one another, nodded, then looked back at Lisa. "We're listening," Arata said, he and Raiden both intrigued over the number.

"Dere's a pyaa pyaa family in Sao Paulo, Brazil dat got a' least five hunnid pounds 'a dat boy stored in a warehouse dere," Bidgette disclosed. "I waan it for not just mi self but fah errbody dats here tuhday, but I need queffas to do the job."

Arata and Raiden deferred to Lisa for interpretation.

"There's five hundred pounds of heroin that a weak family in Brazil is in possession of and Bridgette wants to take it and share it with us here on American soil, but she needs gunmen to get the job done," the federal agent translated.

"Tha' agent is right," Bridgette admitted. "Dis family has a farm dat grows the poppy seed. Wi kill dem? Wi own a' entire poppy field in Sao Paulo, Brazil that can produce five hunnid pounds a' boy every month. Wid yuh product coming in from Japan and duh farm we take in South America? Wi can dominate dat heroin bidness on both coasts here in America."

"Who is this family, Bridgette?" Arata asked, fascinated over the prospect.

"Deveraux is dere name, and dey have non protection 'cuz I killed dere boss mi self in the New York Citay," Bridgette sang in her accentuated voice. "I cut off him head and express it back to him wife in Sao Paolo, Brazil to send mi message, which was to stay away from New York Citay. Fuh payback the people who left Brendah behind in jail kill my brothers in New York for wut I do in Sao Paulo," she added in a voice that suggested pity on her plight. "Now me have to hit them back and take dere heroin, but only mi don't have enough queffas like I said buhfore."

"Queffas are soldiers," Lisa translated. "These people in Cincinnati are behind the deaths of your sister, Arata. And the Devereaux family ordered a hit on Bridgette's brothers in New York."

"We must hit dem both back tuh even da score." Bridgette followed.

"On listening, it seems as if these people in Brazil killed your brothers in retaliation for what you did to their father, am I correct, Bridgette?" Raiden inquired.

"Yah inquire too much about duh past! Yuh men do tha' job in Brazil and take care of the people in Cincinnati fuh us!" Bridgette snapped. "Yuh git mi sum soldiers and I show 'em where dere's a warehouse in Sao Paulo wid sixteen million dollars' worth ah' heroin. Tuhgether, we distribute dat boy on the east and west coasts! If yuh don't waan tha' deal we can part ways tuhday."

"No," Arata casually stated while nodding his head up and down and rubbing his chin as he sat with his legs crossed. "Five hundred pounds is a lot of merchandise for one field to be manufacturing. We know because it's the same amount that we produce back in Japan. We're looking to expand, but we're short of land. If were to take that field in Brazil we would double our production. It's worth looking into."

"How yah' shawt of land and yah from tha' land of dah poppy seed? Why yah comin' up short in Japan like dat?" Bridgette asked while rocking her upper body.

"There's a lot of competition back home, Bridgette. Land doesn't come cheap."

"Yuh should kill all duh ones in yuh way in Japan and take dere poppy fields is wut ya' should do, rude boy."

"That may be the American or the South American way of doing things, but we have a coalition of members back home. We're like members of the stock exchange." Arata countered.

"Huhnn…beware of a' black Friday. Yah shit culd come a' crashin' down very easily, suh." Bridgette mockingly warned. "You men willin' tuh do duh job or nawt?" she then asked.

"Do you have files on the Devereaux family, Agent Vanguard?" Arata asked, brushing Bridgette's remark off.

"I can get them in couple of days at the latest."

"Do that and we'll see about getting some guys lined up," Arata responded as he looked over to Brenda. "How well do know your way around Cincinnati?"

"Well enough to take you to the place where Tanya hangs out." Brenda assured.

"We're going to be putting a lot of resources into this business down in Sao Paulo. You're looking for only one person in Cincinnati." Arata reasoned. "My brother Raiden says he wants to kill Tanya Weinberger. Your job will be to point the woman out. You will need to provide your own protection because Raiden is all that will be needed for the job. We will not send any men to Cincinnati because it will be a sniper attack."

"That's a fair deal," Lisa agreed.

"Y'all puttin' me on the spot here," Brenda reasoned. "I just got out of jail not two weeks ago. Just settin' up and I—"

"No one's feelin' sorry fuh ya', sister gal. Yah have tuh get ya' hands dirty like the resta us." Bridgette interrupted. "Have yuh any queffas from yuh old 'hood in dah Bronx tuh join ya' while yah back east?"

"I got people," Brenda nodded. "And I'm not looking for pity. I know this game just as well as anyone else," she said as she eyed Bridgette, feeling slighted over the remark.

"Yah keep thankin' dat dis issa game and see wut it give back tuh yah while you feelin' rambunctious," Bridgette said with spite in her voice as she slid up to the edge of the seat and gawked at Brenda.

"Do you women have any loyalty amongst yourselves," Arata questioned with delight.

"How we deal wid one 'nother ain't nun yah concern, Asian man. You pry too much, mi already told yuh so," Bridgette sassed as she looked out the tinted windows at the massive freighter resting in port. "How much a' dat boy is on your boat?"

"Two hundred kilograms. Currently, Raiden and I can supply this west coast and Philadelphia with that amount on a monthly basis. Can you women handle the task?"

"The task can be handled if you give us the soldiers." Lisa remarked as she sat back in her soft leather seat with her legs crossed.

Arata eyed the women before him as he eased back into his seat. They seemed capable, only they hadn't enough muscle to push the weight. It was something he felt he could use for leverage. "If we allow you women access to our soldiers, it is me and Raiden who must pull all the strings," he declared. "This will be our organization here in America. You three will have to answer to us and obey our orders in order to receive our help and protection."

"It's a man's world, right?" Lisa joked. She then jumped serious and said, "If you want control, you'll have to complete the Sao Paulo job for us first. Only then will you men be recognized as the leader of this organization we've all formed here today."

"To be frank, we need no recognition to establish a unit here in

America," Raiden countered.

"I don't care if you boys wanna be Frank, Tom, Dick or Harry," Lisa sternly rebutted. "If you want to do business here in this country trouble free, I've given you the terms. If you don't agree, you might as well pull anchor and set sail for your homeland because you two really don't want the trouble I can bring from a legal standpoint," she confidently guffawed.

"We ladies have tha' powah fuh now," Bridgette declared. "We're showin' yah where five hunnid kilogram a' boy at and givin' up tha' woman who killed yah sister! What it is wid yah two akin' like mamapoules?"

Arata and Raiden looked over to one another and spoke briefly in Japanese. With Tammy gone, they had no American influence or contacts was what they said to one another. They would be going into the heroin business blind if they didn't partner up they then agreed.

"How much time will this Sao Paulo job take?" Arata turned and asked.

"A couple of days at the most for me to gather data on the Devereaux family. From there we'll coordinate the hits. Brenda will work on Cincinnati during that time while Bridgette looks into things down in Brazil. Redirect some of your men to Sao Paulo and she'll link up with them."

"We'll send the men if Bridgette provides the artillery and any mechanical equipment and costumes we may need. If everything goes well up until that point, we will do the job," Arata finally agreed as he reached inside his suit jacket and handed each of the women cards with his and Raiden's numbers attached. "In the meantime, give us a day to make arrangements on the merchandise aboard the ship."

"What's on your container again?" Lisa asked.

"Name brand purses…along with sixteen million dollars' worth of heroin. It is to be delivered to this port today and we're waiting for it to offload. Tammy was supposed to help us the rest of the way," Raiden answered somberly.

"I told you we were here to pick up where she left off," Lisa smiled slyly. "I can have your container shipped by rail to

Baltimore. I have a warehouse along a rail spur where it can be offloaded. Your purses will be fine there until you're ready to move them into market. Take eighty kilograms and set them aside for me to distribute here on the west coast. The other one-twenty, leave inside the container and I'll get it over to Baltimore for Brenda to distribute." Lisa responded as she gave Tammy's cellphone back to Raiden and then handed him a business card with her information. "I'll also start lining up your buyers while I gather up the file on the Deveraux family."

"We'll be in touch," Raiden remarked as he tucked Lisa's card inside his suit jacket.

"Good," Lisa replied in a causal tone. "Welcome to America, gentlemen," she added as the Moto brothers began exiting her limousine. Once the Moto brothers had cleared out, Lisa sat back and chuckled. "They never bothered checking to make sure the warrant was legit," she said while shaking her head and ripping up the blank sheet of paper.

"You had me looking around like, who the fuck is FBI out there?" Brenda laughed. "That was a good one."

"I had to get them to reveal what they were up to exactly. I knew they were bringing in a load of heroin," Lisa smirked. "This deal with the Asians must go through, Brenda" she then said seriously. "You have to go through with the job in Cincinnati. Find Tanya, and then get in touch with Raiden when you do."

Brenda looked Lisa off for several seconds before turning back and looking her dead on. "If I do this job on Tanya, Philadelphia belongs to me and me only. I want the main shipment from Brazil to come to my hub in Pennsylvania and I get to set the price on a fifty-fifty split. Otherwise, I walk away and you and Bridgette can figure out how to get at Tanya and off all two hundred kilograms the Moto brothers bringing in today yourselves."

"You help take down Tanya Weinberger, you got Philly," Lisa agreed, knowing she couldn't return to the east coast lest Senator Slack swoop down and drag her before a senate committee to answer questions on her past activities. The two had an understanding that Senator Slack would not interfere in her affairs so long as Lisa stayed away from the east coast. The conniving agent was agreeing to the terms Senator Slack had laid down, even though the deal was one-sided, but nothing was preventing her from entering through Willie's back door by way of Brenda Marshall.

"You got everything set up on this first load coming to Baltimore, Lisa?" Brenda asked, shaking Lisa from her thoughts.

"That I do," Lisa nodded. "And you're on a flight there in a few hours," she added as she pulled open a small leather bag and peeled off a small stack of bills and handed them to Brenda. "Here's some money for you and your people. That's ten thousand dollars."

"Split five ways that's only two thousand dollars," Brenda sniggered. "I done killed men for a hundred thousand dollars by myself back in the day."

If Lisa had her way, she would just as soon kill Brenda this very day. She was important to her at the time, however, because she knew the east coast market just as well as she did. Brenda was expendable in Lisa's eyes, though, for the simple fact that Lisa knew Brenda would never forgive her for killing her husband, Ricky Gross inside a Pittsburgh hotel back in June of 1990 if she were to ever find out. She thought back briefly to the day she'd given herself away as she began to question Brenda's intelligence…

June 1990

…*When Ricky opened the door, a single, gloved-clad hand holding a black wallet came into view. The wallet unfolded and a silver FBI badge dropped down. A slender, red-haired woman then slowly came into view. "Ricky Gross?" she asked with a sly smile on her face.*

"Yeah. That's me." Ricky remarked a little unnerved as he backed into the room. The woman slowly crept inside and stood before Ricky after he'd confirmed his identification. A petite Asian followed, closing the door behind her.

Ricky didn't know how Lisa looked, he was under the impression that he was about to be busted for running guns with the La Rocca brothers given Audi and Austell had been murdered. "I want a lawyer," was all he said with his hands slightly raised, putting the cassette recorder on display.

"A lawyer?" Lisa remarked in a cold manner as she eyed the device in Ricky's hand. The calculating agent was willing to bet her life that she'd found what she'd been looking for ever since the day Audi and Austell had her at that ballgame back in June of '83

where they'd recorded her during a negotiation.

"There isn't a lawyer on this planet that can help you, Ricky," Lisa let it be known as she raised the gun.

Ricky had suddenly picked up on the woman's voice. "It's you on the tape!" he yelled aloud as he charged at Lisa.

Lisa stepped back and fired a round, hitting Ricky in the neck. The shot was intentional because it prevented the man from screaming any further.

Ricky stumbled into Lisa, grabbing her shoulders as he sunk to the floor with blood spurting from the side of his neck. She reached down and gently eased the recorder from the man's grip before kicking him over onto his back and pressing play on the recorder as the man convulsed at her feet.

The conversation where Lisa had admitted to aiding Sheriff Corey Mobley in the killing of Faye Bender's family was heard and she let it play through to the end, if only to assure herself that she'd struck gold. Satisfied she'd obtained the only evidence known that was able to reveal her past crimes, Lisa clicked off the tape. "You're of no longer use to me, Mister Gross," she was happy to confess as she aimed her gun and shot Ricky three times in the face. "Tammy? Hand me your Uzi and go and get the thirty-two you used back at the stadium the other day," she then calmly requested while staring down at her handy work.

When Tammy left, Lisa began a quick search of the motel room as she held onto to the Uzi. She soon discovered the motel's phone receiver laying on the nightstand so she went and picked it up. "Hello?"

"Who's this?" Brenda asked, instantly growing incensed as she believed Ricky had a woman with him inside the motel room. "Where's my man?" she asked agitated.

"Your man is dead," Lisa responded coldly before hanging up the phone and placing the Uzi on the nightstand. Tammy returned at that moment and Lisa had her place the gun she'd used to kill the La Rocca brothers beside Ricky's corpse.

Lisa explicitly remembered saying, 'your man's dead' to an unknown woman the day she killed Ricky. But it wasn't until the day she'd searched Brenda's Range Rover the day Tammy had busted Brenda and Vivian King with 230 kilograms of cocaine back in December of 2008, that Lisa had put two-and-two together.

In that glove compartment, she'd uncovered a picture of Ricky Gross Senior and Brenda Marshall dating back to 1990. Lisa quickly realized that the woman that she'd talk to the day she killed Ricky Gross Senior was Brenda Marshall herself.

For some ungodly reason, Brenda hadn't picked up on Lisa's voice, nor that of any other move made after that. She wasn't too bright was what the agent had concluded. If Brenda hadn't picked up on her voice the past two weeks or so they'd been running together, then she never would. The murder was just too long ago and Lisa doubted if Brenda even remembered the conversation, but Brenda posed another problem for Lisa: she kept asking her to look into the death of her husband Ricky Gross Senior being she'd given up the people related to Tammy's killing.

Lisa kept putting Brenda off, but it would only be a matter of time before she perhaps learned the truth through some other source was Lisa's thinking. And it was because of that possibility, her finding out that she'd killed her husband, that Brenda Marshall would eventually have to be killed. Keeping her busy was the best move for right now, Lisa knew, at least until she could get the forgetful woman to hit back at the Germans. Only then would Brenda Marshall's usefulness become completely obsolete to Lisa Vanguard.

As memories of her killing Ricky ran through her mind, Lisa looked Brenda in the eyes and said, "I've killed men for things way more pricier than a hundred thousand dollars, and for much less than shit on tissue. I'm not paying you for killing Tanya, that's your own deal. I'm only getting you started over in Baltimore. We have two hundred kilograms of heroin to off in the middle of all that's about to go down." Lisa then pulled out a set of keys and pulled three keys off the ring and handed them to Brenda. "These are the keys to my club down in Baltimore called Jonas', and the delivery truck you'll take over to a warehouse I own not too far from there the day I call. The club has a bed and a kitchen on the second floor. You can use it as a base of operations. In between the deals, get you some men and track down Tanya over in Cincinnati for Raiden. Can you manage those things for me?"

"It's a lot, but I can deal with it," Brenda replied casually.

"Good," Lisa remarked. "You take care of things back east and Bridgette will handle this thing with the Devereaux family. My job is to keep us ahead of any investigation and to distribute the remaining eighty kilograms out here. Let's get to work, ladies," she ended as the women began to disband.

CHAPTER TWO

UP IN CHICAGO

"And the Chicago Cubs close out another series with a one run advantage over the Atlanta Braves in a twelve inning game that lasted for just over five hours here at Wrigley Field. It is their second sweep of a series in a row and they're on a roll midway through the 2009 baseball season. Next up, the Cincinnati Reds in a Friday afternoon game," a commentator remarked.

Seventy-six-year-old DeeDee watched the wall-mounted television screen from a bar stool inside a sparsely-filled Cicero Hot Dog Deli as the popular establishment grew near to its eleven 'o' clock weekday closing hour.

It was Wednesday, June 3, 2009. Five days after the meeting that Lisa Vanguard had held with the Moto brothers over in Seattle with Brenda Marshall and Bridgette Fischer. If only for a moment, DeeDee found the need to get away from his condominium overlooking Lake Michigan as it had quickly become a depressing place to call home. Ever since the night Dawk had killed Malik Gomez, his had become a world of tending to an ailing Sharona Benson, whose medical plight had worsened in a short span of time.

Thank God for Irene having traveled to the Windy City to give him a break for the evening was his reasoning, as he just had to get away from it all. Sharona was in constant pain. She was withering away before DeeDee's very eyes and he was powerless to stop her inevitable death. She was on a donor's list, but her chances of receiving a kidney transplant before she succumbed to her ailment seemed impossible. He sat with his hands tucked beneath his chin trying to figure out a way to save his son's mother, but he hadn't a clue as to where to begin as doctors were already doing all they could do.

"Eh, the Cubs won! That's far, few and between with those lovable losers," twenty-seven-year-old Natalia Cannapolis III quipped, shaking DeeDee from his thoughts as he approached the counter and slid a cold twelve-ounce Bud Light across the wooden counter.

"Yeah, it was a good game. Lasted well past the time I planned on being out, though, Natalia." DeeDee groaned as he eased up from the barstool. He rubbed his right knee and said, "I've had my share of beer, son. I have to be alert for Sharona tonight. I'm taking over duties for Irene."

Natalia III knew of DeeDee's concern over Sharona's plight. He knew of a way to help possibly, but he'd been reluctant to mention it; seeing DeeDee in such a downtrodden state over losing a woman he had a long-standing history with, however, had prompted him to hint at the idea. "You can save her, you know?" he said to DeeDee from behind the bar counter in a near whisper as he eyed four patrons inside the deli standing up from a table and gathering their belongings.

"Say again?" DeeDee asked as he looked back at Natalia.

"Your lady Sharona. All she needs is a new set of kidneys. She gets a new set of kidneys that match her blood type and her body accepts it? She can survive this thing."

"She's on a donor's list and I'm willing to pay whatever the cost to see her survive this ordeal," DeeDee admitted. "But until her name is up, there's nothing I can do, son."

"That's where you're wrong," Natalia countered. "If you get the kidneys? You can have them installed."

"Installed? Like spark plugs or new head gaskets on a vehicle." DeeDee questioned as he placed a foot on the brass shelf running along the base of the counter and leaned into it.

DeeDee was being facetious, but the sarcasm he carried hadn't gone undetected by Natalia. "Yeah," the Italian nonchalantly remarked as he rested his hands on the counter and stared back at the aging gangster. "Like spark plugs or a new engine or what have you. It's what doctors do. They're body mechanics that can fix things. If you get the parts? And the right body mechanic to install said parts? You can save your son's mother. We have people in the family who can get kidneys for Sharona. If you find a doctor willing to perform the surgery? They can get her some kidneys."

DeeDee breathed in deeply as he eyed Natalia with open contempt. He could only imagine the processes needed to be undertaken in order to obtain kidneys for Sharona and he wanted no part of it as it was too dark for even a man of his violent history to fathom. "She's on the donor's list," he told Natalia for a second time as he stood upright and buttoned his suit jacket. "That's well enough."

"Okay, DeeDee," Natalia relented while wiping the bar counter. "If you change your mind, though? The offer still stands."

DeeDee extended a hand to Natalia and said, "As much wrong as I've done, the lives I've taken? I can't imagine signing off on something like that. See ya' later, son."

"I understand," Natalia responded while shaking DeeDee's hand. "I won't bring it up again. Let me get a couple of guys to escort you home."

"That's alright," DeeDee objected. "I'm retired and have no enemies. I'll be okay."

"Eh, ya' never know. Could be an old score that needs settling. Stone and Carlos is parked right outside there with my cousins. I'll get them to tail you home," Natalia insisted as he walked from behind the counter.

"Have a good one," was all DeeDee said as he put a hand in the air and pulled one of the doors open and left the building.

The hot dog deli sat in the middle of the block on Twenty-Third Street. DeeDee's caramel 750 Series BMW was parked to the left; behind it was an idling four door, black on black Lexus 350 with tinted windows and chrome wheels. Natalia III's navy blue Expedition on thirty-six-inch chrome wheels was straight ahead, and off to the right was a white, California Edition Mustang with *Cicero Police* painted in black on its sides.

DeeDee stepped out the deli and looked to his right. The doors on the patrol car opened and thirty-one-year-old Renata Cannapolis and her younger brother, twenty-seven-year-old Orlando Cannapolis, exited.

Renata and Orlando were Natalia III's cousins. They were Scoffield 'The Butcher' Cannapolis' grandchildren. Scoffield was the Cicero mobster who'd made Finland Xavier and Lester Sexton disappear. He'd retired from the body disposal business a few years ago, and now that part of the operation was being ran by Natalia III, Renata and Orlando. The three were also moving sixty kilograms a month for the Holland family. The people that were hanging outside the deli, along with Natalia III on this night, were the top members of the Cannapolis family, the Chicago faction of the Holland family. They were DeeDee's people up in Chicago who was like family to the man as he'd been around most of them since the day they were born.

Renata, a well-toned and tanned 5'9" one hundred and seventy pound full-bloodied Italian woman with shiny, short hair dyed a dark burgundy, waved at DeeDee as he stood under the orange streetlight waiting on her to approach him. "Enjoyed your game, sir?" she asked with a gleaming smile over the cackle of her shoulder-mounted radio. She reached over, turned the volume down and said, "We were listening out here. Good win for the cubs!"

"Don't you sir, me, girl," DeeDee chided as he gave the lovely Renata a brief hug and kiss on the cheek. "I enjoyed the time, baby," he smiled. "I needed the break, but I'm on my way home now."

"How's Sharona, DeeDee?" Renata asked, concerned.

"Not, not too well, Renata. If she doesn't get a donor…she may not survive."

"Oh, Christ," Renata sighed as she rubbed DeeDee's arm tenderly. "If there's anything we can do let us know, okay? I'm praying for her now so she'll be okay."

"That's quite conceited of you," DeeDee chuckled as he pulled out his car keys.

"Hey! Can God resist this face?" Renata laughed as she kissed DeeDee's cheek. "Be safe, DeeDee," she smiled.

"And you be safe out here in these streets, pretty lady," DeeDee remarked as he walked over to his BMW.

As DeeDee started to enter his car, Renata whistled and got the attention of the passenger sitting in the black, four door Lexus 350. She made a motion with her hands, signaling the car to follow DeeDee, and it eased away from the curb just as the original gangster pulled off in his BMW and made a right turn onto South Laramie Street.

DeeDee approached I-290 and headed east as he pushed in a CD. The ride down I-290 was uneventful for the most part as Smokey Robinson's song *Cruising* came over the speakers. There was heavier traffic than normal for a weekday night, DeeDee noticed, but it was almost summertime up in Chicago, though, so many around town were out enjoying the warm late spring evening just as he'd done earlier. He relaxed over the music as he took in the sights of the city while cruising up the freeway. People were walking in groups on overpasses, the stations along the El route that ran in the middle of the interstate were all packed and he could see the lights from the downtown skyscrapers up ahead as he rolled past several west side neighborhoods where he once controlled the streets.

Near the I-290/I-90 interchange, the traffic slowed to a crawl as people leaving the Cubs game and heading out to the northern and western suburbs descended on the area. Seventy-six-year-old DeeDee thought about the offer from Natalia as he made his way through the traffic. He kept shaking his head over the process he knew would be taken. Whoever did the job would have to kidnap an innocent human being and remove the organs. As cold-hearted as DeeDee could and had been in times past, he couldn't get himself to go along with the offer Natalia had put on the table.

Traffic died down once DeeDee crossed under I-90. East Upper Wacker Drive was beginning to slow, so he jumped off onto Michigan Avenue where he headed north across the Chicago River and linked up with North Lake Shore Drive.

With Lake Michigan off to his right and rows of condominiums, hotels and restaurants and other businesses on his left, thoughts of his son crossed DeeDee's mind as he pulled up to a red light just up from Oak Street Beach. It'd been a while since he'd seen his youngest boy. Doss III's birthday was coming up in three weeks and the soon-to-be eight-year-old had asked DeeDee for a four-wheeler to ride on the ranch. He sat picturing his boy riding the bike across the ranch down in Oklahoma on his special day, but his smile soon dropped when he remembered that Sharona may not be around to see her son's eighth birthday. His eyes welled up and he bit his bottom lip in frustration while rubbing his temples as the light turned green.

A horn from a car in the lane behind him shook DeeDee from his thoughts and he continued traveling up North Lake Shore Drive for another half mile or so. He made it to his condo and waited for several cars and pedestrians to clear out before he turned left into the underground parking lot of the high rise. A cream-colored Ford Taurus that'd been inconspicuously tailing him kept straight ahead, but the black on black Lexus was turning in behind him.

After riding up three levels inside the garage, DeeDee pulled into a parking spot a bit of ways down from the elevators and shut down the engine. He sat thinking in silence about Natalia's offer until he was startled by a tap on the driver's side window. DeeDee jumped and reached for the .44 magnum he had laying on the seat beside him, but he'd cringed over a sharp pain that shot up into his right knee. Old man discomforts had stifled Doss Dawkins Senior as he looked over to the window and saw a gun in holster.

"Mister DeeDee, I was making my rounds and saw you pull in. You need help with anything tonight?" a young, Caucasian parking lot security guard in his mid-twenties asked, his voice muffled as he stood beside DeeDee's 750 series BMW.

DeeDee let the window down. "I could use a ride over to the elevator, Murphy. I just, my knee kind of gave out on me," he stated calmly as the Lexus that'd been tailing him pulled up.

"Mister DeeDee, everything all right," the passenger inside the Lexus asked.

"I'm fine, Stone. Just a little pain in my knee."

"I'm sure one of your lady friends'll work that out for you, Mister DeeDee," twenty-six-year-old Murphy Harbaugh, stated through a smile. "I was just about to ride him over to elevators, Stone."

"I'll ride too," Stone remarked as he climbed out of the car and hopped onto the golf cart.

"I don't really need all this security. The elevator has a code on it," DeeDee complained as he, Stone and Murphy rode towards the elevator with the Lexus creeping slowly behind.

"Everybody knows that code," Murphy chuckled under his cool demeanor as he drove with one leg out of the cart. "Not you, Mister DeeDee, but all these other old timers around here give the code to their old ladies, they give it to their friends, their friends friends give it to their friends, all the delivery guys that come here has that elevator code," he laughed as he scratched his neck tattoos. "This security company and the guys who run it? They sloppy as shit. They done let a couple of people back here get robbed."

"You security. Shouldn't you be handlin' that shit, Murphy?" Stone asked with a grimace planted on his face.

"The people gettin' robbed not talkin' to the police or anyone," Murphy remarked as he pulled up to the elevator and brought the golf cart to a halt. "And the owners all refuse to report anything because they don't wanna lose tenants. The cameras are outdated so I can't even get a good look at the robbers' faces. The intercoms on some of the floors ain't working either. A lot of people that come here claim to know somebody. All they need is the elevator code and we gotta let 'em in regardless."

"Yo, you hearing this?" Stone asked he looked back at the Lexus. "Why you didn't let us know all this was going on, Mister DeeDee?" he asked as a brown-skinned chiseled-jawed, Black/Italian with curly black hair and a smooth, hairless face and cold, dark eyes looked up from behind the driver's side of the Lexus.

"I'm retired," DeeDee said while shaking his head in disapproval as he slid out of the golf cart. "I have a sick woman I'm dealing with and another woman who's falling out of love with me upstairs. Nobody's worrying about me."

"I'm sure the people who got robbed back here had similar stories, Mister DeeDee," the dark-haired twenty-eight-year-old Black/Italian, whose name was Carlos Aranello, stated from behind the wheel as he ended a phone call. "Stone, ride up there with him and make sure he gets in safe."

"My son be eight in a few weeks fellas," DeeDee smiled as he pushed the elevator button, resolving himself to the security crew.

"Get the fuck outta here!" Murphy laughed from the golf cart. "You got an eight-year-old boy, Mister DeeDee?"

"Yeah, you never met him, Murphy?" DeeDee asked surprised.

"Nahh. You got 'em some pussy yet, though? I know how you get down," Murphy stated, bringing about slight laughter from Stone and Carlos.

DeeDee laughed right along with young men as the elevator door opened. "Not yet, Murphy," he chuckled. "But my oldest grandson brought my youngest grandson a woman when was around fourteen and it's been on since."

"That's about right," Murphy laughed. "Hell, I wish I had a brother to buy me some pussy when I was fourteen. I had to use an alternative measure."

"What you do, Murphy?" Stone asked as he stepped onto the elevator.

"What any horny teenager from Wisconsin would do."

"What's that? Fuck your sister?" Stone asked casually as he held the door back for DeeDee.

"Nahh, I paid your mother ta' suck me off with ya' jive ass." Murphy shot back.

"Yeah? Knowing the type of woman she is, ya' probably did and she accepted that shit, that old skank," Stone said as he pushed the button leading up to the thirtieth floor.

The men chuckled as DeeDee boarded. "I know his mother," DeeDee smirked while shaking his head and rubbing his crotch.

"What's that look?" Stone asked as he stood beside DeeDee, looking him up and down.

"What, Stone? I just said I know your mother that's all, son." DeeDee laughed.

"Nahh, but you had a look in your eye. Like a twinkle or something and ya' rubbed ya' dick while doing it."

"The fuck you watching my moves that close for, boy?" DeeDee chuckled as he leaned up against the back of the elevator and folded his arms.

"He was thinkin' about the time he fucked your mother, Stone," Murphy laughed aloud as the elevators closed.

Carlos eased out of the Lexus at that moment and dusted his dark grey silk slacks straight and shifted the gun he had tucked in his back waistband up under his black, short-sleeved silk shirt. "How is your business in Milwaukee," he asked in a smooth, deep-pitched Italian accent as he walked up and dapped Murphy off.

Carlos Aranello was the main street Enforcer inside the Cannapolis family. He lived in Cicero, but he operated inside Chicago.

"I need another ten bricks," Murphy replied calmly as he sat behind the wheel of the golf cart. "We shouldn't make the deal here because of those robberies. I don't wanna take any chances. It's gettin' a little too rowdy back here."

"We'll do it tomorrow morning at the deli," Carlos let it be known. "Is the security really that bad around this place?" he then asked as he scanned the area over.

Murphy lived inside the condo and stored his cocaine there before shipping it to Milwaukee for distribution. That was the main reason he was concerned over the robberies and the easiness of getting inside the tower, but Carlos was reading something else.

"I'm telling you, bro," Murphy said to Carlos while shaking his head as he pulled out his cellphone. "This place need remodeling from a security standpoint. They plush on the inside. And everybody know you have to have money to stay here, but they also know the security ain't that good. A click from Riverdale just moved in, too. Making money and shit over there on the south side and then coming up here to party," the security guard explained as he texted his girlfriend. "Them mutherfuckas from Riverdale letting everybody they know off the south side up in this camp. Throwing wild parties and shit, having other tenants call in with complaints. We go up there all the time havin' ta' tell they young asses to keep it down. Then they argue, wanna fight and be pulling out guns and shit. They wild as the fuck. This tower ain't nothin' like it was just the year I been here."

"Look out for Mister DeeDee while you're back here tonight," Carlos requested. "We gone have to move him soon."

"He a few floors up from me, but I'll keep an eye on him, bro. Check on 'em and shit. I'll do it until ya' move 'em if need be, but that's only the short time I'm here. I'm gone be leaving this job and this tower. I'm looking for another spot right now. Just texted my old lady about it. Soon as we find another place I'm outta here," Murphy let it be known just as the elevator returned.

The doors popped opened and Stone stepped out. "That son of a bitch DeeDee did fuck my mother!" he snapped as he walked back to the Lexus.

Murphy and Carlos laughed lowly. "What'd you do?" Carlos chuckled.

"Eh, he's in there. Irene is up and Sharona was sleep. I swear if I didn't love the guy I woulda pushed 'em off the balcony for doing that shit to my mother."

"Why? Because he black?" Murphy asked.

"It's not because Mister DeeDee's black! It's because he done fucked every other mother I know in Cicero. You know how many guys I made fun of over that shit? This here gets out and boy it's gone be…" Stone's voice trailed off he slid into the passenger seat and closed the door.

Carlos chuckled as he turned to Murphy. "I'll let my people know about this place. Look after Mister DeeDee tonight and we'll move everybody tomorrow," he remarked to Murphy before he climbed back behind the wheel of the Lexus and pulled off.

DeeDee, meanwhile, had just finished tying a trash bag after entering his apartment and barricading the door. He closed the pantry and walked onto the deck of his immaculate three-story thirtieth floor domicile. The entire first floor was a picturesque scene of quietude. There was a set dinner table off to the right along with a spotless kitchen and a well-organized living room with contemporary style furniture set atop wooden floors and sunk below the marble-floored deck.

DeeDee looked and saw Irene resting on a black suede chaise beside the patio window across the way gazing out over the waters of Lake Michigan under dim lighting. "How's Sharona doing, baby? And why is her medication down here instead of in the bathroom upstairs?" he asked as he descended his theatrical staircase and unbuttoned his silk suit jacket.

Irene bothered not answering right away as she lay on the suede chaise sporting a tight-fitting royal blue leather outfit with powder blue heels and matching accents from earrings to bracelets and a silk scarf. She'd prettied herself for DeeDee and was actually modeling for him to get his attention when he walked into the condominium, but she was now telling herself that she should've known better as DeeDee had looked past everything she'd done not only to herself, but the entire first floor and had asked about Sharona Benson instead.

"I feel like a fool," Irene spoke softly as she gazed out the patio doors with her hand resting beneath her chin.

DeeDee wasn't surprised over Irene's sentiment. Ever since the night he'd introduced Sharona and Doss III to the family, he'd been stressing on how to balance two women he sincerely cared about, albeit for different reasons. He'd been involved with more than one woman at a time before, but never to the depths of the commitments he felt he owed Sharona and Irene. Sharona, he believed, deserved his utmost support. Irene, he felt, deserved the highest respect. Only one of the two women in his life was getting what he knew she deserved from an emotional aspect, however, and DeeDee knew it wasn't Irene.

"I understand your frustration," DeeDee admitted as he placed his silk suit jacket onto a coat rack and walked over to the chaise. "But, let me explain something to you, baby," he groaned as he took to one knee before Irene, who was looking down at him with an apprehensive look.

"What you coming with, Doss? You gone tell me I should just understand what you doing with Sharona because your woman dying, right? She took her medication down here a couple of hours ago and left it on the table if you must know," Irene complained as she sat up on the chaise, placed her heels to the wooden floors and stared into DeeDee's eyes.

"Sharona is not my woman, Irene. She's my son's mother. His dying mother. I know it's not easy on you, but it's not something I can handle on my own. I need you, baby. I really need you to help me get through this."

"Let's say Sharona survives, and I hope to God that she does for her son's sake," Irene confessed as she looked up towards the ceiling with her hands raised even with her shoulders. "But, where would that leave me and you, Doss? Because you did sleep with her," she spoke softly as she searched DeeDee's eyes for answers.

"You come first, Irene," DeeDee admitted as he rubbed Irene's thigh. "This is something I *have* to do. Don't make it so hard on me."

Irene reached out and grabbed both of DeeDee's hands as she rested her forehead to his. "By you asking me not to make it hard on you, you're making it hard on me, Doss," she truthfully stated while massaging the back of his hands with her thumbs. "I have no certainties in this arrangement other than the fact that you slept with Sharona during the time you and I was supposed to be monogamous. I know you were happy to find your son, and you didn't know about Spoonie until after we called. It wasn't because you were stressed is why you cheated on me. You slept with Sharona because of the simple fact that you wanted to. You're still in love with her."

"I fucked up, Irene. I have no excuse for what me and Sharona did that night other than to say I'm sorry. I'm owning up to my mistake—but if you wanna get up right now and walk out those doors I wouldn't blame you for doing so because you don't have to deal with this."

"I think I'm gone do that, Doss," Irene replied as she pushed off from DeeDee and eased up from the chaise. "I'm walking away from this situation."

"You can't be serious, Irene!" DeeDee exclaimed as he eased up to his feet.

"And you can't be serious, Doss!" Irene retorted as she started to walk past her lover. "You askin' way too much of me! I'm takin' on way too much of a responsibility and my acceptance of this insanity can't go any further! I'm worn out over this shit!" she yelled aloud. "You can't even be honest about how you feel about Sharona! So how am I supposed to trust you going forward?"

"I didn't ask you to come here," DeeDee countered as he grabbed hold of Irene's right arm and gently pulled her back. "If you wanna leave go 'head and do it—but what you not gone do is make me feel guilty over a decision you made and you're now finding it hard to deal with your emotions."

"How would you handle it, Doss?" Irene asked as she calmed herself and stepped closer. "How would you handle me sleepin' with somebody else? And then springing some long lost child on you and asking you to accept it," she whispered lowly through her hurt. "And the man I cheated on you with and had this child for? He's dying and I need your help. How would you handle all of that? Would you be happy for me? Would you forgive me?" she asked seriously as she hid her face in DeeDee's slender chest.

"You're not the person I am," DeeDee countered as he held onto Irene. "You're strong enough to not do such a thing. But if ya' did, I'd love you enough to forgive you, baby. I'm sorry for hurting you, Irene. If I could take it all back I would, but not my son. That's something I don't regret."

"I don't regret that either," Irene confessed as she backed away from DeeDee. "I don't regret anything, but I resent what you did to me. I've done nothing but right by you ever since we've agreed to be together. You didn't have to sleep with her...you didn't have to sleep with her, Doss," she told him in a heartbroken, nearly defeated tone of voice as she folded her arms and looked away.

DeeDee reached out and removed a portion of the dyed, permed black hair from Irene's face and stared at her longingly. She kept herself well at age fifty. Her smooth, chocolate skin was soft to the touch. She was a slim, sexy woman with long, curvy legs slightly bowed, and wide hips and had firm breasts. She had a shapely rear that looked good in anything tight, like the leather pants she was wearing on this night.

Irene Charles moved DeeDee. She made him throb over the sheer thought of her presence and was able to stir his every emotion. "It was my one moment of weakness, baby. You know I love you, right?" he spoke tenderly as he pulled Irene close, leaned down and kissed her pouty, lip-glossed covered lips tenderly.

Irene welcomed DeeDee into her, but she wasn't overwhelmed by the moment. She hadn't the inclination to fling herself into his arms like in times past, but she returned the gesture nonetheless and gave it nothing more than what it was worth in her mind's eye: the first of several kisses to come that would bring their relationship to an end.

DeeDee held onto Irene, rocked her slightly and asked, "How about we crack open a bottle of wine and loosen our attire? Make out like old times."

"Loosen our attire? That's a new one from you," Irene laughed as she rocked with DeeDee. "The old times," she then smiled as she reflected on its meaning.

The 'old times' DeeDee was referring to were the days when he and 'Twiggy' would take trips to Cut Bank, Montana in the RV with Francine and Mendoza. The summer of 2008 was a hot season for the two, and one of the most memorable times of Irene's life. The town of Cut Bank was hypnotic and romantic to her. Wheat fields to the north, snow-capped mountains to the west, and blue skies that went on forever. Cut Bank had a spiritual effect on Irene. She and DeeDee had had many a romantic adventure there.

Irene was mesmerized by it all in the beginning. She'd never been to a place as beautiful and peaceful outside of the ranch in Oklahoma, let alone spent time with a man she loved in the way in which she shared intimacy with DeeDee. She was able to reveal her deepest secrets being so far away from home and under nature's spell. The last time they'd made love there, which was the day before they learned of Ben Holland's existence, Irene had shared with DeeDee the time she and Martha slept together down in Vicksburg, Mississippi. She gave him every explicit detail on how she went down on Martha and the two kissing one another afterwards as they lay side by side looking up through the RV's moon roof. The story had made them both horny and before Irene was done, both she and DeeDee had taken off their clothes. They made love under the stars. Irene in the missionary position looking up at the aurora borealis as DeeDee took her over the edge.

"Well," DeeDee asked, still holding on to Irene and shaking her from her thoughts. "What you say, baby?"

"I don't know if that's a good idea, Doss," Irene responded as she walked out onto the patio and looked out into the dark skies.

A feeling of acceptance had washed over DeeDee upon hearing Irene's response. The man hadn't lived seventy-six years to not know the temperament of the woman he was dealing with. Irene was letting go was the vibe he was getting. He straightened himself, walked out onto the patio and looked out over the waters of Lake Michigan as he stood beside Irene. "All things must come to an end," he remarked while looking straight ahead.

"We've outgrown our compatibility, Doss. The circumstances we both have to deal with done put up a roadblock. It doesn't mean I don't love you. I'm just no longer willing to deal with the emotions required in order to be involved in this type of a relationship."

"I understand, baby. We had fun together the time it lasted, though," DeeDee smiled as he gripped the iron railing.

"We did," Irene agreed. "I'm gone miss us. But I think it's best for me, you and Sharona. Doss III, too. He shouldn't grow up under hostility between me and his mother."

DeeDee rested his chin atop Irene's styled hair and inhaled her sweet fragrance. "One last time?" he whispered above her head.

"You're a persistent man," Irene chuckled as she turned and faced DeeDee, her back now facing the sky. "But…yeah. We're consenting adults. In spite of us parting ways, I'd be lying to myself if I said I didn't want to experience us one more tonight."

"What you want done, woman? For this final goodbye?"

"I want the wine you offered, the fireplace lit on this balcony, and you on your knees sucking my pussy while I smoke my weed," Irene answered as she placed a hand to the back of DeeDee's head and pulled him close to rub her cheek to his.

"No music? We used to listen to music over to Cut Bank, remember?" DeeDee asked through closed eyes as his hands drifted down to Irene's soft rear end.

"Yeah, I remember," Irene smiled over DeeDee's touch. "Put something on, babe," she requested as she turned around and rubbed her backside up against DeeDee's crotch. "Let's make it a time we'll never forget."

DeeDee kissed the nape of Irene's neck before he backed away and walked over to the fireplace. "I can do that and more," he said as he pulled a steel screen open on the fireplace and grabbed a bottle of charcoal lighter fluid to spray over the dried logs. "Goodbyes don't always have to be sad affairs."

Irene watched as DeeDee patted his silk slacks and looked around. "Here," she said after going into her leather pants pocket and pulling out a lighter. "My weed is in the curio beside the wine rack."

"Are you going to do anything here?" DeeDee joked as he took the lighter from Irene and put a flame to a starter stick and threw it into the pit.

"I'm gone take a seat before the fire and wait on you to do what I asked you to do," Irene playfully sassed as she eased down into a leather seat and unbuckled her pants. "Go get my weed and wine, man."

"You gone stop ordering me around I know that much," DeeDee mockingly complained as he picked up a fire poker and stirred the flame. "Shoot, I ain't your butler. I' a man with some good dick and you know it."

Irene tilted her head back and laughed as she kicked off her heels. This was a rare moment—a situation where a man and woman were parting ways—yet agreeing to be together for one last time. Some in a similar situation would have expected for the police to be called, and/or the hurling of insults; but this was not

Doss Dawkins Senior and Irene Charles. Both were ending their relationship on not only on a happy note, but going about it with class and dignity as far as they were concerned.

DeeDee turned on his patio stereo, set the volume low and entered the condo just as the Isley Brothers' song *Groove With You* came over the speakers. He returned a few minutes later with two stem glasses and Irene's rolled blunt. He noticed she'd slid the chair closer the fireplace and had removed her pants. She lay on the chair with her legs bunched up close to her body, staring at the orange flames emanating from the fire pit with flames dancing off her gratified eyes. He handed her the weed and set about twisting the cork out of the bottle of wine as Irene pulled a chair up beside her. The roar of a departing aircraft's engine blended in with the music as DeeDee poured.

"I feel a little uneasy about this knowing Sharona's resting," DeeDee stated over the churning sounds of wine rising up in Irene's stem glass.

"I was thinking the same thing, Doss," Irene responded as she took a sip of her wine. "Are we wrong?"

"I don't think so," DeeDee stated seriously as he set the wine bottle down atop a small circular glass table. "Sharona knows about you, baby. We only slept together that one time. There's nothing between us now except for my son and me looking after her."

Irene picked up the remote control to turn the volume up on the patio stereo and the smooth sounds of The Isley Brothers encompassed the entire balcony. "Light me up," she requested.

DeeDee leaned over and lit Irene's blunt. As he did so, he looked down at the silk covering her vagina and started to throb as his manhood grew in length.

"You gonna taste it or what, Doss," Irene asked as she reached down and pulled her panties to the side and put her bald, savory-looking vagina on display.

DeeDee took a seat in the chair on Irene's right side. "I'm gone do that and more," he chuckled as he removed his brown gator shoes and sat them beside the chair. He then stood and unbuckled his silk slacks and stepped out of them.

Irene watched DeeDee undress as she toked on her blunt. Some may wonder what a fifty-two-year-old woman saw in a seventy-six-year-old man. For starters, Irene didn't see an old man in DeeDee. He had low-cut grey hair and thin sideburns. He looked a couple of decades younger than seventy-six, and he was fit for his age. DeeDee was a slender man, 6'4" and one hundred and eighty-five pounds with toned, dark brown hairless skin. He wasn't ripped or anything like that; his age showed in some parts, but overall, he was a handsome, well-kept man to Irene.

Working around the ranch kept him active, plus he also ate well. He was an old-school cat that reminded Irene of some of the mafia-affiliated gangsters her brother Albert Lee used to meet with back in the day when she was growing up on the west side of Chicago in the early seventies. She'd always had a crush on those types, but Albert Lee had always said they were dangerous. When she met DeeDee down on the ranch, she'd met the man of her dreams. It didn't go the way she'd expected, but Irene would always love DeeDee. She just couldn't be his woman any longer after what'd he'd done with Sharona.

While DeeDee disrobed, Irene got up and topped off their glasses. She turned and faced a naked DeeDee and struck a pose in her bra and panties while holding up the glasses. "We forgot to toast," she smiled as she eased over and handed him a Stem glass.

"What are we toasting?" DeeDee asked as Irene sat in the chair beside him.

"Memories. Good memories," Irene smiled as her eyes welled up. "For a while, you were the best thing that ever happened to me, Doss. You made me feel like a real woman. I never got love from a man like I got from you. It took me fifty years to find the love of my life…but after tonight he'll just be my friend."

"To friends," DeeDee toasted while smiling down his nose at Irene. "My memory of you will be, if someone were to ask, my memory of you would be that of a fun-loving, adventurous woman all the way around. I love how you used to get in the RV and just drive Francine and us all up to Cut Bank without even using a map," he said before sipping his wine.

"Me and Francine making a drive up there next month." Irene smiled and sipped her wine as DeeDee moved and sat beside her. "She holding true to Mendoza's last wish on taking his great grandkids to Montana before he was killed. Malaysia and Malara love it out there too. And it'll always be a special place for me," she blissfully declared.

"Maybe after all this has come to pass I can ride out there with you and Francine again. Me and Doss III and Tacoma."

"Maybe so," Irene smiled as she sat her glass aside and ran her fingertips over DeeDee's smooth lips. "But if I remember correctly, these sexy lips of yours were to be busy someplace else."

DeeDee leaned over and kissed Irene's full lips. He set his wine glass down and cupped her mound gently and rubbed her vagina through her silk panties. She spread her legs wider and nudged his head downward while reaching for her blunt and relighting it. Just as his tongue touched her inner lips, she inhaled the smoke and tilted her head back, sighing as she shook her head slowly with her eyes closed. "That's right. Suck that pussy, baby," she couldn't help but to longingly moan out as she and DeeDee both gave way to their heart's desire.

THE HOLLAND FAMILY SAGA

CHAPTER THREE

THERE'S STILL ANOTHER WAY

Sharp pains in her back forced Sharona Benson to sit upright in the king-sized bed on the second floor of the condominium, abruptly ending her slumber. "Irene!" she called out as she stumbled out from under the silk sheets and mink comforter and wobbled over to the bathroom in her disheveled silk gown in search of her pain medication. She pulled the medicine cabinet open and rummaged through it, knocking aside bottles of Excedrin PM and Aleve in search of her morphine pills. "Downstairs," she mumbled to herself upon remembering where she'd left her doses. The time she'd moved from in front of the sink, Sharona collapsed to the ceramic floor in agonizing pain. "Irene! I think I need a doctor!"

Getting no response, Sharona dragged herself out of the bathroom and onto the wooden floors of the bedroom. Although feeling as if she was being poked with a thousand hot needles in her back and sides, she still had enough strength to pull herself up from the floor onto her knees. Tears fell from her eyes as she crawled over to the bed and grabbed her cellphone off the nightstand. She leaned up against the mattress inside the dark room as she pressed a button to illuminate the screen. She quickly dialed 911 as she began crawling towards the bedroom's door.

"911 is this a medical or fire emergency?" an operator asked.

"Medical," Sharona panted as she crawled across the bedroom floor. "Irene, where are you?"

"Am I speaking to Irene? Does Irene need help?" the operator asked.

"I need...I need medical!" Sharona cried as she crawled out of the bedroom onto the walkway. "Irene, where are you?" she screamed as she began crawling head first down the staircase leading to the first floor.

"Your name and condition, ma'am?"

"Twelve, twelve fifty-five Garden Towers on Lake Shore Drive," Sharona yelled at the operator. "Irene!" she then called out again.

"Are you Irene, ma'am?" the operator asked casually as she typed in the address and alerted an ambulance unit.

"Just come quick!" Sharona pleaded as she started to pull herself down the stairs while holding onto the steel railing. "Irene, where are you!" she called out as she struggled to pull herself down to the first floor.

Sharona could faintly make out the images of large silhouettes moving about on her right as their shadows bounced off the brick walls out on the patio. When the image of Irene sitting in DeeDee's lap facing him bouncing up and down at a fast and frantic pace came into view through the iron rails, Sharona grew enraged, not over the fact that Irene was fucking DeeDee, but the fact that she was doing it when she needed her help. A few hours ago, before she'd gone to bed, Irene was sitting with her while DeeDee went and watched the Cubs game. Now, here she was having sex with him while she was on the verge of passing out. Sharona let go of the railing and flung her cellphone towards the patio before laying back on the stairs.

"Fuck me, Doss! Fuck me good!" Irene groaned while rocking in DeeDee's lap. His dick was up in her belly and she was out control with passion as she began rotating on his pole with her fists balled up and back arched inwards. "Oh my god," she moaned just as an unknown object came flying through the opened patio doors and popped her on the left side of her head.

Irene fell off to the side and grabbed her forehead. "Fuck was that?" she asked as she checked her hand for blood.

DeeDee looked in the direction the object had come from and spotted Sharona laying on her back on the bottom two stairs in an immobile state. "Baby," he called out as he hurried back into the condominium and took a knee beside her.

Irene, meanwhile, had gathered herself. She had a small opening on her forehead, but it didn't prevent her from running past Sharona and DeeDee in her stockings and blouse. She hurried up the theatrical stairs, grabbed Sharona's morphine pills off the dinner table and quickly returned to her and DeeDee's side as she twisted the cap off the medication.

"She not moving!" DeeDee panted as he cradled Sharona's head in his hands while tilting it to the side.

"Is she breathing?" Irene asked as she set the pills aside.

"I can't tell! Sharona!" DeeDee screamed aloud as he shook the woman's head.

Irene placed a hand to Sharona's neck and found no pulse. She didn't want to frighten DeeDee over her finding, so she kept her analysis to herself and moved forward with her mission. "Let's move her down to the floor," she requested.

Once Sharona been paced on her back at the foot of the stairs, Irene began using the CPR training she'd received down at the Valley Brook Warehouse by tilting her head back slightly. She leaned down and pressed her lips to the unresponsive woman's mouth while pinching her nose. After blowing several breaths into Sharona, she rose, placed the palm of her hand to her chest and firmly pressed down three times before placing her ear back before the woman's nostrils. Warm air flowed over her earlobes, letting her know Sharona was breathing once again. Irene repeated the act several times until forceful knocks on the door sounded throughout the condominium.

"Somebody called for an ambulance?" "Chicago paramedics on hand in lieu of assistance!" "Paramedics, Sharona!" random voices were heard yelling aloud.

DeeDee looked over to Irene then down at his half-naked body. "Go and get yourself together," she said, nodding her head towards the stairs. "I got this," she told him.

DeeDee trotted up the stairs while Irene left Sharona for the moment to answer the door after placing a coat over her body. A quartet of paramedics were on hand, complete with a gurney the time she'd pulled the double doors open.

"Where is she, ma'am? Sharona!" the lead paramedic frantically called out as she rushed into the condominium, blowing past a startled Irene.

This wasn't the first time Sharona had to be rushed to the hospital. Majority of the EMTs in the area were aware of her situation and she was always made a priority. This was DeeDee's old lady after all—and he was a Chicago legend. Anybody affiliated with him warranted top-notch treatment. DeeDee received it, and Sharona was no different.

This entire situation was brand new to Irene, however; she was frightened out of her mind for Sharona and hadn't understood the seriousness of the woman's illness until this exact moment. She was unable to respond as the stepped aside and let the medical team into the home.

"Ma'am, where is she?" the lead paramedic asked again as she walked across the marble-floored deck while scanning the kitchen and dining area, only to find it void of occupancy. "Sharona!" the woman called out again as she trotted down the stairs leading into the sunken living room.

"She's over by the stairs," Irene urged, snapping out of her brief trance as she led the EMTs back into the home. "She had no pulse, but I gave her CPR and she's breathing on her own now."

The EMTs rushed over to Sharona and began stabilizing her. "Tell Mister DeeDee where're taking her to Mount Sinai," one of the medics remarked as he and the other two medics eased Sharona onto the gurney.

Irene backed up towards the patio and gripped her permed hair while watching the paramedics descend on Sharona. She'd been given an order, but she was unable to fulfill it given her astonishment over what was transpiring before her eyes.

"Blood pressure's low, heart rate is extremely slow and weak," the lead female paramedic remarked after taking Sharona's vitals. "We have to get her to dialysis before she goes into complete renal failure," the mid-forties dirty-blonde-haired Caucasian woman noted as the three male paramedics lifted the gurney. "Dispatch, this is Unit 434. We're gonna be enroute to Mount Sinai and I'm requesting a police escort to the front door of ER. We have a kidney failure in progress and we are going to need a nephrologist to be on hand inside the emergency room upon arrival," she radioed in.

"Roger that. Police unit is enroute. ETA is four minutes. Contacting the Nephrology Unit over to MS now," the dispatcher radioed back.

"Four minutes, guys," the lead paramedic remarked as she readied an IV for Sharona. She placed it on the woman in under thirty seconds and she was wheeled back through the home and carried up onto the deck.

Irene remained frozen up against the patio door covering her lower face as she watched Sharona being wheeled out of the condominium. She'd been harboring some doubt as to whether the woman was actually as sick as she'd proclaimed to be, but the truth had just been laid bare before her very eyes. She felt real low about herself having just witnessed what all Sharona had to go through on any given day that could very well be her last.

DeeDee came rushing down the stairs at that moment while buttoning up a silk shirt. "You gonna get dressed, Irene?" he asked calmly as he walked around the living room looking for his keys. "The escort doesn't usually wait. When Sharona gets to Mount Sinai, the nephrologists will take her into the intensive care unit. It's her low blood pressure. Doctors usually stabilize her before placing her back on the morphine. She'll be home in a day or two," he added as he pulled his keys out of the suit jacket he'd worn earlier.

"I never understood just how serious a crisis this was, Doss," Irene sorrowfully admitted with concern in her eyes. "I'm sorry for the both of you that you have to go through this," she said as she walked out onto the patio and began dressing.

"No need for apologies," DeeDee said as he stood near the patio doors waiting for Irene. "Sharona doesn't want the family to see her like this."

"So, what is she gonna just pass away without seeing anyone? I mean, she is going to die from this is what's gonna happen sooner or later if nothing doesn't change. It does her no good isolating herself. What about Li'l Doss?"

"We were hoping to bring Sharona there to the ranch for his birthday, but it looks like we'll have to have Doss III come here. We were going to tell him then."

"DeeDee," Irene said as she straightened her outfit. "This thing is serious. Sharona needs the full support of the family and all the help she can get."

"It's gone be all right, baby," DeeDee assured. "You ready?"

Irene stared at DeeDee with reluctance. "You don't think she's gonna die do you, Doss?"

"I can't imagine it, Irene. You don't know how painful this is to watch."

"Yes I do. I told you about my people," Irene replied as she reflected on the deaths of her brothers Nolan and Albert Lee, and that of her nephew Simone Charles. "They didn't die from disease, but they died before their time nonetheless," she told DeeDee. "Sharona needs help. Let's get over to Mount Sinai and we'll figure out what to do from there."

Once Irene had dressed, she and DeeDee left the condominium. They were met in the hallway by Murphy, who was coming to check on things. "What happened?" he asked as he walked towards DeeDee and Irene.

"It's Sharona. Her pressure's low and the EMTs say she may be going into renal failure," DeeDee answered as he pushed the elevator's down button.

"Oh shit! I'll ride down with you and take you the car," Murphy responded. "I hope she pulls through, Mister DeeDee," he ended.

****

The waiting room was silent as DeeDee and Irene sat awaiting word on Sharona. She'd been in intensive care for over an hour and both were anxious over her welfare. Irene had wanted to call Martha, but she was down in Phoenix, Arizona preparing to take a trip to South America with Ben. The only other person she felt comfortable calling with the bad news was Naomi, who was readying for a flight that would have her in Chicago come dawn.

A few more minutes had gone by when Natalia III, Carlos and Stone walked into the Nephrology waiting room. "Murphy called me and told me what happened to Sharona. How is she?" Natalia asked as he sat beside DeeDee.

"We haven't gotten any word yet," DeeDee answered through a sigh. "I can't keep going through this, Natalia," he confessed as he agonized over Sharona's plight.

"Yeah. It's a terrible thing to have to experience," Natalia III responded as he picked up a magazine and thumbed through the pages. "My mother's sister died from the same thing over in Sicily two years ago. The same thing used to happen to her until she went in and never came out," he admitted to DeeDee as he rubbed his neatly-trimmed black beard.

"Way to make us feel better," Irene remarked as she shook her head.

"My apologies, Miss Charles," Natalia III said as he closed the magazine. "I just know the seriousness of this type of disease," he said as he looked at the doors leading into the Nephrology operating room. "You go back there and look at all those people, young and old, withering away and moaning in pain? Sounding like ghosts in the night and it stays with you. You wouldn't wanna wish that on no one. And you most certainly wouldn't want your loved ones to have to go through it."

"Sometimes it's the will of God," DeeDee remarked.

"That's a cop out answer," Natalia III retorted as he leaned in closer to DeeDee while staring directly into his eyes. "Sometimes you have to take matters into your own hands because God? Well, He might have other things going on and can't get to you right away, understand me?" he asked in rhetorical fashion as he looked DeeDee off.

"That's the sort of advice you gone give your kids when have some?" Irene asked, bringing about a smirk from Natalia III.

"Okay," Natalia chuckled. "I didn't mean to dampen the mood and I apologize. I'll be right outside," he said as he eased up from the seat and threw the magazine down.

Another hour had gone by and there was still no word on Sharona. Natalia III had taken the time to talk to Carlos and Stone. Carlos Aranello was new to the Cannapolis family. He'd met Natalia when Natalia had taken a trip to Sicily two years ago to attend an aunt's funeral. Carlos came from a family of black/Italian Sicilians who supplied security for American Mafioso and other high profile criminals throughout Italy. He'd shown Natalia around to the local clubs and turned him on to the Sicily nightlife, the month he'd spent on the island. In turn, Natalia offered Carlos a job in America being he had dual citizenship, and Carlos accepted after getting approval from his family. He'd been running with Natalia III for the past year and a half now.

Stone, whose real name was Salvatore` Duche`, had grown up with Natalia III in Cicero since elementary school. He was a six-foot tall, one-hundred-and-ninety-pound olive-toned Italian with arm tattoos and a brown, bald-faded head of hair. He and Natalia

III had started out in junior high stealing cars and dropping them off at the Scoffield Scrapyard over in Gary, Indiana. Their first racket was a profitable one, and by high school, they'd linked their auto theft racket to another venture: armed robbery. The two had become proficient at holding up credit unions and small banks in Michigan and Indiana during the mid-nineties. By 2002, Stone and Natalia III had become made men inside the Cannapolis family, which was another faction of Twenty-Third Street Mafia.

"How'd the ride go over to the condo earlier," Natalia asked his men.

"We thought we saw like a cream or gold Taurus following DeeDee when he rode up Lake Shore Drive. They kept pushin' up the block when we turned off, though," Carlos remarked.

"Cream Taurus, huh?" Natalia III rhetorically asked. "Think it's something to worry about?"

"Can't say, il mio amico. DeeDee not the only high roller on that stretch. Coulda been anybody," Stone remarked.

"Or it coulda been somebody tryna find out where DeeDee stay," Natalia III countered as he rubbed his chin. "Eyes open on this fuckin' gold Taurus," he then ordered.

"They had some fancy chrome rims that stood out," Carlos noted. "They could be in the game Some jack artists maybe. I'll ask around."

"Okay then," Stone chimed in. "We find this fuckin' gold Taurus and ask whoever drivin' it what the fuck they doing hangin' 'round DeeDee's joint. They don't answer right I give 'em one in the kneecap. They usually talk after that," he shrugged. "Done deal."

"That old school shit," Natalia chuckled. "No kneecap busting until we find out exactly, Stone. Might not even be nothing."

"Or it could be fuckin' something like you just said," Stone retorted.

"It's in our best interest to cover all the angles here, boss." Carlos suggested. "It's gettin' pretty busy over where DeeDee lives from what Murphy tellin' me."

"I know that, okay, Carlos? I just don't want us kicking off shit around town by randomly shooting people. Especially without the family's permission," Natalia countered. "We'll move DeeDee.

He's already out of there, so we'll have 'em stay over to Renata's house for the time being."

"What about Sharona? She gone need somebody to be with her." Carlos replied.

"We'll get a caregiver to help DeeDee if Sharona survives this thing and they let her go home. We gotta a couple of EMTs back in Cicero that can sit with her part time, so she'll be fine," Natalia III stated.

Just then, the doctor operating on Sharona walked out from behind a set of steel doors. Everybody shifted focus as they gathered before the man in order to hear his prognosis.

"How is Sharona, doctor?" DeeDee anxiously asked as the group gathered around the stubby, Indonesian.

"Miss Benson's rapidly losing all kidney function, Mister Dawkins. Over two-thirds now," the doctor stated as he removed a pair of glasses. "She must remain in the intensive care for the foreseeable future. She's on dialysis as we speak. When she pulls through, she'll require round-the-clock medical care. More extensive, and intensive than before. Even then, if she doesn't receive a transplant? Sharona may have only two months to live. And that's being overly optimistic. It may very well be less than two weeks that she has to live," he proclaimed, much to everyone's astonishment.

DeeDee walked off with his hands on his hips and his head bowed as he choked back tears. The powerlessness he felt was comparable to nothing else he'd ever experienced. From afar, he heard Irene ask the doctor could anybody go in and see Sharona, but the doctor declined.

"How long before we can see her?" DeeDee turned and asked with red, watery eyes.

"Maybe in twelve hours or so, Mister Dawkins," the doctor remarked. "We're filtering her blood right now. It is a slow process. I'm sorry for what you people are going through. We'll do our very best to bring things under control with Miss Benson. Excuse me now," the physician ended as he turned and walked back into the operating room.

The group all gathered themselves into a circle, no one sure as to what to do except for to wait the twelve hours and hope for the best. "There's still a way, boss," Natalia III stated in a near whisper as he walked past DeeDee while thumbing his nose. "I'm heading down to the lobby for some fresh air," he then said aloud.

"That sounds like a good idea, Natalia. Come on, DeeDee," Irene suggested. "Let's take our mind off things for a while," she ended as the group walked out of the waiting room in silence.

****

DeeDee was back up in the waiting room having just awakened from a long nap several hours after having an early breakfast. Irene was beside him sipping a cup of coffee and Natalia III was busy working over a cheeseburger while reading the morning paper when Naomi walked into the waiting room.

"Eh, look who's here," Natalia smiled as he set his food tray aside, dusted his hands and stood up to greet Naomi. "Sharona's not doing so well," he somberly remarked.

"What's her status?" Naomi asked as she hugged Natalia briefly.

"I'll let Mister DeeDee tell you, ma'am," Natalia spoke humbly as he slowly walked off.

DeeDee walked up to Naomi while shaking his head somberly. "My son is going to lose his mother," he disclosed.

Naomi sighed as she hugged Doss. "DeeDee, I know you didn't want me to, but I brought your—"

"Sis-n-law Naomi? That snack machine took my dollar who we call about that?" seven-year-old Doss III snapped as he pushed the lobby door open and peeked inside. "Daddyyyy!" he then sang out loud as he rushed over to DeeDee.

Doss was stunned to see his son. He put on a pretentious smile and took a knee as Doss III ran into his arms. "Aww, my li'l man," he said while gripping his boy. "What are you doing here, son?"

"Sister-in-law Naomi asked me to fly with her because she was scared," Doss III nodded. "I sat by the window the whole time looking at the sky. And when we was landing? I got to see all of Chicago. I never saw it like that the last time me, you and momma flew to the ranch. I been down there for a long time. When are you and momma comin' home?"

Doss III had been on the ranch for nearly six months. He'd

attended homeschool classes while there and was given his own bedroom. He'd gotten comfortable with his father's people and was now calling the ranch home. The seven-year-old hadn't a clue that the main reason he was being kept on the ranch was because of the fact that his mother was suffering an illness.

DeeDee and Sharona had both agreed that Doss III shouldn't learn of his mother's sickness until it was almost a certainty that she would die. Naomi was getting constant updates. Three times over the past several months, she'd known of Sharona having to be rushed to the hospital. She'd always returned home, and Naomi was able to talk to the woman the same day. The circumstances surrounding this incident, however, had led her to believe that the end for Sharona would soon come after she'd talk to an unnerved Irene. She hung up the phone with Irene the night before and booked two flights with the intent of letting DeeDee finally explain fully what was going on with the boy's mother.

DeeDee understood Naomi's move. He rose and thanked her. "I don't know how to say it," he admitted.

"Neither of us do, Doss. But we have to do it," Irene interjected.

"You want me to sit with you two?" Naomi asked.

"Please," DeeDee requested as he grabbed hold of Naomi and Irene's hand. "Can we sit and talk for a minute, son," he then asked Doss III.

Doss III had sensed that something was wrong as he watched the adults talk. He knew he was in a hospital, but didn't know why. All he understood was that the last time he'd flown on a plane and went to a hospital, someone had been shot. He later found out that it was his niece Spoonie. There was another girl there, he remembered, that was his niece Koko. She'd had her foot run over. That was the day he'd met his entire family, and he loved them all from the very start.

Remembering what'd happened to Spoonie and Koko, Doss III looked at his father, then Irene and Naomi. "Where's my momma?" he asked scared.

DeeDee sat down and had Doss III climb onto his left knee. He placed a hand over his son's heart and said, "Your mother told me you used to have a book about a boy that was friends with a bear."

"Yeah, it's was my favorite story before I got to the ranch," Doss III said as he scratched his leg. "The bear used to meet the boy every morning and walk him to school until he didn't come around anymore. The little boy found the bear sleeping in the forest behind his house and his momma and daddy told him the bear had passed away."

"What happened to that bear happens to every living thing, son. Including us humans." DeeDee spoke. "But sometimes what happened to that bear happens to us human beings faster than others."

Doss III heart dropped. He lowered his arms and dropped his shoulders as he looked up into his father's eyes. "My momma gone die like the bear?" he asked as he hid his face in his father's chest and heaved. "I want my momma!" he yelled out in a muffled voice.

DeeDee held his son and wept with him. Naomi and Irene's faces both were wet with tears as the truth about his mother was revealed to Doss III.

"It's gone be okay, son," DeeDee comforted while rocking his distraught child. "Your birthday's coming up and we're all gonna be there. Your mother, too, I promise."

"What's wrong with momma, daddy?"

DeeDee placed his son back on his knee and said, "We have organs in our body called kidneys. Two of them. Without them? We can't live. Your mother's kidneys aren't functioning properly."

"They're broken?" Doss III asked while wiping tears from his eyes.

"You can say that," DeeDee nodded.

"Can she have one of mines?"

"Doctors say..." DeeDee paused at that moment. The sincerity in son's voice had moved him.

"You're too young, Doss," Naomi replied as she rubbed her brother-in-law's shoulder. "Your mother knows you want to help. You're helping by just being here, son."

DeeDee agonized over the thought of his son losing his mother at such a young age. "Naomi, can I ask you something in private?" he inquired.

"Okay," Naomi replied as she and DeeDee moved to an isolated part of the room and took a seat.

DeeDee took a deep breath and asked, "The doctor that operated on Spoonie, you think she could perform a surgery on Sharona?"

"Doctor Duchene is a talented surgeon, but I can't say whether or not she's ever done a kidney transplant. I'll call and ask her. Did Sharona receive a donor?"

"Not yet," DeeDee said as he began to stress over the decision he was contemplating. "But if we can get the organs and a doctor willing and able to perform the surgery we can save her life."

"Where're you gone get the kidneys from, DeeDee?" Naomi asked puzzled and clueless.

DeeDee leaned over and whispered to Naomi, "There's a racket for that. Natalia says we have people inside the family that can get us a set of kidneys?"

"Perhaps," Naomi remarked while staring up at DeeDee. "You sure that's what you wanna do? Will you be able to stomach it?"

"What other way is there, Naomi?" DeeDee countered. "Sharona has two months to live at best. I'm running out of options to save her life."

"I understand your plight quite well," Naomi replied as she looked down at the floor. "I will not approve of Doctor Duchene, though. Our friend down in Saint Louis that works at Mercy Hospital is the better option. How about you go and book a flight to Missouri while I talk to Natalia? Take Irene and Li'l Doss with you, they both could use some fresh air."

"Be sure and let the doctor know I'm coming. Don't tell him why," DeeDee replied as he turned his attention to his son and Irene.

"Natalia?" Naomi then called out.

"Yeah, boss?" Natalia asked as he walked over and sat down beside Naomi.

"The people you told DeeDee about? You sure they can handle the job? We can do it if you need us to."

"You haven't met them yet," Natalia III realized. "Trust me, they can handle it."

"I know that they're proficient given the Gomez hit, but we're talkin' about something totally different this time around."

"They're butchers," Natalia remarked seriously. "You got me? They're butchers."

Natalia's reply was all Naomi needed to hear as she now knew that DeeDee would be dealing with people just as capable as members inside her own family that would willingly go out and snatch up a body or two in order to save Sharona's life. "How much is this going to cost?" she asked.

"You lookin' at a quarter of a million dollars for the kidneys, plus, you'll have to pay the doctor whatever he charges to do the procedure. And until you find a matching set of kidneys, it's gonna cost fifty grand for each test the harvesters will have to conduct. If the kidneys don't match, they'll have to find another donor. It's gonna cost fifty thousand every time, be it the first attempt or fifteenth rip until they find a match on top of the quarter mill for said product, and the doctor's fee. It could easily run you up to two million dollars or more."

"It'll be money well spent," Naomi remarked while nodding her head. "Don't let DeeDee know, but I'll handle the finances. It's kinda close to home so I'll be able to report anything that shows up in the papers also," she ended as she grabbed her cellphone and made a call down to Saint Louis.

CHAPTER FOUR

LOOPY'S RETURN

"Your wound has healed sufficiently since we've removed the stitching. You may feel some slight discomfort bending a certain way, but it's because of the scarring on your liver. I also recommend that you not drink any alcoholic beverages for at least another month to allow your body to rid itself of the medications you've been under the past six months," seventy-two-year-old Doctor Obadiah Wickenstaff stated to his patient, twenty-two-year-old Guadalupe 'Loopy' Cruz, as she sat on the edge of the bed inside her recovery suite.

It was now early Friday morning on June 5th, two days after Sharona had been taken to Mount Sinai Hospital up in Chicago. Loopy had been confined to inpatient care after being shot through the side six months ago. She had a lot of time to put the pieces together on what'd gone down while she recovered from her wound. She remembered her and her cousin, Sweet Pea, were headed up to her friend Pepper's home in Louisiana, Missouri with their other friend, Simone Cortez, when they were ambushed. Simone was killed as she drove, and the Hummer she was driving had flipped over. Bullets started raining down on the jeep, Loopy remembered. She also remembered being unable to move as she watched her cousin Donatella crawl out the rear of the destroyed SUV holding onto a Mac-10 Uzi.

Pepper and Simone had done a lot of wrong in the game, and Loopy and her cousin Donatella were right along with them. Things had kicked off Halloween night in East Saint Louis back 2008 when seventeen-year-old Pepper had robbed Tito and Toine, known on the streets as the Charles brothers, out of two kilograms and forty thousand dollars in cash.

Tito and Toine worked for Toodie Perez. She went to East Saint

Louis the day after the robbery, investigated, and found out that Loopy and Sweet Pea, who lived on the same block as the Charles brothers, was inside the house that night with Pepper and they were in on the set up. Toodie and the Charles brothers then put out a bounty on Pepper and her crew, including Loopy and Donatella.

Loopy remembered her and Donatella having to move their Aunt CeeCee from the neighborhood when they found out about the bounty. She also remembered Pepper going to Malik and asking him for help in going up against the Charles brothers. A week later, in early November of 2008, Tito and Toine along with one of Toodie's Enforcers, Big Bounce, were killed inside of a bar-b-cue restaurant over in East Saint Louis. Whoever killed the Charles brothers and Big Bounce, was sent by the Holland family themselves, Loopy knew, and before she'd even realized, she'd been drug into a war between the people she and Pepper were working for and Toodie Perez. Loopy didn't expect to be in the game so deep, but she and Donatella had gone too far to turn back. They jumped in the game headfirst without having officially met the people they were working for.

Toodie eventually lost the war between her and the Holland family, but another Enforcer of hers by the name of Ya Murder, had survived the violence. And she'd gone to the group of Germans over in Cincinnati, Ohio, who were supplying Toodie's cocaine and reinstated the contract on Pepper for fifty thousand dollars. Malik Gomez was going to hide Loopy and her people out at a hotel in Saint Louis until the family could find out who Ya Murder was working with, but Pepper had insisted on driving up to Louisiana, Missouri to pick up extra clothes and money the night before.

Loopy thought back to the conversation she and her cousin Donatella had with Pepper just before they walked into Bangin' Heads Salon, and how the decision to follow Pepper up to Louisiana had changed the course of her and Donatella's lives forever…

…*"What Malik say to you, Pepper?" Sweet Pea asked the moment Malik pulled away from Bangin' Heads.*

"He gone set us up at the Millennium Hotel tomorrow," Pepper answered as she and her girls walked into the nearly empty salon. "Before we do that, though, I gotta go up to Louisiana and pick up some more money and guns. All we have is Loopy Mac-10 stashed in Simone's Hummer and a nine millimeter. We gone need some

paper while we over to the hotel."

"If we going to the hotel tomorrow we should just chill here in Saint Louis until the morning. Malik can give us some more guns and me and Sweet Pea have enough money," Loopy reasoned.

"Y'all got money but I don't. I gave up all my loot paying for that car we lost last night," Pepper retorted. "I got money stashed up there and I need to get it anyway."

"Well, well, well! The dirty trio has arrived," Kantrell dragged as she eyed her friends walking into the building.

Loopy came back to the present as Doctor Wickenstaff raised the sleeve on her red Cardinals t-shirt and placed a blood pressure strap around her left arm. She grieved the loss of her cousin as the last seconds of her life unfolded before her very eyes…

… "Donatella, no se mueven!" (¡Donatella, don't move!) Loopy pleaded, unable to control her arms and legs as she coughed up blood.

Sweet Pea ignored her cousin's request as she emerged from the rear window of the smoking Hummer while blasting her weapon, doing the best she could to stave off an unknown enemy. Bullets from her .9mm fired off into the night uphill and Loopy could only watch in futility as the silhouettes of her crew's attackers casually scattered amid Sweet Pea's gunshots while firing back at random.

Loopy heard a yelp spill forth from one of the gunmen as her cousin continued dumping off rounds as she stood outside the fallen Hummer. She could see the figure, who she believed was a female, given her scream, lunge up against the front of the Caprice while clutching her leg before she scurried off to the driver's side, her chrome rifle draping her side as she shielded herself.

Everything went silent at that moment as both parties had run out of bullets and had to reload. Sweet Pea threw the .9mm aside and knelt down at that moment. "Guadalupe, donde el Mac diez?" (Guadalupe, where's the Mac ten?)

Loopy tried to answer, but she now found herself unable to speak. She had wanted to tell her cousin to just lie down and play dead, but she couldn't utter a word. Blood continued dripping from her mouth, and now her nose. She tried to move her arms and reach out to Donatella, but she simply couldn't as she'd lost all control of her movements below her neck. She watched helplessly as Sweet Pea crawled around the Hummer on her knees looking for the Uzi.

Another jolt back to the present was brought about for Loopy when Doctor Wickenstaff removed the blood pressure strap. She remembered wishing Donatella hadn't found that gun she was searching for that night because when she did, she backed out the SUV and started shooting. Loopy remembered being shot just before her seatbelt gave way and collapsing onto the roof of the upturned SUV. It was the way her cousin's body stiffened that will forever haunt Loopy, because at that moment, she had just witnessed her cousin die before her very eyes. "*Usted debe haber me escuchó, Donatella.*" (You should've listened to me, Donatella.) she whispered lowly as she sniffled.

"Do you have a question, ma'am?" Doctor Wickenstaff asked in his deep-pitched, gracious voice as he set the blood pressure strap aside.

"Just thinking out loud," Loopy responded as a slender female dressed in tight-fitting denim Capris, a white, tight tank top and white Jordan's walked into the room and leaned up against the wall.

"Ahh, your friends and family are arriving, Guadalupe," Doctor Wickenstaff smiled. "Remember, no alcohol for thirty days at least. Your body is still absolving itself of the numerous medications you've been on the past six months so take it easy," he counseled.

"What about bud? Can I smoke marijuana?" Loopy asked as Doctor Wickenstaff pulled out a notepad.

"Off the record? I recommend the bud to aide in discomfort. Unfortunately, I can't write you a prescription for the Kush," Obadiah joked as he scribbled on his notepad. "I can, however, write you a prescription for codeine. You'll have sixty, five hundred milligram pills with no refill. One every eight hours is the recommended dosage, but I'm prescribing one every twelve hours for you because you've recovered well. If you should experience discomfort at any time don't hesitate to call or come back here so one of the other neurologists can reassess the situation," the doctor remarked as he ripped the prescription from his tablet and passed it on to Loopy.

"What I do now, doctor?" Loopy asked.

"You gone get up off that bed and we gone go get some real food! And some fuckin' marijuana like the doctor said!" seventeen-year-old Nancy Cottonwood snapped as she pushed off the wall. "You been cooped up in this joint long enough and it's time ta' get back to it!" she happily exclaimed.

"Get back to it is right," Loopy declared as she looked around for her fitted cap. "As far as I know shit's still on."

"Where's your Aunt CeeCee," Doctor Wickenstaff asked as he stood and looked down at Loopy. "I thought she would be here on this happy day."

"She had to go and see her social worker," Loopy replied as she reached over and grabbed her fitted Saint Louis Cardinal baseball cap and placed it on her head.

"Well, you have your friend Nancy waiting at least," Doctor Obadiah said just before he turned and headed for the door. "If ever you need someone to just talk to...you have my number. Take care of yourself, Guadalupe," he ended before pulling the door open and stepping out of the room.

"Doc gettin' all sentimental and shit with a bitch," Nancy laughed as she skipped over to Loopy's side and pushed the chair Obadiah was sitting in aside. "What you wanna do, homegirl? See your Aunt CeeCee and shit before we go and smoke some weed? I got some fire back at the house in Saint Charles," she said as she walked around the room checking out the suite. "From there we can head over to the New Orleans Café` and eat some gumbo and shit. After that? We gone head 'cross the street to Club Indigo and listen in on my brother new act. He signed this band called Jane Dow. They gone make us a lotta loot if they ever remember the fuckin' songs. Something off about 'em but I can't put my finger on it. But, anyway, a lot done happen since you been laid up! I done had birthday and shit. That chick Ya Murder got killed outside of Kirk's. You already know all that, but the biggest shit was with your boy Malik and that nigga Max that just happened not too long ago. Them niggas laid up there and tried ta' set Dawk up to be..."

Nancy's voice and everything she was talking about faded into the back of Loopy's mind as she eased up from the bed and looked her appearance over in the wall-mounted mirror. She'd never been too confident over her looks. She felt her face was too thin and her skin was too light. She didn't like her smoky eyes, which were drab to her. Her facial features made her look like a ghost was how she felt about herself, and she resented her appearance more than anything else in the world.

The way Loopy felt about herself wasn't her main issue, however; all that was on her mind at the present time was revenge for what'd happened to her cousin Sweet Pea and Simone. Pepper's death she could forgive. She was growing reckless and careless anyway. But in spite of those truths, Pepper was still Loopy's girl. She may not have agreed with how she operated, but she would've never killed her girl no matter what. Whoever was in the lime Caprice with the Boogie tag, they were going to get dealt with in quick and orderly fashion was Loopy's thinking.

Reason being was because the last time Loopy had talked to Bay and T-top was six months ago, when she'd told them that the people who'd done the job on her people may have been from Ohio. Loopy was offered the rank of Lieutenant and she'd accepted, but Bay and Tiva had left before she was able to discuss with them her wanting to retaliate. No one had gotten back to her on what'd gone down since then, so Loopy was just picking up where she left off. She was planning on putting a team together and asking Bay and T-top to allow her to hit back at whoever the click was up in Cincinnati that'd killed her people if they were indeed behind it. "Where's Bay and T-top?" she turned and asked Nancy.

"Yo, the feds is all over them two right now," Nancy let it be known as she snapped her fingers to a particular song that she'd been listening to during her ride over to Mercy Hospital while rocking in place. "The twins know you coming home today. Soon as they can get at you, they gone do that. Whatever you need until they get here I got you, though."

"You're just a baby. How can you take care of me when Jay-D and Dooney take care of you?" Loopy asked in an acrimonious tone as she went and grabbed a large cloth handbag out of the closet.

Nancy stopped dancing in place as she looked over to Loopy from across the room. "I'm doing what was asked of me. I got orders directly from Bay and T-top to look after you until they able to get here," she boasted.

"And that's something to be proud of?" Loopy gawked back at Nancy while placing Get Well cards and a few stuffed animals into the oversized bag.

"Hell yeah. Mean I'm moving up, homegirl." Nancy replied she resumed humming the song in her head and dancing in place.

Loopy grabbed a picture of her and Donatella and their friend Jessica 'Jessie' Suede from back in early March of 2004 and stared at it. The three had just won back-to-back championships over to McKinley High School down in Fox Park. Loopy and Sweet Pea were sixteen at the time. They'd had aspirations of earning scholarships to college through sports, but at the end of their senior year, their grandmother had moved across the Mississippi River into East Saint Louis, Illinois where the rent was cheaper and had opened up a taco stand.

A year later, Loopy killed a man after he'd robbed her Aunt CeeCee back in 2005. She and Donatella had been involved in the streets ever since. Now, four years later, Loopy had lost most of her friends and her cousin, and was recovering from a gunshot wound that'd pierced her liver and had nearly taken her life.

"You that down now, Nancy?" Loopy asked seriously. "Things done changed outside that much in six just months?"

"Fuckin' A!" Nancy confirmed. "Shit popped off after Pepper got killed. You remember everything. I was telling you what was happenin' every time I came and visited. What, you wasn't listening?"

"I heard what you said—a little bit," Loopy responded as she nodded her head and headed for the door. "Take me to your block. On the way I need you to call Malik and have him meet me there."

"You ain't heard shit I said!" Nancy boomed. "Malik ass is dead! Max is dead, girl! Shit done changed 'round here! Not just in the past six months, but in just the past six weeks!"

Loopy turned away from Nancy and placed her hands on her hips. "No one bothered telling me," she reasoned. "All my friends are dead. My cousin is dead. Pepper, Simone, Malik, Max. What good am I to the streets without a crew?" she asked as she looked back over her shoulder at Nancy.

"My brothers and me got you. You can roll with us," Nancy

suggested. "Yo, we'll work it out, homegirl. Come on, let me show you somethin'. I bought me a new whip for my birthday. A old school drop top seventy-eight Caddy," she said as she checked the time. "It's still morning out. The sun ain't blazing yet, so we can let roof back. Let's head over to the club where my brothers at and they can run everything down to you."

"Whatever," Loopy said dryly as she walked out the room.

Nancy rolled her eyes and followed Loopy out of the room. "I know you going through a lot," she remarked as she ran and caught up with Loopy and pressed the down button. "But if the family didn't care? They wouldna sent nobody. Everybody busy right now so they sent me. I'm just doing what was asked until the family can get at you."

"I know," Loopy replied casually as the elevator door eased open, allowing the two to step inside. "I'm not mad at you, but I am mad," she ended before pressing the down button.

CHAPTER FIVE

THE PACT

DeeDee had just stepped out of a separate set of elevator doors inside the Nephrology Unit just as the doors containing Nancy and Loopy closed on the opposite side of the reception hall. He looked around the area, eyeing several nurses moving about in their light blue scrubs while replenishing workstations and scribbling onto clipboards. He walked over to the counter and asked the whereabouts of Doctor Obadiah Wickenstaff, and was directed back down the hall he'd just walked up.

After greeting Obadiah's secretary and learning he was in, DeeDee was escorted back. Wickenstaff was sitting at his desk filing medical reports when the recognizable face walked into his upscale office. He stood and extended his hand and said in his slow-pitched, deep voice, "Haven't seen you in over two years I'd say, Mister Dawkins. I talked to your daughter-in-law Naomi the day before yesterday so I was expecting you. She said you had a matter you wanted to discuss?"

"I do," DeeDee remarked while shaking the doctor's hand. "And I appreciate you takin' the time to talk to me."

"What can I help you with, Mister Dawkins?" Obadiah asked as he moved to close his office door. "Sit," he kindly requested as he nodded towards a chair while grabbing two glasses and a clear, thorny crystal jar off his bookshelf. "I was preparing to have a morning glass of neat scotch as I am officially on vacation the next couple of weeks after I file these reports. You're welcome to one if you desire."

"I'll have one," DeeDee replied as he sat down in a leather chair before the doctor's desk. He crossed his legs and ran a finger over his lips in deep thought. "Where're you're going for vacation?" he asked.

"Ahh, I haven't the desire to travel abroad this time. I'm just going to enjoy a few of the golf courses here around the city. Enjoy the company of a woman for a date or two, and ride my horses. Maybe fish in my lake," Doctor Obadiah smiled while pouring drinks. The liquor churned into the glass on the desk as he poured in silence while eyeing Doss, wondering what it was exactly that had sent him his way. "I'd be amiss if I didn't ask about your call on this day when your family and I have concluded all business. Guadalupe Cruz was released minutes ago and I was just drawing up the final bill for Naomi to cover the costs. I don't expect any problems there, or are you here to tell me otherwise?" the doctor inquired.

DeeDee took a sip of his scotch and said, "This has nothing to do with Bena or Guadalupe, Mister Wickenstaff. I came to ask you a question."

"I see," Doctor Wickenstaff nodded as he rounded his desk while holding onto his glass of scotch. "What is it that you would like to know, Mister Dawkins?"

"You've worked on my granddaughter's brain. Did a miraculous job."

"Thank you," Obadiah remarked as he took a sip of his scotch before sitting down across the desk from DeeDee. "Bena, Bena helped me because she was willing to fight for her life. I've seen many gunshot victims succumb to the shock. That sometimes kills them rather than the actual shooting. Bena is a strong woman."

"It runs in the blood," DeeDee stated as he took another sip of his scotch and set his glass down on the marble desktop. "My question is, is how good are you in performing other types of surgeries. Or are you just a lobotomist?"

"You have your terminologies mixed up, Mister Dawkins," Doctor Obadiah disapproved as he leaned back in his chair and crossed his legs. "A lobotomist operates on the brain and makes one tranquil and lethargic. I'm a neurologist. I give my patients back their vigor. I'm far from a lobotomist, a person who can also be labeled as a quack."

"I meant no insult, Doctor," DeeDee apologized. "I guess I'm asking can you do an organ transplant. Can you give a person back their vigor that way?"

"I've done nine heart transplants, five lung transplants and a handful of kidney transplants," Doctor Obadiah boasted before taking another sip of his scotch and looking out over the hospital parking lot. "I've also assisted in several brain operations, removing part of the cerebral cortex in one instance. The patient is perfectly fine as of today."

"Amazing," DeeDee said as he sipped his scotch. "How're your kidney patients doing, Doctor?" he then asked.

"The thing with transplants of any nature is that one has to adhere to a healthy lifestyle and take daily doses of medications to prevent the body from rejecting the donated organ," Doctor Wickenstaff unpacked. "I'd be fabricating a story if I told you every person I've operated on is alive today, but I can say, no one has ever died on my operating table during a kidney transplant or any other preordained surgical procedure. As I said earlier, I give people back their vigor, some take that vigor for granted and resort back to the same lifestyle that landed them on my operating table in the first place—be it drugs, alcohol or some other high-risk venture. Some of my kidney recipients have since died, but it was not because of what I did in the operating room."

"That's good to know," DeeDee nodded. "I'm gone spell it out for you, Doctor. My son's mother is in need of a kidney transplant. I need you to save my son's mother's life. And money is no object."

"Money would not be my major concern, Mister Dawkins. Can I ask how long your son's mother has to live?"

"Two months at the most," DeeDee answered.

"Has she been given a donor? Are the organs approved by the Organ Procurement and Transplantation Network and ready for delivery?"

"No. She hasn't been through any of that, Doctor," DeeDee admitted. "We, we'll have to find a matching set of kidneys."

"How far down is she on the donor's list?" Obadiah inquired as he took another sip of his scotch.

"The donor's list doesn't matter!" DeeDee snapped as he slammed his hand down onto Obadiah's desktop, catching the doctor off guard. "You're making this hard on me, man!" he exclaimed as he stood up and paced the floor with his hands on his hips.

"How am I making things hard on you, Mister Dawkins?" Doctor Wickenstaff asked perplexed as he set his glass down and rose to his feet.

DeeDee walked over to Obadiah and calmly said, "I wanna bypass standard procedure. If I get the organs, will you do the surgery? And if so, how much will it cost me?"

"This thing you're asking of me is unscrupulous at best, Doss." Doctor Wickenstaff began as he leaned over his black marble desktop. "Where and how will the kidneys be obtained matters. You cannot just deliver me slabs of meat and expect me to perform godly miracles with defective product. There's a lot involved in that kind of an undertaking."

"What can be so hard about it, Doctor?" DeeDee questioned as he sat back down in his chair.

Obadiah downed the last portions of his morning scotch, sat back behind his desk and said, "I can interpret the fact that you don't know all what you're asking entails. I suggest you keep it that way for the sake of your sanity as it is a most ungodly business."

"So, you'll do the surgery?" DeeDee asked while looking over to Obadiah.

"The surgery I will perform," Obadiah conceded. "But I will not be able to do it here at Mercy Medical Center being there will be no way to legally lay claim to the organs. You'll have to provide a place for me to operate *and* the organs in order for me to do it."

"How will we know if we've found a match?" DeeDee inquired.

"Through a blood test," Obadiah replied matter-of-factly. "A blood test I can conduct here inside Mercy. What I need for you to do is provide me with a sample of your son's mother's blood. A full tube. Once you have found a donor, I'll need you to send me a sample of their blood. From there, I can run tests and see if the patient is compatible with the donor by doing a cross-match with your son's mother's blood. That is what must be done each and every time until we find a match. And that is the reason why I ask that you not inquire into how this donor procedure will unfold, Mister Dawkins."

"All I am is the front man. I don't wanna know nothing about it," DeeDee declared. "What's your rate on this job?"

"Three quarters of a million dollars is my price. Expect to use another quarter of a million dollars at the very least to secure the merchandise. Shall you go over that amount, my price still stands, I will not lower it no matter the circumstances because I very well may need it and more to obtain lawyers should this deed be uncovered."

"My people can be trusted," DeeDee confidently stated as he eased up from his chair and stood opposite Doctor Wickenstaff.

"The blood samples will be an indicating factor. We'll go from there," Obadiah let it be known.

"We have a deal, Doctor," DeeDee agreed as his hand stretched out across Obadiah's black marble desk.

"One more thing," Doctor Wickenstaff added as he gripped Doss' hand tightly and drew him in closer. "I want seven hundred and fifty hundred thousand dollars paid up front. Otherwise, we have no deal. I'm placing my entire life's reputation on the line for your son's mother, so it's only right that I have some form of insurance going forward."

"You'll receive payment when the donor is found, Doctor. Just be ready to do what needs to be done when the time comes."

"And may you be ready to deal with the results of the pact you've just made, Mister Dawkins." Doctor Wickenstaff cautioned as he let go of DeeDee's hand. "Contact me when you're ready to transfer payment and have the first sample available," he ended as he eyed DeeDee walking out of his office.

DeeDee made it over to his suite inside the Millennium Hotel an hour later and adjoined to his room. All was quiet inside the domicile as he removed his suit jacket and hung it up on a coat rack just before walking into the vast opening of the luxurious layout. He looked over the room, staring at the furniture before him as he pondered what all he was signing up for exactly. Never had a man felt so alone. To calm his nerves, he went over to the mini bar inside the suite that overlooked the Saint Louis Arch, grabbed a pint of Jack Daniels and poured himself a dry shot of whiskey. He downed it quickly as he dialed Natalia III. "We're on," he stated once Natalia III picked up. "Call your people and tell them they have the greenlight."

"You've made the right decision, boss. I'll get right on it," Natalia remarked before ending the call.

CHAPTER SIX

THE MESSENGER

"*...pick up the phone...I'm always home...call me anytime... just ring...three six two...four three six...hey...I lead a life of crime...dirty deeds...done dirt cheap...dirty deeds...done cheap...*" Rock band AC/DC's song *Dirty Deeds Done Dirt Cheap* blared from the interior of a maroon 2008 Ford-350 quad cab pickup with dual rear wheel axle as it sped up Paul Patterson Memorial Parkway, a dark, two-lane road bordered by tall corn stalks on either side. The vehicle was being driven towards Patterson, Iowa, a sleepy, backroads town in south central Iowa that lay thirty miles west of I-35. Patterson was a German-controlled town that harvested wheat and had a population of just over one hundred.

Behind the wheel of the quad cab sat twenty-eight-year-old Delilah Mobley, daughter to current Iowa Governor Mary Beth Mobley. She was a petite beauty with curly brown hair that flowed freely and she had slender, sleepy brown eyes. Coy and innocent looks was her appeal, but she was, at her core, a devious and downright scandalous woman. She dialed a number up in Chicago, but got no answer. When the voicemail picked up, she left a message: "*I need your crew down here to Bevington as soon as possible!*" She then ended the call, tossed the phone aside and sunk back into the leather seat with one hand draped over the steering wheel as AC/DC coated her ears.

It was just past ten on a warm Friday night, the same day of DeeDee's meeting with Doctor Wickenstaff over to Mercy Hospital earlier in the day. Delilah just had pulled off from the Gas Station/Inn that had been in her family for over forty years now. The medium-sized red and white single-story structure dissolved into the background of the pickup's rear window as the road grew more narrow and the surroundings grew darker.

"Bye, bye, store! Bye, bye!" Delilah's brother, Dillon Mobley, said like that of a young child, despite his being thirty-one years of age. He hung out the window waving back at the fading building while flailing a worn-out Kansas City Royals baseball cap into the air as his brown curly hair flapped in the wind. "Patterson that way!" he then happily stated as he turned around and faced the front of the truck while clapping his hands like a happy toddler.

"Place your seatbelt on, Half Dead!" Delilah counseled as she powered up the passenger side window and drove on while bumping AC/DC at a near deafening level.

"He's gonna wake up soon!" a daft-natured Dillon Mobley yelled aloud over the music as he pointed towards the bed of the pickup through the back window.

Delilah looked over her shoulder at the lumpy black plastic bag in the bed of her truck as she turned the volume down. "He's not gonna wake up," she remarked calmly as she gently squeezed her brother's shoulder. "Good job back there."

Dillion shook his head wildly in protest. "They gone know!" he blurted out.

"The guy was raping me and you walked in and killed him," Delilah counseled. "You did nothing wrong, Half Dead. If anybody asks, you say nothing. You tell them you don't know anything, you hear me?"

"Why can't we tell anyone?" Dillon asked as he dropped his head and looked over to Delilah through sad, grey eyes.

"Because no one will ever believe us," Delilah confessed lowly as she drove up the dark, isolated road. "Don't worry. I'll take care of it when we get home so you won't get into trouble. I just need for you to do a couple of more things for me over to our rail spur and the fire pit at the house, okay?"

"Yes, ma'am," Dillon said as he clapped his hands happily. "I saved you from a bad man," he added as he put on his seatbelt. Delilah smiled at that moment. She was proud of her manipulation as she continued driving towards Patterson while replaying what she'd just done…

…*Two hours earlier, Delilah was counting sales inside the convenience store when a brown Cadillac Escalade pulled up. A young white male in his mid-twenties with a close-cut fade and trimmed wide beard wearing a tight pair of jeans, cowboy boots and a button up short-sleeve shirt stepped out. Delilah didn't* recognize the guy so she set the bills down and placed her hand on a .44 Desert Eagle she had resting on the counter. "Can I help ya'," she asked in a perky, country voice.

"I'm Corey Belfast from CESRA," the young man remarked casually as he looked the place over.

"Well looka here, they done sent me a blue-eyed prince," Delilah said while smiling slyly. Corey had taken the statement as a compliment, but Delilah was giving the rank of the guy inside of CESRA that she was going to kill on this night as she knew he was their leader's son by the name he'd given. "I'm Delilah Mobley," she smiled. "Let me close the gas station and have you pull up to the room over to the inn where my truck is parked. It's the only one over there," she remarked as she set about closing the store. When she was done locking the store up, Delilah and Dillon began walking the short distance over to inn under the sky as night approached.

"I want you to do something for me, Half Dead," Delilah said as she walked beside her brother across the dirt lot. "When we get over there, me and my friend are going to go inside the room to talk for a while, okay? I want you to wait in the truck for me."

"Okay," Dillon nodded as he skipped across the lot in his denim jumper.

When Delilah made it over to the room, Corey was standing outside his Escalade. She reached for the keys to the room and said, "The money's inside. Bring the weapons."

"Hey, mister man," Dillon smiled as he jumped up onto the sidewalk. "I'm Dillon Mobley. What's your name, sir?"

"I told you back at the store. I'm Corey," the guy replied in an agitated manner. He then smirked a little as he looked Dillon up and down. "Are you okay, son?" he asked with his head tilted to the side as he spit out a wad of chewing tobacco.

"He was in a farming accident at home when he was a boy," Delilah intervened as she unlocked the door and flicked a switch that lit up a lamp on a nightstand beside a full-sized bed. "It left him with the mind of a little boy."

"Christ," Corey remarked somberly as he went to the rear of his Escalade and grabbed a few of the twelve gauges.

"It's been a rough go. My mother died in that accident and all we have is farmers from around town pitching in," Delilah stated sadly. *"He doesn't know what we're doing,"* she then whispered while biting her bottom lip and smiling seductively at Corey as he walked past her and entered the small room that had furniture dating back to the early nineties.

"Well, that may just work in our favor," Corey smiled as he laid three shotguns down on the shiny turquoise comforter covering the single, full-sized bed and returned to the entranceway. He rested his arm up against the threshold and asked, *"What's a sweet and petite young thing like you doing buying guns from a bad man like me?"* he asked as Dillon looked on.

Delilah smiled up at Corey, admiring his ruggedly handsome features. *"You married?"* she asked as she walked back towards the Escalade.

"Single as the day is long." Corey smiled as he followed Delilah back to his SUV.

"From the looks of things, something else is long," Delilah grinned as her slender, brown eyes drifted down to Corey's crotch.

"You keep that up you just may have to find out now," Corey playfully remarked as he pulled the rear door open on his Escalade and grabbed three more twelve gauges.

"A woman can only hope," Delilah smiled as he grabbed the last twelve gauge and led Corey back into the motel room. Once inside, Delilah went into the bathroom and returned with a duffle bag full of hundred dollar bills. *"Count it,"* she said as she threw the bag onto a small wooden table that had wood bubbling up across its surface.

"Where're you going?" Corey asked as he unzipped the bag and began spreading the stacks of money out onto the wooden table.

Delilah slowly tilted her head, smiled and said, *"To put the kid away of course. He doesn't need to witness what things adults do. And you can unzip something else if you want,"* she added as she turned around and showed Corey the zipper on the back of her paisley sundress.

Corey took in Delilah from behind as she stood in the doorway with her back to him. He could see a small bubble butt poking out *from under her sundress, and her tan skin looked soft to the touch. He kept getting whiffs of her perfume in the air whenever she was near him, and he began to imagine what she looked like naked. He went on counting the money as Delilah smiled back at him and slid out of the room.*

Once outside, Delilah dropped her act. "Half Dead," she said as she walked back to her truck.

Dillon was sitting on the ground pulling piles of dirt into a mound and packing it tight. "You want pie, momma?" he asked, never looking up at his sister.

"Get up from there," Delilah ordered as she placed a hand under one of her brother's armpits and attempted to pull him up. "Come on, you're heavy, baby," she complained.

"Okay," Dillon said as he placed two hands to the ground, pushed himself up and dusted his hands.

"Okay, Half Dead," Delilah whispered as she kept an eye on the motel room's open door. She guided her brother to the passenger side of her truck and helped him inside. "Remember when I said me and my friend were going to talk?"

"Yeah," Dillon nodded as he dropped his head and looked over to Delilah.

"We're about to talk and I want you to wait here for me. It's dark out, so," Delilah paused and skipped over to the bed of the truck and removed a hammer.

"Almost done!" Corey yelled out.

"Be right there!" Delilah yelled out in a delightful voice. She then dropped her smile and returned to Dillon's side. "Take this hammer, Half Dead," she ordered. "I'm going talk. You know what to do, don't you?"

"I don't like—"

"He's a bad man, Half Dead. He may hurt me," Delilah remarked sadly. "You don't want anything to happen to me, do you?"

Dillon quickly shook his head to say no.

"Okay," Delilah sighed. "Just stay here and listen, okay?"

"I listen," Dillon nodded.

Delilah closed the door on the pickup after letting the windows down. She went back into the motel room and closed the door, fumbling with the latch to get it to make a rattling sound. She went on and bought seven brand new chrome twelve gauges at $3,000 a pop from Corey Belfast. When they were done, the 6' 1" physically fit twenty-four-year-old white male propositioned Delilah for sex.

This was nothing new for Delilah. The Mobley Inn sat in the middle of nowhere. The place was rarely used because of its location and its dilapidated appearance. It was more Delilah's playhouse than anything as she would oftentimes sell herself for sex at the inn. That was usually just for the thrill. The men and the money meant nothing to her in times past. This particular man, however, was a gunrunner from Minnesota looking to sell weapons in Des Moines and elsewhere around Iowa on behalf of a group called Christians for Equal but Separate Rights in America (CESRA). Delilah didn't take kindly to newcomers, especially those that interfered with her business. CESRA was putting chrome automatic twelve gauges out onto the streets of Iowa, and they'd made their way down into the Kansas City area, which was where Delilah was selling kilograms of cocaine she was scoring from Natalia III.

One of the guns CESRA had sold had been used to rob and kill two of Delilah's drug runners in Kansas City, Missouri. When word got back to her that CESRA was the crew putting the weapons out on the streets, Delilah lured one of men from the Minnesota group to her inn under the guise of wanting to buy weapons. Being she was a white woman from Iowa, Delilah was trusted by CESRA with no questions asked. She kept flirting with Corey throughout the deal, and before long, the two were flat atop the springy mattress inside the inn while Dillon remained outside in the pickup truck with the windows rolled down and the hammer in his hand that was given to him by Delilah.

Dillon was protective of his younger sister, despite his childlike demeanor, and Delilah knew it all-too-well. The 6' 2" two-hundred-pound gentle giant had burst into rooms inside the inn on several occasions to protect his sister upon hearing her cry out. Delilah wasn't in trouble, she was just enjoying good sex at the time, but she began to notice something in Dillon and was willing to bet he'd go a step further if she were to coax him into action.

As Corey lay atop her, Delilah moaned out loud, knowing

Dillon would hear her. She screamed repeatedly as Corey sexed her until Dillon burst into the room through the unlocked door.

"What the fuck's going on?" Corey asked as he rolled off Delilah and stood to the floor in the nude. "Get your ass outta here, boy! I'm busy fuckin' your sister and she'll be right out...when I'm done with her," he laughed as he shoved Dillon back towards the door.

"Half Dead, don't you do it!" Delilah yelled as she rose up on her knees, putting her naked body on display. She knew her brother liked to see her naked. She also knew it made him mad when others saw her naked as well, however.

Before Corey could react, Dillon raised the hammer given to him by Delilah and slammed it down onto the top of Corey's skull. He fell back on the bed before Delilah and she screamed out again, "Half Dead, don't!" all-the-while knowing she was only fueling her brother's rage.

Over and Over again, Dillon hit a screaming, pleading Corey about his head and face at Delilah's urging until he stopped moving. Delilah then cleaned the room and she and Dillon loaded the seven chrome twelve gauges, the mattress, covers and pillows, into the bed of the truck and threw the body on top after wrapping it up in black plastic. Delilah then placed the money back under the counter after removing eleven thousand dollars and climbed into the truck and sped off from the inn...

..."I miss, mama," Dillon said, bringing Delilah's reflection to an end as she drove on into the night.

"Mama has an entire state to run, Dillon." Delilah remarked nonchalantly as she drove.

"She leave us," Dillon whined.

"There are children like us, because of what daddy, Jeremy and Wendell did to us? They just get thrown away," Delilah stated. "Mama making sure we are being taken care of. She didn't leave us, she's just busy. She left me to care for you, and that's all I'm trying to do now—make sure we aren't thrown away."

"No more potty in the bed," Dillon said as he sat upright in the seat. He then stuck out his tongue and leaned over in an attempt to kiss his sister on the lips.

Delilah and Dillon had a past history that was a secret between them. They were an interesting pair to say the least, sharing more of a mother/son relationship rather than that of brother and sister, and Delilah was in charge. The two had been on their own basically up in Iowa since Delilah was sixteen, and that gave the two of them plenty of time to not only let their imaginations run wild, but for the basic sexual desires explored between them to go unjudged or corrected by anyone.

Delilah pushed her brother's head away while guiding the pickup. "When we were younger, I actually thought that was the right thing to do," she somberly admitted while looking straight ahead. "Not anymore, Dillon. It's why you've been sleeping in your own bed for the past six years. And…you've been going potty in your bed for the…for the past six years," she realized as she looked over to Dillion briefly. "You don't miss mama, because she's around from time to time. You miss us sleeping in the same bed, don't you, Dillon?"

"You made me feel good in the same bed," Dillon shyly stated. "It felt good," he confessed before looking away in coyness.

Delilah's eyes watered as anger coursed through her veins. She hated herself for sleeping with Dillon for over five years from the ages of seventeen to twenty-two. She was lucky, and very grateful not to have gotten pregnant, as Dillon was not only her brother, but a half dead man in her eyes, which is why she called him by such an insulting name. What had caused Delilah to stop sleeping with her brother was nothing more than the fact that she knew it was grotesque and it'd begun to sicken her. A killer she may be. A drug dealer she may be, but she could not live with the stigma of sleeping with her own brother.

"I regret that for us, Dillon," Delilah said without blinking as she drove. "But I want you to hear me loud and clear tonight," she remarked while steadily looking straight ahead. "I don't want you to ever mention that again to me or anyone else or I'll take that hammer and smash your head in like you've done to our friend in the back of the truck, understand?"

As brutal as he could be, Dillon's savagery was controlled by Delilah. It was fair to say he feared his sister at times. The dim-witted thirty-one-year-old just looked at Delilah in silence as the truck cruised up the highway. He knew what he'd done to the man in the back of the truck and he didn't want the same to happen to him.

As for Delilah, she wasn't sure whether Dillon had killed Corey because of her manipulation, or for the simple fact that he was a willing accomplice. None of it mattered, though, so long as they got away with it. Dillon didn't have to answer her over her remarks about the two of them engaging in incest either, because Delilah knew he'd gotten the message. She drove on without saying another word as Dillon laid his head back and looked up at the roof of the lavish pickup.

Upon entering downtown Patterson, which was nothing more than a flashing red light, Delilah made a right turn onto Patterson Farm Road and drove for about a half mile. The ghostly silhouettes of six towering grain silos soon appeared and she veered left off the main road onto a gravel road and came up along a set of railroad tracks that had a row of maroon and yellow grain cars perched atop the steel rails. She kept her foot on the gas pedal at an even keel as the heavy-duty pickup bounced, rocked, and rolled over the ballast as it cruised alongside the railcars off to her left.

In glaring, yellow cursive painted lettering on the side of the maroon grain cars were four innocuous words: *Bender-Mobley Railroad Company.* Delilah neared the end of the string of grain cars owned by her and the Bender sisters, and pulled up before a railcar that had a grain elevator on the opposite side of the tracks with four conveyor belts draping over its open lids.

"I'm going to need your help, Half Dead," Delilah declared as she climbed from the truck and went to the back and let down its rear gate. She then went and pulled the rear passenger door open on the quad cab and pulled out a long, thick rope. Dillon climbed out at that moment and followed her to the back of the truck. "Remember the boy scout knot I showed how to tie?" she asked Dillon as she showed him the rope.

"Like a bow," Dillon remarked as he grabbed one end of the rope.

"Right. Like a bow," Delilah repeated as she pulled out a switchblade and jumped up into the bed of the truck while holding on to the other end of the rope. She cut the black bag open and Corey's crushed, bloody skull came into view. She raised the man's torso slightly and threw the rope under his body. "Come here and tie the knot, Dillon," she requested as she laid the corpse back down.

After getting her brother to tie the knot around Corey's waist, Delilah backed the pickup up to the grain car and tied the bloody hammer her brother had used to kill with to the end of the rope and flung it atop the railcar. She then jumped down, ran over to a ladder on the end of the grain car, and climbed up to its steel roof. One conveyor belt was clicked on as she passed it and grain began to flow. She pulled down on the second and then third conveyor as she passed by them, releasing grain, but she paused when she got to the last conveyor. She looked around and found the hammer and rope. After untying the hammer, she tied the end of the rope to the end of the last conveyor belt. Once she'd made sure the rope was secure, Delilah pushed the lever up, sending the conveyor belt in reverse.

Slowly, the battered body in the pickup below began to rise. It banged against the sides of the railcar, leaving a trail of blood behind as it reached its top. Delilah stopped the conveyor, guided the body over the last hole in the covered grain hopper and cut the rope. Corey Belfast's body dropped into the three foot in diameter hole, but his waist had caught the edge. His corpse lay dangling halfway in the hole with its legs protruding. Delilah kicked Corey's lifeless legs several times and the body moved downward slightly. She then leaned down and pushed him off into the grain car completely. His body fell fifteen feet into the steel cavern and hit with a thud.

Delilah pulled down on the lever on the conveyor belt and grain soon began pouring into the railcar. She took her switchblade, cut the rope free, and threw it inside the railcar. It would take ninety minutes to fill the unit, but by then, her victim's body would be crushed beneath the weight of forty tons of wheat bound for China.

While the car was filling, Delilah climbed down from the grain car and went and grabbed a scanner from the interior of her pickup. She powered it up as she walked along the railcars and aimed the scanner at the side of the grain car with the dead body inside and a red bar scan light appeared on its side. A beep was heard several seconds later and a screen opened. The phrase 'REJECTED. Didn't pass inspection.' was keyed in by Delilah at that moment, and she shut down the device. The railcar would be shipped to Lewiston, Idaho where its contents would be unloaded and burned, thereby closing out a chapter in the story of Delilah Mobley and her deal with CESRA for the time being.

"The boys from the union will be here to finish the railcar, Half Dead. They know to wash the outside of it already," Delilah said to her brother, who was busy entertaining himself by hurling railroad rocks into the field across the way. "Who wants hasenpfeffer?" she then asked aloud.

"Oooh! Rabbit stew!" Half Dead cheered as he ran over to the pickup and climbed into the passenger seat.

"Yayyy," Delilah laughed as she climbed back behind the wheel and pulled back out onto Patterson Farm Road.

Another quarter mile or so north on Patterson Farm Road, the road banked right and led to the large, two story white wood home once owned by Faye Bender's dead husband, Franklin Patterson. No matter how inviting Mary Beth, and later Delilah, had tried to make the place by planting flowers and pear trees all around and letting Saint Bernard dogs roam free amongst the cattle, the Patterson home always remained an eerie-looking structure. It was as if one could see the home's tears. Dillon sometimes said he saw the image of a little boy standing on the second floor balcony, and Delilah herself swore she could sometimes hear the faint cries of a woman coming from the master bedroom whenever she was on the first floor.

Nevertheless, the place was home for Delilah and Dillon, as Delilah could no longer stand her deceased grandmother's, Mabel-Sougherbraun Mobley, home on the other side of town for numerous reasons. It was where she and Dillon had engaged in incest for one. It was also where her grandfather and two uncles, Jeremy and Wendell, had raped her mother Mary Beth, but there was much more to the story. Dillon was Delilah's brother Jeremy's son through his own sister, Mary Beth, and Delilah was her grandfather's daughter through his own daughter. Mabel knew all about her and Dillon's mother being raped by her grandfather and uncles was what Delilah had learned from her mother, Mary Beth, and she harbored a constant resentment towards her grandmother Mabel for allowing the rape and incest to go unchecked. She'd never forgiven Mabel, and was glad when the bitch had died a few months back, truth be told, but the tragic story didn't end there.

Delilah's grandfather/father, Corey Mobley, had been killed inside the Mobley home, and a man by the name of Webster Holden had committed suicide there the same night. The Mobley home, much like the Patterson home, had a bad, bloody history. Delilah hated her incestuous family early on. She had sworn to herself that she would never become them, but in spite of it all and over time, she soon sound found herself carrying on an unspoken practice within her family by sleeping with Dillon.

Delilah had her epiphany at age twenty-two and moved her and Dillon out of the Mobley home that same day. She now hated her grandmother's home so much she would rather spend nights inside a house that some around town, herself included, knew was haunted. The fearless German country girl liked living in the Patterson home, however, because it kept people back in town out of her business. And she'd rather live with a couple of benign spirits before she ever set foot inside the Mobley home again.

After pulling up to the dirt parking lot before the Patterson home, Delilah shut the engine down just as her cellphone rang. She answered and heard Natalia III's voice on the other end. "What's going on, guy? I been tryin' to get in touch with you," she said happily as she slid out of the seat.

"Ya' got me now, Miss Lady. I need you to get in touch with your people down the road for me," Natalia III stated.

"And for what?" Delilah playfully sassed as Dillon jumped from the car singing SpongeBob. The smile she sported increased as Delilah listened to the task Natalia III was requesting. "That's great!" she laughed aloud.

"Can y'all do it?"

"I'll go and see them tomorrow. I'm sure they'll be up to it," Delilah responded.

"Good," Natalia responded. "I'm the go-between so have them keep me posted on everything."

"I'll pass your message along, but before I do, I need you to do me a favor, Natalia," Delilah remarked.

"Like?" Natalia asked.

"There's a brown Escalade parked outside of my inn just off interstate thirty-five in Bevington. I need it destroyed as soon as possible."

"It'll take my guys five hours to get down there once they start the trip. Another five hours back over to the scrapyard Gary, we looking at a ten hour round trip minimum," Natalia informed Delilah.

"You guys better get moving," Delilah suggested. "I just offed a guy. His people are gonna come looking for 'em by tomorrow afternoon and I need that Escalade removed from the premises before they do."

"Anybody we know?"

"Gunrunner from Minnesota belonging to some right-wing nut group calling themselves CESRA."

"It is somebody we know," Natalia remarked. "There's gonna be blow back from those guys over this thing perhaps, ya' know?"

"I'm aware," Delilah answered. "Which is why I need your help."

"Okay, my guys are on the way when I get off the phone."

"Thank you, Natalia," Delilah smiled while twirling her hair in her fingers. "Just so you know?" she added. "There's ten thousand dollars in the cabinet up under the bathroom sink. Have your guys go over the room thoroughly before they leave."

"And you want maid service, too," Natalia joked. "You got it, love," he stated before ending the call.

Delilah then turned to her brother. "Hasenpfeffer! Hasenpfeffer! Hasenpfeffer!" Dillion repeated excitedly while dancing around in a circle before the luxurious home's large wooden staircase under the moonlit sky.

"The rabbit stew will have to wait until another time, Dillon." Delilah let it be known as she faced the land to the north where a 2009 white and black Cessna 400 sat parked on an airstrip that ran parallel to the Patterson home. "We have more work to do," she declared as she stared at the plane for several lingering seconds before she went and pulled the rear gate down on the pickup. "Help me move these guns to the plane before we take this mattress and sheets over to the fire pit," she requested as she grabbed two of the chrome twelve gauges and walked towards the Cessna.

CHAPTER SEVEN

DRIVEN BY BLOOD

"We, we have, there's cookies and orange juice for those giving blood this year to the Cherryvale Red Cross' Annual Blood Drive to replenish their strength after giving blood to save other lives, praise God. And for today, and today only, tours of The Bender Museum are free of charge to all interested parties," Sheriff Cooper spoke into the microphone of a news reporter from Wichita, Kansas on a clear Saturday afternoon, the day after Delilah Mobley had talked to Natalia III.

"And how many donors are you expecting this year, Sheriff Cooper?" the reporter asked the elderly officer.

"Upwards of a thousand, maybe even two thousand," the grey-eyed, wrinkly-faced man smiled through his dentures while sporting red slacks with a white short-sleeved shirt and black ten gallon hat with his silver badge pinned over his heart and his hands resting on his thin waist.

"I'm sure your neighbors in surrounding towns and counties will be thankful for what you're doing. It's a very gracious act," the reporter complimented.

"We owe it all to Mayor Bender. This is her baby. I pray none of the blood being donating needs to be used because that would... well, you know. It would mean a bad thing's done happened somewhere and that's never a good thing. Come, let me show you the Bender Museum."

The Cherryvale Blood Drive was a big event in southeastern Kansas. Started seven years prior, during Faye Bender's inaugural year as mayor, nearly seven thousand pints of blood had been donated over the years to help save the lives of hundreds of Kansans and neighboring Oklahomans and Missourians injured in accidents and violent storms. It was the biggest event held in

Cherryvale, and Faye Bender spared no expense. There was a large field behind The Bender Museum, the small, four-walled wooden shack-of-a-building featuring wax statues of Faye and her sister Bonita's ancestors. Out in that field, Faye, along with the Cherryvale Sheriff's Department, headed up by her sister Bonita Bender, would sponsor the town's Summer Fair along with the annual blood drive.

A large stage was set up in the center of the vast field, and amusement rides, from bumper cars to the Ferris wheel, was scattered about. Kids could have their faces painted and then be entertained by magicians and famed television characters from SpongeBob and Clifford the Big Red Dog to an assortment of Disney and super hero characters. The Cherryvale Bar-B-Cue competition featured well-renowned grill masters such as Myron Mixon, Big Moe and Tuffy Stone. The irresistible aroma of smoking beef ribs, chicken and brisket could be smelled for miles around as one hundred contestants vied for a $25,000 dollar cash prize while passing out samples of some of the best bar-b-cue from Texas to Kansas and beyond.

Amid the joyous laughter of scores of innocent children at play and the seriousness of the bar-b-cue competition, a band would usually be on stage. Faye had gotten the classic rock groups Kansas, and The Marshall Tucker Band and the legendary country/rhythm and blues singer Beverly Battle to perform for this year's blood drive. Microbrewers were on hand to sell their homegrown beer and there was a flea market set up where countless goods from peach chutney to wood sculptures were also being sold for profit. The Cherryvale Blood Drive had been a success each of its previous years and 2009 would be no different it seems.

Walking through the crowd under the blazing afternoon Kansas sun in a red sheriff's uniform, black ten-gallon hat and black boots with shades covering her eyes, was forty-nine-year-old Bonita Bender. She eyed the crowd with Cikala Dunbar and Helen 'Boogie' Weinberger following her lead, the three of them looking for rabble-rousers. With the bar-b-cue heavy weights, Beverly Battle, Kansas and The Marshall Tucker Band in town, the crowd was bigger than usual this year and the three were on the lookout for meth, marijuana and cocaine dealers looking to taint their wholesome event.

Cherryvale had a population of just over two thousand, but on this day, there were easily a sum of five thousand, if not more people, who'd come in from surrounding areas to see the groups perform and to sample the bar-b-cue. With the extra-added people came the possibility of drug dealing, which was a no-no for anybody not working for the mayor or the Cherryvale Sheriff's department.

To the outside eye, the three women in the red sheriff's uniforms appeared to be nothing more than public servants out performing their civic duties; but the uniforms were mere costumes for a group of killers perpetrating a badge. They wore 'modeling gear' so-to-speak given the way their red silk pants hugged their curvaceous hips and the heels on their boots hiked up their taut rear ends.

Bonita led the way. Looking years younger than her forty-nine, she sported platinum sunshades while slowly strolling through the crowd with her brown hair draping down the back of her shoulders with her skin tanned to perfection. Her left hand lingered over the handle of a black .44 Desert Eagle, a semiautomatic handgun not in the traditional keeping of most law enforcement officers as she was not your everyday sheriff's deputy.

Forty-six-year-old Cikala Dunbar, a full-bloodied, tan-skinned Lakota Indian from Rapid City, South Dakota, tailed Bonita as the trio patrolled the crowd. Cikala was busted in Iowa City, Iowa with five pounds of marijuana she was transporting for a biker gang back in her home state of South Dakota. She was facing a five-year stint, but had gotten a decade tacked on to her nickel when she crossed the aisle and knocked the district attorney out cold when the woman smirked at her during her sentencing. Cikala was tough. She had been a brawler all her life, often getting into drunken fisticuffs inside of motorcycle bars when she was on the streets back in Rapid City. She was a scrappy somebody at 5'5", but had slimmed down twenty pounds to an even one hundred and forty pounds. She had fluffy cheeks and a head full of thick, coarse black hair that she wore in a single ponytail that nearly touched her spine. She had the most inviting looks, appearing almost Asian with her thin, brown eyes and broad, friendly smile displaying a row of perfect white teeth.

Twenty-five-year-old Helen 'Boogie' Weinberger brought up the rear in her red sheriff's uniform. The slender, 5'10" tan-skinned German-Jew with the nappy tan afro and clear brown eyes took delight in playing cop. All she did was dress up for the occasion and she was handed a black .44 Desert Eagle and a silver badge. Helen wasn't even on the force, but Sheriff Cooper was so blinded by the kind acts of Mayor Bender that he couldn't, nor did he have the mental capacity, to rebuke blatant lawlessness unfolding right before his very eyes.

Certain townspeople knew of the unruliness within the sheriff's department and the crooked mayor, but the Germans had their fangs so deep into the law enforcement and political structure of the county and state, that those citizens were now powerless to protest the cronyism that had taken root in their town. And whether they wanted to admit it or not, Faye Bender was a good and capable politician that brought jobs and money back to a town that was once one of the poorest towns not just in the state of Kansas, but America as a whole. So long as those who knew remained quiet, and let things unfold as they had been since Faye's arrival seven years earlier, they would have no trouble is what they knew to be true, so they accepted the terms, if only to keep food on their table, money in their checking accounts, and more importantly, their lives.

Those thoughts ran through Bonita's mind as she emerged from Bar-B-Cue alley, which was a long row of grills on either side of a dirt walkway where contestants were competing for the $25,000 dollar cash prize. She looked to her left and saw a tall, lanky Caucasian in his late twenties with spiked brown hair slipping a small plastic aspirin bottle to a pudgy white female with brown freckles. Bonita knew the female. She worked at the Pamida Store in downtown Cherryvale. The teen was a known meth addict, and it didn't take all but a split second for Bonita to put two and two together.

The guy was smiling, watching the youngster walk off as he admired her wide derriere while stuffing a wad of bills into his dingy front jean pocket as he took a sip of his beer. He quickly removed the cup from his lips as he caught sight of a tan-skinned, voluptuous woman in a red sheriff's uniform walking his way with her sunshade-covered eyes honed in on his position. The cup of beer slipped from his hands and he walked off in the opposite direction at a harried pace without saying a word.

"This guy," Cikala sighed as she eased past Bonita. "Hey!" she called out, trying to get the man's attention. The man kept walking so she called out again. "I know you hear me talkin' to you muther —"

"Let 'em go," Bonita calmly interrupted.

Cikala raised a hand out towards the guy like, '*You saw what the fuck he just did?*'

"He's not from around here. I wanna know more about 'em," Bonita counseled as she pulled out her cellphone and dialed a number.

****

"...*keeping your head above water...making a way when you can't...temporary layoffs...Good Times...easy credit rip-offs... Good Times...scratching and surviving...Good Times...*"

Fifty-six-year-old Sacha Merkendorf was sitting in the driver's seat of one of Cherryvale Sheriff's Department's black and red Dodge Chargers under the AC preparing to watch another episode of Good Times on her DVD player when her cellphone rang. The blonde-haired, tall and burly German eyed the phone in the console, recognized Bonita's number and looked over to Maggie McPherson, the buxom red head, green-eyed German with a somewhat larger than normal skull. "That call is for you, big head," she said under her raspy voice.

Twenty-nine-year-old Maggie looked down at the phone, flipped her eyes up and said, "That ain't my shit ringin'!"

"I'm on my lunch break," Sascha replied nonchalantly over the ringing phone as she unwrapped a tuna on rye sandwich. "And this is the episode where the little girl's mother gets killed for burning her with that iron the last time. She can't get away with that. J.J. has to kill Penny's mother on this one. It's the only way to make things right for that little girl."

"J.J. ain't killin' a got damn—you know what?" Maggie relented as she picked up the phone and answered. "Yeah?"

"You and Sascha still parked at the front gate, Maggie?" Bonita asked as she, Cikala and Boogie continued walking through the crowd.

"Yeah, what's up?"

"Tall Caucasian, light-blue dingy jeans, spiked brown hair, brown Converse and a grey wife beater tucked inside the jeans with a brown leather belt. Tag the car he go to and get the license plate number."

"What's the deal on the guy?"

"Outta town meth dealer look like. Let 'em go for now, but get that tag and then run a check on it for me."

"Done," Maggie responded before ending the call and focused her green eyes in on the main gate that led to the festivities.

"Who're we looking for?" Sascha asked before biting into her tuna fish sandwich.

"Why're you eating tuna fish when they have a smorgasbord of bar-b-cue ribs and shit over there?"

"The red meat stops me up worse than the toilet inside your rinky-dink diner always is," Sascha replied while looking at the screen on her DVD player. "You should get a better plumber."

"Just watch your show. I got my diner and this," Maggie sighed as she kept her eyes on the main gate.

"Thank you," Sascha replied. "You understand the seriousness of the situation here."

"What situation, Sacha? It's a fuckin' TV show!" Maggie complained.

"But it's a real one," Sascha countered. "I'm still waiting for the good times to start, though. Maybe after they kill Penny's mother the good times will—"

"There ain't no good times," Maggie interrupted. "It's a contradiction of the circumstances the Evans family live under. The good times are the laughter that takes place inside that apartment. The good times are how that family comes together at the end of each episode after facing a crisis."

"See? It is a real show. We do the same thing here in Cherryvale," Sascha smiled. "Let me see what happens to Penny's mother. You, my dear, you have a job to do."

"This bitch," Maggie dragged as she let the passenger side window down and kept a close eye out on the main gate. Barely five minutes in, she eyed the man that fit the description Bonita had given to her. She sat and watched the suspect, who appeared a little on edge given the way he constantly looked over his shoulders. He hurried along and made his way over to a white Nissan Pathfinder jeep with dark tinted windows and overly-large black-mag rims with a lift kit that raised it four feet up off the ground where he hopped in and left the premises.

"It won't be hard to remember this ride at all," Maggie said as she eyed the black running rails running beneath the truck's doors and the matching black head rack mounted to its top. From her position, she was able to see the license tag on the truck once the man backed out. She jotted down the initials R.E.BEL. *"He ain't spell it out completely, but I'm reading 'Rebel',"* she said to herself as she eyed the truck cruising out of the parking lot. "While you waitin' on Janet Jackson momma ta' get murked, I'm gone go and run a check on this dude in another unit because the computer down in this one," she then told Sascha as she opened the passenger side door.

"I'll let you know how they killed Penny's mother when you get back," Sascha said, enthralled in the show as she took a bite of her tuna sandwich. "They should push her down the elevator shaft and make it look like an accident. That's the best way to take her down," she said as she slowly chewed.

"They ain't killin' nobody on that—fuck it, man! Fuck what you talkin' 'bout," Maggie scoffed as she climbed out of the car, slammed the door shut and walked off.

****

"She looks just like Kate Bender. Only more slender. And to be honest with you, the wax statue is prettier," forty-nine-year-old Claire Bailey sassed as she walked around in a circle staring at the woman in the pink and white wide-bottomed dress and white bonnet.

"Claire, that's not nice!" the woman with her frowned.

"It was a compliment to the artists that did the work not an insult to the Mayor," Claire retorted. "Mayor Bender, we'd be remiss if we didn't get a picture with you and us together. Next to your great, great grandmother's wax statue. She was such a brutal woman," she disrespected.

"Look, look at that table before the curtains!" the second woman ogled as she pulled Claire away.

"Umm hmm," Claire dragged. "Unsuspecting guests sat at that table and were hit over the head with a mallet and dropped into that pit underneath that table."

"No, the wood," the woman with Claire remarked, trying to keep the woman from being so obnoxious. "It's the original table used and it's still in pristine condition."

"Kate Bender used to slit the throats of people who sat at that table before the family stuffed them into the pit," Claire disclosed.

Fifty-two-year-old Faye Bender stood beside the waxed image of her great, great, grandmother, Kate Bender, wearing a wide-bottomed pink and white dress with a white bonnet. She sported a pretentious smile as she waited for Claire Bailey and her friend to take their positions beside her for a photoshoot. Her attitude had been that of silent contempt ever since she'd arrived over to the Bender museum several hours earlier for the given fact that she'd become an object of ridicule. The mockery heaped upon her, were remarks she abhorred. But every year, for the past seven years, Faye Bender would intentionally allow herself to be degraded by dressing up in mid-nineteenth century attire in order to bring to life the infamous Kate Bender for the amusement of the Cherryvale townsfolk.

For one day a year, so long as they remained rooted within the confines of an unspoken form of respectability, citizens of Cherryvale were allowed to come out and lament against their mayor in joking fashion. Very few dared, but those who did were given a pass and were expected to never be heard from again until the following year's blood drive. Claire Bailey, however, was going overboard with her putdowns and it was beginning to annoy Faye to the point of anger.

"The law should've caught up with the Benders when they fled seven miles north to my hometown of Thayer and hopped that train to Colorado," Claire remarked in a flippant manner. "Had they done that the Bender Farm would not be—"

Faye coughed at that moment to get Claire's attention. When their eyes met, the woman saw the scorn in Faye's green eyes and got the message. "But how could they know?" Claire laughed through her fright while readjusting her conversation. "We'll take our photo and be gone," she added as she and her friend gathered around Faye, who refused to smile during the picture while hugging the woman who'd berated her family around the neck a little tighter than necessary to drive home her point.

Claire and her friend broke from Faye's grip and said nothing as they left the museum just as two more adults and three children entered the building. "Welcome to the Bender Museum," Faye smiled as she walked behind the counter that sold replicas of the items her ancestors once used to murder their victims. "If you need any help or have any questions I'm here at your service. My name is Kate Bender."

****

"Why aren't you in an officer's uniform like the rest of your crew, Tanya?" fifty-three-year-old Beverly Battle asked as she sashayed over the marble floors of Faye Bender's spare bedroom in her second floor mansion in just her Jimi Choo high heels and white bra and panties while holding onto a half-smoked Camel cigarette.

Tanya poured a glass of water into a vase of red carnations sitting atop an oak and glass cabinet before wiping her hands on the sides of her tight-fitting denim jeans. "I will not spend my downtime playing cop. I just came here to Kansas to relax before I get back to business in Cincinnati," she stated as she arranged the flowers.

Beverly chuckled as she sat before a lighted vanity mirror and dabbed out her cigarette in a crystal ashtray. "I tell ya', Faye got a nice set up here. Mayor of the town, sister running the police force and all. Woman can practically get away with murder if she outright chose," she stated as she looked at her youthful image inside the circular mirror while picking her curls. "You got my wish list?" she then asked.

Tanya shook her head in disapproval as she walked over to the mantle above the stone fireplace and opened a wooden box. "All these years and much hasn't change with you, Beverly. You rock stars are all the same in my book. It's just drugs all day, sex all night, and music everywhere in between."

"What person in their ever-loving right mind wouldn't want to live that life?" Beverly laughed as she resumed picking at her curls. "Say what you want, but if y'all ain't got no booger sugar it's gone be a sour ass performance over to the fair this evening I'm tellin' ya' right now, Tanya!" the fifty-three-year-old woman complained as she picked up a bottle of perfume and sprayed around her neck. "Hell, I let my wish list be known two weeks before this romper room festival and the only thing got fulfilled

89

was the pork ribs and cole slaw when my bus got here last night! I coulda went and seen ole Myron Mixon and got my fill of that shit today, honey. I want the good stuff that was on my wish list stop playing with me now!"

"You're such a diva," Tanya sighed as she placed a half dozen Quaaludes onto the marble counter top situated before Beverly.

"My stars," the feisty, buxom brunette exclaimed as she clasped her hands together and stared at the packages of cocaine that lay before her. "See, that's why I love your ass, Tanya. You," Beverly paused as she opened one of the plastic bags and scooped up a small portion of the white powder with her pinky nail and took a quick sniff. "You know what a woman of my caliber needs to perform!"

"You haven't had a hit song in a decade," Tanya snapped. "The only reason we put up with your ass is because of what you did for Faye to get her off on those bullshit murder charges back in Iowa. We've invested money in you and haven't gotten a single dime in return."

Beverly dipped her hand into the cellophane bag once more with her pinky nail, brought another small pile of white powder to her nose and snorted it into her other nostril. "Insult me if you want, but I always knew Faye was innocent in that entire deal and I was the first one to come to her defense," she declared. "It was me who pegged that state trooper to corroborate the fact that Faye was down in Missouri with a flat tire during the time her family was being killed up in Patterson. And it was me she felt most comfortable reliving that day with and I was responsible for giving her a new life. Do I hold that over any of you all's head? No, I do not! I did what I did because of my friend Franklin, and I knew how much Faye was hurting over that shit! It hurt her so bad she confessed to doing it because she felt responsible for it all. It hurt me as well and I'm not afraid to admit it."

"It hurt you to the point that you had to become a junky and reneged on our investment in you?" Tanya facetiously asked.

Beverly turned and stared up at Tanya and said, "I was a junky long before Franklin was killed. Been ten years sober now, though, and that's why you haven't gotten a return on your investment if you wanna know the truth."

"Why you didn't say anything?" Tanya inquired. "If cocaine was all you needed to give us a hit album all you had to do was say so," she smirked.

Beverly looked to the floor embarrassed before rising to her feet in her $5,000 dollar, five-inch Jimi Choo stilettoes to face Tanya head on. "Let me set you straight on something," she began. "I went through a crisis ten years ago. I did right to stay away from recording anything new because back then I actually needed that shit," the famed singer stated as she pointed back towards the cocaine resting on the vanity. "I got sober by going on a ten year world tour not to make money, but to prove to myself that I could do it without the drugs. I've done that, but I like to party when I play now yes I do. But only when I play. I'm a social snorter."

"Never seen a 'social snorter' in my life," Tanya quoted through curled lips. "Once a junky—"

"Is a junky only once, once they've made their mind up to not be a junky any longer," Beverly interrupted. "I haven't forgotten the hundred thousand dollars you and your family sunk into me to resurrect my recording career. I was broke when you all gave me that money. Used it to get clean and go back out on tour. Now, I'm able to pay all of it back plus interest, or you can allow me to go out and do what I do best and earn a bigger profit off me."

"You're saying you're ready to get back in the studio?" Tanya asked unassured.

"I am," Beverly stated seriously. "Just let me play and do my thing. You gals got a thriving agriculture business and a Mayor in your crew. It's time to move away from selling drugs because it's becoming so passé."

"I'll give you that," Tanya nodded in agreement as she pulled up a chair and sat beside Beverly. "I gotta be honest, though. At fifty-three, it'll be hard to resurrect a fading rock star's career no matter how much money we dump into the venture. I mean no disrespect, but none of the rock bands from your heyday are selling records like the newer artists out there now."

"What I need is a collaboration," Beverly reasoned. "A collaboration would increase sales on my previous albums that have already gone platinum and diamond. I know music, Tanya. There's still a place inside the music industry for me. And I still have contacts. I know a few major players and have their phone numbers stored," she added as she picked up her cellphone and showed it to Tanya just as a rumbling sound was heard coming from the backside of the mansion.

Tanya hopped up from the chair and peeked out the bay window in time to see a white and black Cessna 400 gliding down onto the runway. "We'll talk more about this music business venture later," she said as she walked out of the room in order to greet Delilah Mobley.

****

Tanya emerged from the rear of the mansion onto Faye's back patio just as the Cessna cruised up behind the home. Dust was being kicked up by the propeller so she placed a pair of sunshades over her eyes as the plane nosed around to face the head of the runway. The engine shutdown and the door popped open just before Delilah jumped down from the plane. "Help me with Half Dead, Tanya!" she happily called out.

"Thought you had business in Patterson with those people from Minnesota," Tanya replied as she went around to the opposite side of the plane and pulled the door open.

"I did!" Delilah squealed with delight as she ran up and unhooked her brother's seat belt. "Took care of my little gun problem last night," she added as she and Tanya helped Dillon from the plane. When Dillon cleared out, Delilah reached behind the passenger seat, pulled out a spanking brand new automatic chrome twelve gauge and showed it to Tanya. "Our friend from CESRA left seven of these behind," she said while smiling devilishly.

"Nice," Tanya said as she took the twelve from gauge from Delilah and got a feel for it. "I wonder what the recoil like on this thing."

"Test it out later. Y'all can have all seven of those bastards if ya' want I don't care."

"I'll take three," Tanya remarked. "So what brings you here besides delivering these guns?"

"Me and Half Dead were on our way home to fix hasenpfeffer after dropping the body off when I got a call from our friend Natalia the third."

"He's not in any trouble with the Holland family over that deal with Malik Gomez is he?" Tanya asked concerned as she racked the twelve gauge.

"He's not, but someone close to him is facing a real calamity," Delilah replied as Dillon took off running out into the open field. "Don't you go near the apple orchard, Half Dead!" she admonished before turning her attention back to Tanya. "Natalia has a sick friend in need of a kidney transplant."

"Wouldn't he do better searching for a donor in Chicago?" Tanya asked as she and Delilah started removing the rest of the guns from the plane.

"*She* would…if only the donor was a willing participant."

Tanya froze in her tracks and stared down into Delilah's eyes. "They're paying for body parts," she stated calmly, knowing full well what her German counterpart was hinting at.

"Two hundred and fifty thousand dollars to whoever finds a matching set of organs," Delilah stated seriously as she grabbed two twelve gauges and leaned them up against the plane. "And a fifty-thousand-dollar disposal fee for each body that doesn't match."

"That could easily run up over a half million dollars," Tanya contemplated. "That'll be good for business being we've lost our Philadelphia distributer."

"Until the Holland family establishes a route back to America with the heroin the Devereaux family will supply us, all we have is our legitimate ventures. On the street side, we still have thirty kilograms of cocaine to move," Delilah let it be known.

"I don't like the method, but I can appreciate the bottom line," Tanya replied.

"So you agree to what Natalia is asking of us?" Delilah asked just to confirm.

"I'd sanction it, but it'll be Faye's decision being that matter will unfold in her own backyard," Tanya replied as she looked over towards the apple grove on the far north side of the land. "Me and Boogie won't be around, though. We're leaving for Cincinnati in the morning to oversee some business back on Mulberry Street. Let's bring the guns inside. After that? I'm going shower, slip into a silk robe and watch television with a bottle of wine."

"You're not going to the fair?" Delilah asked as she removed the last of the guns.

"Been there done that," Tanya stated unimpressed as she reached into her jean pocket and came up with a set of car keys. "Beverly Battle's here. Take my Bentley and drop her off over there to the fair once she's ready and fill Faye in on the guns and the kidney matter when you get there. I'll see you all later on tonight," she ended as she scooped up two more twelve gauges and began walking towards the mansion.

CHAPTER EIGHT

ON THE JOB TRAINING

Delilah Mobley, Cikala Dunbar and Sascha Merkendorf were milling about the first floor library of the Bender mansion clamping gun belts around their waists and checking gun chambers in preparation to head out for another shift. It was three 'o' clock sharp on Sunday morning. June 7th, the day after the blood drive, and the women had all dressed up in their black sheriff's deputy outfits after resting up for several hours. They'd gotten word earlier in the day, via Delilah, on a job that needed doing and they were setting about to complete to the task when Faye, Bonita and Maggie entered the marble-floored, three-column immaculate room with lacquered cherry oak walls.

"Okay, meine Damen." (Okay, ladies) Faye stated as she tucked a black .44 desert eagle into her hip holster and placed a silver badge over her heart. *"Wieder einmal sind unsere Dienstleistungen erforderlich. Dieses Mal ist es für das Allgemeinwohl."* (Once again our services are required. This time it's for the greater good.) Everybody with the exception of Sascha Merkendorf chuckled over Faye's remark and it hadn't gone unnoticed. *"Etwas falsch, Sascha?"* (Something wrong, Sascha?) she casually asked.

"Es gibt kein gutes in diesem Geschäft." (There is no good in this deal.) Sascha replied as she stuffed her desert eagle into her hip holster. *"Es riecht nach der Bosheit darüber, wie es geschehen wird. Am Ende des Tages? Ich fürchte, wir müssen dafür bezahlen. Nicht, dass ich es mit irgendwelchen Mitteln wünsche."* (It reeks of wickedness over how it will be done. At the end of the day? I'm afraid we may have to pay for this one. Not that I wish for it by any means.)

Faye walked past Cikala and Boogie and went and stood before Sascha and looked up into her sleepy, green eyes. *"Sie sind willkommen, dieses heraus zu sitzen, wenn Sie wünschen. Ich weiß, dass Ihre Arbeit und Sie dass recht erworben haben, wenn Ihre Gewissenhaftigkeit gestört wird.* " (You're welcome to sit this one out if you want. I know your work and you've earned that right if your conscience is disturbed.)

Sascha was well aware of the people she was running with and what they were capable of doing being she was one of them. Even more, she knew conscience had no place amongst a crew of killers as it displayed weakness, but yet and still she was willing to go against the grain, if only to absorb herself of possible consequences that may befall her crew over such a treacherous undertaking. *"Fur mich gebe ich keinen Fluch, wenn ich durchgeführt erhalte, oder ertrinke oder abstürze in ein Flugzeug oder mich trinke zum Tod. Aber es gibt noch eine Angelegenheit der Ehre in diesem Leben."* (For myself, I don't give a damn if I get executed, or drown, or crash in a plane, or drink myself to death. But there is still a matter of honor in this life.)

"Aber Hitler Sie Zitiert Sind?" (Is that Hitler you're quoting?) Faye asked while standing before Sascha in her black sheriff's deputy uniform.

"It's Goering she's reciting from December 1945 while he was locked up in Nuremberg facing Nazi war crimes," twenty-nine-year-old Maggie McPherson, a Junior Professor with a PhD in World History from Brown University, answered on behalf of Sascha.

"Correct, Maggie." Sascha stated as she looked her crew over. "Faye? It is my belief that we are on the verge of committing crimes against nature from this morning forth and I want to go on record as being against it…although I must by nature…tally my services to the family's Cause because it is who I am—by nature," she earnestly concluded while staring into Faye's eyes.

"Duly noted," Faye nodded as she smiled up at Sascha and placed a hand onto her left shoulder. "I respect your voice, most beloved soldier."

"But?" Sascha questioned.

"No but behind it," Faye stated seriously as she walked off from Sascha. "I just respect it. Your stance places a certain form of humanity at our feet over this matter." She then turned to face Sascha a second time and said, "You're a deadly woman, but the compassion your heart has forced upon you on this morning is what gives me a clear conscience."

"That was not my intent, but if that is my contribution, I can live with it," Sascha stated as the women began to file out of the library. "I wish us all luck."

"This isn't about luck, it's about proper execution," Bonita let it be known as she followed Faye's lead.

"That's what worries me," Sascha said to herself as she followed her crew through the home's open floor and out the front doors. *"We don't know what we're doing just yet, but this job we can learn while on the job,"* she then silently added as she stepped out into the humid Kansas night.

****

An hour later, the gang of six were in three patrol cars in teams of twos posted up and down U.S. Highway 169, which ran north and south just west of downtown Cherryvale. To the south was Maggie and Sascha. The two were parked on side of the road idling their block Dodge Charger that was shielded from northbound drivers by a couple of grain-hauling semis as they sat in the AC.

Welcome Back Carter's theme song was heard playing on Sascha's DVD player by Maggie as she sat in the passenger seat thinking about how she hadn't been fucked in well over seven months. To get her mind off her aroused state, she looked over to Sascha and asked, "What happened to Good Times? You finished that series?"

"That show is so depressing, Maggie," Sascha replied while shaking her head. "How much bad can one family endure in life? I couldn't stick around for the happy ending if there ever was one."

"I could use a happy ending right about now. I need a man. I need some dick in my life," Maggie rattled off through a sigh.

"Dick is everywhere. You can find a dick with ease. Men are suckers for the sweet vagina."

"What you know about sweet vagina?" Maggie laughed. "Your old self."

"My old self gets a lot of action right here in Cherryvale," Sascha sassed from behind the steering wheel.

"From where?" Maggie asked surprised.

"There's the maintenance guy at the Bender museum," Sascha declared for starters.

"He's a creep. He look like one of them wax statues in there." Maggie countered.

"He does, but that turns me on when he takes me in there after dark."

"It's even creepier that you feel that way." Maggie stated as she looked Sascha off.

"Then there's the guy who works on our cars at the patrol station." Sascha continued.

"That dusty, pasty white mutherfucka," Maggie laughed. "You doing his ass a favor big time if you ain't lying."

"I'm not lying about the dick," Sascha stated. "I also have the Greyhound driver. The black guy. He fucks my sweet vagina until it clamps down on his dick every Wednesday when he takes his break at your rinky dink diner."

"Okay, I'll give you him. He's young and handsome, but he's married so that's fucked up on your part."

"His wife is a beauty. She knows of me because they're, they're…swingers is what they call it. We talk from time to time and she is a nice woman."

Maggie looked over to Sascha with a blank stare. "How you managed to snag that brother?"

"I am a cougar," Sascha smiled. "It's where I do some of my best work, trapping a man. Look at me, Maggie," she added as she leaned over and put her thick thigh on display. "My face is lovely, my green eyes, my blonde hair and sexy, raspy voice. I am irresistible to men."

"You probably threatened that man's life to fuck you," Maggie joked just as a white Nissan Pathfinder jeep with dark tinted windows and large black-mag rims passed by headed north while doing the thirty-five mile per hour speed limit.

"There's that guy you were watching yesterday. The one with the Rebel license plate," Sascha remarked in a low tone as she sat up in the driver's seat.

"I got 'em," Maggie responded as she reached for the CB radio to notify Cikala and Delilah, who were posted up a few yards off of U.S. highway 169 watching the road from the north.

Sascha grabbed Maggie's hand to prevent her from radioing the rest of the crew. "What's your deal?" Maggie scoffed.

"He has an antenna in the bed of his truck, Maggie," Sascha observed. "He may be listening to us. I'll use the cellphone instead," she added as she reached down into the console and grabbed her mobile device and dialed Cikala's number.

"'Sup," Cikala answered on the second ring.

"We have us a potential donor," Sascha said. "White Nissan Pathfinder jeep with dark tinted windows and black rims. He has an antenna so stay off the airwaves."

"The guy from the fair. Gotcha," Cikala replied casually as she sat up and looked to her left and saw a pair of headlights coming up on her Dodge Charger from the south. She tapped a drowsy Delilah's left shoulder to stir her awake as she placed the car in drive, swerved onto Highway 169 and got behind the Nissan with the Dodge's red, blue and white lights blaring. The truck eased off the road onto the dirt shoulder and the two women climbed out of the patrol car in their black sheriff's uniforms with their guns drawn.

Approaching the rear of the truck, Cikala could see two silhouettes in the cab. "You know the routine! Shut the engine off and drop your keys out the driver's side window with your left hand, driver! Place your right hand on the rearview mirror while you're doing it, driver!" she commanded as she crept closer to the truck.

Delilah was on the other side of the pick-up with her gun aimed on the passenger. "Both hands out the window! Slowly!" she commanded as flashing blue, red and white lights approached from the north.

Faye and Bonita had been notified by Sascha and they were on hand to make an assessment of the situation before the crew went another step forward with a possible kidnapping. Cikala and Delilah held their guns on the occupants as Bonita approached the driver's side of the Nissan with her hands behind her back. "Where're ya' going, guy?" she asked politely as she eyed the driver.

"Just dropping off a relative after chaperoning a summer party next town over," the man replied as he stared into the officer's green eyes.

"Must've been some party," Bonita remarked as she nudged her chin towards the array of beer cans laid out over the dash. She then looked over to the passenger. She was a tall, slender female with long brown hair and grey eyes around the age of seventeen. "What are you doing with this guy?" she asked the teenager. "You should be home in bed, not hangin' out with some meth dealer."

"I'm no meth—"

"Shut up!" Bonita snapped. She then grew agitated, took a few steps back and said, "You know what? Both of y'all step out the truck for me."

"What did we do?" the young woman whined. "He's my uncle and he was taking me home to Thayer just seven miles from here!"

"We have reasonable suspicion to believe the driver is driving under the influence and because of past surveillance there may be drugs on board." Bonita clarified as she pulled the driver's side door open.

"I had a few beers over in Independence while sitting in the truck. They're old cans. This is harassment," the man complained as he and the female climbed out of the pickup.

"Driver's license," Bonita remarked, ignoring the man's declaration.

On the passenger side of the pick-up, Faye was busy patting down the young female as Delilah stood by watching. "It's nearly five in the morning and you two just coming from a party?" she whispered into the paranoid teen's ear. "What is your uncle up to really? Is he moving meth through my town?"

"I, I don't know, ma'am," the girl mumbled as she began to cry.

Faye could smell the fear jumping off the teenager and she was aiming to work her over to gain a bigger advantage. "If I search that truck and find any drugs whatsoever, you'll go down right alongside your uncle for a very long time. Trafficking drugs is a serious offense, but I'm willing to let you go if you just be honest with me. Now," she whispered as she leaned in closer to the teenager, "if you don't want to end up in a state prison doing ten years flat, tell me, does your uncle have any drugs inside that truck?"

The young female looked back at the officer standing behind her and said, "He told me not to say anything, but…yeah. It's behind his CB radio in the dash."

"Good girl," Faye smiled as she waved Delilah over. "Place her in the back seat of your patrol car for the time being," she whispered. "Sascha," she then called out. When Sascha neared, Faye whispered into her ear, "We're gonna take her back to the barn."

"What about her male companion?" Sascha asked.

"That's her uncle. She says there's drugs in the truck. If she's telling the truth? We can run the guy in, but if she's a donor match he'll be sure to tell someone that we were the last people seen with her once she disappears."

"Maybe we should let them both go and find someone traveling alone," Sascha suggested as a couple of sets of headlights from the north came into view.

"This guy's been selling meth in my county and I don't like that." Faye rebutted as she placed her hands on her hips and looked to the ground. "But more importantly, we may have a young fresh set of kidneys here and I don't want them to go to waste. That's even more reason enough," she added as she looked through the interior of the truck and saw Bonita and Cikala administering a DUI roadside test to the man.

"Got some smokies up ahead on the left, driver. Some unlucky soul done landed himself a DUI test this early morning," one of the approaching truck drivers up ahead was heard reporting over the radio inside the pickup truck.

The women all took notice as two eighteen-wheeler tanker trucks hauling gasoline passed by, making sure to slow their speed as they rode past the scene. To the truckers, it was just another routine stop in a small town. Three police cars with lights blaring on a dark road and giving some unfortunate citizen a hard time on a hot and humid late spring night after he'd partied a little too hard. "Gotta love the law, right?" one of the truckers was heard laughing over the CB radio as the two semis rolled on.

Faye listened as the truckers resumed conversation about making a stop once they crossed over into Oklahoma while eyeing her sister and Cikala conducting the field sobriety test. Given the way the man was wobbling while trying to walk a straight line, he was obviously going to fail. More cackling from the radio forced her to lay eyes on the CB radio inside the truck. She wasn't sure if the CB was cued up, so she remained silent as she leaned over to try and pry it from the dash in order to dismantle further radio contact. The CB slid out with ease and a Ziploc bag filled with crystal meth came into view.

A quick whistle from Faye caught Bonita's attention. She looked over through the interior in time to see Faye giving a nod of approval as she held up the bag of crystal meth.

"You're under arrest for possession of crystal meth!" Bonita said aloud as she aimed her gun at the man once more.

The man made a sudden move, turning around to face the officer who was going to arrest him and Bonita fired three rapid shots that landed dead center in his chest. He dropped to the ground and Cikala rushed over, rolled the man onto his back and began checking to make sure there wasn't any blood on the asphalt. Upon seeing no blood, Cikala placed a scarf over the man's wound to absorb what blood trickled from his chest cavity as he died beside his pickup.

The man's niece was beyond shocked. After witnessing her uncle get shot, she pissed her pants and passed out in the backseat of the patrol car. The crime scene was cleared in less than five minutes. The man's lifeless body was rolled up into plastic, placed into the trunk of Sascha and Maggie's patrol car and the six outlaws were headed back to the Bender farm with Cikala behind the wheel of the Nissan. During the ride, Faye powered up her laptop to get the background information on Sharona Benson's potential kidney donor.

****

Her name was Piper Bailey. A seventeen-year-old soon-to-be senior at Montgomery County High School back in Cherryvale, and daughter to Claire Bailey, the woman who'd mocked Faye the day before inside the Bender museum to the point of angering her. Faye had never known the child was related to Claire, it was just a coincidence in itself. She walked to and fro before Piper, who was now tied to a chair inside the barn and mumbling lowly in a daze, as she contemplated on the matter. Had she known who the teenager was, she would've let her go, but it was too late to turn back now because she'd witnessed the shooting of her uncle.

Getting down to business, Faye donned a pair of black leather gloves and slapped Piper about the face several times. She snapped out of her trance and found herself sitting before six women in Montgomery County sheriff's uniforms staring down at her with cold expressions on their faces as they stood before her in a semicircle.

"Please," Piper beseeched as she looked around at the women. "I won't say nothing about my uncle! He was a drug dealer and tried to get me to help him, but I told him to bring me home! I just wanna go home to my momma!"

"You're not going home to your mother no time soon so stop pleading," Faye remarked in nonchalant manner. "You have something we need, and you should've stayed your ass sleep for it," she added as she grabbed a handful of the seventeen-year-old's shiny, brown hair and tilted her head back.

"What did I do wrong? What do you want from me?" Piper cried hysterically.

Faye answered Piper's questions by hauling off and punching the teenager in the right temple. She knocked her out cold and backed away while shaking out her stinging left fist. "Okay, Sascha, take a sample," she then commanded.

Sascha grabbed a syringe and went and stood beside Piper and drew a vial full of blood from the unconscious young woman's left forearm. "I don't think we're doing this right," she stated as she handed the vial to Bonita.

"Why you say that?" Bonita asked as she placed a seal over the vial and placed it into a small Styrofoam box lined with hot ice in order to preserve the specimen. "If the blood matches, the doctor in Saint Louis will have his donor. It's as simple as that."

"The woman in need of kidneys is a mid-forties black woman. This is a seventeen-year-old white female. It'll take a miracle for this child's blood to match our client let alone the organs. This is what I was getting at before we set out to do this thing this morning," Sascha explained.

Faye and Bonita stared at one another, speechless over Sasha's observation. Neither of the two, nor anyone else inside the crew, for that matter, had ever taken what Sascha had just said into consideration upon agreeing to the deal they'd made with Natalia

III. Things had carried on way too far, however. Piper and her uncle now had to disappear in order to prevent the heinous act from being uncovered.

"You…you don't need somebody to be of the same race or age to be a match for an organ transplant…right, girls?" Delilah asked, unsure of her statement as she eyed Faye, Bonita and Sascha with a look of doubt displayed upon her face.

"There's only one way to find out now," Faye reasoned as she looked down at an unconscious Piper. "No matter which way it goes, we'll have to keep this girl hidden for the next day or so until that doctor can confirm or deny her usefulness. Her mother will come looking for her I'm sure, so we'll have to figure out what to do with her also."

"And if Piper isn't a match?" Sascha asked. "We could be fishing for weeks for kidneys and we haven't that much time. We have to be more proficient in this endeavor. This teenager is useless to us I'm willing to bet. What are we going to do with her after we learn she's of no value?"

"We'll kill her. And then we'll kill her mother Claire," Faye remarked nonchalantly as she turned and walked off from Piper. "We have a little bit of time to get this thing on track the way it should be. We'll find a donor soon enough," she let it be known as she headed for her bungalow inside the barn to do research on kidney transplants online.

CHAPTER NINE

SPECIAL DELIVERY

Tanya had awakened around eight Sunday morning, a few hours after Faye and company had killed a man and kidnapped his niece. After washing up, she dressed for the day, sporting a pair of high-cut denim jeans, tank top and sneakers. She grabbed her coffee mug and headed for the stairs leading down to the immaculate kitchen inside the Bender mansion. While walking across the balcony, she spotted Beverly Battle sitting before a grand piano just up the hall. She walked over to the open area and asked, "What're you doing?"

"I'm writing this new song that came to me last night in a dream. I don't think it matches my voice, but some youngin' with a sort of an alto pitch can wing it." Beverly replied as she scribbled into a notepad.

"Is it a ballad or straight rock?" Tanya asked.

"It's a rock ballad, sugar. Along the lines of Paul McCartney and Wings' song Let Me Roll It. The guitar riff is killer and I hear this slow, but pounding drum pattern." Beverly said as she wound her hand while tapping her feet and mumbling lyrics. "That talk we had and my performance yesterday lit a fire under my ass, Tanya," the feisty brunette quipped as she hummed the tune in her head.

Tanya wasn't all that moved by Beverly Battle's enthusiasm as she'd this before; not from the famed singer herself per se, but from rock stars in general who sober up and get bit by the creative bug, only to turn around and relapse. Some go back to their old lifestyle, become worse than they were before they got sober and never recover. She was about to leave Beverly be, but she suddenly had an idea. One that could maybe keep the singer focused on making a full return to recording. "Where're you goin' when you leave Cherryvale?" she asked while staring at the back of

Beverly's head.

"Back down to my home in Nashville and work on some music, honey," Beverly joyfully stated as she wrote a lyric down. "I am feeling this song here!"

"I'm gonna be staying put in Cincinnati for the foreseeable future. Why don't you come back with me and Boogie and set up in our home and work on your song there," Tanya suggested. "We have eight bedrooms so there's plenty of room for you. Boogie has a dance room with a piano and an amplifier in there, too."

Beverly set her notepad down, turned and smiled. "I've never been to you and Boogie's place, Tanya! I remember I played Paul Brown stadium with Stevie Nicks back in '99. Honey, we lit that joint up let me tell ya'! I did this twenty-minute riff right beside her while she sung? And both of us was lit up like the sun in front of seventy-five thousand screaming heads."

"You can do it again, you know?" Tanya smiled. "You're still great, Beverly."

"I was great yesteryear, but I see myself as only being good today. I prefer to be modest in my thinking to keep from going overboard and getting too big for my britches. Been there done that."

"So, you're going to join us in Ohio?"

"I'll give it a whirl, I sure will!" Beverly laughed. "I'm packed and ready to go, sugar, just say when you're ready."

"Good. I'll notify you when we're ready to leave," Tanya stated. "The caffeine calling me now this early Sunday morning," she ended as she sauntered across the marble floors and trotted down the stairs where she caught a glimpse of Faye and Maggie sitting at the breakfast nook with a woman who was dabbing her eyes and crying incessantly. She politely spoke and went and took a seat beside Boogie at the island counter in the kitchen. "Who's the guest?" she asked her daughter as she poured herself a cup of brew.

"A woman whose daughter is missing," Boogie casually replied as she combed out the kinks in her tan afro with an iron pick. "She won't ever find her, though," she added as she eyed the troubled female sitting across the way before a window that gave a clear view of the apple groves on the north side of the property.

"Piper would never just up and runaway!" Tanya heard the

woman cry out loud. "And my brother," the distraught woman added as she rolled her eyes in disgust. "He was always trying to influence her to get her to go along with his…" the woman's voice faded off as she refused to divulge her brother's illegal activities.

Whether the woman spoke on the affairs of her brother nor not, Faye knew the deal. "We know about your brother dealing methamphetamine," she let it be known. "But that's not the important issue here. What matters to me and my law enforcement team is that Piper is found alive and returned to your safety, Mrs. Bailey."

"Did Piper have any friends out of state? Or maybe your brother?" Maggie chimed in as she sat in her deputy's uniform with her legs crossed.

"It's true my brother peddled drugs, but I don't know how he does it or who he does it with," Mrs. Bailey stated. "Given his reputation, I should've never let him take Piper to that party in Independence," she cried lowly.

"I can assure you that we're using all of our resources to find the whereabouts of your daughter, Mrs. Bailey," Faye stated as she stood up from her chair. "We have your number and you have ours. Feel free to contact me directly if you have any questions or remember anything that could help us in our endeavors to find Piper," she said in a comforting tone of voice while tucking her hands into the back pockets of her jeans.

Mrs. Bailey looked over to Faye with reluctance and she could tell right away that the woman wanted to ask her a question, and she knew what that question was. "If you think your daughter's absence is because of the way you talked to me yesterday inside the Bender Museum, then you really don't know me, Mrs. Bailey. I'm not a bitter or petty woman to stoop so low as to attack your family in that manner."

"My friend said something similar before I came here, but I wouldn't be able to sleep if I didn't have your reassurance, Mayor Bender. If I learn anything, I'll let you know," Mrs. Bailey confessed.

Faye held her stare on Claire for several seconds. She really was regretting the fact that she'd run across Piper, but it was too late for the teenager. And Claire, sadly, would have to face the same fate eventually. "Okay. No harm done," Faye smiled. "My daughter Maggie here will escort you back to Thayer now, and we'll get back to work on tracking down your brother and daughter to get them back safely."

Faye stood facing the main double doors of her home as Maggie and Claire Bailey left the house. She watched as the two climbed into separate cars and rode off. Her eyes then shifted over to the right where the barn lay. "What time are you and Boogie leaving for Cincinnati, Tanya?" she turned and asked once the cars were out of her line of sight.

"Within the hour," Tanya replied before sipping her coffee. "I have a meeting with our buyers over to Mulberry to set the new prices on the heroin once the Holland family secures the deal with the Devereaux family in a couple of days so I need to get back there."

"Your route back to Ohio takes you through Saint Louis," Faye stated as she walked over to her S-patterned island counter inside her high-ceiling kitchen with the platinum and diamond-cut chandelier. She handed Tanya a card with a number on it and said, "You and Boogie will be able to deliver a package to a doctor over to Mercy Hospital at that number. He'll be there until six this evening to meet you. Don't ask his name," she counseled.

"Not a problem," Tanya casually replied. "I saw you eyeing the barn while Maggie was leaving the farm. Something over there?" she inquisitively asked.

"Your package is over in the barn…amongst other things," Faye replied with a sly smirk. "When you're ready I give you the dime tour. How's Beverly doing?"

"She wants back in on recording. I'm taking her back to my home so she can work on this song she's writing," Tanya replied.

"Really?" Faye replied through raised eyebrows as she stood opposite Tanya from across the granite counter. "Maybe we can collect on our hundred-thousand-dollar investment and then some."

"I don't know about all that," Maggie chimed in. "I heard her performance last evening and she's lost some of her voice."

"She's really good with the guitar, though," Tanya countered. "She suggested a compilation album yesterday and just told me the song she's writing would work with a younger voice. Could be something there. If she can get up with a hot act and do a feature?

That'll pave the way for another album. I mean, Beverly still has 'it'. She just needs a revamping of her career."

"We all have the desire to go legit someday and leave this business behind." Faye admitted. "Maybe it's something to look into."

"I'm a looking," Tanya sighed. "If we can get her back in the music business we can definitely ride that ticket. Me and Boogie are all packed. We'll grab our things after I finish my coffee."

"Meet me over to the barn," Faye remarked as she headed for her the main doors to ride over to the west side of the property.

****

The ride across her land on this sunny late spring morning was a picturesque one for Faye as she rode west. Off to her right in the wheat field lay her massive combine, the machine used to harvest acres of grain. Further north lay the infamous apple groves where countless bodies had been disposed of in the most horrific fashion imaginable. In her rearview mirror, she could see the airstrip dividing her land in half behind her mansion. To her immediate left, secured by barbed-wired fence lay dairy cows clustered up into a heap under the morning sun as Mustang horses roamed free. Shiny steel silos near the edge of the land further left stood strong as grain was being funneled from the silos into several rigs she and Bonita owned in preparation for transport to a rail depot in Kansas City, Kansas. There, the bushels would be transferred to the railcars owned by her and Delilah Mobley and shipped to Lewiston, Idaho with the rest of their harvest wheat from Patterson, Iowa, along with one dead body that was to be burned.

To the outside eye, the Bender Farm was nothing more than a family-owned agricultural business located in America's heartland, but for those who knew the truth, it was clear to see that something sinister was transpiring on this fertile, paradisiac land that lay in southeastern Kansas. The clacking of one's heels three times over could not save them from the ghoulishness as this was no fairy tale, and it was most certainly not a place to call home for those who didn't belong.

Faye pulled up to the large, closed double doors on the barn and climbed out of her quad-cab pickup while laying down on the horn. A small wooden door was pulled open a minute or so later. Sascha poked her head out briefly and looked around in all directions while still sporting her sheriff deputy's uniform. She looked Faye off and disappeared back into the cavernous structure while waving her inside.

After securing the small door, Faye walked across the dirt floor of the barn, passing in between a couple of shiny, green and yellow John Deere tractors, and the Nissan they'd stolen the night before. As she rounded the large wheel of a piece of farm equipment, she laid eyes on Piper Bailey. She sat at a small, circular table handcuffed to its top in a wooden chair with a bowl of oatmeal, an apple, crispy bacon and orange juice before her.

"*Sie weigert sich zu essen,*" (She's refusing to eat) Sascha stated as she stood behind the crew's captive. "*Ich weiß nicht, wie der Mangel an Nahrung ist, ihre Nieren auswirken, wenn Sie eine Übereinstimmung.*" (I don't know how her lack of nutrition is going to impact her kidneys if she's a match.)

"We're trying to negotiate the terms on returning you back to your mother, Piper Bailey," Faye stated in a caring tone as she walked over and stood opposite the terrified teenager. "We don't need you getting sick on us. And how you not get sick on us is by eating what's given to you," she added as she picked up a plastic spoon, dipped it into the oatmeal and stirred the hot cereal.

"I'm, I can't eat!" Piper cried aloud as she stared up at the woman who'd knocked her out hours earlier. "I been vomiting since I got here! Ask her," she added as she stared back at Sascha. Faye looked over to Sascha, and she nodded her head in agreement over Piper's remark.

"You've seen what we've done to your uncle during that stop. It wasn't our choice, but we had to defend ourselves." Faye calmly stated as she pulled out a chair and sat beside Piper and hugged her. "Your uncle tried to pull a gun on one of my officers and she was forced to kill him. I talked to your mother just now and she knows you're safe. Once your uncle's body is identified and your mother lays claim to his remains, you will be released. There's no need for fright and refusal of our kind acts."

"But I still don't know what you people want from me!" Piper cried. "What does anything my uncle did in the past have to do with me? What is that you want me to do? Whatever it takes to save my life I'll do it!" the terrified teenager pleaded over the roar of a chainsaw being started from behind a small wooden door inside the barn.

"What we want is for you to agree to not file a lawsuit against Montgomery County Sheriff's Department over the wrongful death of your uncle. This county is already broke as it is, a civil lawsuit would bankrupt Cherryvale and the town of Thayer where you live. We're trying to avoid that scenario." Faye replied.

"You're holding me hostage over the county going broke?" Piper asked through her tears. The seventeen-year-old had grown comfortable enough to put up a minimal effort of protest over her plight given the way Sascha had been treating her the past few hours, but if she only knew the truth, Piper would've been more terrified than she already was over what was to come.

"To answer your question? Yes." Faye stated over the chainsaw's buzz. "All we want is to not be sued. It would be bad for jobs and businesses. You agree to that, you get to go home. You'll be a hero."

"And if I don't agree?" Piper inquired.

"Then life as you know it will cease to exist," Faye stated in a cold, yet sincere manner. "I will kill you and then I will ride up to Thayer and kill your mother and vanquish your family from this county forever before I even sit down for lunch today. Make the right decision today. Forget about your uncle and take you and your mother's life into consideration."

"You're going to kill me anyway I know it!" Piper cried aloud. "This is a nightmare!"

"You'll make it a nightmare if you don't comply, young Piper," Sascha chimed in. "Do as the Mayor has asked and nothing bad will happen."

"I just wanna go home. Can I talk to my momma, please? Can she come and get me if I agree not to file a lawsuit?"

Faye was sniggering on the inside over Piper's request. As if she would willingly let Claire Bailey walk into her barn and hold discussions with her daughter. Piper was being held hostage over not suing the county and the police force had killed her uncle was the story. No way would Claire be so understanding, even if what Piper was being told was the actual truth. Piper's thought process didn't run that deep, Faye understood. For one valid reason or another, if Faye had to tell it, Piper was on the verge of checking out shortly—kidneys intact or not—and Claire herself would soon follow suit.

Faye hadn't the patience it took to have to deal with Claire for an undetermined amount of time trying to figure out what happened to Piper while knowing all along she was behind the woman's daughter's disappearance. Once Piper was eliminated, Mrs. Bailey would only become an agitation for Faye, so she decided to rid herself of a budding thorn in her side before it ever took root. "I'll have your mother brought here tomorrow morning so you can talk to her," she told Piper as she stood up from the chair.

"How can I trust you?" the wary teenager asked in return as tears dripped from her chin.

"I'm Mayor of this town," Faye reassured as she ran the back of her hand over Piper's wet, flushed cheeks. "City Hall opens at eight tomorrow morning. All your mother has to do is go there and sign documents that she will not file suit against Montgomery County. I'll bring her here so you can sign the documents and from there, you'll be set free. But, before all that happens, I just need you to put something on your stomach. Eat," she urged.

"I'll eat, but I'll believe what you're telling me about my mother only when I see her," Piper replied.

"Okay, I'll let you see her—tomorrow," Faye stated in a serious tone while staring down into Piper's eyes. "Free her hands so she can fill her belly," she then told Sascha as she walked over and pulled open another small door that led into the home she and Maggie once lived in inside the barn as the grind of a chainsaw coated her ears.

Faye walked down the spotless, well-lit hall, sliding past the door on the left that led to the sleeping quarters inside the enclosed cavern. She opened another wooden door that was straight ahead and entered a second corridor. This second hall was darker and narrower, and lined with machetes and other cutting utensils. There was a hook where a chainsaw hung, but the spot was vacant, as well as two hooks where hacksaws were once positioned. The hall soon opened up into a four-cornered, low-ceiled room with red lighting. Faye entered and looked around as the chainsaw died down.

Bonita looked over at that moment. She wore a white butcher's outfit that was splattered with blood and bits of flesh. "I was just finishing up, girl," she told Faye as she removed a pair of bloody goggles and wiped blood from her forehead.

Faye walked past her sister and stood before a wooden table unnerved. Before her lay the severed remains of Piper's uncle. His hands and feet were detached from his arms and legs and his head was disconnected from his body. It lay on its side with its eyes open staring off into empty space. "Wrap everything in plastic to conceal the body parts before taking them out to the apple groves. Save the hands. Put them in the freezer inside the apartment and I'll move them at a later date," Faye ordered just as Tanya walked into the chamber.

Tanya had seen this scenario before and she was unfazed by the sight of it all. She herself had chopped up a victim for Faye over a quarter century ago. Hers was a male victim that'd gotten too close to Faye and had tried to bribe her after learning of her murder warrant back in Iowa during that period of time back in 1983. "Where're the kidneys?" she asked as she eyed the man's body parts neatly laid out on the table.

"They're still with the young girl having breakfast in the barn," Faye answered. "Your package is a blood sample from her that we need expedited over to Mercy Hospital in Saint Louis this morning. I have the vial stored in the refrigerator inside the apartment. Follow me," she added as she left the dimly-lit dungeon and walked down to the apartment.

Tanya paced the wooden floors behind Faye with her hands tucked into the back pockets of her tight-fitting shorts and walked into the apartment. It hadn't been changed at all over the years. In fact, it'd become a haunting relic that was outdated with old furniture and had a musky smell to it.

"You have everything set up in Cincinnati, Tanya? We'll have two hundred and twenty-six kilograms of heroin comin' in ten days or so," Faye asked as she went into the old refrigerator and handed her friend a small Styrofoam box containing Piper's blood sample. She then grabbed a container of cream cheese and set it on the table.

"I'm meeting with the dealers in a couple of days," Tanya answered as she held onto the box. "We're renegotiating price and territory. Upping the price and expanding into Chicago. It's a big heroin market up there."

"Good deal. But, before we set up in Chicago, let me talk to Ben first. We'll need him to put Natalia on to what we're doing." Faye stated as she opened a bag of bagels and popped one into the toaster inside the small kitchen.

"Why? It's not like we answer to the Holland family. We make our own moves," Tanya retorted.

"That is true," Faye nodded in agreement as she grabbed a butter knife and popped the top off the container of cream cheese. "But we have an alliance with the Holland family. What happens to us affects them and vice versa. Let's be smart on how we move is all I'm saying."

"You doubt me and Helen," Tanya stated as she eyed Faye seriously.

"I don't doubt you, sister. I just don't want any unnecessary animosity to occur between us and our allies," Faye remarked as the bagel popped up. "We want the Holland family on our side when we move on Chicago. We'll need Natalia to help us take down any crew or crews that stand in our way and to turn us on to some major players up there. It's good that we have the Holland family's approval on that matter," she added as she placed her bagel onto a saucer and sat at a small table before a dingy curtain. The table and curtain was a replica of her great, great, grandmother, Kate Bender's murder chamber from the late 1800s. Faye hadn't put the area to use as of yet, but she was looking forward to the day, which wasn't far off in her mind.

"We can handle that ourselves," Tanya bit back. "And let's not forget that the Holland family needs our political contacts, which makes us equal partners in the deal you made without even consulting me."

Faye was spreading cream cheese onto her bagel when Tanya spoke. She paused and said, "I figured you would understand and agree with my decision being I'm an equal partner in our arrangement."

"I understand well," Tanya replied casually. "And when I agreed to allow you to form the alliance with the Hollands, I expected you to understand that we fall under no one's umbrella. We operate according to our own laws and do whatever we want."

"But any move our family makes may affect the Holland family nonetheless. It should be my decision to make being it was my idea to move in on Chicago after the deal with Malik Gomez. I figure the Holland family would do us that favor and back us so let me handle it my way. You just line up the suppliers in Cincinnati. Be careful while you're at it. I'll handle Chicago for us," Faye reasoned.

Tanya plopped down beside Faye and smiled at her. Faye, in turn, cut her eyes over at Tanya while spreading cream cheese over her bagel and noticed her snickering. "What's so funny?" she asked as she began to giggle herself.

"You care about me," Tanya smiled as she laid her head on Faye's shoulder. "I promise to be careful, girl."

"So long as you promise," Faye said in a tender tone as she kissed the crown of Tanya's skull. "I just don't think it's a good move to keep the Holland family in the dark over our actions. We said we were going to do good business together and this is good business. Don't you agree?"

"You're right, and I agree. You really like those people don't you?" Tanya asked seriously.

"The Holland family is a real organization. One of the best ones I've seen since we've been in this line of work. We can make a lot of money with them. This first score is worth ten million dollars at least wholesale after expenses."

"Yeah. They are a money pit," Tanya nodded in agreement. "I'm on my way to Saint Louis, I guess, once you finish your bagel and walk me out," she ended.

CHAPTER TEN

THE DAY NOBODY WANTED TO GO TO JAIL

"Step by step...hearts of hearts...left right left...we all fall down...like toy soldiers..."

The studio on the first floor inside Club Indigo was lit up with the sounds of the Jane Dow Band as they began their opening rendition to Makita's song *Toy Soldiers*, a rock ballad that was a number one hit for the singer back in 1989. It was just after the noon hour on Sunday, and several hours after Tanya and Boogie had left Cherryvale.

Club Indigo was empty save for the four members of The Jane Dow Band, Jay-D, Dooney, Nancy Cottonwood, Loopy, Kree, and a couple of engineers Jay-D had put on his record label's payroll to get the ball rolling on his first project, which was the Jane Dow Band's first album. The album was to be a cover album Jay-D and Jane had initially agreed to title *Cover Art*, as Jane was going to cover twelve number one hit songs ranging from Paul McCartney and Wings to Yarbrough and Peebles. Jay-D had sent out cover song clearance requests and contract agreements to all the artists and bands needed for the project. He was prepared to sink a quarter of a million dollars into Jane for a shot at the big time, so getting everything right and professional was of the utmost importance.

From behind Plexiglas, Jay-D and the crew listened as Jane played her drums inside the darkened studio. The keyboardist strung the chords and the bass guitarist strummed his electric guitar while the acoustic player moved about with his guitar strapped to his back as he hadn't a part in this particular song except for the chorus. To Jay-D, Toy Soldiers was missing something his ears couldn't quite decode. He sat before the mixing board with his head bowed listening with his eyes closed as Jane sung the last verse before sliding back into the chorus while pounding her drums...*"When you hear temptation call...it's your heart that takes...takes the fall..."*

"Won't you come out and play with me..." a group of female college students from Lindenwood University sung aloud inside the recording room before Jane sung aloud... *"Step by step... hearts of hearts...left right left...we all fall down...like toy soldiers...bit by bit...we never win...torn apart...for toy soldiers..."*

"That's not how the lyrics go," Jay-D humbly complained as he reached out and powered down the mixing board and hopped up from his seat. He walked over and snatched the door to the recording room open and stepped inside where he eyed all the artists with contempt. "Jane, we done rehearsed this song over twenty times and you still having the same problem with it. What's, what's the deal?" he asked, slightly frustrated. "This the third take on this song now."

Jane removed her sunglasses after setting her drumsticks aside. "Jay," the nineteen-year-old, brown-eyed chubby Lakota Indian stated lowly. "I'm appreciating the opportunity you're giving me and all, but this is not how I do my thing, man."

"What you mean?" Jay-D asked as he walked over to Jane.

"We're a band, man. A rock band. This, this no drug policy you got all of us on is taking us out of our element. At least it's takin' me outta *my* element. I can't get into the groove of things like I want to being sober. I mean, this, this is music, dude," Jane reasoned. "The Beatles, Rolling Stones, N.W.A., Outkast, everybody, all the artist we're using on this project? They recorded with their minds in some other place on occasion and they would admit that. I'm not saying we have to do it every day? But for this first song? I need my bud. You wanna know what's missing? It's not the voice, it's not the band or the instruments, it's the *bud*."

Nancy Cottonwood walked into the recording room at that moment. "What the deal? That shit was getting hot before you stopped it, Jay. I mean, they started off a little flat, but they was picking it up, Big Unc."

"Jane say she need some bud," Jay-D stated as he nodded over to his artist.

Nancy looked the entire group over. "Hell, I know them girls from Lindenwood. They smoke weed like a mutherfucka. Everybody in here except for Kree smoke weed. I don't know about them two mutherfuckas you got running the mixing board, but they ain't singing on this hot ass song. We puttin' a lot of money into this shit and definitely don't need to fuck it...up... like..." Nancy's voice trailed off as she refused to speak about the night her uncle Dooney had killed a man by the name of Alonzo Milton, which led to Jay-D becoming owner of the record label he now ran. "Let 'em have they weed, man." she suggested. "Fuck we got to lose on that?"

Jay-D took his niece's remarks into consideration at that moment. "Let's umm, let's all take a break and head 'cross the street to the New Orleans Café for lunch and we'll get back to it. Y'all want some bud? I'm gone get y'all some bud. But I want this song finished today so we can move on to the next one," he ended before walking out of the recording room.

"Thank you," Jane mouthed to Nancy with a wide smile on her face as she grabbed her drumsticks and filed out of the recording room with the rest of the artists.

****

Meanwhile, over to Mercy Hospital, Tanya had just dropped the blood sample off to a nameless doctor and was climbing back into the passenger seat of her Bentley Arnage after a five-hour drive completed by Boogie. "Doc say we'll know something in a few hours on the sample," she let it be known as she pulled the passenger side door shut. "Umm, I could use a bite to eat before we get back on the road. Y'all girls hungry?"

"Yeah. I know a spot over in Saint Charles," Boogie replied casually as she pulled out of the parking slot.

The trio turned onto Elm Street thirty minutes later and parked down the street from the New Orleans Café. Tanya scanned the block cautiously as Boogie pulled over just down from the New Orleans Café. She could see a navy-blue Navigator and white Maxima parked in front of the diner just up ahead, and a red, drop top Caddy on chrome wheels with all-white interior was parked across the street before a canopy attached to a Club Indigo. Tanya leaned forward, looked across Boogie's lap and read the announcement splayed on a side canopy above the caty-cornered double doors of the club on the corner. "Performing live tonight The Jane Dow Band," she stated lowly as she eyed Boogie.

"That was the band that played the night we met up with Natalia and Malik," Boogie remarked as she placed the car in park. "They were pretty good."

"Sounds like a rock band. Do they play rock?" Beverly asked a little excited as she climbed from the car and stretched her legs.

"They played umm, they played Fleetwood Mac song, World Turning that night and got themselves a record deal. It's a recording studio inside the Holland family club." Boogie told Beverly just before the singer closed the back door.

"The Holland family," Tanya remarked dryly. "You brought us into hostile territory, Boogie."

"How, momma? We don't have no animosity with the Holland family since we made the deal after giving up Malik," Boogie stated after she shut down the engine. "We're doing business for 'em right now. So how we in hostile territory?"

"We're okay with the bosses in the Holland family, Helen," Tanya counseled. "But no one has a complete understanding of how the crews feel about losing their Enforcer in Malik, not to mention the deal with Peppi Vargas and her crew."

"Let's go find out then," Boogie replied as she eased the door open and stepped out of the car.

Tanya had in mind to order Beverly and Boogie back inside the car and have her daughter drive away, but Beverly had crossed the street and was peeking into the tinted windows of the club while pulling on the locked door handles. She threw her arms up and climbed out of the car after placing her Glock .40 in her back waistband.

Beverly, meanwhile, was backing away from the club's entrance with her hands on her hips while staring up at the canopy. "I wanna see what's in there! Who owns this building?" she asked as she walked backwards and stepped out into the street.

"Eh, yo that's our shit!" a male voice boomed out from the café on the opposite corner. "Fuck you doing over there?"

Beverly trotted over to the overweight, yellow-skinned young man with long braided hair. "I'm Beverly. Beverly Battle!" she smiled as she extended her hand.

The young man stood before the entrance to the New Orleans Café and grimaced, flashing a platinum grill as he mean-mugged Beverly's outstretched hand. "You, you saying your name like I'm supposed ta' know you or somethin'. What, you famous or something, Beverly Battle? But fuck all that! Why you over there spyin' on our shit is the question of the day?"

"Dooney, who you talkin' to like that?" another voice, that of a female was heard by Beverly as she stepped out of the café's doors holding onto a blunt and a lighter. When her eyes fell upon the middle-aged woman standing before Dooney, she let the drug paraphernalia slip from her hands. "Oh my god! Oh my god! Dooney, you know Beverly Battle?" she exclaimed as she covered her lower face with her hands.

"This your brother or somethin'?" Beverly asked the young woman. "Because if he is you need to teach this booger some manners about himself!"

"No, he's a teddy bear," the young woman laughed, unable to believe who she was talking to at the moment. "I'm Jane Dow and this is my label manager Dooney!"

"Jane Dow? On the sign over there!" Beverly smiled. "Ole Boogie back there said ya' pretty good at what ya' do! I may just have ta' find out for myself now!"

Loopy had walked out of the New Orleans Café on the tail end of Beverly's remark and she'd heard what was said. *"Boogie?"* she said to herself as she looked to her left.

"There that bitch Loopy go right there," Boogie said to herself as she eyed Loopy staring directly at her just up the sidewalk as she walked beside her mother. She watched as Loopy pulled down on her fitted red cap and smoothly ducked back inside the café. "I forgot my driver's license, momma. I think I'm gone have a drink since you driving the rest of the way back to Cincy," she said. "Wait here and I'll go and get it."

"I'm not liking this move, Helen," Tanya sighed as she pulled out her cellphone and took the time to text Faye and let her know that the sample had been delivered and she should get word back on whether Piper was a match or not by late evening.

Boogie, meanwhile, had went back to the Bentley and pulled a . 45 caliber from underneath the driver's seat the time she opened the door. She tucked the gun into the back waistband of her baggy jeans and pulled her blouse down to conceal the weapon before rejoining her mother.

While the tension was mounting over to New Orleans Café, on the opposite end of the block inside the Cottonwood home, Jay-D and sat talking with Kantrell Luckett, who was furious over not knowing the whereabouts of Malik Gomez.

"It's been nearly a month since Malik disappeared and ain't nobody tellin' me shit!" Kantrell boomed as she stood before Jay-D, who was sitting at his kitchen table with Kree at his side.

"You saw the news the same way we saw the news, Kantrell," Jay-D remarked calmly. "They found Malik jeep last week with a body burned up inside."

"It wasn't Malik inside the jeep, Jason! It was Max!" Kantrell retorted as she slammed the autopsy report down onto the table. "Malik left his ride with Max before he took off for a trip to God knows where! Now Max dead and Malik missing. Word on the street is that the people you work for put a hit out on Max, but that's not my gripe. I wanna know what happened to Malik!"

"People just talking, Kantrell. Because they saying it don't mean we had anything to do with any of that stuff," Kree stated matter-of-factly.

Kantrell cut her eyes at Kree. "We?" she asked through a scowl. "All of a sudden you a gangster?" she bucked through curled lips. "You Jason spokeswoman now? The way you used to run around Fox Park and everywhere else scared out your rabbit ass mind a couple of years ago I think you way outta your league tryna get involved with this shit right here, sister."

"I just made an observation," Kree sassed.

"When you wasn't even being spoken to! Back the fuck up and stay out this shit and keep your mouth shut! And just ta' let ya' know? Your ass fired!"

"What?" Kree exclaimed.

"You heard me, bitch! You fuckin' fired! We off tomorrow being it's a Monday so you can ride up ta' Bangin' Heads and unload all your shit up out my spot!"

"You overreacting, yeah?" Jay-D remarked coolly as he eyed Kantrell.

"No I'm not!" Kantrell objected. "You and that hoe right there know damn well what happened to Malik and neither one of y'all sayin' shit about it!'"

Jay-D eyed Kantrell as she paced his kitchen floor in anger and said, "Your nigga tried to set your boy Ben cousin up to get killed in Chicago. That's what happened."

"Now ya' lyin' to a bitch! That don't even sound like Malik!" Kantrell scoffed as she threw her hands up in an exasperated manner.

"I let you talk shit long enough and we through with all that there," Jay-D stated. Although his voice was low and he was soft-spoken most times, everybody knew when Jay-D was serious. His voice had emanated a certain strength that'd paused Kantrell and now had her listening while biting her lip nervously. "I don't know how you dealt with Malik and how you talked to that fuck boy, but that shit don't fly with me. Malik gone. How it happened, you don't need to know all that there, but I already told you why and I'm not gone repeat myself. What you decide to do with the information gone determine your whole future," he ended as he stared up into Kantrell's eyes from his seated position as his hands drifted down to his waistband.

"You thinkin' about going to the police?" Kree asked as she removed a .45 caliber from her over-sized leather purse and set it on the table.

Kantrell was no novice to the business Malik Gomez was involved in; she herself had aided and abetted him by moving cocaine from location to location on occasion, stashing bricks and holding re-up money for him while he was getting down. The two had even dodged death when Toodie Perez had tried to kill Malik the year before while he was over to her home. He was 'that dude' in her eyes and she loved him dearly. Him not being around ailed her to the core, but given the business he was in, Jay-D could've been telling the truth, only Kantrell wasn't sure at the moment.

Having realized she'd perhaps lost out on love over the possible missteps of her man, Kantrell made the smart decision and opted for diplomacy. She knew of Jay-D's rep as a killer and wouldn't dare upset him any further. The gun Kree had placed on the table had told her all she needed to know about her friend of five-plus years as well. It was now plain to see that Kree was coming under Jason's control and was willing to do whatever it took to have a man love her.

Kantrell looked to ceiling while running her hands through her short, cropped brown hair and said, "I need to know everything that happened, Jason. In order for me to accept this shit and move on? I need to know what it was exactly that Malik did to get himself killed if that's the case."

Jay-D nodded and came up with his cellphone. "You still gone fire my old lady?" he asked as he set the phone on the table.

"No," Kantrell responded as she eyed Kree. "We cool, but I need to speak to someone over you, brer," she told Jay-D. "I feel I'm owed that there if y'all want me to get past this shit. Send Ben my way so we can talk and get some things straightened out."

"That's what it is then," Jay-D said as he picked up his cell phone and dialed a number.

****

"What you think wrong with Sosa, baby?" Oneika asked Dawk as the two sat with Siloam and another ranch hand inside the lobby of Ponca City Hospital.

"I don't know," Dawk responded somberly as he shook his head while sitting with his hands beneath his bearded chin. "It's respiratory, though, I believe. Could be the fresh lacquer on the wooden floors in our house, the wall paint...I just don't know, sweetheart," he declared just as the doctor treating his and Oneika's son, Sosa Holland, walked into the waiting area.

Oneika jumped up and ran towards the doctor when she saw the doctor approaching. Dawk followed, just as his cellphone buzzed in his slacks. Agitated, he answered upon recognizing the number. "Yeah?" he asked hastily as he walked over to the doctor.

"Kantrell want a meeting over that deal with Malik, boss—with ya' fam, though," Jay-D stated.

"He gettin' ready to leave the country right now. Give it a couple of days and I'm gone send 'em that way when he get back," Dawk stated before abruptly ending the call in order to hear the full prognosis on the health of his son.

"Your people handling some business right now. He be in, in a couple of days," Jay-D told Kantrell upon ending the call. "Until then? We cool on that shit, right?"

"Until then," Kantrell responded. "See you Tuesday. Don't your ass be late," she then told Kree before scooping up her clutch purse and heading for the front door.

****

"Fiteen, punk!" Nancy Cottonwood exclaimed as she slammed a bone down onto the domino table. She then looked over to Dooney and smiled slyly as she wrote down her score.

"Shiddd, let me get some of that money," Dooney said as he slammed a bone down. "Twinny, muthafucka!"

"Oh, we runnin' fives?" DeMarco laughed as he laid out the double five bone. "Twinny-five, chumps!" he laughed.

"See that ain't even right," Nancy sighed as she wrote down the scores.

"You started that shit, ole skinny ass," Dooney complained.

"And your fat ass followed," Nancy bit back. "Play, homeboy," she then said to the bass guitarist of The Jane Dow Band.

Thirty minutes had gone by and all was smooth inside the New Orleans Café. With Jay-D off the scene trying to smoothen things over with Kantrell, the tension between Loopy and Boogie was going unnoticed. The two were watching one another intently as they went about their business inside the near-empty café.

Boogie was at the bar with her mother sipping on a Blue Hawaiian while Beverly and Jane Dow sat at a table near the door talking the day away. Loopy, meanwhile, was sitting at a table in the middle of the bar by herself eating a bowl of gumbo. Every time Boogie took a sip of her drink, she eyed Loopy out the corner of her eye, and every time Loopy scooped a spoonful of gumbo, she eyed Boogie.

"Sie wissen, wer das ist, sitzen am Tisch dort drüben, Mama?" (You know who that is sitting at that table over there, momma?) Boogie whispered.

"Sie sagte einer von Peppi Vargas' Menschen überlebt der Hit. Angesichts der Spannungen zwischen Ihnen beiden, ich schätze und sagen Guadalupe Cruz?" (You said one of Peppi Vargas' people survived the hit. Given the tension between you two, shall I guess and say Guadalupe Cruz?) Tanya asked as she sipped club soda with a basket of crackers before her as she looked over in Loopy's direction.

"Sie erraten, rechts. Sie weiß, wer ich bin, aber ich glaube nicht, dass ihre Freunde wissen, was los ist. Ihre Führer Jason Cottonwood nicht hier ist. Diese Leute wissen nicht, wer wir sind außerhalb von Guadalupe." (You guess right. She knows who I am, but I don't think her friends know what's going on. Their leader Jason Cottonwood isn't here. These people do not know who we are outside of Guadalupe.)

"Sie toting?" (You're toting?) Tanya asked in a whisper as she bit into a saltine cracker.

"I am," Boogie replied lowly while looking Loopy off.

"Also i bin Wenn alles untergeht, werden wir sie alle heraus nehmen." (So am I. If anything goes down, we'll take them all out.) Tanya remarked casually as she leaned over and dusted her hands over the floor.

Boogie looked the entire café over at that moment. Waitresses were milling about with smiles on their faces offering drinks, the chef on duty was happily fulfilling meal tickets. Everybody seemed to be getting along, but was completely unaware of what was on the verge of going down.

"Es gibt keinen Grund für die Schießereien." (There's no reason for gunplay.) Boogie told her mother as she looked over shoulder while anxiously biting her nails. *"Wir haben keinen Konflikt mit der Holland Familie als Ganzes. Diese Sache ist zwischen mir und Guadalupe."* (We have no conflict with the Holland family as a whole. This thing is between me and Guadalupe.)

"Turn your back and see what she does then," Tanya remarked as she sipped her ginger ale.

"I'm going to leave her alone," Boogie replied over Otis Redding's song *Sitting On The Dock of The Bay.* "But never will I turn my back on her."

Loopy, meanwhile, was eyeing Boogie with disdain. Several times, she'd gotten up under the guise of having to use the rest room, but she was actually searching for a handgun inside the café's office in order to confront Boogie. She returned unsuccessful after a third attempt and resumed eating. As the seconds ticked by, she and Boogie continued to eye one another until Loopy, believing she would have the backing of her crew, jumped up from her seat. "She killed my cousin, Donatella!" she yelled aloud as she ran towards Boogie and the woman sitting beside her.

Boogie jumped up from her seat and pulled her .45 caliber and pointed it at Loopy, stopping her in her tracks. At the same time, Tanya pulled her Glock .40 and aimed it at Loopy while remaining seated in her barstool.

"Yo!" Dooney boomed as he hopped up from the booth at the back of the café and stormed towards the front of the establishment. He shoved Loopy back and stood before the barrels of the two guns he was facing as the music went silent. "Fuck going on here?" he asked aggressively over the deafening silence while eyeing the women. He recognized Boogie and said, "Y'all bitches crazy? Last time we saw you, you left here under a agreement of peace between you and my people, Boogie! What the fuck you doing?" he followed up as Nancy and DeMarco walked up beside him.

Jane Dow was now crouched behind the table peering out at Dooney. When she'd first met Beverly Battle and introduced her to him, she'd called him a big teddy bear. Whenever they were in the studio, Dooney would always be joking with her before her sessions and while she was working with the engineers. He made her laugh a lot and she was always hugging him. He was a big friendly guy in her eyes. She liked Dooney, enough to want to be his girlfriend. The brown-haired, brown-eyed freckle-faced Lakota Indian was seeing a different side to Dooney this day, however; no longer was he a teddy bear. He was tough. A man of the streets. She liked him even more now.

The current situation came back into focus for Jane as the person Dooney was talking to calmly remarked, "I ain't doing shit, Dooney. Me and my people just stopped through for lunch. We ain't come to start trouble."

Dooney remained in the middle of the aisle with Nancy and DeMarco at his side clutching their weapons. He pulled up on his baggy brown jean shorts while thinking. He knew Loopy was upset over Boogie killing her cousin and two best friends. He couldn't blame her; because if the same people had done something to Nancy or Jay-D, he would be having a hard time accepting what the Germans would have done to his family. He would obey the family's order, though, which was to keep the peace. If Loopy wanted to go after Boogie he wouldn't stop her, but he also wouldn't want to know about it, because he would have to kill her for going against a family order. "Alright we need, we need ta' talk this shit out, Boogie," he said while bumping his fists together. "Lower y'all guns for me."

"You first," Helen smirked, deciding to be petty.

Just then, Jay-D walked into the café with Kree following his lead. He looked at the two women aiming guns and knew what was up right away. He knew Loopy was gone be a problem all along. "I talked to you the day you got out the hospital and told you the case was closed on that, Loopy," he unpacked.

Loopy stared at Jay-D with a heartbroken expression on her face. "My people don't mean nothing to this family," she stated through her tears.

Jay-D knew Loopy was going to be taken care of by the family soon enough over the work she'd put in, but discussing the matter further out in the open was not a good idea. "We gone talk about that later," he said. He then looked over to Boogie and asked, "What you doing here? You ain't even got permission to be around here."

"So, that's where we at with it, Jay-D? I thought our families had a truce. Didn't know I needed permission to come here under the truce," Boogie said as she held her gun steady.

"The truce extend out to Indianapolis. Anything west of Indianapolis you violating."

"We can go wherever we *chose*," the woman beside Boogie said to Jay-D in a disgusted manner as she kept her gun aimed. "We're respecting the deal made. We only came here to have lunch because we *thought* we would be in the presence friends."

"Ain't no friends in this business. Only allies," Jay-D remarked calmly as he looked back at Dooney, Nancy and DeMarco. "Put the guns down. Ain't nobody gone shoot nobody in here today."

Sirens off in the distance was heard at that moment, disrupting the conversation. "Nancy, DeMarco, go in the office and close the door," Jay-D said, jumping into action. "Dooney, go in the kitchen and let the staff know it's all good out here and ain't nothing happenin'," he added as he walked over and knelt down before Jane Dow and extended his hand. "Everybody come from under those tables and take a seat! Take a seat! Turn the music back on, Dooney!" he yelled out while assisting Jane to her feet. "We all having drinks and eating ain't nothin' happenin' but a good time!"

With the police approaching, everybody inside the New Orleans Café was now scrambling to recreate the friendly atmosphere that was going down before the argument erupted in order to make things seem as normal as possible, in spite of the bloodbath that had nearly taken place. Everyone inside the café, from the bold gun-wielding merciless gangsters, to the innocent bystanders and curious witnesses alike, moved into position as the music kicked up for a second time.

Jane's three bandmates crawled from under a booth, took seats and began mixing bones as the four backup singers sat back in their seats and picked up menus. Tanya and Boogie had tucked their guns back into their back waistbands and had taken seats at the bar, the high back chairs they were sitting in concealing their weapons as they picked up their drinks and took sips.

Loopy went and sat at a table with Beverly Battle, Kree, and Jane Dow, who was now worried again. The nineteen year-old had a half-smoked blunt in her sweat pants pocket. The police may search everybody in the place was what she was thinking. Someone inside the café had obviously called the police. That meant they saw the guns Nancy and DeMarco had pulled on the two white women and the guns the white women themselves had pulled. She looked over to Jay-D. The calm look he displayed put her at ease as a lone officer eased into the café with his service pistol pointed outwards.

"We got a call of a disturbance that came from inside this place. Somebody said people was ready to shoot one another," the officer stated as he eyed Jay-D over Otis Redding's whistling on his song *Sitting on the Dock of the Bay*.

From his viewpoint, the officer could see a couple of Caucasian women sitting at the bar having drinks talking amongst themselves. An older white woman, a young Native American female, and what he believed were two Hispanic females, were sitting at a table to his immediate right. They were all looking off in different directions and avoiding eye contact, but it was the older white woman that'd caught the officer's attention over everybody else. "You Beverly Battle?" he asked. A wide, surprised smile crept across his face as he lowered his gun barrel down to his side.

"I sure am, officer. What brings you 'round this day? Is there a problem?" Beverly asked in a perky manner as she smiled up at the officer.

"Yeah, and you're probably in on it. I know your music. It's outlaw music and I love it," the officer smirked back at Beverly. He then looked further down the bar's main aisle. Over to his far left sat four young females. They were debating over ordering the gumbo entrees or the boiled crab legs. At the end of the aisle, he could see that a game of dominos was unfolding between three Native Americans. "Okay, enough of the charade. What's going on here, Jason?" he asked as he eyed the crowd, which seemed to be more calm than necessary.

"It wasn't nothin', Captain Jones," Jay-D calmly stated as he stood before the officer in his light grey silk suit and black leather shoes. "Somebody turned the music up a li'l too loud and everybody got ta' talking over each other."

"I can see how that could happen, but you sure it wasn't more to it, son?" Captain Jones inquired. "I mean, nobody's brains weren't about to get blown out inside this lovely establishment is what I'm asking here?"

"Nah, it wasn't nothin' like that," Jay-D stated, laughing lightly as he extended his right hand out towards the officer. "With the music and everything poppin' people just started talking louder to hear themselves that's all."

"Okay, can we shut down the soul music then?" Captain Jones requested as he shook Jay-D's hand.

"Yo, kill the music!" Jay-D called out towards the kitchen.

The music died down several seconds later and Captain Jones continued. "Someone called and said they saw guns on display. Anybody in here got guns on 'nem?" he asked as he eyed the two white women sitting at the bar, who were refusing to look in his direction. He looked back over to Jay-D and nudged his chin towards the two women. "I know every face in this neighborhood," he stated. "Who are they?"

Jay-D was now in a position to place Tanya and Boogie in a world of hurt given they were packing heat. The guns they were concealing were probably unregistered he surmised. They probably had bodies on them as well, and he knew that at the very least that Tanya and Boogie would have to give up their names along with proof of identification while Captain Jones ran a background check. It wasn't his intent to cause trouble for the Germans, however, so he downplayed it. "I don't know 'em," he told Captain Jones. "This is a new business and all. I see new faces in here all the time."

"So, I guess it's no need to have my guys come in here and do a pat down on everybody inside this joint and take down names?" Captain Jones asked seriously.

"No need for that," Jay-D calmly replied. "You know I run a tight ship. If my businesses or my customers' lives were in jeopardy today I'd be the first to say so. We good up in here."

"Okay," Captain Jones, a short and stout, hairy-armed and slightly-balding officer replied while dabbing the corner of his left eye. "I'll get out your hair now. But before I do, we need to talk outside."

Kree was listening to the entire conversation. She turned and peered out the tinted windows and watched as Jay-D and Captain Jones came into view once more and stood at the edge of the curb. She gasped as she witnessed several more patrol cars arriving on the scene with lights flashing as they surrounded the corner. Eight officers jumped from four cars with guns drawn and Kree could faintly hear the men yelling for Jay-D to get down on the ground. Scared that her lover was going to get killed, she jumped up from her seat and ran towards the door. "They gone kill Jason! Jason!" she yelled.

Tanya jumped up from her bar stool at that moment and grabbed what she thought was a petite tan-skinned female before she'd made it to the café's front doors. "If you run your over dramatic ass out there you'll only agitate them! They just talkin'!" she hissed under her breath as she prevented whom she assumed was Jay-D's girlfriend from running out onto the corner by taking her down to the marble floor.

Back outside, Captain Jones stood with his jaw agape and wide eyes, stunned over the way his men were rolling up onto the corners of Lindenwood Avenue and Elm Street. "I got it, guys! Lower your weapons! I got it I said!" he yelled as he stepped off the curb. Once his men had lowered their guns, Captain Jones turned back to Jay-D. "What's really going on here, Cottonwood?" he asked while sighing and shaking his head.

"Nothin'," Jay-D answered calmly. "Just some people drinking and talking too loud. Kinda got, kinda got the staff unnerved thinking something was about to go down, but it ain't nothin'."

"Okay, but I'm gonna have to write ya' a citation to make it look like I'm doing something here because I got some information for ya', young man," Captain Jones replied as he pulled out a citation pad and an ink pen. He then clicked on his shoulder-mounted CB. "Armed confrontation call is secure, no action needed here it was a misunderstanding," he radioed back to dispatch as the eight men in his unit stood down and huddled into groups of twos in the middle of the intersection.

Captain Jones had begun his rapport with Jay-D a week before Club Indigo had opened when he'd gone down to the Saint Charles Deputy Sheriff's Office to request a security detail on the club's opening night. The two were in the Captain's office back in late March when Captain Jones told Jay-D that he knew what he was doing and who he was working for. Jay-D answered by stating that he didn't know what Captain Jones was referring to, but he thanked the Captain nonetheless for agreeing to sign a contract that paid officers $55 dollars an hour whenever they were working security.

Captain Jones, however, knew the history behind the brown-bricked one story building on the corner of Elm Street. The place had been a mob headquarters going back to the forties. There had never been a homicide in the area until his friends Coban Benito and Humphrey Gaggi were killed along with Faustino 'Lucky' Cernigliaro and his wife Mildred nearly five years ago, and the murder of Doss Dawkins nearly two years ago.

Captain Jones was looking to prevent another episode of violence, but he was also looking to help himself, as he knew some things about an ongoing investigation. "I've written down numbers to an offshore savings account," he told Jay-D as he ripped a pink slip from his pad. "You can deposit five thousand dollars in there for me within the next five business days."

Jay-D rubbed his eyes briefly and placed a hand inside his silk slacks. "Why would I pay you five thousand dollars?" he asked while staring down at Captain Jones.

"I got a sister named Darby Jones. She's a robbery/homicide detective over in Saint Louis," Captain Jones replied slyly. "She tells me everything about her job. She has this friend, Sandra Cordova? She's a uh, she's a Missouri state trooper. Says the two of them is looking into the backgrounds of both of Doss Dawkins' daughters—a Bena and Tiva Holland?"

"Okay," Jay-D remarked as he scratched his chin, remembering the name Sandra Cordova, as she was the officer working alongside Laddy Norcross. "Keep going," he added, knowing the officer was correct in what he was saying about Bay and T-top being investigated by Laddy.

"Cordova told my sister Darby that her and Laddy Norcross slept together a time or two," Captain Jones smiled.

Jay-D merely shrugged his shoulders. "How that's gone benefit me and my people?" he asked.

"It's now obvious you don't know legal procedure, son" Captain Jones stated. "Let me school you right quick. Officers sleeping together while working on a case constitutes a conflict of interest, understand? You can have an entire case or cases thrown out under those conditions! And Norcross is a married man! His life and career would be *ruined* if something like that were to get out," the jolly officer laughed.

Jay-D let soak in what Captain Jones had just related to him. How to go about dealing with it left him somewhat perplexed, though. He had an idea, but he decided it was best to talk to Bay and T-top to see how they wanted to play it. "What more you know about Laddy and Sandra?" he asked Captain Jones.

"Darby tells me that the two of thems be making love over to Sandra Cordova's house. I didn't write that address down on that citation. That's why you should pay me the five thousand dollars. Because with that address? Comes the spare key my sister has stored over to her place," Captain Jones confidently stated as he held up a silver key. "On top of that? You'll gain an ally inside the Saint Charles, Missouri Sheriff's Office that has a sister inside of robbery/homicide over to Saint Louis, that can't keep her mouth shut about ongoing cases she knows about for nothing when it comes to her brother," he merrily stated, knowing he was putting a deal too sweet to pass up on the table.

"If you hear any more about that there come see me. We do business," Jay-D nodded.

"Okay," Captain Jones said as he placed the key in Jay-D's hand. "Consider it a down payment on a new partnership, son. When the money drops, I'll give you the address."

"Good looking out. You ain't gone have to wait on a offshore account because somebody be 'round ta' drop that money off to you in a couple hours. We need ta' get on that ASAP before they split," Jay-D ended as he turned and walked back into the club to see if he could resolve the issue with the Germans and Loopy for the time being.

Kree was standing before the table where Beverly Battle, Jane Dow and Loopy were sitting when Jay-D walked back into the café. "You all right, baby?" she asked concerned as she rubbed his elbow and stared up into his eyes lovingly.

"I'm cool, babe," Jay-D assured as he kissed Kree's cheek. "Take care of our guests while I handle some business."

"Okay," Kree smiled, satisfied that her man was safe from the officers. Playing her support role, she turned to Beverly Battle and asked, "Miss Battle, you gone stay and listen to Jane record across the street?"

"I don't know about all that," Beverly answered, slightly unnerved as she looked over to the bar where Tanya and Helen were now talking to the man who'd went out to meet the officers. Jane had said his name was Jay-D and he ran the record label she was on, but in Beverly's eyes, Jay-D was more than just a studio manager. Not that she was bothered over his perceived outside occupation, she was just wondering if Tanya would allow her to stay if that was what she decided to do. She watched as Tanya and Helen climbed down from the bar stools and walked towards the table. "Loopy, come with us," she heard Jay-D remark as he walked past the table.

"Give us a few minutes, Beverly," Tanya paused and stated as she waited for Loopy to exit the table. "Do you know who I am, Guadalupe?" she asked calmly.

"No," Loopy answered while staring into the woman's eyes.

"My name is Tanya Weinberger. I'm Helen's mother. We're willing to talk things over if you are," she stated as Boogie stood beside her.

Loopy was enraged on the inside. All she could see was her cousin and two friends laying in their caskets in a permanent slumber. She couldn't stand the sight of Boogie or her mother. "*Si hubiera podido me habría matado usted hoy, Boogie.*" (If I could have I would've killed you today, Boogie.) she scoffed lowly.

"I know," Boogie relied casually. "*Y si me hubiese matado a usted esa noche me habría hecho justamente eso. En realidad pensé que hice, pero tuvimos suerte. Usted debe dar las gracias a mí, por lo menos usted puede ir y poner flores en la tumba de su pueblo.*" (And if I could have killed you that night I would have done just that. I actually thought I did, but you were lucky. You should thank me, at least you can go and put flowers on your people's grave.)

"Yo, this way!" Jay-D called out from the end of the aisle.

Loopy walked off and followed Jay-D over to the office with Tanya and Boogie loosely trialing behind. After he'd tapped on the door, Dooney answered and went and stood back beside the curved wooden desk with Nancy and DeMarco, who were still strapped and watching as everybody filed into office.

Jay-D locked the door and said, "Now, both sides done took loses over what Ya Murder did. Loopy? That was business. You gotta get past it."

"We got them right now," Loopy stated in a somber tone. "Nancy and DeMarco got the ups on them, Jay-D! Let's just do it and get it over with! Kill them for me!" she shouted.

Jay-D paced the floor with his head bowed and his hands on his hips, pulling back slightly on his silk suit jacket. "You think I'm gone order the killing of two top members of a faction of this organization on your crew's behalf and start a war?" he asked in disbelief as he stared into Loopy's opaque eyes. "If you wanna kill 'em you on your own with that, but you not gone do no shit like that today! I don't even wanna know about it!" he yelled.

"Who's side on you on, man?" Loopy asked through tears of disbelief.

"I'm on the family's side!" Jay-D yelled aloud. "I'm tryna stop you from going out there and gettin' yourself killed, Loopy! You not gone win that war! Ain't *nobody* gone back you on a move like that! Think about what you askin' me to do!"

As much as Loopy hated to, she had to admit that Jay-D was right. Without the family's backing, she would be forced to go out on her own and go after a team of professional killers and try and hit them on their own turf. All she knew was that the Germans were from Cincinnati. She didn't know where they hung, who all they knew or how they operated. If she went out on her own, it stood a good chance that word would get back to Jay-D and he would have her killed for disobeying a family order. Bay and T-top were the ones who put her back in the game, though. She felt she needed an explanation from those two in order to accept what was expected of her. "I wanna talk to the twins," she told Jay-D. "I promise not to do anything....until I to talk to them," she said as she eyed Boogie and Tanya.

"That's what it is," Jay-D replied. He then looked over to Tanya and Boogie and nodded his head. "We good for now," he stated. "Once Loopy talk to my people, I'll be in touch with the word. Leave me a number."

Tanya went and wrote onto a sticky note and planted it on the door right beside Loopy's face. "This is address to the club we own in Cincinnati," she said while staring Loopy in the eyes. "You now know how to find us now, Guadalupe." She then turned to Jay-D and said, "If your soldier wants to come after us? Don't kill her, let her. Just let us know that that is what she's decided to do and we'll take care of it ourselves. We won't hold the Holland family responsible at all because it would no longer be about business," she said as she eyed Loopy a second time. "It'll be a personal matter between rival factions."

Loopy walked off without looking at the note on the back of the door. "I'm not interested in that anymore," she remarked with her back turned and her hands on her hips. "Just go! Go away from me!" she screamed.

"We'll get lunch somewhere else, Jay-D," Boogie stated as she extended her hand. "I'm sorry for rollin' up on y'all set unannounced. My fault. Loopy, I hope we can get past this?"

Loopy didn't respond. She just stood with her back turned while heaving slightly. Boogie could tell she was crying and she could feel her pain. She herself had cried many a time over the loss of RJ. Nevertheless, it was all business and she merely chalked it up to the game once the deal with the Holland family fell into place. Through her hardened heart, Helen found compassion for Loopy. She was sincerely hoping the two could move past their animosity, maybe become friends even and enter some venture.

Boogie laughed the absurd thought off as her mother pulled the office door open and exited the room. "We'll be on our way," she stated as she stepped out of the office while wondering how things would turn out between her and Loopy, as she really didn't want to kill her for the simple fact that she felt a connection to the young woman over the shared emotion of having to deal with the loss of a loved one.

Beverly was sitting at her table talking to Jane and Kree when she eyed Tanya and Boogie rounding the corner. "Is everything okay, girls," she asked from her seated position.

"Yeah," Tanya nodded as she placed seven twenties onto the bar counter and looked out the tinted double doors to make sure that the police had left the area. "The law vacated and the drinks and entrees are covered. Let's get out of here," she said as she hurried off towards the exit.

"Wait a minute now," Beverly objected. "If the matter has been rectified the least we can do is put something on our stomach before we jump back on the road."

"There's a Jack in the Box back out on the main road we can get something from there and be on our way," Tanya replied hastily before walking out of the café with Boogie following her lead.

Beverly jumped up from her seat and ran out the door and caught up with Tanya and Boogie halfway down the sidewalk. "What's the rush?" she asked. "Let's stay a while!"

"A massacre nearly unfolded inside that place just now," Tanya scoffed under her breath as she and Beverly walked side by side. "We're leaving here in one piece after all that shit! It serves no purpose or benefit for us to stay a while. It's best we leave!"

"Go 'head without me then!" Beverly retorted as she paused before the hood of Tanya's black Bentley Arnage and folded her arms.

"Stop being a truculent brat and get your ass in the car," Tanya laughed as she hit the remote start on her ride and walked over to the driver's side.

"Okay, I have no idea what that word means really? But I do know I'm not leaving here until I'm satisfied and ready." Beverly quipped as she stood on the sidewalk staring at Tanya.

"You're defying me is what it means," Tanya stated in disbelief as she eyed Beverly from the opposite side of the car. "If you refuse to leave, you will get left behind today," she added as she pulled the driver's side door open and climbed inside.

"What harm could that do, momma?" Boogie interjected as she went and stood beside Beverly.

Tanya eased back from behind the steering wheel and eyed Boogie and Beverly. She scratched the left side of her face while facetiously laughing and said, "All, all of a sudden everybody 'round this get-up is buddy-buddy and carrying on like we been friends forever. You were in on a hit that killed three members of the crew inside that building, Helen. One of 'em is still alive and if ya' ask me? She ain't over none of that shit that went down."

"Loopy won't go against her crew, momma," Boogie countered. "And what harm could it do if Beverly stay behind? We were thinking about getting her back into a studio anyway. There's a legit recording studio right across the street—a good one at that," she declared.

Boogie had seen how Jay-D ran his studio when she and Maggie had met up with Natalia III and Malik when they were in the process of thwarting Malik's attempted coup. Jane was a damn good artist from what she'd witnessed that night if she had to tell it. She knew her mother was thinking that something would happen to Beverly if they were to leave her behind in hostile territory, but Boogie was willing to gamble that Jay-D wouldn't allow anything to happen to Beverly Battle once she laid down what she thinking of doing. If anything, he would assure her safety once he learned that the once-mega rock star was interested in working with his protégé Jane Dow. Both organizations could benefit from the deal in her eyes, and on top of that, Boogie knew that by leaving Beverly behind, she could keep tabs on Loopy in an indirect way because she would be able to visit Saint Charles on occasion to check in on her family's artist.

Tanya was reading her daughter's motives one hundred percent, but she was apprehensive for the simple fact that Loopy, who she deemed a loose cannon, was now under Jay-D's umbrella. She wondered if Jay-D could keep his soldier in check, because if anything happened to Beverly, and especially Helen, she would declare war on the Saint Charles faction of the Holland family and waste everybody she recognized from the previous encounter, Jane Dow included.

"If anything happens to Beverly, it'll be on your hands, Helen," Tanya let it be known.

"I'm not some commodity that can be negotiated over," Beverly laughed as she moved over to the rear end of the Bentley. "Whether you agreed to it or not I was staying here, Tanya, and it wasn't just to have lunch. I like that youngster Jane Dow back in that restaurant. Open the trunk and let me get my bags and my guitar so I can give my career a second wind."

Tanya had no further recourse. Every instinct was telling her to override her daughter and for Helen and Beverly to both just get inside the car and pull off, but Beverly seemed cemented in her resolve on staying in Saint Charles. She climbed behind the wheel of her Bentley and waited patiently as Beverly and Boogie walked back up the sidewalk with Beverly's luggage bag and guitar and tugged on the front door. The door to the café was locked this time around Tanya noticed, so she took the time to climb out and grab one of the chrome automatic twelve gauges she'd gotten from Delilah from the trunk whilst Boogie knocked on the door. She'd eased back into her Bentley and was able to witness her daughter sliding the clip out of her semi-automatic and placing it into the back pocket of her jeans.

"What the fuck is Helen doing?" Tanya asked herself as the door was pulled opened. Trusting her daughter, she sat and watched as Boogie and Beverly reentered the New Orleans Café while she sat by idly with the twelve gauge laying on the front passenger seat.

****

"Thought y'all woulda been in the drive thru over to Jack in the Box by now," Jay-D said as he let Boogie and Beverly back into the café. "What's up?"

When Jane saw Beverly walking back into the open area of the café, she grew giddy. The rock star had answered Kree's question by stating that she didn't know if she was going to stay and listen to her perform, and Jane herself was afraid to ask the woman if she would do so, even though she wanted it to happen more than anything else in the world on this day. She remained planted in her seat as the conversation unfolded. "Beverly says that she wants to stay behind here in Saint Charles, Jason. Will that be okay?" she heard Boogie ask as her heartrate increased.

Jay-D looked over to Jane and saw her smile through pursed lips while nodding her head up and down. "I think that would be a wonderful idea," the petite female Boogie had witnessed her mother take down chimed in as she walked up and hugged Jay-D's waist.

"This your woman, Jay?" Boogie smiled.

"He wish the fuck he was," Dooney grimaced over from the bar counter as he sat atop a stool. "That nigga there wish he could be somebody girlfriend."

"I'm, I'm not understanding," Boogie remarked as she kept shifting her eyes around the bar in search of Loopy.

"My name is Kree. I'm a part of LGBT community," Kree chimed in. She then rolled her eyes while staring back at Dooney without uttering a word as she knew what type of a tangent he could go on when it came to her being intimate with his brother.

"Oh, you a tranny," Boogie chuckled. "Welcome to the 'community', Kree," she quoted.

Kree reared back in surprise. "You mean your trans—"

"Nah, I was born with a pussy," Boogie quickly interrupted. "I think I got the L part down, though, since we're being open with each other. Jay?" she then stated through a smile as her eyes shifted back and forth from Kree to Jay-D. She threw her hands up like, 'what the fuck' and said, "I woulda never guessed."

"Guessed what? That I'm gay?" Jay-D asked as he bumped his fists together.

"Nah, dude. I just woulda never guessed that your old lady was…a lady boy," Boogie smirked. "Y'all cute together, though. Do your thang, gangster."

"Alright," Jay-D said as he ran his hands over his face. "Why y'all came back in here?"

"I'm gone lay a job on you," Boogie let it be known while speaking with her hands. "I know things are not all copasetic between your soldier Loopy and I, but I'm willing to extend another arm of peace."

"I'm listening," Jay-D remarked as he moved over to the bar and took a seat beside his brother Dooney while hugging Kree around the waist.

"I don't know if you know who this woman is with me or not," Boogie said as she pointed over to Beverly Battle, who waved politely before stepping back to allow Boogie to continue. "She's a multi-Grammy winning musician going back over three decades."

"It's Beverly Battle!" Jane stood up and blurted out. When all eyes shifted over in her direction, she quickly sat back down. "I'm, I was just saying, everybody. She, she big that's all," she added as she shrunk back into her seat, wanting to disappear from sight.

"Jane Dow is right," Boogie admitted. "Beverly Battle is a big deal. Look her up if you must, Jay-D, but she can very much speak for herself and give you her resume`. She wants to stay here in Saint Charles and work with your artist Jane Dow. I'm willing to allow it to happen so long as nothing happens to her. Take this as a second offer of peace and generosity to be expounded upon the talk we had inside your office just now. Peace because I'm willing to place the life of someone my family holds dear into your hands, and generosity because should your artist and my artist come up with a hit song, your record label would explode. We could all benefit from this arrangement."

Jay-D nodded his approval just as Loopy was walking up the aisle. She made eye contact with Boogie, and turned and walked off. "Loopy," Boogie called out.

Loopy kept walking off and Boogie sighed. She was trying her best to keep the peace between the families, only Loopy wasn't cooperating. Whatever it was that was compelling her to atone for what she'd done to Loopy's people, however, she herself had no answer, all she knew was that she wanted things between her and Loopy to be—in two simple words—all right.

"*Si quieres matarme, mátame ahora!*" (If you want to kill me, kill me now!) Boogie boomed as went into her back waistband, pulled her semi-automatic and threw it down onto the marbled floor. "*Usted quiere matarme, Guadalupe? Aquí está tu oportunidad! Hacerlo!*" (You want to kill me, Guadalupe? Here's your chance! Do it!)

Without hesitation, Loopy leaned down and picked up the semi-automatic and aimed it at Boogie. This time around, no one inside the New Orleans Café budged as they'd all realized that this was a personal matter between Loopy and the woman who'd walked in just to have a drink and an entrée at first.

"You kill me today, you die today and you know it," Boogie

calmly stated as she walked and stood in the middle of the aisle and faced Loopy head on.

"At least we would be even," Loopy countered as she gripped the gun tightly.

"We'd both be dead. How would we be even?" Boogie asked in a compassionate manner as she slowly raised her hands to her sides. "It's a better way to handle this, Guadalupe. Please, listen to me," she pleaded.

"You have to die!" Loopy screamed aloud.

"In your mind I know that makes sense," Boogie countered as she stood with her hands extended out from her body. "Someday I may indeed die because of the life I live. But if you were to kill me today? Today, your life would end also. Do you not understand that if Jay-D or his brother or niece doesn't kill you, the Holland family themselves will kill you? And if the Holland family doesn't kill you, my family will hunt you down and destroy everything and everyone you love along the way? This is suicide, Loopy. Think," Boogie said as she pressed her left hand to her left temple. "You don't have to forgive me ever in life, and I doubt that you ever would, but for everybody's sake that's here today and those who are not, you cannot kill me—because everybody would lose."

"Loopy," Kree spoke out softly as she slid along the bar stools and made her way over to her friend. "You don't have to do this. I'm not taking sides, but she's right. You two, you two don't ever have to meet again in life. Think about others," she stated in all out sincerity. "Think about other people today."

Loopy now felt helpless. She looked around the café. Jay-D was the first person she laid eyes on. He had a look of disappointment on his face as he stood at the foot of the bar with his hands tucked inside his silk slacks. Dooney was sitting beside him with a 'what the fuck you doing' look splattered across his face while slowly shaking his head. She then eyed Jane, who was sitting by herself with a pleading look on her face that said, 'don't ruin it for us'. She turned and looked back at Nancy, who was standing behind her gripping a Mac-10 semi-automatic that was aimed at her torso.

"I'm not the one that's gone do it to ya'," Nancy remarked as she set her gun down on the table beside her. "You bust on Boogie you gone get ta' walk outta here today, but you gone have to live with the repercussions, homegirl. Better think," she said as she looked Loopy off.

Loopy now felt she had no other choice left. She racked the pistol she'd picked up off the floor and placed it to her right temple. "Fuck everybody!" she screamed as she squeezed the trigger.

Boogie ran towards Loopy at that moment and grabbed hold of her body. The two fell over onto the table where the four backup singers were sitting as the gun fell from Loopy's hand. Gumbo entrees and crab legs doused summer outfits and the women all scattered as Boogie and Loopy crashed down onto the floor.

Her face covered in spicy roux, Boogie righted herself while snatching Loopy up to her feet and forcing her up against a wooden column. "*Esto es lo que habría elegido para hacer con ella?*" (That is what you would have chosen to do with it?) she asked in a disappointed manner while panting heavily. "*Usted tuvo la oportunidad de matarme y eligió a suicidarse en su lugar?*" (You had the chance to kill me and you chose to kill yourself instead?)

"*La pistola no estaba cargada!*" (The gun wasn't loaded!) Loopy screamed.

"*¿Sabías que...?*" (Did you know?) Boogie asked as she pressed her body up against Loopy to hold her in position. "*¿Sabías que el arma estaba vacía?*" (Did you know the gun was empty?) she hissed under her breath.

"*Ahora que todavía estoy vivo yo!*" (Now that I'm still alive I do!) Loopy replied in a near whisper as she pushed Boogie off her body. She kicked the gun that she'd just attempted to kill herself with aside and walked off, heading towards the office.

Boogie balled up a fist and placed it to her lips as she watched Loopy walking off. Natalia had put her up on the Holland family's loyalty test shortly after the night everything had gone down with Malik and she'd laid it down on Loopy without anyone knowing her intent, nor she herself knowing the outcome. If Boogie had to tell it, Loopy was loyal to the death in the literal sense of the word. They shouldn't fight was her belief and she was aiming to not just patch things up, but solidify things with Loopy. "Who's your favorite singer, Guadalupe?" she asked out loud, having come up with a plan.

"What?" Loopy scoffed as she looked back at Boogie.

"Your favorite singer. Who's your favorite singer?"

Loopy pondered the question for a moment before saying, "I don't have a favorite singer. They all suck."

Boogie eyed Loopy's outfit, the red Saint Louis Cardinals t-shirt and fitted cap she wore. "You like baseball, though," she smiled as she backed away from Loopy while pointing back at her. *"Si un jefe, y ni siquiera lo saben. Tienes, Loopy."* (You a boss and you don't even know it. You have it in you, Loopy.)

Loopy bothered not responding. She went into the office and slammed the door shut and took a seat behind the large oak desk. Why Boogie was so interested in her left her confused, but she'd be lying to herself if she said she wasn't intrigued. Having passed what she knew was the loyalty test, Loopy decided to play things through. She'd requested a meeting with Bay and T-top through Jay-D and that was to be her next move. She was now planning to sit back for the moment in order to see if the people who'd offered her a job and the rank of Lieutenant actually came through to help her along now that she was willing to jump back into the game full time.

Satisfied that things with Loopy were calm for the moment, Boogie walked back to the front of the bar. "Jay, I wanna thank you for allowing that to play out, man. I didn't know what to expect."

"She could've killed you, yeah?" Jay-D remarked.

"If that was her actual intent? I was like, 'let's get it over with'," Boogie remarked. "But she would've pulled the trigger on an empty gun and that would've let me know where I stood with her. A lot of people would've died had she pulled that trigger. I think I played it right in order to learn her heart, don't you think so?"

"That was slick," Jay-D nodded. "I been talking to Beverly. She told us some shit, good shit. My old lady remember some of her songs and Jane damn near gave the woman's whole bio. Jane said Beverly started out in a small town up in Iowa after her car broke down and she needed a tow to a town called Bevington. Played her first gig at this bar called Bandits up there and blew up in Nashville."

"That's what's up. You know my people well," Boogie nodded as she smiled over to Jane. "Here's my stipulation," she then stated as she shifted her attention back to Jay-D. "Beverly must lay her head where you sleep at night because I trust you don't shit were you sleep. If she's with you I'm trusting she would safe."

"My spot on the other end of the corner on this same side," Jay-D let it be known as he slipped Boogie a business card. "Don't worry about it, we got your girl," he stated seriously.

"Okay," Boogie replied. "Beverly, you're okay with this, right?" she asked as she turned towards the singer.

Beverly smiled over to Jane and said, "I'm looking at the daughter I never had, Helen. We're gonna do some wonderful things inside that studio across the street."

Boogie smiled as she leaned in and kissed Beverly by. She shook Jay-D's hand and nodded over to Dooney and Nancy before walking out of the café.

Tanya, meanwhile, was growing anxious. Ten minutes had gone by and she was preparing to grab her twelve gauge and walk back up inside the New Orleans Café. She was climbing out her car when she spotted Jane Dow bursting out of the doors running her way. She clutched her semi-automatic and looked around, prepared to bust shots, until she eyed Jay-D, Beverly and Boogie easing out of the café with smiles on their faces while shaking hands and patting shoulders. She eased back into the Bentley and placed the gun in between her legs as Jane approached.

"Thank you, Miss Tanya!" Jane exclaimed as she ran up to the driver's side of the Bentley. "You don't know how much this mean to me! It's a dream I never asked for!"

"Thank Beverly. She's the one that sees something in you, Jane," Tanya stated from behind the steering wheel in a drab tone.

"And you don't?" Jane asked, sporting an innocent smile while not knowing that she was offending Tanya, who couldn't care less about Boogie's venture at that moment as she was way too concerned about Loopy.

If she'd wanted to, Tanya could've kept the animosity going by shutting Jane Dow down completely, but being petty wasn't in her nature. She was a woman about her business, and when it got down to it, letting Beverly work on her music in Saint Charles inside a professional recording studio with a budding artist wasn't a bad move at all. It was the very thing Beverly said she needed to happen, and Tanya wasn't going to against it. She scanned Jane standing before her all pudgy and happy in her ragged jean shorts and sneakers. "You're from a different time, Jane. Beverly's time," she smiled. "I'm sure you and my friend will work good together. I look forward to hearing your music," she ended as she peeled away from the curb once Boogie had climbed back into the car.

CHAPTER ELEVEN

THE FAMILY COOKOUT

Siloam Bovina was on her way over to Takoda and Regina's home to help her make stuffed devil's eggs for the family cookout that was getting underway on this steamy hot Sunday, about an hour after everything had gone down in Saint Charles. The thirty-five-year-old brown-haired, hazel-eyed full-bloodied Cherokee was no fool, however; Regina had rarely called her for help on anything, especially since the night she'd killed Reynard. Siloam was climbing into Montenegro's Titan when she had an epiphany: Regina may have found evidence she'd left behind the day she killed Bianca Jacobs inside her house.

True enough, Siloam and Montenegro had replaced the bloody wooden floors and Siloam herself had made sure that Bianca had packed all of her possessions before she killed the woman, but there had to be something she'd overlooked was her thinking as she rode off the ranch. She made it over to Regina and Tak's home on the northeast side of town and pulled into the driveway underneath a leafy hickory tree and sat behind the wheel for a few minutes. Siloam was strapped with a .44 magnum. If she was right in her thinking, things may get a little touchy inside the home and she may have to use it to protect herself.

Killing Regina would bring about certain death for her, however; Siloam knew she would never be able to live it down. Furthermore, the family would have her soul over touching one of their own, especially after she herself had fucked up in the beginning by sleeping with Takoda. She removed the gun from her shoulder holster and placed it inside the glove box before climbing out of the truck and removing her short-sleeved denim jacket. She placed a pair of sunshades over her eyes and pulled down on her cowgirl hat as she made her way up the stairs and rang the doorbell.

Takoda answered a few seconds later and Siloam had to do a double take. Tak, all five-foot-eleven of him and his muscular frame stood before her with his long black hair draped over his shoulders sporting a serious black eye. His left eye was closed shut and purple, with red specks mixed in and the left side of his face was slightly swollen.

"What the hell happened to you?" Siloam asked as she leaned back and frowned at Takoda while removing her sunshades.

"I fell," Takoda mocked and sighed. "What you think happened? She found about us," he truthfully stated as he pulled the door open wider and stepped aside.

"Is it safe for me to enter?" Siloam asked she peered inside the home from the porch.

"Yeah, she's in the kitchen," Takoda responded as he extended his hand.

"Are you going to the cookout?"

"Yeah," Tak replied.

"Here." Siloam said as she handed Takoda her sunshades. "You may want to put them on before you get there to save yourself some embarrassment."

Siloam walked into the kitchen where she saw Regina spreading potato salad into egg whites with a butter knife as she stood before the granite counter. "Glad you came," she said to Siloam without looking up at her.

"What do you need me to do with these eggs?" Siloam asked as she stepped off into the kitchen.

Dimples set the knife down and looked over to Siloam in silence while raging on the inside. "Last night Takoda told me what the two of you done inside my home," she began as she picked up the butter knife a second time and began stuffing the eggs. "We made some serious love after that. We started here in the kitchen, and finished up in the spare bedroom. Sound familiar?"

Siloam understood that Dimples had recreated what she and Takoda had done back in September of last year. "I'm sorry, Regina," she remarked somberly as Takoda entered the kitchen. He'd paused behind Siloam, but when he caught sight of his wife scolding him through her squinted brown eyes, he quickly moved past Siloam and stood beside Dimples.

"When we were done, tell her what I did, Takoda," Regina remarked as she began placing the stuffed eggs into a Tupperware bowl.

"She called me back into the room when I walked out and she, umm… she—she"

"I punched him the eye on purpose," Dimples chimed in. "Hopefully it knocked some sense into his cheating ass."

"You plan on doing the same to me I suppose?" Siloam asked as she stood with her hands behind her back.

"If I was a weak-minded woman, I would scar-drag you from this kitchen to the backyard and leave you there to rot. But, Takoda knew better and it was my husband who allowed it to happen, so he's to blame for this emotional rollercoaster you two put me on," Dimples scoffed as she set the butter knife down on the granite counter top.

"I see. So, where do you and I stand? What is it that you want from me exactly, Regina?"

Regina went into her back pocket and pulled out Bianca's keys and threw them at Siloam's feet. "You come into my home, fuck my husband, and then kill my sister inside these very walls?" she angrily asked as she walked over and got up Siloam's face. "I have every right to kill you. I could kill you today and the family would say nothing about it, Siloam."

"Here I am," Siloam said as she spread her arms and stared into Regina's eyes. "I'm just a poor Cherokee Indian. No one would miss me if killin' me is what you want to do today."

"Don't pity yourself," Dimples counseled with disdain. "As scandalous as you were, I can't deny the fact that I owe you my life—me and my mother both," she said as she walked off with her back to Siloam.

Siloam could see Regina moving her hand up under the front of her white and orange Oklahoma State t-shirt. "Would you really do it?" she asked. "Could you do it if I were to run up on you, Dimples? I said I'm sorry. I never meant to hurt you. I was the weak one in all of this not you, not Takoda. It was all my fault."

Dimples pulled a .38 snub nose from underneath her shirt and held it at her side. She stared down at the gun. "You betrayed me, Siloam," she said as her eyes grew angry with tears.

"Baby," Takoda tried to soothe as he stepped closer to his wife.

"Don't you fuckin' touch me!" Regina screamed as she stood in between Takoda and Siloam, staring them both down. "Look what you've done to me! Look how you got me! Both of you! Siloam, I never expected this from you! Takoda? You was the first friend I made when we moved here after Ne`Ne` and Sandy were killed in Mississippi! Two people I loved and trusted the most outside of my family and allowed into my life betrayed me and it hurts all so bad," Dimples cried. "Takoda why would...how...and then my father and the shit he tried to pull? Bianca?"

"Baby," Takoda remarked as he held his hands up even with his shoulders, "Me and Siloam are sorry. We're sorry. Whatever you need me to do to make it up to you I will. I promise."

"Me too," Siloam said through watery eyes while shaking her head in regret. "I don't expect a miracle, but I'll do whatever it takes to earn your trust again, Regina. Whatever it takes, because, because you're the sweetest woman I know. You're just like Mary to me. Innocent and only wanting peace. I brought chaos into your home and I'm sorry for that. I can't apologize enough."

Regina was heavily conflicted over what'd gone down with Takoda and Siloam. She'd been cheated on and lied to, but had those things not occurred, she and her mother would've both ended up dead because Reynard and Bianca were both plotting against her and Mary. She just couldn't get past the fact that two people she cherished had betrayed her trust. "Had not my father and sister been planning to kill me and my mother, I wonder if, I wonder how you two would be behaving now," she pondered aloud.

"Oh noo, Regina." Siloam sighed. "We felt remorse right away."

"Siloam's right, Dimples," Takoda chimed in. "We realized right away the mistake we made. Neither one of us are sorry for getting caught, we're sorry for what we did to you. I'm sorry for what I did to us."

"But neither of you were going to admit any of it," Dimples said as she nodded while looking straight ahead. "Not even after killing my father and sister, Siloam, did you confess what you did. Everything was settled, and you still said nothing."

"Who in their right mind would confess something like that, Regina?" Siloam reasoned. "How could I tell you those things? I didn't know how to explain. Didn't know where to begin even."

"We family, right?" Regina asked as she looked over to Siloam and set the gun down on the counter.

"Always," Siloam declared as she nodded her head.

"Always, Regina." Takoda followed.

Regina cut her eyes at her husband. "You still have a long ways to go with me," she told him. "I'm not sure this marriage will even survive, but I forgive you."

Takoda looked down at Regina and said, "If I lose you, I lose my world, Regina." Tears dripped from his eyes as he sunk to one knee inside the kitchen and tentatively reached out and grabbed one of his wife's hands. "Don't do this to me, please. I'm nothing without you and my son in my life! Don't go!"

"Don't let this ruin your marriage, Regina," Siloam interjected as she removed her cowgirl hat and stepped closer to Dimples. "If you're gonna be mad at anyone, be mad at me. I was the one who did all those awful things. Takoda had nothing to do with anything that happened between me and your family. He knew nothing about it."

"I feel compelled to thank you for what you've done, Siloam, but the forgiveness doesn't excuse your treachery, it just makes it easier to deal with going forward."

"That's a start. I'll take that," Siloam stated seriously. "I'll finish these eggs for you now."

Get up, Tak," Regina spoke softly through her torn emotions. When her husband stood, she looked him in the eyes and said, "I need to be away from here for a while to get my thoughts together."

"You're gonna leave me," Takoda said as he looked his wife off and rubbed the tears from his face.

"I'd be telling a story if I said that weren't true, but it's not at all a given. I still love—look at me, baby," she demanded. When Tak faced her, Regina heaved and said, "You don't understand how much you hurt me. I know I should be happy that this happened because of the end result, but I'm still stuck at the beginning with you and I, understand? I can't get past what happened, what you did to our marriage inside our home. This was sacred ground. Ours. Where we built our life here, raised our son, and had the best of times. You allowed someone else in on that and I can't be here right now."

"What you need me to do to get you back here, baby?" Takoda asked through his tears.

"Be stronger, and never hurt me like this again or you'll live to regret it," Dimples answered before walking off. "We have a function to attend, so, let's get this food contained and just…just make it through the first day of reconciliation," she recommended.

After thirty minutes or so had gone by, the three had contained the food and were walking out of the home. Regina and Siloam were each holding two containers of deviled eggs as they walked under the shady hickory tree approaching the pickup Siloam had ridden up in. Takoda had just closed the door and locked it. He placed the sunshades Siloam had given him over his eyes, picked up on the handles of two ice coolers full of beer and soda, and headed down the stairs.

Regina had just placed her dish into the back seat of the Titan and closed the door. She eased back out of the interior of the pickup and saw her husband walking her way with the sunshades over his eyes. "Where'd you get those from?" she asked with raised eyebrows.

Siloam pulled the driver's side door open while sighing and shaking her head in disbelief. After all that'd been discussed and what little ground had just been gained, Tak had just put himself back at square one.

"Siloam gave them to me. Said I might need them," Takoda answered meekly.

"That was before I knew what all we were going to discuss exactly," Siloam defended. "I meant nothing by it."

"I know," Regina responded as she folded her arms. "But, I'm gone need for you to take those off, Takoda."

"What? Why?" Takoda asked perplexed.

"Just do what your wife says!" Siloam snapped as she jumped behind the wheel of the pickup and pulled the door shut. "You're already in the doghouse, don't compound it. Give me back my shades, too."

"She's right," Regina agreed as she hopped into the passenger seat of the pickup. "I said if you wanted me back you have to be stronger. And that starts by you wearing that dotted eye to the cookout and explaining to any and everybody who asks, what it is that you've done exactly to earn yourself a hickey on your face," she added as she slammed the door shut. "See you at the cookout, dear. Remember, we have to drop flowers off at Ne`Ne`s grave today, so I'll meet you there at the foot of the hill after we leave the grocery store," she added as Siloam pulled out of the circular dirt driveway.

****

Back over to Ponderosa, Naomi had just emerged out onto the back patio under the evening sun dressed in a pair of tight-fitting white sweat shorts, white tank top and blue and white sneakers with a pair of shades covering her eyes with an adult beverage in her hand. She went and took a seat on the patio beside Francine while engrossed in the screen on her cellphone with a wide smile on her face.

Kimi and Koko had been with their mother since mid-morning and she'd been on the phone the entire time texting someone, only they didn't know who. From the grocery store to several clothing outlets, she'd been in a state of elation over whatever she'd been reading for the past few hours. The twins sat a few tables away from Naomi sipping drinks while eyeing their mother with suspicion.

"Look how she show her teeth every time that phone chirp," Kimi sulked. "I'm telllin' ya', she got a new man, Koko."

"I wonder who it is!" Koko stated happily as she cut her eyes over to Kimi while stirring her raspberry margarita.

Kimi looked over to Koko with a blank expression on her face. "This is nothing to be ecstatic over, Koko!" she exclaimed under her breath. "Somebody tryna replace daddy and momma actin' like she cool with that, girl!"

"It's been over two years, Kimi," Koko reasoned. "I think that's fair enough time for momma to at least entertain a man if that's what she wants to do."

"I'm not liking this at all, Koko," Kimi complained. "Not at all."

"Look who talking, Miss Bouta Be Married. Jealous enough?"

"I'm not jealous," Kimi chided. "I just don't appreciate some man trying to steal momma's heart. She been through enough with daddy.

"Ain't nobody gone put momma through nothing, girl. Relax," Koko laughed before taking a sip of her drink.

Naomi, meanwhile, had sent another text. *How far out are you now?*

I'm coming into town from the south. Four miles from route 11.

Okay. See you soon Naomi texted back as she giggled like a high school female.

"Well, now," Francine smiled as she set a copy of The Ponca City News aside and smiled over to Naomi without speaking further.

"Well what?" Naomi smirked as she took a sip of her vodka and cranberry.

"I haven't seen you this happy since the day you married Doss Dawkins Junior," Francine responded. "Who's the new guy?"

"He's a business man that headed his own real estate firm," Naomi replied as she set her glass down. "He owned the malls we closed out a few months back and he's coming over to sign the last of the documents. He's considering doing further business with Holland Dawkins Enterprises should everything go accordingly."

"When will we get to meet him?" Francine asked while smiling brightly.

"Today," Naomi said as she looked over to Kimi and Koko, who quickly turned their heads away when their mother's eyes fell upon them. "I'm not sure how well this is going to go, Francine because there's keepers at the gate," she chuckled.

"You deserve to be happy regardless of what your children think, Naomi. If your heart is content, by all means, do you. I can't wait to meet him," Francine remarked as she picked up a picture of lemon tea and poured herself a glass.

"'Do you'?" Naomi quoted as she smiled over to Francine.

"Learned it from L'il Doss when I mentioned taking him up to the ranch in Montana the other day," Francine laughed. "And while we're on the subject of Dosses, how's Big Doss doing up in Chicago with Sharona? What are doctors saying about her recovery?"

"I talked to DeeDee this morning. Sharona has gotten a little better," Naomi sighed. "They moved her into Renata's home the other day and she's comfortable. But the truth is, she may not make it past the summer if she doesn't have a transplant surgery, Francine."

"Can't she get a donor? Hasn't she any family?" Francine inquired.

"Kidney disease runs in the Benson family," Naomi replied. "Sharona's father died from it. His side of the family produced no matches, and her mother's side of the family in New York aren't interested in anything but running her business. She has a fifty-eight-year-old aunt on her mother's side in Florida, but the woman's too old and weak to go through with the surgery even though she's a match. A transplant would outright kill her and she wasn't ready to die."

"What a shit bath," Francine stated while shaking her head somberly. "What's DeeDee's resolution?"

"He asked me if Doctor Duchene could perform a transplant on Sharona if he got the organs and I refused." Naomi let it be known."

"What did he say after you rejected him?"

"Nothing. I referred him to another doctor."

"I see," Francine stated as she pondered briefly. "Well, if the doctor is going to do the transplant, where're the organs coming from?"

"From a donor." Naomi replied calmly.

"But, Sharona hasn't a donor yet, right?" Francine asked with a puzzled look.

"That's correct," Naomi replied as she picked up her drink.

"But Sharona got a donor anyway," Francine stated while nodding. "My, my, my...the black market. DeeDee's going all out."

"I talked to the people behind it earlier today. They have a donor, just waiting on the results to come back to see if there's a match or not."

"I don't wanna hear any more about it. I understand it, but by God I couldn't condone it."

"What if a transplant could've saved Mendoza?" Naomi asked.

"As violent as my husband was, I know that he wouldn't have signed off on something like that. I'm not judging by any means, I just know Mendoza would've chosen a different route. And he did. I hope this thing doesn't blow back in DeeDee's face."

"I think the main thing is whether Sharona will survive or not," Naomi disclosed. "I'm more worried about that issue rather than some man or woman whom I've never met in life who possesses something that the family needs in order to save my brother-in-law's mother."

Francine laughed at that moment. "I'm sorry, Naomi, but it just tickles me every time I hear you call Li'l Doss your brother-in-law."

Naomi laughed right along with Francine. "He be serious, too, girl. 'Si-n-law Naomi!'" she quoted. "And he always gotta remind my eight how much of an uncle he is to 'em, Francine."

Francine laughed and sighed as she looked over to Doss III, who was running around with Tacoma and a few of the young kids belonging to the ranch hands. "When you take in everything and look at the end result versus the possible outcome of nothing being done, it makes it easier to deal with. If I could've saved Mendoza, I would do the same," she smiled as she squeezed Naomi's arm. "I hope it works out for Li'l Doss' sake."

Naomi's phone chirped at that moment and she read the message. *I have arrived. What stunning property you have me lady!*

Naomi got up from her seat on the patio and walked into Ponderosa. Tyke was coming down the stairs at that moment and she was on the speakerphone talking to Walee, asking when he would bring Spoonie back to the ranch for the cookout. Tyke and the rest of the Oklahoma State Cowboys' softball team had just been knocked out of the playoffs down in Oklahoma City two days earlier by Oklahoma, ironically, and she'd ridden back to Ponca

City with her mother, Kimi and Koko.

Spoonie, Walee and Kahlil, meanwhile, had ridden back to Stillwater after the game in order to allow Kahlil to attend summer football practices as the Oklahoma State Cowboys' upcoming collegiate season was getting underway. With the day off, the three had slept in late, but they were planning on arriving back in Ponca City just in time to eat as they had no real inclination on helping out with the preparations.

"Hold on, Walee," Tyke stated as she held the phone near her right ear. "Where you off to in a hurry, momma?" she asked while descending the marble grand staircase.

"I have to greet a guest," Naomi answered as she went and pulled one of the large, thick wooden doors open and peered out the front of the home. Her eyes fell upon Montenegro, who was walking up the stairs escorting a man in a white leisure short set, black sandals and a white straw hat. The family's top bodyguard behind Flacco Ramirez had an unsure look on his face as he kept looking back at the guy, then over towards Naomi.

"This, this is uhh…this here is a man that says he knows you, Senorita Dawkins." Montenegro remarked. "Is he correct on that?" he asked, somewhat in disbelief.

"Momma, who at the door? Who our guest?" Tyke asked excitedly as she jumped down the remainder of the stairs and ran up to the front door. When she eyed the brown-skinned, tall man with the shiny bald head and slightly greying beard while peering over mother's shoulder, her smiled dropped and she cut her eyes over to her mother as she exhaled in disappointment.

"Yo, Tyke, who at the door? Bay and Tiva made it up there?" Walee asked over the phone, shaking Tyke from her thoughts. "Who momma guest is?" he asked again, this time his voice coming through the phone at a volume audible to Naomi.

"Walee, you ain't gone believe this, man," Tyke stated in a somber tone.

"Believe what? What's hatnin' up there, Tyke?" Walee asked anxiously as he paced the floor inside of Spoonie and Tyke's apartment down in Stillwater with the phone held close to his mouth.

"Walee? Momma, got a boyfriend." Tyke groaned.

"Aww hell nah!" Walee boomed as he pulled his car keys from his pocket and headed for the front door. "I'm on my way back home right now, Tyke!"

Kahlil was sitting at the dining room table eating a bowl of cereal when he heard Tyke's proclamation. "I'm right behind ya', fam!" he declared as he leapt up from his seat and followed Walee out the door.

Naomi just shook her head through closed eyes as she listened to Walee and Kahlil scrambling through the apartment back down in Stillwater. She knew at that very moment that this was going to be one of the most awkward times of her life. "Mister Fraser, come on in," she sighed. "This is Montenegro and my youngest daughter Sinopa Dawkins."

"Nice to meet yuh, Miss Dawkins," Dunkirk Fraser said through a polite smile and heavy British accent.

"Tyke, don't greet that nigga you don't know 'em like that!" Walee yelled through the phone's speaker as he trotted down the stairs and took off running through the grassy courtyard with his double plats flapping in the wind.

Kahlil was running beside Walee, the two of them hopping bushes like track stars in their silk shorts and tank tops as they made a mad dash for the parking lot. He'd heard his brother from another mother say the word 'nigga' and grew wide-eyed as they sprinted across the courtyard. "Momma gone kick your ass, boy!" he laughed aloud as the two ran up to Walee's orange 2009 four door Dodge Charger.

"What Kahlil said!" Naomi boomed over the phone. "Come your—I'll talk to you when you get here, Walee Dawkins! And don't you forget about Spoonie!" she snapped before ending the call.

Walee and Kahlil were hopping into Walee's ride Naomi reminded them about Spoonie. They climbed back out of the car and looked up to the second floor balcony and saw her waving her arms yelling, "Where y'all going all of a sudden? Come back, y'all! Hey!"

"Go get her, fam," Walee said while checking the time on his father's Rolex watch.

"Baby!" Kahlil yelled at Spoonie as he stepped back into the courtyard and spread his arms. "How could I forget my heart?" he laughed as he jogged across the grass towards the stairs.

Spoonie smiled down at the 6'2" muscular green-eyed Albino with red dreadlocks hanging down to his neck, and her heart melted as she watched him ascending the stairs. He had the warmest smile and the kindest heart to her and made her feel protected at all times. "How y'all just gone run off and forget about me, Kahlil," she asked through laughter while shaking her head. "I thought I was special."

Kahlil drew closer to Spoonie and placed his arm around her small waist. She fit him perfectly, and just to be able to touch the petite, dark chocolate-skinned afro-wearing, slender-eyed beauty like no other man could, made him feel special. "If no one else thinks you're special, I think you're special," he told Spoonie as he hugged her tighter.

"Am I really?" Spoonie asked seriously while staring up at Kahlil. "You haven't walked with me up Ne`Ne`s Hill yet and I've asked you twice. You going there with me would mean a lot," she added as she folded her arms and tucked in her chin with her bottom lip poked out.

"We can do it today when we get there," Kahlil assured. "But first, we have to go and see this man that's tryna get next to moms, already."

"My momma got a new man friend?" Spoonie asked as she backed up and placed her hands on her hips. "Aww shucks nah!"

Kahlil chuckled. "Let me help you down the stairs," he said as he went to scoop Spoonie up.

"I'm well enough to walk, Kahlil. I don't need help with that I keep telling you."

"Spoonie, you just got out the wheelchair for good like, a week and a half ago. I'm just tryna make it easy on you, baby."

"I'm fine, Kahlil. Just listen to me, please."

"What is it that you wanna do or say, Spoonie?"

"You'll find out. Just let me take you there," Spoonie responded as she began to descend the stairs with Kahlil following her lead. "Before I meet my mother's new friend, I want us to go to Ne`Ne`s

Hill. Will you?"

"If that's what you want, Shima," Kahlil replied while staring into the face of the most beautiful female he'd ever encountered. He knew not the reason behind Spoonie's request, but to deny her, would be a betrayal of the love and adoration he'd been carrying in his heart for some time now. He was hoping for much more for the two of them, but Spoonie held the reins, and he was simply along for the ride. A young man in love, and following his heart's desire.

"Yooo!" Walee screamed out while standing beside his idling whip with his arms stretched wide, breaking Spoonie and Kahlil's trance. "What y'all doing? Come the hell down from there!"

"It's what I want done first when we get there, Kahlil," Spoonie stated through a smile before turning and trotting down the stairs. "Now come on! We have to get home and meet my momma's new boyfriend!" she shouted out loud and happy as she ran across the courtyard and jumped a row of brushes while sprinting towards Walee's car.

"The hell took so long?" Walee questioned as Spoonie and Kahlil hopped into his ride. "Y'all over there reuniting like Peaches and Herb when we got some real shit going down back home!" he chided as he backed out the parking spot and threw his whip in drive and mashed the gas pedal.

CHAPTER TWELVE

BABY MOMMA DRAMA

"And that's the same guy that sold us the shopping malls?" Bena asked Koko over the phone as she peered out the office window of the Valley Brook Warehouse, located just outside of downtown Oklahoma City. She kept her eyes focused on the sleeper cab off in the distance with its antennae flapping back and forth while shaking her head in repugnance. It was now nearing two 'o' clock on Sunday afternoon.

"Yeah," Koko answered as she paced back and forth at the bottom of the patio stairs. "He just got here and meeting everybody, but I don't know, Bay," she pondered as she looked up towards the patio where her mother's friend was introducing himself to everyone.

"What's the problem? You think he flaw?" Bay asked concerned.

"He legit and all, it's just that Kimi actin' all jealous because she think—"

"Nobody's taking daddy's place. Put Kimi on the phone." Bay interrupted.

"Bay want you." Koko said as she handed her twin the phone.

"Hey, Bay," Kimi spoke in a reverential tone.

"Kimi, we all miss daddy," Bay said in a loving voice. "But has it ever crossed your mind that momma just may be lonely? She's been dealing with a lot ever since the night daddy was killed. She had to deal with my recovery, rearranging the businesses, reuniting with Ben and his family, the deal with Spoonie, trips abroad and —"

"I get it, I get it. She been through a lot the past couple of years," Kimi stated with resentment in her voice.

"What's really bothering you about this guy?"

"When that man walked through those patio doors I thought I was looking at daddy, Bay," Kimi confessed as her eyes watered. "He a little bit taller, but it's his style. He has an accent and talk funny, but I see a lot of daddy in him."

"And that's a bad thing?"

"No it's a frightening thing," Kimi said as her voice began to crack. "I look at that man and I get mad at daddy for not being here, especially on days like this when the family gets together. Then I get mad at the people who killed daddy. Some days I don't know who to blame."

"You blame the people who killed daddy. That's the only people you blame, Kimi," Bay forcefully stated. "You're afraid of that man, aren't you?"

"Because he reminds me of daddy. And I know what happened to daddy," Kimi said as she broke down. "I don't wanna see momma get hurt again," she cried out.

Bay closed her eyes and sympathized with her sister at that moment as tears seeped from their corners. On any given day and at any given moment, the pain of not having their father around would hit either of the siblings hard. Sometimes they cried alone, other times, they shared their pain with one another and cried together like Bay and Kimi were doing on this day.

"How long before you and Tiva get back here, Bay because I need you," Kimi said through her trembling lips.

Bay wiped her blurry, wet eyes. "I'm waiting on Tiva," she sniffled. "Give us a couple of hours," she added before ending the call. She then scrolled down and tapped the screen to call T-top, knowing she wasn't going to get an answer right away.

****

The callous hand palming her ass cheek was driving Tiva insane as she sat astride a stiff, thick dick. "Fuck me, Terrence," she moaned as ran her hands over her lover's wavy, low-cut hair while laying flat atop his muscular chest.

"It's about time you came up off this pussy, girl," Terrence whispered into Tiva's ear as he held a fistful of her short, curly black hair in his large hand. "Been wanting you in my life," he confessed as he kissed her deeply while driving up into her snug opening.

Tiva hissed and sat upright with her hands planted on Terrence's chest as her phone began to ring. She ignored the call as she was in the middle of an intense, raunchy round of sex. "Ooh, this some good dick," she moaned with her eyes closed.

Ever since she'd helped him out of a jam with his baby's mother, Candace, several months back, Tiva had been feeling Terrence. What'd endeared her to the guy was the manner in which he supported his daughter, Tara. She came first in Terrence's life despite the turmoil his baby mother brought into his life on a reoccurring basis over child support payments. To help Terrence keep up with his financial obligation to his daughter, Tiva had allowed him to work Saturday and Sundays inside the Valley Brook Warehouse unloading railcars. More times than not, it was only her, Bay, Terrence and a couple of other warehousemen on the property along with a few mechanics. At the end of the Sunday shift, Tiva and Terrence often sat inside the breakroom and shot the breeze while waiting on Bay to run an inventory report. The two found that they could laugh and talk about anything from the raising of children to past loves.

Terrence's main goal during that time was to get off the warehouse floor and into one of the rigs the family owned in order to earn a bigger paycheck. He wanted to buy a home where he could raise his daughter in a good neighborhood and give her a life he never had growing up on the northeast side of Oklahoma City, where drugs and gangs reigned supreme. Tiva said she would help him any way she could, but Terrence would have to do his part. He upheld his end of the bargain by getting the DUI he was charged with several months back expunged from his license and passing the company's road test. He'd also started delivering a few local loads several times a week, and that was good enough to earn him a set of keys to one of the family's immaculate Peterbilt sleeper cabs two days before after he'd past a second drug test, which was the day DeeDee had visited Doctor Wickenstaff. The truck had just come out of the mechanic's shop, and Tiva and Terrence had both decided to celebrate by christening the rig.

Tiva tilted her head back and moaned aloud as she straddled Terrence. "Yes, God!" she screamed out in ecstasy as she rotated her hips, firmly planted on her new lover's throbbing dick as it sent waves of pleasure coursing through her body. Her entire being had become sensitive to the touch. Sweat dripped from her tan skin, her nipples were dark and rock hard, and her pink, engorged clitoris was fully exposed from beneath its hood and throbbing uncontrollably.

"Terrence! Baby!" Tiva groaned as she rotated her hips in a frantic, circular motion as she neared the edge. The mattress the two were on in the back of the rig shifted over the force of the lovemaking and the truck's rocking became more intense.

"My baby 'bout ta' come?" Terrence growled as he clasped his hands around Tiva's waist and slid her back and forth over his pole. "Come for me, girl! Come on this mutherfuckin' dick! It's good?"

"Yes!" Tiva exclaimed. "What about you? You like it, baby?" she asked while gasping and rotating her hips constantly.

"It's the best I ever had! The best I *ever* had!" Terrence groaned as his eyes rolled to the back of his skull as he jerked up on his hips. "Let me taste that sweet pussy one more time before I bust while you suck my dick!"

Tiva jumped up off Terrence and rolled the slickened condom off his rod, turned around and planted her wet pussy in his face. She could feel his hot breath on her inner thighs as he caressed her outer thighs gently. Simultaneously, they went down on one another. Terrence taking a mouthful of pussy and Tiva deep throating some of the best dick she'd had since Junior. The two were moaning over one another's organs just as Tiva's phone rang again.

Tiva knew it was Bay calling, but she was on the verge of one of the biggest orgasms she'd had outside of stimulating herself with her silver bullet and was refusing to pull her pussy away from Terrence's sucking lips. She rose up, planted her feet on either side of Terrence's head and began bouncing up and down on his stiff tongue. "I'm 'bouta come all over your face, boy!" she hissed while stroking Terrence's rock hard shaft.

Terrence pushed Tiva's head back down and she leaned forward and took him into her mouth once more. His dick stiffened in between her lips and his sucking on her clitoris intensified.

Tiva's pussy started convulsed uncontrollably and she panted in a high-pitched voice. "Dammnn…dam, dam, dam," she moaned, in awe of the ecstasy as she came on Terrence's face while rapidly rotating her hips.

Terrence was on the verge of coming himself when Tiva took his dick and slapped it along the side of her face. Knowing he was clean over his recent drug test, one in which she'd went a step forward and had him tested for STDs, she took her new lover into her mouth just as he erupted and swallowed as much of his fluid as she could down her throat. It was an act that forced Terrence's toes to curl and he had to push her away. "Got damn, baby," he groaned. "What the fuck was that?"

"I know, right?" Tiva laughed as she crawled up the bed and flopped down beside Terrence. The phone rang again, but she ignored it once more as the two kissed and held one another. "You a freak, boy," Tiva playfully sassed.

"I do what you like that's all," Terrence boasted.

"Where my earrings? You done knocked my shits out my ear," Tiva laughed as she rose up and looked around briefly. She gave up on finding her earrings and stretched out beside Terrence once again as her cell rung. "Fuck, Bay! You killlin' my vibe!" she complained as she jumped up and answered the call. "What, girl?"

"We need ta' get up to Oklahoma City," Bay stated casually as she trotted down the office stairs and burst out of the warehouse main exit door.

"Yeah, yeah, the cookout," Tiva responded as she sat up on the mattress. "I just had some...some business to handle before we left," she smirked.

"And now you got bigger things to deal with before we hit the road," Bay let it be known.

"Like what?" Tiva playfully asked as she opened a box of baby wipes and handed a few to Terrence and took some for herself.

"Candace just rolled up on the property," Bay remarked while watching a white, four door '08 Toyota Corolla cruising up the road leading to the warehouse's main entrance. She ended the call and watched as twenty-seven-year-old Candace Godwin, a short, voluptuous high-yellow-skinned woman with cropped brown hair and brown eyes climbed from behind the wheel of her car wearing a pair of sweat shorts, t-shirt and sneakers.

Bay had seen Candace on the property several times before and by all measures, she was a real bitch. She put on a show every time she came around, often disrespecting Terrence by shouting him down and calling him a deadbeat, even though the guy was up on his child support payments and spent time with his daughter on the regular. And that was on a good day. No one up to the Valley Brook Warehouse liked Candace, Bay included. The two had passed words once before and Bay had to have security escort the woman off the premises.

"Where the fuck my man at 'round this bitch, Bena?" Candace asked aggressively as she walked towards Bay.

"If he was your man you wouldn't have to be askin' me that shit, now would you?" Bay retorted as she thumbed her nose and side-eyed Candace while standing next to her old school Lincoln.

"Where your sister?"

Bay merely shrugged as a black, two door 1987 Delta 88 with a white rag top and twenty-eight-inch chrome wheels rounded the corner. "That's who I'm lookin' for right there," Candace remarked as she walked over towards the car as it slowed to a halt. The obnoxious red-bone was readying to go off on Terrence. She was walking around the front end of his tinted window ride when the passenger side door opened and Tiva climbed out.

"What's up?" Tiva said to Candace while giving her a nonchalant chin nod. "You ready, Bay?" she then asked.

Twenty-three-year-old Tiva was 'on that bullshit' when it came to twenty-seven-year-old Candace Godwin and it was all being done on purpose. The only ties the woman had to Terrence was the fact that she had a daughter for him and Tiva knew it all-too-well. Candace was a bitter, controlling woman unable to let go of a relationship she herself had destroyed by emasculating the man she purportedly loved. Seeing Terrence happy and prospering was the one thing she could not see happen ever in life and Tiva knew and hated that fact.

They say misery loves company, and when it got down to it, Candace Godwin was a miserable woman bent on preventing her daughter's father from ever being happy. She couldn't hurt the man's heart, she knew, so she was now using the two most important things in his life as weapons against him: his daughter and his money.

"What the fuck you doing ridin' 'round with that bitch, Terrence?" Candace boomed as she walked up to the driver's side of Terrence's car and snatched the door open.

Tiva laughed the slur off as she walked over and stood beside Bay. She may have willingly gotten herself involved with a man who had a jealous ex, but she knew how to play it. She'd be as many 'bitches' and 'hoes' as Candace saw fit to call her in life so long as she didn't cross the unspoken line she'd set for herself and Terrence.

Twenty-three-year-old Terrence Mays hopped out his car with his jaws clasped tight. "The fuck you doing here, Candace?" he asked through gritted teeth.

"Your daughter need some new summer outfits. I'm taking her to Sea World in San Antonio next weekend and she has to be on point," Candace sassed.

"You know I have our daughter next weekend!" Terrence grimaced. "And the court order is one fifty a week plus day care and health insurance! I'm kicking out over nine hundred, damn near a thousand dollars a month for Tara! The fuck kinda money you think I'm making driving a forklift?"

"You right about the court order," Candace nodded as she licked her lips and pulled an envelope from the back of her sweat shorts and patted it in her hand. "But, see? I got this letter yesterday from this here warehouse where you working, dear. Now, I know you got your own place and all, but you must've forgot to change the address because when I opened it? I saw it was a letter congratulating you on passing some road test. You got a promotion. And with a promotion comes a pay raise. You're holding out on me," she declared as she smiled up at Terrence.

"That's my fuckin' money! I earned that shit on my own merit, Candace!"

"That's *our money*, nigga!" Candace snapped. "Fuck you thinkin'? That you just gone go off and make some money and get with another bitch and live happily ever after without me gettin' my cut? I'm here to get mine early," she sassed while cutting her eyes over to Tiva, who was standing with Bay shaking her head. "That's right, hoe!" she yelled. "I run this here!"

"You ain't gettin' shit from me!" Terrence screamed as he slammed a fist down onto the ragtop roof of his ride with spittle dripping from his thick beard. "I'm doing my part! And when I go to the day care next week my daughter better be there or I'm callin' the police!"

"Really?" Candace laughed. "You bringin' the law into this shit now, Terrence Mays? Okay. Since you wanna play it like that? I'll be at my social worker office early Monday morning to show her this letter. Look forward to another day in court. Bring your pay stubs, too, ole bitch ass nigga."

Candace had just crossed the line with Tiva having called Terrence a 'bitch ass nigga'. During their many talks, he often expressed his anguish over the way in which Candace handled him in private and public. It took everything within him for him to not haul off and smack the mother of his child in the mouth with a balled-up fist and knock her jaw lose over the way she disrespected him was what Tiva understood to be true. Terrence was a man about it, however, and she understood the fact that Candace was acting out because she still wanted him.

With the courts against him, and an ex out to ruin him, Terrence, if Tiva had to tell it, had no recourse or backup—except for her. Terrence may have been unwilling to lay hands on Candace, but there was nothing preventing her from reaching out and touching the woman who was causing her man so much heartache and pain on his behalf.

"You need my help?" Bay asked in a casual tone, knowing what Tiva was about to do.

Tiva curled her lips while staring over at Bay. "For that bitch? Hell no," she sighed before happily skipping off sideways in Candace's direction.

"I'll come anyway!" Bay politely stated as she reached back and secured the .45 caliber in her back waistband.

"That's the last time I stand by and watch your old ass disrespect him like that!" Tiva barked as she charged at Candace.

Candace was standing at the hood of her car when she saw and heard Tiva running her way with an ice grill on her face. Before she could react, twin was all up in her personal space. Blows to her face sent Candace into a backpedal. She tried to right herself, but Tiva was all over her like a rabid pit bull. "Terrence, get her off me!" she called out as she turned and took off running into the openness of the parking lot.

Tiva was relentless in her attack. She grabbed the back of

Candace's t-shirt, ripping it as she snatched up on her and pounded her across the skull. "All that shit you was talkin' and you ain't gone even fight back, bitch?" she growled as she continued to pound Candace's skull with both of her balled up fists.

"Mommy!" a small voice yelled out over the melee.

"Tara!" Terrence called out as he took off running to Candace's car where his daughter was calling out from the backseat.

Bay had reached Tiva at that moment. She pulled her sister off Candace, who was hunched over covering head while absorbing countless blows. When she rose up, her shirt was torn and hanging off her body and her hair was a disheveled mess. "You people are animals! Fucking animals!" she cried out in embarrassment.

Bay couldn't help but to chuckle silently. Candace had a blackened eye and a red knot on her forehead. The battle-weary woman was breathing heavily as she took off running to her car. "Get away from her, boy!" she yelled at Terrence as she snatched Tara from his arms.

"You come up here with that bullshit, brer!" Terrence yelled as he stood in Candace's face.

"Look at me!" Candace cried as she held onto Tara, all battered and bruised. "You let them jump on me how could you let them do that to me?" she rattled off through her tears.

"Ain't nobody jump on your fat ass! I fucked you up on a dolo, bitch!" Tiva boasted as she stood in the background while snapping her fingers and dancing in place. "You lucky that's all you got today!" she laughed.

"Is the baby okay?" Bay asked in a compassionate tone as she walked up to Terrence and Candace.

"Stay away from me!" Candace fretted as she ran around to the driver's side of her Toyota Corolla and pulled the door open. In the process, two-year-old Tara slipped from her arms.

Bay rushed over and caught the toddler just before she hit the black asphalt. Candace stepped her way, but she hopped back and kicked Candace in the pussy while holding onto Tara. "Fuck wrong with you?" she screamed as she held onto a crying, fearful Tara. "Hope I drew blood from that funky-looking mutherfucka, too!"

"This shit ain't over!" Candace yelled as she climbed behind the wheel of her car. Bay pulled her four-fifth at that moment and aimed it at the driver's side of the windshield, believing Candace was going for a pistol. "Bring Tara here, Terrence!"

"Let me calm her down before I bring here over there!" Terrence protested as he eased his daughter from Bay's arms. "Come get her, they ain't gone do nothin."

"I ain't fuckin' movin' with that crazy bitch pointin' a gun at me is you stupid?"

"Hold on, then. Just let me calm her down," Terrence urged a second time as he bounced Tara in his muscular arms.

"Terrence? Bring…me…my…fuckin' baby!" Candace boomed while clapping her hands. The twenty-seven-year-old red-bone may have been bold and brash, but after suffering an ass whipping like no other in rapid fashion from Tiva, and then having been kicked in the pussy by her twin, she was forced to rethink her insolence, especially now that she was staring down the barrel of a .45 caliber semi-automatic. She started her car and yelled, "Tara, momma right here! Come on, baby!"

Bay lowered her gun and walked back over to her ride where she met up with Tiva. "She gone be a problem," she stated as she remote-started her Lincoln.

"I know," Tiva stated lowly as she eyed Terrence placing Tara into the backseat of Candace's car. "I'm gone have ta' figure out how I'm gone deal with her before things get outta hand."

"Things are already out of hand," Bay countered. "We need ta' find out where she stay to keep tabs on her. We can go back upstairs and pull up the address where that letter was sent and go from there."

"Already," Tiva nodded while staring over to Terrence, watching as he strapped his daughter in while Candace constantly berated him until he slammed the door and walked off. "Let me go and get Terrence straight and we'll go and pull her location before we head up to the ranch."

Candace was pulling off when Tiva made it back over to Terrence. "Your daughter was good?" she asked as she rubbed her man's back tenderly.

"Yeah," Terrence glumly responded. "That woman. Damn," he sighed as he ran his hands over his face in frustration. "I ain't gone have shit long as Candace around."

"You thinkin' about killin' her?"

"Killin'...what? Why would I do that, Tiva? I'll never get away with no shit like that. I ain't...I wasn't even thinkin' on that level. I'm sayin' as long as she in my pockets I won't be able to accomplish shit in life. I'm strugglin' as it is. And now she gone take me back to court for more money? Tired of that bitch using my daughter for a paycheck. I should take Tara and just fuckin' disappear somewhere."

"That's what you really wanna do?" Tiva asked as she faced Terrence head on and folded her arms to show off her disapproval.

"I don't know, fuck. At least I won't have to deal with this bullshit, twin! You don't know what it's like! Barely able to buy groceries, having to put something on the bills just to pay the full rent. I'm not living. I'm not even living, bruh." Terrence complained as he threw his hands up and walked off. "I gotta get ready for a run up to Saint Paul, Minnesota tomorrow."

"What you gone do now?" Tiva asked as she followed Terrence around to the driver's side of his car.

"I got a bottle of gin at the crib. Gone have me a drink and fry some chicken. Smoke a blunt and calm my nerves."

Tiva's heart was propelling her to invite Terrence up to Ponca City at that moment, but her mind was telling her it was too soon. Things were far too messy between him and Candace and she didn't want to move too fast on her emotions. Bad enough she would have to deal with Candace later on down the line, which may lead up to her knocking the woman off for own her survival. To invite Terrence to her home under such turbulent circumstances would only complicate matters. There was, however, a way that she could help Terrence along for the time being while she decided on exactly how she was going to deal with her rival.

"When you leave out tomorrow morning I want you to use the computer in your truck and draw down a three hundred dollar Comcheck," she requested.

"For what?" Terrence asked as he leaned up against the driver's side door of his Delta 88. "I would still have to pay it back and it would show up on my pay stub."

Comcheck was a checking system used by CDL drivers to give themselves an advance on their weekly pay while out on the road. The monies would be deducted from said driver's net pay for a minimal fee and the balance would be their earnings for the pay period.

"You won't have to pay it back," Tiva assured. "Just take the three hundred down, and whatever you make next week, the money will be deducted from your net pay without it showing up on the check stub. So, if you make seven or eight hundred, it'll show up as you making four or five. I'll see to it myself that the deduction doesn't show up on your paystub."

"How you gone do all that?" Terrence asked puzzled.

Tiva realized at that moment that Terrence didn't fully understand the caliber of woman he was dealing with. Her family owned the Valley Brook Warehouse along with Holland Express, the trucking company that hauled ninety-five percent of the warehouse's freight. Her sisters, Kimi and Koko guarded the books. It would be nothing for the family to make three hundred dollars a week disappear from the payroll.

Tiva also had money of her own from the entertainment complex she, Bay and Dawk ran back in Ponca City. Three hundred a week was pocket change for her; she was willing to put up six thousand dollars of her own money, twenty weeks' worth of money in order to lower Terrence's pay in order to help earn him a reduction in child support payments. And if need be, she would get him a lawyer to fight for sole custody of Tara on his behalf as she cared about him just that much. She dared not reveal the many ways in which she was willing and able to help the man she found her heart growing fond of save for the fact that he would not have to worry about the advancements showing up on his paystubs.

"You willing to do that for me, Twin?" Terrence asked as his heart grew humble and appreciative.

Tiva's heart fluttered. She loved the way Terrence called her 'Twin'. She loved it every time he called her by that pet name as it made her feel special and wanted by the man. "It's the least I can do for you, Tee," she responded as she smiled and leaned in for a hug. "You deserve better than what you're getting from Tara's mother. Your daughter deserves better, too. Let's see what happens with it, if you're not comfortable with it we'll find another way."

"Thank you," Terrence said as he hugged Tiva and rocked the

two of them to and fro beside his ride. "I won't forget this shit, baby."

"Let's just hope you come on the other side in better shape," Tiva responded as she held onto Terrence. She laid her head in his broad chest and looked off into space, wondering if she was making the right decision regarding love this time around, or was she once again setting herself for heartache. "I better get upstairs. Me and Bay got a li'l bit more work to do before we knock off. Call me later," she ended as she kissed Terrence's lips, backed away from him and headed for the warehouse's main entrance. She entered the building pondering the decision she'd just made as the music on Terrence's ride cranked up several notches over the dual exhausts of his engine as he cruised out of the parking lot.

CHAPTER THIRTEEN

THE DEAD DO TALK

Walee had just turned onto the ranch, an hour or so after the altercation down at the Valley Brook Warehouse had occurred. He cruised up the black asphalt road, riding in between Quebec white pine wood that bordered livestock and produce on either side. Off to the left, one could see that the doors to both of family's barns were wide open. Cows and calves were out grazing in the pasture and the prized Clydesdale horses were roped off in their separate area eating from bales of hay and trotting around under the cool spray of irrigation hoses.

Up ahead lay the immaculate Ponderosa. Two stories of caramel-colored stone and vanilla marble columns and stairs spread out over fourteen thousand square feet. Naomi's bulletproof Phantom, Kimi and Koko's candy apple red Maserati, and four black, dark-tinted Suburbans, similar to those owned by the Secret Service, were parked out front giving off an unintentional royal appearance.

Off to the right lay Mary's field of tomatoes and onions. Twenty-plus acres of unspoiled, fertile land splashed with vibrant colors of brown, green and orange with a two-story colonial-style home with a large front porch and overhang sat strong beside a tree-lined hill to its left. That tree-lined hill was where Spoonie wanted to be on this day. "Walee, turn off here for me," she said as the gate leading to Mary's land neared.

"We gotta get ta' the house and find out who this dude is pushin' up on momma, Spoonie!" Walee retorted as he rode past the opened gate.

"I don't care about that right now, Walee!" eighteen-year-old Spoonie snapped. "Momma got a man so what? Why you upset? Just let me out if you not gone take me and Kahlil over there!"

"Kahlil?" Walee repeated as he looked over the backseat and stared his homeboy down while slowing the car. "You knew about this, fam?" he asked as he brought his ride to a halt.

"She been asking me to go over to Ne`Ne`s Hill with her, bro," Kahlil stated from the backseat while staring Walee directly in the eyes. "I think momma can handle her own until we get there, don't you? Not like the family gone need us to rush in and save the day."

"What's the deal with you going over there, Spoonie?" Walee asked as he placed the car in reverse.

"Just a couple of things I wanna get off my mind that's been with me ever since the night I got shot," Spoonie replied as Walee backed past the gate leading onto Mary's property. He put the car in drive and turned onto the property and rode over a dirt road in between squared off patches of onions and tomatoes.

Spoonie sat in the front passenger seat and eyed the tree-lined hill. She could see the white tombstone and white marble benches that sat upon the hilltop to the left of the forest's clearing. The cousin she'd never known, yet had been loving as if she'd known her all her life lay in rest under six feet of soil, her marked place of heavenly slumber overlooking the land like that of a proud angle.

"She came to me," Spoonie confessed lowly as Walee drove towards the guest house.

"Say what?" Walee asked as he looked over to Spoonie with his left hand draped over the steering wheel while leaning back into his soft leather seat. "Who came to you?"

"Our cousin Rene`," Spoonie answered as her eyes watered. "She came to me when Doctor Duchene was operating on me. She told me, she told me to 'go back'. She, that's what she told me. To 'go back'," she quoted.

"The dead don't talk, Spoonie," Walee responded, minimalizing his sister's belief as he eased through the field.

"Were you on that gurney?" Spoonie boomed, catching Walee by surprise. "You don't know what all I been through since that night! Nobody know what I been though since that night!" The car was moving at a slow enough pace to afford Spoonie the opportunity to open the front passenger door and hop out.

"Spoonie!" Walee called out as he watched his sister round the rear of his car and take off running through Mary's onion patch on a direct path towards Ne`Ne`s Hill without looking back.

"She need our support, fam," Kahlil stated from the backseat.

"You too, Kahlil? You believe what she sayin' about talkin' to Ne`Ne`?" Walee asked as he brought his car to a halt in the middle of the produce field.

"I'm not saying all that, but it's obvious that whatever she believed happened that night mean something to her, man. Discrediting it ain't gone help none," Kahlil stated as he eased the back passenger side door open. "Spoonie asked me to go up the hill with her today and I'm gone do that for her. If I'm violating, you can say it right now, but I'm going up that hill. We can deal with the consequences later. I just know I need to be there with her, bruh."

Walee looked out the window of his ride and stared on in silence as Spoonie ran across the land. To a degree, he was jealous. Jealous over the fact that Spoonie had chosen Kahlil over him to go and visit Ne`Ne's Hill. That patch of land was sacred to the family he knew and understood. It was where the family went to talk to their members that lay in eternal sleep. It was where family members would go to in order to apologize to those they believed they'd failed, and to also share their joys and triumphs.

Many an accomplishment and defeat within the family had been shared with Ne`Ne` Holland and Doss Dawkins Junior. No matter the circumstance, Ne`Ne's Hill was where one could go and lay all of their sins, regrets and joy bare without being judged. Confession. Walee now understood that his sister was ready to lay her heart bare six months after nearly losing her life and she'd chosen this day, and Kahlil Jamison, to do so. Given the magnitude of what he now realized was going down with Spoonie, Walee put up not a protest. He looked over the seat at Kahlil and said, "Don't ever break my sister heart, fam. You do that you got problems for life."

"I got her, fam," Kahlil remarked as he dapped Walee and eased from the car and trotted through the onion patch.

Spoonie was kneeling before Ne`Ne's grave under the shade trees when Kahlil made it up to the hilltop. It was quiet out, save for a few birds chirping up in the white, leafy, sweet-smelling canopy of surrounding Cleveland Pear trees. He walked over and sat down on the marble bench to the right of Spoonie, who'd sensed his arrival early on. She sniffled a couple of times and said,

"I just wanted her to know that I heard her, Kahlil."

"I know. She hear you, baby."

"You believe me? You believe I saw Ne`Ne`?" Spoonie asked, looking over to her right while wiping tears and resting on her knees before her cousin's grave.

"If you believe, I believe, Spoonie. It don't matter what I think anyway. You know what you went through on that operating table and nobody else."

"That's the thing. Nobody knows, but I want somebody to know. I want you to know because Ne`Ne` changed me."

"How she did that?" Kahlil asked, intrigued over Spoonie's thoughts. She went silent momentarily as she replayed that awful night in her mind.

****

Back down the hill, Walee had driven over to the foot of the hill. He was now on the phone discussing business with Jordan, who was down to his pad in Oklahoma City editing a few videos the two had recorded a week earlier, while leaning up against his ride. "You got all the models to sign off on the one-time payout, right?" he asked his partner in crime.

"Yeah," Jordan responded as she watched the film on a Mac computer. "They had their tests and everything handed back to 'em and shit. I had to cut one chick loose before the shoot over to the Skirvin because she had chlamydia, though. It's just some interracial two-way action on some cheerleaders from Oklahoma State. Strap-on sex, sixty-nine, face-riding, shit like that," she remarked nonchalantly. "Plus we got a club scene where this dude busted out a stripper from the back in the bathroom."

"You got permission from the club to use that footage?"

"Nah. They did it on a whim knowing I was recording the shit for a flick," Jordan laughed. "But you ain't gone be able to tell where it's at once I cut out the background. I can change up the colors on it. Nothing major, we good."

"Alright. What's that about sixty minutes?"

"Yeah, once I add the other two scenes."

"Cool," Walee remarked as he looked over his shoulder and saw Montenegro's Titan, and Takoda's tow truck headed his way from the direction of the guest house. "Let me hollar at my people. Call me back if you got a issue," he said before ending the call.

Walee waited for his family to exit their cars. He watched as Regina went into Takoda's tow truck and pulled out a basket of yellow roses, a roll of paper towels and a bottle of Windex. "My bad, cousin. I forgot today was the day for flowers with Ne`Ne`. Spoonie and Kahlil up there right now."

"For real?" Regina smiled. "Awww, they're courting," she sighed proudly as Takoda and Siloam walked up behind her.

"Yeah, I'm just gone lay low and hang out down here and let them—boy, what happened to your face?" Walee laughed when he saw the black eye Takoda was sporting. "Somebody at the bowling alley snuck you or something, fam? Let's go whip they ass!"

Regina looked over to Takoda and said, "Tell him what you did," before walking up the hill.

Tak leaned up against Walee's ride and began explaining what he'd done in open fashion, much to Walee's astonishment.

****

Back up the hill, Spoonie was just beginning to explain to Kahlil how Ne`Ne` had changed her exactly. "I was scared at first. But she gave me my life back," she explained as she turned and faced her cousin's grave. "Ne`Ne`?" she whispered. "Thank you. I don't know what it was that happened really, all I know is that I saw you. I thank you, and I thank God even more because, because for whatever reason he sent your soul to me and I wasn't afraid anymore. I love you," the emotional eighteen-year-old said as tears streamed down her face.

Kahlil sat with his head bowed praying in silence as Spoonie talked. When she went silent, he looked up at her. "You okay?" he asked in a comforting tone.

"Yeah, but there's more," Spoonie responded. "Something, something that I have to tell you."

"I'm listening," Kahlil remarked as he looked deep into Spoonie's dark brown eyes.

"I was fighting. I was in so much pain and I wanted it to go away, Kahlil," Spoonie confessed through her tears. "I just wanted to go to sleep, but then I saw Ne`Ne` face. It was glowing and she had a rainbow behind it. All I heard was her tellin' me to go back. And then I suddenly woke up. And I wasn't hurting anymore. I could hear all these people talking and feel their hands inside my body, and all I kept thinking about was staying alive. I wanted to live…because I wanted to be able to see you again."

Kahlil was surprised over Spoonie's remark. "You put me first?" he asked in disbelief. "I thought it would've been your mother, or your brothers and sisters."

"I thought about everybody, but you was the first person that came to my mind. I realized how short life could be during that time. I never imagined something like that would ever happen to me in my life. I never thought about dying. I always used to say to myself, 'There's time. I have time to tell him that I love him and I want him to be my boyfriend.' But, I was always scared and searching for the right moment. When I woke up out my coma? I wasn't scared anymore, but I was still searching for the right time. The right time is now," Spoonie said as she pushed herself back and leaned up against the bench beside Kahlil. "I felt your lips touch mine that night. I used to fantasize about kissing you every day. It happened, just not how I wanted."

Kahlil eased off the bench and sat beside Spoonie. "I been in love with you for a long time, Spoonie," he admitted.

"When did it happen?"

"Last Christmas," Kahlil admitted. "Remember we were over to the—"

"Skirvin where Walee was with them two nasty girls Jordan and Anquette," Spoonie finished.

"Yeah," Kahlil chuckled. "Remember we made that video off James Brown song?"

"Santa Clause…go straight to the ghetto…" Spoonie sang through laughter as she bumped her head against Kahlil's left shoulder. "And the video we made!" she happily exclaimed.

Kahlil pulled his cellphone out at that moment and pulled up the video Spoonie was referencing and showed it to her as he placed his left arm around her neck and pulled her close. He watched as her eyes lit up and a wide smile crept over her face. "You still have it," she laughed aloud as she leaned back into his cuddle.

"I watch it every day," Kahlil said as he nuzzled Spoonie's neck with the tip of his nose. Spoonie turned her head slightly and parted her pouty, sexy lips as her eyes closed. She exhaled excitedly when Kahlil's lips met hers as tears rolled from her closed eyes. She gripped him tighter as their tongues intertwined.

"Can I be yours," Spoonie asked upon breaking the kiss.

"I'm already yours," Kahlil whispered as he used his thumbs to remove tears from his first ever girlfriend's face. "On everything I love, I promise to never hurt or let anything happen to you again, baby. I'm gone be good to you forever and always."

"I can't wait to tell my mother," Spoonie smiled as she fell off into the strong grip of her first boyfriend ever. She was hoping he would be the last as Kahlil made her feel whole. He completed her, and it was a feeling she never wanted to go away.

"What y'all going tell Naomi?" Regina asked as she ascended the hilltop, coming in on the tail end of Spoonie and Kahlil's conversation. "Hope I'm not imposing on y'all."

"Nah, you not imposing," Kahlil smiled as hugged Spoonie from behind. The two giggled happily while staring up at Regina.

"Aww sookie, sookie now. I knew I was right about you two up here courting," Dimples smiled upon realizing what was transpiring. "I remember my first boyfriend, Spoonie. His name was Jessie Green back in Ghost Town," she disclosed as she walked over and knelt before Ne`Ne`s grave with the basket of yellow roses at her side. She removed the roll of paper towels and pulled off a few sheets and set them aside for the moment.

"Can I have a few flowers to put on my daddy's grave, Regina?" Spoonie asked.

"Help yourself," Regina smiled as she ran her hands over her exposed thighs. "What did you and Ne`Ne` talk about, Spoonie?" she asked while examining her twin's grave.

"I saw her spirit when I was in surgery," Spoonie smiled as she placed the roses atop her father's grave and rested before him on the backs of her heels.

"Really?" Regina asked as she removed several decaying roses and pulled a few weeds from around Ne`Ne`s tombstone.

"You don't believe me," Spoonie said as she eyed her father's tombstone.

"I didn't say that, Shima," Regina reassured. "I'm just surprised because you never mentioned it before."

"Rene` was the first one I wanted to tell. I held it until I felt strong enough to talk to her openly. And even then I wasn't sure. I kept replaying it until I realized that I really did see her spirit that night. Does that make me weird, Regina?"

"What? Noo," Regina declared as she reached out and rubbed Spoonie's right arm. "Death is a mysterious thing to us all. It's painful to those left behind because it doesn't seem natural to the living. Don't worry. I believe you, baby," she smiled as she picked up the bottle of Windex and sprayed some on Ne`Ne`s dusty Plexiglas-encased photo. "You wanna know what's really weird, though?" she asked as she picked up the paper towels and wiped down her twin's picture.

"What's that?" Spoonie asked.

"Sometimes, before I leave home to come here? I look at pictures of myself in the present. I brought a picture of myself from home over to here a few times and laid it across Rene's picture and compared them side by side when I did. My sister's image is always the same, but I've changed a lot. Fluffier cheeks and bigger hair with a motherly appeal," Dimples chuckled. "But what's weird for me is that I'm watching this young person in this grave grow older. I am Ne`Ne` to a degree because as I change, I see how my sister would look now, and she would've been beautiful," she smiled while eyeing her sister's image as her eyes welled up. "Forgive me, y'all. I'm being self-centered today."

"Nahh," Kahlil remarked intrigued as he knelt down and looked at Ne`Ne`s picture, then over to Dimples. He smiled and said, "When people die, that's it. They never change, Regina. But, damn, we know how both of y'all would look today. And you right, Ne`Ne` would've been beautiful," he complimented, forcing Regina to blush.

"I wonder what my daddy would say about me and Kahlil." Spoonie chimed in.

"I think he would tell you that you have good taste in men, cousin." Regina remarked as she wiped her watery eyes.

"Kinda like you, right, Regina?" Spoonie asked.

"I wouldn't say all that," Regina sighed as she sprayed a second round of Windex onto the white marble tombstone and let it soak in for a few seconds. "Men can be fickle," she said as she resumed wiping the marble. "Some advice, to both of y'all...love one another through the good and the bad. Always be honest and avoid temptation," she said as her eyes welled up again. She began wiping harder on the marble as she sniffled and said, "Things always start out good when you first fall in love. It's the best feeling ever, but people have a way of letting you down in life, man. They don't mean to all the time, but it doesn't eliminate the hurt."

"You all right, fam?" Kahlil asked concerned.

"I'm fine, Kahlil," Regina said as she held back a heave. "Just passing on some worldly advice to y'all newcomers to love. God, I never, I didn't expect this today. I'm happy for you two, though," she added as she wiped her eyes with the back of her hand.

"I'm listening to everything you sayin', fam," Kahlil responded. "Show us how to love. What can we expect?"

"Every relationship is different," Regina stated. "But, I know you'll be going to the NFL soon, Kahlil," she continued. "You gone have women throwing themselves at you, you gone have big money, endorsements, the whole world in the palm of your hands. If you gone be with my cousin? You better be with her and her only no matter what. Because the day she come to me crying about you let her down?"

Kahlil chuckled to himself as he rested on one knee in between the graves of Doss Dawkins and Rene 'Ne`Ne`' Holland. "As I kneel before the two deceased people that mean the most to you and Shima, Regina? I promise I'm not gone hurt your family. You got my word on that," Kahlil said as Spoonie knelt beside him and placed a hand on his back. Both youngsters stared at Regina as they knelt beside her, staring with loving eyes. Even in their young age, they'd both had enough understanding to discern that Regina's pains and convictions were deriving from an outside influence.

"You mean that?" Regina asked through her tears as she stared back at Kahlil. "Because this is not a good feeling and I don't want my cousin to experience it ever!" she cried aloud as she leaned down and covered her face. "Don't you ever cheat on her!"

A powerful moment had erupted atop Ne`Ne`s Hill as one

family member, who was suffering through the agony of infidelity from her own husband, still had enough strength and altruism within her heart to shun aside her own pain and pass down sound, strong advice to those new to love, and younger in years, without criticism. Regina didn't know it at the time, but she'd just prepared Kahlil and Spoonie for a whirlwind of emotional drama that would unfold as Kahlil pressed on in his endeavors to make it to the NFL. In the end, she would become a valuable resource, but their story remains to be told.

After spending another half hour atop Ne`Ne`s Hill tending the graves and discussing matters of the heart and life in general, Regina, Spoonie and Kahlil walked down the hill and saw Walee leaning up against his ride. He was on his cellphone, again, but ended the call when he saw his sister and best friend walking towards him hand in hand with Regina following.

"Where my husband and Siloam go off to?" Regina asked as she looked around and saw that the Titan and Takoda's tow truck was nowhere in sight.

"Relax. Relax, cousin," Walee chuckled, having been filled in all that had gone down with Regina, Siloam and Takoda, minus the murders Siloam had committed. "They laid up there, well, Tak decided to get on with explaining what he did, ya' feel me? He back over to Ponderosa. Siloam making her rounds with Montenegro," Walee let it be known. "You good, Spoonie?" he then asked.

"Yeah, Walee," Spoonie responded as she walked up and hugged her brother. "I hope you not mad for not taking you up there with me. I'll tell you what I said if you want."

"Nah," Walee tenderly remarked as he kissed his sister's forehead. "That's between you, Ne`Ne` and Kahlil. I wish y'all the best, baby girl."

"You're not mad at me for going with your friend?" Spoonie asked in an uncertain tone.

"Never. Kahlil my homeboy. I rather see you with him over anybody else because I know he ain't gone do you wrong, ya' feel? Y'all good together. Let's go home," he sincerely remarked as he dapped Kahlil.

CHAPTER FOURTEEN

ROLLING WITH WALEE

The quartet of family rode over to Ponderosa where Walee pulled up to the backside of the mansion. The back patio was filled with family and friends shielding themselves from the blazing sun by sitting at the patio tables under huge umbrellas. Two grills were going, smoke billowing from their stacks and sides, and what Walee knew to be his mother's old school R&B playlist was playing at a comfortable level.

Tacoma, Doss III, Malaysia and Malara ran around out in the open field with some of the ranch hands' children, Tacoma and Doss III engaged in a water gun fight with some of the older kids as Malaysia and Malara popped a basketful of water balloons. Mary and a few of the ranch hands' wives sat at a table talking as Tak, who was looking to avoid conflict, manned the grills with a couple of ranch hands.

Naomi and Francine sat near the left side French doors talking and sipping drinks and an older group of teenagers played a game of UNO while sipping on sodas and tea at another table. Siloam and Montenegro milled about from group to group with smiles on their faces as they guarded all in attendance. This wasn't as big a function as the family would normally hold as many, including Ben's family and team, were busy handling business on the family's behalf and were unable to break away from important tasks.

Walee was climbing from behind the wheel of his car bobbing to Earth Wind and Fire's song *Let's Groove* when he saw Tracey Sanchez, Rolanda Jones and Tracey's daughter, Angel, emerge from the center patio doors. The Dee-Jays were a family favorite down in Oklahoma. Ever since they'd taken the lead in helping to reunite Ben with his father's people, they were always invited to family functions. Most functions they could not make, but

185

whenever they could, they would fly into Oklahoma City and ride up to Ponca City in chauffer driven limousine and chill with people they'd come to admire and love.

"Fam!" Walee yelled aloud with a wide smile on his face as he pointed up at Tracey.

"Homiieeee!" Tracey smiled as she two-stepped over the edge of the marble stairs while holding onto a frozen daiquiri. "What it is, boy?" she laughed.

Walee jogged around his car and trotted up the stairs and met Tracey halfway. He hugged her briefly and kissed her cheek before she mingled off into the crowd to further enjoy herself.

"That's the li'l booger I been waiting ta' see come here and give auntie a hug!" Rolanda Jones said in one breath as she walked down the stairs with her own frozen margarita.

Walee hugged Rolanda around the waist and rubbed her arm affectionately midway up the stairs. When Walee first laid eyes on Rolanda Jones back in October of 2008, he thought the 5'11" dark chocolate-skinned sister with the wavy black hair was one of the most beautiful women he'd ever seen in life. He was shocked to learn that she was HIV positive and was compelled to meekly and respectively ask her how and what happened.

The two had quickly formed a rapport. And given Walee's fondness for women, Rolanda was a wealth of information when it came to disease and sexual practices. He'd learned many things from his father, mother and siblings, but upon talking to Rolanda, as sexy a woman as she was, what he'd gained from the friendship was not to become trapped, or lulled into complacency by a pretty face and sexy body because disease does not discriminate.

"How Vegas treatin' you, Auntie?" Walee asked as he took Rolanda's hand and led her back up the stairs.

"Like royalty," Rolanda playfully stated. "I thought Jane Dow would've been here. Me and Tracey was hoping for an inside scoop on the album she working on back in Missouri. You got somethin' for me? Because nobody seems to know anything about that young lady."

"That's straight up under wraps. Jay-D ain't tellin' y'all nothin'?"

"Just that he done got some big-name artist on his production team now," Rolanda replied as Tracey's daughter, Angel Michelle

Fuller, stood by smiling shyly.

"Yeah?" Walee said as he eyed Angel, his gaze going unnoticed by Rolanda. "Jay-D usually get what he want you know what I'm saying? If he say he got somethin' big planned take 'em at his word. Just give 'em a minute, he gone get at you when the time is right. I'm gone see to it that he do before Jane album drop. Might even fly out to Vegas and drop that info myself," he added while smiling over to Angel, who merely blushed and walked off without saying a word.

Just then, Tyke emerged from the center patio doors. "Walee!" she called out. "Man, where y'all been all day? Momma boyfriend is in daddy's room with Dawk, Kimi and Koko and Dawk and Koko are starting to like him!" she whispered after pulling her brother away from Rolanda.

"Well excuse me," Rolanda laughed as she walked off and mixed in with the crowd.

"What he doing like that?" Walee asked perplexed as he and Tyke huddled.

Tyke shifted her weight, placed a hand on her hip and said, "You know Dawk likes chess the same way daddy loved it. Mister Fraser had just met everybody when Dawk and Oneika pulled up with Sosa. You know Sosa sick and all. Dawk and Oneika had just got the test results back. They was walking up the stairs to deliver the news and Mister Fraser asked to hold our nephew."

"No way," Walee sighed.

"Yes way!" Tyke snapped. "He looked down at Sosa and said, 'this baby has acne'."

"Thought it was chicken pox?" Walee questioned.

"That's what this dumb doctor back in town was saying, but they ran skin tests. Sosa has too much oil in his skin from the pregnancy, and chemicals were showing up. Oneika was using a detergent too strong for his skin, that's why he kept breaking out because the oil and the detergent was blocking his pores."

"So, momma friend was right?" Walee asked.

"Yeah, and now him, Dawk and Koko is all cozy and stuff in daddy private room now."

"He might not be that bad then," Walee surmised. "Let me go and meet this dude. See what his talk game be like."

"It's strong." Tyke stated, much to Walee's dismay. "What? I like him, too, Walee. Kimi the only one have a problem with him," she smiled before walking down the stairs and greeting Spoonie and Kahlil.

Walee was walking into Ponderosa when he heard, "Walee, come here!" He looked over and saw his mother eyeing him with stern eyes.

After making his way through the family and friends out on the patio, Walee, ever anxious, approached his mother's table. He'd brushed off his mother's request when she spoke to him over the phone while he was down in Stillwater. I mean, she'd threatened him with talks before and had waived it off, but he now knew that the words he'd spoken a couple of hours earlier had struck a nerve within his mother and he had to make amends. "I guess I was about three years old when you slapped my legs for using the N-word," he stated in an apologetic tone as he stood before Naomi. "That was the day Kevin and Serena died."

"I'll go and make some more tea," Francine said, giving Naomi and Walee a moment to be alone.

Once Francine had cleared out, Naomi nodded and said, "The deaths of your grandparents had overridden everything I had intended on doing that day, but I came back some time later and explained to you one on one why that word is to never be uttered by anybody inside this family. I can't control how you talk when not in my presence, but you know how I feel about it. You not only degrade and minimalize the person you're talking to, but you degrade yourself and your heritage in the process. You can call the women you deal with bitches and hoes or whatever you chose if they are dumb enough to accept it, but what you will not do, is degrade those whom I chose to bring into our fold whether you approve or not."

"I understand, momma. I got caught up in the moment," Walee said as he sat in Francine's vacated seat.

"'Getting 'caught up in the moment' can have serious repercussions, Walee." Naomi counseled. "When in conflict, son, you state your disagreements in a respectful manner or you say nothing at all, because if it gets to the point in which you have to name call? It means that you have lost control of your emotions.

Your adversaries will take note and use your hostility against you. You cannot run a business in that manner if you expect to last unless you're ready to shed blood in this business. And you're not part of 'this business'—so play your position and stop trying to dictate mine."

"I understand, momma," Walee responded in a reverential manner. "I just," his eyes watered, but he held back the tears by clinching his fist together. "I be thinking about daddy you know? How he would feel about something like that."

"If your father was alive none of this would be, son. I would not have a man friend to keep me company. But now that I do, it doesn't mean that I've stopped loving your father. I'll always love him more than any other man, but momma gets lonely sometimes now."

"What y'all do?" Walee asked as he leaned forward in his seat with his arms resting on his knees.

"That really is none of your business, but if you must know, we talk, and we dance, and we laugh. Nothing more."

"You sure?"

Naomi looked Walee off and laughed. She had every right to get upset with her son, but she understood that she wasn't talking to an eighteen-year-old young man, she was talking to a worried little boy who was afraid his mother would forget about his father, which was the furthest thing from the truth. "You're being protective when there's no need, Walee. You haven't even met my friend. Do you even know his name?"

"Not yet," Walee answered as he stretched and stood up.

"Well, go meet him," Naomi smiled. "His name is Dunkirk Fraser."

Walee had just hugged and kissed his mother when Bay and Tiva walked out onto the patio. "Where that man pushin' up on my momma at?" Tiva joked as she wobbled over to her mother and sat in her lap. "I know you had a long talk with daddy before you made that decision," she said before kissing Naomi's cheek.

"Get off me, Tiva. I don't know where your butt been," Naomi smirked as she jostled T-top off her lap.

Tiva threw up her hands and bounced around. "Come on, momma!" she laughed. "I been wanting a pieca you since I was four!"

"You couldn't handle me back then when I was thirty-five, and ya' still can't handle me at fifty-four," Naomi confidently declared as she leaned back in the chair and stared at Tiva. "Hop on over here if ya' want some and watch ya' feelings get hurt."

"Yep! She like this new man," Tiva smiled as she sat beside her mother.

"What y'all do, momma?" Bay asked as she took a seat at the table opposite Tiva. "He has to be special for you to bring him here."

His oldest sisters' acceptable demeanor and jovial speech gave Walee some solace. He walked into the home thinking he may have indeed been overreacting. He laughed to himself as he reflected on how him and Kahlil had darted out of Spoonie and Tyke's apartment and sped up to Ponca City like Calvary coming to save the day. *"Like my momma need saving,"* he laughed to himself just as Oneika and AquaNina walked into the kitchen. AquaNina was holding onto his nephew, two-month-old Sosa.

"How he doing, y'all?" Walee asked as he walked over and stretched out his arms and took the baby from AquaNina and held him close. The vanilla-skinned, curly black-haired baby cooed and rubbed his face with his mitt-covered hands.

"Doctors gave him a shot to suppress the reaction he was having to the soap detergent Oneika was using and he has this prescribed lotion to put on his body," AquaNina remarked as she stood on her tip toes and smiled down at Sosa, who was wrapped in a soft cotton blanket.

"He'll be fine in a week or so, but he'll be getting ready for a round of tests soon," Oneika chimed in as she walked over and waved a bottle of Pablum before her son. Sosa reached for the bottle at that moment and started fidgeting in Walee's arms.

"Okay, okay, homeboy," Walee laughed as he passed the baby back to AquaNina.

"You don't want to feed him?" AquaNina asked.

"Next time. I'm going meet momma new man friend."

"Ahh she's buff ole chap!" AquaNina and Oneika

simultaneously stated as they giggled at one another.

"What?" Walee smiled.

"Nothin'," Oneika said as she and AquaNina walked off. "Buff is what Mister Fraser told Dawk I was when Dawk introduced me to him. It means pretty. He's a funny guy, man. You'll like him, Walee," she ended as she and AquaNina disappeared into the west hall, headed back towards Naomi's private room.

Walee headed off in the opposite direction, passing underneath the grand staircase and headed towards his father's private room. He was halfway down the wide, marble-floored hall when he bumped into Tracey's daughter, Angel, as she walked out of one of the spare bedrooms. He grabbed her arms and said, "My bad, baby girl."

"Nah, it's my fault. Where you going?" Angel asked softly as she rubbed scented lotion onto her hands.

Walee looked Angel over without answering right away. She was a gorgeous tan-skinned, amber-haired, green-eyed mixture of black, Latina and Caucasian. She blew him away with her beauty, but she was still young and naïve at age sixteen he knew. He'd finger-banged Angel once in the music room on the second floor of Ponderosa back in October of 2008, and he could've gone further, but he opted not to given her age and inexperience.

"How old are you now?" Walee asked as he stepped back and eyed Angel standing in her loose-fitting grey shorts and matching tank top and white sandals. He licked his lips as he pictured himself doing things to and with Angel he would never even consider doing with Jordan or Anquette.

"I'll be seventeen in September," Angel answered, shaking Walee from his thoughts.

"Is that right," Walee stated slyly. "You know I'm diggin' on ya', but you still young, though. Your momma not might not even be down with nothin' like that anyway. I bet she guard you harder than the Secret Service."

"She does," Angel jokingly admitted. "But that still didn't stop us that night last year, huh?"

"You remember that?"

191

"I get horny every time I think about it. You ever think about it?"

"Nah," Walee fabricated. "To be honest, I wasn't all that impressed. You was more scared than anything. I felt like I was molesting you, girl."

"The only reason I was scared was because my mother was sleeping like two doors down, man." Angel whispered through light laughter. "So, what we did didn't mean anything to you?"

"It meant something—just not all that much, ya' dig? So, you saying if we was to do something like that again you wouldn't be scared this time around?" Walee asked while rubbing his chin.

"I'm not saying all that now," Angel laughed. "My mother, if she knew I liked a boy? She would go completely off, but that don't mean I'm not willing."

Walee bumped his fists together and Angel caught a glimpse of the diamond-crusted watch he wore at that moment. She eyed his outfit, which was nothing more than a pair of black sweat pants with a white tank top and a pair of fresh white and black Air Jordan's, but it was appealing to her eyes nonetheless as it hung right on his slim, muscular physique. He looked like a slender chocolate candy stick that she wanted to lick all over, which had been a fantasy of hers ever since the night she came for the first time in her life on Walee's finger inside the music room.

"You tryna sneak out later on tonight after everybody gone to bed?" Walee asked, shaking Angel from her thoughts. To say these two were feeling one another would be an understatement. Both had a burning desire that was becoming increasingly harder to resist with every passing minute.

"That's what you wanna do?" Angel asked coyly.

"It's not about what I want, baby girl. This whole deal between me and you is up to you, ya' dig?" Walee said as he slimmed his eyes to give off a sexier vibe as he stared down at Angel while motioning with his hands. "I'm not gone do no more than what you wanna do, so don't feel like you have to do something just because I ask you to do it. I'm tryna see exactly where we at with it that's all. You runnin' things, baby."

Angel swallowed the lump in her throat as her body temperature rose slightly. "What, where will we go?"

"For a short walk."

"What will we do?" Angel asked while staring up at Walee in a trance-like state.

"We gone pick up where we left off," Walee responded as he stepped closer to Angel and ran a hand along her right hip. Angel moaned and placed a hand on Walee's shoulder to balance herself. "You like that?" he asked as he leaned down and hovered his lips before Angel's.

"I do, Walee," Angel panted.

Just then, the door to the private room opened and the Commodores' song *Zoom* blared out into the hallway. "Mister Fraser, you ain't right! I'm going out on the patio on that one!" Koko laughed as she emerged from the room while holding onto a half-full bottle of champagne.

Angel and Walee's spell had been broken by the sudden intrusion. They separated, Walee walking towards Koko with his head bowed and rubbing his chin as Angel walked towards the main floor while running a hand through her hair. Whether the two knew it or not, however, Koko had seen them nuzzled up against one another. She'd never paid the two any mind, but she knew Walee all-too-well. "You makin' a move on Angel, huh?" she asked through a sly smile as Walee passed her.

"What happened, girl?" Walee laughed.

"Don't 'what girl' me, boy," Koko whispered over the music. "You pushin' up on Tracy daughter. That woman gone kick your ass if you turn Angel out."

"I ain't gone, I ain't turnin' nobody out, Koko," Walee laughed slyly. "We was just talkin'."

"About settin' somethin' up later on tonight I bet. I ain't gone say nothin'. Do you," Koko remarked while shaking her head. "You going meet momma new friend already?" she asked as Kimi emerged from the room sporting a cynical look.

"What he be like, y'all?" Walee asked.

"Hilarious!" Koko answered.

"Not impressed!" Kimi quickly followed.

"Why you say that, Kimi?" Walee asked puzzled.

"He trying too hard if you ask me." Kimi chided.

"Girl, hush! That man just being himself," Koko interjected. "We going outside, Walee. Go on in and introduce yourself, playboy," she ended while smiling slyly at her younger brother.

"Nah, he gone introduce his self to me. I live here he don't," Walee remarked.

"The way momma diggin' on him that may change, li'l brother," Koko quipped as she and Kimi walked off.

CHAPTER FIFTEEN

THE GOOD AND RICH BRIT

"And I walk up to the guy and says, I says to the lad, yuh may have fired me from this job, but yuh wife is at me home fixing me dinner right now. Anything yuh want me to say upon me arrival, sir?" fifty-five-year-old Dunkirk Fraser laughed as the Sunday evening wore on.

Dawk chuckled as he sat behind the bar eyeing a chessboard with a cigar in his hand and a neat whiskey at his side. "That took a lot of nerve saying something like that to the man you were working for," he added as he moved a piece on the board. "What he do?"

Dunkirk countered Dawk's move and said, "Now mind you, I was a young chap working as a butcher for this guy, he was harmless to me, so I thought. Anyhow, he reaches down and I swear I thought he was going for a sidearm or something. Instead, he comes up with a stack of papers as a heavy mob stood behind me and he says, 'Yes, tell my wife she's no longer my wife. I've frozen her bank account and she's banned from the properties I own. You can have her.' I says back to the guy, 'Blimey! Yuh must have a screw loose! What on earth do I want with the hacky bike now? Take her back she's your bike, yuh uphill gardener!' I woke up three days later wrapped in bandages because those hard-nuts beat seven shades of shit out of me that night. After I healed? I upped the sticks and used the money I saved to start me own real estate company. Opened me first office in the South of Wales at age thirty and never looked back. Been a good and rich Brit ever since."

Dawk was laughing as he flipped through Kimi and Koko's British slang dictionary. Dunkirk had basically slept with a man's wife and admitted it. He then called the man's wife a dirty whore before giving her back and calling the man a homosexual in the process. He then woke up three days later after getting his ass whipped and skipped town.

"You ever got back at 'em for doing that to ya'? Dawk asked Dunkirk.

"To be honest with you, Dawk, I..." Dunkirk's voice trailed off when he saw a slender male with his hair in two thick plats braided to the back walking into the room looking around like he owned the place. "Ahh, this must be Walee Dawkins. Naomi's youngest son! I'm Dunkirk Fraser!" he introduced of himself as he set his drink down and extended his hand.

"What's up, man?" Walee replied cautiously as he took in Dunkirk's demeanor. The guy seemed cool upon first impression, and he carried himself well on first appearances, but Walee was apprehensive out the gate so he held back on the handshake.

Dunkirk withdrew his hand and said, "Dawk, yuh younger brother, I sense he's eggy by my presence, but I think he's a corker. How do I chum up to him?"

"You just insulted me, bruh?" Walee asked as he side-eyed Dunkirk.

"Nah, li'l brother," Dawk laughed as he flipped through the dictionary. "He said you kinda upset over him being here, but he think you a good person."

"Oh, alright," Walee nodded. "Nah, I'm not upset or nothing like that, big dog. I just don't know you, Mister Fraser."

"Mister Fraser is too formal, but I understand it's early doors, or, too early to be informal. So, I'll call you Mister Dawkins to keep along the lines of respect."

"Alright then," Walee nodded. "Who winning the game?"

"It's even," Dawk responded as he eased off the barstool. "You wanna take over for me? I'm gone go and check on Oneika and Sosa."

"Yeah, I got it." Walee replied as he sat before the board.

"You gone need this," Dawk said as he handed Walee the British slang dictionary and walked out of the room.

"Naomi tells me you're a lover boy, Mister Dawkins," Dunkirk remarked as he moved a pawn forth.

"I do okay with the ladies," Walee replied as he moved a knight and took Dunkirk's pawn.

"I was a lover boy me self many moons ago, but now I'm just a wealthy oxygen thief chasing after a wickedly buff woman whose heart I fancy big time."

"Oxygen thief?" Walee smirked as he looked up, then read the definition of oxygen thief in silence. "You can't be actin' like an old man dealing with my mother, Mister Fraser."

"I don't intend to, Mister Dawkins. But I do hope to earn yuh favor without mucking the matter. Your mother invited me here to allow you all to get to know *me*, and for *me* to schmooze up to *everybody*, but it's not in me to be a great pretender. Yuh take me as I am, or yuh don't take me at all, but either way, I will not stop pursuing your mother's heart unless she asks me to. I told Dawk the same thing, and Kimi, and Koko."

"I can respect that, Mister Fraser, don't mean I have to agree with it, though."

"That I respect, Mister Dawkins. Let me fancy yuh a story, though. When I was a boy of thirteen or fourteen, me mums was single by then because dear old dad had gotten himself knocked off in an industrial accident. He drove a forklift right off the dock and it fell atop and crushed him when I was only six."

"I lost my father back in September of '06," Walee remarked as he engaged Dunkirk by resting his elbows on the bar counter. "I was fifteen at the time. It broke my heart. Broke all our hearts," he added as he poured himself a quick shot of whiskey and downed it.

"We lost our fathers in different ways, but the affect was the same on us both, Mister Dawkins. You had plenty of people around you to avenge you and you were more of an age that allowed yuh tuh understand. Me? I had to deal with a mum who became promiscuous and allowed any man into her life. She wanted a father for me, but she chose scum for a mate time and time again. I can't tell yuh how many nights I spent awake as a young boy listening to me mums having a dicky fit or getting beat by some basket case that meant her no good. Yuh mother has never allowed that."

"True," Walee remarked. "To be real, you the first man any of us ever met that she had an interest in. So, what happened between you and your mums?"

"Mums?" Dunkirk smiled. "As I got older, I got bigger and stronger. But me mums still brought these schizzos around and I couldn't take it anymore. The last bloke she was with for about two years. He used to beat her bum six ways from Sunday. Used tuh to beat me, too, until I called foul for the very last time."

"What'd you do?"

"I killed the man." Dunkirk responded bluntly. "Beat him to a permanent slumber with the claw end of a hammer."

"You got away with it, or you did time?" Walee asked while staring at Mister Fraser.

"I was seventeen at the time. Was working in a butcher's shop. So, I knew what to do with the guy. Use yuh imagination on that one. My mother, on the other hand, she lived a peaceful life from that point on. She died right after I opened me first real estate office."

Walee remained silent after hearing Dunkirk speak.

"You're the only one I've told of this matter, Walee. Your mother doesn't even know."

"Why you tellin' me this story?" Walee questioned.

"I heard yuh say the n-word over the phone and yuh mums wasn't too pleased in the least. Yuh seem a hard ass. I tell yuh that story not to scare you, but to let you know that I've been worse the lad you are and can handle me self fairly well if need be. You have me permission to chastise me should I ever disrespect Naomi. I've learned from the flawed men of my mum's past how to treat a woman I care about. And yuh mother I care about. I hope to make that clearer as time wears on."

Walee slid a bishop over the board and said, "Checkmate, Mister Fraser."

Dunkirk laughed as he grabbed the bottle of whiskey and poured a shot for him and Walee. "Last one," he said as he quickly downed the drink. "You're a smart man, Mister Dawkins. And I understand your concern over yuh mums. I was the same way for a while, but my fears were justified. Yuh shouldn't fear the change Naomi is going through now. I'm not the bad guy. I'm just a man who digs yuh mother and seeks yuh respect. Everybody's respect."

"I know my moms," Walee replied. "Whether we approve or not, if she wants you around, you'll be around. I'm not gone act like a spoiled brat or even try and talk her out of it. I don't think none of us will. I appreciate you sharing that story with me, we just gone chill and see what happens. Make yourself at home, bruh," he ended as eased up from the barstool.

"Not another game?"

"Nah, let's go chill with the family, Kirk."

"Kirk?" Dunkirk chuckled. "I like that name. My friends call me Kirk."

"I ain't saying all that there, but it's all good for now," Walee replied as he extended his hand and gave Dunkirk a firm handshake before the two walked out of the private room.

CHAPTER SIXTEEN

WET PISTOLS

Back out on the patio, the atmosphere was still good-natured and relaxing as the sun began to sink low in the sky. Bay and Tiva were sitting out on the hood of Bay's Lincoln discussing the issue with Candace when Bay's phone rung. "Yo," she answered upon recognizing Jay-D's number.

"What up, fam? How soon can somebody from upstairs make it back this way?" Jay-D asked as he stood before Kree's dining room table sipping brandy while loading shells into various magazines, his hands covered with latex gloves.

"What's up?" Bay asked as she snapped her fingers to get Tiva's attention. The two climbed into Bay's Lincoln and sat behind the tint as Bay started the engine and placed the phone on speaker.

"The Germans came through earlier today," Jay-D let it be known as Kree placed a polished chrome .44 semi-automatic and two black steel .45 calibers onto the table before him and began assisting with the loading of the magazines, she herself wearing latex gloves in imitation of her tutor/lover.

"Who it was, Jay?" Tiva asked while looking down at the phone.

"That chick Tanya, and her daughter Boogie. Loopy was on hand and shit damn near popped off. After everything got settled, Loopy asked to talk ta' you and Bay specifically, T-top. And Kantrell been wanting to talk to Ben over that deal with Malik."

"Dawk already told us about Kantrell. Ben gone get at y'all in a couple of days. What them feds be like down there, though?" Bay asked.

"Got some new info on that. Laddy and his partner having an

affair. If we can get proof of that there, we can shut his investigation down."

Bay and Tiva eyed one another seriously and nodded simultaneously. They'd just been given a potential out that could allow them to start moving freely in Saint Louis once again. "Twenty racks for anybody that can get photos of them together." Bay remarked.

"And at worse, if Laddy was to land a bust, we can get the lawyer to ask him under oath about the affair with Sandra Cordova." Tiva added.

"I already paid the sheriff who put me up on it off with five racks, so just drop another fifteen for the chick I'm gone get to set everything up. I'm gone have her go in Cordova house tomorrow while her and Laddy out in the field so we good on that. When y'all be through, though?" Jay-D asked as Kree pulled back the chamber on one of the .45s, clicked on the infrared beam and held the gun out sideways.

"Ben out the country right now. Just keep your phone lit and we gone let you know when we swoop down. Should be in a couple days or so like I said," Bay replied. "You gone have to be ready to rendezvous that day wherever we meet because we gotta be in and out until we get things straight with Laddy and Cordova."

"Gotcha," Jay-D responded coolly before ending the call. He then dialed up another number to get the ball rolling on Laddy and Sandra.

"Jay-D, what up, homeboy?" twenty-four-year-old Jessica 'Jessie' Suede, a slender sister standing 5'8" with skin the color of milk chocolate, answered as she sat out on the basketball court in Fox Park.

"I got a job for ya', fam. You can make a quick fifteen racks if you down."

"Yeah," Jessie replied seriously as she drooped her head. "What all I gotta do like that?"

"Easy," Jay-D replied. "I got a key to a house where I need you to set up some cameras. The good shit ya' feel? High def, motion detectors and everything."

"Who these people is?" Jessie asked as she leaned forward and rubbed her chin.

"Come see me today and I'll put you up on it. Meet me behind the long warehouse off Saint Claire over in East Saint Louis in about an hour."

"I'm on my way," Jessie remarked nonchalantly as she hung up the phone.

Jay-D ended the call, looked over to Kree and said, "What I told you about holding a gun sideways like that, girl?"

"It feels better this way, babe," Kree answered as she set the .45 down and picked up a .44 semi-automatic. "Unt, unt. This one too big," she complained as she quickly set the .44 back down onto the table.

"I heard that before from you," Jay-D smirked.

Kree nudged Jay-D playfully with her elbow as she slid before him. "That gun you got in your pants I can handle, love," she cooed. "But why I can't hold it sideways? And why I can't use my .380 still?"

"That shit for the movies, holding the gun sideways. And I told you we had ta' get rid of that .380 because you got a body on it now. These guns you got from the pawn shop yesterday gone serve you right once you get used to the recoil, baby," Jay-D said as he stood behind Kree and picked up one of the black .45 semi-automatics. He pressed up against her rear as he clasped his hands around hers, the two of them holding onto the gun as he raised it.

Kree shook her head to remove strands of her pinned up, curly black hair from before her brown eyes as Jay-D held the gun and righted it in her hands. "Will I have to kill somebody else again?" she humbly asked.

"Look at 'em," Jay-D whispered into Kree's ear. "That's that boy Max down there. He tried to kill your man that night. What you gone do with it?" he asked as he kissed the nape of Kree's neck and removed his hands from the gun.

Kree held the gun steady, aiming it at the picture on the wall at the end of her hallway as she clicked on the infrared beam. "If he's tryin' to hurt you what you think I'm gone do?" she asked in sexy voice as she closed her right eye to get a better aim on the picture at the end of the hall.

"It's kill or be killed when you rollin' with me, baby. You down enough to do another job like you did on Max a few weeks ago for daddy if need be?" Jay-D asked as he palmed Kree's ass cheeks.

"Anytime you need me to, Jason," Kree answered lowly as she reflected on the night she'd taken a life for the first time ever, nearly four weeks ago, at Jay-D's behest...

...*"I don't know how...someone controlled you...they bought and sold you...I look at the world...and I notice....it's still turning...while my guitar...gently weeps..."*

The melodic piano and pounding drums to Eric Clapton's song **While My Guitar Gently Weeps** *played even inside of Kree's Maxima as she sat parked just down from the entrance to Malik's Grill. It was nearing eleven 'o' clock p.m. on this early May 2009 night and the block was void of pedestrians in this working-class neighborhood. Kree's car and Malik's Benz jeep that was parked directly in front of the door and other cars were parked along the street, but activity was nonexistent as most were home in bed asleep preparing for the next work day.*

A few minutes earlier, Jay-D had gone inside the closed diner to talk to twenty-one-year-old Maximillian 'Max' Zamora. Kree sat nodding her head to the classic rock song with her .380 resting in her lap while thinking deeply about what she'd co-signed onto barely an hour before.

The end result, however, was all that mattered to her at this point in time, because Jay-D had promised her something special during their ride over to see Max. He'd called her while she was over to her home in Saint Charles relaxing in bed watching TV and told her he needed her help over to Malik's Grill. Eager to get next to her budding love, Kree dressed in a pair of tight-fitting jeans and blouse and low heels and met up with Jay-D over to his home just a few miles away in the same city. He emerged from his home on Lindenwood Avenue and climbed into the passenger seat of her Maxima and set a duffle bag down in between his feet.

"Hey, baby," Kree smiled as she leaned over to kiss Jay-D. Jay-D responded by leaning over and French kissing Kree, allowing their tongues to move smoothly over one another as he cupped her soft lower jaw and ran his hands through her silky, black hair.

Kree was always testing the boundaries with Jay-D. True enough, they'd had sex, but Kree was really trying to be Jay-D's one and only. She didn't have all the lady parts, which went without saying, but everything she did, was in the true essence of a real woman. She wasn't sure how Jay-D would take her gesture as they'd only kissed during the few times they'd had intercourse, but the way he'd tenderized the moment had her head up in the clouds. "Where're we going, love?" she asked upon breaking the smooch.

"Head over to Malik's diner," Jay-D replied as he leaned down and unzipped the duffle bag.

Kree pulled from in front the Cottonwood home and rode down the well-lit block. She bent the corner at the end, making a right turn onto Elm Street as she cruised past the New Orleans Café and Club Indigo. "So, what we doing, Jason?" she asked happily as she headed down to North Kingshighway Street.

Jay-D came up with a tightly-wrapped white package. "You know Dawk, right?" he asked casually as he held up the brick.

"Yeah," Kree responded a little unnerved as she made a right turn on red and left the suburb. "Did he do something to you?"

Jay-D looked over to Kree and said, "Nah, baby. Somebody did something to Dawk. He called me and asked to handle some business for 'em tonight."

"You need me to help you make a sell tonight," Kree nodded as she rode onto First Capitol Drive. "Where's Dooney and Nancy?"

"They at the house," Jay-D responded matter-of-factly as he kicked back with the gun in his lap. "But I wanna know how down for me you really are. You already know what I do for a living so it ain't nothing new to ya'. You and me? We good for each other. I been looking for a chick that could get down with me. Somebody willing to ride for me, understand?"

"So that's the stipulation in this relationship, Jason? I have to prove my love by helping you deal drugs?" Kree asked a little disappointed as she reached the junction of First Capitol Drive and I-70.

"Nah," Jay-D replied calmly as he held onto the package. "This here a costume, baby. You gone have to help me kill a nigga tonight," he let it be known.

"Really?" Kree asked slyly as she cut her eyes over to Jay-D. "And what makes you think I'm capable of helping you do something like that, Jason?"

205

"You already got the life in you, you just ain't been taught right," Jay-D explained as he pulled out a half-smoked blunt.

"You gone teach me how to kill somebody, Jason?" Kree smirked as she merged onto I-70 east, headed towards downtown Saint Louis.

"That's right," Jay-D nodded as he eyed Kree out the side of his left eye while lighting his stogie.

Kree swallowed deeply as she sped up and caught up with the flow of traffic on I-70 eastbound. Her question was meant to be taken in a joking fashion, but she knew right away that Jay-D was dead serious in his speech.

"Why me? Why you wanna bring me into your lifestyle, Jason? You don't know if I would rat on you under pressure from the law or just run my mouth on whatever it is that you doing out here while doing hair over to Bangin' Heads."

"Why you held them bricks for me when I got back on?" Jay-D asked as he toked on the blunt.

"'Cause you needed my help."

"And?" Jay-D followed up with as he exhaled smoke through his nostrils.

"You asked me to." Kree confessed as her dark-tinted Maxima on chrome wheels floated down I-70.

"I'm gone be honest with you, baby," Jay-D said as he sat up in the seat and set the doctored-up kilogram of cocaine back inside his duffle bag. "If what I'm about to do gone mess with your head you ain't gotta do it. You can jump off at the next exit and take me back to my house and me and my people could just handle things."

"What, you think I can't go through with it? You think I'm not woman enough to kill somebody?" Kree sassed.

"Shit, I don't know," Jay-D chuckled as he kicked back in the passenger seat once more and took another toke. "Show me something, girl. I'm tryna put you on some game. You brought your .380 with you like I asked you to?" he asked through a raspy voice while blowing smoke out his mouth.

"Yeah, I brought it. But, what if I don't wanna do it? Would that change things between you and I?" Kree asked as she drove past the exit Jay-D had offered up to her in order to allow her to back out of the deal.

"*It wouldn't change a thing, baby. Real talk,*" *Jay-D responded as he reached out his left hand and rubbed Kree's right thigh.* "*But look at this,*" *he said as he extended his right hand.* "*We riding, you and me, going do some gangsta shit. And we gone get away with it. I'm gone kill Max tonight whether you home fixing me dinner in one of them sexy ass negligees you be wearing, or where you at right now—taking me to do a job—because it's what I do for a living. You gone be my Bonnie, or you gone go on back to the house and play wifey? I'm good with ya' either way.*"

Kree's eyes welled up at that moment. Jay-D was kicking some real shit. His resume` was made known the night he'd killed her ex-boyfriend Alonzo Milton and had taken over his record label. She kept quiet on that deal out of fear in the beginning, but her fear had quickly turned to adoration the more she observed Jay-D. She loved him. Plain and simple. Not only that, she trusted Jay-D with her life and believed in her heart that he would never put her into harm's way. What he was asking was dangerous, no doubt, but Kree would only be lying to herself if she said she wasn't curious about her man's lifestyle. Kantrell had told her a few days after the conversation inside Jay-D's home where she confronted him about Malik, that Jay-D was bad business, but Kree didn't see it that way. Jason David Cottonwood's lifestyle was exciting to her. It was a life she wanted to explore, if only for one night in order to get a taste of what her man was involved in.

"*You wanna ride through downtown before we head to Malik's spot?*" *Kree asked.*

"*That's cool. But, you down with me on this here thing, though?*" *Jay-D asked while continuously rubbing Kree's thigh.*

"*I'm down, baby.*" *Kree blushed.* "*You're, you're arousing me with your touch and it's embarrassing, Jason. I'm 'bout to bust out my jeans over here.*"

"*What's new?*" *Jason chuckled as he reached for the zipper on Kree's jeans. He sprung her organ free and began stroking it slow and sensual as he toked on the weed while the two of them floated down I-70 headed east.*

In the same manner in which Jay-D was seducing Kree into a homicide, Kree had the same ability to seduce him into her world each and every time. His attraction to her was intoxicating, and she knew how to do and say the right things each and every time.

207

Tonight was no different as these two went back and forth in their romantic dance that had a violent backdrop.

"You always rub it, but you never kissed it yet," Kree playfully pouted as she lay back in the driver's seat and hunched her hips forward just a little bit while guiding her Maxima into downtown Saint Louis.

Jay-D cracked the window and flicked the blunt out with his right hand while removing his left hand from Kree's stiff dick. "We need to get into focus on what we doing," he remarked. "You do this thing with Max, I do that for you after we done."

Kree looked Jay-D off with a sly smile on her face. "Are...are we really trading sex for murder?" she chuckled as she looked back over to her beau. "If that's the case you gone have to lick and kiss me everywhere down there and then make love to me while I'm on my back. I wanna stare up into your eyes and kiss you over and over again while you're taking me."

"If that's what you want, you got that, girl," Jay-D responded as he righted himself in the seat.

"Really?" Kree smiled as she drove past the Saint Louis skyline with her rod poking out from her unzipped jeans. "We'll see how serious you are. I never liked Max anyway," she added as she straightened herself and jumped onto I-44 west and took the Jefferson Avenue exit, which led to McKinley Heights, where Malik's Grill lay.

Kree sat watching and waiting for Jay-D ad Max to emerge from Malik's Grill. The plan was for her to tail Jay-D and Max in Malik's jeep over to Gravois Park, a rundown neighborhood south of Fox Park that could be accessed via the infamous Jefferson Avenue. Jay-D was going to drop off four bricks to a customer just off Potomac Street and needed Max for muscle. Once the deal was done, Jay-D would jump into Kree's car and he and Max would split up from there was the story. Kree was to walk up and put two in the back of Max's head while he sat behind the wheel and Jay-D would handle the rest.

When Jay-D emerged with Max, Kree's stomach churned. She was now in on a murder plot and wasn't sure if she had the guts to go through with it all. She'd said she never really liked Max, but truth was, the guy was harmless in her eyes. She coughed and tried to put on a calm face when Jay-D began walking her way. He opened the passenger door and grabbed his duffle bag that *contained four tightly-wrapped plastic bags of flour made to look like four bricks of cocaine.*

"He gone pull up in an alleyway on Potomac," Jay-D explained. *"When he do, I'm gone climb out and walk off with this here bag. All you gotta do is get out and make small talk while he sitting behind the wheel. He gone be loose, so all you gotta do is point and shoot. You can handle that?"*

"I th—yeah. I can do it." Kree mumbled while looking Jay-D off.

"Baby," Jay-D called out. He then looked back over to Max, who'd just locked up the diner and was pulling out the keys to Malik's jeep while walking towards the driver's side of the SUV. *"If you get nervous and can't go through with it, just get out your car and stretch and stay put. I'll handle it, and I won't even be mad at you. Don't even think like that. But this nigga a light weight, though. I know you can do it. That boy coulda set me up like Malik tried ta' do Dawk. Think about that there. How would you feel if he killed your man instead?"*

"I don't wanna think about that," Kree said as she turned and looked Jay-D directly in the eyes. *"I'll be okay. And if not, I'll do like you say and stretch."*

"We on point with it then," Jay-D said as he threw the duffle bag over his shoulder, closed the door and trotted over to the passenger side of the idling jeep and hopped into the passenger side.

The SUV pulled off a few seconds later and Kree placed her car in drive. She tailed Jay-D with anxiety, wondering if Max was on to her man's plan as she made a left turn onto Park Avenue and followed the Benz jeep down to Jefferson Avenue and made another left turn. The trio rode under I-44 and cruised past the infamous McDonald's in Fox Park and crossed over Cherokee Street and entered Gravois Park. Neglected, boarded up brownstones lined the block and d-boy cars, the souped-up Crown Vics and Cutlasses and big-body Cadillacs on oversized rims, were parked on either side of the street inside this dilapidated neighborhood that was infested with drugs and crime.

Rows and rows of abandoned homes whizzed by Kree's window as she followed her man into the realm of uncertainty. The brake lights on the jeep lit up and Max made a right turn onto Potomac Street. Kree's palms grew sweaty as she gripped her .380 with her eyes focused on the seat where she knew Jay-D was sitting. Over and over again, she kept telling herself to just point and shoot.

"Point and shoot. But what if Max see my gun?" Kree asked herself as Max turned left into an alleyway. She pulled in behind the SUV and shut her lights down and racked her pistol just as Jay-D emerged from the passenger side of the SUV with the duffle bag. The alleyway was dark, save for a lone light from a pole that had piles of trash and a dingy, velvet chair sitting underneath it. The backyards of homes were on either side, but Kree could tell that most were empty given the wood covering the windows. Several cats scurried as Jay-D rounded the rear of the SUV and eyed Kree seriously over the hood of her Maxima before disappearing behind a wooden fence.

When Jay-D cleared out, Kree climbed from her car with her . 380 in her left hand. "You okay up there, Max?" she asked in a humble, low tone.

Max looked out the driver's side window back at Kree and smiled. "You and Jay got something going on, boy? What the fuck he doing leaving with your faggot ass for tonight?" the muscular twenty-one-year-old Mexican asked while laughing and gripping a .357 magnum.

"I worked late at Bangin' Heads. You know we live in the same town," Kree chuckled as she waved Max off with her right hand.

Max knew what Malik had been up to on this night up in Chicago. As far as he knew, Dawk had been killed in the Windy City. Had Jay-D brought along Dooney and Nancy, he would've suspected something. Kree being with Jay-D, however, had him under the belief that the Cottonwoods knew nothing about the coup underway. When Jay-D returned, he was going to check for the money, and then kill him inside Malik's Benz once they got to rolling again. He would then pull off in an inconspicuous area and wave Kree over and kill her, too, before placing both of their bodies inside of Kree's Maxima and leaving them dead on the spot.

Max's plan went unbeknownst to Kree as she neared the driver's side of the Benz jeep. The Mexican noticed how stiff her left arm was and began raising his pistol slowly. "What y'all doing when we leave here, Kree?" he asked through cautious eyes while hanging out the window.

It was the way Max had posed the question, as if he was trying to keep her calm, that had forced Kree into action. She could see his right arm coming out the window with a bulky object in his hand so she raised her gun and fired off three rounds in seemingly slow motion. A bullet hit the driver's side mirror, shattering it as Max fell off inside the jeep. Kree stumbled over a garbage bag and caught her balance while shuffling sideways with her brown eyes honed in on the interior of the Benz. She could see blood splatter on the windshield, and Max slumped over in the driver's seat, so she knew she'd hit him at least once over her three shots.

"Oh my god," Kree whispered as she held on to her .380 and peered inside the SUV, only to see Max draped over the console with blood spurting from the left side of his neck.

Jay-D emerged from behind the fence at that moment and walked up on the driver's side of the jeep. "You got 'em," he told Kree in a calm voice as he threw the duffle bag over into the passenger seat. He then removed a can of lighter fluid and doused the interior of the jeep with the flammable liquid, making sure to drench Max's body, and the seat where he sat in order to destroy any remaining DNA evidence he'd left behind. "Get back ya' car," he commanded Kree as he pulled a butane lighter from his pocket.

Kree trotted back to her car on wobbly legs and climbed into the passenger seat. She was way too nervous to drive and now wanted Jay-D to take charge as she'd given him every ounce of strength she had to offer upon killing Max. She sat with her legs trembling and watched as Jay-D tossed the lighter into the jeep's interior. Yellow flames lit up her face and the interior of her car and she watched stone-faced as fire danced off of Max's slumped-over corpse. When Jay-D climbed inside and sped off, she exhaled and laid her head back. "I can't believe we just did that!" she exclaimed in a shocked voice.

"But it was easy, right?" Jay-D asked calmly as he wheeled the car out of the neighborhood.

"I guess." Kree remarked lowly. "What now?"

"Shit, you hungry? Let's go home and fix dinner. I owe you something remember?" Jay-D smirked as he reached out and rubbed Kree's thigh. "You did good back there, baby. You did damn good."...

...Kree reflected on that night as the feel of Jay-D's hands on her butt cheeks brought her back to the present. "You gone start something touchin' me like that, boy," she cooed while licking her lips and gripping the .45 with both of her latex-covered hands.

"Like that's a bad thing," Jay-D responded as he ran his own latex-covered hands over Kree's flat stomach. He then moved his hands down to her Capri pants and tugged on the zipper.

Instantly aroused, Kree set the semi-automatic down, removed her latex gloves and assisted Jay-D with the removal of her pants. Naked from the waist down, she spread herself over the table before the loaded pistols and felt the head of Jay-D's pole sliding up and down her crack. "Jason," she moaned as her head rested in her folded arms. "Get it wet for me, baby."

Two smacks on either side of her cheeks forced Kree to twerk a few times while waiting to be penetrated. Jay-D spat onto the fingertips of one of his latex gloves and ran his hand up and down Kree's crevice, coating her opening with his slick saliva as she reached back and spread herself. She grimaced in slight pain as she was slowly filled with her lover's stiff pole.

Pain turned to pleasure as Kree impaled herself on Jay-D's dick, pushing all the way back until her cheeks rested up against his hips. *"Dios mío. Te sientes tan bien dentro de mi, Jason."* (Oh, my god. You feel so good inside me, Jason.) she said as she reached a hand down began stroking herself to arrival.

Jay-D pulled off the gloves, his polo shirt, and then gripped Kree's hips. The two rocked together as he hunched over her petite frame and tongued her from behind while stroking her long, slow and deep. *"Te quiero bebé."* (I love you, baby.) Kree had taught Jay-D how to say those four specific words to her in Spanish, and it was no lie. The adept killer meant it each and every time he whispered it into her ears during their lovemaking.

Jay-D's pace quickened and so did Kree's. She removed her hand from her organ and rose up and bent her legs, sitting down in her man's lap as he took her from behind. Her opening grew damper the more Jay-D stroked her as he was hitting her spot. With her mouth agape, and her hair matted over her face, Kree tilted her head upwards and raised her hands to palm the back of Jay-D's braided hair. *"Vas a hacerme venir tan duro. No dejar de joder a mí, bebé."* (You're going to make me come so hard. Don't stop fucking me, baby.) she moaned while kissing him passionately.

"You there?" Jay-D said as he bit his bottom lip and drove harder and deeper. "I'm coming in this mutherfucka!" he groaned as he flooded Kree's insides while steadily stroking her deep.

"Yes, just like…like that! Like that! Like that! Like…like that!" Kree screamed aloud as she froze in place and erupted, spitting semen halfway across the table.

"Damn," Jay-D laughed as he slid out of Kree and moved to her right. "You came all over the pistols, girl."

"I guess I was fully-loaded," Kree said out of breath while resting on her elbows and looking over to Jay-D laughing. She leaned in with puckered lips and he met her with a passionate, wet kiss while running his hands through her sweaty hair. "You ready to go and meet Jessie?"

"You ready ta' learn how shoot these guns right?"

"Yeah, love. I'm ready to bust some iron," Kree smiled as she rose up from the table. "I'll run us a shower. You need me to iron you some new clothes?" she asked as she sashayed off naked from the waist down with her lover's liquid running down the inside of her thighs.

"Nah, but you get this DNA up off this steel before we leave, girl." Jay-D playfully chided.

"Whatever," Kree laughed as she disappeared into her hallway.

Thirty minutes later, Kree was following Jay-D out of her home with a loaded .45 in her left hand. They climbed into her Maxima with Kree behind the wheel and began making their way over to East Saint Louis in order to meet up with Jessie after a hot shower and a fresh change of clothes.

"You gone have to get use to the recoil on this one here," Jay-D counseled while putting the .45 caliber on display as Kree sped down I-70, headed east.

When Kree didn't respond, Jay-D looked over to her. "You all right, baby?"

"This the same way we went that night we did that thing," Kree stated in a somber tone. "Every time I come this way I think about that night."

"What you think about like that?"

"How easy it was, believe it or not. He died quick."

"Nigga had a gun on him, though. He was gone shoot you that night."

"I know. That's why I don't feel bad about it," Kree remarked as she rode into downtown Saint Louis.

"What you do if nigga shoot back at you, though? Or the police run up screaming and yelling and shit for you ta' lay the fuck down?"

"I would hope that I would have a chance to shoot back in the first instance," Kree reasoned as she merged onto I-55 and began crossing the Mississippi River. "The police, though? I'm surrendering and I ain't even lying to you. I'll take my chances at trial if I make it there."

Jay-D merely smirked over his lover's remark as he looked down at the muddy waters of Ole Man River. He could've gone deep with it and talked about what Carmella Lapiente` had done the day she killed Coban, Gaggi, Lucky and Mildred, but she wasn't on that level yet by a longshot, and he wasn't about to set her out like that knowing she wasn't ready. The bricks she held for him and the job on Max was work enough for her to have put in, but just in case the fuck jumped off, he was intent on steadily teaching Kree how to handle guns in order to defend herself if ever the occasion warranted itself.

The duo made it over to East Saint Louis and exited off Saint Claire Avenue and rode underneath the pylons and pulled into the old warehouse complex where Dawk had unloaded the last shipment of cocaine with Natalia III. The place had a lot of history as it was once the same locale where Carmella Lapiente` had once operated.

The abandoned warehouses of Saint Claire Avenue was still a well-hidden place to conduct business. It was also a good spot to bust off rounds, which was Jay-D's plan for Kree for a spell while he met up with Jessie. He guided her through the dirt and gravel parking lot in between the two red-bricked, worn out warehouses on his right and left and had her drive down the left side of the long hulled-out three-story warehouse that spanned the parking lot and round the bend.

When she did so, Jay-D saw twenty-four-year-old Jessica 'Jessie' Suede facing him while sitting on the hood of a navy blue 1984 tricked-out Cutlass T-top with twenty-eight-inch chrome wheels and dark tint. The decrepit rail flatcars that Dawk Holland had maneuvered past the night he met up with Natalia III were still in place along with the rusted-out engines that were still anchored to the bed. The place hadn't changed at all since the last deal was made here several months prior, which was a good thing in Jay-D's mind's eye. He climbed from passenger seat of the Maxima under the bright spring evening sun with Kree following his lead.

"When you get this whip, bruh?" Jay-D asked as he walked over to Jessie and gave her a fist pound.

Jessie removed her sunshades and said, "Had it for like two months now, fam." She was sporting a pair of powder blue nylon shorts with white spandex underneath, a white tank top, spanking new powder blue and white Jordan's with white wave cap covering her wavy hair while holding onto a freshly-rolled blunt in her left hand.

Jessica 'Jessie' Suede was a stud. She had an insatiable appetite for women and could run game with the best of them. Besides dishing out fresh fades over to Bangin' Heads, she was a tech-savvy woman who, in times past, had bribed women that were on the downlow by recording their sexual escapades and threatening to reveal it to the world if said woman didn't pay her to keep quiet. She'd been up against an attempted murder charge for breaking a woman's neck back in 2007, but Loopy and Sweet Pea had sprung her when they'd killed a witness who was going to testify against her in that particular case.

Jessie also had a history with Kree Devereaux. The two had shared an apartment in Fox Park before Kree got her own place. She was actually Kree's first, and best friend, but a lot had changed since the day Kree was shot by her previous lover's wife back in May of 2007. Kree began searching for love, and she'd found it in Jay-D.

Jessie, on the other hand, had returned to her hustle, but she'd put a twist on it after facing a forty-year stint for attempted murder. She now slept with strictly married women with money willing to pay her for her services. Everything was out in the open with Jessie and her chosen lovers, but she still had the ability to set up surveillance if need be. When Jay-D called, and put a $15,000 dollar job on the line, the slender, chocolate sister with the fresh bald fade and dark, slender eyes couldn't resist.

"What's up, Kree?" Jessie asked, her broad, slender lips parting to produce a wide, beautiful smile sporting pearl white teeth. "With your new love and shit. I'm happy for you, girl," she added as she lit up her blunt.

"Ain't nothin'," Kree answered as she looked around while picking at her curls.

Jessie took a deep toke off her blunt while eyeing Jay-D and Kree. "Y'all two mutherfuckas look like y'all just got through fuckin'," she laughed as she snorted while holding the smoke in.

"Jay, where I'm gone shoot, baby?" Kree asked, slightly embarrassed. *"Is it that obvious?"* she silently wondered.

"Shoot?" Jessie laughed as she released a cloud of bubble gum Kush in to the air. "What you gone shoot like that with your scary self? You plan on bodying somebody, Kree?"

Kree looked over to Jay-D and blushed before walking off. Knowing she'd gotten away with murder was an exhilarating feeling in its own right, but she would never acknowledge it as that was her and Jay-D's secret for all times. One of the flatcars had a stack of wood chained down, Kree noticed. "I'll aim at the wood while you two talk," she told Jay-D as she walked back over to her Maxima and grabbed the .45 from underneath the driver's seat.

"Yeah, y'all fucked before comin' over here," Jessie laughed as she dapped Jay-D. "Take care my girl, homeboy," she added as she passed him the blunt.

"Ion know where your mouth been like that, girl." Jay-D smirked.

Jessie reared back with curled lips and chuckled. "My mouth been on some clean pussy, nigga. If you give head like I do, where your mouth been, bruh?"

Jay-D took the blunt from Jessie took several pulls before handing it back to her just as gunshots from Kree rang out. "You can handle the kickback, baby?" Jay-D looked back and asked.

"Yeah," Kree smiled slyly. She then tilted the gun sideways.

"This ain't the movies, bitch!" Jessie blurted out. "Tilt that shit upright and fire it off!"

"Just messing with him," Kree smirked as she righted the gun and let off a few more rounds.

"So, what's this shit you got going on, my dude?" Jessie asked as she toked on the weed stem.

"My people got the feds all up in they shit, ya' feel me?" Jay-D disclosed. "One Time I got on the payroll laid some shit on me about how I can get 'em off my family ass."

"The feds fuckin'?" Jessie asked through laughter as she jumped off the hood of her Cutlass. "Niggaaaa," she sang as she walked to the rear of her ride and used a key to unlock the truck. "I'm gone do them hoes dirty like they do everybody else out here. Check this shit out!"

Jay-D walked to the rear of the Cutlass just as Jessie raised the trunk and took a step back. He peered over into the bucket and eyed a chrome laptop with three, small black buttons in an even row laid across the top. "What's all this?" he asked curiously as Kree let off a few more rounds.

"That's a Mac computer and the latest remote control motion detection cameras. Them shits is small enough to place out in the open and they pick up everything in hi-def. Voices and all. You can link them shits up together, ya' feel me? Whenever the cameras pick up motion? I get a notification on the laptop and it start recording the shit no matter where I'm at and whether the laptop in use or not."

"How much this shit it cost, Jessie?" Jay-D asked while smiling and nodding his head in approval.

"You don't need ta' know all that. I got a bitch work for a security company that gave me this shit a couple of months ago. They put ADT and CPI asses to sleep. This some spy shit, fam. I ain't never had use for it, but for fifteen racks? Just say I'm offering you top-of-the-line shit and gone get the job done."

"Alright," Jay-D nodded as he went into his baggy jeans and pulled out a key with a sticky note attached. "The address on there, already. I told my people you be in there tomorrow with the setup so you gotta get it installed tomorrow."

"If they out the house we in business, bruh," Jessie nodded as she eyed her equipment. "This here for those two twins Kree told me about?" she then asked.

"What's it to ya'? What she told you like that?" Jay-D asked as he cut his eyes over to Jessie.

"Nah, it ain't like that. Kree down like a mutherfucka, man," Jessie laughed. "She just told me about the day her and Kantrell rolled up on the set when these twins was out there. She said one of 'em was eyein' her like she wanted to get down but she didn't know Kree was transgendered and had eyes for you. One of them twins swing the other way, Jay?" she asked slyly.

"You gone have to find all that out for yourself. Ion know about that shit there," Jay-D remarked in a serious tone.

"If I see 'em, I'm gone get Kree to point her out, bruh—just lettin' you know what my incentive is on top of these fifteen racks," Jessie replied as she eased the trunk down and locked it in place.

"If that is what it is? She gone be all the way up on who you is and what you do and did," Jay-D let it be known as he walked back to the front of the car.

"Tell that bitch. That's what I want you to do, Jay," Jessie stressed while smiling proudly and following behind Jay-D. "If it's what I think it is, she gone wanna fuck with me on the strength of what I done, my nig'. I know it's all business, but a celebration be in order if I knock the feds off that chick ass. I wanna see who she is. Tell her about me when this shit all said and done 'cause I'm gone come through without fail, homeboy," she disclosed as she took a toke off the blunt and passed it back to Jay-D before resting up against the hood of her ride.

Jessie didn't know it, but she was planning on making a move on Bena Holland. Kree had described her as being that of a statuesque, tan-skinned black woman with short, curly black hair and dark, glistening eyes, pink lips and the most beautiful smile she'd seen in quite some time. She knew Bay was attracted to her until she learned her true identity through Jay-D that day.

It was a conversation in mere passing between Jessie and Kree the day after she and Kantrell had rode up on Club Indigo, the way people often just conversate over much of nothing, but Jessie had never forgotten the portrait Kree had painted the day after she had the twins. Jessie now had to see for herself this woman Kree had described to her, if only to end her burning curiosity, and see if she herself could bag what she'd deemed as that of a gangster bitch as she'd never achieved such a conquest. She knew of the Holland family's reputation nonetheless having ran with Loopy, Sweet Pea,

Pepper and Simone not too long ago, and to sleep with one would be just a notch under her belt in her eyes and nothing more.

"You think you can fuck every chick in the world, huh?" Jay-D chuckled as he rested up against the hood of the Cutlass beside Jessie and passed the blunt back to Jessie.

"My game just that tight, fella," Jessie boasted as she put the blunt to her lips and sucked in potent dope.

Bay was supposed to be at the Club Indigo on opening night, Jessie knew, but the feds had thrown a monkey wrench into her plan. She was disappointed not to have met the woman Kree described to her, but she believed if she came through for Jay-D, she would finally get to meet the woman who'd been dancing through her mind for some time now, even though she'd never met her in person. The money didn't matter for Jessie, although it was a nice addition. Her main driving force was one of sexual conquest. The job ahead was a mere formality in her mind's eye as Jay-D wasn't one to play games and she knew the money was good.

"We see what happen with it after I do this lick," Jessie said as she exhaled smoke from her lungs. "Let's help your shorty with this gun, though," she ended as she pushed off the hood and walked over towards Kree, who was busy placing another magazine into her .45 caliber.

CHAPTER SEVENTEEN

GET YOURS

While Jay-D and Kree parlayed inside of Kree's home, back over to the ranch, the party was in full swing as the exciting Sunday rolled on. The sun had dipped behind the trees atop Ne'Ne's Hill and the summer's heat was giving way to a cool breeze as the family and friends milled about on the patio and out in the open field. To the far right of the patio sat Dunkirk and Naomi. The two were enthralled in delightful conversation while watching the family enjoy themselves as they signed the last of the documents in order to formally close out on their deal on the shopping malls the family now owned.

"I think this will be a good investment for your family," Dunkirk said as he signed a document that turned over all tax responsibilities to Holland-Dawkins Enterprises. "Being we're nearing the end of our business arrangement, Naomi, I'm inclined to ask where do we go from here?"

Naomi signed off on the final document and said through a smile, "You know where I am, Fraser. If ever you want to see me, all you have to do is pick up the phone. I'll be here to greet you stateside."

"I'd like things much better if I were to call you from a home in Oklahoma City and ride over and have lunch with ya', me lady." Dunkirk countered.

"You have a place in Oklahoma City?"

"Not yet, but I'm sure it's nothing I can't accomplish through the aide of yuh real estate company now. We've just closed out on a fifty million dollar deal today. My take is thirty million dollars, Naomi. As of now? I'm retired from the business. I haven't any obligations."

Naomi leaned back and stared at Dunkirk seriously. She'd be lying to herself if she said she wasn't feeling the man, but she didn't want to move too fast. "I'd love to see you further, Fraser."

"But?"

"A home so close would mean, well, I have a lot going on and I'm not sure that I can commit to a relationship at the moment."

"I'm too forthcoming," Dunkirk smiled while nodding his head. "Forgive me forcefulness. It's just that when I want something, I tend to put me all into it. I didn't mean to impose."

"I'm flattered, Fraser. Tell you what? I'll have my realty staff look into some properties around the country and put together a list of homes in various cities. I'd rather start out on neutral ground."

Dunkirk spread his hands and said, "I'm already in hostile territory having come under the scrutiny of yuh kids, Naomi. I understand your concerns, though, so I'll abort my plan and follow your lead. I'm curious to know what city here in America you fancy to be a good place for us to see one another."

"I'll be sure to make it worth your while," Naomi remarked through a coy smile. It'd been a long time since she'd felt butterflies, let alone had her center grow moist through mere conversation with the opposite sex. Dunkirk hit all the sensors within Naomi. He gave off good vibes and was a powerful, successful man that held his own and knew what he wanted out of life.

While Naomi occupied herself with stacking the documents, Dunkirk caught sight of Bay, Tiva and Kimi sitting at a table on the other side of the patio. "Excuse me, Naomi. I have got yet to win the hearts of yuh oldest three."

"Bay and Tiva aren't your problem." Naomi chuckled as she shuffled papers.

"Kimi wasn't too fond of meh back inside. But I love me a good challenge." Dunkirk nodded. "Yuh sure this will work now? It's rather bold, Naomi."

"Just do like we discussed and I'll dance with you on the Solomon Islands," Naomi assured.

"Yuh know your offspring, right? Be right back, love."

Dunkirk smiled as he eased up from the table and took in the dozen or so pairs of eyes focused in on him. He strolled across the patio, stopping on occasion for a few seconds to speak to family members as he made his way to the opposite side of the patio where contention lay. As he neared Bay, Tiva and Kimi's table, he could see the three staring at him as they took bites of food. They looked like three lionesses guarding the pride, but there was only one he knew would attack if ever he stepped wrong so he had to handle the situation with tact based on the what he'd been told. He brushed away his anxiety, clapped his hands twice and put on a smile as he approached the table. "Can I sit for a spell, ladies?" he asked politely while tipping his hat.

"The seat empty ain't it?" Kimi sassed.

Dunkirk laughed louder than necessary as he sat beside Kimi. She eased her chair closer to Bay when he did so and picked up two of Regina's stuffed eggs and bit into one while setting the other on her plate.

"I have to ask, Kimi," Dunkirk said as he removed his straw hat. "I've been seeing everyone on the patio eating these little white balls with the yellow mush in the center. What are they?" he asked curiously.

"You never heard of deviled eggs?" Kimi asked dryly while flicking her eyes up and down at Dunkirk.

"Deviled eggs?" Dunkirk smiled. "Why do they call them deviled eggs, Kimi?"

"Because they make ya' shit fire sometimes," Tiva laughed as Bay looked off and chuckled.

"Is that true Kimi? Is that so?"

"Look man," Kimi complained as she set the half-eaten egg down. "You didn't come over here to ask me about no deviled eggs—and what concern of it is to you whether these white balls of yellow mush make me shit fire or not? Don't ask about my ass. What you really wanna know is why I don't like you. And I don't have to answer that question so go on somewhere."

"You're right in all that you say, Kimi, but I will not just go on somewhere." Dunkirk remarked seriously. "I find it hard to understand why a woman as intelligent as yuh self would fancy me a bad guy tuh yuh mums? Do you think I would hurt her heart? Why would I travel thousands of miles and let me self be known tuh everybody to just put up a front for what? I'd be thick as two short planks tuh treat yuh family thataway."

"Thick as two what?" Bay asked. "Translate that, bruh."

Kimi crossed her legs while picking up the deviled egg again and said, "He said it would be very stupid of him. And he ain't even lying."

"I knew it!" Dunkirk laughed. "You've been reading the British slang dictionary I suggested during the shopping mall deal."

"Only because it was necessary at the time." Kimi retorted as she bit into the appetizer.

"Yuh had to dig pretty deep tuh know the terminology. I find it funny that yuh know the meaning of two short planks, but can't answer why these eggs are called deviled ones."

"I thought the deal was stupid in the beginning. And deviled eggs originated in Rome if you must know, Mister Fraser."

"Impressive! But, you were able to get top whack price on the sale in spite of thinking it was stupid. Yuh saw a good deal and yuh leapt on it."

"Top whack mean she got the best price, right?" Bay asked.

"How'd yuh know?" Dunkirk asked as he helped himself to one of the deviled eggs.

"Context clues, man." Bay smiled. "Kimi, you like the dam that's holding back momma's heart, sister. I told you over the phone that no one is going to take—"

"Bay!" Kimi interrupted.

"Yuh fancy meh movin' in on Doss Dawkins Junior." Dunkirk said to Kimi through a nod of understanding after hearing Bay's partial remark. "From what yuh mother's told me he was an exceptional man, Kimi. I couldn't walk a mile in his shoes, and I won't even try."

"Why not? You loving on my momma, right?" Kimi asked as she crossed her legs and eyed Dunkirk.

"I love me Naomi," Dunkirk admitted. "But I've always cut meh own path in life. If the people here are going to like meh? It'll be because I came onto the scene as being that of my own man and not in imitation of the man before me. I'm not here to play daddy. Doss did a fine enough job of raising his children. I'm just another chapter in yuh mother's life. An important one hopefully, but I can only be me."

"You went to charm school in England or something because you smooth, man," Tiva asked through light laughter.

"It comes natural, T-Top. When you're a gentleman and conduct yuh self with respect and treat others the same? It bothers yuh when someone doesn't quite fancy yuh and it forces yuh to get to the heart of the matter. Especially when one hasn't been given the opportunity to prove their worth. I don't think that to be fair treatment." Dunkirk stated as he eyed Kimi.

"I don't have 'tuh' like you." Kimi quoted as she wiped her mouth with a cloth napkin.

Dunkirk nodded. "But can yuh at least respect me?" he sincerely asked.

"I don't have to do that either." Kimi snapped.

"What is it with yuh, Kimi?" Dunkirk asked in a low, but earnest tone. "Sometimes we—"

"This my family," Kimi interrupted. "If I want to feel—"

"Yuh father gave Chablis a chance." Dunkirk interjected, forcing not only Kimi, but Bay and Tiva as well to look over in his direction. "I'm an American collegiate sports fan," he admitted. "It's fascinating to be able to sit up at two or three in the morning and watch some of the best sports ever live from the United Kingdom with a drink and cigar, or something a little extra if that's what one prefers. I saw the report on ESPN the morning everything happened over here. I remembered Shima's last name being mentioned. When me and you all's mother talked off the record, I asked her because I knew her last name was Dawkins as well and se had children in college. She told me the story. I understand the concern, Kimi, but I'm not here to hurt yuh mother. That's all I can say. Take me as I am."

"Through all that, I'm reading that you ain't going nowhere," Bay chimed in. "*With your bad self*" she silently smiled and quoted.

"You're correct, Bena. But this discontent between Kimi and I matters greatly to me. I truly understand her heart. It's a strong, loving one that hates change, but, she's going to change soon when she herself marries. If she's willing to change her heart for love's sake because it makes her happy, why can't she be happy for her mums? Naomi is only looking for the same thing her daughter is due to receive after having lost it once upon a time. One shouldn't be selfish with their happiness when others around them truly deserve it—especially when they've given all they could give to their family without asking for nothing in return but for them to be happy. Why is it a problem when the one who's given the most, asks for just a little bit of happiness in return after sacrificing so much?"

"What *didn't* my momma tell you about us?" Kimi asked as she rolled her eyes to the sky.

"Me Naomi didn't tell me that getting Kimi Dawkins to like me would be easy that's for certain. Yuh mother knows all eight of yuh. I didn't believe her, but she had you all pegged," Dunkirk remarked seriously. "Everything she told me to expect was realized today. Tyke wasn't going to be happy. Spoonie would shrug it off because she was in love with the football player Kahlil. Walee would object, but come around after a conversation. Koko would be all for it. Tiva would be happy. Bay would accept it. And Dawk would have a man-to-man over chess in his father's room before giving his approval based on the man that I am."

"Okay, that's seven. So, what my momma said about me?" Kimi asked.

"She said you would be the one who would take it the hardest because I would remind you of your father and you would be afraid of me for doing so. But she told me to tell you that you would have nothing to fear because I would never take your father's place. And honestly speaking? I have not the desire." Dunkirk confessed as he picked at one of the deviled eggs and took a tentative bite.

Kimi looked over to her mother at that moment as her eyes welled up. Naomi was staring back at her as she sat across the way with a pair of sunshades covering her eyes. The two had traveled onto the same wavelength, speaking with their eyes. Kimi apologizing for being a pretentious self-absorbed bitch, and Naomi accepting her daughter's apology while silently admitting that she could've forewarned her offspring that she had a male friend she'd wanted to invite into their home.

"I just miss my daddy so much," Kimi exhaled through tears and trembling lips as Bay placed an arm around her neck and pulled her close.

"You said you needed me when we talked on the phone while me and Tiva was down to the warehouse in Valley Brook," Bay whispered into her sister's ear. "You know me, Dawk and Tiva's resume' already. If we thought this guy was flaw, you think the three of us would be so nonchalant about him being here? You think Dawk and T-Top would be cool with dude if they suspected something over me?"

"No," Kimi admitted while twirling her thumbs with her head lowered into Bay's bosom in a worshipful manner. "But I wanna know what *you* think, Bay? You think Dunkirk good for momma?"

"Me and the rest of your brothers and sisters all think that Dunkirk is good for momma, Kimi. I already said it and I'm gone repeat it again—you the dam that's holding momma back. Let momma, breath, sister," Bay stated, knowing Kimi valued her opinion above everybody else.

Ever since Kimi could remember, Bay had been her heart. She admired her sister's courage and conviction to be herself no matter what others around Ponca City and elsewhere thought of her above all else. True enough, Bay had often antagonized her when they were younger by stealing her baby dolls, but as she grew older, Kimi realized that Bay had made her durable. And at the same time, she understood that Bay merely wanted her attention. She just didn't know how to say the words she carried on her heart for Kimi, which was that of, 'I love you.'

Bay was not only Kimi's sister, she was her closest sibling and best friend outside of Koko. The odd thing, however, was that, no matter who it was within Naomi's eight that had a problem, there was always a sibling on hand to pick up the slack when one fell weak. They were all best friends when it got down to it. And when one hurt, they all hurt if it was brought out into the open. But at the same time, when one was in the wrong, or going off-kilter without all the siblings being involved, they would be reprimanded and put into their proper place by those in the immediate know. Kimi was being put in check on this day by Bay and T-Top and she knew it. She had a strong enough mindset to go against the grain if need be, but this go around, she could clearly see that she was going overboard with the theatrics, much in the same way as Walee had overreacted and had blurted out the N-word. She wasn't won over just yet by the Brit, but she was willing to give Dunkirk a chance on the strength of her siblings, and more importantly, that of her mother. Still, her position had to be made known.

"It's not that I don't like you, Mister Fraser. Just don't hurt my momma," Kimi stated while looking into the man's eyes. "This isn't about me."

"Yes it is," Tiva retorted as she reached down and grabbed a cordless microphone. "We all knew you would be the one to have the hardest time accepting the fact that momma at least tryna move on."

"Don't take this as a denunciation, Kimi," Bay lovingly stated with a satiated smile on her face while smiling over to Tiva. "Just give the man a chance that's all. Can you do that?"

"At least until yuh marry," Dunkirk chimed in as Tiva inconspicuously passed him the microphone. "Give me 'til yuh marry day in September. If I don't win yuh over by then? Well, we just gone have tuh figure out another way because I have no plans on going anywhere."

"I see that now," Kimi smiled while staring at the handsome British man. "I'm sorry, Mister Fraser. To be fair, I'll give you a chance to win my conviction."

Just then, the piano intro to Marilyn McCoo and Billy Davis Jr's song *You Don't Have to Be a Star* came across the patio speakers. "Blimey! I haven't heard that song in scores and blows!" Dunkirk laughed as he leapt up from his seat and clicked on the cordless microphone that was synced up with the speakers. "Kimi? You must dance and sing with me right now!" he yelled aloud.

"Mister Fraser, no!" Kimi gasped. She then smiled through her tears and hid her head in Bay's shoulder while waving a hand in the air in humble protest. "I'm sorry everybody!" she screamed out loud.

"Don't be a downer, girl! You know you over your self-absorbed rant! Come on here!" Bay laughed as she and Tiva eased up from their seats and tugged on Kimi's hands.

"This one of the songs I want played at my wedding and y'all know it! Me and Udelle gone sing this to each other!" Kimi laughed as she let her sisters guide her to her feet as Naomi made her way over to the table.

"You need to hear this from your family," Naomi let it be

known as she leaned up against Fraser, who opened up the song with... *"Baby come as you are...with just your heart...and I'll take you in... though you're rejected and hurt...but to me you're worth, girl...what you have within..."*

Naomi followed with... *"Now, I don't need no super star...'cause I'll accept you as you are...you won't be denied...'cause I'm satisfied...with the love you inspire..."* she passed the microphone to Bay at that moment, who let loose with...

... *"he don't have to be a star, Kimi...to be in your show..."* Bay quickly passed the microphone to Tiva, who sang out...

... *"he don't have to be a star, Kimi...to be in your show..."*

"Udellleeee! I love you, baby! You should be here with us today, man!" Kimi screamed aloud to the heavens with one hand raise in the air while stepping in place, although knowing her man was down in Norman, Oklahoma and couldn't hear her jubilant cry. "This is a fun song! Thank you, everybody! I's gettin' married soon!" she jubilantly exhaled as the family surrounded her and danced and sang with her in order to further calm her spirit.

The true essence of the Holland family was being displayed on this day down in Ponca City, Oklahoma in dealing with Kimi. They were an adaptable, determined people whose love was based on complete loyalty as they could ill-afford to take any more loses at this point and time given their violent, bloody history. The family was way too deep in the game, and Kimi knew it all-too-well. Her reluctance towards Dunkirk was an instinctual reaction based on her recollections of the recent past, none more than the loss of her father down in Saint Louis, Missouri. Everybody had to be vetted to the fullest extent was her belief. And if one had a problem, they all had a problem was what she knew to be true. Kimi had a problem with Dunkirk. She feared he would hurt her mother because he was just like her father in her eyes, but all she needed was reassurance. She'd placed her judgement into the hands of Bay and Tiva, who were beasts in their own right and they had given their nod of approval. With Kimi on board, all of Naomi's eight had finally come to the conclusion that Dunkirk Fraser was all right. If the Brit was playing a game, they all had to admit that he was damn good at it, but by all accounts, and past interactions, Dunkirk was nothing more than a man who had a fond affection for Naomi. And that was something that they all could live with, unless he proved otherwise.

****

Later that Sunday night, after the family had all settled in, Naomi and Dunkirk where over in her private room. Both had showered and changed outfits and were now comfortably resting and having a nightcap while sitting side by side on Naomi's suede couch as the eleven 'o' clock hour approached.

"I haven't enjoyed a time like today in such a long while, Naomi," Dunkirk confessed before taking a sip of his neat whiskey.

"I took a trip to Mexico a few months back and had a grand time," Naomi followed as she held onto a glass of red wine. "I danced, ate good food and enjoyed a warm night out under the stars."

"Well, I hope I was able to add tuh your enjoyment. It has to be hard losing a man like Doss under those terrible circumstances."

"I replay that day every day," Naomi admitted before taking a sip of her wine. "Not a moment goes by I don't think about the love I lost, but it doesn't stop me from going forward," she added as she placed a hand under her chin and smiled over to Fraser. "What are we doing?" she asked seriously.

"I think we're establishing a bond, me lady," Dunkirk responded as he set his glass down on the walnut coffee table and looked over to Naomi. "If I'm wrong, stop me now," he added as he leaned in closer to Naomi and placed an arm around the nape of her neck.

Naomi paused Dunkirk's attempt to kiss her and stood up from the couch. "I would like to," she stated as she moved about before her walnut-lacquered Ponderosa wood desk. "God knows I would like to, Dunkirk, but I feel like an adulterous woman wanting to go through with this."

"I was only going in for a simple kiss, Naomi," Dunkirk countered as he stood up and stared down at the woman he adored.

"I know," Naomi remarked as she set her wine glass down atop her desk and leaned up against it. "But a simple kiss will not suffice, Dunkirk. I need and want so much more from you tonight. It's been nearly three years, and my body is screaming, *screaming* for an orgasm not brought on by some dream or a shower nozzle—and I'm ashamed of myself for feeling this way. Ashamed for the emotions I'm carrying right now because I feel as if I'll be betraying Doss, but on everything I love—I want for you to just take me in your arms, strip off my clothes, kiss me all over and make love to me like I know you could."

"Then why deny yourself the pleasure?" Dunkirk asked as he stepped closer to Naomi.

Naomi blushed as she looked around the dimly-lit room with her arms folded. "You can't take me here, Dunkirk. Not like this," she said in sexy voice before displaying an inviting smile.

"I most certainly can take you here and like this, me Naomi," Dunkirk smiled while licking his lips as he stepped towards Naomi with his hands behind his back. "This is what you need, what yuh want to happen this night and I know it to be the truth."

Naomi eyed the bulge in the front of Dunkirk's cotton shorts as she rested up against her desk. Her mind was saying no, but her moist mound was saying, '*what the fuck are you waiting on, get yours*'. As Dunkirk approached her with a lustful hunger in his eyes, Naomi paused him once more with a raised finger while picking up her Stem glass. "You can come back tomorrow for breakfast," she said as she took a sip of her chilled red wine.

Dunkirk was at a loss for words at that moment. He was prepared to enchant Naomi, but he'd just been shut down was his belief. "Well, I…I umm…I guess I'll be going now. Return to me hotel room for a spell until later. What time is breakfast?" he dolefully asked as he downed the remnants of his whiskey neat.

Naomi had to be the aggressor in this budding love affair because she didn't want Dunkirk to feel as if he was persuading her into doing something she had no intentions on doing. She couldn't concede that much control to the handsome Brit, not just yet. She was a grown woman who knew what she wanted, however. And what she wanted, was to be fucked on this night. That was the most she was willing to allow to transpire between her and Dunkirk for the moment as waking up beside him in her bed with him spooning her and nudging her for morning sex the way Doss did, and then emerging from her suite some time later while her children and grandchildren perused the home was not an image she wanted to project, nor a moment she cared to recreate

231

just yet. Making it official would be some ways off, and things would have to transition more smoothly, but for the time being, for the moment, there was nothing preventing the two from becoming intimate was Naomi's reasoning.

"Breakfast is when you say," Naomi replied as walked up to Dunkirk and nudged him backwards. "But before you go, I need you to do something for me."

Dunkirk nodded slightly with his eyebrows raised. "Whatever you desire, Naomi."

"Have a seat," Naomi requested as she extended her hands out towards the couch.

Dunkirk made sure to remove his shorts and drawers and spread his shorts out on the suede before taking a seat. His thick dick poked at his navel as he sat back on the sofa.

Naomi laughed at that moment, tickled over Dunkirk's actions. She also grew moister over his confidence. He was able to read her, pick up on her vibes, and keep up with her erratic emotional flow on this night and she was loving every minute of it. "You could've made a complete fool out of yourself by exposing yourself," she joked as she walked over to her desk and picked up the remote to her surround sound system.

"First times can be awkward, but I know it's not the size that stifles yah," Dunkirk said in confidence as he smiled up at Naomi while stroking his dick as Stephanie Mills' song *I've Learned to Respect the Power of Love* came through the speakers.

"You're that confident? Can you handle me?" Naomi asked as she grabbed hold of a clear jar and walked over to the walnut coffee table and picked up his glass. She stood before Dunkirk and poured him another glass of whiskey while pointing her right hip outwards in his direction. He began to tug on the cotton while easing them over her thighs.

The smooth tan skin his eyes fell upon once Naomi had stepped out of her shorts caused Dunkirk's heart to palpate over her partial nakedness. She had curves in all the right places. Wide hips that guarded a mound of neatly-trimmed, silky black hair and skin soft to the touch and smelling sweeter than a basket of fresh strawberries.

"You like that?" Naomi asked as she danced in tune to the music in a slow circle before Dunkirk, putting her firm bubble butt on display. "What are you going to do with all this woman, mister?" she asked as she completed her dance and sashayed over to her desk and picked up her glass of wine. She sipped with her back to Dunkirk, giving shot after shot of her voluptuous ass.

Dunkirk stood up from the couch. "I'm going to make love to you like never before," he stated as he set his glass down and removed his t-shirt.

Naomi set her glass down, turned around and removed her over-sized t-shirt. With the both of them now fully undressed, she and Dunkirk melted together in the nude and slow danced while staring into one another's eyes with lustful appreciation.

"This feels right all of a sudden," Naomi admitted as she rocked inside of Fraser's strong grip.

Dunkirk let his freehand slid down to Naomi's soft ass. He palmed one of her cheeks tightly and drew her closer, his stiff dick now pressed in between their bodies. "Yuh, the most beautiful woman I've ever met, Naomi. Yuh fascinate me," he said in a smooth, tender voice.

Not bothering to respond, Naomi tilted her head upwards and kissed Dunkirk deeply. "Take me," she pleaded as she pressed harder against the Brit's firm body.

Dunkirk pulled Naomi back with him towards the couch where he fell over to his side and lay behind her as he kissed her deeply while running his hands through her coarse, black hair.

Naomi could feel Dunkirk's dick poking at her moist slit from behind. While kissing him deeply, she reached behind her and grabbed hold and placed his head at her opening and eased down slowly. "Ooh," she moaned softly upon being penetrated for the first time in over three years. Right away, passion took complete control. Dunkirk stared into Naomi's closed eyes, determined to deliver to her the love she'd been missing for what was to her an eternity. "Feels good going in doesn't it?" he whispered as he held Naomi's right thigh up in the air.

Naomi was literally frozen with pleasure. It'd been so long since she'd been made love to that she'd forgotten just how good it felt. She lay on her left side with her fists balled and her legs spread and her right leg up in the air. "Fraser," she moaned through closed eyes of ecstasy.

Dunkirk stroked Naomi long, slow and deep while kissing her all over her neck, face and closed eyes as he thumbed her stiffened nipples. She couldn't utter a sound as the pleasure was too intense and unforgiving. Unforgiving in a good way. Her entire body shuddered as an uncontrollable orgasm shot up from her pussy to her brain. "Fraser!" she cried out again as she placed a hand to back of Dunkirk's head and pulled him in for a powerful, deep French kiss as she sunk deeper down onto his dick. "Faster, baby! Go faster!"

Dunkirk placed his right hand on Naomi's right ass cheek. He rose slightly and drove down into her as she lay on her left side. He spread her right leg open further and stroked her fast and hard, but in order to gain a better angle, he rolled her onto her stomach completely on the couch and lay on top of her, removing his dick for the moment.

"Baby, put it back in," Naomi pleaded as she lay on her stomach. "Yes, God," she gasped the moment her throbbing, wet vagina was greeted with her lover's thick, hard and hot dick.

"Yuh throw it back for me now, Naomi," Dunkirk coaxed as he hovered over Naomi's body as if he were doing pushups. "The dick is there for yuh pleasure. Fuck it as yuh please."

Naomi had her hands tucked underneath her body and her legs crossed at the ankles as she lay underneath Fraser. She could feel every inch of his length and girth as he hovered over her ass with the tip of his dick resting just inside of her opening and tickling her clitoris. Wanting more, she thrust her hips upwards and impaled herself on Dunkirk's dick, her ass cheeks planted firmly against his pelvis. "Fraser, yes!" she screamed as she repeatedly threw her ass back on Dunkirk's dick in rapid motion.

"Yuh takin' me there!" Dunkirk grunted as he drove down into Naomi, forcing her body into the soft cushions.

"Fuck me!" Naomi cried aloud. She had to clutch one of the suede pillows to conceal her squeals as she surrendered completely to Dunkirk.

Dunkirk took heed and began ravishing Naomi. He placed his right foot to the floor to gain leverage and began handling her like a rag doll as he dug deep off into her insides. He was slapping her ass checks with one hand with his other hand pressed down on her back while humping her like a man possessed. "I can't take no more!" he growled as he gripped Naomi tightly in his arms and slammed down hard into her opening.

"Fraser!" Naomi shuddered as her body tensed under Dunkirk's firm weight.

"Dammit, Naomi what are yuh doin' tuh me, woman?"

"You fuckin' me good," Naomi cried out as she thrust back on Dunkirk's dick.

"It's too good, me Naomi! I'm losing it, love!" Dunkirk exclaimed.

Ugly faces were made at that moment. Naomi's eyes were shut tight and her face was wrinkled up in agonizing ecstasy as her juices streamed down her thighs. She shuddered over the feel of Dunkirk's dick deep inside her, flooding her insides before he collapsed onto her back while kissing her deeply as their sweaty and satisfied bodies became intertwined in a heap of disarray.

"Blimey," Dunkirk panted as he rolled off Naomi.

"You keep that up you just may get you some breakfast in bed, mister," Naomi joked as she lay on her stomach with her eyes closed.

"I would not complain," Dunkirk smiled as he lay beside Naomi. He removed hair from her face and stared into her dark brown eyes and said, "You're the most wonderful woman I've ever known. I want yuh in my life, me Naomi."

Naomi turned to face Dunkirk and hugged him close while draping her left leg over his leg. "I want the same, Fraser," she confessed before closing her eyes and smiling contentedly.

"I sense a but coming on again, Naomi."

"No but," Naomi smiled. "The statement stands on its own. I want you in my life."

"Hi," Fraser remarked in a sensual tone as his lips neared Naomi's.

"Hello," Naomi replied before the two kissed passionately.

"One for the road?" Fraser remarked as he moved atop Naomi.

"Thought you'd never ask," Naomi replied as she spread her legs and welcomed Fraser a second time while splayed out on her back.

CHAPTER EIGHTEEN

GARDEN GRINDING

While Naomi and Fraser were enjoying one another's company, Angel Fuller was laying in one of the family's beds on the first floor beside her sleeping mother. She looked over to the nightstand and saw that it was nearing one-thirty, now Monday morning on June 8th. She grabbed her cellphone in order to check and make sure that it was on silent as she lay in wait. An unspecified amount of time had passed before she was awakened by the buzzing phone laying on her stomach. She turned away from Tracey and checked the screen.

Step out in the hall and look left the text message read.

Angel eased out of the bed in her shorts and tank top and crept over to the closed wooden door. Her mother shifted up under the covers and she paused momentarily. When she heard her mother snoring lightly, Angel eased the door open, stepped out into the hall and looked left as requested and saw Walee standing before a set of tinted double glass doors bordered by wood. He opened one of the doors and beckoned her before allowing the door to close behind him.

Angel peered back at her sleeping mother one more time before easing out of the room and pulling the door shut. She walked down the hall briskly in her bare feet and pulled one of the doors opened and quickly ducked inside. A wave of warm air coated her skin and the stone beneath her feet was damp and warm. She looked around the room and was hit with a thing of beauty. All around were islands of colorful flowers three feet off the ground and encased in circular brick borders. A winding, stone walkway disappeared into the greenery and she could see the top of a small waterfall in the back of the large, humid room. There was a stream flowing alongside the winding pathway and green plants ran up the sides of the brick walls surrounding the entire garden. A couple of toucans and a grey parakeet were perched along branches in a couple of Japanese maple trees in the garden's center. The entire area was coated in a reddish hue emanating from heat lamps that hung from the high ceiling.

"You never seen our indoor garden," Walee asked as he walked over and grabbed Angel's hand.

"I thought these doors led outside or something so we can walk."

"We still gone walk," Walee replied. "We gone walk through this garden like we Adam and Eve. Let me show you around, Eve," he joked as he began walking with Angel along the stone path through the garden, which had a paradisiac appeal. "My moms, and especially my grandpa, they like to grow watermelons in here. That's about all they grow besides some cantaloupe."

"I like this room, Walee," Angel said as she leaned in closer. "What kind of flowers y'all grow?"

"White tulips, yellow carnations and red and blue roses."

"They don't have any blue roses, boy," Angel laughed.

"What?" Walee said through raised eyebrows as he paused along the stone pathway. "You never seen a blue rose before?"

"Nah," Angel replied as she knelt down and placed her hand into the stream's flowing water. "Where does this water come from?"

"From an aquifer beneath our land. We have to get it tested on the regular because of the livestock, but it always come back good."

"They have like permeable rocks that filter it naturally," Angel replied while running her hands through the water.

"Look at you. Nerd 101," Walee kidded. "You right, though, shorty. We use it to cook with and drink it straight like that from the fountains."

"What you do around this garden to help out?" Angel smiled as she stood up from the stream and shook her hands free of water.

"Gardening not my thing. I used to feed the chickens when I was younger, though. Then I slopped hogs. We ain't have as many ranch hands back in the day as we do now so we all took care of the land, ya' dig?"

"I bet that was fun," Angel said as she walked ahead of Walee into a clearance and stood before a small pond that had three lounge chairs situated before a rock wall that had water seeping down from its cracks. "This is really beautiful, Walee. Your mother is an architect."

"She do aite. You want a drink or something?" Walee asked as he stood behind Angel and pulled a half-smoked blunt from his silk jogging shorts.

"Some orange juice if you have it."

Walee walked over to an area on the far left side of the garden where there was a white granite counter, steel sink, and refrigerator with a gas grill. He pulled down a glass from a cabinet and poured a glassful of freshly squeezed orange juice. He then used the gas stove to light his blunt and returned to the indoor patio area where he sat beside Angel in one of the lounge chairs and took a couple of tokes. He picked up a remote and aimed it at the rocks and Shemekia Copeland's voice came across the speakers.

"I like her," Angel said in a perky tone as she began nodding her head to Shemekia's song titled *Ghetto Child*.

"She real fly. The only time I really listen to her is when I be back here parlaying by myself, though. My boy Kahlil be ragging on me whenever I play it in the ride, so me and Shemekia kick it solo back here sometimes. This here a good place to think about shit when you don't feel like leaving the house."

"What're you thinking about now?" Angel asked as she took a sip of her orange juice while cutting her eyes at Walee.

Walee blew smoke from his nostrils and said, "The same thing you been thinking about since earlier in the hall." He leaned up, faced Angel with his bare feet to the floor and placed a hand on her thigh. "If I remember correctly, I had my hand here, and my face here," he said as he leaned in closer.

Angel spread her legs slightly and pulled Walee's hand up to her hip. "Your hand was there if I remember correctly," she retorted in a sassy tone. "And I was about to do this," she added as she leaned forward and let her lips touch Walee's.

The two kissed deeply against the backdrop of the waterfall

over Shemekia's voice. Walee moved down to Angel's neck and she tilted her head back as he kissed her lower jaw and moved further down. She raised her tank top and freed her pert breasts and exhaled over the warmth of Walee's tongue as it flicked over her erect pink nipples. When she felt his hand easing up under shorts, she spread her legs instinctively parted wider to allow Walee's probing finger better access.

Walee pulled away at that moment.

"Why you stop?" Angel asked as she opened her eyes in disappointment.

"We been there already," Walee said as tugged down on Angel's shorts. "This time you gone get the whole nine, ya' feel me?"

"Walee, I don't know about this," Angel said as she eased up and pushed down on her shorts and kicked them aside. She spread her legs and placed a finger to her bottom lip and stared at Walee with portions of her amber hair covering her face.

Walee knew the deal. Angel may have been saying no, but that was what she was supposed to say to avoid the appearance of giving it up so easily and readily. Ignoring her mocked protest, he knelt before the lounge chair and waved Angel forward. She went willingly, as if in a trance and sat before him while running her hands over his two thick plats. She moaned softly when she felt his hands on either side of her waist as he leaned down and kissed her navel before moving his tongue down to her slickened vagina.

"God," Angel panted as she fell back into the lounge chair. After several seconds had gone by without sensation, she raised her head. "Why you stopped?" she asked.

Walee chuckled to himself as he knelt before Angel and took a toke off his blunt. "Wait here for me," he said as he stood and walked off.

"Walee? God!" Angel complained as she slapped her hands to either side of head with her legs quivering in anticipation over Shemekia's bluesy, sexy song that continued to play over the speakers.

After a couple of moments of silence, Angel rose and looked to her left in the direction Walee had gone. She was startled when something soft landed on her right arm. She gasped and sat up in fright believing her mother had found her, but she was quickly put at ease when she saw Walee standing beside her with a posy of six blue roses.

"You said you never seen these color roses before. I told you they were real," Walee said as he laid the flowers beside Angel.

"They're beautiful, Walee." Angel responded as she picked up the bouquet.

"Just like you, baby girl. Blue roses can mean many things. They can mean love, prosperity or immortality. Now, we can't live forever, no man or woman can do that, but the other two sho nuff a possibility, ya' dig?" he said as he knelt before Angel once again and began rubbing her inner thighs.

Angel sniffed her blue roses and looked up at the stone and wood ceiling as she felt her legs being pushed back. She waited. Waited for what was an eternity until she felt that warm sensation on her outer lips, but that was only the beginning. Walee's pointed tongue touched her clitoris and she was forced to bite down on the silky rose petals to keep from screaming out in ecstasy. He was palming her ass cheeks now, pulling her up from the lounge chair as he lapped at her virgin sex. She rotated her hips, smothering his face with her mound until her entire body shook and a wave of pleasure washed over her.

Angel was swallowing hard and in near tears as Walee stood before her and removed his jogging shorts. She now knew what he meant when he said that she was going to get the whole nine. Walee sat in the lounge chair beside her and lay back with his feet planted on either side of the seat while stroking his pole. "You ready for this?" he asked confidently.

Angel replied by easing up from her lounge chair and kneeling beside Walee. She replaced his hand with hers while staring at the first dick she'd ever seen with her natural eye yet alone touched. It was hard and soft to the touch simultaneously as it throbbed in her soft, stroking hands. "What you want me to do, Walee?"

"Don't matter just don't bite it," Walee chuckled as he took another toke off his blunt.

"Excuse me?" Angel asked perplexed.

"Nothin...nothin'," Walee laughed to himself realizing Angel hadn't picked up on his reference to N.W.A.'s song *Just Don't*

Bite It. "Just suck it if you wanna, baby. You ever thought about sucking my dick?" Angel blushed at that moment. "What?" Walee laughed. "Don't get scared now. It's me and you. After what I just did to you, you gettin' scared on me?"

"I ain't scared," Angel laughed in a shy tone. "I just, I just wonder how you gone look at me after all this."

"The same way I looked at you before all this. Like li'l wifey material."

"Really?" Angel asked as she removed hair from her face. "You not gone think I'm a hoe?"

"Not unless you put yourself in a hoe position. That's real talk right there. You suck my dick, you down with me one hundred always. Show me you down for me," Walee persuaded as he placed a hand to back of Angel's head and gently helped her along.

Angel closed her eyes and opened her mouth and tasted her first dick ever in Walee. Being a novice, she knew only to move her head back and forth slowly. Walee helped her along by moving her hand up and down and she soon got the picture.

It wasn't a good experience for Walee, however; Angel's teeth kept getting in the way. She was scratching his dick with every slurp and he'd had about all he could take after only a few minutes. Her willingness was more than enough for him as he really wasn't too interested in getting head from Angel as he wanted the prize that lay between her legs. "You good, baby girl," he stated as he pulled back on Angel's hair. "Just sit on this dick for me."

Angel was a pure novice in all areas of sex. She was awkward in movement and void of technique, but she was obedient and had the unfailing desire to please. "Like this?" she asked Walee as she stood with her legs on either side of the lounge chair with her vagina hovering above his raw dick.

"Yeah," Walee responded. He licked his lips and placed his hands around Angel's waist and began lowering her down. "Grab it with one hand and put it to your pussy hole. Then just sit down on it," he tutored.

Angel did as instructed. She gasped and immediately creamed when she felt the head of Walee's dick touch her opening. Nothing more than her index finger and Walee's tongue had ever touched her there, but the 'dick feeling' was matchless in pleasure. "I'm doing it right, Walee?" she asked as she eased down on her first dick ever. "Ooooh," she moaned as the first inch went in and the girth began to be realized.

Walee had his mouth agape as he watched this sexy sixteen-year-old lowering herself onto his tool with her head tilted back and hair pouring down her face as sweat dripped off her perfect body. "Keep going," he said as he eased up slightly to gain further pleasure. "You tight than a mutherfucka, girl," he smiled while biting his lower lip.

Angel let out a guttural groan and tilted her head forward. She placed her hands on Walee's chest as he stroked up into her at a steady pace. "Walee," she whispered. It hurt, but felt good at the same time for Angel, and with each thrust, Walee went deeper and deeper. Angel's nails dug into his flesh and she began panting heavily as Walee picked up the pace. "Walee!" she called out again. "Walee! Your dick! Your dick good! It feels so good!"

"Fuck yeah!" Walee growled as he raised up and braced his self with one hand on the lounge chair and the other on Angel's waist. He was holding her down on his dick as he drove up into her in an uncontrolled, lust-filled rage of passion. "This my pussy now! Who this pussy for?" he asked as his face wrinkled.

"This your pussy! This your pussy!" Angel screamed aloud.

"What's my fuckin' name?" Walee asked as he flipped Angel onto her back and placed her legs over his shoulders.

"Walee!"

"And who this pussy for?"

"It's your—"

"Say this Walee pussy!" Walee commanded as he pummeled Angel atop the lounge chair. "Niggas in Vegas ask to fuck what you gone say?"

"This Walee pussy! I'm gone say this Walee pussy! Whatever you doing to me you need to stop because I don't know what you doing to me Walee you need to stop because…"

"Ahhh shit!" Walee growled as he drove forward and shot deep off into Angel while pounding the back of the lounge chair.

Angel was blown away over the experience. She lay atop the lounge chair trembling uncontrollably while kicking her legs about wildly as her body thrashed about. "Ohhhh," she cried out with her mouth wide open total awe.

Walee pulled out of Angel and sat on the edge of the lounge chair with his back to her breathing hard. "You good?" he asked as he reached for his blunt.

"Umm hmm," Angel answered as she rolled over onto her side.

Walee nodded and walked over to the gas stove to relight his blunt. When he returned, Angel was sound asleep on the lounge chair. He'd thought about waking her up for another go at it, but they'd been in the garden long enough. He kicked the lounge chair while gathering Angel's shorts and tank top and she stirred awake.

"Me and Walee ain't do nothin', momma," Angel moaned as she rose up and looked around.

"You better say that shit just like there if she ever ask," Walee smirked.

"How long I been sleep?" Angel asked as she reached for her shorts.

"Not even a minute. You better, umm, you better get back to bed before somebody come looking for ya'. I'm gone see you later on today." Walee stated as he dressed.

"I'm a mess, Walee," Angel said as she stood and did a quick self-check. "My hair, and look at my clothes. They're damp from the floor. And I'm sore between the legs," she added as she rubbed her forehead in condemnation of herself.

"Hey, hey," Walee comforted as he walked over and hugged Angel. "This our secret garden," he joked. "Just go in the bathroom and wash up, and climb back in bed after changing your clothes. Your moms ask what happened tell her you ate too much and was in the bathroom that's all. She probably won't even wake up after all them daiquiris she had, though, so we good."

"What's gone happen now, Walee?" Angel asked in all sincerity.

"We got plenty of time to talk about that, Angel. You need to get back to bed."

"We leaving later in the morning, Walee. When will we talk? Because I didn't do this just to do it. It meant something to me. I hope it meant something to you too."

"It did, and it does. I'm just trying not to get caught tonight, ya' feel?"

"You sure?" Angel asked as she stared up into Walee's eyes.

"Yeah," Walee nodded as he nudged Angel towards the front of the garden. "Go 'head and I'll clean up here. Make it look like nothin' happen."

Angel was a little disappointed in the way Walee was now brushing her off. She'd wanted to spend more time with him, but suddenly had the feeling that she was being put off after she'd given him what he'd wanted. At the same time, however, he was right. She'd been gone from her mother's side far longer than she'd anticipated. She left the garden with the hopes of being able to tell Walee exactly how she felt before she and her mother and aunt Rolanda left the ranch to return to Vegas.

CHAPTER NINETEEN

JUST KICKIN' IT WITH THE FAM

Several hours after Walee and Angel had parted ways found Tiva in her bedroom sound asleep with Malaysia and Malara slumbering at her side. All was quiet inside her lavish, large bedroom when her cellphone began ringing nonstop. She let it go to voicemail and rolled over and snuggled up to her babies, but the phone rang again. This time, she reached down and answered groggily. "Yeah?"

"Yo, did I wake you, Twin?"

"Terrence," Tiva sighed. "What's up, bae?"

"Yo, man. Candace trippin' again. She—"

"Come on, man," Tiva complained as Malaysia and Malara stirred awake. "It's early on Monday and you callin' me with some shit about that bitch?"

"Bitch," Malaysia whispered.

"Shut up, girl!" Tiva snapped as she threw the covers over her daughter's head. Malaysia laughed, moved the linen off her crown and rolled over to shake Malara awake.

"I know it's early, but I need your help, baby."

"What kind of help? I done beat the bi—I thought I put Candace in check yesterday. What she do now?" Tiva asked as she sat up in her king-sized bed as Malaysia and Malara began jumping up and down on the mattress.

"She brought Tara over this morning and dropped her off. She know I got this run up to Minnesota today. I can't get on the road with Tara because she not old enough to travel with me under the company insurance policy."

"So what you asking of me, man? I'm dispatching from the house today so me and Bay not even in the office. Irene in there today."

"I know it's a lot, Tiva…but I'm still on probation. Irene done already threatened to fire me if I fuck up. I don't wanna call her and tell her I have to sit out on this load and get a service failure out the gate and risk my job."

"Okay. But what you need, though?"

"I'm gone be gone for like four days, umm…you think you can look after Tara until I make it back from Minnesota?"

Tiva rolled her eyes at that moment. Terrence was becoming more and more of a burden on her psyche and beginning to crowd her space with his baby momma problems. Deep down, though, she believed he was sincere in his endeavors. Candace was just complicating his life right now by using every tool in her war chest to make things difficult on the guy was her reasoning. "How long before you leave out?" she asked as she eased out of bed.

"I'm ready to roll now. I can meet you at the warehouse when I pick up the trailer."

"Nah…nah…Irene might see you over there. You ridin' up thirty-five when you leave out, right?"

"Yeah, straight that way."

"Alright, when you get about forty minutes out, hit me back and I'm gone meet you at the highway sixty interchange. You have a car seat for Tara?"

"Yeah, yeah, I got one. Twin, I swear on my daughter when I get right I'm gone make all this up to you. It's just that Candace be all—"

"No need to go into all that, man," Tiva interrupted. "Just get yourself together and I'll do the same on this end. Call me forty minutes out," she added before ending the call and tossing her phone aside.

"Come on, momma! Jump!" Malara laughed aloud as she and Malaysia jumped around on the large, cushiony mattress.

Tiva climbed onto the bed like a prowling panther and crept towards her daughters in her silk teddy. "Grrrrr," she grunted. "Momma mad and she's going to…pounce on her little kittens!" she laughed as she tackled her twins and began wrestling with them.

Bay walked into the room at that moment. "Tiva, you seen the claw comb? It was in my room last—ooh a fight! Get her, nieces!"

"How, how you sidin' with them?" Tiva laughed as she rolled onto her back and shielded herself with a pillow as Bay pounced onto the bed where an all-out pillow fight/wrestling match ensued.

****

Meanwhile, on the first floor of Ponderosa, Kimi, Koko, and their friends Affinity and Katie, along with Oneika, Dawk, Angel, Tracey and Rolanda were having breakfast and milling about the first floor kitchen as mid-morning approached. Dawk was holding Sosa, standing before the counter, when Oneika walked up and sprinkled a few dabs of Pablum onto her wrists. "It's perfect," she said as she handed the bottle to Dawk.

"Mister Dawk, can I feed Sosa? Please, please, please?" Angel begged with her hands clasped together.

"Alright," Dawk responded as he walked around the island counter and eased Sosa into Angel's arms with Oneika at his side holding onto the bottle.

"Aww, he's so precious," Angel purred as she cradled Sosa in her arms.

"He just go to anybody," Koko laughed as Lee Sato, Udelle and Devin, Udelle's friend and classmate, walked through the back patio doors in the middle of a heated debate.

"I'm tellin' both of y'all there's no way I'm gonna sign off on something that ridiculous!" Lee complained. "That's a big part of the wedding budget and it's unnecessary. Kimi not even tryna make that kind of a statement and I know I'm right on that. Udelle, you're gettin' caught up with that wedding planner's outrageous ideas and I'm pushin' back on you and her!"

"What's the matter?" Kimi asked as she and everybody else ate a breakfast consisting of hash browns, pancakes and homemade sausage patties.

"Your wedding planner is the problem, Kimi." Lee complained as the trio walked over to the island counter. "We spent hours with that dense woman down in Oklahoma City last night trying to convince her that we do not need lobster shipped to the Solomon Islands from Maine on a private jet amongst other things. It's a waste of time and money."

"I told you that blonde heifer was too extravagant and was gone run through that money, Kimi," Koko said as she eased up from her seat. "You want a plate, Lee? Devin?"

"I'm here too, yeah, Koko?" Udelle said as he extended his hands.

"And your fiancée right there staring in your face," Koko snapped back through a smirk as she grabbed a couple of plates.

"Lee, I know she kind of outlandish, but she was the only one in town that could handle such a large event," Kimi stated.

"How much the lobster costing, Lee?" Rolanda asked curiously.

"Twelve thousand dollars," Lee remarked, much to Rolanda's shock.

"That's a lot," Angel agreed as she held Sosa in her arms and fed him his Pablum.

"Those lobsters draped in diamonds or something," Rolanda asked with her chin tucked in.

"They must gone spin some albums and pour up drinks for everybody before jumping into some hot water, too," Tracey added while shaking her head in disapproval. "Tilt Sosa's head up a little bit, Angel, so he can digest it properly," she counseled her daughter.

Lee extended a hand out to Tracey and said, "These ladies agreeing to do the music on the strength of family. All we have to do is pay for the flight and set them up with a couple of rooms, no big deal. But this wedding planner is asking for four percent of the budget to be used on a private jet to fly some overgrown cockroaches halfway around the world first class just to be smothered in butter and garlic sauce. No way that's happening. Not on my watch."

"I agree with Lee on this one, homeboy," Devin remarked as he sat at the counter and began slicing his pancakes. "What kind of food they have on the island, though?"

"It's a mixture of Spanish and Thai," Lee answered. "A lot of the food has spice in it. The fish, the chicken. There's porridge and a lot of dishes made with bananas."

"I want ribs and seafood. Creole stuff like Katrina be making." Kimi stated.

Lee looked over to Udelle while curling his lips. "Told you," he declared.

"What happened?" Kimi asked.

Udelle shook his head and said, "The whole ride up here Lee kept saying Katrina should cater the wedding and just let the wedding planner handle the flight reservations and book the rooms."

"And to be honest? We can handle flights and reservations ourselves." Lee quickly followed.

Koko laughed and said, "Sound like you wanna X this wedding planner out altogether, Lee."

"Why not?" Rolanda chimed in. "We'd be happy to help you out, Kimi, if you want. We can get the rooms together through our staff at the radio station."

"And I already know a catering service down there in the Solomon Islands that can set us up with tables and chairs and everything we need to make this wedding the best one ever," Lee added. "No sense in paying that woman twenty-four thousand dollars to do what we can do ourselves. Let's keep the money in-house."

"I thought Katrina was busy with her new café over in Saint Charles," Kimi remarked.

"Nah, she has a staff in place down there," Lee countered. "I'm tellin' ya', Kimi, she'd be perfect for this job. If you gone pay anybody, it should be Katrina. You'll get better food, better service and a lower price and she has her mother there to help her out. It'll be a good thing for them."

"No, no," Kimi protested. "I was willing to pay the old planner twenty-four grand, so that's what I'll pay Katrina. Talk to her and see if she wants the job for that price and let me know before the day end so I can call and terminate the contract with the old planner."

"Thank you," Lee sighed as he clasped his hands together. "Now I can eat my breakfast and keep it down. That woman was driving me insane," he ended as he sat at the counter and began to enjoy his breakfast.

"I need salt on these eggs. Affinity, can you pass me the salt, baby?" Devin then politely asked his gorgeous, ebony-skinned girlfriend.

"You shouldn't use raw salt on food. It contributes to high blood pressure, stiffening arteries and gout." Katie, the petite and loquacious twenty-one-year-old brunette remarked, thus sliding the young bunch off into another discussion.

Devin set the salt shaker down as twenty-year-old Affinity chimed in with, "Salt doesn't change its chemical composition whether you cook with it or not, Katie. Good ahead, Devin, it's okay."

Devin pointed to Affinity, picked up the salt shaker and went to dab his eggs, until Katie stopped him and said, "Using raw salt can cut your life span by seven years. You don't wanna die seven years early do you? I know you don't, so put it down."

Devin set the salt shaker down and scooped up eggs with his fork until Affinity said through her dazzling broad smile, "You're referring to cigarettes I believe, Katie? People used raw salt to preserve meat before the invention of the refrigerator so how can salt be harmful? Douse your eggs, Devin, it's perfectly fine, baby."

Devin pointed to Affinity and gave a nod and a wink as he scooped up the salt shaker once more, but Katie quickly countered with, "The average life expectancy during that period of time was forty-five years. People died early because of raw salt."

"Good point," Devin said as he set the salt shaker down.

"People died early because of tuberculosis, the Spanish flu and undetectable cancer back then, not salt. Go ahead, love," Affinity countered.

Devin picked up the salt shaker again, until Katie shot back with, "If raw salt isn't harmful, how come they make food accents like Mrs. Dash and No Salt for popcorn and things like I'm telling you both that salt is not healthy in raw form. You're going to kill Devin by enabling him in such a terrible habit, Affinity, and you know I'm right."

"It's all politics with Mrs. Dash and No Salt. They petitioned the American Medical Association and got them to diagnose people as having high cholesterol from the usage of raw salt. So now they put people on medication, and recommend a no salt diet and suggest using Mrs. Dash. I bet Mrs. Dash is married to a doctor and they in cahoots to make millions of dollars together."

"Mrs. Dash ain't real, and I ain't tryna die early. I'm siding with Katie on this debate, sweetheart." Devin told Affinity as he set the salt shaker down and shoved a spoonful of eggs into his mouth.

"But it was a compelling argument I made!" Affinity laughed as she kissed Devin's cheek and high-fived Katie.

Rolanda sat smiling as she listened to Affinity and Katie have an inconsequential debate over the mere use of salt. They reminded her so much of how she and Lubby used to engage in word play back in the day. It was good to be young was her thinking as she reflected on days lived long ago.

And as far as Kimi and Koko and their friends, Katie and Affinity were concerned, life was drifting along on an even keel. Naomi's eight had been sheltered for years when she and Doss were building their wealth, but they both understood the importance of having their children interact with the world outside of the ranch. Sheltered kids were dangerous kids. Naïve kids. Naomi and Doss wanted their children to be as well-rounded and normal as any other child despite them growing up surrounded by opulence. The seeds sown were now paying off and it showed, as Kimi and Koko, as well as the rest of the siblings, were about as down to earth as one could be despite having millions of dollars at their fingertips. The conversations held inside the kitchen on this day were nothing more than a peek inside the lives of the young ones inside the family who were merely broadening their horizons and allowing a select few to become part of their inner circle. But, as always, when dealing with the Holland family, bones of contention always lurked about, whether they were noticeable or not. This particular Monday would prove to be no different as they day wore on.

Over the clinks of forks and spoons scooping food up from sterling silver plates, Walee walked into the kitchen with Kahlil following his lead. Angel's eyes lit up and she was about to speak to him until a tall white girl skipped into the kitchen and hugged Walee's neck from behind. "Y'all ready to go shoot some guns in the back, baby?" the young woman asked as she clung onto Walee.

"Chill out, Jordan. Trigger happy self," Walee laughed.

"Hey, Walee," Angel smiled as images of the night before danced through her mind.

"What's up?" Walee asked nonchalantly as he went over to the refrigerator and grabbed a bottle of orange juice.

Angel was disappointed in the way Walee had brushed her off; she also began wondering what kind of relationship he had with the girl Jordan as he'd never mentioned her before. Sosa complained at that moment because he began sucking air out of bottle, and Angel redirected her attention. She watched as Walee, Jordan and Kahlil left the mansion through the back patio as she began burping Sosa.

"Koko, remind me to call my dress designer out in California to let her know that she doesn't need to wait any longer on altering the dress measurements," Kimi stated. "I thought it would be confirmed that I would be pregnant and would have to send her new measurements, but both my tests came back negative."

"No baby for us?" Udelle asked as he poked out his lips in mocked sadness.

"Not yet. We gone have fun tryin' on our honeymoon, though. Ain't that right?" Kimi laughed as she gummed her lips. "Myum, myum, myum, myum…give momma a kiss!"

"Too much information! Too—much—information and I'm calling for a gag order!" Koko sassed as she slapped the marble countertop.

"Gag is not a good word to use in this context," Oneika smirked.

"What the hell is wrong with you people?" Koko gasped as Tracey placed fingers inside of Angel's ears.

Angel had heard the entire conversation, however; and as she held onto Sosa, she began hoping and praying that what'd happened last night would not lead to her having to do what she was doing for fun with Sosa on this day full time, as it would certainly not be just for kicks. But alas, her heart and soul was telling her different.

****

While Kimi and company parlayed in the kitchen, Bay and T-top left the home through the front door with Malaysia and Malara in order to meet up with Terrence. Upon stepping outside, they saw their mother out in front of the home on the opposite side of the asphalt driveway. Naomi was wearing a denim jean suit and a white cowgirl hat and white boots with a pair of sunshades. She was tying a couple of Clydesdale horses to the wooden fence that bordered the pastures on the northeast side of the ranch where the barns lay.

"Grandmaaaaa!" Malara screamed out as she stood on the stairs and pointed. "Horseeee!" she stated happily as she crawled backwards down the stairs and darted across the asphalt.

"Hey, momma sugar," Naomi laughed as she climbed under the fence and scooped Malara up into her arms the time the toddler met her. She reached into her denim jacket, handed Malara an apple and said, "You and your sister going for a ride in the car?"

"Yesh! To the store!" Malara said as she held the apple before one of the horse's mouths.

"Not the store," Tiva corrected as she and Bay walked over to Naomi. "Momma, we going get my friend Terrence's daughter and keep her for a couple of days while he on the road."

"Oh, okay. Looks like you and Malaysia gone have some playmates, Malara." Naomi smiled.

"No!" Malara snapped as she dropped the apple and folded her arms.

Malaysia picked the broken apple up and was attempting to eat it, but Tiva stopped her. "That's the horse's apple, baby. And we don't eat off the ground," she laughed as she picked Malaysia up and let her feed a portion of the apple to the friendly stallion.

Bay walked over and rubbed the tan horse with the white mane. "Why two horses, momma?" she asked.

"I'm waiting on my friend Dunkirk. His flight leaves tonight so we're going to ride the horses over the land for a while have lunch and then—"

"Do the do!" Bay laughed.

"Stop!" Naomi blushed. "We're gonna slaughter a hog and then grill some pork chops and relax before he leaves. I'll take him in my car and Siloam is going to tail us down in his rental car."

"I thought he would've spent the night," Bay smiled.

Naomi blushed again as the previous night replayed in her mind briefly. "He most certainly could have," she snickered. "I can share that with you two because I know this conversation will not go beyond us three," she said as she placed Malara back on her feet. "You girls be careful out there on that highway."

"One, two, three, four…five!" Malaysia corrected.

"Girl, hush!" Tiva laughed as she grabbed her daughter's hand and walked off. "We be right back, momma," she ended as she and Bay loaded the kids into the backseat of the Lincoln.

"Where y'all going, Bay?" Tyke asked as she ran out of the front doors.

"Pick up somebody right quick off thirty-five. Wanna ride?" Tiva answered on behalf of her twin.

"Already!" Tyke laughed as she trotted down the stairs and jumped into the backseat in between Malaysia and Malara.

Bay hadn't driven off the land completely when rapper Devin the Dude's song *Boo Boo'n* came over the speakers. "You heard back from Jay-D on Laddy, Tiva?" she asked as she turned onto the main road.

"Nothing yet, girl," Tiva sighed over the music. "I be glad when all that die down, though, because the longer I hang down there at the warehouse in Valley Brook, that's the closer I'm gone get to hurtin' that bitch Candace."

Bay made a right turn onto the two-lane road leading down to State Highway 11 as she and Tiva continued discussing the situation with Candace. The music was down in the front of the ride, but Bay's speakers were thumping in the back. Tyke was busy texting one of her friends from the softball team, but Malaysia and Malara were enthralled in the song as they rode in what was to them, a bedroom that floated. The car had large soft seats and televisions they could watch cartoons on; television was the furthest thing from the twins' mind, however, as they were getting their kicks out of the song with its vulgar words and melodic beat. They kept repeating the words Boo Boo'n every time the rapper said it, along with the cuss words.

"*I'm a bitch I'm a hoe,*" they repeatedly lowly as the car cruised up the highway and made a right onto Highway 11 and headed towards town. "*…early in the mornin' bitches knockin' at my momma door,*" they laughed.

"I was thinkin' if it came to that how would we handle it," Bay remarked as the Lincoln slid past Mary's produce store. She blew the horn at Mary and Dimples, who were out front filling baskets with produce as the car rode onto the westbound side of Kaw Lake Bridge.

Back in the backseat of the ride, Malaysia and Malara where still vibing to the song. They had a couple of fingers in their mouths while rocking back and forth, dripping drool as they repeated in unison…"Wait for me I'm in the bathroom boo boo'n!"

"Lord, these li'l girls!" Tiva laughed and turned the music down completely. "What y'all know about that song?" she asked as she peered over the front seat.

"Him boo boo'n!" Malaysia yelled out as she raised her legs and pointed at her butt. "Take a shit!"

Bay, T-top and Tyke laughed together at Malaysia. "No, well, you're right, but a boo boo could also mean somebody messed up," Tiva counseled. "Like when you waste a drink or something, okay, Malaysia? That's a boo boo, too. It's like a mistake, baby."

"Okay," Malaysia yawned as Malara quickly followed and drooped her head.

"They gettin' sleepy already," Tyke said as she used a remote to turn on the television for her nieces and continued on texting while enjoying the ride.

****

Back inside Ponderosa, Angel had just finished packing. She and her family were leaving in under an hour and she still hadn't gotten to talk to Walee about what the two had done the night before. After she was done packing, she walked back into the kitchen and out onto the back patio where she saw Walee walking with the entire group from the kitchen. They were headed to the back of the ranch as Angel stood and watched through sad eyes as the love of her life engaging in horseplay with the girl Jordan. Her heart was broken at that moment upon realizing Walee had a girlfriend, or at the least, another woman he was close to.

"Why don't you go and join them before you leave," a female voice was heard by Angel, startling her briefly. She looked around and saw Francine walking over to one of the shaded patio tables with a newspaper tucked under her arm and a picture of tea and a couple of glasses in her hands.

"By the time I get there to see Walee, it'll be time for us to leave. And I don't wanna get all sweaty before the flight," Angel remarked dejectedly.

"I see. Come and have a glass of tea with an old lady before you go, then. Did you enjoy your stay here in Oklahoma?" Francine asked as she set her items down and pulled out a couple of chairs.

Angel walked over to the patio table and flopped down in her seat with her head down.

Francine was an observant woman. Most of her days were spent minding everybody's business. And at the age of seventy-six, she was all-wise, able to decipher problems within others without being told the situation. Looking at Angel's demeanor, she knew right away that the teenager was experiencing young love. "Men can be such a pain in the ass sometimes," she remarked as she grabbed a glass and poured Angel a cup of cold lemon tea.

"Tell me about it," Angel sighed as she grabbed the glass and took a sip.

"You give your heart, show 'em how much you care through actions and they crap all over your feelings. That's how they do. But, it's different if they don't know that you care." Francine remarked while rocking slightly.

Angel looked over to Francine and smiled slightly. "Is it that obvious, Miss Cernigliaro?"

"Not really, but I noticed you singled out Walee out that entire group. Is he causing you trouble?"

"Not trouble," Angel confessed. "I just wish I knew about him before we…before I started to like him."

Francine squint her eyes at Angel while pouring her own glass of tea. "It's you and me here, sugar. You can tell Aunt Francine anything. Now, have you and Walee been intimate?"

"No," Angel quickly answered.

"Well, what's the fret?"

"I don't wanna talk about it, Miss Cernigliaro."

"You know," Francine began as she leaned back in her chair and crossed her legs. "When I was your age, maybe a little older, there was this man that I liked up in Brooklyn, New York. This man I loved. He was such a smooth talker. Good looking fella, too. He used to come around and walk past me like I never existed—until I spoke to 'em one day. He said to me, 'Eh, how you doin' in this heavy Italian accent."

"What happened after that?" Angel asked curiously as she sipped her tea once more.

"Everything," Francine remarked. "From that day forth, I made it known that I wanted him. This was the late forties early fifties, you know? During a period of time when sex before marriage was frowned upon. But I didn't care what people thought about me. All I knew was that I wanted that man."

"Did you get him?"

"No," Francine remarked. "But he most certainly got what he wanted from me let me tell ya'. And it was because I allowed it to happen. I couldn't be mad at him. I did it to myself, understand? Besides, the guy was a bum and I met my husband some time later and he was the everything I was looking for in that chump who I thought I loved."

"You're saying Walee isn't worth it, Miss Cernigliaro? You're callin' him a chump?"

"By all means no," Francine chuckled. "What I'm saying is, if you want Walee, you have to let that be known. Don't just sit there with your head bowed feeling sorry for yourself. Do something about it!"

Gunshots off in the distance forced Angel to turn and look across the land where Walee and company were firing off weapons. "You're right," she smiled as she looked back over to Francine. "I'm going tell him what I have to say right now," she added as she hopped up from the chair.

"Angel Michelle Fuller?" Tracey Sanchez called out as she stepped out onto the patio and looked around. "Oh, there you are! Come on, baby. Everything's loaded up and we're headed out."

"Aww, momma! Let me go say goodbye to my friends!"

"You had all morning to do that, Angel! We're already behind and can't miss this flight. Don't worry, it's not the last time you'll see them. Our limousine is waiting on us so, chop, chop! Thank you for everything, Miss Cernigliaro," she said as she ran over and hugged Francine briefly. "We'll see y'all later."

"I'll be right there, momma," Angel remarked in a somber tone. When Tracey cleared out, she turned to Francine and asked, "Any advice for a young woman in love?"

"Listen to what your mind tells you and not your heart. The heart can be a vacillating organ."

"My heart is not indecisive, Miss Cernigliaro," Angel said seriously as she gazed out to the thick forest where she knew Walee was with Jordan. "I really am in love with him," she added as she walked off with a sorrowful spirit encompassing her entire being. "I hope he feels the same when I tell him over the phone one day soon. But I do have a memory to take with me," she ended through a half-hearted smile.

"He got what he wanted from you so that may be a challenge, sweetheart," Francine bluntly stated. "Not to ruin your moment, but remember my story. It's how men do sometimes. Take that with you on your way out."

"*Old hag,*" Angel said to herself as she walked off.

"Yeah, life's a bitch and so am I at times, Angel," Francine said in a nonchalant manner. "Better one truth than a thousand lies to yourself. But, good luck with it all." she ended as Angel disappeared from sight.

Angel left the ranch dejected over what Francine had said to her for one, and also because she didn't accomplish all she wanted to accomplish with Walee, which was to kiss him goodbye and tell him she loved him. Those things meant the world to the sixteen-year-old, and would mean the world to any sixteen-year-old so young, and so in love. She couldn't wait to see Walee again as she was determined to make him hers. She smiled over her heart's desire, looking to the future with optimism and brushing Francine's remarks aside as she replayed the night before in her mind while trailing her mother through Ponderosa to the front of the home where their limousine was waiting.

****

Bay and T-top, meanwhile, had went on and picked up Tara without much fanfare and were now headed back home. They approached the intersections of highways 11 and 77 from the south preparing to stop for the light and make a right turn onto Highway

11. Bay and T-top were just kicking it, enjoying a lovely Monday afternoon with Tyke, Malaysia and Malara. The whole ride back, the family had been listening to fun songs that Malaysia and Malara could sing to in order to keep the children entertained as Malaysia and Malara didn't take kindly to a stranger their size being in their presence. They'd actually tried to fight Tara the time she was placed in the backseat. On several occasions, they'd kicked out at Terrence's daughter, making her day a living hell.

Bay pulled up to the light playing The Seekers' song *I'd Like to Teach the World to Sing*. Tiva would play the song on occasion for Malaysia and Malara as it was easy to remember and helped expand their vocabularies. The family stopped at the intersection, Bay bouncing her shoulders behind the wheel as Tiva turned around and faced the babies and Tyke. "Come on Malaysia and Malara! Sing for Tara, y'all!" she said in joyful mood as she bonded with her daughters and sang aloud... *"I'd like to build a world a home...and furnish it with love..."*

"...grow apples trees and honeybees...and snow white turtle doves..." Malaysia and Malara sang as they rocked back and forth with wide smiles on their faces and their arms reaching out for their mother.

Bay made a right turn on red singing...*"I'd like to teach the world to sing...in perfect harmony..."*

The family had a perfect chorus going as they approached Kaw Lake. Malaysia and Malara were singing happily, Tyke was rocking while texting, and Tara was giggling away as Tiva made funny faces at her. No one inside the car was paying any attention to four men on black and red Harley Davidson Sportsters with chrome and red wheels that had suddenly ridden up behind them as Bay drove in the right lane.

The bikers, wearing black denim and red leather jackets, followed closely and fell in behind the Lincoln in the right lane as it rode onto Kaw Lake Bridge. Just before the lead biker pulled out an Uzi and was preparing to move into the left lane, a convertible Mazda Miata sped by and pulled up alongside the Lincoln blowing its horn furiously.

Bay looked over through her tinted windows and went for the AP-9 she had resting in the console. "Tiva!" she called.

Tiva jumped to attention moment. "What's up?" she asked as she looked around.

"This man here," Bay suddenly sighed as she let the window down upon recognizing the man driving the convertible. "Dunkirk? What you doing, man? You was 'bout to get it, dude!" she laughed as the two rode side by side over Kaw Lake Bridge.

"I was wanting tuh get some flowers for me Naomi! Does Mary's Produce up ahead sell flowers?" he yelled out into the wind.

"I'll take you to our indoor garden on the ranch so you can pick some tulips! She loves those!" Bay yelled back as she caught sight of four black and red choppers tailing her car. An ominous feeling overcame her at that moment as she took note of the bikers, but she brushed it off when she saw Kimi and Koko's Maserati pull up behind her car.

"Righteous! Follow me!" Dunkirk shot back as he sped past Bay's ride and jumped into the right lane.

Bay slowed behind Dunkirk and let the bikers pass, taking another glimpse at the quartet as her sisters' car pulled up on side her. "Wassssupppp!" Udelle laughed from the passenger seat.

"We havin' a family reunion on this bridge or something?" Bay screamed aloud. "First Dunkirk and now you and Lee, Udelle!" she said as she held the car steady.

"We comin' from the hardware store!" Lee yelled from behind the wheel. "Naomi needed some new grates for the bar-b-que grill! Let's race!"

"You don't want none, boy!" Bay laughed as she mashed the gas. The front of her car rose up off the ground and she left Lee in the wind on the bridge.

"Bena, we got the kids in here, girl!" Tyke exclaimed from the backseat as Lee and Udelle shot by like a bullet.

"Y'all lucky, punks!" Bay yelled out the window as she slowed her car.

When the family's cars cleared the bridge, the motorcycles, who'd been tailing them for a time, turned off into Mary's Produce and made a U-turn, headed back to Ponca City. Bay had paid some attention to them, but for the most part, they'd been ignored by the family their first time out.

A few minutes later, Dunkirk, Bay and T-top, and Lee and Udelle were all pulling up onto the ranch. Tiva had plans on taking her two daughters and Tara into the theater room to watch a movie and feed them before taking them out to play with the farm animals. Bay had taken Malaysia and Malara inside ahead of Tara because things had heated up again once the music stopped.

Tiva entered the front doors of Ponderosa a few minutes later guiding Tara by the hand while calling out for Malaysia and Malara, her voice echoing through the cavernous first floor of the mansion.

"They right here, T-top!" Bay called out as she backpedaled out of the main dining room with a jubilant Malaysia and Malara tagging behind.

"Movie time!" Tiva exclaimed as she knelt down beside Tara.

"Yayyyy, mov—" Malaysia went silent.

"Yayyyy, mov—" Malara, too, went silent as she turned her head to the side.

Malaysia and Malara both had ceased their speech when they saw their mother with what was to them 'that stranger' again. They looked at one another in a puzzled manner before Malara asked, "Who?" while pointing to the stranger standing beside her mother.

Whatever was going through their three-year-old minds, it'd forced them to yell out, "Noooo!" as they ran towards Tiva.

"No, momma!" Malaysia screamed.

"That's my momma! My momma!" Malara yelled as both twins ran towards their mother at a frantic pace.

Tiva was caught by surprise. Her daughters were charging at her like two bucking calves on a rampage and she was forced to scoop Tara up into her arms to keep her out of harm's way. She'd just stood back up on her feet when Malaysia and Malara made it over to her. Malaysia had attacked her mother legs, biting her kneecap before she twirled around and slid down onto the marble floor onto her stomach.

Malara, meanwhile, stood before her mother slapping at her legs while pointing up at the stranger in her arms. "My momma!" she cried out.

"Hey now!" Tiva said in a commanding voice as she knelt down with Tara in her arms. "Don't act like that! Y'all was nice in the car until the music stopped! This our friend and she's going to stay with us for a little while, okay?" she asked as she put the toddler on display.

Malaysia picked herself up from the floor and Malara was wiping her tears as the twins stood before their mother staring at the stranger. Tiva could read her daughters' hearts through their worried blue eyes. She could easily discern that they felt threatened by this new intruder and had to be reassured. "Tara here for a movie party today. We gone have us a slumber party with popcorn and soda and your favorite movie."

"Up!" Malaysia and Malara exclaimed happily, citing their favorite animated movie.

"You wanna watch a movie, Tara?" Tiva asked in a high-pitched voice as she placed Tara onto her feet in order to let her get a feel of her new environment. The high-yellow skinned toddler with brown, curly hair and brown eyes looked around wide-eyed, peering out into her unfamiliar surroundings before she turned and put her snaggle-toothed smile on display for the two little people standing before her. "Heyyy," she waved softly.

Malaysia and Malara merely frowned at Tara before walking off while holding hands. Neither had any interest in being nice at this particular juncture. "Up!" Malaysia declared as she and her twin headed for the hall that they knew would lead them to the cartoon they now wanted to watch.

Once inside what they knew to be the movie room, Malaysia and Malara playfully jumped down the carpeted stairs. Tara tried to follow and join her new friends, but Tiva held her back, not wanting her to stumble as her daughters knew the layout of the room all-too-well. The twins had climbed into seats on the front row by the time Tiva made it down the stairs with Tara. She turned on the projection screen and dimmed the lights, placed Tara in one of the large leather seats and trotted back up the stairs to start the popcorn machine out in the hall. She called out for Tyke, who was nearby, and had her go and set up drinks and bring the popcorn in once it was done as she darted back into the theater room to oversee the children.

When Tiva returned, she sat beside Tara, who was on her right, with Malaysia on her left and Malara two seats away. The distance from her mother didn't sit well with Malara, however; the disgruntled toddler scooted out her seat, wobbled past Tiva, and pushed Tara aside and climbed up into the leather seat. "My momma!" she yelled in Tara's face before leaning up against her mother.

"Alright, alright," Tiva laughed as she picked Malara up and placed her in her lap. "Now, we all comfy, right?"

"Yes," Malara responded softly as she lay back on her mother. She looked over to Tara and said again, "My momma!" to reinforce her point.

The movie had been playing for ten minutes when Tyke walked in with a tray containing two bowls of popcorn and four cups of grape soda. "My nieces didn't seem so happy when they first saw your boyfriend's daughter. They okay now?" she asked as she passed out the refreshments.

"Yeah, they good," Tiva smiled as she laid back in her seat under the belief that she'd quelled the animosity between her daughters and Tara.

Tyke handed Tara a cup of grape soda. The toddler went to drink it, but the lid had fallen off and the grape soda spilled all over her clothes and the seat she was sitting in.

"Bitch made a boo boo!" three-year-old Malaysia yelled as she jumped up from her seat and stomped off with her hands clasped to her curly head of black hair.

"She said a bad worrrdddds," Malara sang as she lay back on her mother while pointing over to her twin.

"This gone be a long ass four days I can see that already," Tiva sighed as she moved to help Tara out of her dilemma.

****

Back over to Ponca City, the four biker men were pulling up to Sheriff Nimitz's garage located behind his one level brick home on the west side of town. He slid from under his '79 Chevy pickup and stood to his feet as the lead biker, a man who went by the name of Vaughn Nobles, climbed off his chopper.

"How'd it go on the bridge?" Sheriff Nimitz asked as he

reached down into a cooler and threw a can of beer to Vaughn.

"It's the perfect spot, but, you didn't tell us they all travel in packs."

"What you mean?" Nimitz asked as he tossed beers to the three other bikers and grabbed one for himself.

"We had one car, but two more pulled up. It was too risky out there. I mean, no one was on the bridge, but with all those other cars around? We couldn't hit 'em all."

"We should just bum rush the ranch," a second biker stated before downing his beer.

Nimitz laughed and took quick squib of his beer. "Let me know how that works out. If ya' couldn't hit 'em on the bridge, ya' don't stand a chance gettin' to 'em on the ranch. They're a close bunch, alright?" he fretted as he looked to the ground. "Remember, Hakiba wants someone close to Naomi hit to avenge the loss of her son."

"What's the next move?" Vaughn asked. "Because time is ticking on how long we're gonna be here in Oklahoma. We have business with the club back in Sturgis we need to be tending to if you didn't know."

"I know about the business in South Dakota," Nimitz sighed. "Okay, the bridge still stands, but I know another place we can stake out," he remembered as he gave the biker crew another target in the family to go after outside of Bay and T-top. "Just give it another week or so. I'm sure the moment will present itself, gentlemen. And it's a lesser hassle," he said as he knelt back down and slid back under his raised pickup truck. "Be patient. We'll get us a Holland soon enough," he ended as he went on to enjoy the rest of the day working on his beloved pickup.

CHAPTER TWENTY

BACK TO BUSINESS

"Gacha knows about the land you got down in Brazil, Ben," Swan said to me as we sat inside a limousine on the runway at the airport down on Grand Cayman Island. It was around eleven 'o' clock on a Monday morning. I had a lot of moves to make before day's end so I was looking to wrap things up with Swan and Monty quick-like so we could continue on our journey and settle down in Sao Paulo before it got too late, ya' dig?

"Any idea how he found out about it?" I calmly asked as I slid him two briefcases full of cash.

"The ambassador to Venezuela picked up on a land purchase and did a little digging. Traced the sale back to Holland Dawkins Enterprises," Swan said to me. "But, Gacha's not upset about it. He says if you can offer a replacement crew and not operate in the territories he controls back in the United States, the peace between both families would remain intact."

I wondered at that moment why a man as powerful as Rafael Gacha would be willing to renegotiate terms so suddenly and easily after we'd basically slapped him in the face and went behind his back and forged our own business. My family had pull, but not as much pull as Gacha. Maybe he realized the strength we had being we was able to purchase three thousand acres of land, but something was telling me that there was more to the story, and his reasoning. I had the Asians in place to take over the family's cocaine operation out west, and in the meantime, we was already working on moving our own operations further east through Pensacola, Florida and into cities like Atlanta, and the Carolinas. I'd made the right move by not stepping on Gacha's toes, but it was the ease of his consent that was bothering me because I was bracing for a war south of the border.

"I can work with Gacha's request," I told Swan. "The thing that got me worried is he too calm given our moves. What he up to?"

"Your guess is as good as ours, Ben," Monty answered. "The guy been a little unsteady the past couple of months. I tell ya', something has his undivided attention, but it's not the moves you and your family are making."

"We'll see what else I can dig up, but for now, we still have the go 'head to conduct business as usual," Swan added. "As it stands, we'll keep going for now. If something changes I'll let you know."

I shook Swan and Monty's hand and exited the limousine under the warm morning sun and trotted back over to the waiting jet where Samantha, Martha, Vic, Tre` and Amber were waiting. I'd just dropped 4.5 million dollars off for the next delivery, which was ten days out and our next stop was our land down in Boa Vista, Brazil. Before I boarded the plane, I pulled my phone out and called Dawk. He updated me on the situation over in Saint Charles. When I got back, me, Bay and T-top gone have to fly in and assist Jay-D with reorganizing the crews over in Fox Park and getting Loopy on the same page with everybody else. I climbed the stairs after ending the call and the door was raised. Five minutes later, the six of us was in the air readying for a six hour flight.

"How'd it go down there?" Martha asked once we'd leveled off.

"Gacha know about the land," I told her. "He want another sit down, but Swan say he cool with it all."

"Just like that?" Martha asked with her lips curled while shaking her head.

"I'm not sure about it myself, auntie. It's not the expected move a kingpin would make knowing one of his factions was settin' up shop in his backyard."

"You trust those agents, Ben?" Victor asked me.

"I do, fam, but I know this high up, crosses can get thrown like a mutherfucka. They might be settin' us up. If that's the case? Why keep doing business with us, though?"

"To keep us at ease until they find the right time to hit us?" Martha reasoned.

"Perhaps, but Gacha let me walk away today. If he had something up his sleeve he coulda had Swan and Monty kill me right there on the runway. I don't think that's what he got planned, but something definitely up with dude," I pondered out loud.

"Don't umm," Victor snapped his hands repeatedly. "The white chicks over to Kansas," he said. "Don't they have like a Senator or somebody? Maybe they can look into it."

I nodded. The Germans could be a source of information, but it's gone take a minute to get at 'em. My next call to them gone be when that ship over to Sao Paulo leave the dock. "I'm gone look into it, fam. You might be right," I told Victor just as the seatbelt light went off in the plane, letting us know we were free to move about.

Six hours later, me and the family was approaching a private air strip tucked in a valley down in Boa Vista. It was 2:35 in the afternoon when Amber, who was commandeering the plane, got on the radio. "Altoona, Altoona, you got a copy?" I heard her say.

The radio on the ground cackled and I heard a rustic voice with a slow drawl come over the waves. "Si, is this uhh…is this the uhh…Ponchartrain One?"

"I'm gone need you to speed up a little for me, guy," Amber remarked as she cruised over a forested, lush green mountain top. "Ponchartrain One looking to land. Is the runway clear?"

I looked out the window and saw a vast, green valley come into view. The land my family owned was tucked in between two massive mountains covered in trees and brush. In the valley below was field after field of cultivated land cut into neat squares that resembled a checkerboard. I could make out farm equipment and tractor trailers parked on the roads that ran in between what I knew to be the orange trees resting in the valley. Nestled in amongst all the greenery, I could see a winding dirt road and a narrower, grey strip of land that led to a small field that had a grey airplane parked at the end.

"The runway is clear as soon as I get an acknowledgement on who's flying thee plane, no?" the voice was heard over the radio again. "Come on, tell Hollywood who's in thee air today," the man stated in joking tone.

"Runway's clear Ponchartrain One," I then heard Flacco remark. "Come on home, Senorita. Ignore my uncle."

"Whaaattt?" we all heard the guy named Hollywood remark

269

over the radio as they readied for landing.

Amber guided the jet over the mountain tops and circled the valley once before bringing the plane down onto the runway facing south. We came to a halt before a black, grey and white camouflaged cargo plane. Three black Navigator limousines were off in the distance where six men toting machine guns stood waiting. Over a dozen more men soon emerged from the hangar, each of them toting black machine guns.

Flacco walked out to the plane unarmed, wearing a black on black airman's uniform, black boots and a black skull cap. Me, Vic and Tre` emerged from the plane unarmed and walked up to him and exchanged pleasantries.

"Welcome, amigos," Flacco stated. "We have everything up and running here, Senor Holland. How're things back in America?"

"Okay for now, brer. We have a few things to deal with, but nothing the family stateside can't handle," I remarked as Martha, Samantha and Amber walked down the plane's stairs while looking the valley over.

"Good. As you can see we've cleared the land as Naomi requested. It's hard to get to this place by highway and that's a good thing. Let me give the family a tour of the place," Flacco stated as three open top jeeps pulled up.

"Who that was talking sporty on that radio, Flacco?" Samantha asked as she gave the man a quick hug.

"Me! Why?" a short Mexican with jumpsuit pants one size too big snapped as he jumped from behind the wheel of one of the jeeps and walked up and stood beside Flacco with an AK-47 strapped to his back.

"This is my uncle Altoona Ramirez, Samantha, everybody. We call him Hollywood," Flacco chuckled as he greeted Martha and Amber. "More of the family is guarding the Devereauxs over in Sao Paulo."

"That's right I'm Hollywood. Ladies' man, and pilot extraordinaire," the short, muscular, raspy-voiced man laughed as he pulled up on his baggy, black jeans. "Annddd…I was talking, as you say…'sporty on the radio'."

"Pilot?" Samantha laughed as she stared Hollywood up and down. "You fly for real?"

"Si. There's my plane right over there, senorita."

Samantha and Amber looked over and saw a hulking grey, black and white mass of metal. I'd seen the plane the time I stepped off the jet. It looked like a antique to me. I guess Hollywood sensed our apprehension because he spoke up by saying, "That bird may look like something the Wright brothers flew in the early nineteen hundreds, but that is the bird that will be transporting your cargo, no?"

Flacco got in between the group and said, "Let me show you around before we enter the next phase of your trip abroad, Senor Holland."

"You shouldn't be so serious, nephew," Hollywood remarked as he tailed the group. "I was just getting the girls to warm up to me and you kill my thunder."

We climbed into the three jeeps, me, Samantha, Amber and Martha riding with Flacco and a soldier while Vic and Tre rode in the second jeep. The third jeep was filled with more of Flacco's soldiers. Looking back on the matter, I never pictured being this high up in the game, but I'd be lying if I said I wasn't loving the power and prestige. I rode with a pair sunshades over my eyes looking at acres of cocoa leaves that were soon to be processed and shipped stateside. As we rode, we passed dozens of field hands, about a hundred or more, with shotguns strapped to their backs who were out picking oranges and dumping them into baskets situated in the back of a pick-up truck. Once full, the pickup was driven to the edge of the grove and the fruit was dumped into waiting semis to be driven to Sao Paulo.

"These field hands are paid one hundred dollars a day for their labor, Senor Holland," Flacco said to me as he wheeled the jeep through the groves. "They make more in a month than they could make in an entire year working elsewhere. That in itself will keep them loyal."

"How you get them here if this place is inaccessible by road?" I asked over the blowing wind.

"They're flown here on Hollywood's plane. They come from our hometown of Paraiso back in Mexico and now have homes in Boa Vista further south of here. For anybody to hit this place? They'll need the support of the Brazilian government and a small army. We'll see both coming over the mountains. We have outposts set up atop both mountains with radar and infrared along with rocket propelled grenades. The only ones that can penetrate this place is the United States, and here? They leave us alone."

"Did the Devereaux family come through with their government contacts?" I asked.

"That's what we're flying to Sao Paulo to receive. They also have the first shipment of heroin ready to go."

"Phillip and Grover's ship is waiting at the port as we speak," Martha remarked from the backseat of the jeep. "I have everything set up with the port in Pensacola also," she added.

I nodded my head over Martha's words. She was indeed up on her game. The cocaine wouldn't be ready to be processed for another month or so, but today was to be dry run. Two thousand pounds was what we were going to ship each rip for starters—a solid ton. We was gone use Hollywood's plane to fly from the valley to Sao Paulo, land and offload a shipment off oranges to test the flight and the process. During that time, we would load five hundred pounds of heroin onto Phil and Grover's waiting freighter and ship it to Pensacola and put it in the hands of the Germans. That would complete the deal Naomi had made with the Devereaux family for putting the Germans up on the hit against the Fischer brothers up in New York.

We cleared the orange groves and came up on a field of cocoa leaves. There were at least three dozen armed men walking amongst the cocoa plants. Small tents were set up all throughout the acreage and each had two plastic barrels and a table with a sack of Levamisole on top. I climbed from the jeep and stood before the vast field looking at nothing but money. Millions upon millions dollars were on the verge of being made. We had the logistics, the men and the firepower to run this here thing and it wasn't a doubt in my mind that we would reap large profits from this next racket before it's all said and done. I stood looking over the fields as Samantha walked up beside me. We talk a lot about what we're involved in, ya' dig? Samantha know what's up one hundred. She know how I move, my plans and my worries. I share things with her I don't share with Katrina sometimes. She like my Consigliere in this business.

"What you think about this here set-up, sister?" I asked her as she stood beside me wearing a pair of mirror-tinted shades and a baggy camouflage jumpsuit with black boots.

"I think the set-up is perfect, brother. What we gone have to worry about is transportation. I think the loose end gone be over in Sao Paulo during the loading process."

"I trust Flacco people, though. Speaking of trust, how things going with Amber?"

Me and Samantha had a couple of conversations about getting Amber so involved in the business, but truth be told, we needed her. DOT protocol wouldn't allow Samantha to fly on her own, and I wouldn't want to have her flying twelve or thirteen hours straight by herself anyway.

"She know what's up, Ben," Samantha said to me. "I ran checks on her, Katrina ran checks on her, Naomi did, too. Amber just wanna be up under me," she smiled. "So long as she receiving royalties from Slovak Vineyards back in Flagstaff, she'll be good. And even if she wasn't, she just as much of an adventurer as I am. She on board with us."

"It's dangerous down here, sis. I hate putting y'all out on the front lines like this, but y'all the only ones I trust to fly us around."

"We do it because we want you to be comfortable, Ben. You have enough to deal with when you having these meetings. The least we can do is put you at ease when you up in the air. Don't worry about me and Amber. We know what we're involved in and we're prepared for whatever may go down."

Satisfied with what my eyes were witnessing, and what I was hearing from Samantha, we returned back to the jeeps and rode over to the runway where two semis were backing up to Hollywood's plane. We watched as workers formed a line at the back of the plane and tossed sacks of oranges inside its cargo bay.

"What kind of plane is this?" I asked Hollywood.

"It's a C-2 cargo plane," Samantha answered on Hollywood's behalf. "It's used for military transport mainly."

"Your sister's right, amigo," Hollywood chimed in. "This plane can carry twenty-six men, but of course I load it down to the max with around forty when I bring the workers in because they're light in the ass, you see?" he added, bringing about a giggle from Samantha and Amber.

"This plane can hold up to ten thousand pounds, so forty men

273

wouldn't even be a problem," Samantha chuckled. "He messin' with you, Ben."

"You know a little something I see, Samantha." Hollywood smiled. "When we take to the air, I'll see how well you handle that tin can y'all landed earlier."

"You sure you wanna do that, bruh?" Samantha chuckled.

"What is a bruh?" Hollywood asked perplexed.

"And you call yourself a ladies' man," Amber smirked.

"I'm not well informed on young lady lingo. School me, baby!" Hollywood said as he took in Amber's appearance.

Amber looked Hollywood up and down and said, "You probably have daughters my age, man."

"I have four daughters your age, but they share my blood and you don't, Amber. We can't have any retarded children at all."

"I beg to differ," Amber chuckled as she walked off from Hollywood.

"I'm not retarded I'm stupid, Amber! There's a difference in the two!" Hollywood retorted as we all laughed a little.

CHAPTER TWENTY-ONE

THE LOGISTICS BEHIND IT ALL

An hour or so later, Ben and company were all aboard the planes. Hollywood was flying a two-propeller medium-sized plane that had a big hydraulic door on the back big enough to drive a Hummer or a tank into it. He and Flacco, along with four soldiers, were aboard the plane as its propellers began spinning, kicking up dust everywhere as it taxied onto the runway ahead of the G-550 Samantha was piloting with its tail dipping low to the ground.

"Samantha, you just follow my lead once we get in the air, okay?" Hollywood said over the radio.

"Copy that, Hollywood. We looking at a seven-hour flight I suppose?" Samantha radioed as she revved up the engine on the corporate jet.

"This plane gets up to three hundred and fifty miles, so yeah! You have a uhhh…you have a handle, Samantha?"

"Something tells me I'm in for an adventure before we settle down. I'll give you my old Navy handle. Call me Wild Child!" Samantha radioed back as she taxied onto the runway.

"Ohhh, you're ex-Navy! Well, I'm gone test your skills this flight, Wild Child!" Hollywood radioed from the pilot's seat as his plane thundered over the runway, bouncing over the concrete. "A little music for us, no?" he asked as Steppenwolf's song *Magic Carpet Ride* came over the radio.

Samantha flicked her shades down over her eyes and looked over to Amber as she hit the throttle. This was right up both pilots' alley. They were thrill-seekers to the core and wouldn't dare miss an opportunity to party in the clouds. The black G-550 moved forward and was quickly up to one hundred and fifty miles. It zoomed past orange trees and workers waving their sombreros in a blur, leaving a trail of dust in its wake as it slowly lifted up off the ground. Samantha banked the plane right, avoiding the mountainside and began flying down the center of the valley.

Hollywood clicked on the radio and Steppenwolf's song was heard loud and clear. He began singing the lyrics at that moment as he guided his plane down the center of the valley at a low altitude… *"You don't know what…we can find…why don't you come with me little girl…on a magic carpet ride…"* he sang over the radio.

"I'm a comin'!" Samantha yelled as she hit the throttle and sped the plane up. "Take me for a ride, boy!"

"We'll follow the river! Right down the middle of the valley!" Hollywood yelled over the music as he swung his plane to the left, avoiding a cliff. The pathway soon narrowed and the two renegade pilots found themselves in a gorge bordered by craggy cliffs and waterfalls with a white-capped rushing river at the bottom.

"Scared yet?" Hollywood radioed as he skirted a cliffside off to his right.

Samantha was with Hollywood every step of the way, flying about a mile off his tail. The trees on either side were a haze and the cliffs were coming up on her at a rapid pace. She had to swing the plane left and then quickly bank right to avoid slamming into the mountainside as she flew at half speed. "I'm yawning back here, man!" she radioed back to Hollywood. "Amber's takin' pictures! This is not even a challenge!"

"Hey, you try flying this heavy bird through this gorge!" Hollywood laughed as he went up and over a large dam and popped out over a large lake. "On the other side is your challenge!"

Samantha dropped the plane about three hundred feet off the lake's surface and could see a gorge up ahead. She'd flown for nearly fifty miles in a canyon, but this gorge was much narrower as it had an overhang in which two rocks connected. She would either have to fly over the overhang, or fly underneath it in order to clear it.

Amber had been enjoying the flight up until that point. She looked back out into the cabin and could see Ben, Martha, Tre` and Victor strapped to their seats. The ride was smooth, but she could tell they were a little unnerved. "I don't, I don't think that's a good idea," she whispered to Samantha.

"What's going on up there?" Ben asked.

"Nothing, Ben. Just pilot talk!" Amber shot back. She then closed the cockpit door and whispered anxiously to Samantha while smiling, "Are, are you gonna do it, girl?"

"If he do it, I'll do it," Samantha told Amber as she guided the plane towards the overhang.

The two watched as Hollywood's plane dipped below the overhang. Once it cleared, it shot up like a balloon as it was hit with a gust of wind. "Hahaaaa!" Hollywood laughed. "It's like being shot out of a cannon!"

Samantha and Amber looked at one another stunned. Hollywood's plane was much heavier than theirs and it was still forced up by the wind blowing up from the valley below. The G-550 corporate jet they were flying in would undoubtedly be tossed further and more wildly, maybe even blown up into the overhang before clearing the rocks. As much of an adrenaline junky as Samantha could be, she didn't feel safe flying the jet underneath a rock canopy where the wind was uncertain. Such a gamble would be asinine just to prove a point. She guided the plane to the right, circled around the lake and went up and over the wall of rock and flew high above a vast, swamp-filled valley with specks of black water.

"Nice try," Samantha radioed over to Hollywood as she turned off the seatbelt light and settled in for the flight to Sao Paulo.

"You're scared of a little wind?" Hollywood laughed.

"No, just crashing into a wall of rocks, slamming down into a river and falling off a half mile high waterfall. That's kinda hard to survive," Samantha remarked nonchalantly as she set her coordinates for the Sao Paulo airport.

"Okay, mami," Hollywood radioed back. "Just to let you know, if ever you have to fly out of Boa Vista with a load, that is the route you should take. It bypasses any radars that may be honing in the area because the signals can't penetrate the mountains."

"I'll keep that in mind. See you on the ground, Hollywood." Samantha replied through a slight chuckled and a head nod.

The rest of the flight went unhinged. Nothing was said about the daredevil ride through the gorge or the encounter with the overhang and the risk Samantha had nearly taken. She and Amber disembarked from the plane and met up with Ben and company on a small runway of Sao Paulo/Guarulhos Airport just after ten at night. There were a dozen armed guards and three H-1 Hummers out on the runway waiting for the family to approach. The front passenger side door on the third Hummer opened and out stepped Flacco's older brother, fifty-nine-year-old Juan Camilo.

Juan Camilo was a mean-looking, tall, slender Mexican with a thin beard and sunken eyes and jowls. He pulled down on his sombrero and walked over to Flacco and the family. "We have loaded five hundred pounds heroin for thee Devereaux la Familia hour ago in Santos, Senor Holland," he told Ben in a heavy Spanish accent upon meeting him for the first time. "We try wait for you to show the entire procession, but time was of an essence."

Ben nodded while shaking Juan Camilo's hand. "It was a longer flight than expected from Boa Vista," he remarked as the four walked over to Hollywood's plane.

"Si," Juan Camilo replied. He then looked the plane over before turning to Flacco. "Are there oranges aboard?"

"We're good," Flacco responded as the rear door of the plane began to slowly descend. "Do we have the container?"

"It is on its way with the men to unload the plane, hermano," Juan Camilo stated as he turned to Ben. He wasn't too fluent in English and he sometimes grew frustrated expressing himself, so he returned to his native tongue. "*¿Señor de Holanda? De lo que Camilo y yo podemos ver, el punto débil aquí transferir la cocaína desde el avión y moviendo a través de Sao Paulo sobre a Santos. Estaremos vulnerables a un highjack durante ese tiempo.*" (Senor Holland? From what me and Camilo can see, the weak point here will be transferring the cocaine from the plane and moving it through Sao Paulo over to Santos. We'll be vulnerable to a highjack during that time.)

Flacco translated for Ben, who in turn asked Juan Camilo, "How fast can you do the transfer?"

"*Dos horas. Aquí preferentemente por la noche. Como ahora.*" (Two hours. Preferably done here at night. Like now.) Juan Camilo replied just as a black Escalade and a tractor trailer pulling a red container pulled up before the hangar. The semi swung around and backed up to the rear door of the plane as eight Mexican men with guns strapped to their backs climbed out of the SUV.

Again, Flacco translated. Ben then eyed the setup and gave a nod of approval. Eight men strapped with AK-47s was sufficient enough to offload the cocaine the family would ship. If they were hit, there would be enough men to battle, and two hours was quick enough time to offload a ton of cocaine was his belief. "Let's move on to the next phase," he ordered as he began making his way over to the waiting Hummers. The family all climbed into the bulletproof SUVs and made their way down to Santos, a major port city on the outskirts of Sao Paulo that rested on the Bay of Santos, which opened up into the Atlantic Ocean.

Samantha was in the back of the middle Hummer with Tre, Martha and Ben taking in the city. Sao Paulo was a beautiful town. It reminded her of New York with its tall skyscrapers and heavy vehicle and foot traffic. With a population of over twelve million, it was nothing more than another major city she was visiting for the first time, but a far cry from the dense jungles where the family's cocoa leaves grew.

A full moon was hanging heavy in the sky as the crew made it down to Santos. The town's port was where the freighter owned by Phillip Tran and Grover Kobayashi was docked. The family rode past the cargo ship and turned into a large, well-lit cargo area filled with containers. A large crane was unloading cargo containers from a single line of flatbed railcars and swinging them around onto the deck of the ship.

Ben and Martha climbed from their Hummer and took in the sight. The oranges that'd been flown in would have to be loaded into a container at the airport and driven the short distance from Sao Paulo to Santos and loaded onto the freighter. Martha was heading up the American side of the logistics behind the movement of the freighter and its precious cargo of drugs. "I'm gone need the names of the crew members aboard this ship to see if they match the manifests I got from Phillip and Grover," she told Ben as the two leaned up against the hood of Hummer watching the activity unfold under the clear night's sky.

"Barbara should have all that ready," Ben replied. "What you think, Auntie?"

"I trust Hollywood flying skills," Martha replied as she looked to the ground in deep thought. "It's an easy flight from Boa Vista to here, too. If they can offload and move it safely to the ship, it's

A-one, nephew, but nothing guaranteed. This Brazil, man. Me personally? I wouldn't do that shit," she lightly laughed.

"I feel ya'. It's open season down here," Ben agreed. "But, we got men capable enough to handle the job."

"I believe that," Martha replied. "And I can keep some heat off 'em if the Devereauxs come through with the right information."

"Let's go and see what they talkin' about," Ben remarked as he and Martha climbed back into the Hummer to continue putting together the logistics behind the family's movement of product.

Four miles or so from the Santos port, the caravan slowed before an iron gate at the end of a long, winding road bordered by rows and rows of thick palm trees. Three men in silk suits toting Uzis walked along the front of the cars, squinting their eyes over the headlights as one unlocked the gate and pushed it open.

Flacco paused the lead Hummer and let the window down. *"¿Por qué no está la puerta ya abierta, cristiano? Llamé cinco minutos antes para hacerle saber que estábamos llegando."* (Why isn't the gate already open, Christian? I called five minutes earlier to let you know we were coming.)

Christian Devereaux, a twenty-five-year-old Brazilian with muscular arms and legs, leaned down and said, *"Mi tía Bárbara pidió que la puerta permanecerá cerrada hasta el momento de su llegada. Su padre allí hablando con ellos ahora sobre ella."* (My aunt Barbara requested that the gate remain closed until your arrival. Your father's in there talking to them now about it.)

Flacco leaned back and squeezed his eyes in frustration. He slowly raised his head, looked up at Christian with a scowl on his face and yelled out, *"Esta no es la organización de Barbara! Alguien podría haber sido en nuestro culo, que es la razón por la que me dijo que tener la puerta abierta! Tienes que escuchar a las órdenes y me están dando a la familia si desea permanecer vivo en este negocio!"* (This is not Barbara's organization! Someone could've been on our ass which is why I told you to have the gate open! You need to listen to the orders me and the family are giving if you want to remain alive in this business!)

"Si, Senor Ramirez. I'm sorry," Christian meekly replied as he nodded over to the gate.

"Que esta sea la última vez que desobedecer una orden familiar. Este negocio no es para tomarse a la ligera." (Let this be

your last time disobeying a family order. This business is not to be taken lightly.) Flacco admonished as he eased up off the brake and allowed the SUV to roll slowly through the opened gate. "*Fuck fuera del camino!*" (Fuck out the way!) he boomed to a couple of Devereaux soldiers as the SUVs began to slowly roll through the opened gate.

"What's up with that, Flacco?" Ben asked.

"This Devereaux woman is a pain in the ass for everybody, Senor Holland," Flacco responded in an exasperated tone. "She thinks she still runs her family, but she doesn't understand that she works for the Holland family and answers to us now. We give an order, she overrides it when we're away and it causes problems."

"All that's gone change tonight. Your people tryna keep her alive and she actin' like a spoiled child that done had her toys taken away." Ben remarked as he eyed the exquisite, sprawling villa up ahead.

The caravan of Hummers rode through a botanical garden dotted with stone rose beds and pulled up before four stone arches that lay before the Devereaux family's three-story white stone villa just off in the distance. The beautiful home was lit up with glass-encased streetlights and climbed out under the humid night sky. The Devereauxs may have been inexperienced when it came to the life, but they knew how to make money was Ben's assessment.

The stone villa was immaculate. Just beyond the arches lay a large courtyard with a swimming pool encased in white marble. The villa itself sat at the edge of a cliff that overlooked the Santos port just a few miles away. A few armed guards walked along the pool's edge and several more stood on the marble stairs just outside of the entrance. Ben could tell right away how important the Ramirez family was to the survival of the Devereaux family. Their home was wide open and ripe for the taking giving its numerous excess points from the main road, but the soldiers had an advantage because the home rested up against a cliff. Only the front needed guarding because of the steep hillside behind it.

With the lights of the Santos port at their backs, Ben and company walked alongside the pool towards the front of the villa. Along the way, they met Juan Camilo Ramirez Junior, Juan Camilo's twenty-four-year-old son, whom everybody simply called Camilo. Juan Camilo and Camilo oversaw logistics and

281

security for the Devereaux family with their team of eight henchmen. They were violent, fearless soldiers who would fight to the death if necessary.

"You knew about the gate, Camilo?" Flacco asked.

"I just came on duty. Me and grandpa Edgar tried to tell them. And Barbara, too, but they wouldn't listen," Camilo responded while shaking his head.

"Take Christian's place down at the gate and have him stand poolside until morning," Flacco replied. "We want the family well-protected their time here."

"Si," Camilo responded as he threw an AK-47 over his shoulder and headed for the main gate with two henchmen following his lead.

The group continued on towards the villa's entrance where they were greeted by Edgar Ramirez Senior, Flacco's father, and Barbara Devereaux herself.

"Mister Ben Holland," sixty-four-year-old Edgar Ramirez smiled as he extended his hand. "Welcome to Brazil. You like what you've seen over to Boa Vista?"

Ben was familiar with Edgar through conversations with Flacco. He greeted the man and said, "I'm very pleased with the organization, Mister Ramirez. I hear you having problems with getting the Devereaux family to follow orders, though," he stated as he eyed Barbara.

Ben took in the woman's appearance briefly. From what Naomi had told him, she was in her late-fifties, but she looked years younger to him. Her brown hair flowed down her shoulders and she had perfect tan skin and crystal grey eyes. Barbara also dressed sexy. She wore a tight-fitting all-in-one white silk dress with a split up the thigh and white leather, heeled sandals. She gave off a bold vibe, but Ben knew she posed no real threat having learned what went down at the Ramirez villa, which was the day her family was conscripted into the Holland family.

Barbara hadn't the fight in her like some of the women inside his family, Ben knew. He was willing to bet Mary would give her a run for her money. Nonetheless, Barbara was a woman worthy of respect given the business she had chosen to become involved in; she just needed more coaching. "I'm Ben Holland," he said to the woman as he extended his hand.

"The Ramirez family has been here for four months now, Mister Holland. If someone were wanting to hit us, they would've done so by now. I'm trying to get them to ease their security." Barbara remarked, getting right to the point as she greeted Ben.

"Then why have them keep the gate closed when you knew Flacco was returning with lead members of the family?" Ben asked as he stared down at Barbara. "You're contradicting yourself."

"I can't leave this place without armed guards tagging along and breathing down my neck, Mister Holland. If I want to go shopping, or just pick up fruit from the open market, I have to have these men around me watching my every move."

"What we do is for your own protection, Misses Devereaux. If the Holland family didn't deem it necessary, we wouldn't be here." Ben counseled.

"I'm sorry, where's my manners?" Barbara remarked, changing the conversation. "You have family with you and I'm sure they're tired and wanting to eat and rest. Savio! Show our guest around! Make them comfortable while I talk with Mister Holland and Edgar. Come on in, everybody," she stated as she stepped aside. Barbara's youngest nephew, Savio, a slender twenty-two-year-old Brazilian with brown hair and big brown eyes that held hints of fear, greeted Samantha and company humbly. He guided them through the villa while Barbara, Ben and Edgar Senior convened inside a large living room with dim lighting that had an open balcony overlooking the waters.

The first floor of the Devereaux villa was made of natural stone and built into the hillside that the home rested on. The walls and floors were smoothened out in some areas, but for the most part, it was left in its natural, jagged state. There was an elevator in the left corners of the fancy villa whose glass gave a clear view of the Bay of Santos. Stone arches leading into wide, long halls were scattered about and there were three separate staircases in the home.

This was opulence to the max where the Devereaux family resided. They were sitting on a money pit, only they hadn't the ability to understand the danger the business they were involved in had to offer. They had the ability to move sixteen million dollars' worth of heroin on a monthly basis. And Ben's family was soon to be moving eight hundred kilograms of cocaine a month—twenty million dollars' worth of merchandise wholesale. The man wasn't in town just to have drinks and commiserate with the Devereauxs as the stakes were way too high on this level. Fallibility could lead to death. If his family was going to succeed, Barbara had to get her shit together was Ben's thinking as he, Edgar and Barbara convened inside the living room.

"Make yourselves at home, gentlemen," Barbara said as she walked over to a marble bar and extended her hand. "You men care for a drink?"

"Beer would be fine," Ben answered as he sat on a suede couch. "Edgar?"

"Beer is okay," Edgar remarked as he sat beside Ben. "Now, Madame Devereaux," he unpacked. "Senor Holland is right. You can't let your guard down in this business. You've ordered a hit in New York that was successful against the people who've killed your husband. You can't assume that there won't be any retaliation."

"There's nothing to worry about here in Brazil," Barbara stated as she handed the bottles of beer to Ben and Edgar. "I doubt if the people we hit will be able to reach us here," she added as she eased down onto a velvet chaise.

"I was told they mailed your husband's head back to you, Miss Devereaux. That should cause you some concern," Ben remarked as he twisted the cap off his beer.

"And we retaliated by killing the men responsible. I'm no longer concerned about the hit in New York, Mister Holland," Barbara responded as she lay back on the chaise smiling at Ben and Edgar Senior. "My main concern now is establishing a pipeline back to America for the heroin we possess. Let's focus on that, okay?"

"We'll focus on both," Ben remarked. "Until further notice? What the Ramirez family says goes. That's the way the family wants things done. Even if we didn't have to worry about the hit in New York, your family still sittin' on a large amount of heroin. And in this town? You're a potential target. Let the Ramirez family do their job."

"Okay, okay!" Barbara laughed as she tilted her head back. "We've been working here you know? Five hundred pounds were loaded on the ship you sent here just today. It leaves tomorrow morning and arrives in Pensacola, Florida in one week."

"I'll need the ship's manifest records, and the names of the crew so my people can see if it all checks out," Ben requested.

Barbara smiled and nodded. "I have them up in my office. I'll get them for you, Mister Holland. Make yourselves at home. There's plenty to eat and drink," she ended as she eased up from the chaise and left the room.

When Barbara cleared out, Ben looked over to Edgar. "What you think about that woman?" he asked.

"She takes the business too lightly, Senor Holland," Edgar remarked as he sipped his beer. "She thinks the one hit she ordered, and moving a few hundred pounds of narcotics makes her invincible now."

"She probably shit her pants if a hit was to go down here," Ben followed.

"We can run the business without Barbara, you know, Senor Holland?"

"You thinkin' about killin' Barbara?"

"No, no, no, Señor Holland. I would not do such a thing against the family interests. I'm thinking of buying her out maybe?"

"How much you think something like that would cost?" Ben asked as he stood and removed his silk suit jacket and sat down with his legs crossed t-style.

Edgar took another sip of his beer and pondered while looking down at the stone floor. "They have an entire heroin processing plant on the next island in Sao Vicente that can generate five hundred pounds of month with a street value of sixteen million dollars wholesale."

"My people gettin' three million off the top just for delivering the Devereauxs' product to the United States, Edgar," Ben countered. "We don't have to worry about processing the heroin or distributing it. And we get a cut of what our distributors back in America make on the gross without having to touch the product. We'll make over thirty million dollars in a year's time without major risk. But, to buy them out mean we would have to take over processing, transportation and distribution. We would have to set up an organization here in Brazil and offer 'em at least a quarter billion dollars upfront."

Edgar nodded and said, "That is a lot of logistics and finance when you put it that way."

"And that would all be on top of what we have going on back in Boa Vista. We push cocaine, Edgar. Let the Devereaux family run the heroin here in Brazil and take that risk. We'll provide security and lend some assistance with it until they come on line fully and get stronger. If they can't handle it? We'll revisit this conversation."

"Si, Senor Holland," Edgar agreed just as Barbara returned to the living room with the files Ben had requested.

CHAPTER TWENTY-TWO

ONE NIGHT IN BRAZIL

While Ben was holding discussions with Barbara and Edgar, Samantha, Amber and Tre` had just settled down on the third floor of the villa on a beautiful Monday night down in Santos. Theirs was a brown marble open floor grotto with a low ceiling made of natural brown stone. There was a small kitchen stocked with wine, seafood and steak, and a whirlpool tub big enough for six people filled with turquoise bubbling water that had steam pouring up from its swirls. Behind the tub were four marble arches that led out to an open semi-circle balcony that overlooked the waters of the picturesque Bay of Santos that lay a hundred feet below.

A king-sized canopy bed draped in a see-through mosquito net was off to the right of the tub that was sunk three below the bed, and a flat screen with the latest PlayStation console was mounted on the footboard. There was an island bar and stereo behind on the right with a box of cigars and a cellophane bag on top of it. The room had no lighting save for burning propane torches planted sparsely along the stone walls that gave off dim lighting.

Samantha and Amber had wasted no time indulging themselves in such a sexy layout. They'd grabbed two bottles of chilled wine and cranked up the music, blasting some sexy guitar blues as they stripped beside the whirlpool while smiling over to Tre`, who was flipping through a stack of PlayStation games. He had his back to his wife and Amber, but just over his shoulder, the two women were dancing up against one another beside the hot tub. They were putting on a show for Tre`, the tub's three-foot rise off the floor making it seem as if they were atop a stage in a strip club.

Samantha draped her left arm over Amber's shoulder while slowly gyrating to the sexy blues guitar music as Amber let her blonde hair fall down over shoulders. She placed both her hands on Samantha's hips and rocked with her in the nude.

"Tre`, what you think, baby?" Samantha asked as she ran her left hand through Amber's blonde hair. Tre` hadn't a clue what was going on behind his back, let alone what Samantha and Amber had planned on this night.

Several months earlier, Samantha and Amber had tried to have a threesome with Tre`, but he'd backed out. Samantha thought Tre` was scared at first so she had let the situation rest, but she later learned from Victor that Tre` felt that if he'd slept with Amber, he'd be cheating on his wife. It wasn't about being with another man ever with Samantha, though. She just had a thing for beautiful women. Loved having sex with them, and she felt it was only right that she shared her love for Amber with her husband so as not to have her bisexuality viewed as infidelity. Now that the three of them were down in Brazil spending one night inside a place that was to Samantha, a paradise, she and Amber had decided to give it another go.

"Tre`, can you come and unhook my bra, please?" Samantha called out over the music.

"Damn, they got the new Resident Evil game," Tre` said happily as he popped open the game disc cover and powered up the game console.

"Tre`!" Samantha called, giggling over her husband's obliviousness. "Tre?" she called out again, this time a little louder.

"Say what, baby?" Tre` asked as he looked over his shoulder.

Samantha laughed aloud and said, "Do you not see what your wife is offering you tonight? Put that game down and come over here."

Tre eyed Samantha. She was gorgeous, downright exotic to him. Five-foot-nine and a fit one-hundred and forty pounds with tan-skin and pert c-cup breast. She had the sexiest lips; pouty, pink and slender, and they produced most beautiful, brightest smile he'd ever seen in his life. Her grey eyes sparkled night and day and her shoulder-length black hair was naturally curly and shiny. She always wore it above her neck hanging down in curls in various styles like she was wearing on this night.

Tre` then eyed Amber as she danced with his wife. She was a few inches shorter than Samantha with perfectly tanned skin, d-cup breasts, and long blonde hair. She was fit herself when she'd first gotten out of the Navy, but she'd put on a few pounds since returning home to Flagstaff, Arizona, albeit in all the right places as she was now a sexy, voluptuous woman.

Tre` licked his lips and walked over to his wife's side. "You really want this to happen, don't you?" he asked as he smiled up at Samantha.

"Yeah," Samantha said as Amber rubbed her shoulders softly. "You like what you see? We're gonna bathe and we want you to join us. *I* want you to join us. Come on, it'll be fun," she added just as Amber reached around and began to unclamp her bra.

"I be right back, baby," Tre` smiled as he walked over to the bar counter where he'd seen a bag of weed and a box of cigars. He scooped the items up and returned to the tub, by then, Amber had unhooked Samantha's bra and both had removed their panties and were climbing into the steaming hot water.

"Take your clothes off and get in with us," Samantha smiled sexily as she lay back in the tub and spread her arms, putting her pert, pink, rock hard nipples on display.

Amber was standing up in the nude as she walked around the tub uncorking a bottle of wine. She made sure to put her taut ass on display when she bent down to pick up a couple of stem glasses. "You gone join us or you gone just stand there and be a spectator, Tre`," she chuckled as she rose, flipped her curly blonde hair and began pouring drinks for her and Samantha.

Tre` laughed over Amber's mocking him and said, "Okay. We gone…we gone make it do what it do. Y'all must think I'm scared or something like that." He sat the weed and cigar box on the stone ledge and used a razor blade that was inside the box to slice his cigar open.

"I can't tell you aren't. You're still dressed!" Samantha sassed.

"Okay," Tre` nodded confidently towards Samantha. "Let me roll this smoke so I can get into this here. Talk that shit when I'm off in it. Amber, fix me a drink," he requested as he sprinkled bud into his cigar.

"What are the rules, Samantha," Amber smiled as she grabbed another stem glass and poured Tre` a glass of wine.

"There are no rules is the rule," Samantha laughed out loud. "You heard that, Tre`?"

"It's whatever y'all ladies want. Hold that for me," Tre` coolly replied as he set his rolled blunt atop the cigar box and slid it over to Samantha. He then removed his clothes and climbed the stairs.

Amber took a seat beside Samantha and watched Tre` as he slowly entered the waters. She admired his slim, muscular physique, sexy, dark eyes and tatted-up arms. He'd cut his braids out and now sported a bald-fade cut with a diamond ring in either ear and a platinum herring bone chain around his neck.

Tre` was handsome to Amber, but the thing that impressed her the most was the length of his veiny, semi-hard circumcised dick. She'd felt it the night they tried to have threesome, but she'd never seen it, but now that her green eyes had fallen upon it and she was welcome to it, she was going to fulfill her fantasy of knowing what it would feel like with Tre` inside of her as she'd been attracted to him for quite some time. She'd never stoop so low as go behind Samantha's back. She was actually more into Samantha than Tre`, but she saw nothing wrong with him joining in if that's what Samantha wanted, and she could fulfill a fantasy of her own at the same time, which was to have uninhibited sex with Tre` and Samantha both at the same time.

Samantha sat back proudly watching Amber gawk her husband with a contented smile on her face. She knew had Trudy been alive, this very same thing would be happening on this night, if it wouldn't have happened earlier in their relationship. And whether she and Amber remained an item or not, Samantha would always include her husband, and at the very least, let him know that she was involved with a female and he was welcome to join in as he saw fit. She relinquished her thoughts as Tre` climbed into the tub and eased up beside her and picked up his blunt and lighter.

"Let us bathe you, baby," Samantha said as she picked up a soapy sponge and began rubbing her husband's chest and arms.

Tre` sparked his blunt as Amber came up on the opposite side of him and began rubbing his dick with another sponge underneath the water. Smoke mixed in with the stream rising up from the tub as Samantha and Amber bathed Tre` in the bubbling water while sipping their wine. Tre` was blowing out smoke from his mouth when Samantha leaned in and waved her nose before his face. She absorbed some of the secondhand smoke and leaned back, catching an immediate contact that had her light in the head.

Amber rose and stood before Tre` with her shapely legs on either side of him. She placed her hands on his knees, flung her blonde hair back over her shoulders, leaned down and said in a sexy voice, "Samantha doesn't smoke, but I love it because it makes me super horny. Blow me a charge, Tre`."

Tre` leaned up with the blunt in his mouth in reverse and blew hard. Amber puckered her lips and sucked in the potent dope for nearly a minute straight before pulling back. She held the weed and coughed with her mouth close, making a snorting sound as she pounded her chest. Several seconds later, she exhaled the smoke slowly. "Acapulco gold," she remarked as she picked up a soapy sponge. "I haven't smoked that in so long. There's nothing like that back in Arizona," she added as she continued to wipe herself clean.

Samantha bathed herself and Tre` clean and then slowly eased up and sunk into a dancing Amber's arms. Tre` sat and watched his wife party with her lover while toking on the weed. They danced in a circle while sliding up against one another. It wasn't long before the two embraced and entered into a deep, lingering kiss.

Amber was palming Samantha's bubbly but while gently nudging her back towards Tre`. The two were now right before his face, Samantha with her back to her husband as she leaned down and began sucking on Amber's d-cup breasts. Amber reached a hand down and grabbed one of Samantha's cheeks. Samantha reached back with the other and spread herself with her other hand on Amber's shoulder to balance herself.

"You know what your wife likes just as much as I do, Tre`. Lick her ass. She wants you to lick her ass. Ain't that right, Samantha?"

"Yes," Samantha panted as she pulled her sucking lips from Amber's breast. "Lick me, Tre`. Lick my ass."

Amber grabbed the single iron rail leading into the tub, leaned back and spread herself and tilted her head back. There was no need for instruction as these two had been here many times before. Samantha moaned as Tre`s tongue slid into her crack from behind. At the same time, she leaned forward and smothered her mouth over Amber's bald pussy and drank from her lover. The three had a perfect semi-daisy chain going, sucking and licking one another just as the melodious electric guitar and smooth bass of Carlos Santana's song, *Blues Magic* came over the surround sound system.

Amber sucked in air and let out a moan as she thrust her hips forward, and then in a circular motion as her hair began to fall over her face. She rose up on her tip-toes in order to gain better leverage as Samantha flicked her tongue over Amber's clitoris, kissing it tenderly on occasion before rubbing the tip of her nose across it and taking it back between her sucking lips.

"Baby," Amber moaned as she palmed the back of Samantha's head and drove harder into face.

"Lick it, Tre`!" Samantha called out as she pushed her ass back into husband's face.

Tre` was making love with his mouth to his wife's ass. He had a slow, sensual rhythm going with his puckered lips planting soft kisses on Samantha's cheeks before flicking his tongue over her asshole.

"Damnnnn," Samantha moaned out in ecstasy as she removed her lips from Amber's pussy and looked back over her shoulder. In the eighteen months they'd been married, Tre` had never licked her anus. It was something she loved having done to her, though. Trudy used to do it, and now Amber, but to have her husband do it was magical for Samantha as she'd always fantasized about Tre` licking her back there. "That feels sooooo good, baby," she moaned sexily over the music as she turned and planted her face back into Amber's pussy.

After several minutes had gone by, Samantha eased away from Tre` and walked behind Amber. She rubbed her pussy on her friend's ass while palming her breasts from behind. "Your turn, Tre`," she said as she walked Amber closer to her husband.

"Oh my," Amber smiled as her pussy hovered near Tre`s sexy lips. She spread her legs while leaning back into Samantha and said, "Your wife loves how it tastes, Tre`."

Tre` looked up at Samantha for approval. "I brought her to you, baby. It's okay, Tre`. Taste my girlfriend," she offered as she eased down Amber's backside while planting kisses on her spine. She then kissed both her butt cheeks before spreading them open.

Amber's lips trembled over Samantha's tongue sliding over her rear opening. She was really getting into it when Tre` leaned forward and flicked his tongue across her clitoris. He could taste his wife on the woman's slickened vagina as he licked her pussy while his wife licked her ass.

Amber was lost in ecstasy. She raised her hands and grabbed handfuls of her curly blonde hair as she stood in between husband and wife and had both of her holes orally serviced simultaneously. She spread her legs and sunk lower, opening herself as she rode two tongues in her saddle, rocking back and forth as waves of pleasure shot up her spine and churned her stomach.

"I don't wanna...fuck it!" Amber groaned as her body tensed. She came quietly over Samantha and Tre`s tongue while gripping her hair and frozen in place for several seconds that seemed to last an eternity.

"Sit up on the side of the tub, Tre`," Samantha requested as she slid from behind Amber and crawled through the waist high, bubbling water.

Tre` eased out the water and lay back on the edge of the tub as his wife and Amber knelt before him with their eyes fixated on his erection. Amber grabbed hold of his totem-pole-hard dick as he rested up on his elbows. She was preparing to go down on him, but Samantha snatched her up by her hair, flung her head back and shoved her tongue down her throat.

"You wanna suck my husband's dick?" Samantha asked when she finished her sensual, yet forceful kiss.

"Yes!" Amber moaned. "Please. Let me suck it, Samantha," she pleaded.

Samantha grabbed her husband's dick and eased Amber's head forward. The hades hot blonde went down on Tre`, her lips spread wide over his girth as she slid her mouth down until her lips touched Samantha's hand.

Samantha snatched Amber up again. She gasped for air as Samantha kissed her wildly for a second time before forcing her head back down onto her husband's dick. After a minute of sucking and gagging, Samantha snatched Amber up by the hair and kissed her again. She did that repeatedly, and each time she did, she drove Amber and Tre` crazy with anticipation. In her last move, she held Tre`s dick in her hand and let Amber barely kiss the tip of it, and it drove them both crazy. Amber kept trying to grasp Tre`s dick into her mouth fully, and Tre` kept thrusting his hips to put it there.

"Let's go over to the bed," Samantha requested as she stood up and walked out of the tub.

Tre` and Amber followed Samantha like two lost puppies, completely under her spell. When they were out of the tub and down the stairs, she turned and faced them both and placed her arms around either of their shoulder and pulled them in for a three-way kiss. Their tongues touched at random and they smacked on one another's lips while standing in a group hug flicking their tongues wildly.

Samantha, the master of ceremony over this hot and raunchy ménage a trois, grabbed Tre` by the dick and took Amber's hand and guided them over to the king-sized bed where they fell atop the mattress still soak and wet. "Now where were we?" she asked through a devilish grin as she removed a clamp and let her hair shoulder-length coal black hair fall down to her shoulders. "I know," she smiled as she crawled up the mattress. "Amber was sucking my husband's dick. Lay down, Tre`, because I need for you to do something for me while she does that to you."

Tre` laid on his back at Samantha's request. She crawled up his body and straddled his face in reverse with her hands on his firm chest, her pussy hovering over his face.

Amber laid next to Tre` and began kissing him tenderly while stroking his dick. She gave Samantha a few licks before sliding down the bed and taking Tre` back into her mouth. At the same time, Samantha sunk her pussy down onto Tre`s eager lips.

"This some hot shit," Tre` moaned he as he lapped at his wife's pussy while face-fucking Amber.

"You like this, baby? You're having fun aren't you?" Samantha smiled as she looked down and back at her husband while sliding her pussy all over her his lips and face.

Amber could see Samantha's pretty, pink pussy meeting Tre`s lips. She leaned up and joined in briefly, licking Samantha's clitoris from the front while Tre` fucked her opening with the tip of his tongue. She slid back down and took Tre` back into her mouth and sucked him like a woman possessed, only her matted hair able to be seen as she swallowed him whole while gagging. After a few minutes, she rose and looked into Samantha's grey eyes while stroking Tre`s rock hard dick.

Samantha knew what Amber wanted without her having to ask. She eased off her husband's face, crawled down to his feet and got into the doggy-style position. Amber followed, placing her ass high in the air with her face planted in the mattress. The two looked one another in the eyes as the seconds ticked by, wondering who would get the dick first as they held each other's hand.

Samantha exhaled and her grey eyes grew wide then slowly closed. "I love you, Tre`," she cried out as she pushed back and impaled herself on her man's dick.

Amber quickly leaned over and kissed Samantha before rising up to kiss Tre`. "Fuck her!" she coaxed.

Amber had her back to the opening of the grotto and Tre` was busy fucking his wife when Edgar Senior poked his head into the room. Samantha had seen him, but he quickly left the room without uttering a word. "Oh my god," she moaned. Her phrase had a double meaning, but it was fair to say that at this point it was more over the pleasure than having possibly being seen.

Tre` was now fully into the grove of things. He began fingering Amber's upturned pussy while stroking his wife, sliding two fingers in and out of her snug opening. He removed his fingers and presented them out to Samantha, who turned her head and sucked on them like a Popsicle.

"You like being nasty, don't you, baby?" Tre` asked as he slammed forward and held his dick in place while his wife sucked his pussy-soaked fingers.

"I am loving this," Samantha moaned over Tre` fingers as she drove back and flexed her vaginal muscles over his dick. "Take me, Tre`. Use me, baby. Use me, please," she panted while shaking her head from to side as she moved back and forth over her husband's rock hard dick.

Tre` began a slow circular motion as he reached out and gave Amber a couple of slaps. She wiggled her ass for him and placed a deep arch into her back, one that put her pink, moist slit on full display. Samantha was clamping down on his dick, though, slowly sliding forward and then slamming down, rubbing her ass against his pelvis as she took his full length. She was creaming all over his dick as she picked up the pace. "Get your dick, girl!" he growled as he grabbed Samantha's waist and drove into her deep, hard and fast, fucking her so hard her knees began to come up off the bed.

Samantha began moaning deeply as her pussy was rocked into submission. "No!" she screamed as she clawed at the silk sheets.

"What?" Tre` grimaced as he smacked Samantha hard across the ass and pulled Amber up by the hair and kissed her deeply. "This what y'all wanted, right?"

"Yes!" Samantha and Amber cried out together.

Tre` picked Samantha up, pulling her up while still impaled inside her. She was now on her feet with her hands to the mattress as Tre` took her from behind. Her hair was matted to her skull and her voice had dropped a couple of octaves. "Ung! Tre`, please! No!" she grunted while shaking her head in protest over the pounding she was taking. "Please!" she said again before swallowing hard and gasping for air. "Aww, shit! Awww shit you finna make me come!" she screamed as she stood with her ass up in the air and her hands planted down into the mattress and her head up against the headboard.

"That's right! Come for me, girl!" Tre` commanded as he fucked Samantha relentlessly.

"Mutherfucka!" Samantha laughed as she began coming uncontrollably. "Okay! Ookayyy! You got me! You fuckin' got me, man!" she conceded as she jumped off Tre`s dick and slid down the headboard and lay out of breath.

Tre` then knelt down on the mattress and placed Amber on her back. He grabbed both her ankles with one hand, pinning her feet to the headboard right beside Samantha. He slapped his dick over her clitoris for several seconds and then eased into her while resting back on his knees.

"Oh shit!" Amber groaned as she lay bent up like a pretzel. "Slow down, baby! You're, you're…ahhh!" she cried out as Tre` suddenly stood up in her like he was doing pushups.

"Say what?" Tre` mean-mugged as he began grinding down into Amber. "Say what?"

"Shit!" Amber grunted as she thrust her hips back up into Tre`. She fought hard to get him to lower her legs.

"Oh," Tre` laughed. "You don't wanna be fucked. You wanna be made love to, huh?" he asked as he held his dick deep inside Amber.

"Yes," Amber moaned through closed eyes as she rocked beneath Tre` with her hands on his hips to guide him slowly. "Make love to me, baby. That's what I want," she cooed.

Tre` lay flat atop Amber and grabbed her ass cheeks. He began rotating his hips in a circular motion while kissing her tenderly.

Amber raised her arms around Tre`s back and held him close as she lay on her back with her legs fallen open to the side. Samantha was at her head, her freshly fucked pussy just inches from her face. When she laid her head on Samantha's thigh, Samantha got the picture. She scooted down a bit and draped a leg over Amber's head.

While laying on her side getting her pussy licked, Samantha placed her lips at the junction of her husband's and Amber's lovemaking. Tre` rose up slightly and she removed his dick and placed it in her mouth, sucking Amber's juices and using her mouth like a pussy. She coaxed Tre` by grabbing his nut sack and gently pulling him forward so he could fuck her mouth. After a couple of minutes, she took her husband's dick and guided it back into Amber's waiting pussy.

"Oh God, yes," Amber moaned as she threw her arms back and began rotating on Tre`s dick.

Samantha crawled up the bed and straddled Amber's head facing Tre` and sunk her pussy down into her face. She leaned forward and knelt before her husband and Amber's union. The three were in a tangled heap of pleasure. Samantha licking her husband's dick and her lover's pussy while they made love, the room now heated up with passion and the sounds of sex as the three lovers approached their crescendos.

Tre`s pace began to excel and he began grunting. "Damn this some good pussy," he groaned as he fucked Amber hard and fast.

Amber was right where she wanted to be: on her back with Tre`s dick inside her and Samantha's pussy in her face. It was enough to drive her over the edge. "I'm coming! Y'all good! Y'all goooodddd! I'm coming! I'm fuckin' comin!'" she cried as her body began jerking uncontrollably "Fuck!" she moaned as she dove back into Samantha's pussy and tongued it deep.

Amber was spent, but Tre` continued to stroke her deep. His pace quickened as he held her legs up in the air by the ankles. "No!" Amber pleaded, her voice rising several octaves as Tre` handled her like a rag doll while fucking her mercilessly. "Why, baby? Samantha, ya' husband, please! Make…him…please! Tre`!

No!" she rattled off as she nudged Samantha off her.

Samantha rolled off of Amber's face and laughed over her incoherence. "Finish up in me, baby," she told Tre`. "I think…I think Amber tappin' out."

Tre` eased out of a tired Amber, threw her limp legs aside and hovered over Samantha. He was about to enter her until she grabbed him by the waist and nudged him up a bit. "Let me suck it some more," she said in a seductive, sexy voice.

Tre` did as requested and knelt beside his wife. She took his slickened dick in her mouth and gave him one long slurp, sucking some of Amber's juice off before she grabbed his ass cheeks and drove him forward, wanting him to fuck her mouth again. Back and forth her head went as Amber lay beside her in a limp state.

Samantha could feel Tre` tensing up in her mouth, his organ growing stiffer and throbbing at the back of her throat. She pulled away and lay back while staring up at her husband, biting her bottom lip with a wide smile on her face. "You…were…fantastic! Come on home, boy," she coaxed as she pulled Tre` down on top of her.

Amber did the honors by guiding Tre` home to his wife. She placed his dick at Samantha's entrance and cradled her friend's skull and kissed her deeply as her husband made slow love to her. The three shared another three-way kiss that was all so sensual that they'd become a force of one. "I love you, Tre` Mitchell," Samantha said as she hugged her husband tightly. She raised her legs and spread them wide at that moment, giving herself completely to her husband as his pace increased. "Come in it!" she said as she pursed her lips and looked down at the dick driving into here. "Come in your pussy, Tre`! This…god this your pussy!"

"You ready?" Tre` asked as he rotated his hips in rapid motion. "I'm finna come in this mutherfucka!"

"Give it to me, baby!" Samantha pleaded.

"Samantha!" Tre` groaned out loud as he ejaculated into his wife. Both gripped one another tightly, never wanting to let go as they tongued each furiously while moaning into one another's mouths over the indescribable sensation.

"You're the best, baby. Oh boy here it comes!" Samantha screamed through a shuddering orgasm.

After catching her breath, she kissed Tre` and scooted over to let her him lay in between her and Amber.

"Wow," Tre` laughed as he lay in between the two women with his arms around their necks while breathing hard.

"Next time we have to record it," Samantha said as she lay staring up at the ceiling.

"I'm down," Tre` remarked. "That shit…that shit was fire. Where my weed?"

"Over here," Samantha replied as she eased up from the bed and went back over to the whirlpool to grab Tre`s blunt and a wine bottle. No need for glasses as they would drink from the tap after all that'd gone down.

"Thank you, guys," Amber smiled as she pecked Tre` on the lips.

Samantha returned to the bed and slid onto it knees first. She lit Tre`s blunt with one of the candles beside the bed and handed it to him and fell in beside Amber giggling as they lay side by side staring into one another's eyes lovingly. Before long, sleep had taken over, leaving the three to slumber in the nude while hugged up against one another after the weed had been smoked and the wine had been drunk.

CHAPTER TWENTY-THREE
THE COST OF BUSINESS

The sun was peering over the waters of the Bay of Santos to the east on Tuesday morning, June 9th, as Juan Camilo walked along the side of the swimming pool out in front of the Devereaux villa under the rising sun's orange hue. He'd just completed a check of the close exterior of the home and was now making his rounds on the outside premises. He approached the stone arches at the front of the property and was met by his son Camilo and his uncle Hollywood.

"*Todo está a la altura? Cualquier cosa fuera de lugar anoche, hijo?*" (Is everything up to par? Anything out of place last night, son?) Juan Camilo asked as he held onto an AK-47.

"*Nada fuera de lugar la última noche, papá. Hay una empresa de construcción estableciendo unos doscientos metros abajo de la colina desde la puerta esta mañana, aunque.*" (Nothing out of place last night, dad. There's a construction company setting up about two hundred yards down the hill from the gate this morning, though.) Camilo answered with his great uncle Hollywood at his side. "*Tres vehículos utilitarios y un camión volquete.*" (Three utility vehicles and a dump truck.)

"*¿investigar, Hollywood?*" (Did you investigate, Hollywood?) Juan Camilo asked with the sun to his back.

"No. It's a work day." Hollywood shrugged as he tugged on the front of his one-too-big silk suit jacket as he held onto an M-4 carbine rifle. "Just some guys getting an early start I assumed."

"*No asuma, Hollywood.*" (Do not assume, Hollywood.) Juan Camilo counseled through his sunshades as he scratched his greying five 'o' clock shadow. "*Senor Holland y su familia estará saliendo dentro de la hora. Ir y comprobar en esos muchachos y asegurarse de que son lo que son y me informará. La familia de Holanda no dejarán hasta que todos los puntos son seguras."* (Senor Holland and his family will be leaving within the hour. Go and check on those guys and make sure they are who they are and report back to me. The Holland family will not leave until all points are secure.)

"Si! Be right back with a report," Hollywood quipped as he and Camilo headed for the botanical garden that led to the front gate.

The sun had just broken over the horizon completely as Hollywood and Camilo neared the front gate at the far edge of the property. "Open it up, amigos," Hollywood commanded towards the six men standing on the outside of the barricade.

One of the men pushed the gate open and Hollywood stood in between his team of six henchmen while removing his M-4 carbine rifle from his shoulder. *"Mi sobrino no confíe en los chicos en el camino. Tampoco yo ahora que él ha mencionado. Vamos a ir y asegúrese de que no están aquí para interferir en nuestro negocio."* (My nephew doesn't trust those guys down the road. Neither do I now that he's mentioned it. We're going to go and make sure they aren't here to interfere in our business.) he casually remarked as he racked the rifle and looked downhill towards the men setting up the construction site.

About six hundred feet down the forested road was about a dozen or so men wearing bright orange jackets and black pants. A couple of the men were setting out orange cones while a few others rolled orange and white barrels out onto the road, narrowing it down to one lane.

"No me gusta el aspecto de esta." (I don't like the looks of this.) Hollywood remarked. *"Tomemos dos jeeps allí abajo y pagar nuestros nuevos amigos una visita."* (Let's take two jeeps down there and pay our new friends a visit.) he ordered as he walked over and climbed into the back seat of a black on black Cadillac Escalade with Camilo and two of the Ramirez family's goons in the front seat.

A lead Escalade pulled forward with four soldiers inside and all four windows rolled down. Hollywood and his crew tailed them slowly with their windows rolled up as the team traveled down the palm-tree-lined road with the Bay of Santos off in the distance to their right as they descended the hill. The men up ahead working construction all paused their actions when they spotted the two SUVs rolling their way. A few walked behind the dump truck while one guy wearing a white construction hat walked out into the open road waving an orange flag, signaling for the two SUVs to stop.

Hollywood sat up at that moment and placed a hand on the headrest. He watched out the back driver's side window as the lead SUV slowed to a halt. Two Mexicans in lavish silk suits hopped out from the backseat of the lead SUV and approached the man waving the orange flag with AK-47s draping their sides.

****

Meanwhile, Ben was up in his suite having just finished getting dressed. The itinerary was to fly eleven hours up to Oklahoma to drop Martha off in Ponca City and spend the night on the ranch. From there, him, Victor, Bay and T-top were going to fly over to Bowling Green, Missouri, a small town ninety miles north of Saint Louis, and meet up with Jay-D, Loopy and Kantrell to resolve a couple of issues that had arisen over the weekend. He tied his tie, grabbed his suit jacket and walked out the room and headed for the elevator where he pushed the down button.

The elevator descended from the third floor and Ben met up with Samantha, Tre` and Amber when the doors slid open. "What's up?" he casually asked as he stepped onto the elevator while putting on his suit jacket.

"Nothing!" Amber and Tre` responded in unison while looking off in different directions.

"Why you ask what you heard like that?" Samantha rattled off as she bit her bottom lip while eyeing her brother as the elevator began moving down.

Ben looked over to Samantha, then Amber and over to Tre` as the elevator descended and merely shook his head while straightening his collar. "What the hell y'all got into last night up there? Don't even answer that shit," he added as the doors opened and the four of them stepped out onto the first floor.

Edgar Senior and Flacco were sitting having coffee with Martha, Victor and Barbara. Flacco eyed the family walking his way. "Senor Holland, we have a slight delay," he remarked as he stood up.

"What's going on?" Ben asked as he looked around.

"Some strangers blocking the road. We're looking into it now. Have some breakfast while we wait."

"I'm sure it's nothing," Barbara downplayed. "Here, you all sit," she said as she began pulling out chairs. "You should eat before you take to the air."

"Yes!" Samantha sighed. "After last night I'm starving. Tre`, Amber and I had…had slept like a baby," she then said, changing up her statement quickly before she went any further.

****

Back outside, downhill from the main gate, Hollywood's two goons stood before the lead construction worker. "Who are you? What are you doing here?" one of the men asked over the rumble of the dump truck.

"Cable wire!" the man called out with his head bowed.

The second henchman leaned in for a closer look at the construction guy. "He's Asian!" he said as tapped his counterpart's chest while raising his gun.

"Hit them now!" the construction worker yelled as he turned and ran.

Two figures in black ski masks rose up from the bed of the dump truck and began firing over its sides as the truck began rolling forward.

Hollywood watched stone-faced as his two soldiers exchanged gunfire with the gunmen in the back of the dump truck until both men went down and were rolled over by the semi. The two remaining soldiers inside the lead SUV were climbing out with their guns, but their SUV had been pushed aside by the dump truck. The metal crushed one man, and the other had absorbed a hail of bullets as the semi rolled by.

"*Volver arriba! Volver arriba!*" (Back up! Back up!) Hollywood yelled as the front of his Escalade began to be sprayed with bullet shells from men running alongside the dump truck.

The windshield shattered and both the driver and the passenger in the front seat were struck in the face. The driver died with his foot on the gas pedal, sending the SUV into a tailspin and forcing it up against one of the palm trees lining the road off to the left. As glass shattered all around them, Hollywood and Camilo looked up and saw the dump truck lumbering their way. They rushed out the passenger side back door and scurried up into the cover of the dense, dewy cover of palm trees just before the dump truck bogarted its way through the wrecked SUV and continued uphill.

Together, Hollywood and Camilo ran in between the trees and the thick, damp brush in their silk suits. They had to shield themselves from bullets by pausing every few yards or so in order to allow a burst of gunfire to slam into the wood and penetrate the dirt at their feet before they continued on.

****

Back uphill on the property, Juan Camilo and four soldiers were storming towards the front gate, having heard the gunshots. They were running through the botanical garden when they witnessed a dump truck crashing through the front gate like that of the Taliban on a suicide mission. Nine maniacal ski masked gunmen fired automatic machine guns over the bed of the semi as it went up over stone beds of roses, bouncing furiously, and crushing stone and flowers in its path. The rampage had forced Juan Camilo and his men to take cover just as the dump truck crashed through the stone arches that led into the courtyard of the Devereaux villa.

Whether it was accidental or done or purpose was uncertain, either way, the semi stormed through the courtyard and drove off into the deep end of the swimming pool and quickly sunk down into ten feet of water. Its campaign of destruction was brought to a halt, but the nine gunmen in the rear rose up again and began firing off rounds as they hopped over the rear gate of the dump truck and landed on the ground beside the poolside. A lone gunman ran back towards the botanical garden as the other eight ran towards the villa's entrance.

Back inside the home, Ben, Edgar Senior, and Victor were all strapped with AR-15 automatics and taking cover behind the stone arches on the first floor. They'd sent Samantha, Martha, Amber and Barbara up to the second floor with Flacco, Tre`, and Barbara's two nephews, Savio and Christian to keep them safe as they knew the gunfight was going down in the courtyard and would soon spread to the first floor of the villa.

Out in the courtyard, meanwhile, Juan Camilo was peeking from behind a stone rose bed that hadn't been touched by the dump truck. He could see the lone gunman shooting away from his location over towards another rose bed where two of his men were shielding themselves. The assassin had been firing for nearly a minute and Juan Camilo knew all he had to do was wait. Several seconds later, the gunman's gun went empty. The mistake he'd made was not shielding himself in order to reload.

Juan Camilo rose at that moment and released a gun spray that ripped through the man's skull and neck, just in case he was wearing a bulletproof vest. "*A la casa!*" (To the home!) he yelled out to his four-man team as he took off running through the rose garden back towards the villa.

Hollywood and Camilo, meanwhile, were busy running through the forest. They were trying to make it back to villa to join the battle, but they had troubles of their own for the moment as four gunmen were hunting them down. The two were forced to exchange gunfire with the men out to kill them while making a hard run uphill. Both had the advantage, however, because they were able to see their attackers before they themselves could be spotted. The two were running side by side when a burst of rounds hit close by. The men hunting them were firing in their general direction, but couldn't land an accurate visual. They only fired when hearing crushing sticks, something that occurred every time Hollywood and Juan Camilo moved.

"*Nos estamos acercando a una depresión, Camilo.*" (We're coming up on a depression, Camilo.) Hollywood said as he leaned up against a tree and peeked back downhill to his left while breathing hard. "*Yo sé donde dos de los pajarones sobre nuestras espaldas están en a la izquierda de aquí. Puede ver los otros dos a su lado?*" (I know where two of the assholes on our tail are at on the left over here. You see the other two on your side?)

"*Que a mi derecha abajo aproximadamente cinco 'o' reloj.*" (They're on my right downhill about five 'o' clock.) Camilo whispered as he looked downhill to his right with his tongue hanging from his mouth and a slight smile on his face.

"*Bien, vamos hasta doce 'o' clock para que podamos matar a estos chicos.*" (Well, we're going up to twelve 'o' clock so we can kill these guys.) Hollywood huffed while watching the two men hunting after him creep through the thick brush. "*Lo único es que, cuando nos movemos, ellos van a empezar a disparar de nuevo. Si uno de nosotros va hacia abajo, el otro viene de vuelta. Moriremos juntos hoy, bueno, sobrino?*" (Only thing is, when we move, they gonna start shooting again. If one of us goes down, the other comes back. We die together today, okay, nephew?)

Camilo stared at his great uncle seriously with his back up against the tree. He looked to his right downhill and could see the two men hunting him down wading through the woods, gently brushing branches aside as their eyes darted to and fro with rifles extended. *"Lo haremos con la depresión."* (We will make it to the depression.) he whispered.

Hollywood nodded and held up three fingers. He lowered one, then the second. He paused for a split second before lowering the last finger, and he and Camilo took off running uphill. A foreign tongue, that of Asian was heard at that moment and gunfire immediately followed. Shells nipped at the feet of Hollywood and Camilo, kicking up dirt and shredding leaves as they ran in a snake-like pattern uphill until the two hit a depression that sunk five feet down below the palm trees.

"Aquí, el tío de Hollywood!" (Here, uncle Hollywood!) Camilo whispered as he slid into the pit and quickly peered out over the top of the ledge.

"Sólo tengo un clip a la izquierda despué"s de este!" (I only have one clip left after this one!) Hollywood whispered in a panicked state while gasping for air as he slid in his second-to-last magazine. *"Estamos en una situación de ventaja todavía?"* (Are we at an advantage still?)

"Somos. Si lo hacemos bien vamos a matarlos a todos." (We are. If we do this right we'll kill them all.) Camilo stated through heavy gasps as he leaned up against the dirt sides of the pit and placed the barrel of his gun over the ledge. *"Ir al otro extremo y apunta su arma hacia el otro lado. Disparar a las piernas si alguien corre por."* (Go to the other end and point your gun towards the other side. Shoot for the legs if anybody runs by.) he requested as he peered back over the ledge and saw four pairs of legs running his way.

Camilo scooted over to his left inside the pit and waited for several seconds. When the men neared, he opened fire with his M-4. Two men went down immediately and he crawled out the pit as the other two men ran past him. He ducked behind a palm tree just as the remaining two men turned and shot back at him. Hollywood opened fire on the men from the opposite side of the depression and both men shooting at Camilo went down. He climbed out from the pit at that moment and nodded. Both men then took off running back towards the villa.

CHAPTER TWENTY-FOUR

A GUNFIGHT IN PARADISE

Why I'm not surprised over this shit? Talking to Barbara last night showed me just how weak these people were inside this business, now we out here tryna keep us and them alive. It's like Vietnam around here. Whatever happened outside done died down, but I know the shit ain't over. I'm hiding behind a stone arch deep off into the home next to a staircase. Victor on my left up ahead and Edgar Senior out in front of us of both ducking down in the living room off to my right. We all eyeing one another anxiously, nodding in agreement that we ready to do this as we wait for the inevitable. Right about now, the only place we have to run is up to the second and third floors. If it come to that, it mean we would be on the verge of losing the battle.

Flacco had insisted that I stay upstairs up with Samantha, but I ordered him up there instead. I didn't feel right letting the Ramirez family wage this battle all by themselves. Juan Camilo and his son Juan was already out there with Hollywood, and Edgar Senior was down here with us. If we get run over, somebody from the Ramirez family had to be on hand was what I knew, so I had Flacco fall back. This was where we at with it now, though, out on the front lines in the midst of a fierce battle.

I swallowed hard as the gunfire outside kicked up, this time it was closer than before and getting closer to the point that the gunfire had grown deafening. The front doors were suddenly blown open by a blast. Four men rushed in and all hell broke loose. Me, Edgar Senior and Victor opened fire simultaneously and one man went down right away. The other three scattered off in all directions, but I swear I just saw a ball fly through the air.

"Grenade! Everybody get down!" Edgar Senior yelled as he ran out into the open floor area.

"Vic! Get the nigga hiding behind the counter in the kitchen!" I yelled as I opened fire on the area where the other two men had run. Edgar Senior was out in the open and I wanted to keep him covered. It's been I while since I'd bust to kill, but now that I'm back in it, it feel just like old times, but I'd be lying to myself if I said I wasn't scared as shit.

Shells jumped from my AR-15, Victor's, too, as we held these guys at bay for Edgar Senior. I saw the old military vet scoot across the floor and pick up the grenade and throw back in the direction of the two men I was firing on before he ran back into the sunken living room. "Get down!" he yelled as he dropped from sight.

The two men ran out from behind the stone partition and I was able to cut 'em down. They didn't even hit the floor before an explosion erupted. I ducked back behind the stone arch as smoke and particles shot past me over the sounds of slabs of meat falling back down onto the stone floor.

"I got the one in the kitchen! He dead in the kitchen!" I heard Victor yell out.

The side door was kicked in at that moment and four more gunmen rushed into the kitchen. These guys were right up on Victor. The only thing separating them was the island counter as they engaged in close quarter contact. I could see Victor's silhouette in the morning sun and him back peddling wildly in his suit as he opened fire at nearly point blank range over the counter. The assassins returned fired and Victor let out a yelp of a scream before he ducked down and scurried out the kitchen on his hands and knees. One gunman gave chase as the other three rushed up the stairs.

"*Samantha!*" I said to myself just as Victor emerged from a hall and fell up against the ledge breathing hard with blood dripping down his right pants leg.

"They all over this mutherfucka!" Victor yelled through heavy gasps as he slid another clip into his rifle and looked back out towards the kitchen.

I could hear the gunman approaching, so I stepped out from behind Victor and fired while hunched over. Bullets slammed into the wall behind me and I fell to the floor while exchanging gunfire. I fired off another burst of bullets and hit the mutherfucka in his head three times, cracking his skull.

Screams were heard from the second floor at that moment. The voice that stood out was Martha's. "Here they come!" she screamed out in a terrified voice.

"Samantha, go upstairs!" I heard Tre` yell just as heavy gunfire erupted.

"*Christian, tomar cubierta, usted está en la línea de fuego! No puedo dispararte en el camino!*" I heard somebody scream out in Spanish.

"*Savio, me pegué! ¡Me dieron! ¡Madre de salir de aquí! ¡Vaya! ¡Vaya! ¡Vaya! ¡Vamos hijos de puta!*" Barbara screamed in terror as the gunfire on the second floor intensified.

"*¡Conseguí uno! ¡Caer, Savio! Y quedo con los otros dos! ¡Las mujeres son en el tercer piso con Tre`!*" I heard Flacco yell.

I hurried up the stairs with my weapon over the slew of Spanish banter and thunderous gunfire, not knowing what was being said, nor what I would encounter. Halfway up, the gunfire ceased and I made eye contact with Flacco. He was crouching behind a fallen Christian and a knocked over wooden table that that was cratered with bullet holes. Christian was facing away from me, but I could tell he was hit because the entire backside of his suit jacket was torn and soaked in dark red blood and his M-4 lay in a death grip inside his bloody hand.

Flacco placed a hand to his lips and held up one finger as he made a slicing motion towards me. He then held up two fingers and pointed to the opposite side of the room.

One man down and two more on the other side of the room was what he was telling me. He then pointed back down the stairs and made a curve with his hands and held up ten fingers and began removing them one by one, telling me to go around to the opposite staircase and wait ten seconds.

I nodded and backed back down the stairs and met up with Victor and Edgar Senior. Together, we ran through the destroyed living room as sporadic gunfire continued outside over wild, Spanish yelling.

"*¡No permita que nadie más entre en la casa! ¡Mata a todos los que tenemos uno vivo!*" I heard Hollywood yell over the gunfire.

"Hollywood may have one captured, Senor Holland," Edgar

said to me as we trotted through the kitchen headed towards the second staircase.

"Okay! Flacco, gone lay down some gunfire to distract 'em and we gone come up from the back," I told Edgar and Victor. I'd been counting down in my head as we made it over to the staircase… *four…three…two…one…*more gunfire ensued and three of us climbed the stairs with me leading the way.

I waited at the top of the staircase out of sight for a few seconds as bullets ricocheted off the stone walls. When the lull hit, I peeked out and saw the legs of the two remaining assassins walking across the marble floor. I pointed up and Victor and Edgar came up over my back as I fell out from the stairwell. We unloaded together and our bullets hit the two remaining gunmen in their backs. They froze in place and let off bursts of gunfire into the ceiling before collapsing to the floor.

From across the room, Flacco and Savio Devereaux slowly emerged. Savio ran over to his cousin as I headed up to the third floor to check on my aunt and sister.

When I got up to the grotto, I yelled out, "This Ben! This Ben! Where y'all at?"

The room was dead silent and no one was in sight. Tre` finally peeked out from a crevice and sighed as he held on to an AR-15. He stepped forth and pulled Samantha and Amber out with him. Samantha was gripping a M-4 rifle and Amber had a twelve-gauge shotgun. Martha emerged from the balcony and she ran across the room into my arms, followed by Samantha.

"Ben, you okay?" Martha asked relieved. "What the fuck happened? Who hit us?" she asked with an AK-47 draping her side.

"Clear inside!" I then heard Edgar Senior yell out. "Outside clear?"

"Outside clear says Juan Camilo Senior!" I heard another voice call out from the first floor.

"Second floor is secure!" Flacco yelled down. "Everybody on the third floor is safe?"

"Everybody good!" I called out as I held on to my sister and aunt back. They were all a little shook, but untouched.

"He didn't say everyone was safe on the second floor," Barbara fretted as she emerged from behind the island counter in her silk robe and slippers. "Where're my nephews? Are Christian and Savio okay?" she asked me. Not waiting for a reply, Barbara began walking slowly towards the stairs with her hands on her hips and sobbing lowly. "Savio! Christian!" she weakly called out as she began walking down the staircase. *"Dios, no dejes que mi corazón diga la verdad hoy!"* she cried out.

I didn't know what Barbara had said, but I knew what she would witness once she hit the second floor. I was also thinking that the head of the Devereaux family may have to witness the downside of this business firsthand to understand the seriousness of it all. There was a moment of silence as Barbara's head disappeared from sight. I broke away from Samantha and Martha and walked over to the stairs and could see her descending slowly in her robe as she held onto the rail while staring blankly out the bay window that overlooked her destroyed property. I trotted down the stairs and caught up with her just as she made it to the second floor and looked to her right.

I joined Barbara's side as both our eyes fell upon the carnage. There, on the opposite side of the room, laying on his back surrounded in a pool of blood with his eyes wide open was Christian Devereaux.

"¡No, no mi sobrino! ¡Cristiano! ¡Qué te han hecho! ¿Qué han hecho, Dios mío?" (No, not my nephew! Christian! What have they done to you! What have they done, Dear God?) Barbara screamed as she took off running across the room and dropped down beside her murdered nephew.

I didn't know what was said by Barbara Devereaux, but it was no doubt that she was grieving the loss of her family as she cradled his head in her hands. I stared somberly as I looked over to Flacco. I could tell he was thinking the same thing as myself: that Barbara had just learned what a high price could be paid in this life and she wasn't as safe as she thought.

"Oh, my god," I heard Samantha gasp as she, Amber, Tre` and Martha descended the stairs.

This was a bloodbath. On both sides. Across the second floor lay four dead men. The place had been ripped to shreds by bullets. Furniture was upturned, and blood, guts and brain matter was scattered all around. We were literally walking on shells and had to balance ourselves to keep from slipping on the blood.

Samantha held my hand as we walked out of the carnage with no tears shed. My sister was just relieved that I was still alive, I knew. We were the lucky ones out this ordeal. No one from my family had gotten wasted, but the Ramirez family had suffered serious losses in defense of the Devereaux family, and Barbara herself had loss a family member. Whoever was behind it had some serious muscle. Enough manpower to hit us head on.

My first guess was that it was a local crew looking to overtake the Devereaux family's heroin operation, but when Victor pulled off one the dead men's ski mask, I was left puzzled. I rushed over to the second dead man and pulled his mask, then the third man's mask. I stood looking at these men and right away Phillip Tran and Grover Kobayashi came to mind. I was under the impression that we'd been hit by some Brazilians, but these guys were Asian.

Phillip and Grover knew about the heroin shipment, and the Devereaux family's warehouse as well. They'd also sent the cargo ship over to move the product back to America. Flacco walked up and stood beside me as he eyed the dead man at my feet. "What are you thinkin', boss?" he asked me.

"That Phillip and Grover set all this up, but…"

"It doesn't fit," Flacco interrupted, finishing my thought. "The Asians have no reason to stage an attack like this. But on the other hand…"

"They could've turned a crew out in San Francisco on to what was doing." I finished up Flacco's thought as I grabbed my cellphone. I was going to call Phillip direct and ask him was he behind it.

"Boss," Flacco said just before I hit the call button. He leaned down and pulled down on the dead man's front collar and then ripped his shirt open completely. Tatted on his chest was an evil smiling flaming skull. "Yakuza," he stated. "This was not our own. The Japanese mafia is on to us," he added as he knelt on one knee and stared at the dead body.

"We have prisoners from the pool! We have two alive!" Hollywood yelled out from the first floor at that moment.

"Go on down there, Ben," Martha said as she removed Victor's shirt and tie. "Me and Tre` gone get Victor taken care of. Samantha, you and Amber go over there and check on Barbara."

Martha was in control of things here so I left her to tend to the business on the second floor. "Come on, Flacco," I said as I trotted down the stairs with my assault rifle at my side.

We got down to the first floor and saw Hollywood and Camilo standing in the bombed out living room before two bloody-faced Asians who were down their knees with their hands tied behind their back. I walked down the stairs leading into the living room, stood before the two men and pointed my AR-15 at one, and asked the other, "Who sent you?"

"Sucka me dick!" the Asian laughed as he spat blood onto my shoe.

I switched the gun to the guy who'd spat on my shoe and asked the other Asian, "Who ordered this job?"

"I have family in Japan!" he cried out.

I squeezed the trigger and shot the guy who'd spat on my shoe in the face three times, sending him on his way with the quickness. "You wanna see your family again? Talk! We'll send you on your way when done," I told the lone Asian.

"The deal was made in Seattle!" the Asian declared. "That's all I know!"

I backed away and looked over to Hollywood. "Put the pain on him. Get everything out of 'em, then kill 'em. Send some people to check on the Devereaux family warehouse while you take care of that," I ordered as I walked off to go back upstairs and check on Barbara and get my family ready to leave for America.

"Give us an hour, boss. We'll have everything up to his great, great grandparents' name, address and their occupation back in Japan, or wherever he's from," Hollywood said as he and Camilo pulled the guy up to his feet. "And Juan Camilo?" he then called out.

"Yes, sir?" Juan Camilo answered.

"You asked me to report back to you before I left the poolside. I'm just able to get back to you on that. Those guys down the hill? Come to find out, they weren't construction workers like I thought after all," Hollywood ended as he and Camilo dragged the Asian deep into the home in order to torture him for information.

CHAPTER TWENTY-FIVE
THE SPLIT

It was five hours after the hit over in Sao Paulo, Brazil. Tuesday afternoon. Bridgette Fischer had just returned to the cliffside mansion on the Margarita Islands that she shared with her husband Rafael Gacha. Theirs was a stone and marble two story mega mansion set atop a four-hundred-foot cliff with the Caribbean Sea to the east, and a valley filled with orange groves to the north, south and west. A long, winding mountain road led up the property, and Bridgette had just made it back to the refuge. She climbed from the back seat of a stretched Mercedes limousine, slammed the door shut, and leaned up against the car in frustration.

Nothing had gone right down in Santos. The hit on the Devereaux family had backfired. Bridgette had been warned not go through with the hit by Rafael, but she'd gone against his wishes nonetheless and it had ended in unmitigated disaster. The Moto brothers had lost thirteen men they'd brought in from Japan to do the job. On top of that, the warehouse Bridgette herself had raided with six of her husband's men Sao Vicente had been emptied out. There was no heroin to be stolen; she was lucky to dodge a team of Devereaux henchmen approaching the warehouse by jumping into a speedboat and traveling up a river back into Sao Paulo where she caught a flight from back to Venezuela in order to hide and figure out her next move.

The driver of the limousine climbed from behind the wheel and Bridgette said to him, "Yah stay inside tha' car. Wi won't be here much longer," before she pulled out a cellphone she'd bought from the airport back in Caracas, the capital of Venezuela.

****

From his private balcony on the opposite side of the mansion, Rafael sat at his marble desk trimmed in gold and watched his wife on the security cameras with Swan and Monty, his most trusted Enforcers, surrounding him. She seemed frustrated as she leaned up against the limousine running her hands through her dyed black hair while making a series of phone calls that seem to be going unanswered.

"Things did not go well for her, in Sao Paulo," Rafael remarked as he eyed the camera.

"You think she'll go on to her next move, boss," Swan asked while staring at the cameras and sliding a scope onto a M110 semi-automatic sniper rifle.

"We're about to find out," the forty-two-year-old muscular Colombian with a head full of curly black hair answered as he eased up from his high-back leather chair and tucked a .45 caliber semi-automatic into his front waistband. "You guys know what to look for," he said as he walked across the large room and pulled his steel double doors open. The Boss of Bosses was met out in the hall by four armed soldiers standing at attention. He walked in between the men as they held their AK-47s at their sides while straightening his suit jacket as they followed his lead down his wide, winding marble staircase.

****

Bridgette, meanwhile, had tried to call Lisa Vanguard, Arata and Raiden Moto without success. She was calling from an unsecure phone with an unrecognizable number so she figured her three partners were playing it safe, which was a move she understood. Her thoughts then drifted over to Rafael and the plans she had for him on this day.

"How'd it go in Sao Paulo?" Rafael asked, catching Bridgette by surprise. She looked up to see her husband walking down the marble stairs of his mansion with a scowl on his face and four goons tailing him.

"Tings didn't go well," was all Bridgette said as she stormed off from Rafael.

"You get back here!" Rafael screamed out as he rushed down the stairs and grabbed Bridgette by the arm. "You purposely went against me? You jeopardize all I have built to try and start your own family? Right under my nose you do this!"

"I do it fuh us, Rafael!" Bridgette defended.

"You should have never gotten Jaffrey and Theron involved in heroin! That is not what we do! Not what they knew *how* to do! They died because of what you did in New York when you chopped a man's head off and mailed it back to his family!" Rafael boomed. He then lowered his voice and said softly, "And then you go a step further by hitting the Devereaux family on their own turf today? How'd that work out?"

"I under estimate tha' Devereaux family! Dey had a' army," Bridgette confessed as her eyes watered. "I make mistake but I make id up tah yah Rafael! Just give mi one more chance tah prove I can run tings!" she pleaded.

"That family in Sao Paulo is run by the Holland family! Friends of mine! How long you think it'll be before they find out that my wife was behind the hit? How would that look, Bridgette?"

"And waan if dey do find out it was mi, Rafael! I'm yah wife!" Bridgette sassed and seethed as she pointed to herself. "Yuh fine with dem settin' up bidness in yah backyard down in Boa Vista and yah gon' do nuthin' 'bout it? Yuh wuld choose Holland ova me?"

Rafael shook his head somberly. He had his reasons for allowing the Holland family to set up their own cocaine operation in Boa Vista, but he dare not let anyone inside his organization in on that secret unless he be dethroned.

"You're no boss," Rafael said as he stared into Bridgette's cold, green eyes. "You're a reckless, dangerous woman incapable of running a family!" he yelled out. "Leave the wars and the cocaine to me! Do as I say! End this alliance you've made with those Japanese and whoever else is involved with it!" he demanded as he turned and walked off from Bridgette.

"I cawnt do dat eva, Rafael," Bridgette protested as her hands drifted down to her back waistband.

When Rafael turned around, he saw his wife holding onto a .40 caliber. "This is how you make things right for disobeying me?" he asked as he opened his suit jacket and placed his hand on top of his .45 caliber.

"Yah finissed, Rafael!" Bridgette stated as she held the gun at her side. "Tha' presadent a' Venezuela is dyin' and yah gon' lose powah soon!"

"You knew?" Rafael asked surprised as he chuckled. He removed his hand from his silk suit jacket and began walking around in a circle with his hands extended out over this unexpected epiphany. "I, I was under the impression you were going to kill me because you knew I was going to be angry at you over your fuck up in Brazil. But…but now I see that you not only had it in for those people, you had it for me as well," he stated seriously as he watched his four soldiers walk past him and stand beside Bridgette with their AK-47s aimed back at him.

"Wid out politic backin' yah have no powah, Rafael. Tha' next man hasn't yah favor," Bridgette disclosed as she patted her gun against the side of her thigh.

"The next man?" Rafael questioned through a serious gaze as he eyed his treacherous wife and the four men who'd just betrayed him. "After me there is no man, dear wife. Venezuela is my country. I run this country, and I kill those who disagree with me in my thinking. You put faith in any other man but me and you will…be…disappointed in the outcome. I'm all you've got and will ever have in this world."

"Yah wuz all I had once ago, Rafael! All I had before—"

"Before what?" Rafael boomed, cutting Bridgette off. "Before you ran off on some wild and crazy dream of starting your own heroin business with your two incompetent brothers who were more into throwing parties for Wall Street hippies than making money? Jaffrey and Theron were just as careless as you are! Look what's happened to your dream! Your brothers are dead, and you're now left with no one! No one but me! Where're your friends now?"

"They be 'round. Wi all be 'round. Only yah won't be, Rafael," Bridgette scowled as she raised her gun.

Two of the gunmen beside Rafael went down at that moment over sniper fire. The drug lord took advantage of his wife's and the other two men's astonishment and pulled his .45 caliber.

Bridgette saw the play and ran towards the back of the limousine while wildly shooting back at her husband. One of her gun's bullets inadvertently hit one of the men who'd joined her in her staged coup de tat and he fell back screaming out in agony.

Rafael opened fire on the lone gunman, taking him down as he ran and hid at the front of the limousine. From opposite ends of the bulletproof limo, husband and wife rose at the same time and exchanged gunfire with one another in a violent attempt to end one another's life as they danced around the car from opposing ends. Back and forth they went, ducking down and raising a few feet from their previous stance to fire off rounds with their freehand guarding their faces as they sought to eradicate one another, Bridgette looking to seize power, and Rafael desperately trying to hold on to it.

Gunfire from the left side of the limousine forced Rafael to duck for cover. He looked over the hood and saw a half dozen more of his soldiers running to Bridgette's aid. Outnumbered, he ran from behind the safety of the limousine out into the open, headed for the cover of the marble stairs that led back into his mansion just a short distance away. He ran with his suit jacket covering his head as a hail of bullets were hurled in his direction. Shells bounced off the sides of the staircase, barely missing him as he dove onto the stairs.

At that moment, Swan and Montgomery, who'd fired on the four men with Bridgette just minutes earlier, appeared on the second floor. They'd set up a fifty-caliber machine gun on the front balcony with an eight hundred round belt of ammunition attached and let loose on the men protecting Bridgette. Seven more men from inside the home ran out onto the long balcony and joined in on the gunfight with AK-47s.

One of the men on the ground fired off a rocket propelled grenade towards the second floor, sending Rafael's seven soldiers scattering for cover as Monty and Swan continued firing off with the fifty-caliber machine gun. The grenade hit fifty feet away from the ex-narcotics agents, detaching half of the front balcony and killing three of Gacha's men.

Swan and Monty continued firing over the dust and ash encompassing them underneath the balcony's overhang. Through coughs and gasps, they took down the guy who'd fired the grenade. They then quickly came under gunfire and had to take cover inside the mansion briefly.

"Yah nawt tha last man, Rafael! Yah cawnt handle yah wife even let a' lone tha' next man!" Bridgette mocked over the gunfire as she climbed into the backseat of the limousine. The car peeled out in reverse just as Swan and Monty returned to the balcony and aimed the machine gun in its direction. The front of the limousine absorbed blasts of bullets as it swung around and sped off the land under the blazing summer sun with five men giving chase, begging Bridgette not to leave them behind.

Rafael slowly rose in the wake of the carnage his wife had left behind as several of his soldiers not in on the coup ran past him firing off rounds. He stood on his marble staircase and watched as his loyal subjects waged battle out in the open with the men Bridgette left to fend for themselves. A wave of gunfire from Swan and Monty at the enemy's feet quickly ceased all activity. The five men in with Bridgette were quickly rounded up and ushered back before Rafael Gacha at gunpoint and placed onto their knees before him.

With his team of loyal soldiers behind him, Rafael slowly walked down the stairs while staring at his betrayers and placing a fresh magazine inside his .45 caliber. *"Le dio a los hombres el mundo."* (I gave you men the world.) he somberly stated while looking each of the Colombian men in the eyes. *"Salimos de Bogotá en Pablo Escobar's wake y hecho millones de dólares juntos. Y usted me paga en este juego por aliarse con una perra ingrata sobre mí en su lugar. ¿Qué hago aquí?"* (We left Bogota in Pablo's wake and made millions of dollars together. And you pay me back in this game by siding with an ungrateful bitch over me instead. What am I to do here?) he rhetorically asked as he spread his arms and let the gun dangle from his right forefinger.

Swan and Monty came up on Rafael's left side at that moment. "We got three men dead back inside the house. Your wife got away, but I guess it's no need in letting you know that," Swan remarked as he eyed the five men on their knees. "Who put Bridgette up to this?" he asked as he ran up and kicked one of the men in the face with the hard heel of his leather shoe. The guy fell back covering his bloody face, saying nothing.

"I have a better way," Rafael interjected. He gripped his pistol and walked to the first man in line on his right. *"¿conoce los nombres de los hombres con Bridgette? Quiénes son estos japoneses?"* (Do you know the names of the men with Bridgette? Who are these Japanese?) he asked as he pressed the gun to the man's forehead. *"Me dicen y voy a matar al resto y le permiten vivir."* (Tell me and I'll kill the rest and let you live.)

"No sé, señor Gacha! Ella sólo nos dicen acerca de Chávez!" (I don't know, Senor Gacha! She only tell us about Chavez!) the man stated in fear.

Rafael squeezed the trigger and blew the back of the man's skull out. He then moved to second man, placed the gun to his forehead and asked, *"Quiénes son estos japoneses está involucrado con mi esposa? Me dicen y me voy a matar al resto y le permiten vivir. Regresará a Bogotá rompió un hombre, sino un live."* (Who are these Japanese my wife is involved with? Tell me and I will kill the rest and let you live. You'll return to Bogota a broke man, but a live one.)

"No sé, señor Gacha! Ella sólo nos dicen acerca de Chávez!" (I don't know, Senor Gacha! She only tell us about Chavez!) the man remarked while breathing heavily.

Rafael squeezed the trigger a second time, blowing the brains out of another man as he moved over to the third man. He was the one Swan had kicked in the face and he had to be placed back onto his knees. *"Le pido que, al igual que las otras dos...quiénes son las personas Bridgette está involucrado?"* (I ask you, like the other two...who are the people Bridgette is involved with?)

"No sé, señor Gacha! Ella sólo nos dicen acerca de Chávez!" (I don't know, Senor Gacha! She only tell us about Chavez!) the man coughed through his pain.

"Scripted answers they're giving me," Rafael said to Swan and Montgomery. "Bridgette's a thoughtful one. Even though she doesn't know what she's quite doing, she's smart enough to think ahead. These guys know nothing." He bothered not asking the other two men the question as it was plain to see that they weren't going to talk even if they knew what all his wife was up to. All three remaining men were killed seconds apart by a furious Rafael with a single bullet to the forehead.

"What now, boss?" Monty asked as he stood before the five murdered men.

"Get a message to the Holland family, preferably Ben. If not Ben, then Dawk or Naomi," Rafael said as he walked off from before the bodies of the five men he'd just killed. "Tell the Holland family that it was my wife who was behind the hit in Sao Paulo. Give them her name, and tell them that someone from their family has to come here for a face-to-face meeting. Our organizations have been having a lot to discuss since the Sheinheimer hit in Boca Raton anyway and now's the time we come clean with all of the dirty little secrets we've been keeping from one another," he ended as he dropped his gun and slowly walked up the stairs.

CHAPTER TWENTY-SIX

A TWIST IN THE PLOT

Samantha had just landed the G-550 on the runway down to Ponca City Airport as dusk set in over America's heartland on Tuesday evening. The corporate jet rolled to halt before Bay's Lincoln and one of the family's Suburbans with its front wheel banked left as the side door floated down on the right side.

Dawk, Bay and T-top stood at the front of the Lincoln watching their family descend from the plane. Ben trotted down the stairs and gave the big three a hug before Bay and T-top broke off and ran up the stairs to greet Samantha and Martha.

"I couldn't call you from the air, fam," Ben said to Dawk as the two climbed inside the backseat of Bay's bulletproof Lincoln. "Shit went sour in Brazil."

"I heard about it," Dawk nodded as he sat beside Ben in a tailor-made silk suit and removed a pair of sunshades from his eyes.

"What happened down there might be over what happened with Tammy Moto," Ben told Dawk. "We caught one of the gunners and he gave up a name—Arata Moto."

"Tammy's last name," Dawk nodded. "You ain't heard about Gacha because you was up in the sky, but he got hit today too," he told Ben.

"I thought he woulda been in on the shit. Who hit Rafael?" Ben asked as he looked over to Dawk.

"Your boy Swan called me from Margarita Island and told me what went down. He said Gacha wife Bridgette Fischer was behind the hit in Sao Paulo earlier today. She done made an alliance with some Asians somewhere here in America."

"Fischer?" Ben asked surprised while rubbing his chin. "You

sayin' Rafael wife was the sister of the two brothers the Germans hit up in New York back in April?"

"That shit coming back on us, fam," Dawk acknowledged. "Gacha say Bridgette been here in America since that job we did on her brothers. Bridgette and her two cousins from Montego Bay, Jamaica killed some chick in the Bronx who was in on that job, but Gacha don't know who it was that Bridgette killed up there. Gacha don't know who Bridgette dealing with either. Only that they Asian."

"Me and Flacco thought it was Phillip and Grover at first," Ben remarked as he sat on the edge of the seat rubbing his chin.

"Nah," Dawk remarked coolly as he looked out the front of the window and watched his sisters and his cousin and Amber take turns snapping pictures before the jet. "Phillip and Grover looking to take over once we step aside."

"They gain a bigger advantage by supplying the ships to the outfit since we won't be shipping by rail much longer," Ben followed.

"Sho nuff," Dawk agreed. "Since we know it's not a inside job, that mean they got some new players done jumped in the game," he unpacked. "Whoever the fuck these Asians is they have to be out there on the west coast, though."

"Why you say that, fam?" Ben looked over and asked.

"That's where most Asian outfits set up their business," Dawk answered. "Bay and T-top killed a couple of Asians up in Seattle back in 2002. They was selling heroin—just like the Devereaux family. If we look around Seattle? I bet we find out who Arata Moto is."

"They Yakuza ta' begin with," Ben revealed.

"That there mean they can't strike on American soil if they true to the game," Dawk disclosed.

"So they need somebody to pull the strings for 'em stateside," Ben deciphered.

"Which might be Bridgette Fischer since Gacha say his wife linked up with a Asian click back over here," Dawk added.

Slowly, the pieces of a puzzle were coming together for Ben and Dawk as they sat and talked. Both could foresee a major problem on the horizon over what'd gone down in Brazil, only they hadn't all the necessary ingredients needed in order to stifle the threat just yet.

Ben leaned back into the seat and weighed the issue. Rafael's wife had tried to kill him after a failed job on the Devereaux family. Given the thirteen Asian men who'd been killed in the failed attempt, whoever was backing her had to have an influence in the game. And if they were Yakuza, that meant that they would have more soldiers at their beck and call to fight overseas. Whoever was backing Bridgette could go after them over and over again in Brazil if they wanted to being they were Japanese mafia was his thinking. *"We need a major sit down,"* he thought to himself.

"Gacha say he wanna sit down to renegotiate some terms," Dawk stated, shaking Ben from his thoughts.

"I was just thinkin' that, fam," Ben replied. "We do it next month. Until then? Everybody need to be protected. I got people watching my family back in Phoenix and I know we good here," he added.

"Saint Louis protected and Chicago straight," Dawk followed.

"Only problem we gone have is with the Devereaux family." Ben stated. "They ain't gone have no protection once the—"

"Ramirez family move over to our coca field in Boa Vista," Dawk finished up.

Ben and Dawk had a gangster's rapport whenever discussing business. They were so close in their thinking that they often finished one another's thoughts. Ben was the oldest by ten years nearly, but he would readily admit that he wasn't prepared to head an organization as big as his family's in the beginning. Mendoza, had been showing him the way up until his demise, but he was steadily adapting well to the position with Dawk at his side.

Dawk was a laidback country boy from Chicago. And although he'd been raised in Ponca City for eighteen of his twenty-five years, he had not only his father's blood, but the spirit of the old Cicero mafia bosses running through his veins. He thought from an organizational standpoint. He was a street CEO able to predict the actions of a rival from a deeper level than most of his counterparts. Ben on the other hand, was a fearless negotiator. He would willingly stand amongst cold-hearted killers and speak on behalf of his family unnerved, and he was just as much of a killer as the people he dealt with inside the business. Ben was always on the lookout for a setup as well, which was why he wasn't too surprised over what'd gone down in Brazil. He and Dawk were a good team that ran the family proficiently with Naomi at the helm.

"Who you think we can get to replace the Ramirez family once they move over to the coca field in Boa Vista?" Ben asked, breaking the silence.

"I really don't know right now, Cuz. Loopy coming back on line soon," Dawk replied. "I'm thinkin' she could take over things in Saint Louis and we move Jay-D down there for a minute."

Ben snapped his fingers at that moment. "You just reminded me, fam," he stated. "Barbara Devereaux said she got a son named Kareem Devereaux that live over in Saint Louis. He call his self Kree."

Dawk looked over to Ben with raised eyebrows and asked, "Barbara Devereaux is Kree mother?"

"That's the only Kree in Saint Louis I know," Ben said. "Her cousin got killed this morning. Barbara saw him laying dead and I guess she got some kind of change of heart or something. She told me she hated her son at first, but losing her nephew like that there, she asked me to see if I can find dude."

"Small world," Dawk remarked.

"Ain't it, man? Barbara wanna see her son again back in Brazil, but I told her it was too dangerous."

"Might not be, fam," Dawk reasoned. "I know Jay-D gone wanna make that trip with Kree. I'm thinkin' it might be good for those two to fly down there while the Ramirez family still there, ya' feel me? That way Kree can make amends with her mother and Jay-D can decide if he want the Brazilian job or not."

"I got ya'. That's the perfect setup for that." Ben nodded as he kicked back in the passenger seat. "I gotta call Faye and put her up on this deal with Arata Moto when we get to the house," he added.

"The Germans may be able to add insight on this thing with Bridgette and these Asians," Dawk followed. "We talk more at the house."

"How ya' son doing, fam?" Ben asked, changing the subject.

"Man, Sosa got an ear infection now," Dawk sighed. "I mean,

he been fighting off sickness since he was born April past. He got some shots lined up next week and another round next month."

"Ben Junior had some health issues early on, brer. Sometimes the first year be real rough for a newborn, then it's smooth sailing from there. I guess it be the shock of coming into a world with so much bullshit going on, ya' dig," Ben chuckled. "Baby be thinkin', 'man, I shoulda stayed my ass wherever the fuck I was at'."

Dawk laughed lightly. "I don't know what Sosa be thinkin', cousin," he remarked as his eyes lit up. "But, my li'l man barely sleep," he proudly stated. "First, he be aggravated, but he like being around people, man. Get along with everybody, everybody, Ben. I'm building a pier out behind the house on Kaw Lake. When Sosa get older? We gone sit out and catch some of that catfish out there."

"My boys be trying to grab at the fish Samantha got flowing through her yard," Ben smiled as he looked out the window. "You gone have fun raising Sosa, cousin. I'm enjoying the hell outta raising my boys. By the time they hit grade school hopefully this phase of our life be over and done with."

"I said back in Vegas when we met up with O'Malley that we was in it for life," Dawk stated seriously. "Sosa startin' ta' change my mind about things, fam. I don't want him to grow up without a father. I hope you right."

"About what?" Ben asked as he looked over to Dawk.

"That it'll all be behind us by the time our sons hit grade school."

"One hundred," Ben nodded. He gave Dawk a fist pound just as Samantha and company began making their way over to the vehicles for the ride home.

****

While Ben and company made their way back to the ranch, over to Ponderosa, Kimi and Koko were inside their mother's bedroom suite removing ten thousand dollar bands of hundred dollar bills from the family's large safe and gun locker and spreading it out over her marble desk top. They'd been working from home the past few weeks being they hadn't any classes over to the University of Oklahoma. With the books in order, the twins now had the job of counting out $150,000 dollars that was going to be delivered to a woman by the name Guadalupe Cruz by Bay and T-top the following day. They were nearly through with the count when Bay and T-top walked into the room after returning from the airport.

"Ben and Samantha downstairs," Bay remarked happily as she walked ahead of Tiva.

"That's what's up. Who cooking tonight?" Kimi asked as she banded a stack of hundred dollar bills.

"I got it! I got it! What y'all want?" Tiva asked as she skipped sideways up to the desk.

"Momma and Dunkirk slaughtered a big ole hog Sunday past," Koko looked up and answered as she slid a stack of hundred dollar bills into a money counter. "They cut some one-inch thick shoulder blades and baby backs. We can grill those with some baked macaroni and cheese and fry some fish for Spoonie and Tyke."

"That sounds good," Bay responded as she sat down in her mother's executive chair. She looked up at Koko, squint her eyes and said, "Girl, you missing an earring."

"Lee probably knocked it out when he had her in the buck," Tiva quipped.

"Like that boy Terrence knocked your earrings out right before you beat up his baby momma Sunday past?" Koko shot back as she grabbed her cellphone and texted Lee.

Tiva looked over to Bay at that moment and curled her lips as she began rocking her hips.

"What?" Bay giggled.

"You couldn't keep your mouth closed on that, huh? I told you not to tell nobody." Tiva scoffed.

"I don't know why you shamed," Bay playfully defended. "And I ain't tell nobody I told Kimi and Koko."

"I'm not ashamed," Tiva retorted. "I like Terrence. His messy ass baby momma just don't know her fuckin' place."

"Her *fuckin'* place!" Kimi playfully mimicked while wobbling her head and banding money.

"That's right," Tiva laughed. "I had that bitch hunched over hittin' her in the head and shit like this here, Kimi," she added as she frowned and imitated the way she'd fought Candace.

"Lord," Koko chuckled as she watched her older sister fight with herself.

"And then I smacked her cross the face two times before Bay pulled me off the li'l pitiful hoe," Tiva continued demonstrating as she fanned her hand out two times. "Whap, whap! And then two-stepped on that bitch," she added as she danced in place briefly while snapping her fingers.

"What if she come back, Tiva?" Kimi asked as she placed a bundle of money on top of a neat pile of cash.

"What?" Tiva grimaced. "I wish that bitch would! And watch me throw her ass in the trunk of a car and bury that bitch alive somewhere."

"And I'll drive," Bay followed.

Kimi and Koko looked at one another seriously and said not a word.

"We just playin', y'all," Tiva laughed. "Bay you scared 'em."

"We ain't scared," Koko sniggered while banding the last stack of bills. "We just know y'all two crazy enough ta' do something like that to that woman."

"Fuck that bitch Candace," Tiva remarked lowly.

"You got that all counted up?" Bay asked as she stood up from her mother's comfortable chair.

"Yeah," Kimi answered as Koko threw the last stack onto the pile. "Hundred and fifty large. Somebody gone be happy," she smiled.

"Happy wouldn't be the word or the emotion behind this here, Kimi," T-top corrected. "Fifty racks is for one of our soldiers that one on the job. The other hundred thousand is a life insurance payout to the surviving family."

"Oh," Kimi stated somberly, bothering not to inquire any further. "Well, it's all there. Anything else y'all need done?"

"We gone need another two hundred thousand set up in an offshore account. That's for two more of our people that got killed," Bay replied as she and Tiva began placing the money into a duffle bag, leaving Kimi and Koko stunned over the business their sisters were handling.

****

While Bay and T-top were handling business on Loopy's behalf, Ben and Dawk were down in Doss' private room. Dawk was discussing with Ben a problem he was dealing with in town when Lee walked into the room looking down at the floor. "Welcome back, boss," he said when he caught sight of Ben. "Now where is it?" he then asked as he moved pillows around on the leather couch.

Ben and Dawk both watched as Lee rearranged the pillows on the sofa. He raised the cushions and then knelt down on the floor and ran his hands underneath the couch before standing up and placed his hands on his hips and looking the shelves over. "It's probably over here," he said as he jogged around the sofa and began sliding his hands along the bookshelf.

"Place been swept for bugs already, homeboy," Dawk remarked while chuckling at Lee.

"I know," Lee said as he returned to the sofa and raised the cushions a second time. "Found it," he said as he came up with a diamond-studded earring. "Koko left this in here."

"What y'all was doing on that couch like that?" Ben asked through laughter.

"Nah, boss," Lee chuckled. "We was sitting in here looking over pictures of Doss earlier today. Koko got nostalgic. She wanted to remember the good times she had with her father in light of her mother having a new friend," he stated as he straightened the cushions and texted Koko back with "*Found it.*"

"That's what's up. How everything going with the wedding planning?" Ben asked.

"We had a caterer that was hell-bent on spending the entire three hundred-thousand-dollar budget," Lee said as he walked up and gave Ben a quick dap and a hug. "This caterer wanted lobster flown in from Maine, champagne and wine from Napa Valley and some stupid orchestra to play the music."

"What you decide on, fam?" Dawk asked.

"I ain't decide on shit. That broad was planning a wack ass wedding...so I had the bitch fired," Lee answered. "She was gonna fuck Kimi's wedding up and I couldn't let that happen. I'm hiring Katrina to cater the whole thing."

"My wife can handle that," Ben nodded. "And her momma can help her. It'll give her something to do because Faye getting bored down there."

"That's what I know," Lee agreed as he blew onto the earring Koko had lost. "Katrina and Faye can grow closer, and we can save some money on the wedding to put to use on other things like transportation and lodging. Excuse me, fellas. I just came to find Koko's earring. Didn't mean to barge in," he explained while walking out of the room and closing the door behind him.

When Lee cleared out, Dawk turned to Ben and said, "Oneika daddy, August, used to be a city councilman here. He still know a couple of people on the force that don't deal with Nimitz. That thing with Tonto all good from what he say. Police ain't been askin' questions and have no suspect."

"It's good we got somebody with connect inside the police here while that investigation still going," Ben said as he poured another shot of brandy and downed it while sliding the bottle over to Dawk.

"You right. But, sometimes I be thinking about asking August to run again—for mayor, though." Dawk said as he grabbed a shot glass.

"And get that same set up as the Germans up in Kansas," Ben nodded while pondering the move. "What would be the reasoning behind it, though, fam?"

"So August could fire Sheriff Nimitz." Dawk replied. "I think he tried ta' kill Oneika the day we got married. It's too risky killin' em now, but I'm sensing he gone be a problem sooner than later. I'm either gone get 'em fired, or I'm gone kill 'em. Whichever one come first," he declared as he poured himself another shot of brandy. "Tonto momma may be a problem also," he added. "She was the one who went to Nimitz before Tonto was even killed."

"And she been real quiet ever since," Ben remarked. "You think Hakiba and the Sheriff up to something?"

"I would like to think that Kahlil momma have better sense than that," Dawk answered. "I respect her son enough to not kill her, but if she in with Nimitz then I don't have a choice in the matter."

"How you gone play it?" Ben asked he grabbed his cellphone. "You talkin' about a mayor reminded me to call Faye just now."

"I'm gone talk to August about running for mayor next year. We all worried about Sosa right now, so I don't wanna bring it up just yet. But I'm gone put that bug in his ear before summer out." Dawk answered. "It's still early, though, Cuz. We look into it," Dawk ended as Ben began scrolling through his phone.

****

One hundred and twenty miles to the northeast of Ponca City, over to the Cherryvale Farm, Faye Bender and Sascha Merkendorf stood over a sedated thirty-year-old Caucasian woman with black hair and brown eyes as Tuesday night set in. The woman lay on a gurney slumbering while being medically prepped to have her kidneys removed. True to their word, the Germans had come through with a donor for Sharona Benson. It had taken only four days since they'd undertaken the endeavor, and they were all set to go after receiving a phone call from the doctor doing the job that one of the four blood samples they'd sent to him that morning via Maggie McPherson had come back as a positive match. Maggie was now making the drive back to Cherryvale with the surgeon in tow to perform the operation.

With the doctor on his way to do the extraction, the Germans now faced another conundrum: during their search, they'd gone all out the night before and had snatched up four women who'd been traveling alone through the town of Cherryvale, Kansas. Now that they had their donor secured, the three remaining women were now in the process of being disposed of.

Faye walked out of the bedroom that had become a makeshift operating room and stepped out into the open area of her bungalow located inside her large barn. She was dressed in the white and pink dress and white bonnet she'd worn at the blood drive three days prior. The bungalow was being lit with an oil lamp, the same lamp her ancestors had used over one hundred and twenty years ago. She walked over to the replica table that her great, great grandmother Kate Bender had used during her reign of terror and pulled back on the curtain. "You're ready for the next one, Bonita?" she asked while peeking into the small pantry.

"Yeah, bring her on," Bonita stated as she wiped blood from her chin and gripped the mallet she was holding tighter while dressed up in a pair of jean overalls and a white long sleeve t-shirt that was blotted with bloodstains.

Faye pulled the curtain shut and walked over to the small door leading out into the narrow chamber and looked to her right. "Cikala?" she spoke softly before slowly disappearing back into the bungalow.

Cikala Dunbar was standing before two terrified women, a brunette and a black woman, sitting in chairs with their hands tied before them. Each were on their way home, just passing through an inconspicuous town when they were pulled over by sheriff's deputies for speeding. While presenting their license and registration, they were knocked out with a taser. When they awoke, they found themselves tied up inside a slender hall that was lit by oil lamps. It was a place comparable to that of a medieval torture chamber as two strange women wearing clothes from the 1800s, wide-bottomed dresses, denim overalls and worn boots and whatnot, moved about in silence under dim-lighting.

"You," Cikala called out as she pointed to the twenty-something hazel-eyed brunette woman wearing a Kansas State University t-shirt and pulled the woman up to her feet. "Get inside!" the full-figured Lakota Indian ordered.

"No!" the young woman cried out. "What're you going to do? What are you going to do me? I don't wanna go in there!"

Cikala shoved the petrified young woman into the room and pulled the door shut. She fell to her knees and quickly bounced up with her hands tied before her body and began looking around as her lips trembled and tears poured down her brown cheeks. No one was in sight as she leaned up against the door with her mouth wide open, whimpering in fright as her eyes scanned the empty, quiet, low-ceiling room with its old, haunting furniture and yellow hue. A shadow soon appeared over the flickering oil lamp off to her right and she leaned up against the door even further, raising her leg to guard herself.

"Please," the young woman agonized as the shadow grew larger. "I'll do whatever you want just don't kill me!" she cried out as the shadow grew even larger. When the woman who'd stuck her head out the door appeared in her wide-bottomed dress and white bonnet holding on to a long butcher's knife, the young woman screamed out in sheer terror, "Why? Why are you doing this?"

"Shhh," Faye whispered as she crept towards the young woman with the knife at her side. "Are you afraid of me?"

"Yes," the young woman cried. "Yes, ma'am."

"Sit down over there," Faye requested, using the knife as a pointer.

"Okay," the young woman complied as she moved over to the table and sat with her back to the dingy curtain.

Faye walked over and stared down at the woman seriously with her head tilted to the left. "Thank you for playing along," she smiled as a white hand pulled back on one of the curtains, the move going unnoticed by the frightened young woman.

"Thank, thank you? Thank you for what? Playing along with what?" the young woman yelled. "Just let me—" the young woman paused her speech when she noticed the blood and bits splattered on the table before her. "Oh my god! This is what you did to the other two!" she gasped. "Miss Bender, please! Just let me—"

The young woman went silent when a mallet slammed into the back of her skull, fracturing it in the process as her upper body fell onto the tabletop face first. Faye completed the job in complete imitation of her great, great grandmother Kate Bender by walking up to the woman and slitting her throat, nearly decapitating her skull. Blood began to ooze from the woman's neck as she stepped back and admired her handy work.

Bonita moved from behind the curtain, snatched the woman up out of the seat, pulled her back into the pantry and quickly closed the curtain. "I'm ready for the last one," she said as she stood in between the two dead women with the bloody mallet looking around at the gore she'd produced. Faye smiled as she walked off. This had been a dream of hers and Bonita for years, to replicate what their great, great grandmother Kate Bender had done over a century earlier.

Killing for the sake of killing made Faye moist in the center. It was an exhilarating feeling to be able to get away with cold-blooded murder just for kicks. DeeDee had given her an outlet, and she was taking full advantage of the moment right along with her sister Bonita. Just before she grabbed hold of the doorknob leading out into the hall, Faye's cell rung. She recognized Ben number and answered. "Mister Holland, how's everything?"

"We had some problems down in Brazil," Ben remarked. "I was wondering if I could fly up there in the morning and run some things by you?"

"Now's not a good time, Ben," Faye stated seriously. "I'm in the middle of something here. Can we discuss this over the phone?"

Ben gave Faye a brief rundown of what'd transpired in Sao Paulo over a period of five minutes and she was put on alert. "I'll call Tanya and let her know what's going on. Thank you for letting me know all of this, Ben," she stated as she ended the call. She then stuck her head out into the hall and called for the last victim, the black woman, as she walked back into the folds of her bungalow to begin her routine of terror for the final time.

CHAPTER TWENTY-SEVEN

THE BOSS AND THE BITCH

"Still smokin' bud...still smokin' weed...still smokin' bud...still smokin' weed...still smokin' weed...still smokin' bud...still smokin' weed..."

The dance hall on the second floor of 3600 Mulberry Street was filled with marijuana smoke, and the sounds of Mystikal's song *Still Smokin'* thumped loudly from two fifteen-inch floor woofers. It was still Tuesday night, a few minutes or so after Faye had talked to Ben. A red light bulb painted the room in a sexy shade of red as Boogie danced in the middle of the floor in a black fish net leotard and five-inch stilettoes. She moved with the grace of a gazelle before Popeye and his three goons. Popeye wasn't too pleased, but his three homeboys were admiring the hip-hop ballerina performance.

Popeye sat and watched nonchalantly as Boogie bowed her head and stood facing him and his men as they sipped brandy. She slid her feet from side to side, spread her arms, and slowly raised her head to the left while nodding her head and snapping her fingers in rhythm with Mystikal's song. Her hips rocked slowly as she leaned back with one foot before her. A hand went up over her nappy, tan afro as she twirled slowly and bent at the waist then rose quickly over the men's howls. With her back to the audience, she moved slowly across the wooden floor in her heels, making her cheeks bounce separately while looking back at twenty-seven-year-old Popeye and his team.

Popeye and his three goons had flown into Cincinnati earlier in the day to discuss business with Tanya Weinberger. They were the newest addition to the German crime family. The three men with Popeye were Fordham 'Ford' Nelson, Drake 'Bell' Bellamy, and Tyson 'Big Ty' Drought. They were street men with large prestige that hailed from the west side of Baltimore who dubbed themselves

The Educated Thugs.

Ford, Bell and Big Ty all had degrees from Georgetown University in biochemistry. They specialized in intelligence gathering and forensics. Their careers, along with Popeye's, had been guided by Senator Slack herself and after years of preparation, they were ready to take on their first venture: the distribution of one hundred kilograms of heroin into the cities of Baltimore and D.C.

Willie was the main driving force behind the new unit inside the German crime family. This was her deal, albeit a risky one. If it were ever to be discovered that a sitting Senator was the lead member of a heroin drug ring, it would undoubtedly be one of the biggest political scandals to hit Washington. Even more, the drugs were being peddled into D.C. itself, the Senator's own backyard, which would only compound the disgrace. To be certain that insurrection would not rear its ugly head, Willie had trained her son and three handpicked colleagues of his to head her portion of the crime family. Having gotten their priorities in order as far as shipping, dealers and distribution locales, Popeye and his team were now parlaying with Boogie on the second floor of 3600 Mulberry Street.

Boogie ended the routine and walked over to Popeye. "How'd you like it, William?" she asked as she stood before him with her hands on her hips and nearly out of breath.

Popeye stood up in his baggy black Prada jeans and white Airforce Ones and grabbed both of Boogie's hands and pulled her to the side. Boogie went willingly, sashaying across the wooden floors while holding on to Popeye's hand. The 6'1' black/Lakota Indian with high-yellow skin and braided jet-black hair and brown eyes was dreamy to her. She adored him to the max and would do anything to make him happy. They'd slept with one another several times some years earlier, but theirs had become more of a business relationship as of late.

Boogie wanted more, and Popeye knew that to be true, but he couldn't get past what he deemed whorish behavior on Boogie's part. He also knew she'd slept with RJ in times past, which made her a loose woman in his mind's eye. Yet, in spite of her being perceived as 'easy', twenty-seven-year-old Popeye adored Boogie. She was someone he could see himself spending his life with if she only slowed her roll to a degree.

"What the fuck was that, Helen?" Popeye asked in a

condescending tone.

"What was what?" Boogie laughed, unaware of Popeye's disdain over what she'd done.

"You way too beautiful to feel like you have to shake your ass before a group of men to earn their approval, girl," Popeye reprimanded. "That was unnecessary and skanky on your part."

"Unnecessary and skanky?" Boogie asked as she let go of Popeye's hands and backed up a few paces. She placed her hands on her hips and said, "You didn't have a problem when I offered to perform for you."

"That's right," Popeye agreed. "You agreed to perform for me."

"Nur sagen Sie Helen und Stop fucking herum spielen." (Just say you want to date Helen and stop fucking playing around with it.) Fordham 'Ford' Nelson, a bald-headed, physically fit dark-skinned brother wearing a silk suit, blurted out as he, Bell and Big Ty stood up and laughed.

"Ist es wahr, William" (Is this true, William?) Boogie asked through a sly smile as she stepped closer to Popeye. *"Sie möchten mich für selbst ist, warum haben Sie sich mit mir heute Abend aufgeregt?"* (You want me for yourself is why you have become agitated with me tonight?) she asked as she neared his face with her hands behind her back.

"Lassen Sie mich Ihnen für heute Abend. Zeigen Sie mir Cincinnati." (Let me take you out for dinner tonight. Show me Cincinnati.) Popeye smiled as he pecked Boogie's lips and stepped back from her.

"Er ist für immer der Herr, meine Brüder." (He is forever the gentleman, my brothers.) Ford chuckled as he, Bell and Big Ty headed for the door leading back down to the first floor of the club. *"Wenn es mir war, obwohl, ich begleiten sie in die Dusche, während meine Kleidung."* (If it was me, though, I'd be escorting her to the shower while taking my clothes off.) he added just before pulling the door open and leaving the dance hall.

Boogie walked off from Popeye once the door had closed and paced the floor in a coy manner while rubbing her arms with her back to him. *"Ich bin verschwitzt."* (I'm sweaty.) she stated lowly while picking up a towel from a bar stool and wiping her face.

"Wenn wir gehen zum Abendessen, ich muss zuerst zu einer Dusche." (If we're going out for dinner, I need to shower first.) she added as she pulled the top of her leotard down and rubbed her apple-sized breasts free of sweat with her back steady to Popeye.

Popeye walked up behind Boogie, placed his hands on the back of her hips and shoved her forward towards the shower stall in the corner. She tilted her head back and rubbed her face up against his as the two erupted into laughter. *"Sie wollen mir Ihre Frau zu sein, nicht wahr, Popeye? Sie wollen mich ganz für sich, also können Sie mir jede Nacht haben und ein Lächeln auf meinem Gesicht?"* (You want me to be your woman don't you, Popeye? You want me all to yourself so you can have me every night and put a much needed smile on my face.) Boogie stated as she slid her soft ass over the front of Popeye's baggy jeans.

"Wollen Sie mir zu geben, Helen?" (Do you want to give yourself to me, Helen?) Popeye asked as he pressed Boogie up against the wooden door leading to the shower stall. He held her hands up over her head against the door with his tented jeans crushing up against her leotard, forcing the linen into the folds of her crevice.

"Ja, Baby, ich weiß." (Yes, baby, I do.) Boogie hummed as she began rocking her body by bending either knee beneath Popeye's weight. *"Sie können tun, was auch immer Sie wollen, wann immer Sie wollen, William. Ich bin dein."* (You can do whatever you want to me anytime you want to, William. I'm yours.) Boogie confessed in low, sexy tone of voice. The two had a perfect rhythm going under the red light bulb amid the quiet of the dancehall as they rocked in unison up against the wall.

Unable to resist the tempting, sexy woman before him, Popeye turned the knob on the door and he and Boogie fell off into the shower stall. She turned and faced him head on inside the small room that was laced in grey granite with a sink and a toilet and double-headed shower. A passionate round of kissing ensued as Boogie reached back and turned on the hot water and backed off into the shower stall and removed her torn attire. The glow of the red light bulb out in the dance hall illuminated the small room as Popeye removed his clothes and stepped into the shower stall and gripped Boogie tightly under the water's rising temperature.

****

Back down on the first floor of 3600 Mulberry Street, Tanya had just ended the call with Faye Bender. She'd just learned that he

Holland family had been hit down in Sao Paulo, Brazil by someone belonging to the Moto family. She was on her way up to the second floor to put Boogie up on game when she ran into Ford out on the main floor inside the half-full bar.

"Ford, where's Helen?" Tanya asked.

"Her and Popeye upstairs mapping out a late-night dinner," Ford replied as he walked behind the bar and grabbed a bottle of Ace of Spades. "We gone sit over at a table in the corner and parlay until they come down and tag along with 'em. You good, boss?" he asked.

Tanya's intent had been shifted with Ford's presence. Her plan in the beginning was to go up and inform Boogie of the rising threat, but she now decided to walk out to her ride and grab the three automatic twelve gauge shotguns she'd gotten from Delilah in order to have extra firepower once the club closed in a couple of hours. "Follow me outside, Ford. We need to get some more guns," she requested.

"Sure, boss," Ford replied. "Yo, brothers? Get the drinks ready and we gone go and smoke in the corner when I get back," he added as he hurried behind Tanya.

"*Seit fast zwanzig Jahren diese Frau hat die Deutschen im Rhein wohlhabende Spieler im Spiel.*" (For nearly twenty years this woman has made Germans in The Rhine wealthy players in the game.) an octogenarian World War II German-Jew war vet that'd fought alongside the British said aloud as Tanya walked past him.

Several more German-Jews in their mid to late eighties nodded in agreement while smiling over to Tanya. These were a few of the men Tanya had first dealt with when she and Boogie's father, Alfredo Lowes, first set up shop in Cincinnati back in the late eighties. Over the Rhine, or The Rhine as it is called, is a main German outlaw hub where drug trafficking reigned supreme; 3600 Mulberry Street was headquarters when it came to the German underworld and Tanya Weinberger sat at the head of table. Cincinnati was her home base and stronghold. A place where she was respected for her prowess and ability to stave off competition from those not affiliated or in alignment with the German Cause.

Tanya thanked the man in the funny flower hat by shaking his hand and kissing his wife before walking off. The two got up and followed her, preparing to leave the club. Once outside, the group of four parted ways. The old man and his wife heading to their car parked to the right up the street, and Tanya and Ford rounding the corner headed towards her car. Tanya was driving a champagne four door Maybach 62 that was parked just to the left of the caty-corner entrance two cars down from Boogie's lime Caprice and Popeye's black on black Suburban. With Ford walking beside her, she pulled her key pad from her tight-fitting leather shorts and popped the trunk.

"I have three shotguns I need brought inside for when we close later," Tanya told Ford as she walked past him and raised the trunk up on the Maybach.

Ford was walking up to the trunk of the car when a hail gunfire erupted from the rooftop of the three-story building situated directly across the street from 3600 Mulberry Street. "Boss!" he yelled as he ran up and grabbed Tanya and pulled her down beside the Maybach, closest to the sidewalk. Bullets ricocheted off the ground and slammed into the rear of the vehicle as he lay on top of Tanya to shield her from the gunfire.

Up on the second floor, meanwhile, Popeye and Boogie were still in the shower stall. Popeye was taking Boogie from behind underneath the steaming hot water when he heard what was to him, faint gunshots. "Yo," he said as he slowly slid out of Boogie. He eased out onto the dancefloor and looked around and heard the rat-ta-tat-tat of semiautomatic gunfire.

Boogie heard the gunfire before she'd even exited the shower stall. "*Mutter!*" (Mother!) she screamed as she ran past Popeye dripping wet and naked. She snatched the doors open on a wall-mounted cabinet on her immediate right and grabbed a Sturmgewehr 44 automatic assault rifle and slid in a hundred round magazine. She racked the rifle as she took off running towards the door leading down to the first floor.

"My boys got it down there! The gunfire coming from the roof across the street! Follow me!" Popeye yelled out as he grabbed an AK-47 and slid in fifty round clip. He ran over to the emergency staircase that led up to the roof of 3600 Mulberry Street while sliding in his magazine. Boogie followed his lead ready to spray as the two rushed up the stairs.

Back outside on ground level, Tanya and Ford were coming under heavy gunfire. Tanya's Maybach had been shot up to the point that both the passenger side tires had been flattened and all its windows were shot out. The two were pinned down beside the bullet-ridden car crouching away from shells landing all around them when gunfire from the front of the club broke out.

Ford looked back over his shoulder and saw Bell and Big Ty shooting up at the two-story building directly across the street from the front side of the club before running for cover. Whoever was attacking the crew had the advantage being posted up on top of two buildings that looked directly down on the club from two vantage points he quickly understood. He and Tanya both were going to get killed if they didn't get back into the fight and back whoever it was off him and Tanya's ass was what he knew. "I'm going for guns," he told Tanya as he began looking and listening for a lull in the gunfire.

"You see that nigga? You sure somebody was up there, dog?" Bell casually asked as he looked up at the roof with his Mark 23 . 45 automatic draping his side.

"You better get your head back in here, boy!" Big Ty, and overweight dark-skinned brother standing an even six feet with a thick beard a low cut, gasped as he leaned up against the wall while holding onto a chrome Mac-10 semi-automatic.

"We gotta get on the other side by Ford, though, my nig," Bell said in a slow drawl while looking back at Big Ty. He looked back up at the roof and said, "We should just run to the other side, bruh."

"If we run out there we gone die. Whoever it is on that building is a fuckin' sniper," Big Ty said as he gasped for air. "He hit one of them Germans, old dude with that funny ass hat on. He hit dude right in the forehead two times. And then hit his wife. He plucking muthafuckas off. I'm down like a mutherfucka, but I ain't committin' suicide. Run your retarded ass out there if you want to," he laughed lowly while steadily gasping for air. "I'm a tell 'em we couldn't get to 'em because of the fuckin' sniper. And they got two bodies out front the building to back me up. They gone have ta' ride with that one."

Bell looked back down the alley behind him. It was lit up on his left with bright orange light from the baseball field that lit up the whole alleyway. "Let's 'head this way and come up on 'em from the other way then," he suggested.

"Was wondering how long it was gone take your ass to figure that shit out," Big Ty said as he crept down the alley.

"I been knew. Your fat ass had ta' catch ya' wind, though," Bell calmly replied as he crept down the alley behind Big Ty, the two of them just missing sight of a black Escalade slowly cruising up the block from the other end of the baseball field.

Back on the opposite side of the block, Ford and Tanya were still pinned down. Tanya was worried to death about Boogie as she lay beneath Ford with her eyes shut as bullets ricocheted all around. She was hoping no one ran up on her and Ford. There were only two gunners as far as she could tell, but this was a hit, she knew. There had to be more shooters either lurking, or on their way. She wanted to call out for Boogie, but it would only make matters worse.

Ford, meanwhile was bidding time. He knew the gunners would have to reload soon. A few more bursts rang out and he lowered his head. Suddenly, the sound of thunderous gunfire erupted from the roof of 3600. Ford looked up and knew it was Boogie and Popeye. The gunfire raining down on him and Tanya ceased at that moment and he and Tanya both scrambled over the pavement to the rear of the Maybach.

They each grabbed a twelve gauge automatic and ducked back behind the tattered vehicle just as gunfire erupted again from both rooftops. Gunshots from the ground level caught their attention as they racked their weapons. They aimed briefly, but quickly lowered them when they saw that it was Bell and Big Ty.

Ford used the distraction to pull Tanya up to her feet. "Let's get back inside!" he said in a raised voice over the gunfire as he led the way, he and Tanya hunched over as they crept along the side of the cars parked beside club. The gunfire died off just as Ford and Tanya made it the last car. Tanya looked down the block and saw a man laying dead on the sidewalk beside his car as headlights from an approaching vehicle lit up the ground beneath it. She then looked over and saw a woman slumped over the hood on the passenger side of the car.

Gunfire erupted and Tanya took cover once more behind Boogie's Caprice. Ford, meanwhile, crept along the cars parked on the opposite side of the club while looking up at the building. When he saw what he believed was a person atop the roof, he began shooting up at the rooftop and the gunman returned fire.

"Tanya, get inside! I got you covered!" Ford yelled out as he shot up at the roof.

Tanya leapt out from behind the car she was hiding behind, and was trotting to the club's entrance when a black Escalade pulled up on her and skidded to halt. She aimed her twelve gauge and was prepared to open fire, but when she saw the face of the person sitting in the backseat aiming an Uzi at her, she paused. Calm reigned for several seconds as Tanya stared her aggressor in the eyes with a shocked, hurtful expression of disbelief upon her face. "We were working on getting you out, bitch!" she scoffed as she held the twelve gauge even with her shoulders.

"This bitch worked herself out since the boss had more important shit to do!" Brenda barked.

With the understanding that nothing said by Brenda could bring about an understanding over the betrayal, Tanya squeezed the trigger on her twelve gauge. Brenda did the same on a semi-automatic Uzi and what sounded like that of multiple cars repeatedly backfiring erupted into the night air.

Bullets whizzed by Tanya as she moved to her right. The chipped, green wood on the building dissolved where bullets landed as she hunched down and fired. Her gun blasts shattered the back window on the Escalade, forcing Brenda to duck down.

Tanya began moving for the club's front door when Brenda rose once again and began waving the Uzi from side to side as she resumed firing off rounds. The tinted windows on 3600 Mulberry shattered and in a hail of bullets, Tanya Weinberger screamed out in a high-pitched voice and went down after being struck seven times in the chest, left arm, torso and both legs in rapid succession. Her bullet-stricken body collapsed back into the doorway of 3600 Mulberry and blood began drenching the concrete as the Escalade sped off the block.

Up on the roof, Popeye and Boogie had waged battle with the two shooters across the way. The gunners broke and ran just as the Escalade sped off, but Popeye was certain he'd hit one of the men. Screams from people on the ground level forced him to look over the edge of the building. He could see a crowd gathering around a fallen victim. Someone was laying on the ground, but he wasn't sure who it was. When he saw the strapped white sandals and the person's pale white legs, however, he knew right away who it was that'd been hit.

"What's going on down there?" Boogie asked as she ran up beside Popeye and peered over the ledge. When she looked down to the ground, Boogie saw what Popeye had seen. She also knew what he knew: that her mother had been shot. She backed away from the ledge with a blank stare and let her assault rifle fall from her grip as tears welled up in her eyes. "Mutter!" she hysterically screamed as she took off running across the asphalt barefoot and naked.

Boogie ran down the stairs while placing a robe on to cover herself. The entire bar had been emptied and the patrons were all outside scattered before the entrance and standing out in the street. Ford, Bell and Big Ty were kneeling before Tanya with their hands on her wounds to try and prevent her from losing blood, but Tanya was in bad shape. Blood was spurting from her nose and she was swallowing hard, making a deep croaking sound as she looked up at the sky.

"Aus meinem fucking! Verschieben Sie die fucking!" (Out of my fucking way! Move out the fucking way!) Boogie yelled as she fought her way through the crowd. She pushed Ford aside and his hands left the wound in Tanya's chest. Ford quickly regained his balance and shoved Boogie back.

"The ambulance is on the way!" Ford screamed as he pressed down on Tanya's chest wounds. "I can't give her chest compressions because she has a hole in her lung! I was forcing blood out of her!"

Boogie rested on her knees as she stared her mother in the eyes. Tanya was in and out of consciousness, caught up in a battle for her life and trying to stay alive. *"Räche mich!"* (Avenge me!) she gasped. *"Helen... mich rächen!"* (Helen...avenge me.)

"Wer war es? Wer dies tat, Mutter?" (Who was it? Who did this to you, mother?) Helen asked through her tears as she leaned over her badly wounded mother. Tanya coughed, spitting blood onto the side of Boogie's face before closing her eyes. Boogie laid her head on Ford's bloody hands and cried aloud as ambulance sirens were heard off in the distance.

Popeye emerged from the club fully dressed just as paramedics were pulling up to the scene. Four medics rushed from the back with a gurney and began administering aide to Tanya and two more ambulances were just down the block tending to the old couple.

Popeye and his crew walked off from the chaos to access the matter. "They hit us from the roof, bro. It was two up there." Ford explained as he pointed to the building across the street.

"The other shooters was on this building here," Big Ty remarked as he pointed to the building across the street from the club's entrance. "One was a sniper, though. He caught them two old folk on the other side the club."

"Black Escalade pulled up and Tanya paused, bruh. It was like she knew the person, ya' know? They sped up the block and picked up three dudes and peeled out. They was too far away to make out." Ford added.

"Tanya passed out before telling Boogie who she saw, too." Big Ty chimed in while shaking his head.

"I think I hit one of 'em," Popeye told his team.

"Let's do some forensics on the shit," Ford said as he began walking out into the street.

Popeye had Big Ty stay back with Boogie while he, Ford and Bell trotted over to the apartment building across from the club. They entered through a back door and crept up the stairs towards the roof with their guns aimed up as the lights of the ambulance glared from below. While the red and white lights traveled down the concrete jungle, the fate of Tanya was still uncertain as Popeye and his team emerged onto the roof and walked slowly towards the ledge while looking down at the asphalt.

Along the way, they'd found empty soda cans, beer bottles and cigarette butts. From the worn colors and dried out butts, it was clear to see that the items had been there for some time. Once they'd reached the ledge facing the club, however, more recently used items were found, including that of spent bullet shells. Ford leaned down and eyed a smoked marijuana blunt and dumped tobacco. Whoever it was that hit Tanya had been waiting a while because they had enough time to roll one and smoke.

The stogie was still burning and the tip was wet, Ford noticed. "You didn't hit nobody, but you scared 'em enough cuz he dropped the blunt he was toking when you shot at 'em," he told Popeye as he pulled out an ink pen and used the tip to put out the joint. A Dutch wrap packaging laying on the ground was used to store the blunt for the time being. "We can get some DNA off this tip, and if we're lucky, whoever it was is in the system already. Can your mother get somebody in DC to run AFIS?" he asked Popeye.

"Yeah," Popeye answered as he took Ford's pen and picked up a bullet shell. "We might get some prints off these, too," he added. "Secure all this shit and get it in my mother's hands ASAP. I'll call and let her know what done happened so she can set up a lab. I'm going be with Boogie and stay here in Ohio with her until we get some results," he added as he walked off.

Popeye made it back over to the club and saw Boogie sitting with her head in her knees in the very spot her mother had once laid. Officers were walking around asking questions, but no one was volunteering any information. The streets would handle the matter soon enough they all knew as that's how business was handled in The Rhine. Popeye knelt down before Boogie and whispered, *"Wir herauszufinden, wer das war. Wir haben einige Sachen auf dem Dach, die helfen können, diese Jungs die Spur. Wie ist Ihre Mutter?"* (We gone find out who did this. We found some stuff on the roof that may help track these guys down. How's your mother?)

"Sie sagte, daß sie nicht ansprechbar war und ich konnte nicht mit ihr fahren." (They said she was unresponsive and I couldn't ride with her.) Boogie heaved as she clutched her knees and rocked back and forth in her seated positon. *"Sie geht zu sterben, William. Wenn ich mich an der Universität von Cincinnati Medical Sie mir mitteilen, dass sie tot ist!"* (She's going to die, William. When I get to University of Cincinnati Medical they're going to tell me she's dead!)

"Sag das nicht, Baby." (Don't say that, baby.) Popeye comforted as he kissed Boogie's temple and helped her to her feet. *"Was wir gegangen, ist erhalten Sie gekleidet, und um das Krankenhaus und für deine Mutter warten durch zu ziehen."* (What we gone do is get you dressed, and head over to the hospital and wait for your mother to pull through.) he ended as he led a distressed Boogie back into the club.

CHAPTER TWENTY-EIGHT

BIG DADDY LADDY

"It's two hundred and forty-two miles to Indianapolis from Saint Louis where this Ford Focus was rented by Bena Holland back in January of this year. The mileage on said rental was five hundred and twenty-two miles round trip," Laddy Norcross said to Sandra Cordova as the two sat at the State Trooper's kitchen table inside her one story brick home located just outside of downtown Saint Louis.

It was moments after Tanya Weinberger had unbeknownst to them, been shot up in Cincinnati. The two law enforcement officers were going over the latest data collected on their budding case against Bena and Tiva Holland. Laddy was trying hard to link the twins to a hit in Indianapolis against Ricky 'RJ' Gross Junior that had gone down outside of the Conrad Inn and Suites on South Meridian Street and he believed he'd found a smoking gun. The agent felt he was getting close enough to at least bring Bena and Tiva before a grand jury for questioning based on the mileage of the rental car and a couple of other things that were more than coincidental.

Sandra placed a glass of wine before Laddy and returned to the stove where she slid a skillet back and forth over gas flames to mix up the sausage, peppers and onions she had going. She poured a little red wine into the concoction before taking a swig right from the bottle. "God, that's delicious," she said as she licked her thumbs, turned the flame down low and stood beside Laddy wearing just a t-shirt with no bra and pair of panties.

"Okay," Sandra said as she leaned over Laddy, "What does that prove, baby?"

Laddy leaned back in the chair and smiled at that moment. He looked Sandra over. She was a thing of beauty to him as he adored

Hispanic women. Standing 5'6" with wide hips, brown hair and hazel eyes. The two had begun an affair a month earlier after constant flirtations. Being miles from home working a case that had him running around in circles left Laddy in need of companionship. Sandra had been there every step of the way with him, and the two had easily established a friendship in the profession. Laddy used to return to his hotel room in the beginning, but the closer he grew to Sandra, the more they began to hang out after work. First it was just drinks in a local cop bar. Then drinks and dinner at different restaurants around town. Before long, there were night caps over to Sandra's house while she prepared dinner.

The two were sitting across from one another a month earlier, enjoying crusted salmon and shrimp pasta talking about much of nothing when their sexual affair began. Laddy briefly reflected back on that night…

…"I think I'll go and get my hair done tomorrow," Sandra remarked as she stirred her pasta. She looked up at Laddy, turned her head to the side and asked, "How should I get it done, Big Daddy Laddy?" while picking at her brown, shoulder-length curly hair.

"Big Daddy Laddy?" Laddy laughed as he cut into his salmon.

"Are you offended?" Sandra asked through a seductive smile.

"Wouldn't change things if I were, now would it?" Laddy asked as he placed a piece of salmon into his mouth.

"Maybe not," Sandra blushed. "You know I want you, Laddy," she sincerely stated. "You wouldn't be entertaining me after hours if you weren't the least bit interested in knowing what it would feel like."

Laddy wiped his mouth and said, "If it's half as good as this fish, then I'm in trouble."

"That's a bad analogy," Sandra laughed as she left the kitchen and walked into her living room. "I know you like jazz, but I haven't any in my CD collection!" she yelled out from the living room. I have this great soul compilation disc I copped from a peddler some time ago. Is that okay?"

"I love soul music!" Laddy said as he poured himself a glass of Dom Perignon. "Almost as much as your cooking, woman," he then said to himself.

"Awesome!" Sandra shot back. "Give me a minute!" she called out over Michael Jackson's song Human Nature.

Several minutes had gone by and Laddy had just finished his meal. He was getting up for a second glass wine when Sandra reappeared. She stood in the doorway wearing a see-through negligee with a white camisole and no panties. She'd wet her hair, making it curl naturally as she stood with her hands on her curvaceous hips. "You like?" she asked as she turned slowly to the music.

Laddy grew an instant erection watching Sandra parade her sexy body before him. "You know I'm a married man," he chuckled as he poured himself another glass of wine.

"I know," Sandra remarked as she walked over to Laddy, picked up his glass of wine and took a sip. "I'm not asking you to marry me, man. Just fuck me like I know you been wanting to since we first met," she whispered as she leaned down and kissed Laddy deeply.

Laddy responded by reaching out and grabbing a handful of Sandra's soft, rotund ass cheeks. He kneaded her breasts with his free hand as he stood to his feet and ripped his shirt open. "You wanna be fucked?" he asked seductively as he turned Sandra around and unbuttoned his silk slacks.

"Yes, Laddy," Sandra panted as she spread herself out over the table, knocking dishes aside as Laddy entered her in a single motion. "Yes," she panted. "I'm a pathetic whore and you like it! You like it don't you, Laddy?"

"I love my wife!" Laddy groaned as he pummeled Sandra's pussy from behind.

"I know! I know!" Sandra panted. "This is our...yes, god! Our secret!" she cried out as she hid her face inside her folded arms and let Laddy have his way with her until he arrived, spilling semen onto her ass cheeks and backside.

A lesser man would blame what happened that night on too much wine, but Laddy wasn't the type of man to make excuses for his immoral behavior. He adored Sandra, had been adoring her for some time, but he was unwilling to make the move being he was a man of reservation. Once Sandra put it out there, however, Laddy did nothing to resist this tempting woman who pushed his buttons.

The two had a lot in common, namely their careers, but Sandra was also a hot piece of ass if Laddy had to tell it. His wife was over six hundred miles away and hadn't a clue what he was up to with his partner down in Missouri, and he and Sandra had agreed to end their affair when and if Laddy either solved the case, or was removed from it and Missouri altogether.

In the meantime, the two went along with things as if they were item. Laddy spent many a night over to Sandra's home and was comfortable enough to leave a few changing clothes and a couple of bottles of cologne on her dresser. He leaned back in the chair wearing a pair of loose-fitting cotton shorts, having showered recently, as he looked over the files he'd collected.

"What this rental proves," Laddy remarked as he took another sip of his wine and hugged Sandra around her thick waist, "what this proves is that Bena and Tiva Holland were in Indianapolis the night RJ was killed. The rental company they rented the car from had a GPS aboard. Printouts show that the car was parked across the street from the Conrad at the Hard Rock Café on the day RJ was killed."

"All you have is circumstantial evidence. A grand jury won't opt to take our case to trial based on speculation," Sandra reasoned.

"You're correct, mami," Laddy nodded. "But, I subpoenaed surveillance footage from the Hard Rock that night a while back and got this back just today," Laddy said as he popped a disc into his government issued laptop.

Sandra placed her hands to the table and watched as a brown Ford Focus pulled up into the Hard Rock Café in Indianapolis minutes before RJ was killed. The car rode past the entrance to the Hard Rock and two figures were seen inside the car. Both were easily distinguished as females identical in body size, although their faces could not be made out clearly due to the glare from the lights and the darkness of night.

"The car went off camera after passing by the entrance, but watch this," Laddy remarked as the footage jumped forward several minutes. "You can see people running out into the street. That was seconds after RJ was killed. And then…"

Sandra watched as the brown Ford Focus came back into view. "This time, there's only the driver in the front seat. You can see somebody in the back and this…" Laddy froze the video and zoomed in on the Ford Focus and let the footage roll in slow motion as the figures inside the car grew even more blurry. "You can see that whoever is in the backseat is removing a magazine from some sort of rifle," Laddy said as he replayed the last few seconds of the video. "There's our assassin," he said seriously as the blurry image of Bena Holland sitting in the backseat of a rented Ford Focus removing a magazine from the rifle she'd just used to assassinate Ricky 'RJ' Gross Junior stared back at him and Sandra.

"I can print these pictures out, present the entire video along with a timeline and send it all to my superiors as evidence. That data, along with the car rental GPS putting a brown Ford Focus rented by Bena Holland in Saint Louis and driven to Indianapolis, should be enough to drag those two before a grand jury."

"They'll deny being in Indianapolis before the grand jury, you know that," Sandra remarked.

"That's what I'm hoping they do," Laddy countered. "The penalty for perjury can be up to five years. With all the evidence presented? It'll be enough to put Bena and Tiva Holland away for five years at least. And I'll earn more funding from the appropriations committee to go after them for the murders of Desiree Abbadando, the Onishi brothers and a police officer that was killed the same night the Onishi brothers were killed. That would place them on death row for sure," the federal agent smiled.

"Big Daddy Laddy on the rise," Sandra smiled as she moved back over to the stove. "Dinner will be ready in about twenty minutes, honey."

Laddy's head was up in the clouds over the evidence he'd gathered on Bay and T-top. In his mind's eye, it was only a matter of time before he bust his case wide open and have all the chips fall into place. In the mood for love, he slid his chair back, stood up and hugged Sandra from behind. "You're the best partner a man could have in law," he smiled as he raised Sandra's silky brown hair and kissed the nape of her neck.

"You want some pussy before dinner?"

"Why of course," Laddy smiled as he turned the stove off and guided Sandra past the table, through the living room and led her into the bedroom.

Along the way, Sandra had cued up her stereo system. The

melodic sounds of Norman Connors' song *You Are My Starship* came over the speakers. Inside the bedroom, the horny Hispanic removed her t-shirt and panties and lay flat on the bed, welcoming Laddy atop her as the two became one. Sandra's creamy, thick thighs were spread wide as Laddy sunk down into her tight vagina. The two moaned and began kissing heavily while quickly getting into rhythm without the intervention of foreplay.

"It's yours," Sandra moaned. "Big Daddy Laddy," she moaned. "Fuck my pussy! Fuck me!" she begged.

"Give it to me, baby," Laddy panted as he stroked Sandra deep and hard while cradling her head on his hands and planting kisses all over her neck and face. He leaned down and suckled her nipples as he began rotating his hips inside of his mistress's sloppy wet vagina. "Damn," he moaned as he humped Sandra relentlessly.

"Where you wanna come? You wanna come in mami's pussy? My mouth? What Big Daddy want?"

Laddy frowned in pleasure as he grabbed one of Sandra's legs and threw it back over his broad shoulder. He clasped his hands to her curvaceous hips and began stabbing her, letting just the tip of his dick kiss her opening before driving back inside.

"Oh, god, you gone drive me crazy," Sandra panted as she grabbed either side of Laddy's biceps and jerked her hips upwards. "I wanna come. Can I come on your dick?"

"Come on this dick!" Laddy growled as he picked up the pace, driving deeper into Sandra with every stroke as his dick began to throb.

"Come with me!" Sandra screamed out. "Yes, Big Daddy!"

"Baby!" Laddy grunted as his hips jerked. He pulled out, scooted up the mattress and placed his dick to Sandra's eager mouth. Before she'd engulfed him fully, Laddy was spewing semen across Sandra's face and broad lips. She lay back and let his fluid coat her face while rubbing his pole over her lips and flicking her tongue across his head, planting soft kisses as she licked him clean, purposely swallowing some of his semen in the process.

"What was that?" Sandra asked as she turned her head away from Laddy and laughed.

"You…you didn't like it?" Laddy asked as he laid down beside his woman.

"What?" Sandra chuckled. "That was amazing, baby. I can't get enough of you. I'm gone keep you working this case for as long as possible, man. You too much fun for one woman," she said as she leaned over and pecked Laddy's lips. "Now I'm ready for some wine. Get yourself together while I pour us up a glass," she said as she eased out of the bed rejuvenated.

"I'll be there in a minute. Let me check on Hermelinda before we continue on with the night," Laddy ended as he reached over to the nightstand and grabbed his cellphone to call and check in with his family.

CHAPTER TWENTY-NINE

THE END OF AN ERA

It was just after midnight back over to DC, early Wednesday morning. June 10th. Exactly two weeks after all the events starting with Lisa and the Moto brothers' discussion over in Seattle, Washington had unfolded, and a few hours after Laddy and Sandra had their sex romp. Senator Willameena 'Willie' Slack had just emerged from the Senate chamber. For the past thirteen hours, she and the rest of the Democrat Senators had been debating Republican Senators over the controversial Affordable Healthcare Act that was scheduled to go up for vote at the end of the year. She was met by several of her aides out in the Senate hall, all of whom had messages for her as she powered up her personal cell. Right away, the Senator's phone buzzed over and over again. She looked down and saw that she had numerous messages from her son Popeye, Fordham Nelson, Sally Irving and Faye Bender.

Willie had never had this happen before and she immediately grew worried over the possibilities. She pressed the voicemail button and heard Popeye say, "Momma, we got hit in Cincinnati. Tanya went down tonight. She up to University of Cincinnati unresponsive. I got Ford on his way with…"

"Senator Slack, do you have any word on the progress of President Obama's healthcare bill? Are you able to sway any republicans into joining you and Senate democrats on its passage out of the Senate?"

"What?" Willie mean-mugged at the reporter after listening to the entire message. She was prepared to go off, but she kept her composure when she saw that she was up against a dozen journalists.

"The healthcare bill? Have any republicans joined you in the pass—"

"Republicans are not interested in joining us democrats in passing healthcare reform for neither their constituents nor any American citizen at this time," Willie remarked, cutting the reporter short and jumping back into political mode. "But, we have a majority here in the senate so it's only a matter time before the Affordable Healthcare Act becomes law. Without republicans, we have the numbers needed to pass the President's bill, but we're encouraging the republicans in the senate to join us in doing something good for the American people by passing this monumental healthcare bill that will benefit millions of citizens, cut costs and lower premiums," she answered over numerous camera flashes.

"The republicans are doing a good job at discouraging their constituency with the talk of death panels. Are there going to be, will the President set up a panel that will decide—"

"It's sick for anyone to suggest that the President will set up a committee that will decide who gets to live and who dies," Willie interrupted another reporter. "It's a scare tactic," she laughed.

"You're polling high back in Louisiana. Sixty-four percent approval rating in a solidly republican state. Are you worried that your joining the President in passing this bill will put you in harm's way for your 2010 reelection bid?" a third reporter asked.

"If I did everything based on how I thought the people would respond, I would never pass a single bill. I'm bound to upset some people even when doing the right thing. The key to good governance is doing what's right even at the risk of one's own political future. I'll risk my Senate seat every day of the week if I knew that what I was doing was the right thing to do. And passing this healthcare bill is the right thing to do. The people will thank me later, win or lose come 2010," Willie smiled. She walked off from the reporters as they continued hounding her with questions as she headed for her Senate office.

Once inside her office, Willie listened to all the messages and learned that her ears were not fooling her. Tanya had indeed been hit over in Ohio and was in bad shape. She flopped down in her executive chair and dialed Popeye's number and was filled in on all that'd transpired. Ford was still about five hours out, so all she could do is wait on his arrival before she began digging into who was behind the hit exactly.

The silence inside the pristine office sent Willie off into a deep, somber reflection. Tanya was her girl from back in the day. They'd become friends back in Davenport, Iowa over thirty years ago. Willie had known Tanya long before she'd ever met Brenda or the King Sisters down in New Orleans. She was responsible for Willie having ascended to Senator, and she'd put in major work on the crew's behalf. None of that mattered to Willie, however; the only important thing was that Tanya pulled through and they get the issue resolved in a quick and orderly fashion. The downtrodden Senator rubbed her temples as she called Faye to see how she was dealing with the matter.

****

Faye hung up with Willie after discussing the Ohio hit and closed her eyes at her desk as she grieved her wounded friend in the early hours of Wednesday morning. Tanya was the sister she never had. It was Tanya that'd looked out for her and Maggie when she was on the run after being accused of murdering her own family by sending her down to New Orleans. It was Tanya who'd helped kill the warden of Mitchellville prison in order to save Bonita's life, and it was Tanya that'd made the organization what it was to this very day by seeing the bigger picture in placing Willie into politics early on.

Without Tanya, the crew wouldn't be as formidable as they were, Faye knew. She also knew that if Tanya were to die, the family would lose half their strength as Tanya had the know-how on how to distribute heroin. She was also the one that met with Willie and discussed important matters. A lot of things would change without her presence, but for business sake, the crew had to press on, no matter how hard the task.

"Momma," Maggie called out as she poked her head inside the room, having just arrived with the doctor needed to perform the surgery on Sharona.

"You're back from Saint Louis," Faye stated glumly as she sat at her desk. "Have you heard?"

"*Über Tanya? Ja. Wird sie in Ordnung?*" (About Tanya? Yes. Will she be okay?)

"*Sie ist aus Chirurgie und in einem kritischen Zustand. Sie ist nicht mehr reagiert und hat innere Blutungen, die Ärzte haben eine harte Zeit zu korrigieren. Wir sind auf das Schlimmste vorbereiten.*" (She's out of surgery and in critical condition. She's

361

unresponsive and has internal bleeding that doctors are having a hard time correcting. We're preparing for the worst.)

Maggie choked back tears and said, *"Ich habe den Arzt im Erdgeschoss warten. Willst du mich zu ihm zurück nach Saint Louis?"* (I have the doctor waiting downstairs. Do you want me to take him back to Saint Louis?)

"No," Faye replied somberly as she rose from behind her desk. "We still have a job to do on behalf of Natalia so let's get to it," she added as she walked out of her office with Maggie on her heels.

"I've called Natalia. He's bringing Sharona Benson here in the morning." Maggie said to Faye as the two descended the stairs.

"Good," Faye stated as the doctor came into view. *"Ich bin mir sicher, dass der Arzt will, um diese so schnell wie möglich, damit er zu seinem normalen Leben zurückkehren können."* (I'm sure the doctor wants to get this done as soon as possible so he can return to his normal lifestyle.) She smiled as she went and greeted the man and said, "Nice to meet you. I was told you want to remain name free, so I'll keep it at that. Doesn't mean I'm being rude, just respecting your wishes."

"I understand well. Nice to meet you," Doctor Wickenstaff remarked as he stood to his feet while holding onto a black satchel filled with cutting utensils and medications. "Do you have everything prepared for today's procedure?"

"I do, but the recipient will not be here until morning. In the meantime, I'll take you to the donor for the extraction." Faye calmly replied.

Faye and Maggie drove Doctor Wickenstaff over the darkened land of the Cherryvale Farm to the barn and led him inside. The narrow corridor was haunting at best to the good doctor with its red lighting and worn wood. He wondered how a woman who lived in such an elegant mansion could have a place as vile and decrepit as the hut he now found himself in as the place was more suitable to primitive times at best. The constant roar of a chainsaw from behind a closed door at the end of the hall unnerved the man enough to make his palms sweaty, and the recognizable smell of death lingered in the air. The stench grew louder when Faye pushed a side door open that led into a windowless abode that was humid and being lit with nineteen century oil lamps.

Doctor Wickenstaff had to hunch over slightly inside the low-ceiled area being he stood well over six feet. He looked around the dingy room and said, "This is neither a satisfactory nor aseptically suitable setting to perform a radical nephrectomy. There should not be any dust present. The room must be completely sterile in order to prevent contamination of the recipient."

"This is where the extraction is to take place, doctor," Faye remarked as she guided Wickenstaff to a small door on the right at the rear of the bungalow. "You'll do the transplant in my home," she added as she pushed the door open.

Doctor Wickenstaff stepped off into the room and looked around stunned at the contrast of conditions. On the walls were images of Sesame Street characters. There was an Oscar the Grouch trash can that had the Muppet character sitting up in it with a frown on its face. In the far left corner was a Big Bird statue. The yellow Muppet was holding onto an empty gumball machine smiling back at the doctor. In the right corner of the room stood a tall Caucasian woman. She eyed the doctor without saying a word as she held onto a silencer-tipped revolver and nodded over to the woman.

"This was my daughter Maggie's room when she was just a child, doctor. We lived here before our home across the way was erected," Faye confessed. "As you can see, Maggie left it untouched."

"I see," Doctor Wickenstaff remarked calmly. "The smiling faces, they help to lighten the mood, I guess. Hello," he then said to the blonde-haired, tall, burly woman standing in the corner with the stern look on her face.

"We've been waiting for you for a while, doctor," she responded in her deep-pitched voice. "Do the surgery so I can kill this woman and do away with what's left of her already. We've been at this for long enough," she stated in a cold and callous manner.

In between Doctor Wickenstaff, Big Bird and the woman with the hostile demeanor was a gurney supporting a naked Caucasian woman in her early twenties. Her dark brown eyes were open and her tan face was red with tears as she lay gagged and bound. Doctor Wickenstaff walked over and looked down at the woman as he set his satchel atop the Oscar the Grouch trash can, crushing the Muppet back down into the plastic bin. "This is where I wanna be!

Grouch paradise!" the Muppet character was heard saying through the closed lid.

Sascha chuckled over the Muppet's talking as she held on to the silencer-tipped revolver. "This procedure…how long will it take, doctor?" she asked.

"Three hours if all goes well," Doctor Wickenstaff remarked as he pulled a syringe and a vial from his bag. He stuck the needle into the glass tube and sucked up a hypodermic full of morphine.

The woman on the gurney began squirming and screaming through the duct tape covering her mouth as the doctor approached with the needle. A weekend spent with friends over in neighboring Missouri summer hiking had devolved into a real-life horror flick for her on her return drive home to Salina, Kansas when she was pulled over just east of Cherryvale and taken captive. The buzz of the chainsaw from the next room over had awakened her and she now found herself in the clutches of evildoers who had no conscience. She tried her best to free herself by wiggling her hands, but she was struck over the head by the woman with the pistol and grew dizzy. A pinch in her arm stung briefly and eyes lowered as she succumbed to the effects of whatever drug she'd been given. Her world soon faded into darkness, a darkness in which she would never see the light of day again.

"You need us to stay with you, doctor?" Faye asked as the woman calmed down and went to sleep.

"I think I'll be fine. What I'll need is complete silence while I perform. Can you, can you delay whatever it is that is going on outside in the other room for a few hours?"

"I'll get that done for you. Come on, girls." Faye stated in a low, respectable tone.

"You and Maggie go on," Sascha remarked. "I want to see how the doctor does this surgery."

Faye and Maggie left and Sascha remained in place. She watched the nameless doctor carefully as he sterilized his hands and then drew dotted lines on the woman's stomach with a sharpie. "Do you have a family, doctor?" she asked.

"I do," Doctor Wickenstaff replied as he pulled out a large scalpel and a bottle of alcohol. "My wife passed ten years ago in an automobile accident and my daughter is a surgeon in the Army overseas."

"Does this bother you? Taking an innocent life? Someone you don't even know in order to increase your bank account?"

"No more than it bothered you to hit her across the head with that gun to keep her subdued for me," Doctor Wickenstaff remarked in a curt tone. "You seem like a woman with a conscience to a degree, maybe one who wasn't in agreement with this decision but went along with things for loyalty's sake," he added as he poked around in his bag.

Noticing the doctor's hands were full, Sascha took a step forward and used one of his scalpels to pick up a rag and hand it to the man. "This woman means nothing to me," she told the doctor as she resumed her stance in the corner. "I believed this was a bad act that will beget us bad karma when we first started. Something happened to a friend of ours today and she will die soon. I see that as the bad karma. I did not want to be right in what I was thinking about this being a bad act."

"A life for a life?" Doctor Wickenstaff asked as he donned a pair of latex gloves.

"Yes. My friend will die tonight, and this is why," Sascha said as she nodded over to the gurney. "But someone will live... maybe."

"I can't assure you that someone will live. This world, this life is always uncertain," Doctor Wickenstaff remarked as the chainsaw went silent. "You can sit still and quiet and trouble will still find you somehow, however. Don't think that this, this undertaking here, wherever we are, is the cause of your friend's demise."

"Wherever we are? Did you not read the signs along the way?"

"I was clever enough to sleep the whole ride so as to not know where I was being taken," Doctor Wickenstaff replied as he leaned down and began making an incision in the woman's side. "When I'm done here I hope I never see you people again in life. I care not to know where I am and who you people are. This job tells me all I need to know about the people in my midst. No offense."

"None taken," Sascha smiled. "I'm here to assist you if you need any help, doctor."

"I feel comforted," Doctor Wickenstaff replied in kind. "I take back what I said, but only for you, ma'am," he then added.

Sascha tilted her head and looked at the doctor perplexed. "What makes you say that?" she asked.

"I may want to see one of you ladies again. Preferably the one who stands in the corner like an observant student," Wickenstaff smiled through his surgical mask. "You intrigue me, lady. I'd like to invite you to play a round of golf someday once this all passes."

"This is no longer cougar territory. I have now become a hunted bunny," Sascha blushed as she watched the doctor work. "We'll see, doctor," she ended as she kept her stance. "We'll see."

****

Over to the room opposite where Doctor Wickenstaff and Sascha were, Faye and Maggie were standing before the wooden table inside their torture chamber staring at countless body parts that had been cut up by Bonita and Cikala, who were now working on their last victim with the aid of a hacksaw. Up on the shelf sat a prized possession for Faye: the severed heads of Claire Bailey and her daughter Piper. The skulls sat upright, mouth and eyes open staring back at her. The Baileys had been the first to be conscripted into her and Bonita's reenactment of their ancestors' treacherous deeds and it'd culminated with the death of an innocent black female.

Faye stared at Bonita as she cut into the arm of the black woman she and Faye had killed several hours earlier. She hadn't heard the news about Tanya just yet and Faye knew it would break her heart. Deciding to reserve the news about their for for later, she walked up beside Bonita and said, *"Heute Abend ist die letzte Nacht diese Scheune stehen wird. Wir müssen es zerstören."* (Tonight is the last night this barn will stand. We'll have to destroy it.)

Bonita continued sawing the woman's arm with her tongue hanging out the side of her mouth and said, *"Ich kenne. Es gibt keine Weise, können wir alle die DNA der sieben Menschen, die wir die letzten drei Tage getötet haben, entfernen. Was müssen Sie beachten?"* (I know. There's no way we can remove all the DNA of the seven people we've killed the past four days. What do you have in mind to do with it?)

"Sammeln auf der Feuerversicherung." (Collect on the fire insurance.) Faye remarked as she picked up Claire's head, dropped it into a wheelbarrow full of severed arms and legs and began

wheeling it to her pickup truck for discarding inside the apple groves.

Several hours later, Doctor Wickenstaff and Sacha emerged from the bungalow out into the barn where Faye, Bonita, Maggie McPherson and Cikala were sitting quietly listening to the police scanner. All was quiet in the small town being the main perpetrators of violence were idle now. The crew's half dozen or so other paid soldiers not in on the deal were patrolling and had orders to stand down for the night and conduct normal traffic stops and to answer all calls that came in.

Sascha was holding onto a Styrofoam box containing a set of extracted kidneys. "You can discard the donor now that we're done," she told Faye and company.

Bonita sat crying silently as she smoked a joint. Faye had finally broken the news and it'd crushed her. She'd wanted to rush to Cincinnati, the same as Faye, but the crew had to remain in Cherryvale until Sharona Benson was out of harm's way. It could be up to a week before she could leave the farm. Bonita wondered if she would ever see her friend alive again, but given the latest report that Tanya was still in critical condition, the chances were grim at best.

In the hours that it had taken Doctor Wickenstaff to perform the surgery, there was some good news: Ford had touched down in DC and the evidence he'd gathered was now in the hands of Senator Slack. Right around the time Sharona Benson would be leaving the Bender Farm would be close to the time when the results would be made known. The crew would be clear to go after whoever it was that was behind the hit on Tanya, and that was enough comfort for the time being. The immediate task ahead, however, was to prepare the barn for its final phase.

Faye and Bonita went to work on the donor after dragging her corpse into their butcher shop. They chopped her remains up into small, movable parts while Maggie and Cikala removed valuables from the bungalow and stored them over to the mansion. The Bender sisters emerged from the barn with the last remains of their murder victims an hour later and set the black trash bags they were toting into the back of Faye's dueler before walking back into the barn side by side in a somber mood with their heads to the ground.

The once lively place had become a desolate wasteland in a

short manner of time. Even the walls seemed to be weeping over what was to come on this night. One large combine and a tractor remained in the open area of the barn and a cow had been brought in for added affect. Tools remained in place, lining the walls and giving off a reverential aurora as Faye and Bonita slowly walked past them in their 1800s attire, Faye in her pink and white wide-bottomed dress and white Bonnet and Bonita in her denim overalls and boots.

The Bender sisters entered the bungalow and looked around in silence. *"Wenn ich hier zurück, dies war das erste Hotel in dem Maggie und Ich nach Hause. Ich wurde eine Mutter hier für eine Weile."* (When I returned here, this was the first place Maggie and I called home. I became a mother here for a while.) Faye told Bonita as she walked around the open area with her hands on her hips.

"Es war immer ein Platz für mich zu töten, aber ich verstehe Ihre Stimmung, Schwester. Ich hasse es zu sehen zu gehen." (It was always a place to kill for me, but I understand your sentiment, sister. I hate to see it go too.)

"Es ist das Ende einer Ära." (It's the end of an era.) Faye smiled through subtle tears as she looked back at Bonita.

"Könnte gleichen sagte für Tanya. Es ist wie zwei Epochen in der Familie heute zu Ende kommen." (Same could be said for Tanya. It's like two eras in the family are coming to an end today.) Bonita respectfully replied as she wiped tears from her eyes and walked over to the gas stove. It would be fair to say that the Bender sisters were more in sorrow over the possible outcome of Tanya than the fate of the barn, but it seemed as if both affairs were now working hand in hand.

"Wir haben unsere Vorfahren im Einklang Tradition stolz getan." (We've done our ancestors proud in keeping tradition.) Faye stated, breaking the brief moment of silence as she walked over to the stove.

"Und wir werden das Gleiche für Tanya. Auf einen neuen Anfang." (And we'll do the same for Tanya. To a new beginning.) Bonita remarked as she turned a knob, releasing gas into the air.

"Auf einen neuen Anfang." (To a new beginning.) Faye followed as she herself turned a knob on the gas stove. She gave the place a final look over before she and Bonita left the bungalow for a final time with the oil lamps still burning.

Maggie McPherson, meanwhile, was standing out on the mansion's second floor balcony looking over to the barn when she saw her mother and Bonita emerge for what she knew would be the last time. She looked at the windowless wall where the bungalow lay and reflected on her childhood briefly. It all seemed so normal to her back then, growing up in an enclosed dungeon with no friends with only the company of books and TV to keep her entertained while her mother 'worked' in the room just outside the lone door. She'd become accustomed to homicide over those tender years. Her Sesame Street bedroom made things seem typical, but Maggie knew there was nothing ordinary about the way she was raised, nor that of the life she now led. When it got down to it, however, she wouldn't have it any other way as crime, murder itself, was all she'd ever known outside of receiving the best education money could buy.

Cikala emerged out on to the balcony at that moment. She and Maggie stood side-by-side and watched Faye's dueler creep through the darkness over towards the apple groves. The body count was up to over two dozen in the seven years or so Cikala had been around, and there were more victims before she'd arrived, she knew to be true. She herself was sad to see the barn go, and just like Faye, Maggie and Bonita felt, to Cikala, it seemed as if the doors were closing for Tanya as well. She pulled a rolled blunt from her t-shirt pocket and sparked it up. After a few puffs, she passed it on to Maggie and used a remote to cue up a wireless speaker back inside the observation room.

Maggie toked as she watched her mother and Bonita place the final remains into a wood chipper just as Bone Thugs N Harmony and Tupac's song *Thug Luv* shot through the speaker. She bobbed her head to one of her favorite artists in Tupac just as her cellphone buzzed. Filled with anxiety, she tentatively looked down and read the group text from Boogie and slowly bowed her head in sorrow.

Cikala checked her buzzing phone, read the same message and was forced down to one knee in stunned grief.

With tears in her eyes, Maggie looked out to her mother's dueler as it made its way back to the mansion. She was wondering if Faye and Bonita had gotten the text. Her question was answered when she saw the pickup come to a sudden halt. The interior lit up as Faye and Bonita both climbed out. Maggie watched as her mother dropped to her knees while Bonita leaned up against the side of the truck and began pounding the hood repeatedly.

Maggie looked down at the message from Boogie a second time and read it again: *She died.*

Stunned, Maggie walked off in seemingly slow motion just as the barn off in the distance exploded, vibrating the mansion's foundation. She threw an arm up in the air and shook her head with her eyes closed as she danced in place, mourning Tanya as Tupac rapped on…*"Until they stop me…bury murder me or drop me…I got… thug luv for my nationwide posse…feel me…"*

CHAPTER THIRTY

ONWARD

A shaking hand signed a death warrant inside the morgue over to University of Cincinnati Medical Center around ten 'o' clock Wednesday morning. Boogie handed the clipboard back to the Medical Examiner and stood before her deceased mother as Popeye fell back and tucked his hands into his silk slacks, giving her a moment alone.

After a twenty-seven-year run that began in March of 1982 in Des Moines, Iowa at the age of nineteen, Tanya Weinberger's criminal career had come to an abrupt halt on June 10, 2009 at the age of forty-seven. The revered leader inside the German crime family lay with her eyes closed in a peaceful slumber atop a cold, steel table. Her blonde hair was neatly combed and the seven gunshot wounds had been cleaned, leaving behind only that of red dots that blotted her flesh. The autopsy report said she'd died of internal bleeding from bullets that had pierced both of her lungs and had torn up her intestines. Tanya's body had been so badly damaged that there was much of nothing that doctors could do to save her life without a lung transplant. Hers was a similar fate that Sharona was facing, but whereas Sharona had a fighting chance, a transplant for Tanya simply could not be completed in time enough to save her life.

Boogie closed her eyes and pressed her lips together as tears dripped from her chin onto her mother's heart. Although she was grieving the loss, her mother's last words, '*Helen...rache mich*', were etched into her psyche and she would not rest until her mother's dying wish was fulfilled. Only then would Boogie be able to go forward with the remainder of her life. "*Alles, was von deiner Mutter?*" (Anything from your mother?) she asked Popeye in a somber tone as she swallowed the lump in her throat.

"*Noch nichts, Liebe. Prüfung ist im Gange, aber. Wir sollten*

371

etwas in ein paar Tagen wissen." (Nothing yet, love. Testing is underway, though. We should know something in a few days.) Popeye answered in a loving tone.

"Was mache ich jetzt, William?" (What do I do now, William?) Boogie turned and asked with hints of fear and uncertainty in her voice. *"Ich kann nicht... Ich weiß nicht einmal, wenn ich umgehen kann was zurückbleibt. Cincinnati ist jetzt meine Aufgabe, aber ich habe um ehrlich zu sein..., dass mein Herz jetzt nicht in den Straßen ist. Ich habe gerade... Ich will sie wieder lebendig zu sein!"* (I can't...I don't even know if I can handle what's left behind. Cincinnati is now my responsibility, but I have to be honest...my heart is not in the streets right now. I just...I want her to be alive again!) she blurted out through her tears as she turned and stared at her mother's corpse. *"Ich bin ohne sie verloren, Mutter!"* (I'm lost without you, mother!) she cried out as she leaned down and gently cradled her mother's head in her arms.

Popeye walked over and slowly pulled Boogie back. She screamed to the top of lungs at that moment and kicked wildly, knocking over a steel cart filled with medical utensils.

"I can give her something to make her sleep if you'd like," the Medical Examiner stated as she held up a bottle of codeine.

Popeye took the medication and ushered Boogie from the morgue. He pushed her up against the wall just outside the room and looked deep into her eyes. *"Ich bin mit Ihnen!"* (I'm with you!) he grimaced. *"Ich weiß, dass das scheiße Weh! Ich bin verdammt weh!"* (I know the shit hurt! I'm fucking hurt!) he said through gritted teeth as tears filled his eyes. *"Aber ich bin nicht gegangen, dass sie geben! Sie geben nicht auf ihre Mutter, mich oder diese Familie! Wir über diese Scheiße zusammen gegangen!"* (But I'm not gone let you give up! You not giving up on your mother, me or this family! We gone get through this shit together!)

Boogie stared at Popeye for several seconds before hugging him tightly. *"Ich will die Schmerzen weggehen, William! Aber es geht nicht weg!"* (I want the hurt to go away, William! But it's not going away!)

"The hurt not supposed to go away right now...if ever at all," Popeye let it be known as he held on to Boogie. "You loved her, that's why it hurts, baby. We been here for a while. Let me take you home so you can rest. We'll get back to it when we wake up. Come on, baby," he said in a comforting tone as he escorted Boogie towards the exit where he placed her inside of his

Excursion and drove her home.

Several hours later, while Boogie lay sleep, Popeye received a phone call as he sat at her bedside reading an advanced copy of Colin Powell's novel, *My American Journey*. He didn't recognize the number, but figured it was probably Ford calling from a different number. "Hello?" he answered.

"Yo," the voice stated. "I called Kansas and they told me what happened and gave me this number. I need to get in touch with somebody over that way."

"They told me you was gone call. Helen unavailable right now, brer, this Popeye you talkin' to. Don't worry 'bout talkin' 'cause the line secure. What can I help you with?"

"You know where Lumpkin airport at, right?" Ben asked.

"Yeah."

"Okay. I'll call you with a time to meet up later on today. I got some info to drop on ya'."

"Gotcha," Popeye nodded before ending the call.

****

Ben had just hung up the phone with Willie's son, Popeye, and was now sitting in the G-550 with Bay, T-Top and Lee before a hangar at a small airport in Bowling Green, Missouri around one 'o' clock on Wednesday. The family was waiting on Jay-D and his people from Saint Charles to ride through, and all were caught up in their own thoughts about what had happened to one of the Germans last night. Ben had only met Tanya Weinberger once. That was when he dropped info about Iiayad Sheinheimer on her. She and Faye had done that job and their crew had also taken down the Fischer brothers in New York back in April. In two month's time, though, things had come full circle for all involved. Now the family was left trying to put all the pieces together before more bodies started to drop. Ben sat looking over the files he had for Popeye when he saw Jay-D's blue Navigator approaching the hangar.

The doors opened up on the jet and Lee got up to escort Jay-D and Loopy onboard. The two walked onto the plane and Loopy sat before Bay and T-top at a small table as Ben and Jay-D remained standing. "First off, I wanna welcome everybody," Ben stated.

373

"We would've liked to have had this meeting back at the club in Saint Charles, but with the feds in town, I know y'all understand."

"It's nothing, boss," Jay-D remarked. "From my perspective ain't no problem, ya' feel me? I'm only here to help Kantrell and Loopy get past whatever animosity they have with certain people in the family and some things that went down not too long ago."

"That's what it is, then," Ben replied. "We gone leave the ladies to talk in here, and I'm gone hollar at Kantrell while you and Lee stand guard," he told Jay-D.

Once Ben and Jay-D cleared out, the meeting between Loopy, Bay and T-top got underway aboard the plane. "Loopy," Bay remarked. "*Hemos escuchado acerca de lo que sucedió en el café. Jason dice usted y Helen son bien ahora?"* (I heard about what happened at the café. Jason said you and Helen are fine now?)

"Si," Loopy sighed as she looked away. "*Quiero preguntarle algo."* (I want to ask you something.) Bay nodded, and Loopy asked her, "*Si se tratara de cualquier otra persona, la gente no se ocupaba de la familia, usted habría matado a Helen, sabiendo quién es ella ahora?"* (If it were anybody else, not people the family was dealing with, would you have killed Helen, knowing who she is now?)

Bay looked Loopy square in the eyes and said, "*Tendríamos que haber estado en una gran guerra, pero sí. Incluso sabiendo que ella es ahora, habríamos matado Helen Weinberger...para usted."* (We would've been in a huge war, but yes. Even knowing who she is now, we would have killed Helen Weinberger...for you.)

Loopy looked down at the tabletop in silence. She then raised her head and said, "*No quiero ser parte de esto ya."* (I don't want to be a part of this anymore.)

"*Decir qué?"* (Say what?) Tiva frowned as she looked over to Loopy with her chin tucked in. "*No salir hasta que nos diga que salir en este momento. Aceptó el empleo de teniente en Mercy Hospital y esperamos mantener fiel el trabajo acordado hacerlo en nombre de la familia."* (You don't get out until we say you get out at this juncture. You accepted the job of lieutenant back inside Mercy Hospital and we expect you to hold true to the job you agreed to do on behalf of the family.)

"Hold on. Hold on, Tiva," Bay interceded. "What's your reasoning, Loopy?" she asked concerned.

"*Es mi tía CeeCee. Donatella no estar aquí es matarla y ella está preocupada por mí ahora. ¿Cada vez que salgo de la casa? Ella ora por mí y frota esta ceniza en la frente. ¿Cuando regrese? Ella lo hace para limpiar de malos espíritus, pero es molesto.*" (It's my aunt CeeCee. Donatella not being here is killing her and she's worried about *me* now. Every time I leave the house? She prays over me, and rubs this ash on my forehead. When I return? She does it again to cleanse me of bad spirits, but it's annoying.)

"*Los espíritus malos sólo que sé es en vino amargo. Necesita volver a centrarse, Loopy.*" (The only bad spirits I know is in some sour wine. You need to get back into focus, Loopy.) Tiva scolded.

"Tiva?" Bay sighed. She was getting agitated with her twin's lack of compassion over the circumstances with their soldier and was looking to quiet her as she felt there was more behind Loopy's wanting to leave the business. "*¿Cómo es tu vida, Loopy? Además de CeeCee te molesto por bendecirte cada día, ¿cómo usted vive?*" (How's your home life, Loopy? Besides CeeCee annoying you by blessing you every day, how are you living?)

"*No tenemos dinero.*" (We have no money.) Loopy remarked somberly. "*El tiempo que estaba en el hospital mi tía tuvo que cerrar su camión de tacos. Vendemos platos de comida fuera del apartamento para conseguir por ahora. Ella quiere abrir un restaurante mexicano algún día. Tengo que conseguir un trabajo para ayudar hacia fuera con eso porque no puedo seguir esperando cosas sucedan con la familia de Holanda.*" (The time I was in the hospital my aunt had to close her taco truck. We sell food plates out of the apartment to get by now. She wants to open a Mexican restaurant someday. I have to get a job to help her out with that because I can't keep waiting for things to happen with the Holland family.)

Bay leaned back and looked over to Tiva without cracking a smile, believing she'd gotten to the heart of the matter.

Tiva curled her lips and cut her eyes at her twin. "Okay, you were right and I was wrong to assume, Bay. Sorry, Loopy," she sincerely remarked as she leaned down, picked a duffle bag up and placed it on the table.

"I understand the business and how it goes, T-top," Loopy answered. "I wasn't expecting you to understand so easily, but, I accept your apology. No harm done."

Bay reached down into the bag and came up with several thick bundles of hundred dollar bills. *"Cuidamos de los nuestros."* (We take care of our own.) she told Loopy as she placed the money on the table. "This is one hundred and fifty thousand dollars. Donatella's insurance policy payout, and the payout for you taking one on the job. There's another two hundred thousand dollars. One hundred a piece that was to go to Simone Cortez and Peppi Vargas. They have no benefactors. The money, therefore, goes to Guadalupe Cruz per street law." (This is one hundred and fifty thousand dollars. Donatella's insurance policy payout, and the payout for you taking one on the job. There's another two hundred thousand dollars. One hundred a piece that was to go to Simone Cortez and Peppi Vargas. They have no benefactors. The money, therefore, goes to Guadalupe Cruz per street law.)

Loopy leaned back and widen her eyes as she stared at the money. *"Las oraciones de mi tía."* (My aunt's prayers.) she said in disbelief. *"Trabajaron!"* (They worked!)

Tiva and Bay looked Loopy off at that moment. Neither believed that CeeCee's prayers had been answered. The money being handed to Loopy was blood money after all. Three people had died for three hundred thousand dollars, and that didn't come about because of prayer, it came about because of the business Peppi and her crew were involved in was their belief.

"We've put the rest of your money into an investment fund that will accrue over the years," Bay stated as Tiva handed Loopy a bank statement and small portfolio. "You wait a year, and you can pull down your interest. Should be somewhere around forty thousand dollars."

"With the one hundred and fifty large you have now, and forty thousand a year on interest you'll have enough to take care of your aunt CeeCee, Loopy," Tiva chimed in. "We're setting you up to be in a boss position. You still wanna back out the shit?" she asked.

Loopy picked up one of the money stacks, sniffed the bills and then thumbed through the money. "Can I ask you something?" she requested humbly. Bay and T-top nodded, and Loopy continued. "Say...say I want to do my own thing. My grandmother opens her restaurant and I want to...I want to help her run it. Can I do that and still be a part of the business?"

"We would encourage it," Bay remarked as Tiva nodded in agreement. "Look," she then said as she scooted to the edge of her seat, "we understand the losses you've taken. You've earned every right to walk away. We want you with us, but it would be selfish to make you stay. If you stay? You do it because you want to, not because you feel forced."

Loopy nodded as she threw the money stacks into the duffle bag and zipped it. "¿Cuál es mi siguiente paso?" (What's my next move?)

Tiva came up with a chrome .45 caliber semi-automatic and two fully-loaded magazines. *"Queremos que vender nuestros cocaína."* (We want you to sell our cocaine.) she stated seriously. *"Tenga cuidado de CeeCee hasta que estamos llamados. Podrá sentarse afuera los primeros envíos por Jay-D tiene por ahora. Tomar ese dinero y abrir el negocio de su tía. Una vez que termines con eso, llámenos. Usted tiene hasta el primero de septiembre para manejar su negocio en nombre de su tía."* (Take care of CeeCee until you're called upon. You will sit out the first few shipments because Jay-D got it for now. Take that money and open your aunt's business. Once you're done with that, call us. You have until the first of September to handle your business on your aunt's behalf.) she ended as she gave Loopy a card with her and Bay's personal number attached.

"Voy a estar listo en septiembre." (I'll be ready by September.) Loopy said as she extended her hand. *"Gracias por ello."* (Thank you for this.)

"We have a real estate company that can help find a location for you," Bay chimed in as she pulled out her cellphone to contact Koko, who would lead the business venture on Loopy's behalf with Kimi. "You know how to reach us if you need us," she ended.

****

Back outside in Jay-D's Navigator, Ben sat in the driver's seat with Kantrell in the passenger seat as Jay-D and Lee chopped it while standing at the back of the SUV. Ben had relayed to Kantrell the fact that Malik was killed up in Illinois over trying to have Dawk killed in a hostile takeover several minutes earlier and she was left to digest the hard truth. Jay-D had given her the facts days earlier, but hearing Ben speak on it had settled the matter because Ben was what she deemed a 'real nigga'. The two had a rapport going back to New Orleans in the mid-nineties and Ben had always been truthful in her eyes.

Kantrell had some info of her own to drop on this day. She'd been holding onto it for some time after Malik's disappearance and had been wanting to tell what she knew, only she didn't know who she could trust. She'd had Jay-D under suspicion for some time as being behind Malik's disappearance, but Ben had cleared the matter up. She had to hear from a 'real nigga' before she could accept Malik's death, and now that he'd spoken, she was ready to tell what she knew.

"The feds been staking out my salon, Ben," she revealed as she looked him in the eyes. "This agent gave me his card two weeks ago. Said call him if I found out anything about Malik. He asked me if I knew Bay and T-top, too. I told him I didn't know who your people were and left it at that," she added as she handed Ben the card given to her.

Ben took the card and read the name aloud. "Laddy Norcross," he sighed in frustration as he crushed the card in his hand. "What all he asked you?"

"Malik's diner? Laddy asked me about it. I been handling things over there since Malik been…since he been gone. I told DeMarco not to say nothing about the business your people doing inside there because I think there might be bugs inside the place."

"Nobody put Jay-D up on that?" Ben asked surprised.

"He swept it two times that I know of," Kantrell confessed. "But he been busy with his record label lately with that girl Jane Dow. Laddy could've gotten one in there by now. Jay-D tryna get legit money and I can respect that. DeMarco, though? That boy not on that level 'cause he too young and inexperienced. He might bust a gun, but he not ready to run that spot. You need ta' put somebody else in a position to run that spot or else close it down. I say close it down, because I refuse to run that joint for Malik bitch ass."

Ben eyed Kantrell as he rubbed his chin in deep thought. She was true to the game by all measures in his mind's eye. In the nearly twenty years he'd known her, she'd never changed her ways and had always kept it real with him, and Manny and Oscar when they were alive. He began formulating a plan to get Laddy off his cousins, and it all lay with his next stop over in Ohio. "Put some chains on that diner when you get back to Saint Louis," he ordered. "Close it down."

"What about DeMarco?"

"I'm gone let Jay-D know what to do with that boy there," Ben answered. "Either way, I'm putting you in charge of closing down Malik's Diner. If the feds ever come back," Ben emphasized as he slammed a balled-up fist into the palm of his hand, "if the feds *ever* come back you let me know that same day. I wanna know what they ask, I want their names, and the date. If you can nail it down to the exact minute that'll be even better."

"What I get out this deal, Ben?" Kantrell asked as she stared into Ben's eyes.

Ben chuckled and licked his lips. "If I was a cold-bloodied nigga I'd tell you that you get to live," he sincerely remarked. "You and me not there with it, though. So what you need done for tellin' me this and keepin' an eye out for the feds?"

"Obama done pissed off a lot of people, brer," Kantrell replied as she exhaled. "The recreational center where my salon at done lost its funding. They sold out to a construction company that's coming through to build luxury condominiums. I have to move to a new spot."

"How long you got?"

"About four months. I have to be out by the first of October."

"You been here for what? Four years or something like that? You ain't got no money saved, girl?"

"I paid cash for everything, Ben," Kantrell explained. "My house hit for three hundred, my Escalade was another sixty tricked out. I paid off a hundred and thirty thousand dollars in college and business loans. I'm debt free, but I don't have the money to buy a new salon. With the recession going on? I can't even get a loan for a new spot."

"Malik didn't leave behind no money?"

"Me and my girl Jessie gutted that boy house over in Maplewood a week ago," Kantrell answered. "Ain't nothin' there. I called his people down in New Mexico to see if they knew where he was, asking subtle questions to try and get a feel on whether they knew if he had money stashed and they said Malik wasn't their concern. They put his house on the market so I can't even cop nothing off that there. I'm assed out, brer."

"How much money you need for another spot?"

"Fifty thousand. I need twenty percent upfront to get in on this new spot," Kantrell remarked as she showed Ben the lease on a place she was looking at in downtown Saint Louis. "It's a new strip mall opening up in October. It's in a busy spot with heavy foot traffic and plenty of parking. I can rack up down there...if I had the money to get in."

"How soon you need the money?"

"By the first of September."

"Okay," Ben nodded as he looked out the front windshield of Jay-D's Navigator. "I'm gone front you that money the first week of September, but you know what you gotta do for me, right?"

"I'm not fuckin' you if that's what you thinkin', brer. Katrina my girl, man. You fly and all, but I even tryna—"

"Whoa, whoa, hold up, baby," Ben laughed. "I'm not asking you for no pussy, Kantrell. I need you to watch the crew for me. Let me know if you think somebody talkin'."

"Oh, okay," Kantrell responded as she rocked back and forth in the passenger seat. "I'm just saying, dudes on your level be tryna hook hoes by buyin' them shit and I'm not that type of woman, ya' dig? I'm gone pay you back soon as I can."

"You ain't gotta do all that," Ben stated as he looked Kantrell off and smiled, tickled over his long time friend's assertiveness.

"I want to, Ben. This all business, homeboy," Kantrell retorted. "I'm gone watch the crew as much as I can and look out for the feds, and you help me get back on my feet. That's the deal. I'll do all I can to keep them boys off you and your people ass."

"Okay," Ben nodded. "They gone play you hard, fam. They might even know about your spot closing and gone try and offer you some money to help you out. Refuse all that shit there and deny knowing everything. Let them talk and ask questions. Laddy a rookie at this shit."

"Yeah," Kantrell nodded in agreement. "That white boy drop names and shit and try and use it for intimidation, brer. He know Jay-D because Jay be on the block over to Saint Charles. Jay-D ain't gone talk, but the rest? Ion know."

"That's why you gone close Malik spot. I'm gone put Jay up on game before I cut out. Y'all two work together on this thing with the feds," Ben remarked as Jay-D and Lee walked up to the driver's side of the Navigator. "Write your number down for me so we can keep in contact," he said as he eyed Jay-D.

Kantrell wrote her number down and Ben exited the Navigator. He stood before Jay-D and said, "I got a message for Kree, fam."

"What's that?" Jay-D inquired.

"Her cousin Christian was killed yesterday down in Sao Paulo. Her mother say they been talking online?"

"Yeah?" Jay-D remarked a little surprised. "What happened, fam?"

Ben briefly ran down to Jay-D what had transpired in Sao Paulo. "Kree momma named—"

"Barbara Devereaux," Jay-D interrupted. "They can't stand each other, though."

"That's what I gathered at first," Ben replied. "But Barbara done had a change of heart, ya' dig? The family asking that you tell Kree about her cousin, but say nothin' about her mother wanting to see her just yet. We gone set something up some time in September so they can meet."

"That's what's up," Jay-D replied as he went into his suit jacket and handed Ben a DVD disk. "This a disc with that federal agent and that state trooper together, ya' feel me? Tell Bay 'nem my people came through and I handled the payment on it for the family."

"Gotcha," Ben responded as he patted the disk in his hands.

After getting things straight with Jay-D, Ben climbed back aboard the plane while dialing up Popeye, and the family was on to their next stop, which was Lumpkin Airport over to Cincinnati, Ohio.

****

An hour and ten minutes later, Samantha was wheeling the G-550 onto a side spur at Lumpkin Airport over in Cincinnati, Ohio. Ben saw the same Bentley Arnage that Tanya had driven up in earlier in the year and knew it was Popeye approaching. He and Lee emerged from the plane as the car cruised up beside the runway. Ben could hear music jumping from the sunroof of the ride and recognized the song right away. Either Popeye was from

New Orleans, or he was heavy into rap because the song, *Ward Bangin'*, by New Orleans rappers L.O.G. and Fila Phil, was a hometown hit.

Ben waited in between the car and the plane with Lee at his side for Popeye to exit. He stepped out in a pair of red nylon shorts, red and white Jordan's and a white tank top. He gave a head nod to the light-skinned brother he assumed was Ben Holland since the other guy was Asian. Ben had given him his name when he called him back with the flight time.

"You got some info for me I heard," Popeye remarked as he closed the door and stood beside the Bentley bumping his fists together.

"That's right, whoa," Ben remarked, intentionally using a New Orleans slang.

"Whoa? You from the boot?" Popeye asked while cracking a sly smile.

"Ninth Ward Desire. Born and raised, brer," Ben remarked as he walked up and extended his hand.

"Seventh Ward Hard Head," Popeye stated seriously while shaking Ben's hand.

"I never did business there, dude. But we got some business today," Ben said as he opened the manila folder he was carrying and handed Popeye a sheet of paper.

Popeye looked down at the sheet and read the name out loud, "Moto," he said. "This wouldn't be connected to Tammy Moto would it?"

Ben nodded and said, "We believe so. Our people down in Brazil with the heroin connect, the Devereaux family? They got hit yesterday morning, ya' dig? We lost a few soldiers, but we wasted the hit squad and got the name Moto from one of the Asians down there after it was all said and done. We gone try and track down who these Asians are and may need your people help, but we have another name to lay on ya' first," Ben remarked as he pulled out a second sheet and handed it to Popeye.

"Bridgette Fischer," Popeye sighed as he crumbled the paper and turned away from Ben. "You tellin' me the hit in Brazil and what happened with Tanya here in Cincinnati last night is connected?" he asked with his back turned.

"We think so. Bridgette Fischer married to our Colombian connect, ya' dig? She tried to kill 'em yesterday afternoon, but she failed and now she on the run. We think she with whoever Moto is, but if the two hits is related, Bridgette had to have help from somebody here in America. That's the missing link right now."

Popeye turned and faced Ben and said, "My name is William Slack."

"Senator Slack's son," Ben nodded.

"That's right, fam. Tanya was the go-between and head of the family here in Cincinnati. Helen up next with that job, but you know she not too well right now given what happened last night so I'm filling in for now."

"The family sends their condolences. Let us know when the funeral is and we'll send a few representatives."

"Boogie said she wanted a private ceremony and I agree. Tanya gone be cremated and kept on a mantle here in Cincy," Popeye let it be known. "We hold something big and the feds'll be all over that joint once it get out. Last thing any of us need is the feds taking pictures and matching names ta' faces, ya' feel me? My people know the respect your family has so don't take it as a slight on your people. We just looking at keeping future moves safe and under wraps."

"I got ya'," Ben nodded. "What you can do with that info, though?"

"I got the names memorized and I'm gone hold onto 'em for now," Popeye remarked as he handed the papers back to Ben. "Me and my boys collected some evidence last night and it's in my mother's hands now. We got people analyzing the data as we speak and should know something in a few days. Until the names come down ain't much we can do but speculate on the situation."

"Next order of business is the five hundred kilograms of heroin that's gone be touching down a week from today," Ben remarked as he placed the papers back inside the folder. "We got the trucks ready to roll, just need a dropoff point. Tanya was supposed to give us that some time this week."

"I'll call you in a couple of days. We have a spot here in the city for the drop off. The buyers still in play so we good," Popeye remarked.

"I suggest you put a security detail on the load when it leave port," Ben counseled. "Have somebody follow the merchandise all the way from the port to the dock, ya' dig? With all that went down, it's a possibility somebody working with Bridgette may try and hijack the load."

"I appreciate that tip," Popeye remarked while looking straight ahead with his hands inside his shorts. "The driver in on it?"

"Nah. He just a man with a load, brer."

"Okay. I'm gone put a team on the trailer and the driver once the product ship. Just give me the info off the manifest with the arrival date and we good from there."

"Not a problem," Ben nodded. "Last order of business," he added as he went into his inside coat pocket and handed Popeye a disc. "This here the federal agent looking into my people. We got 'em recorded fuckin' his partner in the investigation." he told Popeye. "Was wondering if your mother or somebody could get them off my people ass with that there?"

"I'll get it to my mother ASAP and get back to you, bro."

"Cool," Ben replied as he shook Popeye's hand. "Everything straight for now. You got my number, fam. Call me once the evidence come back so we can put this all together. If I can be of service, let me know."

"Done," Popeye ended as he climbed back into the Bentley and rode off.

Ben, meanwhile, returned to the plane for a flight back to Arizona to spend time with his family.

CHAPTER THIRTY-ONE

PEOPLE WITH NOTHING BETTER TO DO

Katrina was in the kitchen inside her mansion down in Mesa cutting up fresh onions to sprinkle over the T-bone steak she was preparing for Ben once he arrived home after dropping Samantha and Amber off over to Samantha's house, just a few miles away. She hadn't seen her husband in three days and was looking forward to spending time with him. The champagne was chilling and the food would be ready in an hour or so, enough time for her and Ben to unwind together over a glass of bubbly.

"Girl, you got it lit up like the day time in here," Faye Sanders chuckled as she walked into the kitchen wearing a silk robe and slippers while squinting her eyes. "Ben must be on his way home," she smiled as she poured herself a cup of coffee.

"How you know, momma?" Katrina laughed as she rocked to Keith Sweat's song *Make It Last Forever*. She was dipping and sliding from side-top-side as she sprinkled fresh onions over her husband's steak.

"Because you haven't been this excited since the day he left," Faye smirked as she sipped her brew.

"I'm always happy, momma!" Katrina giggled as she wiped her hands on her apron and stirred the Italian cut string beans and potatoes simmering in a crock pot.

"You sure, baby?" Faye asked concerned. "You're never worried about what Ben does when he flies out of town with Samantha?"

"Of course I worry, momma, but I can't think like that," Katrina frowned. She really didn't appreciate her mother dampening her mood, but Faye was asking a question no one had asked her in quite some time.

"I'm not trying to spoil anything for you, child," Faye reassured. She then looked away and said, "I guess I picked a fine time to be a mother, huh? After all these years, here I am questioning you about the man you've married when your father is doing life and I have nothing to call my own."

"My father put himself in jail—his words," Katrina remarked in a wry tone. "I wrote him another letter and sent pictures of me and the babies telling him I was going to visit soon. He wrote me back and said he can't have visitors right now, so I cancelled the trip we had planned at the end of the month."

"The way he actin' up back there you may never get to see 'em, Katrina. It's all my fault. We should've went and seen him the day after we reunited. I can't get it together," Faye sighed. "I have the worst luck, and it's spillin' over into your life."

"Why you always downing yourself?" Katrina grimaced as she backed away from the stove. "I'll see daddy when the time is right. I know who he is, and I know where he's located. I love him. Him and Eddie both and I wrote them and told them that."

"What about your brothers and niece in Missouri?" Faye asked as she took another sip of her coffee.

"We talk everyday almost. I'm tryna get those three out here, but Jay-D busy working on an album he say. It's nothin' for me to fly out there, though. I just have to make the time, but I been so busy lately."

"You have all these things going for you, Katrina. I'm proud for you. I wish I had as much as you have by way of family."

"What are you babbling about?" Katrina frowned, not understanding her mother's complaint. "You have me, momma. I'm the most precious possession you have. Me and your grandsons. You have plenty of assets in us."

"I know, baby," Faye smiled as she looked down into her coffee. "But I've been here for some time now and I don't have nothin' to call my own. You know how I spend my days?"

"Eating me out of house and home," Katrina said as she curled her lips.

Faye laughed and walked over to Katrina and rubbed her shoulder. "Besides that, girl," she said. "I tutor Ben Junior and Kenyan after feeding them breakfast, work out in the gym, check the mail, read the internet and play Bid Whist with Henrietta."

"Umm hmm, I know," Katrina remarked as she grabbed a sterling silver pot from the cabinet. "Henrietta told me you took her tutoring job, girl."

"See? That's what I mean!" Faye laughed. "I'm going around knockin' people out of position and shit, girl," she dragged for herself. "I need something to do, Katrina. Henrietta don't mind, but Celeste already said if I fuck with her job she gone fight my fat ass."

Katrina bent over laughing at that moment.

"I'm serious, Katrina!" Faye said while leaning up against the counter with her coffee mug held to her lips. "That old Mexican woman pulled me to the side yesterday and asked me what I was doing when she saw me washing y'all clothes. Got ta' talking that Spanish shit....clebella miamata webatta juballa rigamatta gatta mutherfucka nada take a my fuckin' job or whatever she was saying that day! I understood when she said I wasn't gone take her job, though, you can believe that shit!"

"Momma, you stupid!" Katrina said, laughing and in tears now as she leaned over the counter.

"Shiddd! I respected that mutherfucka right then and there, ya' heard me, Katrina? Celeste ain't gone shank me and fly back to guata-gauta or wherever the hell she from, shiddd," Faye remarked as she sipped her coffee.

Katrina had a hand resting underneath her chin while leaning over her marble countertop with her eyes closed as her body heaved. This was a side to her mother she had never known, her sense of humor, but she loved Faye Sanders to life for bringing it into her world. It was one of the things that had prompted her to give Faye enough respect to start calling her 'mother' all over again as that was what she'd become over the short span of the time the two had rekindled their mother/daughter relationship.

In the beginning, Katrina was uncertain as to how things would go with Faye being around. She actually thought they would clash, that Faye would be nothing more than a drain on her finances and psyche, but to the contrary, Katrina's mother was an asset and a pure joy to be around. There were problems true enough, but nothing out of the ordinary within any mother/daughter relationship. The major conflict between the two was that of Faye constantly nagging Katrina about not having something to do, but happily, an opportunity had presented itself.

Still laughing, Katrina righted herself and leaned up against the counter beside her mother. "You really want a job?" she asked with a wide smile on her face.

"You gone fire Celeste for me?" Faye joked.

Katrina walked off and waved her hand in the air. "I can't deal with you, momma," she laughed. "No," she said as she turned to face her mother. "Ben's friend Lee Sato called me the other day. Ben's cousin Kimi, you met her in Saint Charles the day we reunited remember? She getting married in September and wants me to cater her wedding in the Solomon Islands."

"Solomon who?" Faye asked as her face wrinkled. "Where in the world is a Solomon Island?"

"It's a bunch of islands in the middle of the Pacific Ocean somewhere. It's tropical."

"A tropical island," Faye asked as she grew enthused. "Besides Illinois I never been anywhere. Can we go to the wedding if we cater it?"

"Yeah," Katrina smiled. "It pays twenty-four thousand dollars too."

"Really?" Faye said seriously as she set her coffee mug down. "Baby, you...you're..." her eyes watered at that moment. "You've become more than I ever wished for you to become in life, Katrina. When I saw this home, I was wowed. Your businesses left me breathless, baby. I'm proud of you, child."

"You tell me that every day and it feels good each time, momma. Now, let me be even prouder than what I am of you for making all the right changes in your life."

"Whatever I have to do, baby," Faye said seriously as she picked up her coffee mug.

"Okay, then, momma. I want you to be my assistant. You and I will manage this twenty-four-thousand-dollar budget and make the necessary arrangements to have food prepared for this wedding. Are you up to it?" Katrina asked meekly while biting her bottom lip.

"No," Faye quipped. "But, with you leading the way and me putting a mother's touch on it? Humph! I'm sure we'll be okay," she assured. "I'm not good with money, so you handle that and just tell your fat ass assistant what she has to do to make things run smoothly. Deal?"

"Deal," Katrina said as she hugged her mother tightly and kissed her cheek. Headlights out front signaled Ben's arrival.

"Umm," Faye said as she swallowed a sip of coffee and drew up spilled liquid with her fingertip and licked it. "Man of the house home now and it's about to be on and poppinnn'," she sang. "Let me go and see what I can learn about this island we going to, baby. You two youngsters have fun!"

"Get outta here, ole gal," Katrina joked as she threw a dishrag at her mother as she skirted out the kitchen toting her coffee mug.

When Ben walked into the home, Katrina was there to greet him at the door. He smiled down at his wife as he removed his silk suit jacket while taking in her appearance. Katrina always dressed down when she was home. In public, it was always power suits and high heels with her hair done to the max. Around the house it was tight-fitting jeans, her hair down and no make-up. The woman had a natural beauty that Ben found irresistible. It made him feel good to come home to a loving, loyal wife, and adorable aunt and two sons that made him the proudest man alive.

"I have a beautiful family," he said as he took Katrina into his arms, leaned down and kissed her lips tenderly. "You miss me as much as I missed you or what, baby?"

"You know I did," Katrina replied as she melted into Ben's strong, warm embrace. "Ooohhh," she sighed as she rubbed up against his muscular frame.

"Come on," Ben suddenly said, tugging Katrina by the hand.

"What, baby?" Katrina laughed. "I was preparing you dinner."

"I'm holding dinner," Ben said as he reached down and palmed his wife's mound through her tight denim shorts.

"Well...alright," Katrina happily relented as Ben scooped her up into his arms.

"How my sons?" Ben asked as he carried Katrina through the home towards the gym on the first floor.

"They've been fed and put to bed, baby," Katrina said as she reached out and turned the knob on the door leading into the gym.

Ben pushed the door open with one of his wing tips and kicked it shut with his heel. "You ready to work out, woman?"

Katrina just giggled as she held onto Ben's neck. "How, how're we gonna do this, man?"

Ben responded by walking over to his weight bench and sitting down while still holding on to Katrina. She sat atop him sideways, watching as he loosened his tie and unbuttoned his shirt as she grabbed a remote and turned on the surround sound. Ben had told her to have it ready for him and she was just that. Freshly showered and scented all over. Ben slid down the bench and said, "Bring it here," just as the rap song *Front Porch* by Twista and The Speedknot Mobstaz, the last song he'd playing before he left for Brazil, came across the speakers.

Katrina responded by removing her shorts and straddling her man's face facing away from him with her feet planted into the soft carpet on either side of the bench. She moaned when Ben grabbed her hips and rotated her pussy over his tongue. His pleasing her was prompting her to want to return the favor. She'd managed to unbuckle her husband's slacks and free his hard dick, but the pleasure she was receiving simply wouldn't allow her to focus. Giving away to pleasure, she sat up and rocked over Ben's probing tongue while rubbing his broad, muscular chest.

"Baby," Katrina moaned as she raised her t-shirt and began tweaking her hardened nipples.

"Sit on that mutherfucka," Ben commanded as he nudged Katrina up.

Katrina eagerly eased off her husband's face, turned and faced him and grabbed hold of his dick and placed it at her entrance. She moved it back and forth over opening before leaning down and engulfing it fully, taking Ben to the back of her throat and gagging over the depth in which she'd swallowed him whole. "Damnnn," she sighed as she raised her head and began flickering her tongue across the tip before taking the head in her mouth and sucking softly while stroking the base.

"Oh shit," Ben groaned as he palmed the back of his wife's head and drove her deeper down onto his dick. "Suck it hard and fast, girl. Suck that dick like you know it's yours."

"Yes!" Katrina panted as she rose and slapped the dick against the side of her face. "I love how your dick taste, baby. I love you," she said before going back down and sucking like it was the last dick ever.

Katrina could feel Ben tensing up in her mouth so she pulled away. While biting her bottom lip, she wiggled her way up to his waist with her legs on either side of the weight bench while Ben undressed. After Ben had kicked off his shoes and pulled off his pants completely, Katrina leaned forward and eased down slowly onto his dick. Her eyes instinctively closed, allowing pleasure to take over. After a couple of minutes, Katrina leaned forward and kissed Ben deeply while running her hands over his wavy, ponytailed hair. She began bouncing up and down while kissing him hungrily as her orgasm neared.

Katrina's tight pussy was driving Ben wild with passion. He gripped his wife, holding her close to his body as the two made love atop the weight bench while kissing, sliding tongues back and forth and rubbing cheeks. Katrina sucked in air and began trembling.

Ben's body tensed as his dick hung deep inside wife, throbbing as semen bubbled in his loins. "Aww shit!" he growled as he began thrusting up into his wife, the bench now rocking and creaking under the violent assault.

"Fuck yeah," Katrina panted as she bounced up and down on Ben's dick while flicking her tongue against his. "Yeah, yeah, yeah! Ben, yeah!" she cried out as her body tensed.

"Aww fuck! Fuck, Katrina!" Ben laughed as he rose up slightly and busted off deep inside his wife.

The two lovers collapsed on the bench seconds after, Ben laying on his back and Katrina splayed out over him with her head resting on his face. "Wow," she sighed through closed eyes. "How was your dinner, baby?" she chuckled.

"Get better every time," Ben said as he ran his hands through his wife's hair, cupped her face in his hands and kissed her repeatedly while telling her much he loved and adored her.

"Let me get cleaned up and fix you something to put on your stomach. I'll run you a bathe in our bedroom before I go back in the kitchen. Steak and green beans okay, bae?"

"Yeah," Ben said as he lay back on the bench. "See you in a minute," he ended as he did a few reps with the three hundred pound weights he kept locked in before he headed upstairs.

****

It was nearing the noon hour when Samantha's eyes opened. Ben had dropped her and Amber off the night before and the two went in and showered and hopped in the bed with Tre`. He'd left early in the morning to open House of I.D.E.A.S., and Amber was still sleep up under the covers Samantha noticed.

"Wanna fuck?" Samantha asked playfully while shaking Amber from her slumber.

"Sure, why not," Amber replied half-sleep as she rolled over onto her back.

Samantha laughed as she climbed from the bed naked. "Maybe later, girl. I have to check on Gabby and Tabby," she remarked.

"Okay, love," Amber remarked as she rolled back onto her stomach and pulled the covers over her head.

After showering and throwing on a pair of cotton shorts and t-shirt, Samantha left her master suite and walked downstairs. She found her twins sitting in their highchairs at the dining room table with Xiang and Asa Spade. The two were staying with Samantha per her request and had an entire side of the second floor to themselves. They were an asset because they were able to give Henrietta a break whenever she flew out of town with Ben.

"Samantha, you're just in time for lunch," Xiang smiled as she placed bowls of homemade ravioli before Gabby and Tabby and quickly grabbed a yellow sheet of paper off the table.

"Mommyyyyy!" the twins blurted out in unison.

"Hey my apple bunchkins," Samantha delighted as she kissed the tips of her daughters' noses. "You, too, dad. You're my apple bunchkin too," she added as she skipped around the table and hugged Asa Spade.

Samantha went to hug Xiang, but she felt a little uneasiness within the woman. She looked down and saw Xiang hiding a yellow sheet of paper behind her back.

"Let me have that, baby," Asa said to Xiang.

"What's that?" Samantha asked as her grey eyes fell upon the yellow flyer Xiang was holding onto.

"It's nothin'," Xiang laughed. "I'll just go throw it away," she added as she went to tear the sheet up.

Samantha snatched the flyer from Xiang and read it aloud, "Homeowners Association Annual Presidential Campaign Meeting. Why y'all hidin' this from me?" she asked as her eyes darted back and forth between Xiang and Asa.

"It was his idea not to tell you, Samantha." Xiang playfully snitched. "I was going to give it to you," she said as she pointed back to herself, "but your daddy thinks it's a mistake for you to run."

"Why, dad?" Samantha asked curiously.

"Because you're running out of spite against that old white woman stay next door," Asa admitted. "Knowing you and your mouth? You gone end up upsetting a whole bunch of people and embarrassing yourself in the process."

Samantha shoved Asa playfully and sat across from him and began feeding her twins. "I am not running out of spite, dad," she defended. "I have some good ideas."

"Like what?" Asa said as he leaned back and folded his arms.

"Like...like, umm...like not letting dogs take shits on other people's lawn."

"That's what you gone run on?" Asa laughed.

"You should go to the meeting, Samantha," Xiang encouraged. "Listen to what your opponent has to say and challenge every single thing you do not like. You need a platform that's all."

"You would encourage her with all that foolishness," Asa said as he shook his head in protest.

"I like how you talkin', girl. You wanna be my campaign manager, Xiang?" Samantha asked through a smile as she spoon-fed her babies.

"I'd love too, Samantha!" Xiang quipped. "Asa, will you come to the HOA meeting with us? We can ride bikes over there to the rec center."

Asa shook his head through closed eyes as he stood up from the

393

table. "I'm not ridin' a bicycle through this neighborhood with you two crazy ass women, have me looking like some suburban square ass white dude," he laughed. "Y'all have it at. I gotta meet Dougie over to Ben's shop anyway. Let me know how that work out for y'all," he added as he grabbed the keys to the BMW Ben had given him and eased out of the home, leaving Samantha and Xiang behind with the kids.

"What's up with my daddy?" Samantha asked Xiang as she took a bite of the ravioli.

"Bored," Xiang said matter-of-factly as she pulled a laundry basket close and sat down beside Samantha.

"I can understand that," Samantha nodded. "Ace a man of action. Not much to do here in Phoenix since he been out."

"And that's the way I like it, Samantha." Xiang stated as she began folding towels. "I like the normal life. I wish he would do some of the things I want to do."

"Dad is not a HOA type of man, Xiang. And he's definitely not a home body."

Xiang flipped her long, shiny black hair and smiled over to Samantha, her green eyes twinkling. "Wouldn't it be wonderful if Montoya was an HOA home body guy, though? Just the opposite of what he is now?"

"That, that would be a real change for my daddy," Samantha chuckled. "I don't know if Ace even got it in him, though."

"Well, I have it in me," Xiang sighed. "While Asa gallivants around in the streets like a king without an army in search of something that makes him feel like the man he's used to being, I will be here with you. We're going to kick that old woman's ass next door," she laughed.

"Okay," Samantha nodded in agreement. "I think you're more excited about this thing than I am, Xiang. We'll head to the meeting after I feed the babies and put something on my stomach as well. So, what should our campaign slogan be?" she asked as she and Xiang set about their day.

****

"Now, if you looking for quality and style for a low price, you might wanna go with these twenty-two-inch Executive Chrome wheels. They gone run ya' 'bout two grand—but you put 'em under that Mustang, you gone be sitting nice!" Dougie stated to a male customer that was browsing Ben and Tre's shop this warm, sunny Thursday afternoon.

While Samantha and Xiang readied themselves for the HOA meeting, Dougie was hanging over to House of I.D.E.A.S. in the rim shop. In the three months since he'd been on the streets, Dougie had gotten cool with Tre` and the rest of the team inside the detail shop. Cool enough to the point that he was able to use a whip at the end of the day. He was also making a couple dollars over to the shop from washing cars and changing flat tires. The thirty-two-year-old gangster was using the money to parlay at some of the four star hotels around Phoenix. He also spent nights in the homes of a few females he'd met that was lacing him with cash.

Dougie didn't actually work at the detail shop. He wasn't on the payroll. He was one of those OGs that hung around dudes making legitimate bank and had their respect to the point that they allowed him to make money while hanging around the joint by doing jobs they themselves weren't interested in, or willing to let go so Dougie could earn a few dollars. His latest hustle found him trying to get a customer who'd been looking at rims to score a set so he could make a couple of hundred dollars, but the guy seemed reluctant.

"Two thousand dollars is a lot of money," the guy, a Mexican who appeared to be in his late twenties stated as he looked at a lower costing set of rims.

"You got a 2008 Ford Mustang, you need these rims right here, dawg." Dougie stated as he pointed to the rims. "Look at 'em! You can see your face in them mutherfuckas!"

"I can see two thousand dollars in them suckas!" a young woman with the Mexican guy replied as she smiled a little.

"Look, hoe," the man stated in an aggravated tone, "whatever I decide ta' put on that dam car is my business!"

"Say, pimpin'," Dougie stated, a little agitated as he turned his attention to the man, "why you gotta be talkin' to your shorty like that?"

"'Cause she a hoe and she need ta' stay in a hoe place." the man replied.

Dougie looked back to the female. She smiled and looked to the floor in embarrassment as she walked away, "I'm gonna go sit down." she stated lowly.

"Stay your ass right in there, too!" the man remarked just as Tre` entered the sales room from the body shop.

"What's up, Elroy?" Tre` yelled from across the room as he wiped his hands on a shop rag. "You gettin' them rims today, homeboy?" he asked as he laughed lightly to himself.

"We still tryna' decide, player. Maybe next week." Elroy replied as he walked back towards the lounge. "I'm a chill for a while before I stab out, amigo," he said to Tre` as he left the sales room.

"That nigga was talkin' stupid to this li'l chick that was with 'em brer." Dougie stated as he walked over to Tre`.

"A li'l Mexican chick?" Tre` asked.

"Yea. Baby girl was tight! Short with brown hair, thick thighs and a phat ass."

"That's Juanita," Tre` stated. "She a bad mamma jamma, too. That boy Elroy be stuntin', though. He been supposed to buy Juanita some rims for her Mustang, but he ain't tryna do that," he told Dougie as he looked around behind the counter, which held numerous speakers and speaker boxes in various sizes.

"*Her* Mustang? I thought that was his whip!" Dougie stated in disbelief.

Tre` turned around laughing as he shook his head. "Elroy deliver produce. Katrina sent him over here when they got ta' talkin' one day. I thought that was his whip, too, at first. All summer Elroy been comin' in here stuntin' like he gone buy the li'l chick some rims. Me and the boys peeped it out, though. He just wanna drive her car on the weekends. He about twenty-eight or twenty-nine, Juanita around twenty-three. Elroy got the li'l chick head swollen and kinda playin' her, bruh." he stated as he grabbed a speaker box from behind the counter and walked back towards the body shop. "You play it right you might can get that, Dee. Juanita don't really like Elroy. She more scared of 'em than anything," he ended as he walked back towards the workshop.

Dougie now had it on his mind to get up with Juanita after hearing Tre`s last remark. By all accounts, her man was a phony who was taking advantage of her and she deserved better was his take on the matter. He brushed his white t-shirt flat and walked through the showroom and entered the lounge where he saw Juanita sitting on one of the C-sectional sofas by herself watching BET, which was running rapper Dorrough's video *Ice Cream Paint Job*, as she sang along with the lyrics... *"Cream on the inside...clean on the outside...ice cream...ice cream...ice cream paint job..."*

"Where ya' boy?" Dougie asked as he picked up the remote control and turned down the volume slightly.

"He went to get some hot wings from down the street." Juanita asked while bobbing her head to the music and looking around the lobby.

"You like them rims I showed Elroy, huh?" Dougie asked he walked over to Juanita while licking his lips.

"Yes, sir. They are real nice wheels and would like good on my car. It was a college graduation gift I bought for myself. Elroy is not going to buy those rims for me ever. He has been bringing me here all summer and it is the same story every time—we are going to see." Juanita replied in a dejected tone as she picked up a Lowrider magazine and began flipping through its pages.

"Look, I can help you out, but you gotta keep it on the low, ya feel me?" Dougie stated as he sat beside Juanita.

"What are you going to do? Do you work here or something like that?" Juanita asked as she looked Dougie in the eyes.

Dougie, for the first time could see just how pretty Juanita was; she had big, round brown eyes, and beautiful smile that showed off her pearl white teeth. She smelled like raspberries, and her golden-brown skin looked soft to the touch. She talked proper and it turned Dougie on to the highest degree as it's been a while since he'd dealt with a straight-laced chick. On top of that, Juanita had to have a little bit of money, or damn good credit at worst, being she was able to sponsor her own California edition convertible Mustang.

Dougie, believing he'd found a possible keeper, decided to move on Juanita, despite knowing she was involved with somebody else. "Nah, I don't work here," he told the twenty-three-year-old, "but I could get my people to hook you up, ya' feel me?"

"Why are you doing this to me? You know I have a man already."

"You got a lame ass boyfriend is what you got." Dougie countered. "You can do way better than fuckin' Elroy."

Juanita laughed lowly and looked back towards the TV. "He is my lame ass, though." she remarked.

"You didn't say that you couldn't do better," Dougie chuckled. "But if you wanna be with a stunt dog instead of rolling with a real nigga, that's on you. If you change your mind, though, hit me up." he added as he grabbed Juanita's cellphone.

"What are you doing?" Juanita asked through a curious smile. She'd never encountered a man like Dougie, who was smooth, yet forceful. She liked it.

"I'm givin' you my number so we can hook up," Dougie answered seriously as he fumbled with the phone.

Juanita had her phone locked, so Dougie gave it back to her and asked her to open it, and she did so. The OG knew right then and there that she was willing to get down with him. He was putting his number in Juanita's phone when Elroy pulled up in front of the shop.

"Here he comes." Juanita whispered as she leaned over and looked out of one of the tinted front windows.

"Forget that dude." Dougie said nonchalantly as he sucked his teeth and continued to enter his number and then typed in a name.

Dougie was looking to start some shit. He was intentionally fucking with Juanita's nerves, and at the same time, trying to spark a confrontation with Elroy to separate him from the youngster. He was a fake in Dougie's eyes and he was looking to expose an older cat that hadn't enough street in him to combat the animosity that a real OG brought.

Dougie was nearly done, but he could tell Juanita was getting nervous because Elroy was about to climb from her car. "I'm putting my name in as it is. I'm, Dougie," he said as he typed.

When Elroy walked into the lounge, he saw Dougie handing Juanita back her phone. Dougie had actually done it purpose just to see what Elroy would do, and by all accounts, he'd started something.

Elroy tossed the bags of wings aside and dropped the sodas he was carrying and rushed over to Juanita. "I leave your ass for ten minutes and you talkin' to another man, Juanita? You disrespect me like that?" he boomed. "You ain't shit but a fuckin' hoe!"

"Why you worryin' about her if she a hoe?" Dougie asked as he pounded his balled-up fists together.

Elroy noticed Dougie's stance. The twenty-nine-year-old 5' 9", one hundred and eighty pound bald-headed Mexican walked over in his direction. "You want some of me, esse?" he asked as he rushed Dougie.

Juanita hopped up and stepped in between the two. "Elroy, you need to calm down!" she yelled as she faced her boyfriend.

"Get the fuck out the way, bitch!" Elroy snapped just before he slapped Juanita in the face, knocking her to the ground.

Dougie met Elroy head on and the two males began fighting inside the crowded lounge near the front doors. The fight spilled back onto the sidewalk with Dougie grabbing the front of Elroy's shirt and forcing him back up against Juanita's Mustang as patrons filed out to watch the melee.

Juanita picked herself up off the carpet and ran out the front doors screaming wildly for Dougie and Elroy to stop fighting.

At the same time, Asa Spade and Ben were approaching the detail shop from opposite directions. Both had laid eyes on the melee happening out in front the business and had different reactions. Ben didn't like no shit going down at his business given all he was involved in, but Asa was bored out of his mind and was looking for some action. He sped up and pulled over to the curb and jumped out his BMW bumping Eightball and MJG's song *Mr. Big*.

"Fuck 'em up, Dee!" Asa Spade yelled over the music as he trotted over to help his boy. He'd gotten to the ruckus before Ben and joined Dougie, who was fucking Elroy up to the point that he had the Mexican covering his face as he waylaid away on his arms and body.

Ben approached from the opposite direction and pulled up in the middle of Buckeye Road. "Dee, what happened?" he asked aloud as he climbed out his Mercedes S-class and ran up on the two wild swinging males. "Y'all fightin' in front my shit drawing heat!" he scoffed as he rounded the Mustang.

Elroy had grown weak-kneed. He was dropping to the ground when Asa Spade ran up and kicked him in the stomach. The Mexican released his bowels and cried out in a high-pitched voice, "Oh my God!"

Asa Spade and Dougie backed up laughing at that moment, Dougie gripping the crotch of his baggy burgundy Dickies as he and Ace slapped hands. "You heard that nigga calling on Jesus?" Dougie laughed.

Ben ran up at that moment and shoved Asa and Dougie inside. "Fuck wrong with y'all" he boomed. "Tre`, take 'em to my office and—"

"Gun!" Asa Spade yelled aloud when he witnessed Elroy righting himself and reaching up under his shirt. He charged past Ben and ran up on Elroy and grabbed both arms just as the embarrassed Mexican raised the gun and fired off a round.

The bullet had just missed Ben's left side. It whizzed by him and shattered one of the large pane windows on the detail shop as patrons scattered off in all directions. Asa punched Elroy's wrist and the gun dropped from his hands. Ace then pinned him to the ground face down with a knee in his back.

Juanita stood by screaming hysterically. She never thought Elroy would go so far as to try and shoot somebody. "You crazy! No wonder your baby momma got a restraining order on your ass! You crazy!" she repeatedly cried.

"What the fuck wrong with you, nigga?" Ben asked loudly as he shoved Asa Spade aside, picked Elroy up and threw him up against another window of his shop.

"Dougie was fuckin' with my hoe, Ben! You want him, Juanita?" Elroy asked angrily as he struggled to free himself, only to be held back by Ben. "I'm a kill that boy Dougie!"

Ben took Elroy's words to heart. He may have been pissed with Dougie, but he was not about to let Elroy threaten his people. He tightened his grip on Elroy and looked him square in the eyes and said, "Elroy, I'm a tell ya' stuntin' ass like this, stay the fuck from 'round my shit! You threaten my people, then you threatening me. And believe me dog, you don't wanna go there with it," he ended just as three squad cars pulled up to the scene.

"Ben, you and me is cool, amigo."

"Don't give me that amigo shit, nigga! What the fuck you bringin' a gun 'round my shit for? You was gone shoot my people in front my face, nigga? You coulda fucked up and hit me, boy!"

The more Ben thought about the situation, the angrier he grew. Had Asa not been there to accost Elroy, Elroy may have gotten off a few shots instead of one. He could've been killed this very day. With that thought in mind, Ben let go of Elroy and hit him in the face one time and knocked him out cold. "Don't ever fuck with my people, nigga!" he shouted as the police ran up and grabbed hold of him, Dougie, Asa and Juanita and began to clear the scene of on-lookers.

After taking reports, and hearing the details of the incident from the parties involved and comparing them to witness statements, Ben, Asa, Dougie and Juanita were let go. Elroy's gun was confiscated and he was arrested for battery, destruction of property and illegally discharging a firearm in city limits and hauled off to jail.

After everything had settled down outside, Ben, Asa, Dougie and Juanita reentered the lounge where Ben apologized to his customers. For a brief moment, Ben had reverted back his old ways. He was mad at himself for losing his cool, but Elroy had crossed the line. Ben had never let anyone pull a gun without retaliating back in the day, and it was hard for him not to do so at the present time. After he explained to his customers that it was a big misunderstanding involving family and friends, he told them all to order themselves food from the place of their choice and it would be on the house. He then walked into his office with Asa, Dougie and Juanita following behind him. He closed the door once everybody was inside and turned and said, "Juanita, I don't know you that well, but I know you smart enough to know better than to be fuckin' with somebody like Elroy. Everybody in this shop been tellin' you he nothing but trouble."

"I know, Ben, but Dougie pushed up on me, you know?"

Ben looked over to Dougie with a serious gaze. He then turned back to Juanita and asked, "You feelin' Dougie?"

"I don't know," Juanita said as she pouted her lips. "I mean, it's not like this is all my fault anyway, Ben. That fight was between Dougie and Elroy."

"Over you, though," Ben countered. "Look," he then said. "Your ride still out front. I don't know what's gone happen between y'all two after this, but you welcome to stay. Let me talk to my boys and you can figure out what you gone do later. You know where Dougie at if you want him, but I'm a tell you this here —If you deal with Elroy when he get outta jail, don't ever come 'round here again."

"I'll be in the lounge," she remarked meekly while looking over to Dougie.

"I be out there in few, shorty," Dougie smiled.

Juanita merely nodded before walking out of the office. When she cleared out, Ben, Asa and Dougie sat and talked. They all knew how outrageous jealous males could get. Elroy had attempted to shoot Dougie and there was nothing stopping him from trying again if he wanted to do so upon his release.

"What you think Elroy gone do when he get outta jail, Dougie?" Ben asked.

"If he make bail he gone go see—"

"That shit was rhetorical, bruh," Ben remarked nonchalantly. "I know you and Ace been idle the past few months, but intentionally kicking up dust because you ain't got nothing else better to do ain't the way, ya' dig?"

"You right, fam," Dougie agreed as he leaned forward and rested his elbows on his knees. "I'm just not use to sittin' 'round, blood. Ain't much to do down here in Phoenix but fuck with some hoes, though."

Ben leaned back in his chair and crossed his legs t-style. "So, y'all ready get back in the family business, huh?" he asked while staring Asa and Dougie in the eyes.

"I'm up for whatever," Asa Spade remarked.

"Okay," Ben nodded. "We got another shipment of cocaine coming in next week—one hundred kilograms. I'm gone give y'all the keys to the warehouse we use to remix it up and the formula that go with it. Everything you need is in the warehouse."

"Cocaine," Asa sighed as he threw up his hands.

"What it is exactly you wanna do then, brer?" Ben asked Asa Spade somewhat frustrated. "The family tied up in a lot of things right now and I'm tryna fit you and Dee back in where I can down here."

"You don't think I'm hot after what went down in Colorado, Ben?" Asa reasoned. "Lisa and Laddy know my ass out. Who's to say they won't start tailing me again down here?"

"Laddy in Saint Louis right now. You know that," Ben countered. "And Lisa Vanguard is who knows where. The warehouse up in Flagstaff. It's in the open so you can easy spot a tail on the way up there. You gone link up with Phil and Grover the day of, too. The Asians won't let nobody near the place that don't belong."

"How much the job paying?" Dougie asked.

"Fifty thousand apiece to turn one hundred bricks into two hundred using the formula we have. Me and my boys did it in three hours," Ben answered. "From there y'all can free-lance," he bargained.

"Free-lancing might work. I can get back into pimpin' down here." Asa thought aloud.

"I got something better for ya'," Ben countered as he got up and grabbed a bottle of Louis XIII and three glasses. "I got a cousin been tryna get into the pornography business out in the Midwest. He got a team of women he use for his videos and shit, ya' dig? But he don't have licensing or proper distribution. I'm gone talk to 'em, tell him he got a willing investor."

"Pornography," Asa nodded as Ben poured him and Dougie a drink. "Now, I can deal with that, blood," he nodded as he took a sip of his cognac. "Only thing is, I can't set up back in Vegas."

"Van Nuys, California would be the better place, fam," Ben let it be known. "It's all legal out there."

"Hmm," Asa thought while holding onto his drink. "Los Angeles, where I know the lay of the land, a few hours from base here in Phoenix, and it's still close to baby girl. Xiang gone surely wanna stay here because this place starting ta' grow on her ass, too."

"And the shit legal," Dougie followed as he took a sip of his own cognac.

"My boy Lee laying low after a hit he did for the family, but he be back online after my people wedding in September," Ben stated. "He can take back over the warehouse in Flagstaff, and you two can move on to Van Nuys. Use the downtime to get everything going with the adult film company in the meantime. I suggest you get Dante` O'Malley to help draw up the legal documents."

"That's what's up," Asa nodded.

"So, we got a deal?" Ben asked.

"Deal," Asa responded as he and Dougie stood and shook Ben's hand.

"Alright, fam. Next order of business is this deal with Elroy," Ben said, moving the meeting forward. "Juanita might be in some trouble. If Elroy don't kill her, he damn sure gone hurt her. And he might come back here for me knockin' 'em out. Dude gone be a problem."

"That was my fuck up, so I'm gone handle it," Dougie chimed in. "Nigga jump stupid he get dealt with. Especially for touching my shorty," he added as Ben and Asa chuckled.

"What? Shiiddd, that's my hoe, now," Dougie let it be known.

"Katrina know people on the force. I'm a call her and let her know what's up so she can get somebody to call her the moment Elroy make bail," Ben remarked. "So, we straight now, right? No more wild ass scenarios, right?"

"We good, big dog," Dougie nodded as Asa agreed. The two left the office and Ben leaned back and sighed. It's hard keeping street dudes out of trouble, but he was able to give Asa Spade and Dougie a job worthy of their potential to keep their heads level being they had nothing else better to do at the time except to get into some bullshit. They were straight for the moment, but he knew Elroy would soon be a problem and he was already making plans to deal with him whenever that time arose.

CHAPTER THIRTY-TWO

THREE CHUMPS

"This is the request for funds from the Governor of Louisiana concerning Hurricane Katrina relief funds. Another two hundred million dollars. It made it out of committee and all that's missing is your signature, Senator Slack," Popeye remarked as he slid a manila before his mother as she sat behind her desk inside her Senate office.

"David Gregory's people from NBC are on the line," another assistant remarked as she held her hand over her cellphone. "They want to know if you're available to do Meet The Press at the end of the week? You can do it from your home, Senator Slack."

"How long will the interview last?" Willie asked as she signed the bill and handed it back to her other aide.

"It's an eight minute segment on the progress of the Affordable Care Act. You'll follow Paul Ryan in the second segment," the aide answered.

"The Army Corps of Engineers is requesting that you add an additional ten million dollars to the Louisiana Governor's federal budget request to settle their debt with Caterpillar before they began the next phase of the Lake Ponchartrain levee heightening in New Orleans," a third administrator said to Willie as he handed her a single financial document. "I'll need a signature and your personal seal at the top of the letterhead before I fax it to their corporate office in Moline, Illinois," the young man added.

"Hand me back that folder with the Governor of Louisiana's request, Popeye," Willie requested of her son. "Tell NBC I'll be fine with the segment so long as they allow me to go on before Congressman Ryan. I want to state my case, not rebut the rhetoric from the opposition," she then told the second aide.

The aide placed the phone to her ear and walked a ways off as Willie signed off on a ten million dollar loan payment. She handed the folder back to the young man with her personal seal attached just as another aide walked into the office and handed her a sealed envelope.

"Is this the Senate revision to the Affordable Care Act?" Willie asked her aide as she spread out several more bills needing her signature.

"No, ma'am. It's a sealed document from FBI headquarters in Quantico. Also, the President is requesting a mid-day meeting with the leading Democrat Senators supporting the Affordable Care Act on Thursday in the West Wing. Shall I confirm?"

It was now the Monday after Tanya's funeral over the weekend and five days after Ben had linked with Popeye over to Cincinnati. June 15th. Since the night Tanya was shot, Willie had been waiting for the data to come back on the specimens Popeye and Ford had collected as she went about her government duties. Over the swirl of activity unfolding inside her office with her staff, which consisted of a constant flux of government lingo, name-dropping and ringing phones, she swirled around in her chair and unsealed the envelope she'd just been handed. She read the names of three men, one who had a listed address on 156th Street over in the South Bronx, the same address as Zelda and Vivian King.

"Not those three chumps," Willie thought to herself. *"But who put 'em on?"* she questioned through further silence. "Popeye?" she then said aloud in a smooth, casual manner as she held out the folder.

Popeye took the folder from his mother and read the names. He knew the names listed, but was left stunned. "This all true, momma?" he asked in disbelief as he leaned down and whispered into his mother's ear.

"Our people in Quantico are infallible and you know that, son," Willie responded as she looked out over Capitol Hill.

"That they are," Popeye agreed. "You got a chance to look at that CD I got from Ben Holland the other day?"

"Yeah, I watched it—twice—with a glass of wine and a joint the second time around," Willie chuckled. "For real, though," the hip Senator stated as she dropped her smile. "I can do this for Ben Holland. When the time is right, I'll get up with Agent Norcross."

"Okay," Popeye responded seriously. "What you want me to do with this information we received today?"

"These people did not make this move on their own," Willie remarked seriously, getting down to business. "Go there to the Bronx and find out who was behind the hit on Tanya and kill them all," she whispered into her son's ear.

Popeye patted the folder against his mother's shoulder. "I'm on my way to pick up Ford and the crew in Baltimore," he said before turning and walking out of the office.

"It's a go from NBC on Meet The Press. You're scheduled for a nine 'o' clock taped interview Saturday morning with NBC can you confirm?" an aide asked as Popeye left his mother's chaotic office.

"Senator? The mid-day meeting with the President on Thursday morning in the West Wing can you confirm?" another aide asked Willie.

"Yes and yes," Willie acknowledged through a sigh as she rotated her chair back around to her desk and began pouring over the next rounds of government business. "Somebody get Congresswoman Georgette Grayson from Mississippi on the line. I want to know her thoughts on the Senate revision of the Affordable Care Act before I do Meet The Press," the Senator requested as she began looking over two more bills deriving from within the Senate that needed her allegiance or opposition.

CHAPTER THIRTY-THREE

HOW TO KILL FIVE PEOPLE AT ONE TIME

It was two days after Popeye had met with his mother. June 17th, 2009. He'd linked up with Ford, Big Ty and Bell on Monday night and the crew arrived over to the New York area the night before and had camped out over in New Jersey. The four were cruising through the Bronx in a freshly painted cargo van with *Maintenance* painted on the side early Wednesday morning. They rode under the Bruckner Expressway and pulled up to Zelda's old apartment, located on West 156th Street, dressed in light blue jumpers. It was just past nine in the morning, the time when kids were in school and adults were on the job or on their way to work, and the late-night hustlers were still slumbering or just stirring awake.

Popeye sat staring at the three-story brownstone for a few seconds. "Everybody know the deal, right?" he asked while screwing a silencer onto a .380 handgun.

"Yeah," Ford answered as he bit into a pickle. He sucked his teeth and said, "We go in there, secure the joint and let the other one come in and do her business. I hope she ain't get that rental car in her name, though."

"She used an alias on the flight and the rental," Popeye let it be known as he checked his watch. "She should be here in another hour so let's get to it."

"We gotta be sure them dudes in there first, though," Big Ty remarked from the back of the van while buttoning his jumper.

"We gone do that by going in to tune up the a/c and fix the door," Bell coolly followed as he placed a pair of garden shears and two iron spikes into a couple of toolboxes and closed the lids. "Everything she asked for in here, Popeye," he said as he looked down at a list of tools. "These some wicked items, though. Wonder what she gone do with all this shit."

"Use your imagination, homeboy," Popeye said as he eased the door open and stepped out into the morning sun. He led the way up to the third floor of the building with his boys and tapped on a door just up from the apartment where Zelda and the Puerto Rican twins once lived.

"Who's there?" an old woman was heard calling out from behind the door as the four men stood in a semi-circle placing latex gloves onto their hands.

Popeye leaned in and said, "Maintenance, ma'am. We're here to tune up the a/c unit."

The door wiggled several times before the woman said, "Can you push it open for me, son? I have bad wrists and it jams sometimes."

Big Ty used a boot to kick the door open. He stepped back and Popeye slowly entered the apartment and looked around while gripping his toolbox. "Morning," he said in a nonchalant manner. "We're the maintenance crew today."

"Nice to meet you, young man. I'm Margaret. Miss Margaret what everyone calls me."

Popeye bothered not responding. He walked off from the woman without saying a word, walking past a dining table on his left, and a small kitchen with a humming refrigerator and rickety gas stove on his right where he eyed two men up ahead sleeping on the sofa. One was stirring awake, but the other was still knocked out sleep. He looked to his left and saw a dresser lined with perfumes and the old woman's picture sitting atop the wood structure. A door down the hall on his left was closed, so he headed that way after setting his toolbox down. "We good," he called out to his crew.

"The a/c unit is on the other side of the apart—"

Ms. Margaret was cut off in her speech when Big Ty placed a gun to her forehead. "Sit down," he calmly commanded as Ford and Bell entered, closing the door behind them. The guy stirring awake on the couch rose up, but Bell and Ford rushed into the living room with guns drawn and he flopped back down on the couch.

Popeye, meanwhile, was at the end of the hall. He could hear moaning coming from behind the door as he twisted the knob, discovering that it had been left unlock. He peered through the crack and saw a thick, dark-skinned female sitting atop a dark-skinned brother with dreads. The man's head was to the door, but the woman was startled to see a light-skinned man staring at her while gripping a chrome pistol. "Bae!" she screamed out just before a bullet slammed into her chest, knocking her back onto the mattress with her knees pinned beneath her naked, lifeless body.

The man on the bed rolled over and reached for a Mac-11 resting on the floor, but Popeye had run up and kicked it aside. A powerful blow to the head dizzied him as Popeye snatched him up by the hair and forced him back up the hall towards the living room. "What's this shit, son?" the man asked while being guided through the hall in the nude.

"We need some questions answered from you and your crew." Popeye declared as he approached the end of the hall with the gun pressed to his captive's back.

Ford and company had Ms. Margaret and the other two guys secured in the front of the apartment. The men sat on the sofa with plastic ties securing their hands behind their backs while Ms. Margaret sat at the dining room table sobbing heavily.

"Good," Ford smiled as he sat down before a flat screen television and picked up a PlayStation joystick upon Popeye entering the living room. "The gang's all here," he smiled. "Yo, homie," he looked over to one of the men. "What kind of games you got for this PS three, fam?"

The guy Ford was talking to raised his chin high and asked, "Ain't shit, nigga! The fuck y'all want from me and my people?"

Ford leapt up from his seat and smacked the young man across the head with his .45, drawing, blood from his temple. "I'm askin' the questions here, B," he scolded. "See? That's how that shit work. I ask, you tell. Now, what kinda games you got for my PS three? And it better be some good shit or we gone have some real problems in this dump this morning, ya' feel me?" he mean-mugged.

"Oh, lord, don't hit him no more, mister, please," Ms. Margaret pleaded from the dining table as Big Ty sat across from her with a gun aimed at her chest.

"Mister?" Ford scoffed as he walked over to Ms. Margaret. "I look like a senior citizen to you, old lady? Call me mister again I'm gone smack your...that...what he is to you?" he asked the terrified woman while biting his bottom lip and pointing back towards the man he'd smacked with the steel.

"That's my grandson," Ms. Margaret cried aloud. "Lord, he always in some kind of trouble. What he do now, Jesus?"

"You askin' me or Jesus?" Ford chuckled.

"This ain't right! This ain't right at all!" Ms. Margaret cried.

"Lay off her," Popeye ordered as he placed his captive on the sofa beside the other two young men.

Ford was the type to play crazy mind games with his victims. He was all action, but could put on an even bigger act, going from friendly to aggressive on a dime. It was a tactic he used to keep his prey off balance; but it was more terrifying than anything because more times than not, the people he would accost had committed some form of transgression against the organization and knew what their fate would possibly be in the end.

"Okay," Ford nodded as he backed away from Ms. Margaret. "Yo, homie," he then said to the man he was talking to seconds before as he skipped back into the living room. "Sorry about, about how I went at your gram's over there, aite? But she offended me. You should make her tell me she sorry. Help set matters straight between us two," he said as he waved the gun constantly before the man's face.

The man looked up at Ford with blood streaming down over his eyes. He then looked over to his grandmother and was about to speak. "Hol, hol, hol up," Ford laughed. "You was really gone do that shit? Yooo, this nigga pussy!" he laughed as he sat back down and looked through the stack of video games and came up with a Call of Duty disc. "Yo, Bell? You up for a game, my dude?"

Drake 'Bell' Bellamy was a twenty-seven-year-old skinny, dark tan-skinned brother with low-cut, wavy hair and thick eyebrows hailing from the east side of Baltimore. He talked low and slow, even in the midst of drama, as he was calm cat under pressure. He had an inquisitive mind and could sometimes ask questions to the point of annoyance, but he was the type of gangster that left no stone unturned when putting in work. "I ain't for no games right now, Ford," he remarked in a low tone as he walked over and looked down at the young man sitting in between the two young men on the couch.

The guy couldn't have been no older than eighteen to Bell. His braids were in a disarray and he wore a school uniform and fresh leather sneakers with a platinum chain around his neck. He'd been quiet and compliant the whole time the people around him were getting beat or worse and seemed to be terrified out of his mind. Bell quickly surmised that the youngster was in way over his head, so he decided to walk him through what was about to go down as he obvious had no clue what he was involved in. Sometimes, lessons are learned the hard way to those who dare to enter a deadly game without fully understanding the consequences. And what this particular youngster would experience on this day would come to serve as a warning to others who thought the 'game' was just for kicks.

"How old you is, bruh?" Bell calmly asked the youngster as he patted his silencer-tipped Mark 23 .45 on the side of his jumper.

"Sixteen," the youngster meekly replied while staring at the gun without blinking.

Bell looked down at his gun, then back over to the teen. "Why you running with these dudes here?"

"They my friends."

"You know what your friends into?" Bell asked as he set his gun down on the coffee table and folded his arms while staring at the youngster.

"Not everything."

"Well, let me tell ya' since you wanna play innocent. They killed a woman last week in Ohio. You knew that?"

"No, bruh."

Bell stared at the young man for several seconds as he lowered his eyebrows. "I think you lyin' to me, fam. I think you know exactly what they did. So, I'm a ask you again. You know what they did?"

"Yes, sir," the young man admitted.

Ford looked up from the PlayStation at that moment and jumped up. "The fuck I said about calling people—"

"Nah…nah, he good," Bell calmly interjected, holding Ford back. "What's your name, homie?" he asked as Ford backed away.

"Nashawn."

"Alright, Nashawn. We know the names of the people that was on that building cross from the club, and you not one of 'em. You was on that other building?"

"Nah, I was…I was driving the Escalade."

Bell looked over to Popeye at that moment and nodded. He was getting to the bottom of who was all involved in the hit, but his main focus was on schooling the sixteen-year-old. "Okay," started up again. "You know who you helped kill that night?"

"They told me it was just some white chick."

"She wasn't just some white chick, bruh. She was a big timer that dealt heroin. She was our boss. We all worked for her. If you know people around here who bang their veins, they probably sucked up some of her product," Bell remarked as he placed his hands behind his back and took a casual stance. The youngster looked up at Bell with a stunned look. "That's right, dude. Wayyy from Cincinnati her shit was pumping up here in the Bronx. So, you know she was a major player now."

"I swear, man I ain't know nothing. I was just told to drive that's all."

"How much you got paid?" Bell asked curiously.

"Two racks."

"And they low-balled the fuck out ya' with two thousand dollars," Bell remarked as he shook his head somberly. "You probably thought that was a lotta money. You look like the type that just like to dress fly and fuck around with some hoes at school, huh?"

"Yeah," Nashawn remarked as he continued to grow anxious.

"I used to be the same way at your age, Nay. Sell me a couple of ounces, re-up and hit the mall. But, I ain't never killed a big timer when I was your age. I ain't let the niggas I ran with put me in some shit I knew nothin' about, ya' feel me?" Bell asked casually as he moved and looked out the window and stared down at the piles of brick and mounds of junked furniture across the way.

Nashawn nodded his head and said, "I fucked up, mister. I'm sorry."

"How I'm gone tell my boss you sorry? She ashes now, fam," Bell stated as he walked over and sat on the coffee table and picked up his .45 caliber. "If you kill a big timer, right? If you kill a big timer, and her people get back at you, what you think her people gone do? What you think should happen when you kill a big timer and her people catch up with ya'?" he asked while waving the gun with the barrel pointed downward.

"Come on, man," Nashawn pleaded.

"What?" Bell asked calmly as he checked the chamber on his semi-automatic. "I just asked a question, Nay. What you think should happen to somebody who killed a boss and her people catch up to ya'?"

Nashawn began palpating as he let soak in what was going down. In the beginning, it was all fun and games for him. He'd been able to travel with a click down to Cincinnati and hang out, drink and smoke while riding around the city. He'd never been out of the Bronx, let alone New York state itself. The two grand he'd gotten, he'd used to buy new Jordan's and outfits. Today, he'd skipped high school and was planning on getting his hair braided up before heading over to campus to show off his new gear and do. A couple of females were going to meet up with him after school let out and they were going to chill over to his mother's home and smoke while she was at work. What'd he'd done in Ohio had quickly been forgotten, but it was now understood that his actions had severe repercussions.

Bell looked over to the naked guy sitting to Nashawn's right. He was a slender, older cat around twenty-one or so and tatted up. "You was fuckin' back there, homeboy?" he asked seriously.

"Fuck you, nigga!" the older guy boomed.

"Yeah, he was fuckin'." Popeye remarked as he paced the floor and checked the time on his watch while making a call.

"That's my sister back there," Nashawn remarked.

Bell scratched one of his thick eyebrows and said, "Your sister back there dead, Nay. My boy over there killed her, and I'm gone kill you after while."

Nashawn leaned forward and vomited onto the floor.

"That's what happen when you kill a big timer, young one," Bell stated as he held a hand just below his wide, downward curving lips. "Next time around? Know the business you in, son. This shit ain't a game at all," he ended as he grabbed his gun and went and sat beside Ford where he picked up a controller. "Reset it so I we can kill all these mutherfuckas," he told Ford.

While Bell and Ford messed around with the game, Popeye had just snapped his phone shut after making a call. "She be here in about ten," he told his crew.

"I smelled bacon on the way in," Ford said as he reset the game. "Yo, bruh," he said to Ms. Margaret's grandson, who was sitting to the right of Nashawn with a bloody face. "Gram's cooked breakfast, you have guests, and ain't even offer nobody none! If I didn't know any better I'd think you didn't like me."

"Yo," Ms. Margaret's grandson called out to Popeye, "what's this all over, bro?"

"You knew the girl Zelda stay a couple doors down on the other side the hall?" Popeye asked as he went and stood before the three men.

"Yeah. Somebody killed her a month or so ago. Shot her ass up on Beck Street outside the Chinese joint."

"You know who did it?"

"Nahh," Ms. Margaret's grandson said as he looked away from Popeye.

Ford looked over to the guy and curled his lips. He sat the joystick down and picked up his .45 and began easing up from his seat. "This boy 'bouta make me smack his ass 'cross the—"

"Okay, okay!" Ms. Margaret's grandson spoke up. "Everybody saying some Jamaicans done that shit! That's all I know, man."

"You ain't have to kill my old lady, yo," the naked guy Popeye escorted into the living room suddenly blurted out.

"They gone kill us all! They gone kill us!" Nashawn fretted through a wall of tears.

"Shut the fuck up over there!" Big Ty screamed just as a knock appeared on the door. He got up and peeped through the peephole. "It's her," he told the crew as he snatched the door open. "You heard anything from the outside?" he whispered.

"Neine," the woman replied in as she walked into the apartment and looked the place over.

Nashawn and the two other men sitting on the couch recognized the woman right away. She'd been with Zelda and the Puerto Rican sisters over to the Chinese restaurant some months back and they all remembered jostling her playfully as she spoke German to them.

"Krause," Ms. Margaret's grandson said in desperate tone from across the room. "These your friends? Help us get out of this shit!"

Sascha eased pass Big Ty and walked into the living room wearing a green mechanic's uniform. "Who was it that sent you three to Cincinnati?" was all she asked as she went and stood before the men while donning a pair of leather gloves.

"Krause, you remember me, right?" Nashawn smiled. "We was joking and shit the night Zelda came through, remember? We friends!"

Sascha looked at Nashawn with a cold, dead stare as she slowly shook her head from side to side. "When did I ever say I was your friend, little boy?" she asked in a cold tone, her lips in a downward frown and her hands tucked behind her back.

"Krause, Krause," Ms. Margaret's grandson pleaded through his bloodied face, "I think you was diggin' me. I wasn't makin' fun of you that night. Help us, please?"

Sascha took a step to her left and stared down at the young man. "I remember you," she said in wry tone. "I said I would have sex with you because I am a cougar. Maybe in the next life," she casually remarked before scooting two places to the right and staring down the naked guy. "You were the one who spoke to me first and made fun of me. I told you I would kill you in your sleep that night, but it looks as if you will be wide awake for this," she stated as she walked over to the tool boxes sitting beside the dining room table. "Where are my shears, Big Ty?" she asked with her back to the three young men and her hands behind her back.

"Yo, she getting ready to unleash some medieval type shit on y'all ass," Ford remarked while steadily playing the game with Bell. "If I was either three of y'all? I'd tell everything I know, then ask me to put one in y'all temple. Get it over with quick—because ain't nobody leaving here alive today, you can bet your life on that shit right there."

Ford may have been clowning around, but he was dead serious —and the people inside the apartment on 156th Street knew it as well. Ms. Margaret, Nashawn were merely caught up in something way bigger than they could imagine. The old woman had no idea what her grandson was involved in, and Nashawn had went along for the sheer thrill of it all. None of that mattered, however, as the two of them, and the other two young men who'd led the job were now up against it.

A job done over 650 miles away down in Cincinnati, Ohio was a job that they'd never thought would come back to haunt them, but the game was merciless, and the people they'd cross weren't the type to just let a matter rest. Tanya had to be avenged. Boogie was still out of her mind over the loss of her mother, whose death was a serious blow to the organization, but the Germans still had more than enough strength to retaliate. Faye had sent her most brutal soldier to even the score up in the Bronx on Boogie and Tanya's behalf in Sascha Merkendorf. And whether the people knew what had happened or not, everyone that was caught inside the apartment would have to pay with their lives.

Nashawn cried out, "We'll help y'all get the people who hurt y'all if y'all want! Just don't do this to us!"

Sascha knelt down and grabbed the garden shears while ignoring the pleas for mercy. They were so new and sharp, that shards of metal jumped off the blades as she clamped the blades together. "Yo," Big Ty sighed as he grabbed a roll of plastic and spread it out before Sascha. "Squeeze 'em on this plastic so we can collect those shards. FBI got a way of tracking shit down to where the blades was manufactured. They keep a catalog of purchases. We don't need any evidence left behind after this here," he added as he dabbed the floor with his latex gloves to collect the loose shards.

Once the blades were free of particles, Sascha went back and stood before the three terrified men. "I'm gonna ask one more time," she stated in a serious tone. "Who sent you guys to Cincinnati?"

"I don't know!" Nashawn cried out. "But I wasn't on that other building! We met a Asian man before everything happened and he said he wanted to kill that white chick his self! He had a sniper rifle! We dropped him off down the street and he climbed up on the roof with that gun! I'm tellin' you the truth, Krause, please don't kill me," he cried out with his head bowed.

"What was the Asian's name?" Sascha asked calmly as she eyed the three men. Neither of the young men replied at that moment. They couldn't because they knew not the Asian's name. They all just bowed their heads and shed tears.

Sascha looked the men over. It was clear they weren't understanding the seriousness of the situation, so she had to reinforce her position. "*Der härteste Teil zu sterben, die sich mit dem Schmerz, manchmal zusammen mit ihr geht.*" (The hardest part to dying is dealing with the pain that sometimes goes along with it.) she stated as she walked over to the naked man.

The guy began moving his head and tried to jump up from the couch, but Popeye and Big Ty held him down. At that moment, Ms. Margaret, who was closest to the exit, tried to escape. She leapt from her chair and ran up to the door and tried to pull it open. "They're going to kill us! Help me! 911! 911!" the petrified old woman screamed out while trying to pull the door open. The door was stuck once again, however, and Ms. Margaret was forced to grab her arthritic wrists in agony.

Big Ty rushed over and grabbed Ms. Margaret around the neck. He flung the frail woman to the side and she fell off into the kitchen, hitting her head on the edge of the counter before she crashed down onto the linoleum in an unconscious state.

"Grandma!" Ms. Margaret's grandson screamed out as he leapt from the couch. He was knocked back by the cold steel of Ford's pistol and he, too, now lay unconscious with another wound to his skull.

Sascha eyed Nashawn as she stood before the naked guy with the shears in her hands. "Watch me, little boy. If you want to die quick, because you are going to die today, tell me what I want to know," she remarked as she placed the shears to the naked man's face and sliced off his lips and his nostrils in one fail swoop.

Nashawn gasped in shocked horror as his friend fell back on the couch with blood spurting from his face as cartilage slid down his bare chest. His teeth were on display and a thick, red, milky substance was oozing out of two slats where his nose had been just seconds ago. The way his friend writhed about in pain while sticking out his tongue had Nashawn's heart skipping beats. Little did he know, however, that the horror show was just beginning.

While the guy whose face she'd sliced writhed in agony, Sascha looked up at the wall behind the sofa and tapped it with her knuckle. "Sheetrock. Good," she nodded. "Drag him over there," she ordered as she pointed to the man with part of his face sliced off.

"Pleashhe! Krau—pleashhe!" the young man began to beg through ragged gurgling and snorting. "I'll shell what sha wanna know! I'll shell!" he declared though garbled speech as Ford and Popeye pulled him up from the sofa.

"Who was it that sent you?" Sascha asked as she placed an ear to the man's face.

"Shlark-shinned woman!" the young man cried out in agony.

"Dark-skinned woman?" Sascha asked to confirm.

"Yesh," the guy hissed through his pain.

"That could be anybody. Not good enough," Sascha responded in a casual tone. "Untie his hands and put them up to the wall," she commanded as she walked over to her tool chest and pulled out the two iron spikes. "Ford, put one of these spikes up to his hands," she added as she opened a second toolbox and came up with a large hammer.

"Krause! Come on, man!" Nashawn whined while watching his friend being placed up against the wall. "I said he was Asian!"

"Do you know this dark-skinned woman? Who is this Asian?" Sascha asked as she tightened her grip on the hammer.

"I don't know her! I don't know their names!" Nashawn cried out.

"*Du lügst mir!*" (You're lying to me!) Sascha screamed aloud as she turned to the naked guy Popeye and Ford was holding up to the wall and drove a spike through his right hand with the mallet she was gripping. The guy was in so much pain he couldn't scream out. He vomited onto the floor as Sascha grabbed his other hand and drove the second spike through it, crucifying him fully to the wall and letting his body hang free. She wiped blood from her chin while panting before she stepped closer and grabbed her latest victim around his neck. "Speak to me if you can! Who am I? Say that I am your god. Call me god," she hissed.

"God, pleashhe," the man choked. "Pleashhe, god."

"*Guter Junge.*" (Good boy.) Sascha said in a serious tone as she ran a bloody glove through the man's dreadlocks while staring deep into his eyes. "*Guter Junge. Jetzt für mich sterben.*" (Good boy. Die for me now.) she then whispered in a soothing voice as she placed both of her glove-clad hands over the young man's nose and smothered him to death, forcing him to drown in his own blood while crucified to the wall. She then pulled a knife from the front pocket of her jumper and slit the guy's throat. With her job done, the Germans' angel of death bowed her head, turned and walked away from her latest victim to let the rest of the crew finish the job.

"Yo, Nay," Bell casually remarked as he aimed his .45 at Nashawn's forehead. "You saw that there? That was the toughest man in your crew, bruh. Which it ain't saying much because all y'all pussy. But, you can check out fast, or we can grab some more spikes from the toolbox ya' feel me?"

"I swear on everything I love I don't know the woman name, Bell. She was locked up with Zelda down in Philadelphia was all she said and she wanted get back at some people who left her stuck out! Short, thick ass woman with a bush!" Nashawn confessed through his tears.

Bell looked over to Popeye and tilted his head while nodding it up and down. Short, thick woman with a bush locked up with Zelda? He knew right off top that it was none other than Brenda Marshall who was behind the hit on Tanya. When Popeye gave the order through a mere nod, Bell turned and said, "It was good talkin' to ya', Nay. Remember what I told you about this game, though. Shit ain't a joke, fam."

"Bell, please! My sister already dead! We my momma only two children! Please! My momma gone be hurt over—" Nashawn went silent when Bell fired three shots into his chest with his silencer-tipped .45 caliber. He fell back dead on the sofa with his eyes wide open and a look of stark terror planted on his face.

Popeye got on the phone at that moment and called his mother back down to DC. "Check the books down in Philadelphia and see if Vivian and Brenda still locked up on that case," was all he said before ending the call.

"What the fuck we gone do now?" Ford asked as he slowly paced the floor in deep thought with his hand beneath his chin. "If Brenda done switched sides, she know some of our moves, Popeye. Shit can go south real quick for the family."

Popeye nodded and said, "If Brenda out, and she came here to put these dudes on, she had to set up somewhere."

"The King Sisters' house over to Long Island!" Ford realized as he snapped his fingers.

"You, Bell and Big Ty take the van and go and check it out," Popeye ordered as he looked around the apartment at the carnage they'd produced. "I think we got all we gone get from these people. Y'all go on, whoa. Me and Sascha gone take care of Ms. Margaret and her grandson and link up with y'all on the other side. The security code was 2035 last I remember, but it could've been changed since then. That mean y'all may only get sixty seconds to find some intel. Move fast, move careful," he ended as his team prepared to leave the apartment.

CHAPTER THIRTY-FOUR

KNOW YOUR PLACE

Willie had just arrived home to her Church Falls, Virginia mansion around noontime, a couple of hours after Popeye and company had completed their task up in New York. She'd been on hold for nearly ten minutes with the Philadelphia Department of Corrections and had just gotten in touch with the prison's deputy warden. "Sorry for the delay. How can I help you, Senator Slack?"

"There's an ongoing case with the Federal Bureau of Investigations," Willie said as she entered her lavish domicile that was adorned with indoor plants, Greek statues and marble columns. "Brenda Marshall and Vivian King have been requesting to see their attorney. Now, their barrister has been in contact with the prison system, but is unable to see or talk to her clients. Before another technicality is thrown into this case, I need to know when Brenda Marshall and Vivian King will be available to meet with their attorney specifically."

"The next collection of flight records you requested from LaGuardia and JFK arrived, Senator Slack," Willie's assistant stated to her as she trotted down her marble staircase and entered her great room.

"Brenda Marshall was released from holdings five weeks ago, but Vivian is still here," the Deputy Warden remarked as Willie took the files from her assistant and began disrobing while walking to her indoor pool.

"What? How is Brenda free?" the Willie frowned. "I need you to fax Slack and Irving the copies of Brenda Marshall visitors' list for the past two months. Do it ASAP!" Willie ordered as she ended the call. She then dialed a number down in Miami as he entered her indoor pool lounge in the nude.

"Slack and Irving, how can we be off assistance today?" thirty-eight-year-old Sally Irving asked as she sat at her desk inside a high rise down in South Beach.

"Sally, did you know that Brenda was released last month without Vivian? How could you get Brenda off without Vivian when they were in on the same—"

"I didn't get anybody off yet, Willie!" Sally interrupted. "The trial for Brenda and Vivian hasn't even been scheduled and I was in the process of securing a bond for the two. Neither has an address in Pennsylvania, so I was looking to get the D.A. to allow them to come here to Florida under a secured bond until the trial while on house arrest. How'd Brenda walk?" Willie's longtime friend and law partner for the past six years asked perplexed.

"That's why I'm calling you, Sally!" Willie scoffed as she sat at her patio table and flipped the pages of the airport manifests open to the day of the hit on Zelda King. "You were supposed to keep an eye on those two! Be lookin' for a fax from the Philly DOC shortly! You need to find out who all visited Brenda and help me get to the bottom of this shit!" she ended as she cut the call off.

Willie then scanned the names on the airport manifest and one name stood out—a name Popeye had dropped on her by way of Ben Holland: Bridgette Fischer. From what the Senator knew, Bridgette was in with Arata Moto. Her phone rung again and it was Popeye calling.

"Talk to me," she said upon answering.

"Got a name from the King Sisters' house—Arata Moto." Popeye let it be known.

"Thank you, son. I got some info here myself. Let me put this shit together and I'm call you back with your next move. Everything cool in the Bronx?"

"It's done."

"Get outta there. Head down to Baltimore and I'll get back to you," Willie said before ending the call.

The shrewd Senator sat back in her patio chair before her heated pool in the nude trying her best to put to the pieces together. Bridgette Fischer was married to Rafael Gacha, but by all accounts, they were at odds, so he couldn't be behind the hit was her assumption. Yet, Bridgette had traveled to the Bronx in order to kill Zelda King. That could be chalked up to Bridgette merely putting the pieces together on the hit against Jaffrey and Theron

Fischer, but the hit on Tanya in Cincinnati was another story. If Arata Moto was in with Bridgette, then someone had to put him up on the hit against Tanya was Willie's belief, only she didn't know who the go-between was.

Sally Irving, meanwhile, was down in South Beach looking at a dead phone in her hand with her chin tucked in. She was left just as puzzled as Willie as to how Brenda Marshall had been freed when a deal hadn't been struck. She decided to make a call herself to the Philadelphia Department of Corrections to see if she could decipher just how Brenda had been released. She was able to reach the deputy Warden himself, and had requested that she be allowed to talk to Vivian King.

"You know I can't allow that freely, Counselor," the deputy Warden guffawed. "You may be a partner in Senator Slack's law firm, but even those perks come with a price."

"If you're recording this call, I'd like to inform investigating officers that you've accepted cruise tickets for you and your wife, season tickets to the Philadelphia Eagles' home games, and free nights over to Palm Springs on the dime of myself," Sally said, being sure to omit Senator Slack from the bribery payments.

"There's no recording," the deputy Warden said seriously as he pulled his door open. "Get me Vivian King out of solitary confinement," he requested of his secretary.

"Okay," the secretary replied. "Here's the backlog on the visitation records you requested for Brenda Marshall as well," she added as she handed the Warden a manila folder and walked off to retrieve Vivian.

"What did King do to land herself in solitary confinement?" Sally asked annoyed. "You're supposed to inform me of these things, Warden."

"I've been away the past week or so," the Warden reverentially replied. "King will be here in a couple of minutes. She can explain it all."

Sally was on her computer booking a flight to Philadelphia when Vivian came to the phone several minutes later. "Vivian, what happened up there? Did Brenda turn state?"

"I think so, Sally," Vivian nodded in disgust. "Somebody

visited Brenda a couple of days before she was released. I asked her who it was, but she brushed me off. The day she was released, guards found my cellphone during a shake down. I had it hid in the wall behind my shelf, but the guards found it under my mattress and sent me to the hole. Brenda was the only one who knew where my phone was," she angrily confessed. "That bitch set me up for solitary confinement while she got out and I don't know what the fuck is going on!"

"Calm down, calm down," Sally soothed as her fax machine beeped. She grabbed the visitation's list the Warden had faxed and quickly scanned the names. "Oh, my god," she gasped.

"What happened?" Vivian asked.

"Not—nothing, Viv," Sally remarked, doing well to remain calm. "Look, you going back to the hole until I get there tomorrow, alright? I wanna keep you safe because Brenda done lost her ever-loving mind. Put the Warden back on."

"Yeah," the Warden answered as he sat on the edge of his desk with a leg planted to the floor.

"If anything happens to my girl Vivian King? Slack and Irving will reign down fire on the entire penal system of Pennsylvania. You keep her safe until I get there!"

"I understand," the Warden nodded. "We'll discuss payment when you arrive."

Sally hung up the phone and dialed Willie's number. When the Senator answered, she asked, "Are you sitting for this shit, girl?"

Willie was preparing to take a dip in her indoor pool when she heard Sally speak. She sat at a table and asked, "What did you find out, Sally?"

"Lisa Vanguard visited Brenda the day before Zelda was killed and two days afterwards. On the third day? Brenda was released and had her charges dropped. Brenda got Vivian thrown in the hole by making sure the guards found her cellphone to keep her in jail while she went free. Vivian was unable to call anybody the time she was in solitary confinement and nobody notified us because the Deputy Warden on our payroll was away. Brenda cut a deal with Lisa Vanguard, Willie," Sally seethed.

"I told that bitch not to fuck with me or my people!" Willie screamed as she jumped up and kicked her chair.

Now it had all made sense to Willie. The missing link had all fallen into place on this day and she'd summed it up in mere seconds. Popeye had told her that one of the guys in New York, A Nashawn character, had described a short, back woman with an afro as being the one who'd put them up on the hit on Tanya, and Ford had found a number on a pad belonging to an Arata Moto inside the King Sisters' home. To go along with those facts, white Jamaicans had been behind the killing of Zelda and an Asian sniper was said to have been in Cincinnati the night of the hit on Tanya. Bridgette Fischer was a white Jamaican with the same last name of Jaffrey and Theron Fischer, and she'd flown out of LaGuardia the day Zelda King was killed according to the airport manifests the Senator had just obtained.

"Lisa Vanguard, Brenda Marshall, Arata Moto and Bridgette Fischer. That's who's behind the hit on Tanya and who we're up against," Willie mumble to herself.

"What you say?" Sally asked.

"Nothing," Willie remarked. "You need to get up to Philadelphia and spring Viv—"

"Flight's already booked and I'm on it," Sally interrupted.

"Good. You handle that, and I'll take care of this federal agent who doesn't know her place," Willie said as she began formulating exactly how she was going to take down Lisa Vanguard, the main person she held responsible for the deaths of Zelda King and Tanya Weinberger.

CHAPTER THIRTY-FIVE
DIRTY POLITICS 101

It was now late Thursday evening, the day after Willie had learned that Brenda Marshall was released from prison in Philadelphia. Laddy Norcross had just arrived back to his home in Alexandria, Virginia after being summoned back to FBI Headquarters down in Quantico. He walked into his 4,000 square foot two-story brick home and was greeted by his blonde-haired Mexican wife inside the foyer.

"How was your flight, love?" Laddy's wife, Hermelinda, asked as she removed his suit jacket and handed him a glass of wine. "How's your case going in Missouri?"

"The flight was fine, and the case is moving ahead," Laddy proudly answered as he took a sip of wine and pulled his voluptuous wife close for a quick kiss. "I've brought with me the evidence I believe will bring the people I'm investigating before a grand jury," he smiled as he held up a small briefcase containing the data he'd collected the time he'd been down in Missouri.

"That's wonderful! So you should be coming home soon? Your daughter will be glad to have you around if you are."

"How old is she now? Five?" Laddy joked as his kissed his wife a second time.

"Don't give her an extra year," Hermelinda laughed. "She's already begging to go to school at four. She's writing her name now, dear!" she exclaimed.

"I really hate missing those moments, Hermelinda," Laddy said seriously. "When this case is over, I'll make it up to you and Ashleigh. I promise."

"I know," Hermelinda smiled as she walked into the great room. "Dinner will be ready soon, Laddy!" she yelled out from deep within the home. "Oh, there's a DC number left for you on your desk inside your office! You're to call as soon as possible was the message from a Senator Slack!"

"Is that your famous spinach lasagna and fried chicken I smell?" Laddy asked aloud as he sniffed the air and set his briefcase down beside his desk inside his office.

"Yes, it is! I bet you miss home cooked meals while out in the field!" Hermelinda called out from the kitchen through light laughter.

"I do, sweetie!" Laddy declared as he thought about the many nights he'd spent over to Sandra's house enjoying her cooking and lovemaking. "I'll be in there shortly, dear!" he called out as he picked up the yellow sticky paper and dialed the number he'd been left.

"Senator Slack," the voice stated upon answering.

"Senator," Laddy remarked, surprised to be speaking to one of the Senators that sat on the appropriations committee, the commission that funded his investigations. "How can I help you tonight?"

"Actually, I was needing to help you, Agent Norcross," Willie remarked as she sat on the patio behind her Falls Church mansion enjoying the warm night air and its clear skies.

"Help me how?" Laddy asked curiously as he sat at his desk.

"You're calling so I take it you're home?" Willie asked as she motioned towards one of her housekeepers. "Have the chauffer bring my limousine around, please, ma'am?" she requested.

"I am. But I was under the impression that I would be meeting my superiors in the morning to discuss setting up a grand jury on the Holland case," Laddy stated as he leaned back in his office chair. "What do we have to discuss that's so important that it can't wait until morning, Senator?"

"You may want to hear this off the record first before we convene formally down in Quantico," Willie replied casually. "I'll be there within the hour," she added before ending the call.

Under the warm night sky, Willie, dressed in a black pant suit and heels, scooped up her briefcase just as her BMW limousine rounded the backside of her home. She climbed in and was whisked away in the night. There was light traffic out as the limousine cruised down East Broad Street. Willie rode in the backseat with her legs crossed in deep thought as lights from the city reflected off the tinted windows. She arrived over to Laddy house forty minutes later. His was a neighborhood lined with row houses sitting atop hills and lined with bushes and brick mailboxes at the foot of steep driveways.

"Wait here," Willie told the driver as she exited the limousine and walked up the steep stairs. She rang the doorbell and Laddy answered a few seconds later and welcomed her in. "Me and my wife and daughter were just about to have dinner. Care to join us?" the agent asked politely.

"It smells delightful," Willie said as she sniffed the air.

"Good evening, Senator. Can I get you a coffee? Wine? Come on in!" Hermelinda welcomed.

"Wine is perfect. Thank you," Willie smiled as she stepped off into the foyer. She peered out into the open area and eyed exposed brick on the walls that held several oil paintings and a few plaques handed out by the FBI. Contemporary-style furniture sat atop marble floors along with vaulted-ceilings and crown molding. "Well," Willie smiled. "Someone has good taste."

"This is all Hermelinda's doing," Laddy declared. "I haven't the knack for art or any kind of decoration."

"He's being modest, Senator Slack." Hermelinda laughed.

"Please, call me Willie," Senator Slack remarked as she shook Hermelinda's hand.

Just then, a toddler with blonde hair like Hermelinda, and brown eyes like Laddy, skipped into the living room. "I'm Ashleigh," she smiled. "And this is momma, and this is daddyyyy!" the four-year-old sang as she ran up and hugged her daddy's legs. "Puppy," she said as she poked out her bottom lip.

"She's adorable!" Willie smiled as she knelt down. "And what kind of puppy do you want, Ashleigh?"

"A big one!" Ashleigh laughed as she held her hand above her head. "One I can ride like a pony in here!" she added as she pointed back towards the living room and took off galloping.

Willie laughed as she stood up. "They are so precious at that

431

age!"

"They are," Laddy smiled.

"Senator Slack, it's an honor to meet you. I've never…we've never had a Senator in our home. Can you stay for dinner?" Hermelinda asked.

"I'm sure the Senator has plenty of work to accomplish before the night is—"

"I'd love to stay!" Willie interjected. "Before we do, do you mind if me and Laddy discuss a couple of issues?"

"Oh no, it's why you're here, I'm sure," Hermelinda smiled. "His office is right over there. I'll go and set an extra plate and bring your wine in a few minutes," the happy wife added as she grabbed Ashleigh by the hand and headed for the kitchen.

"Right this way," Laddy said as he extended his hand to allow Willie to walk ahead of him.

The two entered the office and Willie got down to business. "You're probably wondering what the hell am I doing here," she chuckled as she held onto her briefcase.

Laddy merely nodded. "I'm all ears."

"This case you have against Bena and Tiva Holland? You have to end it," Willie let it be known as she stared Laddy in the eyes.

"End it?" Laddy repeated without smiling as he tucked his hands into his silk slacks. "Now why would I want to do that, Senator?"

"Let's just say it'll be good for your career," Willie replied as she laid her briefcase flat on top of Laddy's wooden desk.

"What'll be good for my career is when I haul those twins before a grand jury in the upcoming days."

"You're presenting your evidence to your superiors tomorrow, correct?" Willie asked as she tilted her head slightly.

"That's right. I have enough probable cause to put Bena and Tiva on the bench. They'll deny questioning, but I'll nab them on perjury. That's five years easy. And then I'll come back with evidence that they've committed murders across the Midwest and the Pacific Northwest once I receive further funding. I'm expecting full cooperation from the committee you sit on in this endeavor."

"Okay," Willie nodded as she opened her briefcase, "But when you come before the committee tomorrow, or the day after? I have evidence of my own that I will present pertaining to the Holland case."

"What evidence is that, Senator?" Laddy smirked, believing nothing Senator Slack could produce could ever get him to back out of the case he had against Bena and Tiva.

"You're laughing at me," Willie smiled as she pulled out a disk and looked across Laddy's desk. "Can you power up your laptop for me, please?"

Laddy powered up his laptop and took the disk from Willie and placed it inside the slot and closed it. A few seconds later, he heard a familiar tune. It was the opening melody to Norman Connors' song *You Are My Starship*. The upstanding federal agent watched stunned as an image of him and Sandra, who was in only her bra and panties, waltzed across the screen hugging and kissing.

The disk then skipped forward to the bedroom. "It's edited, but I have the full version prepared to present to the committee when you get there tomorrow...or the day after," Willie chuckled over the sounds of Sandra and Laddy having sex.

Laddy scrambled to close his office door before hurrying back to the laptop to see what all the disk held. "*Oh, god, you gone drive me crazy,*" he heard and watched as he and Sandra went at it inside her bedroom. "*I wanna come. Can I come on your dick?*"

"*Come on this dick!*" Laddy heard himself moan, watching himself on video as he picked up the pace. He was fucking Sandra six ways from Sunday and both were enjoying every minute of it.

"*Come with me!*" Sandra screamed out on the video. "*Yes, Big Daddy!*"

"*Baby!*" Laddy heard himself yell out as he witnessed himself scoot up the mattress and ejaculate over Sandra's face and lips.

"There the money shot!" Willie applauded. "Shit, I came twice watching y'all two horny devils go at it...Big Daddy Laddy," she stated with a sly grin.

Laddy stood behind his desk staring at Senator Slack with his jaw clasped. He was turning beet red, mortified over having his adulterous affair presented back to him in raw form.

"Welcome to Dirty Politics 101, Agent Norcross," Willie said, breaking the silence as she closed the laptop. "You're in the big leagues now...Big Daddy Laddy. The people you're investigating, as you can now see, have friends in very high places. Now, you will go to Quantico tomorrow and say you have nothing by way of evidence concerning the Holland case and you will shut your investigation down. Need I explain the consequences if you don't?" she asked just as Hermelinda opened the door and walked into the room with a glass of wine.

"Here you go, Senator," Hermelinda smiled. "Dinner's all set if we're ready?"

"Give us a few more minutes will, you, darling?" Laddy requested as he folded his arms and placed a hand beneath his chin.

"Okay. I'll warm the garlic bread," Hermelinda replied as she left the office, closing the door behind her.

"You would ruin my marriage and my career to save two killers from going to jail the way they deserve?" Laddy asked through clinched teeth once his wife had cleared out.

"You damn right. Think about how that lovely wife of yours heart will crack if this were to get out. Think of the public embarrassment you would endure and having to explain to that gifted daughter of yours why mommy and daddy aren't together anymore," Willie countered. She then smiled and said, "But, I will reward you for doing me this favor, Laddy."

"Reward me how? By not presenting this to the public?" Laddy asked disgustedly as he pointed at the laptop.

"That, too. I mean, pornography has ruined so many here in DC," Willie said as she kissed her teeth. "But you? You deserve a better fate, Agent Norcross. I'm going to keep you in the game by lobbing you a homerun," she said as she pulled out a thick manila folder and another disk and plopped them down before Laddy.

"What is all this?" Laddy asked with his hands extended.

"Your first career case. Take that video out and play this audio disk," Willie requested as she briefly went into detail on what all she needed Laddy to do while presenting him the needed evidence.

What lay before Laddy was something he'd never fathomed in life. Had Senator Slack not had the substantiated evidence to support her claim, he would've never believed her. "This is epic," he remarked as his eyes glazed over while listening to audio Willie had offered up to him.

"You agree that this is way bigger than the Holland case?" Willie asked with her lips pressed into a smile.

"This is out of the solar system," Laddy remarked amazed. "One request," he said.

"What's that?" Willie asked.

"I want Sandra with me on this. She deserves it."

"You got a deal," Willie agreed as she extended her hand. "This is to go down Monday morning. That'll give me time to put everything in place over the weekend. Laddy," she then said seriously, "don't you backdoor me. I swear if anything leaks before Monday, that video will become public. No questions asked."

"I'm on board I assure you, Senator," Laddy replied seriously. "I'll have everything ready to go Monday morning."

"Good. Now, let's go have dinner with the family...partner," Willie replied. "Keep that video disk. I have my own copy to jerk off to," she joked, much to Laddy's disapproval.

CHAPTER THIRTY-SIX
HOW SNAKES OPERATE

The Friday morning after Willie's meeting found Brenda Marshall over to Highlandtown, located just east of Baltimore. She was inside Jonas' running around the top floor in a panicked state. A story had just run on Good Morning America that detailed a quintuple murder that had taken place in the Bronx. She'd called Mrs. Margaret's grandson on a throwaway phone and a homicide detective answered, letting her know that her crew had been eradicated. The news report described a scene of horror—mutilated bodies that had been tortured before being executed, and mangled corpses scattered throughout. Tenants inside the building said they never heard a sound and were left perplexed as to how five people could be killed inside of an apartment inside a crowded complex. The massacre had all the makings of a mafia hit from the twenties and authorities were left shocked and clueless as the how five people could be murdered without anyone hearing a thing as it unfolded.

Brenda knew exactly how five people could be killed, and she also knew who was behind the murders. Fearing she was next to face the wrath of the Germans, she immediately hung up the phone and began gathering what all she could. Once she was done, she headed down the stairs with two duffle bags full of hundred dollar bills and a fully-loaded Uzi. Through the tinted front window, she could see a black Excursion she knew Popeye to drive on occasion, pulling up across the street. She backed up the stairs while watching as Popeye and Ford climbed out and looked around carefully before making their way over the side entrance like lions on the prowl.

Deciding not to engage the Senator's son and his partner, Brenda ran back up to the second floor and pushed the fire exit door open on the opposite side of the room. She escaped out the rear of the building just as Popeye and Ford knocked on the front door to pay her a visit.

Back downstairs, Popeye stood guard as Ford used a screwdriver to try and pry a side door open when he heard an engine starting. He back peddled to the front of the building, pulling out a .50 caliber in the process. When he peered around the corner to his left, he saw a white Escalade on large chrome wheels pulling off from the opposite end of the club headed east on Eastern Avenue. The SUV was headed away from him, and he was reluctant to open fire as several cars were passing and there were a few pedestrians out as well. He whistled back to Ford upon catching a glimpse of Brenda behind the wheel and the two ran back to their Excursion.

"That bitch know what the fuck she did that's why she running," Ford stated as he hopped behind the wheel and sped off after Brenda.

Brenda was gripping her Uzi as she made a left turn onto Grundy Street, headed north towards East Lombard Street. She slowed her Escalade and waited for the Excursion to emerge from behind the buildings with her gun pointed out the driver's side window and her right hand on the steering wheel as she let the vehicle cruise while in drive. When the Excursion appeared, she opened fire, unleashing a rapid torrent of bullets into the morning air.

"Aww fuck!" Popeye yelled as he and Ford ducked down in the front seat. The front of the Excursion dropped down and the windshield shattered as the two hopped out of the SUV and scattered for cover.

Brenda emptied her thirty-two-round clip in under fifteen seconds and mashed the gas. She could see Popeye and Ford running up the block behind with their guns out, so she leaned down and sped up to East Lombard Street, running stop signs in the process as she neared the main road. She banked right on East Lombard and jumped onto I-895 headed north of Highlandtown.

Back on Eastern Avenue, Popeye and Ford were left in the middle of the intersection with an incapacitated ride that was leaking radiator fluid and had two flat tires. Popeye called Bell and Big Ty, who were over to Lisa Vanguard's Highlandtown home, and had them ride back over to Eastern Avenue upon learning that the house was void of occupancy.

Senator Slack had given every single detail on what'd gone down with Tanya and Zelda King to her team the night before and the hunt was now on for Brenda Marshall. The crew had tried to strike early, but had come up short. Brenda Marshall was their priority, but she'd gotten away on this day. It was only a matter of time before the woman was flushed out into the open, however, being she was now on the defense.

Forty-five minutes later, Brenda was pulling up to a Flying J truck stop in Elkton, Maryland, a small town fifty miles or so north of Baltimore just off I-95. She pulled in amongst the big rigs riding through the large parking lot and parked before the Iron Skillet restaurant and went inside. She'd left her two duffle bags of money behind, but had concealed her reloaded Uzi in a large purse as she went into the convenience store and purchased a new cellphone. After taking a seat at a booth inside the restaurant before a window that was right before her Escalade, she powered up the phone and dialed Lisa Vanguard's number as the nine 'o' clock morning hour approached on the east coast.

****

Lisa Vanguard was nearly done dressing for the day in her high-rise apartment over in Seattle, Washington when her cell rang just before six in the morning. She walked over to her nightstand in her $4,000 dollar light-brown Canali linen pant suit and looked at the unfamiliar number and let it go to voicemail. A minute or so later, she received a notification. She sat on the edge of her king-sized bed while placing a pair of black $2,200 dollar Manolo Blahnik stilettos onto her feet as she listened to the message while picking at the curls in her freshly-cropped head of red hair.

"Pick up! I'm calling right back!" she heard Brenda say in a near whisper.

The phone rang again and Lisa answered just as she stood and tucked her .40 Glock into her hip holster while checking her appearance in a wall-mounted mirror as she put the phone on speaker. "What is it now, Brenda?" the federal agent asked through a sigh as she stared at her image and smiled.

"I was almost hit today," Brenda whispered. "Willie sent her son after me today. They know it was me behind the hit in Cincinnati. My crew was taken out in the Bronx. You need to get in touch with Arata and Raiden and have them send more men so I

439

can fight this shit off."

"How did they get to your crew, Brenda?" Lisa asked as she picked up the phone. She cut off the speaker and walked out of her room and strolled over to her gourmet kitchen with the phone to her ear.

"I don't know. Maybe they left something behind. Popeye and his crew do that forensics shit, ya' know? I thought it would be best if we split up and lay low for a while until things died down so I sent them back up to the Bronx. They got made up there." Brenda nervously unpacked as a waitress appeared before her.

"Coffee, ma'am?" the woman asked through a polite smile.

"That's fine," Brenda replied as she brushed the woman off. "Lisa?" she then spoke into the phone as static was heard.

"Where are you now?" Lisa asked as she placed the phone back on speaker and stood beside Raiden and Arata Moto. Brenda's voice grew distorted and Lisa could no longer hear the woman. "Are you there?" she asked, getting no reply.

Arata and Raiden had arrived over to Lisa's place an hour earlier and the three were making preparations for their next container of heroin scheduled for delivery on Monday afternoon. It was a Friday, so containers had to be ordered before day's end, and soldiers were needed on hand in order to break down the product to have it shipped to their preordained locations.

Lisa had put the Moto brothers up on a Gangster Disciple click up in Chicago that was able to score twenty kilograms of heroin. With the move she was planning on making against Brenda Marshall, she knew she would need another avenue to fill in on the one hundred and twenty kilograms of heroin Brenda would lose, so she'd used her federal resources to find another set of dealers that could pick up the partial slack. The federal agent had only made a preliminary contact with the Chicago gang and was expecting to meet with them later in the week, but in the meantime, there was much work needed to be done in Seattle.

Brenda Marshall, if Lisa had to tell it, was only getting in the way as her value had been all but exhausted. She was now searching out a way to rid herself of the woman and the baggage she carried completely.

"Brenda, are you there?" Lisa asked again after several seconds had gone by.

"I'm in some town called Elkton with Bridgette's Escalade. My phone went out for a minute," Brenda replied. "Can you...can you get in touch with the Moto brothers and tell them to send men? I'll need back up on the next shipment up to Philly and protection against Tanya's people."

"The Moto brothers are out of the country right now," Lisa remarked dryly as she moved about her kitchen. "Look, we're going to put a halt on the shipments to Philadelphia for now, Brenda. Do you have the re-up from the last shipment?" she asked as she put on a pot of coffee.

"What?" Brenda exclaimed. "We had a deal. I was to kill Tanya, and you was to give me Philadelphia. I killed my best friend to make this deal and now you playin' me short?"

"No one's getting shortchanged. How can I ship merchandise when your crew has been eliminated? I'm not going to ship one hundred and twenty-five kilograms of heroin to Philadelphia when you have no backup on the east coast."

"I'm askin' you for backup, bitch!" Brenda seethed as the waitress slid a cup of coffee and several napkins before her.

"Are you ready to order, ma'am?" the woman asked.

"Look bi—I'm good with my coffee, thank you," Brenda exhaled while fanning the woman off.

At the same time, Lisa was preparing to grab a mug out one of her cabinets when Brenda called her out her name. The narcissistic agent froze momentarily and looked over to her phone through cold-hearted green eyes. In an instant, her mind had been made up as to how she would deal with the woman as Brenda's demise had been long overdue given her stupidity. Her usefulness had finally run its course.

"What did I tell you, Brenda?" Lisa asked, easily hiding her disdain for the woman. "The Moto brothers are out of the country. There's nothing I can do right now because we're already stretched thin as it is. Arata and Raiden will be back next week. We'll get you your men then."

"What about this re-up?" Brenda replied. "I'm still in this business, Lisa."

"You are, Brenda. We're just making some new and safer

connections. Bridgette will come through and gather the re-up. She'll be flying in from Los Angeles and will meet you tomorrow evening over to the safe house in Philadelphia."

"I'll find another place," Brenda countered. "After what went down at Jonas' they could be up on that spot here in Philly. I'm at this number for the time being. Have Bridgette call me when she lands in Philly and I'll have her meet me somewhere."

"She'll be in touch," Lisa assured before she ended the call.

"Brenda is supposed to be dead," Arata remarked the moment Lisa ended the call. "She owes us her life for botching that job in Ohio. Raiden was supposed to take the shot not her. And because of what she did, Tanya Weinberger's people may now know who we are."

"Oh, don't I know it?" Lisa sighed as she eyed the Moto brothers. "We have to clean this up and clean it up quick. The people that may be on to us are led a woman by the name of Faye Bender. She was the one who killed your parents."

"How do you know that?" Arata asked curiously.

"Brenda told me in passing. She was in that house that day back in January of '84 as well, but she doesn't remember who you are," Lisa confessed.

"And how long have you known this?"

"Since before I met you guys," Lisa admitted.

Arata and Raiden both stared at Lisa through squinted eyes with scowls on their faces.

"I wasn't keeping it from you forever. I had intentions on telling you guys," Lisa let it be known. "I know it looks deceitful, but the truth is we needed Brenda at the time. She moved one hundred and twenty kilograms, and she was the best shot we had to get to Tanya. But she fucked it up in the end," the agent chuckled in disbelief while shaking her head. "She's of no value to us now. I knew you two were gonna want her dead for botching the Cincinnati job and I'm working on it. I would've told you when she was dead and given you the reason why. It just so happens you asked before the appointed time."

"Is there anything else we need to know?" Arata asked.

Lisa thought briefly and said, "There isn't any more secrets. We will have an even slate once Brenda is eliminated. It'll be done before the weekend is over."

"If not, there will be no 're-up' as you ladies say," Raiden quoted.

"That won't be necessary," Lisa chided as she eyed the Japanese men sitting at her counter with slight contempt. "Don't let Brenda's mistake fool you about me because I'm not her. I always cover my tracks. Excuse me now will you? I have to inform Bridgette of her trip to Philly tomorrow," she concluded as she walked out of her kitchen.

"She has a big ego," Arata remarked once Lisa was out of earshot.

"And she's too assured of herself. How long does she think she can get away with leading a double life?" Raiden asked.

"Are you kiddin'?" Arata said seriously as he sipped his coffee. "She's been getting away with it for over thirty years, Raiden."

"This whole deal with Brenda just has a bad vibe to it, brother," Raiden replied. "It may come back to bite Lisa in the ass. And if it bites her? It affects you and I."

"Lisa is creating the bad vibe, Raiden" Arata stated. "Let's wait and see what she does to rectify the matter."

"What if she doesn't kill Brenda this weekend?" Raiden asked.

"Then we'll do to her on Monday what was supposed to have been done to Brenda over the weekend," Arata declared in a matter-of-fact tone.

"Agreed," Raiden nodded as he sipped his coffee.

CHAPTER THIRTY-SEVEN

QUEEN COBRA

The following Saturday had Brenda pacing the floor as eight 'o' clock p.m. approached. She'd been smoking bud all day to calm her nerves as she'd been having an uneasy feeling about Lisa Vanguard since the call she'd made to the woman the day before from the Flying J Truck Stop in Elkton. If Brenda had to tell it, Lisa was hanging her out to dry on the east coast after she'd betrayed one of her own in Tanya Weinberger. When she'd explained that her crew had been annihilated, Lisa had showed no concern. She'd also denied her access to more soldiers and had halted the heroin shipments to Philadelphia. Her dream of running her own family was falling by the wayside it seems, but she was still willing to hold onto her beliefs that the game would reward her for all the work she'd put in over the past decades. And if she could, she would hit back at Lisa for turning her back on her when she needed her the most. All bets were off with the federal agent as far as Brenda was concerned. At this point in time, she had nothing to lose so she was prepared to go all out in the game.

The chiming of her phone startled Brenda as she paced the dank wooden floors of a cheap one-room studio rental unit in south Philadelphia. She answered and heard Bridgette's voice.

"Wut's yuh locale, sistah gal?" Bridgette asked as she and two well-dressed white Jamaicans climbed into the back of a taxi out in front of Philadelphia's busy International Airport.

Brenda gave Bridgette her address before ending the call. She went and unlocked the door afterwards and sat at a small rickety wooden table that had a perfect bead on the door, and waited in the darkness with her Uzi cocked, only the orange streetlights illuminating her rental as she toked on a blunt. Forty minutes later, she heard a knock.

"It's open!" Brenda called out as she shifted in her seat and raised her Uzi.

The door slowly opened and Bridgette walked in looking around with a nonchalant attitude. She caught sight of Brenda sitting at the table inside the small apartment with her Uzi aimed back at her and said, "Yuh read the play, sistah gal," with two muscular white Jamaican men with long, brown dreads following her lead. "You have the re-up wid yuh?" she asked as she stepped off into the room wearing a red silk maxi-dress with a split up the side and red ankle-boots boots with her braided blonde hair pinned up over her shoulders.

"It's here. Five million dollars," Brenda remarked as she held on to her Uzi. "I figured out on my ride up here to Philly that I was no longer of any value to that bitch Lisa," she added as she exhaled marijuana smoke. "She used me to get to Tanya and then she left me out here to get killed."

"She waan me tuh come kill yuh for fuckin' up the hit on Tanya, but I not come tuh kill yuh for fuckin' the hit up on Tanya, Brendah." Bridgette remarked as she reached back and closed the door.

"What the fuck you here for then?" Brenda asked as her nose flared.

"Tuh let yuh know I waan yuh in my family over in Caluhfornia. And I wanna help ya' take Lisa down for wut she do tuh ya'," Bridgette sympathized as she walked over to the table where Brenda was sitting and eyed two duffle bags resting at her feet. "Dat the re-up?"

Brenda kept her eyes on the two men with Bridgette and said, "Fuck the re-up, alright? How the fuck can you help me? Why should I even trust you knowing you dealing with the bitch who done just crossed me out?"

Bridgette pointed to a chair, requesting to sit, and Brenda nodded. She pulled the chair out and sat across from the angered woman. "Wait fuh me on tha' other side a' tha' door while mi and Brendah chat," she said to the two young men that were with her. When her goons left the small apartment and closed the door behind him, Bridgette turned to Brenda and said, "Lisa Vanguard ah snake, yeh?"

"Tell me I something I don't know," Brenda said through curled lips as she held her Uzi on Bridgette and set her blunt down in an ashtray.

"Okay. I *will* tell yah somethin' yuh don't know yet, sistah gal —Lisa kill yah husband in a Pittburgh hotel in 1990." Bridgette disclosed.

"What?" Brenda snapped as her face wrinkled.

"Yuh heard mi right. Lisa told me yestahday wen I ask why she waan mi tah dead yah. She said yuh husband had sum ting she need and him had tuh be killed for it. She no tell me what it wuz she needed him tuh die for at duh time tho'," Bridgette confessed.

"You're lyin' to me!" Brenda scoffed she tightened the grip on her Uzi.

"If I waan kill yuh I wulda come in a' blastin'," Bridgette remarked calmly. "How do I know yuh ask a woman where yah man was when she picked up duh fon in tha' hotel duh day yah husband Ricky Gross was murked, eh? Lisa kill yah husband, Brendah! She killed tha' La Rocca brothers too...Audi and Austell. And she framed yah dead husband Ricky Gross for erry little ting she did."

Brenda ran a hand through her thick afro as she dropped her head and loosed the grip on her Uzi. Tears welled up in her eyes as she reflected on how Lisa had been lying to her all along. The story Bridgette told her was exactly what the newspapers printed back in June of 1990: that Ricky had killed the La Rocca brothers, Audi and Austell, two days earlier, and he'd been killed in retaliation on the day of their funerals. Brenda never believed that story because the timeline wasn't adding up.

Ricky was found dead with a .32 revolver that was used in the execution-style killings of the La Rocca brothers beside his body. An Uzi used in a 1984 killing down in Cincinnati was found inside the hotel room as well. Ricky was charged posthumously for each of those murders, but Brenda had always known that her husband had been framed. Her man was with her down in New Orleans the day the La Rocca brothers were killed in Pittsburgh. She remembered that time back in June of 1990 because it was a couple of days before Zelda and Vivian were due home after a few years behind bars.

"Zelda," Brenda sobbed. "I got my fuckin' girl killed," she said with a heavy heart. "The fuck I was thinkin'?"

Bridgette sat watching from across the table as Brenda began baring her soul. "Let it all out," she slyly enticed. "I kno' it hurts tuh kno' yah fren do some ting like dat tuh yah, Brendah. I no lie tuh yah tuday. Lisa killed your husband. And she knows something else about yah too."

"What else she know about me?" Brenda asked as her eyes watered.

"There's another reason she waan yah dead." Bridgette said as she cut her eyes over to Brenda.

"What other reason could there be, Bridgette?" Brenda looked up and asked as her nerves began to rattle. "I can't think of no other reason Lisa would wanna kill me other than me fuckin' that hit up on Tanya. What? She crossing me out over Tammy or something? I told her who did that!"

"Tammy has some ting tah do wid it. I won't tell you wud it is, tho'. Fuh ya' tuh join me and my clan I have tuh kno' that you can remember tings. Lisa knows something else about yah and it has tah do with Tammy. Tink. Solve tha' riddle," Bridgette urged.

Brenda continued on putting the pieces together. It hadn't dawned on her until that very moment that Tammy and Lisa had a longstanding history. It could've been Lisa herself who moved that gun from the home in Cincinnati. And if she did, she would've had to have been the one to kill Ricky. Brenda then remembered that brief phone conversation she'd had with a woman she believed had killed her husband. She'd never shared that conversation with no one in her life, but it had always haunted her. She'd always wanted to know who it was on the phone that day and, now, the mystery had been solved. She had no idea that she'd been in the midst of her husband's killer all along, but she couldn't help to feel as if she was missing a piece of the puzzle.

"Are you okay, Brendah?" Bridgette asked, shaking Brenda from, her thoughts.

"You plan on going after Lisa?" Brenda asked as she continued gripping her Uzi.

"Yah! But, yah haven't finished tha' riddle I lay on yah. Don't ya' waan kno' tha' riddle?" Bridgette asked curiously as she tilted her head down and stared at Brenda in disbelief.

"I'll figure that shit out later, okay?" Brenda snapped as she let the Uzi slip from her hands. She left her weapon behind on the table as she went over to the refrigerator and pulled a twenty-ounce Bud Light from the top shelf and began searching for a can opener. "I don't wanna know about a fuckin' riddle. What I wanna know is you gone go at Lisa because I want in on that bitch," she declared as she pulled open a kitchen drawer and began rummaging through it until she found a bottle opener.

Bridgette's green eyes fell upon the Uzi that had been left laying on the table. She looked over to Brenda, who had her back to her, and scooped the gun up into her left hand in the process. "We pretend to go through wid a' deal in Seattle the next time a' ship come in," she said in a sly tone as she aimed the gun at Brenda's back while leaning over the table. "In the middle of it all we blow Lisa Vanguard and the Moto brothas away. Den wi take dere whole shipment a' boy and keep it fuh ah' selves."

"Two hundred kilograms is worth about sixteen...million..." Brenda's voice trailed off when she shut the kitchen drawer and turned around. Across the way, she saw Bridgette aiming her own Uzi back at her. "So you did come to kill me," she stated in a nonchalant manner as she popped the top on her beer and took a sip.

"I nawt come here tah kill yah fuh fuckin' up tha' job on Tanya, but why yah leave ya' gun on tha' table wid mi like dat?" Bridgette asked through a side eye as she welded the gun on Brenda. "Wat yah testin' me ah' some ting?" she asked while waving the Uzi back and forth.

"Hey," Brenda chuckled as she eyed Bridgette without a hint of disdain in her voice "I left my gun because I thought we were on the same page."

"Me no believe wat yah tell mi, sister gal," Bridgette sang as she pointed the tip of the Uzi's barrel towards the seat Brenda had been sitting in. "Yah waan test and see if me waan kill yah? Come an' sidung!"

"Sit down?" Brenda chortled as she sat the bottle of beer down and spread her arms. "If you wanna shoot me, go 'head and do it, Bridgette. I'm damned if I do and damned if I don't at this point in my life. Sometimes I wish I could just leave all this shit behind," she confessed as she began to slowly walk over towards Bridgette.

"I have a way tah leave id all behind yah," Bridgette disclosed as she held the Uzi on Brenda.

"Do it then," Brenda said in a trance-like state of mind as she stared into the barrel of her own Uzi without blinking.

Bridgette laid the gun on the table, freeing it from hands as she leaned back in her chair. "Mi no kill yah fuh fuckin' up tha' job on Tanya," she confessed. "Tha' plan I have iz tah kill Lisa and duh Moto brothers. Do yah' like dat?" she asked as she eyed Brenda.

"I can get with it," Brenda nodded as she picked up her Bud Light and took another sip.

"Good. Yah owe Lisa anyway becuz ah' wat she do to yah husband. Let's not forget dat. And she got yah tah' kill yah own fren Tanya Weinberger in tha' process. Yah owe dat bitch, sistah gal!" Bridgette preached as Brenda took a seat across from her.

"Who else in on this job against Lisa?" Brenda asked as she leaned back in the chair and sipped her twenty-two-ounce Bud Light once more.

"Tha' Moto brothers bring in too-hunnid kilograms a' boy. My two cousins outside dat door will help us. Split four ways, dat's fiftty kilograms each worth four million dollars. Lisa insult ya' some weeks ago when she gave yah a' petty ten tousand dollar. Yuh should kill her ova tha' disrepeck alone!" Bridgette instigated as she looked Brenda off and placed her hands underneath the table.

"You right," Brenda nodded in agreement. "I would take it all back if I could, though."

"Why yah say dat?" Bridgette asked.

"I don't wanna talk about it," Brenda chuckled while waving Bridgette off. Her smile soon dropped and her heart melted as she reflected on the past. "I'm just thinkin'…thinkin' about my husband and son," she unpacked. "It was always Ricky's dream for us to move to an island and retire," Brenda said as she laid her afro into the palm of her right hand and crossed her legs. "I been chasing that same dream for over thirty years and all that's been accomplished is me losing my family."

Bridgette sat and watched in silence as tears began to roll from Brenda's eyes. Once again, she was baring her soul. "Remorse be a weak ting is dis game," she informed Brenda.

"I not remorseful," Brenda retorted as she sniffled and set her beer down.

"Yah lie!" Bridgette snapped as she shifted in her seat. "But yah no lie tah me, yah lie tuh ya' self! Yah feel remorse 'cuz yah kno' yah 'bout to retire after yah kill Lisa Vanguard doncha, Brendah?" she asked as her hand slid up under her red, silk dress.

"I do," Brenda sobbed while looking Bridgette off. "I lost my husband to this game. I lost my son to this fuckin' game," she sobbed. "I was in jail for my son's funeral," the remorseful woman heaved as she lowered her head to the table. "And in the end, the bitch who ruined my life? I been in business with her!"

"Bare yah soul tuh me, Brendah. Wat else ya' sorry fuh wat the game gave back tuh yah, sistah gal?" Bridgette asked as she slid the chair back from the table with the heels of her boots.

"I killed my best friend," Brenda confessed. "That shit about Tanya was a lie. She ain't have nothing to do with Tammy gettin' killed. I killed my best friend for nothin'!" she cried out.

"Wat a pity fuh you," Bridgette facetiously sympathized as she eased up from her seat and strolled over to Brenda with her hands behind her back. "But in dis life yah' can't feel sorry for shid like dat," she let it be known as she looked down at the back of Brenda's head.

"I want Lisa dead!" Brenda yelled out as she pounded the table with her right fist and her head resting in the crevice of her left arm.

"Lisa time will come soon nuff. But your time is now, Brenda Marshall," Bridgette avowed as she came from behind her back with a five-inch blade and drove it into the base of Brenda's skull.

Brenda used what remaining air she had left in her lungs to gasp in horror before she went silent and began chewing on her tongue. Blood began spurting from her ruptured carotid artery as Bridgette backed away from her latest victim's trembling torso. The tip of the five-inch blade she'd driven into Brenda's neck had seared through the base of her skull, and the tip of the blade lay lodged in the wooden table.

Bridgette walked past Brenda while looking into her shocked eyes and said in a cold, callous voice. "Lisa nawt only waan yah dead fuh fuckin' up tha' job awn Tanya, she waan yah dead fuh killin' Tammy's parents, Kazuki and Cho Moto, twenty-five years ago," she sang while leaning down and staring into Brenda's eyes. "Dat is the riddle you did nawt figah out. Lisa Vanguard may be snake, but it is I who be tha' Queen Cobra. First you, now I go fuh Lisa and kill hur too," the conniving white Jamaican remarked as she took a seat across from Brenda and waited for her to die while contemplating her own shattered life.

Bridgette Fischer was about as ruthless as one could be inside the business. She cared about little, and gave no fucks about even less. She enjoyed killing for the sheer thrill of it all—and she was damn good at it. Loyalty was just a word to her, and Causes were nonexistent except for where she was the benefactor. She was a woman bent on proving to her husband that she was capable of running her own empire alongside him. She regretted the day she'd tried to kill Rafael. He was the best thing that'd ever happened to her. He'd given her a life of luxury for over thirty years that she was appreciative of, but he'd refused to let her fly after all she'd done on his behalf.

After all the bloodshed down in Medellin in the late eighties, a planting of a bomb on Rafael's behalf by her in Caracas in 1992, he still didn't deem Bridgette worthy or capable enough of running her own family was what she knew to be true. The job in Brazil against the Devereaux family was to be her come out party. She'd planned the entire thing herself and had hopes of reporting back to her husband the good news. Only, things hadn't gone according to plan down in Brazil. Bridgette knew Rafael was going to find out about the botched job and she felt she'd upset him to the point of wanting to kill her over the mistake, which was why she'd tried to kill him instead.

Rafael wanted a trophy wife, Bridgette knew, but she viewed herself as being much more. She saw herself as a woman of prestige and power rather than an object of a man's desire that would willingly do his bidding without benefitting from it herself. The way Bridgette saw it, she'd given Rafael his start and had willingly took a backseat while he became the biggest cocaine dealer in Venezuela. She was owed her own family was her stance. And it was perfect in her eyes because she and Rafael sold different product.

Bridgette felt as if she and Rafael could own the world if they worked together rather than apart. She knew she'd fucked up trying to kill her husband, but she viewed her willingness to die over something she believed in so much as more proof of her love for the man who'd given her the game. She was doing as he'd taught her, which was to take shit from no one and destroy any and everything standing in your way. Rafael wasn't living up to his own advice in Bridgette's eyes, however, if the estranged wife had to tell it. He was doing what he'd always warned her against by not retaliating against the Holland family. To her, it seemed as if Rafael was allowing the Holland family to surpass him. Bridgette didn't understand his thinking behind it all, but she began thinking about a way to reconcile with her husband just as Brenda's body began twitching as she lay across the table with the knife protruding from her neck.

Bridgette whistled and the door to the apartment was pushed open at that moment. "Take dat bags of moolah and bring dem down to me Escalade Brendah no longer needs. Me right behind yuh," she ordered one guy as she grabbed her cellphone and dialed a number.

"Vanguard."

"Dat job for the Asians is done and we have the re-up," Bridgette stated as she eased up from the chair.

"Good," Lisa said calmly. "I'll need you here in Seattle for the next drop so we can discuss your running Philadelphia. It'll be in Monday morning around six."

"I be dere early Munday morning. Wi drive straight thru," Bridgette replied before ending the call. She then looked over at Brenda who lay dead with her eyes open and stared remorselessly as she slowly turned and walked out of the apartment.

One of Bridgette's cousins greeted her in the hall. "Wud yah waan do with the resta tha' crew on tha' wess coast?" he asked.

"I no truss Lisa. Wi get tah Seattle early Munday and kill hur and convince the Moto brothas dem should deal wid us becuz Lisa cawnt be trusted," Bridgette stated as she began descending the stairs with her family following her lead. "Let's be on tha' road. Wi have shawt time left," she ended as she placed a pair of sunshades over her eyes and walked out of the building.

Brenda Marshall came onto the scene in 1982 at the age of eighteen down in New Orleans, Louisiana. She died on June 20, 2009 at the age of forty-six after a twenty-seven-year run in the game that culminated in her dying a lonely death inside a rundown one-room studio apartment on the south side of Philadelphia, Pennsylvania. To add to her insult, she'd loss her husband and son to the very same business that had taken her life on this day. Hers was a tragic story indeed.

CHAPTER THIRTY-EIGHT

RESSURECTED

The white suede curtains inside one of the bedrooms on the first floor of Ponderosa opened with a swooshing sound when Sharona Benson pulled the rope. It was the morning after Brenda Marshall had been killed in Philadelphia. June 21St. The Sunday morning sun beamed into the luxurious suite as Sharona stood before a bay window overlooking the middle portion of the land. The land and its peoples were just stirring awake, but some were already up and about. Sharona could see Mary and Regina across the way preparing to irrigate their onions, collard greens and tomatoes while Regina's son Tacoma, and a friend of his from school, loaded loose vegetables into a red wagon as the two walked up and down the planted rows.

Life was happening all around Sharona Benson and she was grateful to be on hand to witness it all. Five days ago, she'd undergone a kidney transplant on a farm somewhere in Kansas was all she knew. She was driven to the Oklahoma border on Friday where she was transferred to Francine's RV and driven back by Irene. She'd spent all day Friday and Saturday in bed recuperating and had awakened on the day of the summer solstice reinvigorated. A soft tap on the double wooden doors caught Sharona's attention and she left the bay window and donned a robe before pulling one of the doors open.

"Good morning, Miss Benson. How're we feeling today?" the brown-skinned young woman wearing green scrubs smiled.

"I feel great, Doctor Duchene." Sharona smiled as the doctor and close friend to the family entered her room pushing a steel cart. She sat in a comfortable chair as the doctor approached.

"Wonderful," thirty-three-year-old Daphne Duchene responded as she ushered the cart before Sharona. "I have your daily dose of antirejection medication prepared for you today. How are you feeling?" the doctor asked as she stood before Sharona. "Are you experiencing tenderness in the organs? Any fever or weight gain?"

"No, I'm fine, doctor. I actually have a lot of energy today for the first time in so long. Is it possible for me to go outside?"

"I wouldn't recommend it," Doctor Duchene objected. "You're still open to infection. And with all the dust and livestock around? It'll be easy for foreign bodies to enter the system. Let's give it another week and see how it goes, okay?"

"Alright," Sharona sighed as she prepared to take her daily doses.

For the rest of her life, Sharona Benson would have to take a round of medicines, four different types, in order to prevent her body from rejecting the organs she'd received. Doctor Wickenstaff had prescribed the regiment before leaving Cherryvale, and the records were transferred to Doctor Duchene, who would oversee Sharona's daily dosages until a permanent family doctor could be obtained. Neither woman knew what had gone down behind the scenes in order to save Sharona's life. As far as they knew, the kidneys had been donated from an anonymous person who'd died in a car accident in another state.

"Do you have kids, doctor?" Sharona asked after swallowing her first dose of pills.

"Kids? No, ma'am. I have enough to deal with working in the medical field and paying off debt," Doctor Duchene stated as she readied a second round of immunosuppressants. "Some days I work twenty hours in the emergency room, so it has been a relief for me to come to Ponca City," she said in an appreciative tone.

"The ranch has a way of soothing people's soul doesn't it?" Sharona asked through a bright smile as she took her second round of medication. "I always enjoy coming here."

"It's like a vacation, Miss Benson," Doctor Duchene gushed. "I could use a real vacation, though."

"You, Kimi hasn't invited you to her wedding, girl?" Sharona asked surprised.

"No she hasn't!" Doctor Duchene said as she reared back surprised with her hands on her hips. "She never said a word the whole the time I been here! When and where?"

"This September in the Solomon Islands."

"Way out in the Pacific," Sharona said through light laughter. "I'm happy for her! I would love to go. I wonder what the expense would be."

"Kimi's been so busy making the arrangements she probably forgot to tell you, doctor," Sharona said as she readied for her third round of medications. "Tell you what," she then whispered. "I'll plant a bug in her ear for you later on today. Keep the first week of September open, sister. I'm taking you on a much-needed vacation."

"Really? That would be the nicest thing anyone has ever done for me, Miss Benson."

"Aww...I think the twins would be glad to have you after all you've done, baby," Sharona declared.

"And I'd be honored," Sharona responded in kind. "Your last dose is a steroid. Afterwards, you must put something on your stomach to prevent light-headedness," she ended as she prepared Sharona's last round of medication.

****

"So, dad. I be the big eight come Wednesday, ya' feel me? I was wondering if you looked into that mini four-wheeler I asked you about the other day?" seven-year-old Doss III asked his father as he helped him prepare breakfast inside the first floor kitchen by pulling a basket of farm fresh brown eggs from the refrigerator.

"I told you once...I'm not gettin' you a four-wheeler, son," DeeDee remarked as he cut into a slab of bacon the size of a loaf of bread. "You don't know how to ride, and it's hilly around here. You might tip it over."

"Not if you ride with me, dad. You can drive it, just get it for me so we can ride it together. Pretty please?"

"You really want this four-wheeler for your birthday?" DeeDee asked as he stopped cutting bacon slices and looked down at his son.

"Yeah," Doss III admitted. "I promise to be careful if you teach me how to ride it. I'll watch you drive. You can drive it every day if you want so long as I get to ride with you."

"I'll look into it, okay, son? No promises, though."

"Momma says no so we have to get her on our side, dad. I think a puppy will make her happy."

"More like a puppy would make *you* happy, right?" DeeDee laughed. "You're tryna get a two-for-one, aren't you?"

"Can you blame a kid for tryin' really?" Doss III asked as he placed the basket of eggs onto the counter beside the stove. "Momma says you saved her life. How did you that, dad?"

"Ohh, I just found a good doctor for her, son," DeeDee remarked as he grabbed a large skillet and placed it on the stove and turned on the gas.

"She said she would've died without you, dad. You're a hero," Doss III smiled up at his father and gave him a quick hug. "I don't know what we would do without momma. Who would help me with my homework and stuff?"

"That's all you gathered from that experience?" DeeDee chuckled.

"No. But, it's what I thought about first. I would miss her at that time. And that made me sad."

"You know what I would've missed most about your mother?"

Doss III grabbed his shoulders and began making moaning sounds, much to DeeDee's astonishment. "You gone miss the love, dad," he said through a devilish smile. "The love."

"Your mind ain't right, son," DeeDee laughed. "What I would've missed is your mother's laugh. It's infectious."

"What does infectious mean, dad?"

"Contagious. Like how a cold spreads."

"Is what momma have infectious?"

"Not by any means, son," DeeDee remarked as he knelt down and waved his progeny closer. He took his son in his arms and said, "Your mother will be perfectly fine in a little while, okay? She'll be around to help with your homework, fix your meals, and tuck you in. And she will do it until you're able to do those for yourself."

"What about you, dad?" Doss III questioned shyly.

"What about me? I'll be there, too."

"You're old, dad. How long do humans live exactly?"

DeeDee knew he had more days behind him than ahead of him according to the laws of nature, but he couldn't, nor would he ever tell his son that fact. He was hoping for another ten years at least; enough time to allow his son to grow older and understand death more soundly. "I'll be around long enough to see you ride that four-wheeler," he told his son.

"You're gonna get it for real?" Doss III asked excitedly, quickly forgetting about the last question he'd asked his father.

"Yeah, but it'll be our secret." DeeDee smiled just as Sharona and Doctor Duchene appeared off in the distance.

"Scout's honor," Doss III said as he saluted his father. "You don't have to worry about me saying a damn—"

"Hush your mouth," DeeDee whispered through a chuckle. "Here comes momma. We have to get her to go along with the idea about the four-wheeler, remember?" he asked as he held onto his son's hands.

"How will we do it, dad? How will we tell momma?" Doss III whispered back.

"Let the old man handle it," DeeDee winked as he stood to his feet to greet the two women. "Who's up for bacon?" he asked as the morning continued to unfold.

"Meeeeee!" Malaysia sang aloud as she walked into the kitchen after emerging from the second stairwell.

"You just ate upstairs, greedy!" Tiva laughed at Malaysia as she and Bay entered the kitchen with Malara, Tara, and the twins' three bloodhounds that their grandfather Mendoza had gotten them last Christmas shortly before he met his demise in Chicago.

"Where're you all off to?" Sharona asked as she and Doctor Duchene took seats at the island counter.

"We're going see Sosa this morning over to Dawk house and walk the dogs," Bay answered as the bloodhounds walked through then kitchen with their noses planted to the marble floor.

All three of the black and brown floppy-eared canines walked over to DeeDee and sat before him while staring up and licking their chops. He threw a few pieces of bacon down and the dogs scooped them up and quickly swallowed. They sat again and waited patiently for another treat.

"Nooo, come onnn!" Malara commanded as she ran over and nudged the dogs towards the patio doors. "Outside!"

"Now look at her takin' charge," Bay laughed. "We going, y'all," she added as she and Tiva guided the twins outside.

"When I get my four-wheeler we can ride down to the lake and see Sosa! I'll have it Wednesday for my birthday!" Doss III blurted out.

"Really?" Sharona asked as she eyed DeeDee.

DeeDee placed his hands on his hips and stared down at his son. "What happened to scout's honor, boy?"

"Hey, I...I never took the oath, man," Doss III replied with his hands extended. "I'm only seven! You gone listen to me? I'm excited, dad!"

"Enjoy your breakfast, grandad," Tiva chided as she and Bay left Ponderosa with the dogs and kids in tow.

****

Naomi, meanwhile, was sitting on the patio of her suite on the second floor of Ponderosa before a circular marble table facing Kimi and Koko, who sat with their backs to the land. There was a spread out on the table, a silver bowl filled with cheese eggs, mounds of buttered toast and smoked sausage links cured inside the family's smokehouse along with a picture of orange juice and a jar of lemon tea. It was a lovely Sunday morning down in Ponca City, and while many in the family parlayed, or tended to duties around the ranch, Naomi and her protégés had business to discuss.

"I have the files on your selections of possible interns to bring into the family," Naomi stated as she sat at the table in a white pant suit, white stilettoes and wearing a white sombrero with a pair of sunshades covering her eyes. "Affinity and Katie are qualified. None of their family has any arrests for high crimes, and they themselves are A students. You have the go ahead from me if you want to bring them in on an internship, but I suggest it be a slow endeavor," she told her middle daughters.

Kimi and Koko were soon to be responsible for handling a million dollar per day organization working alongside their mother once the Devereaux family's heroin connection came online in a week or so. The task was becoming a little overwhelming for them both, so they asked their mother for 'additional resources', meaning, could they bring in additional recruits to serve under them in order to further the family Cause?

Naomi saw early on that her daughters would need help. She was expecting this move sooner rather than later, and her protégés had come through without fail by presenting not only the budding problem she herself foresaw, but they'd also brought forth a possible resolution. Through mere observation, Naomi could easily discern that Affinity and Katie worshipped the ground that Kimi and Koko walked. The twins were in the top percentile of their Accounting class and were very professional. At times, it seemed as if they knew more about Accounting than the professor did.

Affinity and Katie hadn't many friends until the met Kimi and Koko, either, but for the past two years or so, their social life had become an active one thanks to the twins. There was always something interesting to do whenever Kimi and Koko were around. They'd been inside Kimi and Koko's office over to HDE and were fascinated by all they'd seen. Affinity and Katie wanted to be around Kimi and Koko at every chance and valued their opinions. They were ripe prospects in Naomi's mind's eye.

"What would be the first assignment handed to your handpicked interns?" Naomi asked of Kimi and Koko.

"Nothing major," Kimi responded as she placed a couple of sausage links onto a silver saucer and scooped up a portion of eggs. "We have this two hundred-thousand-dollar account set up on behalf of Guadalupe Cruz, remember? All that is needed is for someone to watch the interest payments on that investment and move a few stocks around every quarter. Me and Koko was thinking we could have Affinity and Katie manage those records while we upgrade the systems to take on the additional funds that'll be coming in."

"Going from six hundred and fifty thousand dollars per day to one million dollars per day is a hefty increase, momma," Koko chimed in as she poured herself a glass of orange juice. "We just wanna be sure we're handling the monies correctly to avoid an audit."

"Wise decision for the immediate foreseeable future," Naomi replied as she flipped a few pages in Loopy's portfolio. "I'll sign off on giving Affinity and Katie Guadalupe's portfolio to manage, but I want to add my own caveat—this will be a test of their resolve and dedication."

"What you have in mind, momma?" Koko asked. "Me and Kimi both figured that Loopy's portfolio would be enough since it's an offshore account."

"My friend Dunkirk is in the market looking to buy a home here in the United States. Let's give that job to Affinity and Katie as well. I want to compound the revenue and see how well those two handle over a million dollars' worth of finance located in two different parts of the world," Naomi stated as she placed Dunkirk's files before Kimi and Koko. "It's a go on Affinity and Katie," she confirmed. "Good job, ladies."

Just then, Martha emerged onto the balcony. "You wanted to see me, sis?" she asked as she eyed the spread on the table.

"Yes," Naomi replied. "Kimi? Koko? Could you give me and Martha a minute?"

"Sure, momma. We'll go call Affinity and Katie and let them know they have the internship," Kimi spoke on behalf of her and her twin.

When her daughters cleared out, Naomi turned to Martha and asked, "What do you think about the shootout in Brazil?"

Martha leaned back, removed her sunshades and said, "It was a bunch of cowboys looking to take down the Devereaux family as far as we know."

"You don't think there was more behind it?"

"What else could be taken from it, sis?"

"This Bridgette Fischer woman has been quiet as of late. Gacha doesn't even know where his wife is now. Tammy was an agent here in America, and we have the name Arata Moto on our radar. It's a good chance those Japanese are right here in America looking to retaliate over the loss of their sister."

"If they are, we can find them," Martha declared. "But, by right, isn't that a German problem? They did take the hit on Tammy Moto."

"But it was our men, Phillip and Grover, who did the deed, Martha. We also put the Germans on Bridgette's brothers up in New York, so we're just as culpable as our German allies and we run the same risks alongside them. I'm sensing more bloodshed here in America and I don't like it," Naomi pondered as she looked out over the land. "And there's something else that's bothering me about that sting down in Brazil," she added.

"Like what?" Martha asked as she grabbed a silver saucer and helped herself to a few scoops of cheese eggs a sausage patty.

"I told Barbara during our meeting at the Ramirez villa that she was a prospective target for sting kings. I think Bridgette was there to grab those five hundred pounds of heroin the Devereauxs had stored, only she got there too late. The product had already been loaded onto the freighter and she was not expecting the Devereaux family to have a small platoon guarding them. Now the product is coming to the United States in a few days."

"Ben already suggested to the Germans that they provide security for their product," Martha remarked.

"But I'm worried about our people as well. You have drivers in that area?" Naomi asked.

"I have three of my best drivers in northwest Florida. They're running loads from Pensacola to Jacksonville and back right now. Whoever's in town when the ship is unloaded will get the job."

"Okay, good. But I'm going to call Ben and get him to run things by the Germans again to be certain." Naomi replied. "You know, Martha? The higher up me and Doss went in this business I thought it would become easier. It's much harder than I thought when you're pulling the strings, though...especially when you care about the people working for you."

"We'll be okay, sis. We're Hollands. And we always come out on top," Martha ended as she went on and ate her breakfast. Neither Naomi nor Martha knew it at the time, but Naomi's phone call to Ben on this lovely Sunday morning would change the course of many lives over the next thirty-six hours and bring about deadly consequences that no one could have ever predicted nor expected.

CHAPTER THIRTY-NINE

THE COMING ATTRACTION

We boarded the G-550 and had just leveled off over Phoenix, ya' dig? A few hours ago, Naomi had called me and wanted me to run things by the Germans one more time before this shipment of heroin touchdown in few days or so. I called Faye up in Kansas, and she was just about to call me to put me up on some game by inviting me to Cherryvale. I knew she had an airstrip on her property so I decided to fly out. Before we touched down in Kansas, though, I decided to stop over in Ponca City. It'd been a while since my sons visited their people and being I had free time, I was planning on dropping them off with Henrietta at the ranch. I'd thought about bringing Katrina along, but that meant Faye would have to ride and I wasn't feeling that too much just yet. I downplayed the situation by telling Katrina that this would give her and Faye more time to continue bonding while the family went on an excursion for a day.

Don't get me wrong, I have no problems with Faye being around, I just felt it was too soon for her to get close to my people like that. Her time will come soon enough since she was helping Katrina cater Kimi's wedding anyway. I unbuckled my seatbelt and kicked back in the soft executive seats as Amber guided the plane through the clear blue morning skies. I had my sons, two-and-a-half-year-old Ben and ten-month-old Kenyan, with me, and Samantha had brought one-year-olds Gabby and Tabby along.

"You gone have your hands full on the ranch, Auntie," I said to Henrietta. "When all the kids get together you know how they do."

Henrietta laughed as she checked the children's seatbelts. They sat facing her in booster seats dozing off after only minutes in the sky. "Umm, hmm," Henrietta chuckled. "They look so peaceful now, but the floodgates will burst open when they lay eyes on Malaysia and Malara."

"Them the ring leaders right there," I laughed. "What Kimi and Koko call 'em when they all together?"

"The Short Legs Committee," me and Henrietta answered at the same time and laughed aloud.

"I talked to Yiska this morning, Ben. He asked about you again," Henrietta then said to me, changing up the entire mood.

"I know he did, Auntie. I'll make a trip there before the wedding to hollar at him and JunJie."

"Are you okay?" Henrietta asked as she looked over to me from across the aisle.

"Why you ask that, Henrietta?"

"Yiska said JunJie's sons have him worried about some of the things that's going on. They've been there quite a few times since the trip you made to Brazil he said."

"That's not my concern, Henrietta. They're entitled to visit JunJie as much as they like."

"What happened down there, Ben?"

I shook my head and looked away at that moment as I sat with my legs crossed. Henrietta worried way too much, but I'd be lying if I said she was off base each time she did so. This Bridgette Fischer woman may indeed be a problem, and losing a twenty-million-dollar load of product would indeed cause problems for the family if she were to pull the shit off. I couldn't tell Henrietta none of that, though, and I knew Yiska was sending an indirect message for me to be careful. "Nothing went down in Brazil that we need to worry about, Henrietta. Just some business the family gotta look into."

"Is that what this trip is all about?"

"Nahh, Auntie. I had to meet an associate near Oklahoma, so I thought it would be cool for you and the children to fly down to the ranch for the day and chill with the family."

Henrietta just stared at me through those probing brown eyes. "I always worry about you when you leave home, son. If I didn't care, I wouldn't ask, but I can't help myself."

I got up from my seat and plopped down beside Henrietta. "Remember when I was a boy and I first brought my puppy Ralo home?"

"Yeah," Henrietta smiled. "But, what's your point?"

"I remember you telling me that Ralo should sleep in the spare bedroom with you that first night so he won't mess up the carpet in my bedroom. You remember what I said back to you?"

"You said to let you take care of Ralo and not worry about the carpet," Henrietta said while staring at me with a look of uncertainty.

"You had that same look of doubt on your face twenty-seven years ago," I contentedly smiled. "Like you thought I didn't know what I was doing. But what happened with Ralo that night?"

"He pooped on the floor like I knew he was going to," Henrietta remarked with her hands spread. "If you were trying to make a point, you've done nothing but help prove mine, son," she smiled as the plane bounced slightly.

"Point is, you let me make that mistake and then helped me clean up the mess Ralo made to keep me out of trouble," I told Henrietta. "But now, as a man, the messes made are messes that I'm big enough and strong enough to clean up myself. You can't save me like you helped save me back then."

"The 'messes' today are way larger than Ralo, Ben. This is your life we're talking about here, not some doggy doo." Henrietta counseled me through a frown.

"I know, Auntie. I've made many mistakes along the way, but I'm good at what I do," I whispered as I looked into her eyes. "I'm not saying I'm the best, but I understand that I can't allow a mess to be created if I can prevent one. Ralo never dropped a deuce in my bedroom after that because I kept an eye on him, understand? I trained him not to do that on my carpet, or in the house because I realized the mistake I allowed him to make."

"That is the most God awful analogy I've ever heard in my life!" Henrietta exclaimed through a belly laugh. "You have good people around you is what you're trying to say? Is that it, son?" she asked as she dabbed a finger in one of the corners of her watery eyes. "You should read more, Ben. You aren't any good at metaphors in the least bit sense of the word. Go on, Shakespeare, with ya' bad self!"

I laughed and hugged my Aunt. I knew I was delivering a load of horse shit, but I'd accomplished my goal, which was to get her to smile and remove her mind from worrying about me like she always did. "I won't be gone long, Auntie," I said as I kissed her hand gently. "Don't worry about me, okay? I'm always careful. I promise you that."

"Fair enough," Henrietta smiled as she lay her head back and smiled down at her great nieces and nephews.

****

We landed at Ponca City Airport around noon time after a three hour flight. Amber brought the plane to halt before three of the family's black on black Suburbans. The door lowered and I could see Naomi, Kimi and Koko climbing out of one the SUVs wearing blue denim outfits and tan boots as Siloam and Montenegro and a couple more ranch hands stood by watching with shotguns strapped across their backs. I was leading the way, holding Kenyan and guiding Ben down the stairs when Tiva and Bay hopped out from the second Suburban with Spoonie and Tyke.

Tiva placed Malara and Malaysia on the ground and held their hands, preventing them from darting off. "Get the camera ready, Spoonie," she laughed.

"Let it go!" I heard Malaysia cry out as she jumped up and down in place while slapping at Tiva's hands.

"What I told you about bucking up to me? Calm it down!" Tiva scolded.

"But?" Malaysia whined as she pointed back at Tabby and Gabby, who were being held back by Samantha.

"Okay, go!" Bay said as she raised the camera.

Tiva released her grip and Malaysia and Malara took off running in our direction in their shorts and tank tops. "Cousinnnnn!" they yelled out together as they shuffled through the crowd and emerged out in the open.

Tabby and Gabby stood by smiling as Malaysia and Malara approached. Bay caught the images of the toddlers greeting one another. Tiva's daughters were brushing Tabby and Gabby's long, black hair back into place and straightening their clothes and talking toddler as Spoonie filmed the event. "You fly on it!" Malaysia smiled as she pointed up at the jet. "You fly?"

"Yeah, they fly with their momma," Samantha answered on

behalf of her daughters as she knelt down and kissed her cousins. "You wanna get on my plane, Malaysia?"

"No!" Malaysia snapped as lashed out at Samantha. "Hey, Ben!" she then waved at her older cousin.

Two-and-a-half-year-old Ben Junior was a laidback fella, much like his father. He gave a quick wave as he stood beside Big Ben in a pair of slacks and silk shirt, looking every bit the younger version of Ben Holland. He was more focused on all of the bigger folk around him and trying to make sense of where he was and who were the people before him and his daddy. He stepped closer to Ben and laid on his leg while watching everyone move about.

"No 'hey, Ben', you!" Samantha said, pretending to be angry as she raised a hand. "You hit me and we gone fight for real, you ole meanie!"

Malaysia backed away from Samantha and looked up at Spoonie. "Hey? Her not nice," she pouted.

"You was tryna hit me, girl!" Samantha laughed. "Okay, come give me a hug, baby," she said, drawing Malaysia back to her for a warm embrace.

Malaysia spread her arms and made swooshing sounds at that moment. "They fly!" she laughed. "Come on! Home!" she then said as she grabbed Tabby and Gabby's hands. "Come on, Ben!"

Malaysia, Malara, Tabby and Gabby walked amongst the adults patting one another playfully and laughing while being filmed, Ben Junior tailing his female cousins, taller than them all, and sporting a nonchalant attitude as if he'd done this all before.

Kimi and Koko walked up to the group and looked down at the five as they strode by like actors on the red carpet.

"Looka the Short Legs Committee!" Koko laughed. "Hey, y'all!"

"'Sup?" Ben Junior spoke softly.

"'Sup, playa?" Koko laughed aloud as she stood with her hands on her hips watching the children mosey along.

"Ben, y'all staying the night?" Kimi asked as she walked over the jet.

"And you knowwiiiiitttt!" I said through laughter as I hugged Kimi. "I know y'all got a few steaks laying around that ranch y'all not putting ta' use."

"We may be able to work something out, homeboy," Kimi responded as she greeted Amber.

Naomi stood off in the distance leaning up against the hood of the lead SUV as she watched the family. It was always a big deal whenever we flew in from Arizona flew for a visit. These moments were far different from the business trips I made, which could be a little tense at times. The last time I'd flown in, I returned with a wounded Victor and had escaped being killed in an intense gunfight down in Brazil. This time around, it was all about family, so time was taken to allow the members to mingle before returning to the ranch where the festivities would continue.

"Naomi, how're you?" Henrietta called out as the two of us walked over to Naomi.

"Hey, Henrietta. I didn't see you over there, woman. How's everything?" Naomi responded as she gave me and Henrietta a quick hug and a kiss.

"I've been okay. It's good to be here, but this humidity is stifling. Reminds me of Louisiana."

"Wait until you get a taste of the mosquitos," Naomi chided.

"Let me tell you something, girl…I'd rather mosquitos than the scorpions in Arizona any day. One nearly pricked me inside the pool house down there last week!"

"Shut the front door!" Naomi laughed. "There's bottled water in the back seat of the SUV here. Make yourself comfortable."

When Henrietta cleared out, Naomi walked over to the rest of the family. "Alright, everybody!" she said aloud. "Let's load 'em up! Me and Ben will be back in a few hours and we'll prepare dinner!"

Naomi never said she was flying with me to Kansas, but I ain't bother saying nothing about it. We was loading the children up into the SUVs, but Malaysia and Malara insisted on watching the plane once they saw it moving. Samantha was in the process of guiding it down the runway to its turnaround point to take off and the twins were fascinated. Tiva relented and the children were unloaded once again and stood by watching as me and Naomi climbed aboard. They were all waving as the doors were raised and the plane began rolling down the strip of concrete.

Samantha turned the plane around, dropped a pair of sunshades over her eyes and radioed the tower. "Wild Child, ready for takeoff on runway one," she said through her mouthpiece.

"Copy that, Wild Child. Skies are clear!"

"Let's give 'em a show!" Samantha said seriously as she twisted knobs and pushed forward on the throttle. The plane began rolling forward, headed north, and off in the distance to my right, I could see the family standing out before the SUVs. They began waving as we grew closer, but by the time we passed them, they were a blur. I looked back and could now see them waving as we took to the skies, headed for Cherryvale, Kansas.

Once we'd leveled off, I looked over to Naomi and asked, "What's with you flying up to Kansas, Auntie?"

"I've never met our allies, Ben. I figured what day better than today? It was bound to happen, son. No big deal."

I nodded and kicked back the remainder of the flight. It was a short one being Cherryvale was only a hundred and twenty miles northeast of Ponca City. We arrived forty-five minutes later and Samantha circled the property before landing. From the air, I could see a white and blue Cessna parked off to the side. I remember that plane being flown by the Governor of Iowa back in January. There were also a number of patrol cars parked behind the home. The main thing that caught my attention, though, was the barn Faye owned. It was burned down to the ground and the remaining wood was pushed up into a single pile. I wondered what was up with that as we sailed over the property. I'd called Faye while at the airport back in Ponca City and she told me to expect what I was witnessing, except for the barn, and it would be clear to land once I saw someone step out into the runway and wave a red flag.

Samantha circled a second time before receiving the signal. She watched as a lone woman guided a horse onto the runway and waved a red flag before guiding the horse back out into the pasture. We landed and pulled up behind the Bender home where nearly two dozen women from different races, some wearing sheriff's uniforms and gun holsters, milled about on the patio. Two grills were going and there was plenty of liquor circulating. The door began lowering and I went and stood at the exit as music, that of drums and guitars with heavy bass, shit like that, filled my ears…"*…every mornin' before breakfast…I don't want no coffee or tea… just me and my good buddy Wiser…that's all I ever need… 'cause I drink alone…*"

I was greeted by Faye Bender when the doors descended and my eyes fell upon what looked like a rock concert going down on the patio. Faye had this big smile on her face and her cheeks were rosy red as she stood beside the stairs rocking her hips in a pair of daisy duke shorts and sandals. I could tell she was a little lit, as I'd never seen her dance let alone vibe to any kind of music.

"You didn't say I was being invited to a party, Faye," I remarked over the music while walking down the stairs. I looked around at all the revelry with a slick smile on my face. Had I not trusted Faye the way I do, I would've never gave Samantha the go ahead to land. You can't be afraid in this business, though, even in the face of what may seem to be that of uncertain circumstances. The Germans weren't doing nothing more than what me and my people were doing back in Ponca City in my eyes. The only difference was that most of the people here were ruthless butchers. They kill anybody and don't even think twice about it.

"Yes, Ben," Faye laughed as she took a seat on the jet's stairs before me. "This, this is a party like no other and we're only just beginning!" she yelled out over the music as she stood once again and downed the remnants of what I presumed was champagne.

"Our legs need to stretch and it done got hot inside this plane," Naomi said at that moment as she emerged from the plane with Samantha and Amber following her lead.

"Faye, this is my Aunt Naomi Holland, my sister Samantha and our friend Amber."

"Well now," Faye smiled as she shook Naomi's hand. "I apologize for the lack of consideration, Ms. Naomi," she sincerely remarked. "If I knew you were coming I would've been more formal in attire."

"No need to apologize, Ms. Bender," Naomi countered. "It's good to see people in this profession that we're aligned with enjoying themselves."

"You're gonna wanna celebrate, too, Naomi," Faye giddily remarked. "Your nephew provided us with the leverage we needed to finally take down a common foe. I'll fill you in on everything that's going on shortly. There's champagne and bar-b-cue on the patio. Make yourselves at home," she added before walking off.

Me and my family walked up on the patio, where the music grew louder, and were greeted by some of Faye's people. I was handed a cold Heineken by an officer as she stepped aside and let us through. Off to my left I could see a band playing out on the patio. Out in front was a voluptuous middle-aged brunette strumming an electric guitar.

"That's Beverly Battle!" Amber yelled out as she marched through the crowd while wiggling her hips with a hand gripping a Heineken raised in the air. "Whoooo!" she yelled out as she rocked out before the woman as the drummer sung on..."*...yeah, the other day I got invited to a party...but I stayed home instead...just me and my pal Johnny Walker...and his brothers Blackie and Red...and we drank alone...*"

I looked over the crowd and squint my eyes at the drummer. It was Jane Dow performing. "What's that song?" I leaned down and asked Amber.

"That's George Thorogood's song I Drink Alone!" Amber replied over the music. "That drummer and Beverly is jammin'! That drummer can really sing! The whole band rockin' out!" she complimented.

I took a swig of my beer and held it up high, catching Jane's attention. She twirled her drumstick briefly to acknowledge me and continued banging the wood as Beverly Battle rocked on with a solo. There was a saxophonist playing along with Jane and Beverly, and their keyboardist was sitting with a pair of sunshades covering his eyes swaying side to side like Ray Charles as he tapped his feet. It was always a moment to make you pause when Jane was performing. Today was no different. I'd never heard this song before, but everything was on point. The entire was crowd was jamming. Naomi was even getting down with a step or two over the saxophones.

"That's my family over there jammin' got dammit," she said as she danced in place while holding onto a glass of champagne as Jane sung on..."*...yeah, my whole family done gave up me...and it makes me feel all so bad...the only one who will hang out with me...is my dear Old Granddad...and we drank alone...*"

Beverly came back in with her guitar and the bass kicked in. I began nodding my head until the song ended, when it did, Jane hopped from behind her drum set and ran in our direction. "Ben! Naomi! What are y'all doing here!" she asked excited and out of breath as the crowd applauded.

"What you doing here, girl?" I asked as I gave the budding rock star a hug.

"I came here with Beverly Battle to perform! We're taking a break from recording for a couple of days! This is our first single off the album! Jason didn't tell you?"

"Nah, but it's all good." I was glad that Faye was trusting enough to have Jane over to her home. That meant things were still good between the two families in my book. Jane took off running back to the patio and mixed in with the crowd.

"Mister Holland," an older woman said to me as she extended her hand. "Bonita Bender. I'm Faye's sister. I've met you once."

"Yeah, back in January," I responded as I shook the woman's hand.

"You're staying for the celebration tomorrow morning?"

Before I could inquire about this celebration, another voice yelled out over the crowd. "That's Ben Holland over there? I know that ain't Ben Holland over there!" I looked around Bonita and saw a light-brown-skinned woman with pressed black hair walking my way. She was slender and a little on the tall side, and she looked familiar.

"Where I know you from?" I asked unsure.

"You owe me a contract off Techwood in Atlanta from November '92, man," the woman laughed.

"Vivian King," I smiled through a nod as I laughed out loud. "What up, girl?" I asked while hugging her briefly. "It's been almost seventeen years since I last seen you!"

"A lot went down went down, brer. Tanya went to jail that day and we lost touch after that. How you know my people?" Vivian asked as she stared me up and down. "I heard about Manny way after he was put in the ground. I was in Cincinnati back in '99."

"Me and Faye linked up on some old shit, ya' dig? I'll run it down to ya' later on. But, what's the party for, though?"

"Them bitches killed my sister, Zelda, man," Vivian sighed.

"But we gone get us some payback tomorrow, ya' feel me?"

"How so?" I asked curiously.

"That is why I called you here, Ben," Faye answered, still laughing. "Lisa Vanguard is going down tomorrow and it is going to be fun to watch it happen!"

Lisa Vanguard wasn't really a problem for me in the big scheme of things. The woman did do some good in her life from my point of view. I mean, she did help take down Manhattan up in Wichita once we'd found Samantha. But I also knew she'd been looking into Naomi. That's how Laddy latched on to Bay and Tiva. She then threw Asa Spade's trial to get him back on the streets to kill him, and the ultimate was that she'd killed Faye's best friend, son and husband up in Iowa. Those two had been battling one another for decades now, and by the looks of this party, Faye was about to win the final showdown and settle the score once and for all.

"Let's talk inside," Faye suggested, shaking me from my thoughts.

We made our way further through the crowd and I got to see close up how the Germans were celebrating what was to come. Whatever was going down was huge. Pictures of Lisa Vanguard with a Hitler mustache were laying around and torn FBI jackets with the letters crossed out were being worn by some. Everybody was laughing and joking, drinking dancing and eating. There was a large countdown clock on a mantle that was ticking down. The time remaining was fourteen and a half hours, which would land it on five 'o' clock central time tomorrow morning.

Once inside, me, Naomi and Faye talked amid the faint sounds of the party unfolding outside. Faye could barely contain her joy. She was barely focusing on the conversation, but I knew she was alert. "I really wish, I wish we've could've met under calmer circumstances, Ms. Naomi, but this day," she sighed. "I've been waiting over thirty years and I…can…not…not be happy to save my life! I just can't!" she laughed through heaving. "God is good," she said as she placed her hands on her hips and licked her lips while looking away from me and Naomi.

Naomi smiled and said, "We won't stay long, Ms. Bender. We ourselves have a day with the family to enjoy as well. Maybe later on, after everything settles down, we can have a formal meeting of the minds."

"Yes! We, we will do that," Faye said as she dropped her smile and cleared her throat. She tried to remain serious, but she just couldn't manage it as that wide smile reappeared once more. She was almost in tears over the joy she felt and it was becoming infectious to me and Naomi both.

"Quickly," Naomi resumed. "We just wanted to make sure that you have a security team in place for this next shipment. I know you loss an important member in Tanya Weinberger. If you need our assistance we can offer it if you like."

Now, Faye's smile vanished. "I really appreciate you coming here to tell me that, Naomi," she sincerely remarked. "We have a team that's capable enough to handle security, though. Once we get the product moving again, we'll turn our attention to Bridgette Fischer and Arata Moto. That is where we can use your help."

"When you come up with a plan of action, let us know," my aunt responded to Faye. "There shouldn't be any trouble with the first few loads of heroin because it is assumed Bridgette doesn't know the name of the ship or the port of call just yet. But you can never be certain."

"Right. And even if she doesn't know, it won't take long for her to figure it out," Faye pondered while nodding her head in deep thought.

"We're going to put you in touch with the Asians who did the hit on Tammy," I told Faye. "They'll be in a better position to help you track down Arata Moto. Y'all should work together on taking them down."

"I am in agreement with you on that, Mister Holland," Faye nodded. "We'll meet with your people once we secure shipment. Give a few days after delivery. Where's a good place to meet?"

"San Francisco," Naomi chimed in. "We have a base set up there. You can also discuss future shipments."

"Deal," Faye replied as she shook me and Naomi's hands. "Do you two care to stay a while?"

"No" Naomi appreciated. "Go on and enjoy yourself, Ms. Bender."

"Are you early risers, then?" Faye asked as she guided us back towards the patio doors.

"We are," Naomi answered.

"Good," Faye smiled as she opened one of the doors, letting the sounds of the party back into the home. "Have your televisions on CNN at five tomorrow morning if you're so kind to oblige. You can celebrate with us then. We're going to pop popcorn and drink to the occasion," she ended as she walked us back out to the plane to see us off once Samantha had turned it around.

I left the Bender farm under calm spirits. According to Faye, the party had been thrown for Lisa Vanguard. She wouldn't go into detail about it, only telling me and Naomi to be up in time to watch CNN news. I looked out at the blue skies that were creating a picture of serenity above the violence on the ground below and wondered what Lisa was doing at this exact moment. Did she know how different things would be for her come morning? Could she see or feel the impending pressure she would be placed under in a matter of hours? How would she deal with it? This game has a way of sometimes giving back to you all of the horrors you dish out to your enemies and then some. If that fate becomes Lisa's reality, then she was in for fire and brimstone given all the hell she'd raised during her tenure. Only time would tell what and how things would go down with the woman, and whether she knew it or not, Lisa Vanguard had only thirteen hours left before she found herself in a world of shit.

CHAPTER FORTY

DIRTY LITTLE SECRETS

"Okay, it's one fifty west coast time. At last check, our arrestee is home alone at this hour," Laddy Norcross remarked as he stood before eight federal agents inside a small, windowless office located at FBI headquarters in Seattle, Washington. "I have to state that we're apprehending a dangerous suspect and the exercising of caution is a must on this job," he continued as he stood before a wall-mounted laminated map, using a clicker to highlight the downtown skyscraper he and his team were going to storm. "I want three men on the streets, four in the lobby, and I'll go up with another agent to assist me in making the arrest," he told his men as they sat in high school desks inside the cramped office that was more like a classroom.

"What's my position?" Sandra Cordova asked as she sat in the front row before Laddy.

"You will remain in the sport utility vehicle until I emerge with Lisa Vanguard," Laddy answered casually. "Now, this is to be a low key arrest, free of media on our part. We're under the radar and I expect to keep it that way," he continued speaking as he checked the time. "Okay, it is two a.m. and we need to get going soon. Twenty minutes to departure," he declared as he donned his FBI jacket.

Sandra sat and watched disconsolately as Laddy's team disbursed inside the room. There was a long table lined with twelve gauges, and the men began picking up shotguns and shells and loading the artillery while discussing the upcoming job. Over the racking of shotguns, Sandra stood up from the high school desk and pulled Laddy aside. "What are you doing?" she asked lowly.

"What do you mean by 'What am I doing?'" Laddy asked as he calmly slid a magazine into a M-4 rifle.

"You're keeping me out of the action, Laddy," Sandra complained. "You know how much this arrest means to me. I want to be there to see the look on Lisa Vanguard's face when you arrest her this morning!"

"This is a sensitive task, Sandra," Laddy stated. "A dangerous one as well. I'm trying to keep you out of harm's way."

"I can handle myself just fine, Laddy!" Sandra scoffed under her breath. "After all we've learned from Senator Slack? I should be there and you know it! You know how much this case means to me!"

Laddy and Sandra had both met briefly with Senator Slack Saturday morning at her home in DC. She'd given them all the information needed to go after Lisa Vanguard, but she'd left out one thing: the video of Laddy and Sandra together. The State Trooper knew nothing of the coercion Laddy was under, and he refused to enlighten the woman at the present time.

"I know very well how much this case means to you, Sandra. Which is why I don't want you involved initially," Laddy countered as he let the shotgun fall to his side. "You're too emotional under the circumstances. I'm not going to risk having you run in there gung-ho with guns-a-blazing just to see the look on Lisa's face. She'll have her day in court. You can gloat then," he assured as he took a step back and walked past Sandra. "Alright, boys let's make this happen!" he commanded as he draped his assault rifle over his broad shoulders.

Officers out in the main hall stepped aside when Laddy and his team walked through the double doors leading towards the exit. Like Roman soldiers, they walked up the middle of the hall in their green FBI jackets and black slacks with their heads bowed in deep thought over the task that lay ahead with Laddy leading the way. This team of federal agents had been tasked with one of the most difficult jobs inside of law enforcement: that of executing a federal murder warrant on one of their own. Lisa Vanguard was a prestigious member of their community. She had royalty status operating as an agent and prosecutor for the Federal Bureau of Investigations. She'd conducted field operations in all corners of the United States and had taken down some of the most violent and cunning criminals in the nation. All had been tainted, however, given the evidence Laddy had received, and per the law, Lisa Vanguard had to be stripped of power and taken into custody.

Sandra tailed the men with her twelve gauge draping her side.

She sported a frown, disappointed over the fact that she would not be allowed to join Laddy on Lisa's floor to bring her into custody. Rain pelted her black windbreaker as she emerged from the building. Laddy's team was climbing into a couple of black Suburbans as fog rolled across the parking lot. He stood beside the front passenger seat of his SUV as Sandra walked past him and opened the back door. "I'm sorry for downplaying your emotions back there," he told Sandra. "I...I don't want nothing to happen to you that's all," he admitted.

"We were partners in this, Laddy," Sandra whispered as the SUV's engine cranked up. "Whatever we did off the clock? Should be left off the clock and we should just do our jobs. I was good enough to lay beside you the past couple of days here, but not worthy enough to work alongside you today. I think I understand what's going on here."

"No, you don't," Laddy whispered as he stared into his mistress's eyes. "I love you. Understand that, why don't you?"

Sandra had no reply. She was left with a warm, softened heart and a blank stare over Laddy's remark. "My makeup is running, and it's not because of the rain," she confessed.

"We'll talk about it later, baby," Laddy smiled under the light rainfall. "Tell you what?" he then came back with. "I won't handcuff Lisa until I bring her down. I'll let you do the honors by cuffing her as I read her the Miranda rights, but you have to stay in the SUV until I bring her down. Deal?"

"Deal," Sandra smiled. "Thank you," she added as she climbed into the backseat of the Suburban.

"Agent Norcross!" an agent called out as he ran down the stairs. "Agent Norcross?"

"What is it?" Laddy asked as he was preparing to climb into the front passenger seat of his SUV.

"There was a discrepancy on the murder warrant against Agent Lisa Vanguard"

"What kind of a discrepancy?"

"The homicides occurred in Kansas City, Kansas. Somebody documented Kansas City, Missouri. The secretary is preparing a new warrant now. It'll be another twenty minutes before you can leave."

Laddy checked his watched and saw that it was now 2:25 in the morning. It was a twenty minute ride over to Lisa's skyscraper. A twenty minute delay would place him on the block at 3:05 in the morning—ten minutes behind schedule. He'd thought about going ahead without the proper warrant, but Lisa was a savage when it came to the law. This one technicality she would undoubtedly uncover and use to earn herself an acquittal.

"Shit!" Laddy snapped as he eased back out of his SUV. "Sandra has an interview to do in thirty minutes. Let's see if we can expedite this new warrant because it places me and her both behind schedule!" he barked angrily as he trotted back inside FBI headquarters.

****

Lisa was over to her apartment in Seattle, Washington sound asleep when her phone began ringing. She slowly opened her eyes and focused through the darkness to check the time and saw that it was 3:02 in the morning, west coast time. The neon green light lit up her face as she reached out and grabbed the phone. "Vanguard speaking," she yawned as she fell back onto her plush pillow.

Raiden emerged from the home he and Arata shared and trotted over to a waiting BMW 750 series. "We have to leave Seattle this morning, Lisa. We have a jet to take you into Canada. We can hide out there until we figure out our next move," he stressed as he climbed into the backseat, slammed the door and tapped the headrest, forcing the driver to speed off with him and two more soldiers inside.

"Canada?" Lisa questioned as she sat upright in her bed. "What's going on, Raiden?" she asked confused while clicking on her night light. "We're expecting a shipment today."

"You haven't heard," Raiden nodded somberly. "The ship is being rerouted to San Francisco. Arata will handle things there, but you must leave. You need to turn on the television and put it on CNN. Gather your things while you do so and we'll meet you out in front of the condominiums. Move fast because we must leave!" he ordered before ending the call.

Lisa jumped out of bed and used the remote to turn on the television. She flipped through the channels until she found CNN and saw an image of herself sporting sunshades and her FBI badge under the headline *FBI Agents Caught on Tape Discussing*

Murders Committed.

"What," Lisa gasped as she turned up the volume and listened to the recording. "No!" she screamed out as she heard Tammy Moto's voice.

"How did you get back at Gayle McPherson?" Lisa heard Tammy ask as she ran to her closet and snatched down a leather pantsuit. She also grabbed a pair of leather matching boots and began dressing in a panicked state. "She didn't. I trusted that bitch! My best friend sold me out!" she screamed as she listened to what she knew was to come as she remembered the day she and Tammy had discussed the murders over to Tammy's home in New Jersey.

"I killed Gayle's parents in Kansas City, Kansas. Dressed up like an agent, because I was only a cop at the time? And got their address from some guy over to the Kansas City, Missouri police department. A Cordova or some guy," Lisa heard herself say through laughter as she ran over and pressed the code to unlock her safe.

"Do you want more wine?" Lisa heard Tammy asked while sliding into her pants.

"You're trying to get me (beeped) up or something, Tammy?" the stunned FBI agent heard her herself asking.

"You're already (beeped) up, partner. Tell me more of your dirty little secrets," Tammy was heard laughing.

"This is a stunning news story that has been leaked to us this morning," a CNN reporter was then heard remarking as the recording faded into the background. "I can't cite the source because we don't know where or who the source is. And, and, not that we would," she added as she shuffled papers, "but this package landed on our desk an hour ago and we're still dissecting it. We have some more edits to play and a few references listed in the documents that we received along with the recording. One is Sergeant Sandra Cordova, the purported daughter of the officer who met with FBI Agent Lisa Vanguard some thirty years ago. Do we have her? Do we have Cordova on the line?" the reporter asked as she held an earpiece up to her ear.

Lisa was furious, but even more so, she was humiliated. She was dumping piles of money into a briefcase along with extra magazines for her Uzi while listening to her dirty laundry being aired out for all the world to hear and it was crushing her soul. Cameras were set on the Department of Justice and reporters were camped out front waiting to speak with the attorney general or anyone from the upper echelon of the FBI to gain further knowledge of this budding news story that was sure to end her career in government.

"Okay. Cordova is unavailable," the reporter stated. "We have, we have now our CNN law correspondent Dante O'Malley aboard to help us understand the implications behind this stunning revelation. Again, CNN has obtained tapes of a decorated FBI agent discussing murders she's committed alongside her deceased partner and DC is waking up to a law enforcement scandal of epic proportions. O'Malley, are you there?"

"I'm here," Dante` remarked over the phone. Lisa looked up to see the image of her longtime rival as he sat inside his home office up in Boston, Massachusetts.

"Okay, Mister O'Malley. What are the implications behind these recordings?" the reporter asked.

"The implications are severe," Dante` answered as he cleared his throat. "We have a federal agent and prosecutor admitting to murders she herself committed. It is undeniably Agent Vanguard's voice because I received the same recordings and have had time to dissect all of the audio. Her partner Tammy Moto made sure to drop names and I'm guessing that was to be used as some form of insurance on Agent Moto's behalf if ever Agent Vanguard doubled-crossed her in some way."

"And let me state for the record that Agent Tammy Moto was killed in New Jersey a couple of months ago and that case is still ongoing," the news anchor chimed in. "Now, O'Malley, you said that Agent Vanguard was a prosecutor. How will that affect past cases or any arrests she's made as of late?"

"It's all been contaminated," Dante` stated. "It's obvious Agent Moto and Agent Vanguard were engaged in illegal activity from extortion to drug dealing and up to and including murder. This is devastating for past convictions and any upcoming trials. People may very well walk over these circumstances and I'm sure there will be appeals filed across the country from numerous inmates inside of federal holding facilities."

"Jesus," the anchor sighed as she rubbed her temples. "Okay, okay, we have to take a quick—no commercial!" she suddenly blurted out as she looked into the camera. "No commercials! We have Senator Willameena Slack, Democrat Senator from Louisiana who sits on the Foreign Relations Subcommittee. For those that don't know, the FRS oversees in part, investigations into criminal activities throughout the western hemisphere. Cartels included," the anchor was sure to add. "Good morning, Senator Slack."

"Good morning," Willie said as she sat in inside her home office.

"What, what can you tell us about this breaking news story?"

Lisa stood up and rushed to her nightstand where she grabbed a mini-submachine Uzi and racked it. Her phone rung at that moment and she saw that it was Raiden. "Yeah? I'm on my way down," she said as her heart palpated. Lisa was inclined to leave, but she had to pause to listen to the Senator who'd taken her down on this day before she left.

"What I can tell you is that I've received the same information as Dante` O'Malley, CNN, MSNBC and Fox News. This story is breaking across this nation and it is my allegation having listened to the recordings that Agent Lisa Vanguard is a rogue Agent. She has been stripped of her power. Access to all government facilities and websites is hereby denied. She is now a wanted civilian criminal in lieu of five counts of murder on American citizens and she has also been implicated in the death of her partner Tammy Moto," Willie threw in for good measure. "Lisa Vanguard is to be considered armed and dangerous and currently ranks as number five on the FBI's top ten most wanted list as of this morning," she added, doing all she could to hide the smirk and joy coursing through her veins as she derailed Lisa Vanguard's entire career on national television.

"The trust towards law enforcement is already at an all-time low and this does nothing to help stem the tide of public distrust," Dante` chimed in, compounding the matter. "When we as American citizens can no longer trust the chosen best amongst us to uphold the law who can we trust? Agent Vanguard is a disgrace to the badge and must be apprehended. I suggest she turn herself in and save us all the time and expense of having to track her down," he finished.

"We're expecting to hear from Attorney General Eric Holder in the upcoming minutes, but we have more of the recordings to come and it is astounding the level of corruption that this agent was engaged in. Stay with us as we take a quick break and get more from Senator Slack and our political correspondent, Boston Attorney Dante` O'Malley," the anchor concluded as the program went to commercial.

Lisa was shaken out of her boots over the bombshell that had exploded in her lap. In an instant, her entire course of life had been altered. She knew what lay on those recordings per the conversations she'd had with Tammy up in Philadelphia. Senator Slack said she was wanted on five counts of murder. That meant she'd had to have heard the recording of Lisa talking about the hits against the La Rocca brothers up in Pittsburgh and the Ricky Gross murder she'd committed with Tammy Moto at her side. She tucked her mini Uzi into the back of her leather jacket along with several extra magazines and stormed out of her condominium, leaving the television on and everything outside of the $150,000 dollars she had stashed behind in her wake.

****

As Lisa made her way down from her condo, several miles away, Laddy Norcross and Sandra Cordova were leading a three-carload team of federal agents over to Lisa's place to make the arrest on Senator Slack's behalf. They'd been delayed at headquarters awaiting the new warrant, but they were now on their way. The streets of Seattle were empty and dampened with a light ran as the caravan of black on black Excursions with dark tint rounded the corner onto the street that led to Lisa's skyscraper.

Laddy racked his M-4 in seemingly slow-motion as he pondered what lay ahead as he sat in the passenger seat. He knew Lisa was corrupt, but never had he imagined her to be a serial killer toting a badge. He'd heard the tapes Saturday past inside Senator Slack's home office right alongside Sandra and was left in shock over hearing his former partner's confession to countless atrocities. The price for letting Bay and T-top walk on RJ's murder was well-worth it in his eyes as Lisa was one who swore by the law to uphold it and protect American citizens from the criminal element. Now, it was plain to see that Lisa Vanguard herself was the criminal element he'd sworn to protect America from all his life.

Sandra sat in the backseat behind Laddy with a twelve gauge resting in her lap. After thirty-plus years, she was on the verge of solving the mystery that'd haunted her father the remainder of his life right up until his death. He'd been right about the federal agent that had visited him back in 1976 the whole time, although no one had never bothered listening to him. Lisa Vanguard had indeed murdered two people in Kansas City, Kansas and set their bodies afire, however, and today was to be a highlight in her career. A tribute to her father once she got to place the handcuffs on Lisa Vanguard.

****

Just up the street, the elevator doors had opened in the lobby. Lisa had her Uzi cocked and ready, expecting to be greeted by a platoon of law enforcement. She was prepared to go out in a blaze of glory, but instead, she found a serene, empty luxurious area that had one lone clerk and an armed security guard at the front desk chatting it up over the quiet. After concealing her Uzi once again, she stepped off the elevator and hastily made her way through the lobby. She pushed the tinted doors open and looked around, spotting the Moto brothers' 750 BMW parked across the street. A smile crept across her face as she stepped out onto the sidewalk. Headlights off to her left caught her attention at that moment. She recognized the vehicles right away and pulled her Uzi.

Laddy hopped out of the lead Excursion before it ever rolled to a halt. "Lisa!" he yelled out loud as he approached the woman.

Lisa opened fire on Laddy, but he ducked behind a partition. Sandra emerged from the back of the Excursion at that moment with her twelve gauge racked and raised, but Lisa moved to the side and sprayed her with a round of bullets and ducked back inside the building.

"What was that?" the armed guard inside the lobby asked the clerk as he placed his hand atop his Glock .9 and peered out into the street.

Lisa emerged through the rotating door where she and the security guard stared one another down. "Freeze!" the security guard ordered as he pulled his service pistol.

Lisa had the ups on the man, however; she sprayed the security guard while he was pulling his pistol and he dropped to the floor in a mangled heap. "Move!" Lisa commanded the clerk as she motioned her gun towards the condominium's main office and sealed the door shut behind her.

The rogue agent looked around the office, which was more like a penthouse suite with its contemporary furniture, soft carpet and bookshelves. A television was on in the room, CNN, and as Lisa began barricading herself inside the office in preparation for what she knew was now a hostage situation, she was forced to watch as Senator Slack and Dante` O'Malley continued dissecting her criminal career before the world.

"The killings, according to the audio, date back to the time of the Pittsburgh mafia," Senator Slack was heard by Lisa as she guided her terrified hostage past a tall ladder and lighting and forced her down onto the couch.

"That would be the LaRocca brothers, Audi and Austell," Dante` let it be known. "I'm sure Pittsburghers remember the infamous case where the men were found murdered inside their baseball suite. We have audio of Agent Vanguard admitting she killed those men as well."

"What is all this material?" Lisa asked her hostage as she eyed the ladder, tall lighting and long lightbulbs laying on the floor.

"The maintenance crew was replacing the lightbulbs," the hostage answered through trembling lips as she huddled on the couch. She removed some of her blonde hair and asked, "Are you going to kill me?"

"I can't answer that right now," Lisa said, nearly out of breath as she began pacing the floor.

Raiden and his goons, meanwhile, remained idle for the moment as they watched federal agents hop out of the other two SUVs and storm the building. An H-1 Hummer pulled up at that moment and the back window rolled down.

"Lisa's finished," Bridgette Fischer said to Raiden as she stared down into his BMW. "We should leave now."

"We can't just leave her." Raiden countered.

"Yuh strike on 'Murrican soil yuh violate Yakuza law. Yuh can't beat the federal gov'ment hur anway. Feel no way about it 'cuz Lisa Vanguard dun served her purpose tuh tha' crew. Let us move on," she ended as her Hummer rode off smoothly with Raiden following her lead, both gangsters leaving Lisa to sort out the mess she now found herself in over trying to backdoor Senator Slack.

Laddy, meanwhile, lay over a wounded Sandra calling for help, dialing 911. The state trooper was bleeding from her left leg, but she was still coherent. "Did we get Vanguard?" Sandra asked as she clutched Laddy's hands with hers.

Laddy had seen Lisa run back into building, but he knew the woman wasn't hit or captured as of yet. "We'll get her," he told Sandra. "You just hang in there, baby. Don't, don't you die on me! Not after all we've been through!" he cried lowly.

Sandra smiled and said, "She shot my vest first. That saved me. It's just a leg wound. I'll be fine, love. Now, my father can rest peacefully. Go get that bitch."

"I told you to stay in the car until I secured her!" Laddy yelled aloud as the remaining team of agents began to secure the scene and call for a negotiator.

"I needed...I needed something big to say for the interview," Sandra joked. "I'm sorry," she said as she lay in wait for an ambulance.

CHAPTER FORTY-ONE
THE FED PARTY

"Reports are coming from Seattle that a shootout has occurred outside of a skyscraper where Federal Agent Lisa Vanguard is purportedly holed up in the lobby's main office with a hostage under her control," a news reporter from CNN disclosed.

"Keine Möglichkeit, wird sie es dort machen. Ich hoffe, sie stirbt einen langsamen Tod." (No way will she make it out there. I hope she dies a slow death.) Faye Bender said through a smirk as she lined up a shot on the pool table inside the room.

"Tausend Dollar sie aufgeben." (Thousand dollars she surrender.) Maggie chimed in as she dipped her hand into a bowl of buttered popcorn.

"Ich nehme das Wetten und heben Sie weitere Tausend" (I'll take that bet and raise you another thousand.) Bonita answered as she pulled out a knot of money. *"Wenn Vanguard ein Cop shot können Sie glauben, dass Sie raid, Büro und den Kopf abschlagen."* (If Vanguard shot a cop you can believe they will raid that office and knock her head off.)

Cikala sparked up a blunt and blew the tip before passing it to Maggie. "Y'all want some more beer?" she said through a deep cough as she held onto a cue stick.

"Champagne for me," Faye remarked as she sank a cue ball in the middle pocket.

"I'll get it," Sascha chimed in. "The television is boring me."

"What?" Cikala laughed. "This is like the best reality show ever, girl!"

"She's going to kill herself, watch!" Sascha said as she walked out of the playroom.

491

"Und es würde nicht zu einem besseren Menschen passiert, wenn es sich um wahr zu sein! Ich hoffe, dass Sie es!" (And it wouldn't have happened to a better person if it were to be true! I'm hoping for it!) Faye laughed as she walked around the pool table trying to figure out her next shot.

The Germans were having a private party for Lisa Vanguard. They'd stayed up all night carousing, napping on and off along the way, as their time clock ticked down. They were all there to witness the breaking news when it aired at five a.m. on the dot. Smoke was in the air, laughter abounded, and bets were being made over Vanguard's fate. This was by far, one of the happiest days of their lives. To see their mortal enemy holed up like a rat and unable to escape was joy beyond compare. Sascha returned with a cold six pack and a fresh bottle of champagne and the party continued on as the image of a helicopter hovering over the building and shining a light down onto the entrance of the skyscraper in Seattle appeared on the television an hour after the news had first broken across the nation.

****

Over to Cincinnati, Boogie lay in her bed with Popeye at her side. The two had awakened around four in the morning to wait for the appointed time and they'd been rewarded with a sight that now had Boogie smiling through her sorrow. Word had come down that Brenda had been killed in Philadelphia on Saturday past and it'd relieved Boogie a great deal. Her mother's killer had been taken down, and now the crème de la crème was on the verge of getting her comeuppance as she stood by holed up like a sewer rat caught in a PVC pipe with hungry feral cats waiting on both ends.

"Es gibt noch mehr von Ihnen heraus dort, wissen Sie?" (There's more of them out there, you know?) Boogie declared as she lay in Popeye's arms with her head in his bare chest.

"Die Moto Brüder." (The Moto brothers.) Popeye remarked as he ran his hands through his woman's coarse, tan hair while staring at the helicopter circling above the standoff.

"Und Bridgette Fischer." (And Bridgette Fischer.) Helen added. *"Dieser Krieg ist erst am Anfang. Ich möchte Ihnen allen für das, was sie für meine Mutter war tot."* (This war is just beginning. I want them all dead for what they did to my mother.) *"Wake Me Wenn es vorbei ist."* (Wake me when it's over.) she ended as she closed her eyes and dozed off.

"Yeeesss indeed," Martha sang as she sat in the theater room with Naomi and Ben watching the events unfold on CNN. "This like, remember The Brown Hornet from Fat Albert, y'all?" she asked through a smirk. "Whenever something happened, you could hear somebody askin' at the end of the show, 'How he gone get out of this one'? I'm asking the same shit about this bitch here," she laughed as she nudged her chin towards the projection screen. "It's over for the broad, man," she added as she shook her head.

"Lisa ass was tripping fuckin' around with that Senator," Ben replied seriously as he eyed over two dozen federal agents hiding behind SUVs and patrol cars with rifles aimed at the front of the skyscraper where Lisa was holed up.

"Umm hmm. Now she about to get her clock cleaned once and for all," Naomi calmly remarked as she sat and read The Ponca City News, vaguely paying attention to what was happening on television.

Lisa's troubles were bringing about a mixture of feelings within the organization she'd been battling for many years. Whereas Faye and company were ecstatic over what was going down, Helen was melancholy over it all and expecting more bloodshed. The Holland family was more nonchalant about the matter. Lisa hadn't affected them directly, save for Asa Spade and his crew, but all inside the Holland family, including Asa Spade, viewed Laddy Norcross as the greater threat. Still, Lisa's demise was a welcomed sight to behold for all involved.

"But there is something that will be of detriment to us," Naomi remarked as she folded the paper.

"What's that, Auntie?" Ben asked causally.

"At least with Lisa, the family was dealing with someone just as dirty as the people she called herself tryin' to arrest. Vanguard let a lot of things slide. Things that weren't of her concern, she was willing to look the other way," Naomi explained. "Senator Slack may have Laddy in her hip pocket over that video, but how long before another federal agent starts digging into what we all have going on? I'm willing to bet the ranch that he won't be corrupted like this one here," she added as she pointed to the projection screen. "Laddy would become obsolete in the big scheme of things should something like that occur and we would find ourselves up against a legitimate investigation," she further unpacked, leaving Ben and Martha to contemplate in silence the repercussions over the inevitable downfall of Lisa Vanguard as they continued watching the events unfold on live television.

****

Back over to Seattle, Laddy Norcross was kneeling down on one knee behind an Excursion listening in on the conversation that the negotiator was having with Lisa Vanguard. "Agent? Agent, listen to me," the negotiator spoke in a comforting tone as she looked over the hood of the SUV towards the tinted window on her left where the lobby's main office lay. "You've made a mistake, okay? No one is judging you at this moment, Agent Vanguard. Let the hostage go, come on out and we'll talk about it down at headquarters," she added as she turned and faced the mobile phone's suitcase with a hand to her ear to drown out the sound.

"A mistake? Talk about it at headquarters? Are you shitting me, bitch?" Lisa scoffed as she peered out the office's tinted bay window and laid eyes on the dozen or so patrol cars and at least two scores of federal agents that now had the block roped off. "You know my charges! You care to explain to me how I keep myself off death row by surrendering? What guarantees do I have, huh?"

"I am not in a position to offer you a deal, Agent Vanguard. Not under the circumstances. Not while you hold an innocent woman hostage." the negotiator responded as she peered back over the hood at the office where she knew Lisa lay. "Do you know she's married with two sons?" she asked as she once again faced her mobile phone's suitcase and placed a hand over her free ear to better be able hear a reply.

"The fuck I care?" Lisa barked. "I want a car with a full tank of gas! The hostage remains with me until I'm clear of city limits! If my demands are not met within the hour, I will kill this bitch! Goodbye!"

"Lisa, wait! Wait a minute!" Laddy interrupted as he held an earbud to his ear.

"I was wondering when I would hear from you," Lisa seethed. "Are you happy now, Laddy? You've finally gotten the big case."

"We just want the hostage, Lisa. Then we'll talk about getting you a getaway car. We'd just as soon let you go free and hunt you down before we risk having an innocent woman's life taken today. Let her go." Laddy pleaded.

"I can't do that, Agent. You know how this goes, man," Lisa said as her voice cracked. "I wasn't a bad officer. I did good work out there! Right here in Seattle! Remember Agent Jarkowski?"

"I remember Jarkowski. From the Onishi brothers' case," Laddy remarked somberly. Laddy also remembered that Lisa Vanguard had stolen two hundred and thirty kilograms off the Jarkowski case after she'd killed the man when he tried to go for his gun. He chose not to compound Lisa's troubles as he was sincerely trying to free an innocent woman. "You did good work, partner."

"Is Officer Cordova okay?" Lisa asked as tears welled up in her eyes.

"She's out of surgery and resting. No serious damage," Laddy replied in a soothing tone.

"I never meant to hurt her, Laddy."

"I know, Lisa."

"We were a good team."

"We were, partner."

"Everything I've done, all we've done, will be erased. I'll go down as a disgraced officer. I can't live with that stigma, Laddy." The sound of a pistol racking was heard at that moment, and the negotiator jumped in.

"Lisa don't! We're getting the car ready for you!" the negotiator pleaded upon snatching the mobile phone back from Laddy.

"I've had time to weigh the issue and I've come to the conclusion that it is too late for me. You should've disconnected the power. Maybe then I could've been talked into surrendering," Lisa said casually as sat the phone down, allowing the negotiator and Laddy to both hear what she was preparing to do.

****

"This is worse than federal agents taking bribes during the prohibition era," Lisa heard Dante` O'Malley tell the CNN panel of three he sat on.

"The woman makes Al Capone look like a Saint," another

495

commentator remarked while shaking his head. "This is indeed a sad day for the law enforcement community not just in the United States, but for law enforcement around the world."

"That might be a stretch," a third commentator remarked as she chuckled.

"I agree it's a stretch," O'Malley chimed in. "But this definitely ranks amongst some of the worst by all accounts."

Over the last hour and a half, Lisa sat and watched as politicians and analysts alike dissected her career and ridiculed her service to the public. The fallout that would inevitably follow over her corruption was a bitter pill for a woman of Lisa's caliber to accept, and the news reports did nothing to persuade her into surrendering herself and face her past crimes. To the contrary, it only fueled her resolve.

"Get up!" Lisa ordered the frightened clerk. The young woman was of college age and recently married. She'd taken a night job to help pay her tuition, but now found herself in the throes of a woman on the brink of insanity. Over and over she'd requested to talk to her husband, but Lisa had denied the request. She wanted someone to suffer with her, and the best thing she had going was an innocent woman frightened out of her mind.

"Please," the woman begged as she eased off the lone velvet sofa inside the office with her hands raised. "I'll do anything you want me to do."

"I want you to die for me," Lisa said as she pulled out her mini Uzi and racked it and fired off a volley of bullets.

"Move! Move! Move!" Laddy commanded from the street after hearing the gunfire through the phone. He bothered not wanting for confirmation that the hostage was dead as he was certain Lisa was going for suicide by cop.

"They're coming," Lisa remarked anxiously as she ended the call and looked out the bay window where she saw countless federal agents running out from behind SUVs with rifles, headgear and bulletproof vests. She crept over to the ladder as officers began storming the building and sat her gun down on the top step. Her firing the Uzi was a ploy to get the FBI to raid the office so she could unleash her final act and they'd taken the bait.

There was an extension cord beside the ladder in the office that was being used by the maintenance crew to replace lightbulbs. The break they'd gone on shortly before Lisa burst into the office with her hostage, and the equipment left behind, had given her a way out. She climbed the ladder and threw the extension cord over a wooden rafter, tied it in place and placed the noose around her neck before turning to face the entrance doors. "Stand there!" she ordered her hostage as she pointed to a spot before her in front of the ladder.

"Ma'am, please!" the clerk cried out as she moved towards Lisa.

"FBI! FBI! FBI!" Lisa heard echoing out in the lobby.

"Come here now!" Lisa ordered the woman as she stood on the ladder with the electrical cord tight around her neck while tying a rag around the lower portion of her face.

The clerk realized Lisa couldn't run after her being she was on a ladder with a noose around her neck and the gun out of her hands, so she chanced going for the door. At the same time, the FBI agents were raiding the office. The door was blown open with a centralized explosion placed on the locks and agents bombarded the room with canisters of tear gas. Nauseous gas spread throughout its interior as Lisa picked up her mini Uzi and aimed it at the entrance. "Bring it on, mutherfuckas!" Lisa screamed like a woman possessed as she squeezed the trigger on her mini-Uzi.

The clerk coughed and screamed over the hail of gunfire that erupted from behind her as she began dropping to the floor. A burst of semi-automatic from gunfire three federal agents storming the room quickly erupted from the entrance back into the office in return and the clerk went down in a hail of bullets. She was struck nearly a dozen times in her side by federal agents. The men took to their knees and began looking around the room through their thermal goggles as they crept low to the floor while waving their weapons. Neither of the three had bothered to look up, however; a second round of automatic gunfire erupted from deep within the office, sending the agents scrambling for cover as the tear gas thickened. Two members of the three-man team howled out in pain as armor-piercing bullets ripped through their vests.

"Come on! That's all you got for me?" Lisa Vanguard roared aloud over the smoke as she reached into her back waistband and grabbed another magazine. "Y'all must don't know who in the *fuck I am*!" she defiantly sassed as she let the empty magazine drop from her gun before swiftly sliding in another thirty-two round magazine and quickly racked it.

Out on the main floor, Laddy Norcross, with two agents following his lead, rounded the backside of the front desk with M-4 rifles racked and fully loaded. Just feet up ahead to his left, Laddy could see two federal agents being dragged out of the room by their collars by a single agent as another canister of tear gas was tossed into the office by a third agent.

"Tear gas explosion!" Laddy yelled as he and his men turned away. The canister exploded seconds later and another round of automatic gunfire exploded from within the room. The agent that was pulling his partners free of the line of fire dropped down on top of the agents' whose life he was trying to save as the wood on the counter behind him shattered into pieces.

"Stay back!" Laddy ordered his men as he crept towards the office's entrance. He peered around the threshold and could see the red image of Lisa suspended in midair though his thermal goggles. While remaining in a kneeling position, Laddy climbed over the bodies of his three fallen comrades and squeezed the trigger on his M-4 one time and Lisa's silhouette went stiff. He fired again and her body began swinging from side to side with its hands at its side. While rising up to his feet, Laddy fired a total of twenty times and unloaded on Lisa Vanguard, the bay window behind her shattered and tear gas poured out into the open air.

The room was beginning to clear and Laddy could now began to make full sense of it all. He walked amongst the carnage consisting of five dead bodies, that of four federal agents and the lone, innocent clerk. Frayed furniture and devastated glass was all around as he kept his eyes on the body swinging from the ceiling. The closer he drew, the clearer he could see. Through the thinning cloud of tear gas while still wearing his mask and holding onto his M-4 rifle, Laddy stared up at the lifeless corpse of his former partner as her body rocked slightly back and forth.

Lisa had sustained an absorbent amount of bullets to her chest, torso and legs. The pantsuit she wore was darkened with her blood from the chest to the pants legs. She died looking straight ahead with her green eyes wide open and a slight smile on her face, as if she had welcomed death. Laddy looked at the FBI badge his former partner had dangling from her neck and thought about how proud he was the day he became Lisa's partner. He never foresaw this day. Never even fathomed that such a tragedy and twist of fate would occur. If he'd been told that he would be the one to end his partner's life and career just five years after they'd become a team, he would've bet his life that whoever made such a decree would've been dead wrong.

On looking at the badge draped around Lisa's neck, Laddy didn't see a criminal, though, he saw a fallen comrade instead. An officer who'd simply gone astray. And in spite of her being a criminal for over thirty years and nearly killing his mistress, this was not how Laddy wanted to remember his former partner. He reached up and snatched the badge off Lisa's neck just as FBI agents began filing into the office, and he quickly tucked it into his jacket pocket. When he looked up at Lisa again, only then did he see the woman for what she was worth—nothing more than that of a common criminal who'd met a deserved fate in his eyes.

Lisa Vanguard first appeared on the scene in April of 1979 at the age of twenty-two in Bentree, West Virginia. She died just over thirty years later in Seattle, Washington on June 22, 2009 at the age of fifty-two. In her wake, she'd committed a number of homicides, manipulated both men and women into doing her bidding and had gotten an innocent woman killed by the agency she once worked for and had taken out four federal agents before she herself was killed at the hands of her former partner in Laddy Norcross. The fallout over her demise would shake up the Federal Bureau of Investigations for a time unforeseen and place Laddy Norcross in the limelight for a short while. He would be viewed as a hero, the man who'd taken down one of the most corrupt federal agents since its inception in July of 1908, over hundred years prior, but even he held secrets that would hang over his head for the unforeseeable future being Senator Slack had incriminating evidence against him and Sandra Cordova.

CHAPTER FORTY-TWO
A KILLER'S REMORSE

It was two days after Lisa Vanguard had rid the world of her presence. June 24th 2009. Throughout the organization, jubilance abounded. The Germans were over the moon over the recent events and were now readying themselves for their first shipment of heroin. The Asian faction of the family was gearing up for another two hundred kilograms of cocaine and Ben was headed back to Arizona. His job for the moment was to get an appeal underway to have JunJie's fifty-seven-year sentence overturned being he was the last person indicted and prosecuted by Lisa Vanguard. His chances of walking were extraordinary, as his sentence had come about deep into the time in which Tammy had been recording Lisa's confessions.

An enemy to many inside the organization had been vanquished and it was now business as usual for most, but, problems for some still existed, namely DeeDee. The aging gangster walked amongst the cattle pens holding onto a newspaper he'd found the day before that had an article that disturbed him severely. He leaned up against a portion of the wooden fence with a boot on the bottom rung staring at the cows as they lay around in the dirt flapping their tails to ward off flies under the warm morning sun. He'd always stated that he'd never wanted to know the how in which the kidneys were obtained for Sharona Benson, but upon reading the article, he was forced to face the horrors of his decision.

DeeDee opened the front page of the paper and read the heading in The Ponca City News: *Kansas Officials Baffled over Rash of Disappearances*. It was the faces that haunted DeeDee and brought about a feeling of remorse. One man and six women. Seven people in total. These were the faces of ghosts in DeeDee's mind. The smiles they sported, and comments in the article from the worried relatives of some of the victims praying for their safe return was stressing his mind as he knew the missing persons' relatives would never see them again. The victims left in the wake of Sharona's surgery were all young people to DeeDee's age seventy-six. College students, an uncle and brother, daughters and mothers. All had been eliminated. Unwittingly becoming ensnared in one man's self-righteous Cause that'd cost them their mortal existence.

As he looked down at the images of the dead, one face in particular haunted DeeDee—that of the young black woman. Her name was Oleander Francois. Twenty-two and an undergraduate attending Wichita State University. She was returning home from visiting her parents in South Carolina when she disappeared somewhere in Kansas. Her car had turned up in Wichita with her cellphone inside, but Oleander was nowhere to be found was what DeeDee had read.

The Germans were clever enough to take some of their victims' cars and belongings and dump them near their homes in order to make it appear as if the missing had indeed made it to their place of destination. Piper's uncle's fingerprints were found inside a couple of cars, his severed hands having been used to tamper with the evidence and throw authorities off. The Germans had also discarded items taken off their victims out in the middle of nowhere in order to further throw the heat off their tail back in Cherryvale. Throughout Kansas and North Central Oklahoma, possessions belonging to the missing persons were turning up at random. A purse here, a suitcase there, a cellphone left inside a rest area bathroom just off the interstate and the occasional abandoned car that'd been torched in some cornfield. There were no bodies to discover with any of the belongings to help further the investigation and the law was left baffled. Kansas officials believed a serial killer, or a group of serial killers was on the loose in the state, but they hadn't a solid lead to go on save for scant possessions belonging to people who'd mysteriously vanished into thin air.

DeeDee had gotten what he'd asked for in saving Sharona, but the burden that was unintentionally thrust upon him was heavier than he'd anticipated. He folded the paper and began the lengthy walk back to Ponderosa as he pulled out his cellphone and dialed up Will Rogers International Airport down in Oklahoma City.

****

"You ready, baby?" Oneika asked as she walked out onto the front porch of her and Dawk's home located on the far south side of the ranch. She had Sosa in tow and a diaper bag as she stood beside her husband looking over the land. "Is that DeeDee over there?" she asked as she squint her eyes.

"Yeah," Dawk answered while studying his grandfather's body language as he walked up the slight hill leading back to Ponderosa. "It's been a while since he been over that way. Something must be troubling him."

"You wanna stop by the house and talk to 'em before we head to the hospital in town?" Oneika asked as she smiled down at a smiling Sosa.

Dawk eyed his grandfather for a few seconds, wondering what had him in a downtrodden spirit. He was unknowingly out of the loop concerning DeeDee's actions, but his best guess was that whatever it was troubling his grandfather had something to do with Sharona being on the property. Not knowing the true cause, Dawk surmised that his grandfather was trying to figure out how to handle Irene and Sharona at the same time being they both were home now. "Nah," he said to his faithful, loving wife. "We need to get down there because it's gone be a long day with all these tests they have to run. I'll talk to 'em when I get back," he ended as he took his son from Oneika and guided his family down the stairs to the Suburban where Siloam and Montenegro were waiting patiently.

****

"It's been what? Like a week or something, Angel? And you tellin' me you pregnant?" Walee laughed over the phone as he conversed with Angel Fuller, who was over to her mother's home in Las Vegas, while laying back on his king-sized bed. "I'm calling foul on that one, shorty! Unless you wasn't a virgin before we first got down, that ain't my baby, baby."

"I am a vir—I was a virgin, Walee," Angel snapped as she lay back in her plush, queen-sized bed accented with satin and silk covers and sheets and fluffy pillows. "You were my first ever."

"Okay, then. You took a pregnancy test or something? And if you did, tell me where they selling a test that can determine if you pregnant a week after having sex."

"I don't need a pregnancy test, Walee!" Angel reasoned. "Sometimes a woman just knows!"

"A woman? Girl, you sixteen!" Walee laughed to himself as he stared at his cellphone. He placed the yap back to his ear and said, "Alright, I can feel ya' on that, baby girl. Kinda like when Kimi thought she was pregnant, huh?"

"Just like that!" Angel said as she curled her lips.

"What if you not pregnant, though? Because Kimi thought she was pregnant, but she was wrong about that there." Walee reasoned as he threw the covers off his body and placed his bare feet to the lacquered ponderosa wood floors.

"It's my gut, man. I just got a feeling. We need to figure out what we gone tell my momma." Angel paused and waited for a reply. When she got none, she looked at her phone only to see that Walee had ended the call. Her heart dropped to the pit of her stomach and tears leaked from her eyes as she felt she'd been rejected after sharing with him her beliefs. The phone rang again and she sat up and answered in haste.

"My bad, baby. The call dropped."

"Walee?" Angel sighed as she fell back into her pillows. "Walee, tell me you not gone hurt me."

"What exactly you want from me, Angel? We did what two consenting people do when it came to that. What you want me to be your man or something?"

Angel remembered the conversation she'd had with Francine just before she left and the pertinent advice the woman had given her on that day…*"If you want him, you have to let that be known. Don't just sit there with your head bowed feeling sorry for yourself. Do something about it!"*

"I do!" Angel blurted out she wiped tears from her face. "I want you to be my man, Walee. Because…because I'm in love with you. We can be good together I promise if you just give me the chance to show what a good person I am I just want us to be happy I know we in different states and all but we can—"

"Whoa, whoa…baby girl? Slow down some for daddy," Walee chuckled. He'd known from jump that Angel was digging on him major, and truth be told, he was feeling her just the same, only he had to keep his cool over the matter. "Let me tell ya' something, Angel," he began to unpack. "I don't know if you know what it is that I do for a living, but I'm not just a college student, ya' feel me?"

"I know. You with that girl Jordan," Angel stated in a soft tone as she threw the covers off her body and placed her bare feet to the soft, thick carpet in her bedroom.

"I'm not with her, with her. But we do business together, you know what I'm saying?" Walee responded as he went and checked his face and physique in his floor mirror.

"No. Spell it out for me, Walee." Angel requested as she walked over and checked her naked physique in the full-length mirror mounted on the back of her door.

"I thought you knew, Angel." Walee replied as he entered his walk-in closet and selected a pair of jeans, shirt and matching sneakers.

"No, I don't know. What is it that you do with Jordan?" Angel asked as she pulled her closet door open and looked her sponsored Macy's wardrobe over as she had a photoshoot with the famed company for their fall lineup scheduled in a couple of hours out in the desert north of Vegas.

"You really wanna know?" Walee asked as he popped tags on new gear.

"Yeah," Angel replied as she laid out a silk all-in-one dress with a mid-length cashmere coat and ankle-length boots.

"Okay," Walee remarked. "Me and Jordan run a adult video operation. We film people having sex, take the videos and download them on disks and sell—hello? Hello? Angel?" Walee removed the phone from his ear only to see that Angel had ended the call. Believing the call had been dropped like before, he redialed her number. The phone rang a couple of times before going to voicemail. He tried again and the phone rang several times before going to voicemail again. *"That bitch hung up on me,"* Walee smiled to himself while nodding his head.

He threw his phone aside and went on with his day. Angel was pissed he knew, maybe even hurt over what he' just told her, but he wasn't about to fret his nerves over a youngster in love with his dick game. As much as he wanted to finish the conversation with Angel, he wasn't going to give her the privilege of having him calling her back repeatedly, nor was he about to leave a message trying to explain himself. If Angel wanted him, she knew how to reach him. On top of that, shorty believed she was pregnant, and that in itself would give Walee an excuse to call her in a couple of months if he didn't hear back from Angel first.

After laying out his clothes, Walee headed for the bathroom to shower up. He pulled the door open to his room and saw Spoonie and Tyke marching up the hall. Tyke was strumming a violin she'd taken from the music room, and Spoonie was playing an antique saxophone, also taken from the music room. The two were wearing birthday hats as they tried to play, what Walee could decipher as being that of the happy birthday song, only they were mangling the notes.

Out in front Spoonie and Tyke, marching up the floor was Doss III. The fun-loving child had on a red velvet robe that dragged the floor, a gold-plated crown on his head and he was holding onto a gold-plated scepter as he marched up the wide hall, taking a step to the left, then to the right before pausing. He then took a step to the left, then to the right, and paused again. "Hear ye! Hear ye! The king has arisen! I say to all…the king has arisen!" he blurted out before resuming his stately march up the hall with Spoonie and Tyke mangling his song behind him.

"What's going on here?" Walee laughed as he stepped back and let the little king and his royal court march past his bedroom.

Doss III stopped, looked straight ahead and shook his head somberly before slowly turning to face Walee. He held out his scepter and said in a deep voice, "You've forgotten his majesty's birthday is today? I should banish you to the swamps!"

"You been watching too much TV, boy," Walee laughed. "How old you is, though?"

"Your uncle is the great eight! He expects his gift!" Doss III answered in his kingly voice before turning around. "Maestro!" he commanded as he held up his scepter and continued his march up the hall.

"What I told you about that uncle stuff?" Walee laughed as he joined the royal march up the hall.

"The king doesn't make the rules he only lives by them!" Doss III replied as he stopped and knocked on Bay's bedroom door. When she didn't answer, he pushed it open, only to find an empty room. "Where are my subjects?" he asked, continuing on in his king voice.

"What, umm, what that dude trippin' off, y'all?" Walee laughed as he asked Spoonie and Tyke.

"He wanted to be a king for day on his birthday was what he told us. So, we made him a king." Spoonie answered as she resumed blowing her saxophone.

"Who else know about this?" Walee asked as he followed the court up the hall towards Tiva's bedroom.

"Nobody," Tyke said as she strummed the violin while sliding up the hall. "And that's the funny part, getting to watch his reaction. I got the camera taped to the end of the violin recording everything," she smiled. "He a trip, Walee!" she laughed as she watched her uncle push Tiva's door open.

"Aww, man! T-top is missing!" Doss III complained in his normal voice. "Where is everybody, y'all?"

"Let's look on the other side of the house, king! Your other royal subjects may be awash with the king's tasks!" Spoonie said through mocked bewilderment. "We have to find them, your majesty! It's your birthday after all, king!"

"Yes!" Doss III said as he looked up the hall while flaring back on the sides of his velvet robe. "My subjects are near I can sense them near me! Music, please!"

The march continued up the hall, crossing over the balcony that separated the great room from the grand staircase. Doss III dipped a hand into the water fountain across from the grand staircase and scooped up a sip. "I want buckets of this fine water delivered to my castle by morning's end!" he commanded.

"Aye aye, king!" Tyke laughed as she held the violin on Doss III, filming his every move.

Doss III crossed the hall and turned into a hall on his right. He peeked into the classroom on his left and saw Malaysia and Malara sitting at desks before Francine.

"Heyyyy," Malara smiled and waved.

"Dossy!" Malaysia cackled.

"You there! The old one!" Doss III said to Francine.

"Ya' little booger I'm not an 'old one'! It may be your birthday today, but I'm not gonna take your insult. Not today, not ever so can it!" Francine snapped with her hands on her hips.

"Can it!" Malaysia and Malara said in unison.

"Hmm," Doss III said with his lips turned downward. "You must be from another kingdom," and he walked off.

Doss III continued his march through Ponderosa, making his way down to the first floor kitchen where he met his mother and father. He dropped his scepter and ran up to the counter where his parents were sitting. "Momma, today's my day! I get the cake, the four-wheeler and a whole bunch of other stuff, right?"

"Happy birthday, son," Sharona smiled as she eased out of the bar stool and knelt before her child. She kissed his forehead and said, "The family had to work today, but when they get in, where're going to bake you a cake and have your party, okay?"

"Aww! I want cake now, momma!" Doss III complained while holding onto the edge of the granite counter top.

"You may be a king today, but I'm king every day, son. And your mother is the queen and what she says goes," DeeDee laughed as he walked over and picked his boy up. He grunted as he held onto him. "You're getting heavy, boy. This may be my last time picking you up like this," he laughed as he placed Doss III back to his feet. "Well, I'm off, everybody."

"Where're you're going, dad?" Doss III asked.

"Going see a man about a certain gift a certain someone wants," DeeDee smiled as he donned a fedora, took the newspaper he'd been carrying around all morning, and headed for the front doors.

"You want us to come with you, grandpa?" Spoonie asked.

"No, that's okay," DeeDee replied as he grabbed the keys to Bay's Lincoln and tucked the newspaper under his arm pit. "I'll be back later today after a few runs. Just going into town for a spell."

"Okay!" Tyke said aloud. "We'll show you the video we made when you get back, granddad!"

DeeDee climbed behind the wheel of Bay's ride and tossed the newspaper into the passenger seat. The music cranked up the time he started the engine… "…*man you don't know who that is…that nigga work for HPD been selling weed 'round for years…so while you plotting and scheming or whatever the fuck that you doing… hollar at me…I'll be in the bathroom boo booing…*"

"What in the…" DeeDee turned the music down completely and pulled off from in front the home and wheeled his way into town. He made it over to a hardware store located on Highway 177 on the south side of Ponca City, pulled into the parking lot and just sat and stared for a minute. His every inclination was telling him to purchase the four-wheeler for his son and return to Ponderosa, but he couldn't bring himself to do so. A day away from it all was what he was needing as he looked down at that one face, that of Oleander Francois.

Still troubled over the plight of Oleander, DeeDee climbed from behind the wheel and was greeted by a salesman. "What can I do you for, sir?" the man asked as he wiped his greasy hands on a clean rag.

"My son turned eight today," DeeDee stated. "I was wondering if there's a four-wheeler available for a young child that age? One he can drive on his own that has all the necessary safety features. I'm worried about a rollover the most."

"Okay," the guy said as he looked back at a row of freshly painted four wheelers. "We have the Boulder Kids ATV. Has all the features of an adult ATV, single cylinder four stroke engine, a speed limiter with a remote shut off and a steel, durable frame that makes it difficult to rollover, especially with the governor and remote shut off. Cost you about seven hundred and eighty bucks, but it's top of the line as far as safety is concerned," the guy ended as he tugged down on his Chicago Cubs baseball cap.

"What you know about them Cubs?" DeeDee smiled.

"Hell, mister," the salesman smiled. "If it ain't Wrigley it ain't right in my book! Those lovable losers haven't won a damn thing since my great grandfather was knee high to a spider but it never stopped me from loving them sons of bitches none."

DeeDee bent over laughing at the salesman's remark. "Seven-eighty you say?"

"Yes, sir! And we got in all colors too. Any favorite the youngin' prefers?"

"Well," he was wearing a red velvet robe this morning. Calling himself a king. So, how about we get it in red to match the king's wardrobe?"

"Popular color, sir. Delivery's usually extra. Thirty bucks, but being it's for the little one, I'll knock it off. You're in town?"

"Yeah," DeeDee said, still laughing over the salesman's Cubs' remark. "I'll meet you inside with the address and to settle up the bill."

"I have to tell, ya', man. My delivery guy is out and won't be back until around seven thirty. If you're local, I can have it delivered anywhere here in town say about eight 'o' clock?"

"The party isn't until seven. It'll still be light out, so that's fine," DeeDee said as he went into the car and retrieved his checkbook.

After paying the cost, DeeDee continued south on Highway 177, headed down to Oklahoma City. Twenty miles out, he called Walee.

"Yo, what up, grandpa?" Walee asked as he headed down to Stillwater to hollar at Kahlil.

"Son? Are you coming down to Chicag—are you coming down to Oklahoma City today?"

"I wasn't planning on it. Why, grandad?" Walee asked from behind the wheel of his Dodge Charger.

"I'm gone need someone to pick up Bena's Lincoln from in front her condominium and drive it back to Ponca City tonight."

"What, you going somewhere?"

Before DeeDee could answer, his phone buzzed. He looked and recognized Kimi's office number from Holland-Dawkins Enterprises headquarters in downtown Oklahoma City, and was happy as it gave him an easy out. "Never mind, I'll call you back, grandson," he stated as he switched calls. "Kimi, what's happening?"

"Grandad? Before we order this ice cream cake for Li'l Doss, we was checking to make sure Sharona could eat it, or do we need to get a special cake for her?"

"She can have ice cream and cake," DeeDee laughed as he wheeled Bay's Lincoln down the highway. "What time is closing time down there?"

"Five, but we leaving at four to pick up the cake and get my uncle…I hate saying that because he just revels in it," Kimi sighed.

"Anyway, we should be up there around seven?"

"Okay. Before you, when you get off work I need a favor from you, baby?"

"Like what? You tryna sneak off with Irene and need me to cover for you or something like that, man? I'm not doing it! No, sir!"

DeeDee rocked in laughter behind the steering wheel. "No, Kimi!" he exclaimed. "I need for you to pick up Bay's car from her condo in Oklahoma City and drive it back to Ponca City for me."

"Okayyy…and can I ask why?" Kimi sassed, believing her grandfather was creeping on his son's birthday.

"Can I get the benefit of the doubt, Kimi? Just trust me, okay? It's only a favor and I'll be there in time for the party."

"We'll see. You ole…love you, grandad! Don't worry about hiding the key, momma has the spare one."

"I love you, too, sugar." DeeDee responded in a loving tone as he ended the call by blowing Kimi a kiss through the phone.

Fifteen minutes later, DeeDee was pulling up to Bay's condo. A cab was waiting and he'd wasted no time in parking the car and climbing into the taxi. "Will Rogers," he told the driver.

****

A little after four in the evening, Naomi, Kimi and Koko were walking out HDE headquarters. Lee Sato, who was filling in for Flacco Ramirez, was out in front of the matriarch and her protégés as they walked towards the elevators. For added muscle, Lee had recruited Udelle's homeboy, Devin. The job was temporary until Flacco got things straight down in South America, but at 6'5" three hundred pounds with a bald head, thick beard and little to no body fat, Devin was an intimidating brother. Lee was looking to recruit Devin, but Naomi had the final say so. As of now, Devin was considered a willing prospect under the guidance and supervision of Lee Sato.

"Who do you want to drive Bay's car from the condo back to Ponca City, Kimi?" Lee asked as the group paused in front of the elevator.

"I'll do it," Devin chuckled as he pressed the elevators' down button.

"I bet you would," Lee laughed. "That sucka can giddy up, though, homeboy," he acknowledged.

"That's what I'm saying," Devin replied.

Naomi was texting Dunkirk, who was looking at homes up in the Hamptons, when she heard Lee's question. "Why are we driving Bay's car back home? How did it get here?" she asked. "And who drove it down?"

"Grandad drove it down and said he needed somebody to drive it back for him." Kimi answered as the elevator doors open. The family boarded and Lee and Devin stood in front with .45 calibers in the back waistbands of their silk suits and mirror-tinted sunshades over their eyes as the doors closed.

"Where is your grandfather going? To the warehouse?" Naomi asked as she stopped texting Dunkirk.

"Maybe so, momma," Koko chimed in. "Irene is over there."

"I knew that old buzzard was tryna get me to cover for him!" Kimi frowned. "And on his son's birthday for crying out loud."

"Says the overly dramatic young woman," Koko mocked.

"That man," Naomi sighed as she dialed DeeDee's number. She waited until the call went to voicemail. "Mister, you need to call me. What are you doing running off to God knows where? Call me, Doss," she ended. Naomi then dialed the office over to the Valley Brook Warehouse.

"Holland Express, Irene speaking. How can we be of service today?"

"Irene, is Doss with you?" Naomi asked as the elevator doors opened.

Irene rolled her eyes and said, "No, Naomi. I haven't been with Doss like that since the night Sharona fell ill in Chicago."

"Chicago," Naomi said to herself. *"I know this man didn't just up and..."*

"Is the party still on for Li'l Doss, Naomi? Because me and Martha were leaving shortly with his gifts." Irene remarked, breaking Naomi's chain of thought.

"Yes, it is. We'll see you and Martha there," Naomi remarked as the group walked off the elevator. "Call me if you hear from Doss because we can't find him right now," she requested before ending the call.

Once inside her bulletproof Phantom, with Lee behind the wheel, Naomi sat in the backseat in between Kimi and Koko calling DeeDee repeatedly. By the time they'd made the twenty-five minute drive over to Bay's condo, she was at her wits end as DeeDee wasn't answering none of the numbers she had on him. She kept her calm, hiding her anxiety, as Devin climbed from the front passenger seat and used the spare key to enter Bay's ride. He backed out and pulled off and Lee followed.

"What about the ice cream cake, momma? The Kroger's got it ready for us," Kimi asked as five 'o' clock approached.

Wanting to keep things as close to normal as possible, Naomi kept up with the day's plan by agreeing to pick up the cake for Doss III, but deep down inside, she was scared out of her mind for DeeDee as she'd seen this play before. The man had dropped off the radar, and that meant that he was hiding from something, which was the best possible scenario, or someone had gotten to him. If it was the former, DeeDee was still in danger, as he was vulnerable being off his bases. If it was the latter, then, the family was already too late.

In Naomi's mind, DeeDee had simply gone off line. The family hadn't any close enemies in Oklahoma, save for Sheriff Nimitz, but the guy had been quiet as of late. "*Maybe too quiet,*" Naomi thought to herself as Lee wheeled her Phantom into a Kroger's parking lot. "*But why DeeDee?*" she pondered as the driver's side rear door was opened by Lee.

Naomi went in and quickly paid for the cake. Kimi and Koko, meanwhile, had gone into a nearby Dollar General to grab party favors, including candles and birthday hats, which took up a little extra time. It was six 'o' clock by the time the family made it back to the cars. Devin was standing outside of Bay's Lincoln reading a newspaper as the family approached. He laid the paper on the hood, but a gust of wind had sent it flying into the air. It whizzed past Naomi, who was quick enough to grab it off of reflex. Being a reader, she was inherently inclined to fold the paper neatly, and when she did, she saw the heading: *Kansas Officials Baffled over Rash of Disappearances.*

"Where did you get this paper from, Devin?" Naomi asked as the tension coursing through her veins heightened.

"It was laying on the passenger seat when I climbed in back at Bay spot, Miss Naomi." Devin remarked as he and Lee placed the groceries on the back floorboard of the Lincoln. "I can get rid of it, but that was a damn good article in there."

While keeping her composure, Naomi, who'd just figured it all out, walked to the rear of her Phantom. "Let's get to the ranch," she requested as she pulled the back door open for Kimi and Koko. "Come on, babies," she ushered as she looked around the parking lot for anything strange.

****

Back over to Bay's condominium, Walee and Jordan Whispers was just pulling up in front of the home. Walee looked and saw Kimi and Koko's Maserati in the driveway, but not Bay's Lincoln. The condo had a violent history, so Walee wasn't about to take any chances. "Get that thing," he told Jordan before the two climbed out and went and knocked on the door.

Udelle answered a few seconds later. What's up, homie?" he said as he stepped back. "Come on in!"

"Yo, how long you been here, fam?" Walee questioned as he stepped off into the home with his hand up under his shirt placed atop a .40 Glock. Jordan was just to his left with a thirty-two shot tech nine hidden in her hands that was tucked behind her back.

"'Bout ten minutes. Why?" Udelle asked as he grabbed a couple of bottles of tequila from one of the kitchen cabinets. "I had to stop here on my way up to the ranch to get these bottles of liquor, ya' feel? You know how kids' parties turn into adult parties, bruh!" he said happily. "I'm working as a intern over to the local ABC station, yeh, fam?" he said as he clicked off the vent light above the stove.

"That's what's up, dude," Walee remarked as he eased his hand up off his torch. "Look, umm…Bay…Bay car wasn't out there when you got here, Udelle?"

"Nah, I ain't see it." Udelle responded as he placed the bottles into a plastic bag. "Y'all heading up?"

"Yeah," Walee answered puzzled. "Let's umm, let's be out, fam." He checked the time and saw that it was six thirty, which would place him an hour behind the party's seven 'o' clock start time.

As Jordan drove his Dodge Charger, Walee got on his yap and dialed his grandfather while tailing Udelle, who was up ahead in the Maserati, but he got no answer. Wondering what had gone down, because last he talked, DeeDee was asking him to pick up Bay's Lincoln. *"Maybe I misunderstood,"* Walee reasoned as he dialed up Bay.

"Yo?" Bay answered as she sat out on Kaw Lake Park sipping gin and listening to music with Tiva and AqauNina.

"You got your car, sis?" Walee asked.

"Nah, Spoonie say grandpa got it, but he ain't back yet. He went to get Li'l Doss a four-wheeler, but he probably having a hard time finding one."

"You heard from Dawk?" Walee asked while kicking back in the passenger seat.

"He still at the hospital. We went in for a minute, but they just running tests right now. We gone head home when we see Dawk cross Kaw Lake Bridge."

"Alright, I'm on my way up there." Walee stated as he ended the call. He then dialed his mother's number.

"You're back from Stillwater, son?" Naomi asked upon answering.

"Nah, I just left Bay spot about twenty minutes ago. Grandad called and asked me to pick Bay ride up, but when I got there it wasn't in the driveway. I just talk to Bay and she say he still got it."

"We got the car, son," Naomi said, still keeping her composure. "Who's with you?"

"Jordan. I got my burner with me, momma. I'm good. Udelle up the road in Kimi and Koko ride. We on our way back home."

Naomi sighed in relief. "Did your grandfather say anything else?"

"He asked me about the car, but then it was like he was about to say he was going to Chicago, you know? I talked to Bay and she said he was out getting a four-wheeler for Li'l Doss."

"That place closes at nine," Naomi said as she checked her watch. "We'll be in town around seven thirty. I'll stop and check. You, Jordan and Udelle just keep on coming, son," she requested before ending the call.

Upon reaching Ponca City, Naomi had Lee pull off to the right into the gravel parking lot of the local motorcycle shop. It was five minutes to eight when she climbed out the car and was greeted by a salesman wearing a Chicago Cubs hat. "What can I do you for, ma'am?"

Naomi pulled out her phone and showed the salesman a photo of DeeDee. "Did this man come here today?" she asked.

"Chicago Cubs fan!" the man smiled. "Sure did! And he bought a dandy of a four-wheeler. Red one like the one over yonder for his son. And I sure appreciate him because I was able to reach the day's quota in sales. Appreciated him so much, I gave him free delivery. Matter of fact," the guy said as he checked his watch. "I promised him my delivery driver would have it to 'em at eight 'o' clock. Should be pulling up to the address he gave me right about now."

"Do you know the address? He's my father-in-law and he's a little…a little troubled right now." Not everybody in Ponca City knew the Holland family by face, although their name was ringing. Some were just everyday Americans trying to eke out an honest loving, much like the guy who'd sold DeeDee Li'l Doss's four-wheeler.

"That's an easy one…One Ponderosa Drive, right off Furguson Road," the guy remarked, letting Naomi know DeeDee had indeed stopped by. Highway 177 led down to I-40. It was the road the family sometimes used to travel to and from the city. DeeDee could've very well purchased the four-wheeler before heading out of town. Climbing back into the backseat of her Phantom, Naomi tried calling DeeDee again as the family began making their way back to Ponderosa.

****

"Ayeeee! There go momma 'nem!" Bay said as she witnessed her mother's Phantom jumping onto Kaw Lake Bridge with her Lincoln following close behind as the sun began to set over the city as she stood beside Spoonie and Tyke's G35 Infinite. "Damn they flying!" she noticed as she leaned up against the trunk of the ride.

"I bet Lee and Devin driving," Tiva laughed. "You know how

they be tryna race and shit."

"I know that ain't happenin'! Not with my momma!" Bay barked. "Slow y'all asses down over there!" she laughed aloud, knowing her people couldn't hear her.

"Y'all ready to go to Li'l Doss party?" AquaNina asked as she leaned back into Bay.

"We did the birthday thing already with the king," Tiva chuckled as she guzzled wine straight from the bottle. "We waiting on Dawk anyway. We ain't going in until he and my sister-in-law cross that water, ya' heard me? Like Ben be saying, Bay," she joked as the twins laughed.

****

Naomi and company was pulling up to Ponderosa just after eight in the evening. The sun had dipped behind the hickory trees to the west sitting atop Ne'Ne's Hill, allowing an orange hue to coat the land. She could see the small white delivery truck out in front the home and Doss III skipping about happily in his red velvet robe and gold-plated crown with his gold-plated scepter held high in the air. The young boy was overjoyed that his father had gotten his most wanted gift, and when he saw Bay's Lincoln pulling up to the home, he ran up to the car and waited with baited breath for his father to emerge.

The driver's side door on the old school opened and Doss III ran up on Bay's Lincoln. "Daddy! You got my—oh. Devin, where my daddy?" he asked as he looked inside the car. He then ran over to Naomi as she was exiting her car. "Sis-in-law Naomi, where my daddy? He in your car?" the child asked as he ushered past Lee and climbed into the front seat of the Phantom. "Kimi? Koko? You seen my daddy?"

Kimi and Koko looked over to their mother, not knowing what to say.

"He'll be back later, son," Naomi told Doss III. "Come on, let's get this four-wheeler together so you can ride it!" she coaxed in an attempt to take Li'l Doss's mind off his missing father.

Doss III lowered his scepter and said, "No. I told my daddy I was going to ride with him and he was going to drive it first so he can teach me. I'll wait on him to come home."

"You want us to sing happy birthday and cut your cake, Li'l Doss?" Koko asked as she presented the ice cream cake to her uncle.

Doss III raised a balled fist and swung at the cake, but Koko had moved it away. She gasped as she looked over to her mother. "Okay, we'll wait for your daddy," she said as she walked up the stairs while holding onto the cake.

"Sis, what's up?" Martha asked as she walked over to Naomi, who was standing off to the side.

"Doss? I think he went back to Chicago."

"Why?" Martha asked as her face wrinkled.

"Because of Sharona," Naomi responded. "This thing with the kidneys," she added as she handed Martha the newspaper article.

"Kansas Officials Baffled over Rash of Disappearances," Martha read lowly as she eyed seven strangers. "What does this have to do with DeeDee?"

"DeeDee went to the black market to save Sharona's life," Naomi let it be known. "Those are the lives destroyed in the process for a set of matching organs. DeeDee saw it and now he's regretful over it all."

"He in Chicago by his self? Fuck he thinkin', Naomi?" Martha scoffed. "What about the Italians?"

"I'm headed to my office to call them now after I call Kansas to confirm something. Keep everybody calm while I handle this. Wait a few minutes and send Sharona and Li'l Doss up to see me after you tell Sharona what her man has done to save her life. Do so by showing her the article," Naomi ordered as she turned and headed towards the stairs leading to Ponderosa.

****

DeeDee had just made it back to his loft in Chicago. He sat alone in the dimness of his domicile in a state of depression nursing a neat glass of whiskey as eight thirty approached. The images of the seven missing people were still haunting him, none more than the picture of Oleander Francois. Everything about the deal that'd gone down over Sharona seemed wrong now, and for the first time in his life, Doss Dawkins Senior, hardened killer and gangster, was feeling remorse over murders he'd condoned. Oleander could've been Spoonie or Tyke, Kimi or Koko in his mind's eye. He remembered the pain he felt the night he learned Spoonie was shot. And if Tonto had gotten away with kidnapping Koko, she herself could be in a grave this day. For the victims in Sharona's wake, however, there would be no funeral. No answer to the lingering question of 'Where is my family?'

The phone rang at that moment, shaking DeeDee from his thoughts. He got up to answer, but he didn't want anyone to know where he was at the present time so he walked off from the ringing phone until it ceased ringing. A minute later, his cellphone rang. He looked down and saw Naomi's number. "Yeah?" he answered.

"DeeDee, where are you?" Naomi asked as she sat at her office desk inside her suite.

"I'm somewhere safe, Naomi," DeeDee replied calmly. "Just had to get away for a minute after what I've learned."

Naomi sighed through closed eyes and said, "Long before this even got underway I warned you, Doss. You can't take back what's done and I know you understand that. The only thing left to do is to press on and be happy Sharona is still around. Your plan, as devious as it was, it worked, man."

"This has to be the most atrocious thing I've ever done, Naomi. It's hard to sleep now. I keep seeing that innocent young woman, the black one. Knowing what happened to her, what she may have gone through...it bothers me."

"I called Kansas," Naomi remarked. "If it's any comfort to ya', she wasn't the donor."

"She should've been," DeeDee replied somberly. "At least her death would not have been in vain. Somewhere there's a mother and father waiting for their daughter to return home but they'll never see her again, nor will they ever know what happened to her," he stated as tears dripped from his eyes.

"You should be with your family," Naomi remarked as Sharona walked into her office with Li'l Doss.

"I know," DeeDee said as he swallowed deeply. "I'll return tomorrow."

"Someone has something to say to you right now," Naomi responded as she stood up from her chair and handed the phone to Doss III.

"Dad?" the eight-year-old asked meekly. "Why you left us like that? Are you coming back?"

DeeDee smiled and his eyes grew brighter. "Son," he smiled. "Daddy didn't leave you like that, man," he half-heartedly smiled. "I had to fly back home for some, I had to come home for a day. I'll be back in the morning."

"You should've let me fly home with you," Doss III responded as he skipped over Naomi's marble floor in his king's robe. "Kimi and Koko bought me a cake for my birthday and you aren't going to be here to see me blow out the candles!"

"I'll be there tomorrow, son. I promise."

"Okay. I can wait dad. You're worth it," Doss III smiled as he handed the phone back to Naomi. "He's coming home tomorrow, Sis-in-law Naomi."

"That's wonderful, my love. Go down and join Tacoma and the others in the theater room and me and your mother will be right down, okay?"

"Okay. Can we use the popcorn machine?"

"Get Spoonie to set it for you. Tell I said it's okay."

"Thank you," Doss III ended as he walked out of the office.

Naomi placed the phone to her ear and said, "What are you doing back there, man? Did you let Natalia know you were back in town? You were supposed to be staying at Renata's house anyway. Get the hell outta there."

"No need for bodyguards, Naomi," DeeDee responded exasperated. "I just want to be alone can't you understand that? This is my way of dealing with my remorse. Let me heal, please."

"I'm gonna book you a flight for in the morning, Doss," Naomi declared as she began flipping through her cellphone for Natalia's number. "And I'm having Natalia come and remove you from that place because the security isn't any good there. You could've at least let the Cannapolis family know you were returning to Chicago."

Sharona took the phone at that moment and said to DeeDee, "I want you back here first thing in the morning, understand me, mister? It's time to end this pity party you been attending all by your lonesome and enjoy the time you have left with your son. He misses you. We all do."

"That's right! We miss the old Doss, man! Stop whining so darn much!" DeeDee heard Naomi say aloud in the background.

The aging gangster laughed over Naomi' remark, and his heart grew warm having spoken to his son. "I thought I'd be ostracized for what I've done, baby," he told Sharona.

"You did what you did out of love, DeeDee. Had you told me? I would not be here, though. Never would I have condoned it, not even on my death bed, but it is what it is," Sharona declared as she looked at the faces of the deceased displayed on the front page of The Ponca City News.

"That's not making me feel any better, baby," DeeDee admitted. "I just wish I never saw that paper, dammit!"

"Doss," Sharona replied lovingly, "I didn't ask for this. What am I going to do? Rip out my organs and throw them away? I'm sorry for all that had happened to the people involved, but I refuse to throw this chance away. I nearly died...to go from that to where I am today? I'm thankful. I thank God every day for what's inside me and I'm not going to go through life with a heavy heart. Neither should you, baby. Come back to Oklahoma."

"I will," DeeDee smiled. "Naomi's booking me a flight for in the morning. Save the cake until I get there will you, baby?"

"I will, Doss. I'll tell your son you love him on your behalf because he done took off for popcorn," Sharona joked through a worried heart.

"They forget so quickly. I'll make it up to you and him both tomorrow. I promise." DeeDee responded.

"You damn right you will," Sharona joked. "Naomi will call you back with the flight schedule."

"Okay. Bye now. Love you, baby."

"And I love you, Doss," Sharona ended with a smile.

****

While DeeDee milled about in his apartment preparing for a shower, Natalia III, Stone and Carlos were just walking out of The Cicero Hot Dog Deli having received a phone call from Naomi notifying them of the fact DeeDee was back in town.

"We gotta get over there quick," Natalia said as he remote started his Expedition and jumped in behind the steering wheel.

"What's his gripe sneaking into town like this? What he on a contract or something?" Stone asked as he climbed in opposite Natalia with Carlos in the back seat.

"He's...never mind, il mio amico. It's something with his woman Sharona that's aggravating the guy."

"Spill it, bro," Stone requested as Natalia pulled away from the curb without responding. "Alright, never mind about it. Let's just get there at least. I wouldn't take I-290, though there's...never mind," he said as he saw the interstate up ahead.

"It's none of you guy's business about DeeDee, alright?" Natalia scoffed as he jumped onto I-290 headed east. About a mile down, numerous sets of brake lights appeared up ahead along with flashing sirens. "What the fuck's going on?" Natalia grimaced.

"There was a three-car accident," Stone remarked. "Saw it on the news before we left. It's shutdown. Everybody's getting off on South Cicero Ave and heading down to West Fifth Avenue to get around that shit."

"Fan-fuckin'-tastic," Natalia sighed as his SUV began crawling in bumper-to-bumper traffic.

****

Back down in Ponca City, Dawk and Oneika were just emerging from Ponca City Medical Pediatrics Ward with Sosa in tow as the clock struck nine. They'd spent the entire day in the pediatric wing having more tests run on Sosa over his skin ailment. Doctors had no clue as to what was causing the baby to have constant rashes on his arms and back so they'd referred husband and wife to a pediatrician in Dallas, Texas.

"We should head down to Bay's condo in Oklahoma City and spend the night there and get up and drive to Dallas in the morning," Dawk suggested as he and Oneika walked into the lobby where Siloam, Montenegro and two more ranch hands were waiting.

"Before we do, I have a few personal things I need to get from the ranch," Oneika replied as she held Sosa in her bosom.

"If we go back to the ranch, we might as well camp out there and get a fresh start in the morning," Dawk countered. "It is kinda late. Siloam and Montenegro gone have to pack some things too. Let's just go home and rest up, baby."

"Okay," Oneika responded softly. "I'm sorry, Dawk," she added.

"Sorry for what?" Dawk asked as he walked beside his wife with his arm around her waist while looking down at his sleeping son.

"This has to be over something I done when he was first born. The detergent may have triggered a reaction in Sosa. I should've been more alert."

"You couldn't foresee that, baby," Dawk comforted. "We'll get it resolved soon enough," he added as the couple neared the lobby.

"How'd it go?" Siloam asked as she stood and greeted Dawk and Oneika.

"More tests," Oneika sighed. "We're going see a specialist down in Dallas in the morning."

"We want y'all with us when we go, so pack up when we get home," Dawk remarked as the family left the hospital and stepped into the warm night air.

Dawk strapped Sosa into his car seat and he and Oneika climbed into the backseat of the family's bulletproof Suburban, flanking the baby with Dawk on the passenger side and Oneika sitting behind Montenegro, who was driving.

Siloam hopped into the front passenger seat, pulled the door shut, and the family began making their way back to the ranch. They approached the main intersection of U.S. Highway 77 and State Highway 11, and caught a red light. Montenegro slowed, looked around, and then made a right turn onto Highway 11 headed east towards Kaw Lake, just as four men on red and black motorcycles pulled up on U.S. Highway 77 from the north facing south. The lead man eyed the SUV headed down the highway and nodded over to his counterpart as he pulled out an Uzi and racked it. The four outlaws waited patiently for the light to turn green before making a left turn, headed east on Highway 11, carefully tailing the SUV.

All was quiet inside the SUV as it neared the foot of Kaw Lake Bridge. It was dark out, but Kaw Lake Park was lit up with the softball field's lights. The concession stand was open and the parking lot was full of cars on this hot, humid summer night. There were also a few boats out on the water, late night jet skiers daring to slosh through the dark waters.

Dawk looked across Oneika to his left and saw Bay sitting on the trunk of Spoonie and Tyke's Infinite with T-top and AquaNina standing beside her. He could also see Kimi and Koko's Maserati and Walee's Charger. They'd ridden out to the park to be with Bay and Tiva as they waited on Dawk's return.

"Remember you used to work the concession stand over there, baby?" Dawk asked Oneika as the SUV approached Kaw Lake Bridge.

Oneika blushed and said, "During my wilder days? Yes I do." The loving wife looked into her husband's eyes and could see the want. "You wanna go over there with your siblings tonight don't you?" she asked through light laughter.

Dawk leaned back in the soft leather seat and donned a reminiscent smile as he rubbed his chin. "We used to have fun at that park. I ain't hung out like that with 'em in a while."

"Take a car when we get back to the ranch and just go over there." Oneika urged.

"You sure?" Dawk asked as the Suburban rode onto the eastbound side of Kaw Lake Bridge.

"Sosa is down for the night and I have to catch up on Grey's Anatomy. It's still a little early, baby. Go and enjoy yourself. Take your mind off things for a while," Oneika answered as she grabbed Dawk's hand and kissed it tenderly.

Down on Kaw Lake Park, Bay had caught sight of the family's Suburban just before it disappeared onto the twin span crossing the lake. When she saw the motorcycles tailing, she jumped from the trunk of the Infinite and immediately thought back to the day she and T-top were returning home with Terrence's daughter, Tara. Something was telling her to jump in the Infinite and go after her brother, but she remained in place, watching in silence as the motorcycles disappeared onto the bridge.

Back inside the Suburban, Montenegro could see four headlights coming up on him fast. He thought nothing of it as he kept driving. Everyone was in a relaxed state inside the SUV as the headlights grew closer, totally off guard and unaware. One of the motorcycles sped past Montenegro and slowed. The Mexican sped up, shooting past the motorcycle, but it sped up again. When it reappeared, Montenegro could see that the guy had an Uzi pointed at the wheels. "It's a hit!" he screamed out just as bullets penetrated the front and rear driver's side tires, dropping the SUV over to the left.

Oneika covered Sosa. Dawk covered his wife. Siloam grabbed her .45 caliber and racked it as another burst of rounds from the three remaining bikers shot up the engine. Bullets bounced off the front of the Suburban, unable to penetrate its hull, but Montenegro had overcorrected underneath the massive gunfire. In an attempt to ward off the bullets, he swerved the Suburban to the right. The shattered driver's side front wheel became lodged in the concrete and the SUV went topsy-turvy, rolling over one time before crashing through the concrete barricade and plunging off the right side of the bridge nose first into the murky waters of Kaw Lake.

Bay had heard the gunfire and was already in the Infinite with T-top and AquaNina. Boaters had saw what'd happened and were headed that way with bright lights shining down into the water in search of the vehicle. Bay sped past Walee, Kimi, Koko, Spoonie and Tyke, who'd all heard the gunshots, but weren't aware of what'd just gone down. Afraid for the family, the young five jumped into Walee's car and followed suit.

Inside the SUV, Siloam was struggling to free herself. She'd clicked her seatbelt the time the heavy SUV hit the water and was able to escape through the shattered passenger side window. She floated up to the surface of the twelve feet deep water, caught her breath, and sunk back below the surface as speed boats approached.

Dawk, meanwhile, was struggling to find his son. He couldn't find Oneika either. Through gritted teeth he fumbled around in the darkness, but it was too chaotic inside the upside down vehicle as it lay on the sandy bottom of Kaw Lake. He floated out the passenger side window, swam up to the top, caught his breath and dropped back down below the surface of the water a second time.

Siloam, meanwhile, had grabbed hold of someone and had pulled them out through the back passenger side window of the SUV. She swam back to the surface with the limp body and saw that she was holding on to an unconscious Oneika.

Dawk emerged at that moment and saw Siloam swimming on her back with his unconscious wife. "Sosa!" he screamed aloud as he sunk back beneath the murky waters. With his eyes open in the water, Dawk swam twelve feet down. The rear lights on the SUV were still lit, giving him a point of reference as he approached and reached inside where he knew his son's car seat was locked in place. The entire area was empty, however, as all Dawk felt were the leather seats and the loosened seatbelt that once held his firstborn. He screamed under the water as he reached around in a desperate attempt to locate his son. He felt flesh in his hands, but knew right away that it was Montenegro given the body's size. Nearly out of breath, he was forced to resurface.

When he did, Dawk let go of an agonizing cry as he slapped at the water. "My son!" he cried out as boaters approached. "Not my fuckin' son you sons of bitches!"

"Dawk!" Bay called down from the top off the bridge. The entire area was now lit up by three large lights from three speedboats that'd made it to the scene.

"Bay, I can't find Sosa!" Dawk yelled back. He held his breath again and sunk beneath the water for fourth time, but hadn't the air in his lungs to make it down to the bottom. The natural instinct to survive forced him to resurface, and this go around, Dawk knew. Sosa had been down too long to have survived the ordeal. He swam over to the edge of one of the boats and held on to the side as he cried out into the night sky as his body heaved over the heartfelt pain of losing his firstborn child.

****

Back up in Chicago, DeeDee was preparing to shower and go to bed. He'd laid out a charcoal grey silk suit and matching gators, wanting to look sharp for his return to Oklahoma. He'd just thrown a large towel over his shoulder and was headed to the shower when his doorbell rang. "Dammit, Natalia," he sighed as he headed down the stairs to the first floor.

Without thinking, DeeDee pulled the door open. "If Naomi sent you I'm doing just—"

DeeDee went silent when he was struck with a balled up fist across the face. Three people rushed in with blue bandannas covering the lower portion of their faces and locked the door behind them. Two took off to search the home as the third remained with a stunned DeeDee while holding him at gunpoint with a chrome .50 caliber pistol.

"Young punk! Who the fuck are you and what do you want from me? You know who the fuck I am?" DeeDee boomed as he rested on his elbows in the nude.

"I know exactly who you are Doss Dawkins," the aggressor remarked nonchalantly.

DeeDee was surprised to hear a female's voice. He crawled backwards while naked on his back, wondering who the female was. "Did I upset your mother or something?" he asked intrigued. "Who are you?"

The female pulled down her bandanna and knelt before DeeDee. She was a tall, thick, brown-skinned female with short-faded hair dyed blonde and numerous tats on her neck belonging to the Gangster Disciples. She sported a mouth full of diamond teeth and couldn't have been no older than twenty years of age at the latest. "Do the names Clementine Green and Kyle Desmond ring a bell, Doss?" she asked calmly.

DeeDee shook his head to say no, but he knew damn well who the young woman was referring to as a brief flashback to a play-by-play given to him by his deceased son, Doss Dawkins Junior, ran through his mind...

....Just before Kyle entered his home, he was greeted with two . 9mm hand guns that held silencers over the barrels. He stared at the guns that had been shoved into his face just as a gloved hand was wrapped around his mouth from behind. He was guided into his apartment in silence where Junior closed the door and locked it.

Clementine came out the room holding her baby with a smile on her face, but when she saw the three men shoving Kyle towards the sofa, she took off running back into the bedroom and locked the door and hid her baby.

"Do your job, son." Lucky said in a clam manner.

Junior ran towards the bedroom and kicked the door open and aimed his weapon on Clementine. The frightened young woman screamed when her assailant kicked the door in, but she was quickly silenced by a bullet that had entered her chest and exited her back.

Junior then walked over and saw that Clementine was still alive as she lay on the floor beside the bed. She was reaching for her baby as she eyed her assailant standing over her with his gun aimed squarely at her head. Junior said nothing as he looked Clementine square in the eyes and shot her two times in the face. She died on her bedroom floor right beside her crying baby. Clementine Green was Junior's first kill. And he felt no remorse for killing the mother of a newborn child as to him it was just a job that simply needed doing.

Doss and Lucky, meanwhile, were preparing to take care of Kyle, having tied him up and forcing him down on the sofa. Kyle was breathing hard at this moment, unable to believe he was about check out. He asked Doss through panted breath why he was being killed.

"You been hiding out for a reason—because you snitched on your man after you got busted with his drugs. He sent us so you can pay him back with your life." Doss replied in a cool, calm and collective manner as checked the silencer on the barrel of his . 9mm, making sure it was secure.

"I swear! I swear, man! That was all Trenton idea! All we was supposed to do was hold the drugs?" Kyle panted.

"You got the drugs here?" Doss asked.

"Trent kept everything. He played us! Tell, tell that Asian man I ain't had shit ta' do with him gettin' ripped off and I'm sorry."

"I'll give him your message," Doss replied as he and Lucky took aim and shot Kyle in the head and torso a total of twelve times.

As the three men turned to leave the apartment, Doss, remembering he had seen Clementine holding a baby, turned to Junior and said, "You didn't kill that baby did you?"

"No. She won't even remember this shit." Junior replied.

"Now you wanna play stupid with a bitch," the female laughed. "Seventeen years ago your son, Doss Dawkins Junior, killed my mother and father inside Cabrini Green. Clementine was my mother. Kyle was my father. Word on the street is that your son, and an Italian named Lucky and his son Junior killed my people. I can't tell ya' how bad I wanted to touch y'all when I found out, but unfortunately for me, your son and his two goons got murked a while back. But, I have you to get my revenge on," she smiled.

"Your people ratted on a mafia boss," DeeDee defended as he rubbed his throbbing jaw.

"I don't give one good rabbit fuck if they dropped a dime on everybody in Cicero! You had no right to touch my family, nigga! It's a new damn day, Doss! Troi Lynn Green gone make a name of you tonight, boy!" the female boomed through laughter as she stood up and aimed her .50 cal at DeeDee's chest.

"Go 'head then!" DeeDee screamed. "Take me out! It still won't bring your parents back, young punk! Do it! You think I'm scared to die! Hell, I been dead for some time now, mutherfucka!"

Troi Lynn licked her lips and nodded just as her goons trotted back down the stairs. "We good," one of the teenagers remarked.

"Pick him up," Troi Lynn commanded as she walked past DeeDee, kicking him one time in the face before walking over to the patio and pulling the sliding doors open. "Damn this a nice view, bruh," she said as she sniffed the warm air. "Come see this view, DeeDee. Check it out on your way down, fam."

"No," DeeDee struggled as he was jerked up to his feet. "Nooooo!" he screamed aloud in a hoarse voice upon realizing his fate. "Shoot me, dammit!" he said as he planted his bare feet into the wooden floor in an attempt to keep his self inside his condominium.

"Shooting you would be too good. Too quick and easy," Troi Lynn pondered as she stared back at DeeDee from the balcony. She then looked thirty stories down at the passing cars and people walking, looking like ants on a pile. "Heads up!" she said aloud as she laughed. "Yo, handle that," she ordered as she stepped aside.

"Bye, old man," one of Troi Lynn's goons growled as he and his counterpart drug him forward.

DeeDee used a free hand to punch one of the men in the mouth. The youngster let go off his grip and backhanded DeeDee in the mouth as the other punched him in the gut. DeeDee folded over and one of the thugs punched him in the back of his head at the base of his neck. He dropped flat onto his belly and was scooped up again.

"Fuck you," DeeDee whined as he was dragged out onto the balcony butt naked. "Eat my shit! My family will have your souls!"

"But I'll take yours tonight," Troi Lynn clapped back as DeeDee was flung up against the steel rail with his back facing the street thirty stories below.

To the very end, DeeDee fought. He swung again, this time striking Troi Lynn in the face. She stumbled back, looked around and grabbed an iron poker from the fireplace. Her two goons stepped aside and she hit DeeDee in the top of the head, drawing blood from his skull with one powerful blow and buckling his knees.

The seventy-six-year-old gangster was still gagging for air when he was picked up. "No," DeeDee pleaded as he urinated on himself. "I'm naked, mutherfuckas! Let me die in my home with some dignity, dammit!" he groaned.

"You forgot to say please, old man," Troi Lynn stated in cold-hearted manner as she nodded to her goons while holding on to the bloody poker stick.

It was the most awful sound ever. The scream DeeDee made as he was flung off the side of his balcony from thirty stories high in the nude.

"Bring my Taurus around," Troi Lynn quickly ordered once DeeDee had dropped from sight. "Them Italians over to that hot dog deli next up on the list. Starting with that boy Carlos," she ended as she dropped the poker stick and walked back inside the condominium.

To be continued.

Made in the USA
Middletown, DE
21 February 2023